Eleanor Hallowell Abb Collection novels

In this book:
Fairy Prince and Other Stories, 1922
Peace on Earth, Good-will to Dogs, 1920
The Indiscreet Letter, 1915
Molly Make-Believe, 1910
Little Eve Edgarton, 1914
The Sick-a-Bed Lady, 1911
The White Linen Nurse, 1913
Rainy Week, 1921

Eleanor Hallowell Abbott (1872 – 1958), born in Cambridge, Massachusetts, was a nationally recognized American author. She was a frequent contributor to The Ladies' Home Journal. She went on to publish seventy-five short stories and fourteen romantic novels. Being Little in Cambridge When Everyone Else Was Big is an autobiography written by Abbott about her childhood in Cambridge.

In this book:
Peace on Earth, Good-will to Dogs…………......Pag. 3
Fairy Prince and Other Stories……………..…..Pag. 23
The Indiscreet Letter………………….…..……Pag. 74
Molly Make-Believe……………….…………...Pag. 86
Little Eve Edgarton……………….....…………Pag. 124
The Sick-a-Bed Lady……………….…………..Pag. 163
The White Linen Nurse……………..…………Pag. 249
Rainy Week………………….…………………Pag. 304

Peace on Earth, Good-will to Dogs

PART I

f you don't like Christmas stories, don't read this one!

And if you don't like dogs I don't know just what to advise you to do!

For I warn you perfectly frankly that I am distinctly pro-dog and distinctly pro-Christmas, and would like to bring to this little story whatever whiff of fir-balsam I can cajole from the make-believe forest in my typewriter, and every glitter of tinsel, smudge of toy candle, crackle of wrapping paper, that my particular brand of brain and ink can conjure up on a single keyboard! And very large-sized dogs shall romp through every page! And the mercury shiver perpetually in the vicinity of zero! And every foot of earth be crusty-brown and bare with no white snow at all till the very last moment when you'd just about given up hope! And all the heart of the story is very,—oh *very* young!

For purposes of propriety and general historical authenticity there are of course parents in the story. And one or two other oldish persons. But they all go away just as early in the narrative as I can manage it.—Are obliged to go away!

Yet lest you find in this general combination of circumstances some sinister threat of audacity, let me conventionalize the story at once by opening it at that most conventional of all conventional Christmas-story hours,—the Twilight of Christmas Eve.

Nuff said?—Christmas Eve, you remember? Twilight? Awfully cold weather? And somebody very young?

Now for the story itself!

After five blustering, wintry weeks of village speculation and gossip there was of course considerable satisfaction in being the first to solve the mysterious holiday tenancy of the Rattle-Pane House.

Breathless with excitement Flame Nourice telephoned the news from the village post-office. From a pedestal of boxes fairly bulging with red-wheeled go-carts, one keen young elbow rammed for balance into a gay glassy shelf of stick-candy, green tissue garlands tickling across her cheek, she sped the message to her mother.

"O Mother-Funny!" triumphed Flame. "I've found out who's Christmasing at the Rattle-Pane House!—It's a red-haired setter dog with one black ear! And he's sitting at the front gate this moment! Superintending the unpacking of the furniture van! And I've named him Lopsy!"

"Why, Flame; how—absurd!" gasped her mother. In consideration of the fact that Flame's mother had run all the way from the icy-footed chicken yard to answer the telephone it shows distinctly what stuff she was made of that she gasped nothing else.

And that Flame herself re-telephoned within the half hour to acknowledge her absurdity shows equally distinctly what stuff *she* was made of! It was from the summit of a crate of holly-wreaths that she telephoned this time.

"Oh Mother-Funny," apologized Flame, "you were perfectly right. No lone dog in the world could possibly manage a great spooky place like the Rattle-Pane House. There are two other dogs with him! A great long, narrow sofa-shaped dog upholstered in lemon and white,—something terribly ferocious like 'Russian Wolf Hound' I think he is! But I've named him Beautiful-Lovely! And there's the neatest looking paper-white coach dog just perfectly ruined with ink-spots! Blunder-Blot, I think, will make a good name for him! And—"

"Oh—Fl—ame!" panted her Mother. "Dogs—do—not—take houses!" It was not from the chicken-yard that she had come running this time but only from her Husband's Sermon-Writing-Room in the attic.

"Oh don't they though?" gloated Flame. "Well, they've taken this one, anyway! Taken it by storm, I mean! Scratched all the green paint off the front door! Torn a hole big as a cavern in the Barberry Hedge! Pushed the sun-dial through a bulkhead!—If it snows to-night the cellar'll be a Glacier! And—"

"Dogs—do—not—take—houses," persisted Flame's mother. She was still persisting it indeed when she returned to her husband's study.

Her husband, it seemed, had not noticed her absence. Still poring over the tomes and commentaries incidental to the preparation of his next Sunday's sermon his fine face glowed half frown, half ecstasy, in the December twilight, while close at his elbow all unnoticed a smoking kerosine lamp went smudging its acrid path to the ceiling. Dusky lock for dusky lock, dreamy eye for dreamy eye, smoking lamp for smoking lamp, it might have been a short-haired replica of Flame herself.

"Oh if Flame had only been 'set' like the maternal side of the house!" reasoned Flame's Mother. "Or merely dreamy like her Father! Her Father being only dreamy could sometimes be diverted from his dreams! But to be 'set' and 'dreamy' both? Absolutely 'set' on being absolutely 'dreamy'? That was Flame!" With renewed tenacity Flame's Mother reverted to Truth as Truth. "Dogs do *not* take houses!" she affirmed with unmistakable emphasis.

"Eh? What?" jumped her husband. "Dogs? Dogs? Who said anything about dogs?" With a fretted pucker between his brows he bent to his work again. "You interrupted me," he reproached her. "My sermon is about Hell-Fire.—I had all but smelled it.—It was very disagreeable." With a gesture of impatience he snatched up his notes and tore them in two. "I think I will write about the Garden of Eden instead!" he rallied. "The Garden of Eden in Iris time! Florentina Alba everywhere! Whiteness! Sweetness!—Now let me see,—orris root I believe is deducted from the Florentina Alba—."

"U—m—m—m," sniffed Flame's Mother. With an impulse purely practical she started for the kitchen. "The season happens to be Christmas time," she suggested bluntly. "Now if you could see your way to make a sermon that smelt like doughnuts and plum-pudding—"

"Doughnuts?" queried her Husband and hurried after her. Supplementing the far, remote Glory-of-God expression in his face, the glory-of-doughnuts shone suddenly very warmly.

Flame at least did not have to be reminded about the Seasons.

"Oh *mother*!" telephoned Flame almost at once, "It's—so much nearer Christmas than it was half an hour ago! Are you sure everything will keep? All those big packages that came yesterday? That humpy one especially? Don't you think you ought to peep? Or poke? Just the teeniest, tiniest little peep or poke? It would be a shame if anything spoiled! A—turkey—or a—or a fur coat—or anything."

"I am—making doughnuts," confided her Mother with the faintest possible taint of asperity.

"O—h," conceded Flame. "And Father's watching them? Then I'll hurry! M—Mother?" deprecated the excited young voice. "You are always so horridly right! Lopsy and Beautiful-Lovely and Blunder-Blot are *not* Christmasing all alone in the Rattle-Pane House! There is a man with them! Don't tell Father,—he's so nervous about men!"

"A—man?" stammered her Mother. "Oh I hope not a young man! Where did he come from?"

"Oh I don't think he came at all," confided Flame. It was Flame who was perplexed this time. "He looks to me more like a person who had always been there! Like something I mean that the dogs found in the attic! Quite crumpled he is! And with a red waistcoat!—A—A butler perhaps?—A—A sort of a second hand butler? Oh Mother!—I wish we had a butler!"

"Flame—?" interrupted her Mother quite abruptly. "Where are you doing all this telephoning from? I only gave you eighteen cents and it was to buy cereal with."

"Cereal?" considered Flame. "Oh that's all right," she glowed suddenly. "I've paid cash for the telephoning and charged the cereal."

With a swallow faintly guttural Flame's Mother hung up the receiver. "Dogs—do—not—have—butlers," she persisted unshakenly.

She was perfectly right. They did not, it seemed.

No one was quicker than Flame to acknowledge a mistake. Before five o'clock Flame had added a telephone item to the cereal bill.

"Oh—Mother," questioned Flame. "The little red sweater and Tam that I have on?—Would they be all right, do you think, for me to make a call in? Not a formal call, of course,—just a—a neighborly greeting at the door? It being Christmas Eve and everything!—And as long as I have to pass right by the house anyway?—There is a lady at the Rattle-Pane House! A—A—what Father would call a Lady Maiden!—Miss—"

"Oh not a real lady, I think," protested her Mother. "Not with all those dogs. No real lady I think would have so many dogs.—It—It isn't sanitary."

"Isn't—sanitary?" cried Flame. "Why Mother, they are the most absolutely—perfectly sanitary dogs you ever saw in your life!" Into her eager young voice an expression of ineffable dignity shot suddenly. "Well—really, Mother," she said, "In whatever concerns men or crocheting—I'm perfectly willing to take Father's advice or yours. But after all, I'm eighteen," stiffened the young voice. "And when it comes to dogs—I must use my own judgment!"

"And just what is the lady's name?" questioned her Mother a bit weakly.

"Her name is 'Miss Flora'!" brightened Flame. "The Butler has just gone to the Station to meet her! I heard him telephoning quite frenziedly! I think she must have missed her train or something! It seemed to make everybody very nervous! Maybe *she's* nervous! Maybe she's a nervous invalid! With a lost Lover somewhere! And all sorts of pressed flowers!—Somebody ought to call anyway! Call right away, I mean, before she gets any more nervous!—So many people's first impressions of a place—I've heard—are spoiled for lack of some perfectly silly little thing like a nutmeg grater or a hot water bottle! And oh, Mother, it's been so long since any one lived in the Rattle-Pane

House! Not for years and years and years! Not dogs, anyway! Not a lemon and white wolf hound! Not setters! Not spotty dogs!—Oh Mother, just one little wee single minute at the door? Just long enough to say 'The Rev. and Mrs. Flamande Nourice, and Miss Nourice, present their compliments!'—And are you by any chance short a marrow-bone? Or would you possibly care to borrow an extra quilt to rug-up under the kitchen table?... Blunder-Blot doesn't look very thick. Or—Oh Mother, *p-l-e-a-s-e!*"

When Flame said "Please" like that the word was no more, no less, than the fabled bundle of rags or haunch of venison hurled back from a wolf-pursued sleigh to divert the pursuer even temporarily from the main issue. While Flame's Mother paused to consider the particularly flavorous sweetness of that entreaty,—to picture the flashing eye, the pulsing throat, the absurdly crinkled nostril that invariably accompanied all Flame's entreaties, Flame herself was escaping!

Taken all in all, escaping was one of the best things that Flame did.... As well as the most becoming! Whipped into scarlet by the sudden plunge from a stove-heated store into the frosty night her young cheeks fairly blazed their bright reaction. Frost and speed quickened her breath. Glint for glint her shining eyes challenged the moon. Fearful even yet that some tardy admonition might overtake her she sped like a deer through the darkness.

It was a dull-smelling night. Pretty, but very dull-smelling. Disdainfully her nostrils crinkled their disappointment.

"Christmas Time adventures ought to smell like Christmas!" she scolded. "Maybe if I'm ever President," she argued, "I won't do so awfully well with the Tariff or things like that! But Christmas shall smell of Christmas! Not just of frozen mud! And camphor balls!... I'll have great vats of Fir Balsam essence at every street corner! And gigantic atomizers! And every passerby shall be sprayed! And stores! And churches! And—And everybody who doesn't like Christmas shall be *dipped*!"

Under her feet the smoothish village road turned suddenly into the harsh and hobbly ruts of a country lane. With fluctuant blackness against immutable blackness great sweeping pine trees swished weirdly into the horizon. Where the hobbly lane curved darkly into a meadow through a snarl of winter-stricken willows the rattle of a loose window-pane smote quite distinctly on the ear. It was a horrid, deserted sound. And with the instinctive habit of years Flame's little hand clutched at her heart. Then quite abruptly she laughed aloud.

"Oh you can't scare me any more, you gloomy old Rattle-Pane House!" she laughed. "You're not deserted now! People are Christmasing in you! Whether you like it or not you're being Christmased!"

Very tentatively she puckered her lips to a whistle. Almost instantly from the darkness ahead a dog's bark rang out, deep, sonorous, faintly suspicious. With a little chuckle of joy she crawled through the Barberry hedge and emerged for a single instant only at her full height before three furry shapes came hurtling out of the darkness and toppled her over backwards.

"Stop, Beautiful-Lovely!" she gasped. "Stop, Lopsy! Behave yourself, Blunder-Blot! *Sillies*! Don't you know I'm the lady that was talking to you this morning through the picket fence? Don't you know I'm the lady that fed you the box of cereal?—Oh dear—Oh dear—Oh dear," she struggled. "I knew, of course, that there were three dogs—but who ever in the world would have guessed that three could be so many?"

As expeditiously as possible she picked herself up and bolted for the house with two furry shapes leaping largely on either side of her and one cold nose sniffing interrogatively at her heels. Her heart was very light,—her pulses jumping with excitement,—an occasional furry head doming into the palm of her hand warmed the whole bleak night with its sense of mute companionship. But the back of her heels felt certainly very queer. Even the warm yellow lights of the Rattle-Pane House did not altogether dispel her uneasiness.

"Maybe I'd better not plan to make my call so—so very informal," she decided suddenly. "Not at a house where there are quite so many dogs! Not at a house where there is a butler ... anyway!"

Crowding and pushing and yelping and fawning around her, it was the dogs who announced her ultimate arrival. Like a drift of snow the huge wolf-hound whirled his white shagginess into the vestibule. Shrill as a banging blind the impetuous coach-dog lurched his sleek weight against the door. Sucking at a crack of light the red setter's kindled nose glowed and snorted with dragonlike ferocity. Without knock or ring the door-handle creaked and turned, three ecstatic shapes went hurtling through a yellow glare into the hall beyond, and Flame found herself staring up into the blinking, astonished eyes of the crumpled old man with the red waistcoat.

"G—Good evening,—Butler!" she rallied.

"Good evening, Miss!" stammered the Butler.

"I've—I've come to call," confided Flame.

"To—call?" stammered the Butler.

"Yes," conceded Flame. "I—I don't happen to have an engraved card with me." Before the continued imperturbability of the old Butler all subterfuge seemed suddenly quite useless. "I *never* have had an engraved card," she confided quite abruptly. "But you might tell Miss Flora if you please—" ... Would nothing crack the Butler's imperturbability?... Well maybe she could prove just a little bit imperturbable herself! "Oh! Butlers don't 'tell' people things, do they?... They always 'announce' things, don't they?... Well, kindly announce to Miss Flora that the—the Minister's Daughter is—at the door!... Oh, *no*! It isn't asking for a subscription or anything!" she hastened quite suddenly to explain. "It's just a Christian call!... B—Being so nervous and lost on the train and everything ... we thought Miss Flora might be glad to know that there were neighbors.... We live so near and everything.... And can run like the wind! Oh, not Mother, of course!... She's a bit stout! And Father starts all right but usually gets thinking of something else! But I...? Kindly announce to Miss Flora," she repeated with palpable crispness, "that the Minister's Daughter is at the door!"

Fixedly old, fixedly crumpled, fixedly imperturbable, the Butler stepped back a single jerky pace and bowed her towards the parlor.

"Now," thrilled Flame, "the adventure really begins."

It certainly was a sad and romantic looking parlor, and strangely furnished, Flame thought, for even "moving times." Through a maze of bulging packing boxes and barrels she picked her way to a faded rose-colored chair that flanked the fire-place. That the chair was already half occupied by a pile of ancient books and four dusty garden trowels only served to intensify the general air of gloom. Presiding over all, two dreadful bouquets of long-dead grasses flared wanly on the mantle-piece. And from the tattered old landscape paper on the walls Civil War heroes stared regretfully down through pale and tarnished frames.

"Dear me ... dear me," shivered Flame. "They're not going to Christmas at all ... evidently! Not a sprig of holly anywhere! Not a ravel of tinsel! Not a jingle bell!... Oh she must have lost a lot of lovers," thrilled Flame. "I can bring her flowers, anyway! My very first Paper White Narcissus! My—."

With a scrape of the foot the Butler made known his return.

"Miss Flora!" he announced.

With a catch of her breath Flame jumped to her feet and turned to greet the biggest, ugliest, most brindled, most wizened Bull Dog she had ever seen in her life.

"*Miss Flora!*" repeated the old Butler succinctly.

"Miss Flora?" gasped Flame. "Why.... Why, I thought Miss Flora was a Lady! Why—"

"Miss Flora is indeed a very grand lady, Miss!" affirmed the Butler without a flicker of expression. "Of a pedigree so famous ... so distinguished ... so ..." Numerically on his fingers he began to count the distinctions. "Five prizes this year! And three last! Do you mind the chop?" he gloated. "The breadth! The depth!... Did you never hear of alauntes?" he demanded. "Them bull-baiting dogs that was invented by the second Duke of York or thereabouts in the year 1406?"

"Oh my Glory!" thrilled Flame. "Is Miss Flora as old as *that*?"

"Miss Flora," said the old Butler with some dignity, "is young—hardly two in fact—so young that she seems to me but just weaned."

With her great eyes goggled to a particularly disconcerting sort of scrutiny Miss Flora sprang suddenly forward to investigate the visitor.

As though by a preconcerted signal a chair crashed over in the hall and the wolf hound and the setter and the coach dog came hurtling back in a furiously cordial onslaught. With wags and growls and yelps of joy all four dogs met in Flame's lap.

"They seem to like me, don't they?" triumphed Flame. Intermittently through the melee of flapping ears,—shoving shoulders,—waving paws, her beaming little face proved the absolute sincerity of that triumph. "Mother's never let me have any dogs," she confided. "Mother thinks they're not—Oh, of course, I realize that four dogs is a—a good many," she hastened diplomatically to concede to a certain sudden droop around the old Butler's mouth corners.

From his slow, stooping poke of the sulky fire the old Butler glanced up with a certain plaintive intentness.

"All dogs is too many," he affirmed.

"Come Christmas time I wishes I was dead."

"Wish you were dead ... at Christmas Time?" cried Flame. Acute shock was in her protest.

"It's the feedin'," sighed the old Butler. "It ain't that I mind eatin' with them on All Saints' Day or Fourth of July or even Sundays. But come Christmas Time it seems like I craves to eat with More Humans.... I got a nephew less'n twenty miles away. He's got cider in his cellar. And plum puddings. His woman she raises guinea chickens. And mince pies there is. And tasty gravies.—But me I mixes dog bread and milk—dog bread and milk—till I can't see nothing—think nothing but mush. And him with cider in his cellar!... It ain't as though Mr. Delcote ever came himself to prove anything," he argued. "Not he! Not Christmas Time! It's travelling he is.... He's had ... misfortunes," he confided darkly. "He travels for 'em same as some folks travels for their healths. Most especially at Christmas Time he travels for his misfortunes! He ..."

"*Mr. Delcote*?" quickened Flame. "Mr. Delcote?" (Now at last was the mysterious tenancy about to be divulged?)

"All he says," persisted the old Butler. "All he says is 'Now Barret,'—that's me, 'Now Barret I trust your honor to see that the dogs ain't neglected just because it's Christmas. There ain't no reason, Barret', he says, 'why innocent dogs should suffer Christmas just because everybody else does. They ain't done nothing.... It won't do now Barret', he says, 'for you to give 'em their dinner at dawnwhen they ain't accustomed to it, and a pail of water, and shut 'em up while you go off for the day with any barrel of cider. You know what dogs is, Barret', he says. 'And what they isn't. They've got to be fed regular', he says, 'and with discipline. Else there's deaths.—Some natural. Some unnatural. And some just plain spectacular from furniture falling on their arguments. So if there's any fatalities come this Christmas Time, Barret', he says, 'or any undue gains in weight or losses in weight, I shall infer, Barret', he says, 'that you was absent without leave.' ... It don't look like a very wholesome Christmas for me," sighed the old Butler. "Not either way. Not what you'd call wholesome."

"But this Mr. Delcote?" puzzled Flame. "What a perfectly horrid man he must be to give such heavenly dogs nothing but dog-bread and milk for their Christmas dinner!... Is he young? Is he old? Is he thin? Is he fat? However in the world did he happen to come to a queer, battered old place like the Rattle-Pane House? But once come why didn't he stay? And—And—And—?"

"Yes'm," sighed the old Butler.

In a ferment of curiosity, Flame edged jerkily forward, and subsided as jerkily again.

"Oh, if this only was a Parish Call," she deprecated, "I could ask questions right out loud. 'How? Where? Why? When?' ... But being just a social call—I suppose—I suppose...?" Appealingly her eager eyes searched the old Butler's inscrutable face.

"Yes'm," repeated the old Butler dully. Through the quavering fingers that he swept suddenly across his brow two very genuine tears glistened.

With characteristic precipitousness Flame jumped to her feet.

"Oh, darn Mr. Delcote!" she cried. "I'll feed your dogs, Christmas Day! It won't take a minute after my own dinner or before! I'll run like the wind! No one need ever know!"

So it was that when Flame arrived at her own home fifteen minutes later, and found her parents madly engaged in packing suit-cases, searching time-tables, and rushing generally to and fro from attic to cellar, no very mutual exchange of confidences ensued.

"It's your Uncle Wally!" panted her Mother.

"Another shock!" confided her Father.

"Not such a bad one, either," explained her Mother. "But of course we'll have to go! The very first thing in the morning! Christmas Day, too! And leave you all alone! It's a perfect shame! But I've planned it all out for everybody! Father's Lay Reader, of course, will take the Christmas service! We'll just have to omit the Christmas Tree surprise for the children!... It's lucky we didn't even unpack the trimmings! Or tell a soul about it." In a hectic effort to pack both a thick coat and a thin coat and a thick dress and a thin dress and thick boots and thin boots in the same suit-case she began very palpably to pant again. "Yes! Every detail is all planned out!" she asserted with a breathy sort of pride. "You and your Father are both so flighty I don't know whatever in the world you'ddo if I didn't plan out everything for you!"

With more manners than efficiency Flame and her Father dropped at once every helpful thing they were doing and sat down in rocking chairs to listen to the plan.

"Flame, of course, can't stay here all alone. Flame's Mother turned and confided *sotto voce* to her husband. Young men might call. The Lay Reader is almost sure to call.... He's a dear delightful soul of course, but I'm afraid he has an amorous eye."

"All Lay Readers have amorous eyes," reflected her husband. "Taken all in all it is a great asset."

"Don't be flippant!" admonished Flame's Mother. "There are reasons ... why I prefer that Flame's first offer of marriage should not be from a Lay Reader."

"Why?" brightened Flame.

"S—sh—," cautioned her Father.

"Very good reasons," repeated her Mother. From the conglomerate packing under her hand a puff of spilled tooth-powder whiffed fragrantly into the air.

"Yes?" prodded her husband's blandly impatient voice.

"Flame shall go to her Aunt Minna's" announced the dominant maternal voice. "By driving with us to the station, she'll have only two hours to wait for her train, and that will save one bus fare! Aunt Minna is a vegetarian and doesn't believe in sweets either, so that will be quite a unique and profitable experience for Flame to add to her general culinary education! It's a wonderful house!... A bit dark of course! But if the day should prove at all bright,—not so bright of course that Aunt Minna wouldn't be willing to have the shades up, but—Oh and Flame," she admonished still breathlessly, "I think you'd better be careful to wear one of your rather longish skirts! And oh do be sure to wipe your feet every time you come in! And don't chatter! Whatever you do, don't chatter! Your Aunt Minna, you know, is just a little bit peculiar! But such a worthy woman! So methodical! So...."

To Flame's inner vision appeared quite suddenly the pale, inscrutable face of the old Butler who asked nothing,—answered nothing,—welcomed nothing,—evaded nothing.

"... Yes'm," said Flame.

But it was a very frankly disconsolate little girl who stole late that night to her Father's study, and perched herself high on the arm of his chair with her cheek snuggled close to his.

"Of Father-Funny," whispered Flame, "I've got such a queer little pain."

"A pain?" jerked her Father. "Oh dear me! Where is it? Go and find your Mother at once!"

"Mother?" frowned Flame. "Oh it isn't that kind of a pain.—It's in my Christmas. I've got such a sad little pain in my Christmas."

"Oh dear me—dear me!" sighed her Father. Like two people most precipitously smitten with shyness they sat for a moment staring blankly around the room at every conceivable object except each other. Then quite suddenly they looked back at each other and smiled.

"Father," said Flame. "You're not of course a very old man.... But still you are pretty old, aren't you? You've seen a whole lot of Christmasses, I mean?"

"Yes," conceded her Father.

From the great clumsy rolling collar of her blanket wrapper Flame's little face loomed suddenly very pink and earnest.

"But Father," urged Flame. "Did you ever in your whole life spend a Christmas just exactly the way you wanted to? Honest-to-Santa Claus now,—did you *ever*?"

"Why—Why, no," admitted her Father after a second's hesitation. "Why no, I don't believe I ever did." Quite frankly between his brows there puckered a very black frown. "Now take to-morrow, for instance," he complained. "I had planned to go fishing through the ice.... After the morning service, of course,—after we'd had our Christmas dinner,—and gotten tired of our presents,—every intention in the world I had of going fishing through the ice.... And now your Uncle Wally has to go and have a shock! I don't believe it was necessary. He should have taken extra precautions. The least that delicate relatives can do is to take extra precautions at holiday time.... Oh, of course your Uncle Wally has books in his library," he brightened, "very interesting old books that wouldn't be perfectly seemly for a minister of the Gospel to have in his own library.... But still it's very disappointing," he wilted again.

"I agree with you ... utterly, Father-Funny!" said Flame. "But ... Father," she persisted, "Of all the people you know in the world,—millions would it be?"

"No, call it thousands" corrected her Father.

"Well, thousands," accepted Flame. "Old people, young people, fat people, skinnys, cross people, jolly people?... Did you ever in your life know *any one* who had ever spent Christmas just the way he wanted to?"

"Why ... no, I don't know that I ever did," considered her Father. With his elbows on the arms of his chair, his slender fingers forked to a lovely Gothic arch above the bridge of his nose, he yielded himself instantly to the reflection. "Why ... no, ... I don't know that I ever did," he repeated with an increasing air of conviction.... "When you're young enough to enjoy the day as a 'holler' day there's usually some blighting person who prefers to have it observed as a holy day.... And by the time you reach an age where you really rather appreciate its being a holy day the chances are that you've got a houseful of racketty youngsters who fairly insist on reverting to the 'holler' day idea again."

"U—m—m," encouraged Flame.

—"When you're little, of course," mused her Father, "you have to spend the day the way your elders want you to!... You crave a Christmas Tree but they prefer stockings! You yearn to skate but they consider the weather better for corn-popping! You ask for a bicycle but they had already found a very nice bargain in flannels! You beg to dine the gay-kerchiefed Scissor-Grinder's child, but they invite the Minister's toothless mother-in-law!... And when you're old enough to go courting," he sighed, "your lady-love's sentiments are outraged if you don't spend the day with her and your own family are perfectly furious if you don't spend the day with them!... And after you're married?" With a gesture of ultimate despair he sank back into his cushions. "N—o, no one, I suppose, in the whole world, has ever spent Christmas just exactly the way he wanted to!"

"Well, I," triumphed Flame, "have got a chance to spend Christmas just exactly the way I want to!... The one chance perhaps in a life-time, it would seem!... No heart aches involved, no hurt feelings, no disappointments for anybody! Nobody left out! Nobody dragged in! Why Father-Funny," she cried. "It's an experience that might distinguish me all my life long! Even when I'm very old and crumpled people would point me out on the street and say '*There's* some one who once spent Christmas just exactly the way she wanted to'!" To a limpness almost unbelievable the eager little figure wilted down within its blanket-wrapper swathings. "And now ..." deprecated Flame, "Mother has gone and wished me on Aunt Minna instead!" With a sudden revival of enthusiasm two small hands crept out of their big cuffs and clutched her Father by the ears. "Oh Father-Funny!" pleaded Flame. "If you were too old to want it for a 'holler' day and not quite old enough to need it for a holy day ... so that all you asked in the world was just to have it a *holly* day! Something all bright! Red and green! And tinsel! and jingle-bells!... How would you like to have Aunt Minna wished on you?... It isn't you know as though Aunt Minna was a—a pleasant person," she argued with perfectly indisputable logic. "You couldn't wish one 'A Merry Aunt Minna' any more than you could wish 'em a 'Merry Good Friday'!" From the clutch on his ears the small hands crept to a point at the back of his neck where they encompassed him suddenly in a crunching hug. "Oh Father-Funny!" implored Flame, "You were a Lay Reader once! You must have had *very* amorous eyes! Couldn't you *please* persuade Mother that..."

With a crisp flutter of skirts Flame's Mother, herself, appeared abruptly in the door. Her manner was very excited.

"Why wherever in the world have you people been?" she cried. "Are you stone deaf? Didn't you hear the telephone? Couldn't you even hear me calling? Your Uncle Wally is worse! That is he's better but he thinks he's worse! And they want us to come at once! It's something about a new will! The Lawyer telephoned! He advises us to come at once! They've sent an automobile for us! It will be here any minute!... But whatever in the world shall we do about Flame?" she cried distractedly. "You know how Uncle Wally feels about having young people in the house! And she can't possibly go to Aunt Minna's till to-morrow! And...."

"But you see I'm not going to Aunt Minna's!" announced Flame quite serenely. Slipping down from her Father's lap she stood with a round, roly-poly flannel sort of dignity confronting both her parents. "Father says I don't have to!"

"Why, Flame!" protested her Father.

"No, of course, you didn't say it with your mouth," admitted Flame. "But you said it with your skin and bones!— I could feel it working."

"Not go to your Aunt Minna's?" gasped her Mother. "What do you want to do?... Stay at home and spend Christmas with the Lay Reader?"

"When you and Father talk like that," murmured Flame with some hauteur, "I don't know whether you're trying to run him down ... or run him up."

"Well, how do you feel about him yourself?" veered her Father quite irrelevantly.

"Oh, I like him—some," conceded Flame. In her bright cheeks suddenly an even brighter color glowed. "I like him when he leaves out the Litany," she said. "I've told him I like him when he leaves out the Litany.—He's leaving it out more and more I notice.—Yes, I like him very much."

"But this Aunt Minna business," veered back her Father suddenly. "What *do* you want to do? That's just the question. What *do* you want to do?"

"Yes, what do you want to do?" panted her Mother.

"I want to make a Christmas for myself!" said Flame. "Oh, of course, I know perfectly well," she agreed, "that I could go to a dozen places in the Parish and be cry-babied over for my presumable loneliness. And probably I *should* cry a little," she wavered, "towards the dessert—when the plum pudding came in and it wasn't like Mother's.—But if I made a Christmas of my own—" she rallied instantly. "Everything about it would be brand-new and unassociated! I tell you I *want* to make a Christmas of my own! It's the chance of a life-time! Even Father sees that it's the chance of a life-time!"

"Do you?" demanded his wife a bit pointedly.

"*Honk-honk!*" screamed the motor at the door.

"Oh, dear me, whatever in the world shall I do?" cried Flame's Mother. "I'm almost distracted! I'm—"

"When in Doubt do as the Doubters do," suggested Flame's Father quite genially. "Choose the most doubtful doubt on the docket and—Flame's got a pretty level head," he interrupted himself very characteristically.

"No young girl has a level heart," asserted Flame's Mother. "I'm so worried about the Lay Reader."

"Lay Reader?" murmured her Father. Already he had crossed the threshold into the hall and was rummaging through an over-loaded hat rack for his fur coat. "Why, yes," he called back, "I quite forgot to ask. Just what kind of a Christmas is it, Flame, that you want to make?" With unprecedented accuracy he turned at the moment to force his wife's arms into the sleeves of her own fur coat.

Twice Flame rolled up her cuffs and rolled them down again before she answered.

"I—I want to make a Surprise for Miss Flora," she confided.

"*Honk-honk!*" urged the automobile.

"For Miss Flora?" gasped her Mother.

"Miss Flora?" echoed her Father.

"Why, at the Rattle-Pane House, you know!" rallied Flame. "Don't you remember that I called there this afternoon? It—it looked rather lonely there.—I—think I could fix it."

"Honk-honk-honk!" implored the automobile.

"But who *is* this Miss Flora?" cried her Mother. "I never heard anything so ridiculous in my life! How do we know she's respectable?"

"Oh, my dear," deprecated Flame's Father. "Just as though the owners of the Rattle-Pane House would rent it to any one who wasn't respectable!"

"Oh, she's *very* respectable," insisted Flame. "Of a lineage so distinguished—"

"How old might this paragon be?" queried her Father.

"Old?" puzzled Flame. To her startled mind two answers only presented themselves.... Should she say "Oh, she's only just weaned," or "Well,—she was invented about 1406?" Between these two dilemmas a single compromise suggested itself. "She's *awfully* wrinkled," said Flame; "that is—her face is. All wizened up, I mean."

"Oh, then of course she *must* be respectable," twinkled Flame's Father.

"And is related in some way," persisted Flame, "to Edward the 2nd—Duke of York."

"Of that guarantee of respectability I am, of course, not quite so sure," said her Father.

With a temperish stamping of feet, an infuriate yank of the door-bell, Uncle Wally's chauffeur announced that the limit of his endurance had been reached.

Blankly Flame's Mother stared at Flame's Father. Blankly Flame's Father returned the stare.

"Oh, *p-l-e-a-s-e*!" implored Flame. Her face was crinkled like fine crêpe.

"Smooth out your nose!" ordered her Mother. On the verge of capitulation the same familiar fear assailed her. "Will you promise not to see the Lay Reader?" she bargained.

"—Yes'm," said Flame.

PART II

It's a dull person who doesn't wake up Christmas Morning with a curiously ticklish sense of Tinsel in the pit of his stomach!—A sort of a Shine! A kind of a Pain!

"Glisten and Tears,Pang of the years."

That's Christmas!

So much was born on Christmas Day! So much has died! So much is yet to come! Balsam-Scented, with the pulse of bells, how the senses sing! Memories that wouldn't have batted an eye for all the Gabriel Trumpets in Eternity leaping to life at the sound of a twopenny horn! Merry Folk who were with us once and are no more! Dream Folk who have never been with us yet but will be some time! Ache of old carols! Zest of new-fangled games! Flavor of puddings! Shine of silver and glass! The pleasant frosty smell of the Express-man! The Gift Beautiful! The Gift Dutiful! The Gift that Didn't Come! *Heigho*! Manger and Toy-Shop,—Miracle and Mirth,—

"Glisten and Tears,LAUGH at the years!"

That's Christmas!

Flame Nourice certainly was willing to laugh at the years. Eighteen usually is!

Waking at Dawn two single thoughts consumed her,—the Lay Reader, and the humpiest of the express packages downstairs.

The Lay Reader's name was Bertrand. "Bertrand the Lay Reader," Flame always called him. The rest of the Parish called him Mr. Laurello.

It was the thought of Bertrand the Lay Reader that made Flame laugh the most.

"As long as I've promised most faithfully not to see him," she laughed, "how can I possibly go to church? For the first Christmas in my life," she laughed, "I won't have to go to church!"

With this obligation so cheerfully canceled, the exploration of the humpiest express package loomed definitely as the next task on the horizon.

Hoping for a fur coat from her Father, fearing for a set of encyclopedias from her Mother, she tore back the wrappings with eager hands only to find,—all-astonished, and half a-scream,—a gay, gauzy layer of animal masks nosing interrogatively up at her. Less practical surely than the fur coat,—more amusing, certainly, than encyclopedias,—the funny "false faces" grinned up at her with a curiously excitative audacity. Where from?—No identifying card! What for? No conceivable clew!—Unless perhaps just on general principles a donation for the Sunday School Christmas Tree?—But there wasn't going to be any tree! Tentatively she reached into the box and touched the fiercely striped face of a tiger, the fantastically exaggerated beak of a red and green parrot. "U-m-m-m," mused Flame. "Whatever in the world shall I do with them?" Then quite abruptly she sank back on her heels and began to laugh and laugh and laugh. Even the Lay Reader had not received such a laughing But even to herself she did not say just what she was laughing at. It was a time for deeds, it would seem, and not for words.

Certainly the morning was very full of deeds!

There was, of course, a present from her Mother to be opened,—warm, woolly stockings and things like that. But no one was ever swerved from an original purpose by trying on warm, woolly stockings. And from her Father there was the most absurd little box no bigger than your nose marked, "For a week in New York," and stuffed to the brim with the sweetest bright green dollar bills. But, of course, you couldn't try those on. And half the Parish sent presents. But no Parish ever sent presents that needed to be tried on. No gay, fluffy scarfs,—no lacey, frivolous pettiskirts,—no bright delaying hat-ribbons! Just books,—illustrated poems usually, very wholesome pickles,—and always a huge motto to recommend, "Peace on Earth, Good Will to Men."—To "Men"?—Why not to Women?—Why not at least to "*Dogs*?" questioned Flame quite abruptly.

Taken all in all it was not a Christmas Morning of sentiment but a Christmas morning of *works*! Kitchen works, mostly! Useful, flavorous adventures with a turkey! A somewhat nervous sally with an apple pie! Intermittently, of course, a few experiments with flour paste! A flaire or two with a paint brush! An errand to the attic! Interminable giggles!

Surely it was four o'clock before she was even ready to start for the Rattle-Pane House. And "starting" is by no means the same as arriving. Dragging a sledful of miscellaneous Christmas goods an eighth of a mile over bare ground is not an easy task. She had to make three tugging trips. And each start was delayed by her big gray pussy cat stealing out to try to follow her. And each arrival complicated by the yelpings and leapings and general cavortings of four dogs who didn't see any reason in the world why they shouldn't escape from their forced imprisonment in the shed-yard and prance home with her. Even with the third start and the third arrival finally accomplished, the crafty cat stood waiting for her on the steps of the Rattle-Pane House,—back arched, fur bristled, spitting like some new kind of weather-cock at the storm in the shed-yard, and had to be thrust quite unceremoniously into a much too small covered basket and lashed down with yards and yards of tinsel that was needed quite definitely for something else.—It isn't just the way of the Transgressor that's hard.—Nobody's way is any too easy!

The door-key, though, was exactly where the old Butler had said it would be,—under the door mat, and the key itself turned astonishingly cordially in the rusty old lock. Never in her whole little life having owned a door-key to her own house it seemed quite an adventure in itself to be walking thus possessively through an unfamiliar hall into an absolutely unknown kitchen and goodness knew what on either side and beyond.

Perfectly simply too as the old Butler had promised, the four dog dishes, heaping to the brim, loomed in prim line upon the kitchen table waiting for distribution.

"U-m-m," sniffed Flame. "Nothing but mush! *Mush!*—All over the world to-day I suppose—while their masters are feasting at other people's houses on puddings and—and cigarettes! How the poor darlings must suffer! Locked in sheds! Tied in yards! Stuffed down cellar!"

"Me-o-w," twinged a plaintive hint from the hallway just outside.

"Oh, but cats are different," argued Flame. "So soft, so plushy, so spineless! Cats were *meant* to be stuffed into things."

Without further parleying she doffed her red tam and sweater, donned a huge white all-enveloping pinafore, and started to ameliorate as best she could the Christmas sufferings of the "poor darlings" immediately at hand.

It was at least a yellow kitchen,—or had been once. In all that gray, dank, neglected house, the one suggestion of old sunshine.

"We shall have our dinner here," chuckled Flame. "After the carols—we shall have our dinner here."

Very boisterously in the yard just outside the window the four dogs scuffled and raced for sheer excitement and joy at this most unexpected advent of human companionship. Intermittently from time to time by the aid of old boxes or barrels they clawed their way up to the cobwebby window-sill to peer at the strange proceedings. Intermittently from time to time they fell back into the frozen yard in a chaos of fur and yelps.

By five o'clock certainly the faded yellow kitchen must have looked very strange, even to a dog!

Straight down its dingy, wobbly-floored center stretched a long table cheerfully spread with "the Rev. Mrs. Flamande Nourice's" second best table cloth. Quaint high-backed chairs dragged in from the shadowy parlor circled the table. A pleasant china plate gleamed like a hand-painted moon before each chair. At one end of the table loomed a big brown turkey; at the other, the appropriate vegetables. Pies, cakes, and doughnuts, interspersed themselves between. Green wreaths streaming with scarlet ribbons hung nonchalantly across every chair-top. Tinsel garlands shone on the walls. In the doorway reared a hastily constructed mimicry of a railroad crossing sign.

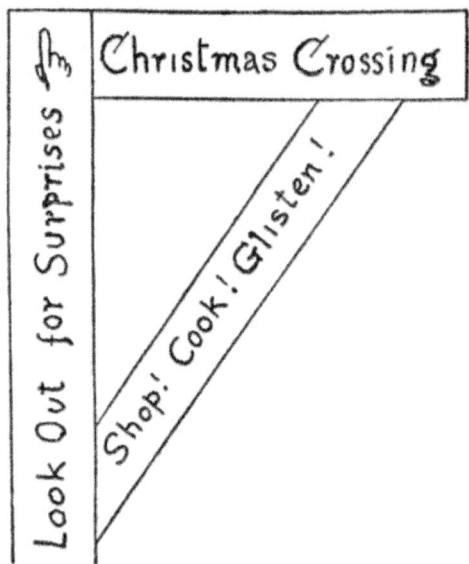

Directly opposite and conspicuously placed above the rusty stove-pipe stretched the Parish's Gift Motto—duly re-adjusted.

"*Peace* on *Earth*, Good Will to *Dogs*."

"Fatuously silly," admitted Flame even to herself. "But yet it does add something to the Gayety of Rations!"

Stepping aside for a single thrilling moment to study the full effect of her handiwork, the first psychological puzzle of her life smote sharply across her senses. Namely, that you never really get the whole fun out of anything unless you are absolutely alone.—But the very first instant you find yourself absolutely alone with a Really-Good-Time you begin to twist and turn and hunt about for somebody Very Special to share it with you!

The only "Very Special" person that Flame could think of was "Bertrand the Lay Reader."

All a-blush with the sheer mental surprise of it she fled to the shed door to summon the dogs.

"Maybe even the dogs won't come!" she reasoned hectically. "Maybe nothing will come! Maybe that's always the way things happen when you get your own way about something else!"

Like a blast from the Arctic the Christmas twilight swept in on her. It crisped her cheeks,—crinkled her hair! Turned her spine to a wisp of tinsel! All outdoors seemed suddenly creaking with frost! All indoors, with *unknownness*!

"Come, Beautiful-Lovely!" she implored. "Come, Lopsy! Miss Flora! Come, Blunder-Blot!'"

But there was really no need of entreaty. A turn of the door-knob would have brought them! Leaping, loping, four abreast, they came plunging like so many North Winds to their party! Streak of Snow,—Glow of Fire,—Frozen Mud—Sun-Spot!—Yelping-mouthed—slapping-tailed! Backs bristling! Legs stiffening! Wolf Hound, Setter, Bull Dog, Dalmatian,—each according to his kind, hurtling, crowding!

"Oh, dear me, dear me," struggled Flame. "Maybe a carol would calm them."

To a certain extent a carol surely did. The hair-cloth parlor of the Rattle-Pane House would have calmed anything. And the mousey smell of the old piano fairly jerked the dogs to its senile old ivory keyboard. Cocking their ears to its quavering treble notes,—snorting their nostrils through its gritty guttural basses, they watched Flame's facile fingers sweep from sound to sound.

"Oh, what a—glorious lark!" quivered Flame. "What a—a *lonely* glorious lark!"

Timidly at first but with an increasing abandon, half laughter and half tears, the clear young soprano voice took up its playful paraphrase,

"God rest you merrie—animals!Let nothing you dismay!"

caroled Flame.

"For—"

It was just at this moment that Beautiful-Lovely, the Wolf Hound,—muzzled lifted, eyes rolling, jabbed his shrill nose into space and harmony with a carol of his own,—octaves of agony,—Heaven knows what of ecstasy,—that would have hurried an owl to its nest, a ghoul to a moving picture show!

"Wow-Wow—*Wow*!" caroled Beautiful-Lovely. "Ww—ow—Ww—ow—*Ww—Oo—Wwwww*!"

As Flame's hands dropped from the piano the unmistakable creak of red wheels sounded on the frozen driveway just outside.

No one but "Bertrand the Lay Reader" drove a buggy with red wheels! To the infinite scandalization of the Parish—no one but "Bertrand the Lay Reader" drove a buggy with red wheels!—Fleet steps sounded suddenly on the path! Startled fists beat furiously on the door!

"What is it? What is it?" shouted a familiar voice. "Whatever in the world is happening? Is it *murder*? Let me in! *Let me in!*"

"Sil—ly!" hissed Flame through a crack in the door. "It's nothing but a party! Don't you know a—a party when you hear it?"

For an instant only, blank silence greeted her confidence. Then "Bertrand the Lay Reader" relaxed in an indisputably genuine gasp of astonishment.

"Why! Why, is that you, Miss Flame?" he gasped. "Why, I thought it was a murder! Why—Why, whatever in the world are you doing here?"

"I—I'm having a party," hissed Flame through the key-hole.

"A—a—party?" stammered the Lay Reader. "Open the door!"

"No, I—can't," said Flame.

"Why not?" demanded the Lay Reader.

Helplessly in the darkness of the vestibule Flame looked up,—and down,—and sideways,—but met always in every direction the memory of her promise.

"I—I just can't," she admitted a bit weakly. "It wouldn't be convenient.—I—I've got trouble with my eyes."

"Trouble with your eyes?" questioned the Lay Reader.

"I didn't go away with my Father and Mother," confided Flame.

"No,—so I notice," observed the Lay Reader. "*Please* open the door!"

"Why?" parried Flame.

"I've been looking for you everywhere," urged the Lay Reader. "At the Senior Warden's! At all the Vestrymen's houses! Even at the Sexton's! I knew you didn't go away! The Garage Man told me there were only two!—I thought surely I'd find you at your own house.—But I only found sled tracks."

"That was me,—I," mumbled Flame.

"And then I heard these awful screams," shuddered the Lay Reader.

"That was a Carol," said Flame.

"A Carol?" scoffed the Lay Reader. "Open the door!"

"Well—just a crack," conceded Flame.

It was astonishing how a man as broad-shouldered as the Lay Reader could pass so easily through a crack.

Conscience-stricken Flame fled before him with her elbow crooked across her forehead.

"Oh, my eyes! My eyes!" she cried.

"Well, really," puzzled the Lay Reader. "Though I claim, of course, to be ordinarily bright—I had never suspected myself of being actually dazzling."

"Oh, you're not bright at all," protested Flame. "It's just my promise.—I promised Mother not to see you!"

"Not to see *me*?" questioned the Lay Reader. It was astonishing how almost instantaneously a man as purely theoretical as the Lay Reader was supposed to be, thought of a perfectly practical solution to the difficulty. "Why—why we might tie my big handkerchief across your eyes," he suggested. "Just till we get this mystery straightened out.—Surely there is nothing more or less than just plain righteousness in—that!"

"What a splendid idea!" capitulated Flame. "But, of course, if I'm absolutely blindfolded," she wavered for a second only, "you'll have to lead me by the hand."

"I could do that," admitted the Lay Reader.

With the big white handkerchief once tied firmly across her eyes, Flame's last scruple vanished.

"Well, you see," she began quite precipitously, "I *did* think it would be such fun to have a party!—A party all my own, I mean!—A party just exactly as I wanted it! No Parish in it at all! Or good works! Or anything! Just *fun*!—And as long as Mother and Father had to go away anyway—" Even though the blinding bandage the young eyes seemed to lift in a half wistful sort of appeal. "You see there's some sort of property involved," she confided quite impulsively. "Uncle Wally's making a new will. There's a corn-barn and a private chapel and a collection of Chinese lanterns and a piebald pony principally under dispute.—Mother, of course thinks we ought to have the corn-barn. But Father can't decide between the Chinese lanterns and the private chapel.—Personally," she sighed, "I'm hoping for the piebald pony."

"Yes, but this—party?" prodded the Lay Reader.

"Oh, yes,—the party—" quickened Flame.

"Why have it in a deserted house?" questioned the Lay Reader with some incisiveness.

Even with her eyes closely bandaged Flame could see perfectly clearly that the Lay Reader was really quite troubled.

"Oh, but you see it isn't exactly a deserted house," she explained.

"Who lives here?" demanded the Lay Reader.

"I don't know—exactly," admitted Flame. "But the Butler is a friend of mine and—"

"The—Butler is a friend of yours?" gasped the Lay Reader. Already, if Flame could only have seen it, his head was cocked with sudden intentness towards the parlor door. "There is certainly something very strange about all this," he whispered a bit hectically. "I could almost have sworn that I heard a faint scuffle,—the horrid sound of a person—strangling."

"Strangling?" giggled Flame. "Oh, that is just the sound of Miss Flora's 'girlish glee'! If she'd only be content to chew the corner of the piano cover! But when she insists on inhaling it, too!"

"Miss Flora?" gasped the Lay Reader. "Is this a Mad House?"

"Miss Flora is a—a dog," confided Flame a bit coolly. "I neglected—it seems—to state that this is a dog-party that I'm having."

"*Dogs*?" winced the Lay Reader. "Will they bite?"

"Only if you don't trust them," confided Flame.

"But it's so hard to trust a dog that will bite you if you don't trust him," frowned the Lay Reader. "It makes such a sort of a—a vicious circle, as it were."

"Vicious Circe?" mused Flame, a bit absent-mindedly. "No, I don't think it's nice at all to call Miss Flora a 'Vicious Circe.'" It was Flame's turn now to wince back a little. "I—I hate people who hate dogs!" she cried out quite abruptly.

"Oh, I don't hate them," lied the Lay Reader like a gentleman, "it's only that—that—. You see a dog bit me once!" he confided with significant emphasis.

"I—bit a dentist—once," mused Flame without any emphasis at all.

"Oh, but I say, Miss Flame," deprecated the Lay Reader. "That's different! When a dog bites you, you know, there's always more or less question whether he was mad or not."

"There doesn't seem to have been any question at all," mused Flame, "that *you* were mad! Did you have *your* head sent off to be investigated or anything?"

"Oh, I say, Miss Flame," implored the Lay Reader, "I tell you I *like* dogs,—good dogs! I assure you I'm very—oh, very much interested in this dog party of yours! Such a quaint idea! So—so—! If I could be of any possible assistance?" he implored.

"Maybe you could be," relaxed Flame ever so faintly. "But if you're really coming to my party," she stiffened again, "you've got to behave like my party!"

"Why, of course I'll behave like your party!" laughed the Lay Reader.

"There *is* a problem," admitted Flame. "Five problems, to be perfectly accurate.—Four dogs, and a cat in the wood-shed."

"And a cat in the wood-shed?" echoed the Lay Reader quite idiotically.

"The table is set," affirmed Flame. "The places, all ready!—But I don't know how to get the dogs into their chairs!—They run around so! They yelp! They jump!—They haven't had a mouthful to eat, you see, since last night, this time!—And when they once see the turkey I'm—I'm afraid they'll stampede it."

"Turkey?" quizzed the Lay Reader who had dined that day on corned beef.

"Oh, of course, mush was what they were intended to have," admitted Flame. "Piles and piles of mush! Extra piles and piles of mush I should judge because it was Christmas Day!... But don't you think mush does seem a bit dull?" she questioned appealingly. "For Christmas Day? Oh, I did think a turkey would taste so good!"

"It certainly would," conceded the Lay Reader.

"So if you'd help me—" wheedled Flame, "it would be well-worth staying blindfolded for.... For, of course, I shall have to stay blindfolded. But I can see a little of the floor," she admitted, "though I couldn't of course break my promise to my Mother by seeing you."

"No, certainly not," admitted the Lay Reader.

"Otherwise—" murmured Flame with a faint gesture towards the door.

"I will help you," said the Lay Reader.

"Where is your hand?" fumbled Flame.

"*Here!*" attested the Lay Reader.

"Lead us to the dogs!" commanded Flame.

Now the Captain of a ship feels genuinely obligated, it would seem, to go down with his ship if tragic circumstances so insist. But he never,—so far as I've ever heard, felt the slightest obligation whatsoever to go down with another captain's ship,—to be martyred in short for any job not distinctly his own. So Bertrand Lorello,—who for the cause he served, wouldn't have hesitated an instant probably, to be torn by Hindoo lions,—devoured by South Sea cannibals,—fallen upon by a chapel spire,—trampled to death even at a church rummage sale,—saw no conceivable reason at the moment for being eaten by dogs at a purely social function.

Even groping through a balsam-scented darkness with one hand clasping the thrilly fingers of a lovely young girl, this distaste did not altogether leave him.

"This—this mush that you speak of?" he questioned quite abruptly. "With the dogs as—as nervous as you say,—so unfortunately liable to stampede? Don't you think that perhaps a little mush served first,—a good deal of mush I would say, served first,—might act as a—as a sort of anesthetic?... Somewhere in the past I am almost sure I have read that mush in sufficient quantities, you understand, is really quite a—quite an anesthetic."

Very palpably in the darkness he heard a single throaty swallow.

"Lead us to the—mush," said Flame.

In another instant the door-knob turned in his hand, and the cheerful kitchen lamp-light,—glitter of tinsel,—flare of red ribbons,—savor of foods, smote sharply on him.

"Oh, I say, how *jolly!*" cried the Lay Reader.

"Don't let me bump into anything!" begged the blindfolded Flame, still holding tight to his hand.

"Oh, I say, Miss Flame," kindled the entranced Lay Reader, "it's *you* that look the jolliest! All in white that way! I've never seen you wear *that* to church, have I?"

"This is a pinafore," confided Flame coolly. "A bungalow apron, the fashion papers call it.... No, you've never seen me wear—this to church."

"O—h," said the Lay Reader.

"Get the mush," said Flame.

"The what?" asked the Lay Reader.

"It's there on the table by the window," gestured Flame. "Please set all four dishes on the floor,—each dish, of course, in a separate corner," ordered Flame. "There is a reason.... And then open the parlor door."

"Open the parlor door?" questioned the Lay Reader. It was no mere grammatical form of speech but a real query in the Lay Reader's mind.

"Well, maybe I'd better," conceded Flame. "Lead me to it."

Roused into frenzy by the sound of a stranger's step, a stranger's voice, the four dogs fumed and seethed on the other side of the panel.

"*Sniff—Sniff—Snort!*" the Red Setter sucked at the crack in the door.

"Woof! Woof! *Woof!*" roared the big Wolf Hound.

"Slam! Bang! Slash!" slapped the Dalmatian's crisp weight.

"Yi! Yi! Yi!" sang the Bull Dog.

"Hush! *Hush*, Dogs!" implored Flame. "This is Father's Lay Reader!"

"Your—Lay Reader!" contradicted the young man gallantly. It *was* pretty gallant of him, wasn't it? Considering everything?

In another instant four *shapes* with teeth in them came hurtling through!

If Flame had never in her life admired the Lay Reader she certainly would have admired him now for the sheer cold-blooded foresight which had presaged the inevitable reaction of the dogs upon the mush and the mush upon the dogs. With a single sniff at his heels, a prod of paws in his stomach, the onslaught swerved—and passed. Guzzlingly from four separate corners of the room issued sounds of joy and fulfillment.

With an impulse quite surprising even to herself Flame thrust both hands into the Lay Reader's clasp.

"You *are* nice, aren't you?" she quickened. In an instant of weakness one hand crept up to the blinding bandage, and recovered its honor as instantly. "Oh, I do wish I *could* see you," sighed Flame. "You're so good-looking! Even Mother thinks you're *so* good-looking!... Though she does get awfully worked up, of course, about your 'amorous eyes'!"

"Does your Mother think I've got ... 'amorous eyes'?" asked the Lay Reader a bit tersely. Behind his spectacles as he spoke the orbs in question softened and glowed like some rare exotic bloom under glass. "Does your Mother ... think I've got amorous eyes?"

"Oh, yes!" said Flame.

"And your Father?" drawled the Lay Reader.

"Why, Father says *of course* you've got 'amorous eyes'!" confided Flame with the faintest possible tinge of surprise at even being asked such a question. "That's the funny thing about Mother and Father," chuckled Flame. "They're always saying the same thing and meaning something entirely different by it. Why, when Mother says with her mouth all pursed up, 'I have every reason to believe that Mr. Lorello is engaged to the daughter of the Rector in his former Parish,' Father just puts back his head and howls, and says, 'Why, *of course*, Mr. Lorello is engaged to the daughter of the Rector in his former Parish! All Lay Readers...."

In the sudden hush that ensued a faint sense of uneasiness flickered through Flame's shoulders.

"Is it you that have hushed? Or the dogs?" she asked.

"The dogs," said the Lay Reader.

Very cautiously, absolutely honorably, Flame turned her back to the Lay Reader, and lifted the bandage just far enough to prove the Lay Reader's assertion.

Bulging with mush the four dogs lay at rest on rounding sides with limp legs straggling, or crouched like lions' heads on paws, with limpid eyes blinking above yawny mouths.

"O—h," crooned Flame. "How sweet! Only, of course, with what's to follow," she regretted thriftily, "it's an awful waste of mush.... Excelsior warmed in the oven would have served just as well."

At the threat of a shadow across her eyeball she jerked the bandage back into place.

"Now, Mr. Lorello," she suggested blithely, "if you'll get the Bibles...."

"Bibles?" stiffened the Lay Reader. "Bibles? Why, really, Miss Flame, I couldn't countenance any sort of mock service! Even just for—for quaintness,—even for Christmas quaintness!"

"Mock service?" puzzled Flame. "Bibles?... Oh, I don't want you to preach out of 'em," she hastened perfectly amiably to explain. "All I want them for is to plump-up the chairs.... The seats you see are too low for the dogs.... Oh, I suppose dictionaries would do," she compromised reluctantly. "Only dictionaries are always so scarce."

Obediently the Lay Reader raked the parlor book-cases for "plump-upable" books. With real dexterity he built Chemistries on Sermons and Ancient Poems on Cook Books till the desired heights were reached.

For a single minute more Flame took another peep at the table.

"Set a chair for yourself directly opposite me!" she ordered. For sheer hilarious satisfaction her feet began to dance and her hands to clap. "And whenever I really feel obliged to look," she sparkled, "you'll just have to leave the table, that's all!... And now...?" Appraisingly her muffled eye swept the shining vista. "Perfect!" she triumphed. "Perfect!" Then quite abruptly the eager mouth wilted. "Why ... Why I've forgotten the carving knife and fork!" she cried out in real distress. "Oh, how stupid of me!" Arduously, but without avail, she searched through all the drawers and cupboards of the Rattle-Pane kitchen. A single alternative occurred to her. "You'll have to go over to my house and get them,—Mr. Lorello!" she said. "Were you ever in my kitchen? Or my pantry?"

"No," admitted the Lay Reader.

"Well, you'll have to climb in through the window—someway," worried Flame. "I've mislaid my key somewhere here among all these dishes and boxes. And the pantry," she explained very explicitly, "is the third door on the right as you enter.... You'll see a chest of drawers. Open the second of 'em.... Or maybe you'd better look through all of them.... Only please ... please hurry!" Imploringly the little head lifted.

"If I hurry enough," said the Lay Reader quite impulsively, "may I have a kiss when I get back?"

"A kiss?" hooted Flame. In the curve of her cheek a dimple opened suddenly. "Well ... maybe," said Flame.

As though the word were wings the Lay Reader snatched his hat and sped out into the night.

It was astonishing how all the warm housey air seemed to rush out with him, and all the shivery frost rush back.

A little bit listlessly Flame dragged down the bandage from her eyes.

"It must be the creaks on the stairs that make it so awfully lonely all of a sudden," argued Flame. "It must be because the dogs snore so.... No mere man could make it so empty." With a precipitous nudge of the memory she dashed to the door and helloed to the fast retreating figure. "Oh, Bertrand! Bertrand!" she called, "I got sort of mixed up. It's the second door on the left! And if you don't find 'em there you'd better go up in Mother's room and turn out the silver chest! *Hurry*!"

Rallying back to the bright Christmas kitchen for the real business at hand, an accusing blush rose to the young spot where the dimple had been.

"Oh, Shucks!" parried Flame. "I kissed a Bishop before I was five!—What's a Lay Reader?" As one humanely willing to condone the future as well as the past she rolled up her white sleeves without further introspection, and dragged out from the protecting shadow of the sink the "humpiest box" which had so excited her emotions at home in an earlier hour of the day. Cracklingly under her eager fingers the clumsy cover slid off, exposing once more to her enraptured gaze the gay-colored muslin layer of animal masks leering fatuously up at her.

Only with her hand across her mouth did she keep from crying out. Very swiftly her glance traveled from the grinning muslin faces before her to the solemn fur faces on the other side of the room. The hand across her mouth tightened.

"Why, it's something like Creation," she giggled. "This having to decide which face to give to which animal!"

As expeditiously as possible she made her selection.

"Poor Miss Flora must be so tired of being so plain," she thought. "I'll give her the first choice of everything! Something really lovely! It can't help resting her!"

With this kind idea in mind she selected for Miss Flora a canary's face.—Softly yellow! Bland as treacle! Its swelling, tender muslin throat fairly reeking with the suggestion of innocent song! No one gazing once upon such ornithological purity would ever speak a harsh word again, even to a sparrow!

Nudging Miss Flora cautiously from her sonorous nap, Flame beguiled her with half a doughnut to her appointed chair, boosted her still cautiously to her pinnacle of books, and with various swift adjustments of fasteners, knotting of tie-strings,—an extra breathing hole jabbed through the beak, slipped the canary's beautiful blond countenance over Miss Flora's frankly grizzled mug.

For a single terrifying instant Miss Flora's crinkled sides tightened,—a snarl like ripped silk slipped through her straining lungs. Then once convinced that the mask was not a gas-box she accepted the liberty with reasonable *sang-froid* and sat blinking beadily out through the canary's yellow-rimmed eye-sockets with frank curiosity towards such proceedings as were about to follow. It was easy to see she was accustomed to sitting in chairs.

For the Wolf Hound Flame chose a Giraffe's head. Certain anatomical similarities seemed to make the choice wise. With a long vividly striped stockinet neck wrinkling like a mousquetaire glove, the neat small head that so closely fitted his own neat small head, the tweaked, interrogative ears,—Beautiful-Lovely, the Wolf Hound, reared up majestically in his own chair. He also, once convinced that the mask was not a gas-box, resigned himself to the inevitable, and corporeally independent of such vain props as Chemistries or Sermons, lolled his fine height against the mahogany chair-back.

To Blunder-Blot, the trim Dalmatian, Flame assigned the Parrot's head, arrogantly beaked, gorgeously variegated, altogether querulous.

For Lopsy, the crafty Setter, she selected a White Rabbit's artless, pink-eared visage.

Yet out of the whole box of masks it had been the Bengal Tiger's fiercely bewhiskered visage that had fascinated Flame the most. Regretfully from its more or less nondescript companions, she picked up the Bengal Tiger now and pulled at its real, bristle-whiskers. In one of the chairs a dog stirred quite irrelevantly. Cocking her own head towards the wood-shed Flame could not be perfectly sure whether she heard a twinge of cat or a twinge of conscience. The unflinching glare of the Bengal Tiger only served to increase her self-reproach.

"After all," reasoned Flame, "it would be easy enough to set another place! And pile a few extra books!... I'm almost0 sure I saw a black plush bag in the parlor.... If the cat could be put in something like a black plush bag,—something perfectly enveloping like that? So that not a single line of its—its figure could be observed?... And it had a new head given it? A perfectly sufficient head—like a Bengal Tiger?—I see no reason why—"

In five minutes the deed was accomplished. Its lovely sinuous "figure" reduced to the stolid contour of a black plush work-bag, its small uneasy head thrust into the roomy muslin cranium of the Bengal Tiger, the astonished Cat found herself slumping soggily on a great teetering pile of books, staring down as best she might through the Bengal Tiger's ear at the weirdest assemblage of animals which any domestic cat of her acquaintance had ever been forced to contemplate.

Coincidental with the appearance of the Cat a faint thrill passed through the rest of the company.... Nothing very much! No more, no less indeed, than passes through any company at the introduction of purely extraneous matter. From the empty plate which she had commandeered as a temporary pillow the Yellow Canary lifted an interrogative beak.... That was all! At Flame's left, the White-Haired Rabbit emitted an incongruous bark.... Scarcely worth reporting! Across the table the Giraffe thumped a white, plumy tail. Thoughtfully the Parrot's hooked nose slanted slightly to one side.

"Oh, I wish Bertrand would come!" fretted Flame. "Maybe this time he'll notice my 'Christmas Crossing' sign!" she chuckled with sudden triumph. "Talk about surprises!" Very diplomatically as she spoke she broke another doughnut in two and drew all the dogs' attention to herself. Almost hysterical with amusement she surveyed the scene before her. "Well, at least we can have 'grace' before the Preacher comes!" she laughed. A step on the gravel walk startled her suddenly. In a flash she had jerked down the blind-folding handkerchief across her eyes again, and folding her hands and the doughnut before her burst softly into paraphrase.

'Now we—sit us down to eatThrice our share of Flesh and Sweet.If we should burst before we're through,Oh what in—Dogdom shall we do?'

Thus it was that the Master of the House, returning unexpectedly to his unfamiliar domicile, stumbled upon a scene that might have shaken the reason of a less sober young man.

Startled first by the unwonted illumination from his kitchen windows, and second by the unprecedented aroma of Fir Balsam that greeted him even through the key-hole of his new front door, his feelings may well be imagined when groping through the dingy hall he first beheld the gallows-like structure reared in the kitchen doorway.

"My God!" he ejaculated, "Barrett is getting ready to hang himself! Gone mad probably—or something!"

Curdled with horror he forced himself to the object, only to note with convulsive relief but increasing bewilderment the cheerful phrasing and ultimate intent of the structure itself. "'Christmas Crossing'?" he repeated blankly. "'Look out for Surprises'?—'Shop, Cook, and Glisten'?" With his hand across his eyes he reeled back slightly against the wall. "It is I that have gone mad!" he gasped.

A little uncertain whether he was afraid of What-He-Was-About-to-See, or whether What-He-Was-About-to-See ought to be afraid of him, he craned his neck as best he could round the corner of the huge buffet that blocked the kitchen vista. A fresh bewilderment met his eyes. Where he had once seen cobwebs flapping grayly across the chimney-breast loomed now the gay worsted recommendation that *dogs specially*, should be considered in the Christmas Season. Throwing all caution aside he passed the buffet and plunged into the kitchen.

"Oh, *do* hurry!" cried an eager young voice. "I thought my hair would be white before you came!"

Like a man paralyzed he stopped short in his tracks to stare at the scene before him! The long, bright table! The absolutely formal food! A blindfolded girl! A perfectly strange blindfolded girl ... with her dark hair forty years this side of white—*begging him to hurry*!... A Black Velvet Bag surmounted by a Tiger's head stirring strangely in a chair piled high with books!... Seated next to the Black Velvet Bag a Canary as big as a Turkey Gobbler!... A Giraffe stepping suddenly forward with—with dog-paws thrust into his soup plate!... A White Rabbit heavily wreathed in holly rousing cautiously from his cushions!... A Parrot with a twitching black and white short-haired tail!... An empty chair facing the Girl! *An empty chair facing the Girl.*

"If this is *madness*," thought Delcote quite precipitously, "I am at least the Master of the Asylum!"

In another instant, with a prodigious stride he had slipped into the vacant seat.

"... So sorry to have kept you waiting," he murmured.

At the first sound of that unfamiliar voice, Flame yanked the handkerchief from her eyes, took one blank glance at the Stranger, and burst forth into a muffled, but altogether blood-curdling scream.

"Oh ... Oh ... Owwwwwwww!" said the scream.

As though waiting only for that one signal to break the spell of their enchantment, the Canary leaped upward and grabbed the Bengal Tiger by his muslin nose,—the White Rabbit sprang to "point" on the cooling turkey, and the Red and Green Parrot fell to the floor in a desperate effort to settle once and for all with the black spot that itched so impulsively on his left shoulder!

For a moment only, in comparative quiet, the Concerned struggled with the Concerned. Then true to all Dog Psychology,—absolutely indisputable, absolutely unalterable, the Non-Concerned leaped in upon the Non-Concerned! Half on his guard, but wholly on his itch, the jostled Parrot shot like a catapult across the floor! Lost to all sense of honor or table-manners the benign-faced Giraffe with his benign face still towering blandly in the air, burst through his own neck with a most curious anatomical effect,—locked his teeth in the Parrot's gay throat and rolled with him under the table in mortal combat!

Round and round the room spun the Yellow Canary and the Black Plush Bag!

Retreating as best she could from her muslin nose,—the Bengal Tiger or rather that which was within the Bengal Tiger, waged her war for Freedom! Ripping like a chicken through its shell she succeeded at last in hatching one front paw and one hind paw into action. Wallowing,—stumbling,—rolling,—yowling,—she humped from mantle-piece to chair-top, and from box to table.

Loyally the rabbit-eared Setter took up the chase. Mauled in the scuffle he ran with his meek face upside down! Lost to all reason, defiant of all morale, he proceeded to flush the game!

Dish-pans clattered, stools tipped over, pictures banged on the walls!

From her terrorized perch on the back of her chair Flame watched the fracas with dilated eyes.

Hunched in the hug of his own arms the Stranger sat rocking himself to and fro in uncontrollable, choking mirth,—"ribald mirth" was what Flame called it.

"Stop!" she begged. "Stop it! Somebody *stop* it!"

It was not until the Black Plush Bag at bay had ripped a red streak down Miss Flora's avid nose that the Stranger rose to interfere.

Very definitely then, with quick deeds, incisive words, he separated the immediate combatants, and ordered the other dogs into submission.

"Here you, Demon Direful!" he ad0ressed the white Wolf Hound. "Drop that, Orion!" he shouted to the Irish Setter. "Cut it out, John!" he thundered at the Coach Dog.

"Their names are 'Beautiful-Lovely'!" cried Flame. "And 'Lopsy!' and 'Blunder-Blot!'"

With his hand on the Wolf Hound's collar, the Stranger stopped and stared up with frank astonishment, not to say resentment, at the girl's interference.

"Their names are *what*?" he said.

Something in the special intonation of the question infuriated Flame.... Maybe she thought his mouth scornful,—his narrowing eyes...? Goodness knows what she thought of his suddenly narrowing eyes!

In an instant she had jumped from her retreat to the floor.

"Who are you, anyway?" she demanded. "How dare you come here like this? Butting into my party!... And—and spoiling my discipline with the dogs! Who are you, I say?"

With Demon Direful, alias Beautiful-Lovely tugging wildly at his restraint, the Stranger's scornful mouth turned precipitously up, instead of down.

"Who am I?" he said. "Why, no one special at all except just—the Master of the House!"

"*What?*" gasped Flame.

"Earle Delcote," bowed the Stranger.

With a little hand that trembled perfectly palpably Flame reached back to the arm of the big carved chair for support.

"Why—why, but Mr. Delcote is an old man," she gasped. "I'm almost sure he's an old man."

The smile on Delcote's mouth spread suddenly to his eyes.

"Not yet,—Thank God!" he bowed.

With a panic-stricken glance at doors, windows, cracks, the chimney pipe itself, Flame sank limply down in her seat again and gestured towards the empty place opposite her.

"Have a—have a chair," she stammered. Great tears welled suddenly to her eyes. "Oh, I—I know I oughtn't to be here," she struggled. "It's perfectly ... awful! I haven't the slightest right! Not the slightest! It's the—the cheekiest thing that any girl in the world ever did!... But your Butler said...! And he did so want to go away and—And I did so love your dogs! And I did so want to make *one* Christmas in the world just—exactly the way I wanted it! And—and—Mother and Father will be crazy!... And—and—"

Without a single glance at anything except herself, the Master of the House slipped back into his chair.

"Have a heart!" he said.

Flame did *not* accept this suggestion. With a very severe frown and downcast eyes she sat staring at the table. It seemed a very cheerless table suddenly, with all the dogs in various stages of disheveled finery grouped blatantly around their Master's chair.

"I can at least have my cat," she thought, "my—faithful cat!" In another instant she had slipped from the table, extracted poor Puss from a clutter of pans in the back of a cupboard, stripped the last shred of masquerade from her outraged form, and brought her back growling and bristling to perch on one arm of the high-backed chair. "Th—ere!" said Flame.

Glancing up from this innocent triumph, she encountered the eyes of the Master of the House fixed speculatively on the big turkey.

"I'm afraid everything is very cold," she confided with distinctly formal regret.

"Not for anything," laughed Delcote quite suddenly, "would I have kept you waiting—if I had only known."

Two spots of color glowed hotly in the girl's cheeks.

"It was not for you I was waiting," she said coldly.

"N—o?" teased Delcote. "You astonish me. For whom, then? Some incredible wight who, worse than late—isn't going to show up at all?... Heaven sent, I consider myself.... How else could so little a girl have managed so big a turkey?"

"There ... isn't any ... carving knife," whispered Flame.

The tears were glistening on her cheeks now instead of just in her eyes. A less observing man than Delcote might have thought the tears were really for the carving knife.

"What? No carving knife?" he roared imperiously. "And the house guaranteed 'furnished'?" Very furiously he began to hunt all around the kitchen in the most impossible places.

"Oh, it's furnished all right," quivered Flame. "It's just chock-full of dead things! Pressed flowers! And old plush bags! And pressed flowers! And—and pressed flowers!"

"Great Heavens!" groaned Delcote. "And I came here to forget 'dead things'!"

"Your—your Butler said you'd had misfortunes," murmured Flame.

"Misfortunes?" rallied Delcote. "I should think I had! In a single year I've lost health,—money,—most everything I own in the world except my man and my dogs!"

"They're ... good dogs," testified Flame.

"And the Doctor's sent me here for six months," persisted Delcote, "before he'll even hear of my plunging into things again!"

"Six months is a—a good long time," said Flame. "If you'd turn the hems we could make yellow curtains for the parlor in no time at all!"

"W—we?" stammered Delcote.

"M—Mother," said Flame. "... It's a long time since any dogs lived in the Rattle-Pane House."

"Rattle-*Brain* house?" bridled Delcote.

"Rattle-*Pane* House," corrected Flame.

A little bit worriedly Delcote returned to his seat.

"I shall have to rend the turkey, instead of carve it," he said.

"Rend it," acquiesced Flame.

In the midst of the rending a dark frown appeared between Delcote's eyes.

"These—these guests that you were expecting—?" he questioned.

"Oh, *stop*!" cried Flame. "Dreadful as I am I never—never would have dreamed of inviting 'guests'!"

"This 'guest' then," frowned Delcote. "Was he...?"

"Oh, you mean ... Bertrand?" flushed Flame. "Oh, truly, I didn't invite him! He just butted in ... same as you!"

"Same as ... I?" stammered Delcote.

"Well..." floundered Flame. "Well ... you know what I mean and ..."

With peculiar intentness the Master of the House fixed his eyes on the knotted white handkerchief which Flame had thrown across the corner of her chair.

"And is this 'Bertrand' person so ... so dazzling," he questioned, "that human eye may not look safely upon his countenance?"

"Bertrand ... dazzling?" protested Flame. "Oh, no! He's really quite dull.... It was only," she explained with sudden friendliness, "It was only that I had promised Mother not to 'see' him.... So, of course, when he butted in I...."

"O—h," relaxed the Master of the House. With a precipitous flippancy of manners which did not conform at all to the somewhat tragic austerity of his face he snatched up his knife and fork and thumped joyously on the table with the handles of them. "And some people talk about a country village being dull in the Winter Time!" he chuckled. "With a Dog's Masquerade and a Robbery at the Rectory all happening the same evening!" Grabbing her cat in her arms, Flame jerked her chair back from the table.

"A—a robbery at the Rectory?" she gasped. "Why—why, I'm the Rectory! I must go home at once!"

"Oh, Shucks!" shrugged the Master of0 the House. "It's all over now. But the people at the railroad station were certainly buzzing about it as I came through."

"B—buzzing about it?" articulated Flame with some difficulty.

Expeditiously the Master of the House resumed his rending of the turkey.

"Are you really from the Rectory?" he questioned. "How amusing.... Well, there's nothing really you could do about it now.... The constable and his prisoner are already on their way to the County Seat—wherever that may be. And a freshly 'burgled' house is rather a creepy place for a young girl to return to all alone.... Your parents are away, I believe?"

"Con—stable ... constable," babbled Flame quite idiotically.

"Yes, the regular constable was off Christmasing somewhere it seems, so he put a substitute on his job, a stranger from somewhere. Some substitute that! No mulling over hot toddies on Christmas night for him! He *saw* the marauder crawling in through the Rectory window! He *saw* him fumbling now to the left, now to the right, all through the front hall! He followed him up the stairs to a closet where the silver was evidently kept! He caught the man red-handed as it were! Or rather—white-handed," flushed the Master of the House for some quite unaccountable reason. "To be perfectly accurate," he explained conscientiously, "he was caught with a pair of—of—" Delicately he spelt out the word. "With a pair of—c-o-r-s-e-t-s rolled up in his hand. But inside the roll it seemed there was a solid silver—very elaborate carving set which the Parish had recently presented. The wretch was just unrolling it,—them, when he was caught."

"That was Bertrand!" said Flame. "My Father's Lay Reader."

It was the man's turn now to jump to his feet.

"*What*?" he cried.

"I sent him for the carving knife," said Flame.

"*What*?" repeated the man. Consternation versus Hilarity went racing suddenly like a cat-and-dog combat across his eyes.

"Yes," said Flame.

From the outside door the sound of furious knocking occurred suddenly.

"That sounds to me like—like parents' knocking," shivered Flame.

"It sounds to me like an escaped Lay Reader," said her Host.

With a single impulse they both started for the door.

"Don't worry, Little Girl," whispered the young Stranger in the dark hall.

"I'll try not to," quivered Flame.

They were both right, it seemed.

It was Parents *and* the Lay Reader.

All three breathless, all three excited, all three reproachful,—they swept into the warm, balsam-scented Rattle-Pane House with a gust of frost, a threat of disaster.

"F—lame," sighed her Father.

"Flame!" scolded her Mother.

"Flame?" implored the Lay Reader.

"What a pretty name," beamed the Master of the House. "Pray be seated, everybody," he gestured graciously to left and right,—shoving one dog expeditiously under the table with his foot, while he yanked another out of a chair with his least gesticulating hand. "This is certainly a very great pleasure, I assure you," he affirmed distinctly to Miss Flamande Nourice. "Returning quite unexpectedly to my new house this lonely Christmas evening," he explained very definitely to the Rev. Flamande Nourice, "I can't express to you what it means to me to find this pleasant gathering of neighbors waiting here to welcome me! And when I think of the effort *you* must have made to get here, Mr. Bertrand," he beamed. "A young man of all your obligations and—complications—"

"Pleasant ... gathering of neighbors?" questioned Mrs. Nourice with some emotion.

"Oh, I forgot," deprecated the Master of the House with real concern. "Your Christmas season is not, of course, as inherently 'pleasant' as one might wish.... I was told at the railroad station how you and Mr. Nourice had been called away by the illness of a relative."

"We were called away," confided Mrs. Nourice with increasing asperity, "called away at considerable inconvenience—by a very sick relative—to receive the present of a Piebald pony."

"Oh, goody!" quickened Flame and collapsed again under the weight of her Mother's glance.

"And then came this terrible telephone message," shuddered her Mother. "The implied dishonor of one of your Father's most trusted—most trusted associates!"

"I was right in the midst of such an interesting book," deplored her Father. "And Uncle Wally wouldn't lend it."

"So we borrowed Uncle Wally's new automobile and started right for home!" explained her Mother. "It was at the Junction that we made connections with the Constable and his prisoner."

"His—victim," intercepted the Lay Reader coldly.

At this interception everybody turned suddenly and looked at the Lay Reader. His mouth was twisted very slightly to one side. It gave him a rather unpleasant snarling expression. If this expression had been vocal instead of muscular it would have shocked his hearers.

"Your Father had to go on board the train and identify him," persisted Flame's Mother. "It was very distressing.... The Constable was most unwilling to release him. Your Father had to use every kind of an argument."

"Every ... kind," mused her Father. "He doesn't even deny being in the house," continued her Mother, "being in my closet, ... being caught with a—a—"

"With a silver carving knife and fork in his hand," intercepted the Lay Reader hastily.

"Yet all the time he persists," frowned Flame's Mother, "that there is some one in the world who can give a perfectly good explanation if only,—he won't even say 'he or she' but 'it', if only 'it' would."

Something in the stricken expression of her daughter's face brought a sudden flicker of suspicion to the Mother's eyes.

"*You* don't know anything about this, do you, Flame?" she demanded. "Is it remotely possible that after your promise to me,—your sacred promise to me—?" The whole structure of the home,—of mutual confidence,—of all the Future itself, crackled and toppled in her voice.

To the Lay Reader's face, and right *through* the Lay Reader's face, to the face of the Master of the House, Flame's glance went homing with an unaccountable impulse.

With one elbow leaning casually on the mantle-piece, his narrowed eyes faintly inscrutable, faintly smiling, it seemed suddenly to the young Master of the House that he had been waiting all his discouraged years for just that glance. His heart gave the queerest jump.

Flame's face turned suddenly very pink.

Like a person in a dream, she turned back to her Mother. There was a smile on her face, but even the smile was the smile of a dreaming person.

"No—Mother," she said, "I haven't seen Bertrand ... to-day."

"Why, you're looking right at him now!" protested her exasperated Mother.

With a gentle murmur of dissent, Flame's Father stepped forward and laid his arm across the young girl's shoulder. "She—she may be looking at him," he said. "But I'm almost perfectly sure that she doesn't ... see him."

"Why, whatever in the world do you mean?" demanded his wife. "Whatever in the world does anybody mean? If there was only another woman here! A mature ... sane woman! A——" With a flare of accusation she turned from Flame to the Master of the House. "This0 Miss Flora that my daughter spoke of,—where is she? I insist on seeing her! Please summon her instantly!"

Crossing genially to the table the Master of the House reached down and dragged out the Bull Dog by the brindled scuff of her neck. The scratch on her nose was still bleeding slightly. And one eye was closed.

"This is—Miss Flora!" he said.

Indignantly Flame's Mother glanced at the dog, and then from her daughter's face to the face of the young man again.

"And you call *that*—a lady?" she demanded.

"N—not technically," admitted the young man.

For an instant a perfectly tense silence reigned. Then from under a shadowy basket the Cat crept out, shining, sinuous, with extended paw, and began to pat a sprig of holly cautiously along the floor.

Yielding to the reaction Flame bent down suddenly and hugging the Wolf Hound's head to her breast buried her face in the soft, sweet shagginess.

"Not sanitary, Mother?" she protested. "Why, they're as sanitary as—as violets!"

As though dreaming he were late to church and had forgotten his vestments, Flame's Father reached out nervously and draped a great string of ground-pine stole-like about his neck.

"We all," broke in the Master of the House quite irrelevantly, "seem to have experienced a slight twinge of irritability—the past few minutes. Hunger, I've no doubt!... So suppose we all sit down together to this sumptuous—if somewhat chilled repast? After the soup certainly, even after very cold soup, all explanations I'm sure will be—cheerfully and satisfactorily exchanged. Miss—Flame I know has a most amusing story to tell and—"

"Oh, yes!" rallied Flame. "And it's almost all about being blindfolded and sending poor Mr. Lorello—"

"So if by any chance, Mr.—Mr. Bertrand," interrupted the Master of the House a bit abruptly, "you happen to have the carving knife and fork still on your person ... I thought I saw a white string hanging—"

"I have!" said the Lay Reader with his first real grin.

With great formality the Master of the House drew back a chair and bowed Flame's Mother to it.

Then suddenly the Red Setter lifted his sensitive nose in the air, and the spotted Dalmatian bristled faintly across the ridge of his back. Through the whole room, it seemed, swept a curious cottony sense of Something-About-to-Happen! Was it that a sound hushed? Or that a hush decided suddenly to be a sound?

With a little sharp catch of her breath Flame dashed to the window, and swung the sash upward! Where once had breathed the drab, dusty smell of frozen grass and mud quickened suddenly a curious metallic dampness like the smell of new pennies.

"Mr. ... Delcote!" she called.

In an instant his slender form silhouetted darkly with hers in the open window against the eternal mystery and majesty of a Christmas night.

"And *then* the snow came!"

END

Fairy Prince and Other Stories

In my father's house were many fancies. Always, for instance, on every Thanksgiving Day it was the custom in our family to *bud* the Christmas tree.

Young Derry Willard came from Cuba. His father and our father had been chums together at college. None of us had ever seen him before. We were very much excited to have a strange young man invited for Thanksgiving dinner. My sister Rosalee was seventeen. My brother Carol was eleven. I myself was only nine, but with very tall legs.

Young Derry Willard was certainly excited when he saw the Christmas tree. Excited enough, I mean, to shift his eyes for at least three minutes from my sister Rosalee's face. Lovely as my sister Rosalee was, it had never yet occurred to any of us, I think, until just that moment that she was old enough to have perfectly strange young men stare at her so hard. It made my father rather nervous. He cut his hand on the carving-knife. Nothing ever made my mother nervous.

Except for father cutting his hand it seemed to be a very nourishing dinner. The tomato soup was pink with cream. The roast turkey didn't look a single sad bit like any one you'd seen before. There was plenty of hard-boiled egg with the spinach. The baked potatoes were frosted with red pepper. There was mince pie. There was apple pie. There was pumpkin pie. There were nuts and raisins. There were gay gold-paper bonbons. And everywhere all through the house the funny blunt smell of black coffee.

It was my brother Carol's duty always to bring in the Christmas tree. By some strange mix-up of what is and what isn't my brother Carol was dumb—stark dumb, I mean, and from birth. But tho he had never found his voice he had at least never lost his shining face. Even now at eleven in the twilightly end of a rainy Sunday, or most any day when he had an earache, he still let mother call him "Shining Face." But if any children called him "Shining Face" he kicked them. Even when he kicked people, tho, he couldn't stop his face shining. It was very cheerful. Everything about Carol was very cheerful. No matter, indeed, how much we might play and whisper about gifts and tinsels and jolly-colored candles, Christmas never, I think, seemed really *probable* to any of us until that one jumpy moment, just at the end of the Thanksgiving dinner, when, heralded by a slam in the wood-shed, a hoppytyskip in the hall, the dining-room door flung widely open on Carol's eyes twinkling like a whole skyful of stars through the shaggy, dark branches of a young spruce-tree. It made young Derry Willard laugh right out loud.

"Why, of all funny things!" he said. "On Thanksgiving Day! Why, it looks like a Christmas tree!"

"It is a Christmas tree," explained my sister Rosalee very patiently. My sister Rosalee was almost always very patient. But I had never seen her patient with a young man before. It made her cheeks very pink. "It *is* a Christmas tree," she explained. "That is, it's going to be a Christmas tree! Just the very first second we get it 'budded' it'll start right in to be a Christmas tree!"

"*Budded?*" puzzled young Derry Willard. Really for a person who looked so much like the picture of the Fairy Prince in my best story-book, he seemed just a little bit slow.

"Why, of course, it's got to be *budded*!" I cried. "That's what it's for! That's——"

Instead of just being pink patient my sister Rosalee started in suddenly to be dimply patient too.

"It's from mother's Christmas-tree garden, you know," she went right on explaining. "Mother's got a Winter garden—a Christmas-tree garden!"

"Father's got a garden, too!" I maintained stoutly. "Father's is a Spring garden! Reds, blues, yellows, greens, whites! From France! And Holland! And California! And Asia Minor! Tulips, you know. *Buster's!* Oh, father's garden is a *glory*!" I boasted.

"And mother's garden," said my mother very softly, "is only a story."

"It's an awfully nice story," said Rosalee.

Young Derry Willard seemed to like stories.

"Tell it!" he begged.

It was Rosalee who told it. "Why, it was when Carol was born," she said. "It was on a Christmas eve, you know. That's why mother named him Carol!"

"We didn't know then, you see"—interrupted my mother very softly—"that Carol had been given the gift of silence rather than the gift of speech."

"And father was so happy to have a boy," dimpled Rosalee, "that he said to mother, 'Well, now, I guess you've got everything in the world that you want!' And mother said, 'Everything—except a spruce forest!' So father bought her a spruce forest," said Rosalee. "That's the story!"

"Oh, my dear!" laughed my mother. "That isn't a 'story' at all! All you've told is the facts! It's the *feeling* of the facts that makes a story, you know! It was on my birthday," glowed mother, "that the presentation was to be made!

My birthday was in March! I was very much excited and came down to breakfast with my hat and coat on! 'Where are you going?' said my husband."

"Oh—Mother!" protested Rosalee. "'Whither away?' was what you've always told us he said!"

"'Whither away?' of course *was* what he said!" laughed my mother. "'Why, I'm going to find my spruce forest!' I told him. 'And I can't wait a moment longer! Is it the big one over beyond the mountain?' I implored him. 'Or the little grove that the deacon tried to sell you last year?'"

"And they never budged an inch from the house!" interrupted Rosalee. "It was the funniest——"

Over in the corner of the room my father laughed out suddenly. My father had left the table. He and Carol were trying very hard to make the spruce-tree stand upright in a huge pot of wet earth. The spruce-tree didn't want to stand upright. My father laughed all over again. But it wasn't at the spruce-tree. "Well, now, wouldn't it have been a pity," he said, "to have made a perfectly good lady fare forth on a cold March morning to find her own birthday present?"

My mother began to clap her hands. It was a very little noise. But jolly.

"It came by mail!" she cried. "My whole spruce forest! In a package no bigger than my head!"

"Than your rather fluffy head!" corrected my father.

"Three hundred spruce seedlings!" cried my mother. "Each one no bigger than a wisp of grass! Like little green ferns they were! So tender! So fluffing! So helpless!"

"Heigh-O!" said young Derry Willard. "Well, I guess you laughed—then!"

When grown-up people are trying to remember things outside themselves I've noticed they always open their eyes very wide. But when they are remembering things inside themselves they shut their eyes very tight. My mother shut her eyes very tight.

"No—I didn't exactly laugh," said my mother. "And I didn't exactly cry."

"You wouldn't eat!" cried Rosalee. "Not all day, I mean! Father had to feed you with a spoon! It was in the wing-chair! You heldthe box on your knees! You just shone—and shone—and *shone*!"

"It would have been pretty hard," said my mother, "not to have shone a—little! To brood a baby forest in one's arms—if only for a single day—? Think of the experience!" Even at the very thought of it she began to *shine* all over again! "Funny little fluff o' green," she laughed, "no fatter than a fern!" Her voice went suddenly all wabbly like a preacher's. "But, oh, the glory of it!" she said. "The potential majesty! Great sweeping branches—! Nests for birds, shade for lovers, masts for ships to plow the great world's waters—timbers perhaps for cathedrals! O—h," shivered my mother. "It certainly gave one a very queer feeling! No woman surely in the whole wide world—except the Mother of the Little Christ—ever felt so astonished to think what she had in her lap!"

Young Derry Willard looked just a little bit nervous.

"Oh, but of course mother couldn't begin all at once to raise cathedrals!" I hastened to explain. "So she started in raising Christmas presents instead. We raise all our own Christmas presents! And just as soon as Rosalee and I are married we're going to begin right away to raise our children's Christmas presents too! Heaps for everybody, even if there is a hundred! Carol, of course, won't marry because he can't propose! Ladies don't like written proposals, father says! Ladies——"

Young Derry Willard asked if he might smoke. He smoked cigarets. He took them from a gold-looking case. They smelled very romantic. Everything about him smelled very romantic. His hair was black. His eyes were black. He looked as tho he could cut your throat without flinching if you were faithless to him. It was beautiful.

I left the table as soon as I could. I went and got my best story-book. I was perfectly right. He looked *exactly* like the picture of the Fairy Prince on the front page of the book. There were heaps of other pictures, of course. But only one picture of a Fairy Prince. I looked in the glass. I looked just exactly the way I did before dinner. It made me feel queer. Rosalee didn't look at all the way she looked before dinner. It made me feel *very* queer.

When I got back to the dining-room everybody was looking at the little spruce-tree—except young Derry Willard and Rosalee. Young Derry Willard was still looking at Rosalee. Rosalee was looking at the toes of her slippers. The fringe of her eyelashes seemed to be an inch long. Her cheeks were so pink I thought she had a fever. No one else came to *bud* the Christmas tree except Carol's tame coon and the tame crow. Carol is very unselfish. He always *buds* one wish for the coon. And one for the crow. The tame coon looked rather jolly and gold-powdered in the firelight. The crow never looked jolly. I have heard of white crows. But Carol's crow was a very dark black. Wherever you put him he looked like a sorrow. He sat on the arm of Rosalee's chair and nibbed at her pink sleeve. Young Derry Willard pushed him away. Young Derry Willard and Rosalee tried to whisper. I heard them.

"How old are you?" whispered Rosalee.

"I'm twenty-two," whispered young Derry Willard.

"O—h," said Rosalee.

"How young are you?" whispered Derry Willard.

"I'm seventeen," whispered Rosalee.

"O—h," said Derry Willard.

My mother started in very suddenly to explain about the Christmas tree. There were lots of little pencils on the table. And blocks of paper. And nice cold, shining sheets of tin-foil. There was violet-colored tin-foil, and red-colored tin-foil—and green and blue and silver and gold.

"Why, it's just a little family custom of ours, Mr. Willard," explained my mother. "After the Thanksgiving dinner is over and we're all, I trust, feeling reasonably plump and contented, and there's nothing special to do except just to dream and think—why, we just list out the various things that we'd *like* for Christmas and——"

"Most people end Thanksgiving, of course," explained my father, "by trying to feel thankful for the things they've already had. But this seems to be more like a scheme for expressing thanks for the things that we'd *like* to have!"

"The violet tin-foil is Rosalee's!" I explained. "The green is mine! The red is mother's! The blue is father's! The silver is Carol's! Mother takes each separate *wish* just as soon as it's written, and twists it all up in a bud of tin-foil! And takes wire! And wires the bud on the tree! Gold buds! Silver buds! Red! Green! Everything! All bursty! And shining! Like Spring! It looks as tho rainbows had rained on it! It looks as tho sun and moon had warmed it at the same time! And then we all go and get our little iron banks—all the Christmas money, I mean, that we've been saving and saving for a whole year! And dump it all out round the base of the tree! Nickels! Dimes! Quarters! Pennies! *Everything!* And——"

"Dump them all out—round the base of the tree?" puzzled young Derry Willard.

Carol did something suddenly that I never saw him do before with a stranger. He wrote a conversation on a sheet of paper and waved it at young Derry Willard. It was a short conversation. But it was written very tall.

"*Phertalizer!*" explained Carol.

My father made a little laugh. "In all my experience with horticulture," he said, "I know of no fertilizer for a Christmas tree that equals a judicious application of nickels, dimes, and quarters—well stirred in."

"Our uncle Charlie was here once for Thanksgiving," I cried. "He stirred in a twenty-dollar gold piece. Our Christmas tree bloomed *everything* that year! It bloomed tinsel pompons on every branch! And gold-ribbon bow-knots! It bloomed a blackboard for Carol! And an ice-cream freezer for mother! And——"

"And then we take the tree," explained my mother, "and carry it into the parlor. And shut the door."

"And *lock* the door," said my father.

"And no one ever sees," puzzled young Derry Willard, "what was written in the wishes?"

"*No one*," I said.

Rosalee laughed.

"Some one—must see," said Rosalee. "'Cause just about a week before Christmas father and mother always go up to town and——"

"Oh, of course mother *has* to see!" I admitted. "Mother is such friends with Christmas!"

"And father," laughed Rosalee, "is such friends with mother!"

"Usually," I said.

"Eh?" said father.

"And then," explained mother, "on Christmas morning we all go to the parlor!"

"And there's a fire in the parlor!" I explained. "A great hollow Yule log all stuffed full of crackly pine-cones and sputtering sparkers and funny-colored blazes that father buys at a fireworks shop! And the candles are lighted! And—and——"

"And all the tin-foil buds have bloomed into presents!" laughed Derry Willard.

"Oh, no, of course—not *all* of them," said mother.

"No tree ever fulfills every bud," said my father.

"There's Carol's camel, of course," laughed Rosalee. "Ever since Carol was big enough to wish, he's always wished for a camel!"

"But mostly, of course," I insisted, "he wishes for kites! He got nine kites last Christmas."

"Kites?" murmured young Derry Willard.

"*Kites!*" I said. "I *have* to talk a good deal. Once always for myself. And all over again for Carol." It seemed a good time to talk for Carol. Perhaps a person who came all the way from Cuba could tell us the thing we wanted to know. "Oh, Carol's very much interested in kites!" I confided. "And in relationships! In Christmas relationships especially! When he grows up he's going to be some sort of a jenny something—I think it's an ologist! Or else keep a kite-shop!"

"Yes?" murmured young Derry Willard.

There are two ways I've noticed to make one listen to you. One is to shout. The other is to whisper. I decided to whisper.

25

"You don't seem to understand," I whispered. "It's Christmas relationships that are worrying Carol and me so! It worries us dreadfully! Oh, of course we understand all about the Little Baby Christ! And the camels! And the wise men! And the frankincense! That's easy! But *who* is Santa Claus? Unless—unless—?" It was Carol himself who signaled me to go on. "Unless—he's the Baby Christ's *grandfather*?" I thought Derry Willard looked a little bit startled. Carol's ears turned bright red. "Oh, of course—we meant on his *mother's* side!" I hastened to assure him.

"It is, I admit, a new idea to me," said young Derry Willard. "But I seem to have gotten several new ideas to-day."

He looked at mother. Mother's mouth looked very funny. He looked at father. Father seemed to be sneezing. He looked at Rosalee. They laughed together. His whole face suddenly was very laughing. "And what becomes," he asked, "of all the Christmas-tree buds that *don't* bloom?" It was a funny question. It didn't have a thing in the world to do with Santa Claus being a grandfather.

"Oh, mother never throws away any of the buds," laughed Rosalee. "She just keeps them year after year and wires them on all over again."

"All unfulfilled wishes," said my mother. "Still waiting—still wishing! Maybe they'll bloom some time! Even Carol's—camel," she laughed out suddenly. "Who knows, sonny-boy—but what if you keep on *wishing* you'll actually travel some day to the Land-Where-Camels-Live? Maybe—maybe you'll own a—a dozen camels?"

"With purple velvet blankets?" I cried. "All trimmed with scarlet silk tassels? And smelling of sandalwood?"

"I have never understood," said my father, "that camels smelt of sandalwood."

Young Derry Willard didn't seem exactly nervous any more. But he jumped up very suddenly. And went and stood by the fire.

"It's the finest Christmas idea I ever heard of!" he said. "And if nobody has any objections I'd like to take a little turn myself at *budding* the Christmas tree!"

"Oh, but you won't be here for Christmas!" cried everybody all at once.

"No, I certainly sha'n't be," admitted Derry Willard, "unless I am invited!"

"Why, of course, you're invited!" cried everybody. Father seemed to have swallowed something. So mother invited him twice. Father kept right on choking. Everybody was frightened but mother.

Young Derry Willard had to run like everything to catch his train. It was lucky that he knew what he wanted. With only one wish to make and only half a minute to make it in, it was wonderful that he could decide so quickly! He snatched a pencil! He scribbled something on a piece of paper! He crumpled the "something" all up tight and tossed it to mother! Carol and mother wadded it into a tin-foil bud! They took the gold-colored tin-foil! Rosalee and I wired it to a branch! We chose the highest branch we could reach! Father held his overcoat for him! Father handed him his bag! Father opened the door for him! He ran as fast as he could! He waved his hand to everybody! His laugh was all sparkly with white teeth!

The room seemed a little bit dark after he had gone. The firelight flickered on the tame coon's collar. Sometimes it flickered on the single gold bud. We cracked more nuts and munched more raisins. It made a pleasant noise. The tame crow climbed up on the window-sill and tapped and tapped against the glass. It was not a pleasant noise. The tame coon prowled about under the table looking for crumbs. He walked very flat and swaying and slow, as tho he were stuffed with wet sand. It gave him a very captive look. His eyes were very bright.

Father got his violin and played some quivery tunes to us. Mother sang a little. It was nice. Carol put fifteen "wishes" on the tree. Seven of them, of course, were old ones about the camel. But all the rest were new. He wished a salt mackerel for his coon. And a gold anklet for his crow. He wouldn't tell what his other wishes were. They looked very pretty! Fifteen silver buds as big as cones scattered all through the green branches! Rosalee made seven violet-colored wishes! I made seven! Mine were green! Father made three! His were blue! Mother's were red! She made three, too! The tree looked more and more as tho rainbows had rained on it! It was beautiful! We thanked mother very much for having a Christmas-tree garden! We felt very thankful toward everybody! We got sleepier and sleepier! We went to bed!

I woke in the night. It was very lonely. I crept down-stairs to get my best story-book. There was a light in the parlor. There were voices. I peeped in. It was my father and my mother. They were looking at the Christmas tree. I got an awful shock. They were having what books call "words" with each other. Only it was "sentences!"

"Impudent young cub!" said my father. "How *dared* he stuff a hundred-dollar bill into our Christmas tree?"

"Oh, I'm sure he didn't mean to be impudent," said my mother. Her voice was very soft. "He heard the children telling about Uncle Charlie's gold piece. He—he wanted to do something—I suppose. It was too much, of course. He oughtn't to have done it. But——"

"A hundred-dollar bill!" said my father. Every time he said it he seemed madder.

"And yet," said my mother, "if what you say about his father's sugar plantations is correct, a hundred-dollar bill probably didn't look any larger to him than a—than a two-dollar bill looks to us—this year. We'll simply return it to him very politely—as soon as we know his address. He was going West somewhere, wasn't he? We shall hear, I suppose."

"Hear *nothing*!" said my father. "I won't have it! Did you see how he stared at Rosalee? It was outrageous! Absolutely outrageous! And Rosalee? I was ashamed of Rosalee! Positively ashamed!"

"But you see—it was really the first young man that Rosalee has ever had a chance to observe," said my mother. "If you had ever been willing to let boys come to the house—maybe she wouldn't have considered this one such a—such a thrilling curiosity."

"Stuff and nonsense!" said my father. "She's only a child! There'll be no boys come to this house for years and years!"

"She's seventeen," said my mother. "You and I were married when I was seventeen."

"That's different!" said my father. He tried to smile. He couldn't. Mother smiled quite a good deal. He jumped up and began to pace the room. He demanded things. "Do you mean to say," he demanded, "that you want your daughter to marry this strange young man?"

"Not at all," said mother.

Father turned at the edge of the rug and looked back. His face was all frowned. "And I don't like him anyway," he said. "He's too dark!"

"His father roomed with you at college, you say?" asked my mother very softly. "Do you remember him—specially?"

"Do I remember him?" cried my father. He looked astonished. "Do I remember him? Why, he was the best friend I ever had in the world! Do I remember him?"

"And he was—very fair?" asked my mother.

"Fair?" cried my father. "He was as dark as a Spaniard!"

"And yet—reasonably—respectable?" asked my mother.

"Respectable?" cried my father. "Why, he was the highest-minded man I ever knew in my life!"

"And so—dark?" said my mother. She began to laugh. It was what we call her cut-finger laugh, her bandage laugh. It rolled all around father's angriness and made it feel better almost at once.

"Well, I can't help it," said father. He shook his head just the way Carol does sometimes when he's planning to be pleasant as soon as it's convenient. "Well, I can't help it! Exceptions, of course, are exceptions! But Cuba? A climate all mushy with warmth and sunshine! What possible stamina can a young man have who's grown up on sugar-cane sirup and—and bananas?"

"He seemed to have teeth," said my mother. "He ate two helpings of turkey!"

"He had a gold cigaret-case!" said my father. "*Gold!*"

My mother began to laugh all over again.

"Maybe his Sunday-school class gave it to him," she said. It seemed to be a joke. Once father's Sunday-school class gave him a high silk hat. Father laughed a little.

Mother looked very beautiful. She ruffled her hair a little on father's shoulder. She pinked her cheeks from the inside some way. She glanced up at the topmost branch of the Christmas tree. The gold bud showed quite plainly.

"I—I *wonder*—what he wished," she said. "We'll have to look—some time."

I made a little creak in my bones. I didn't mean to. My father and mother both turned round. They started to explore!

I ran like everything!

I think it was very kind of God to make December have the very shortest days in the year!

Summer, of course, is nice! The long, sunny light! Lying awake till 'most nine o'clock every night to hear the blackness come rustling! Such a lot of early mornings everywhere and birds singing! Sizzling-hot noons with cool milk to drink! The pleasant nap before it's time to play again!

But if *December* should feel long, what would children do? About Christmas, I mean! Even the best way you look at it, Christmas is always the furthest-off day that I ever heard about!

My mother was always very kind about making Christmas come just as soon as it could. There wasn't much daylight. Not in December. Not in the North. Not where we lived. Except for the snow, each day was like a little jet-black jewel-box with a single gold coin in the center. The gold coin in the center was *noon*. It was very bright. It was really the only bright light in the day. We spent it for Christmas. Every minute of it. We popped corn and strung it into lovely loops. We threaded cranberries. We stuffed three Yule logs with crackly cones and colored fires. We made little candies. All round the edges of the bright noon-time, of course, there was morning and night. And lamplight. It wasn't convenient to burn a great many lamps. At night father and mother sat in the lamplight and taught us our lessons. Or read stories to us. We children sat in the shadows and stared into the light. The light made us blink. The tame crow and the tame coon sat in the shadows with us. We played we were all jungle-animals together waiting outside a man's camp to be Christianized. It was pleasant. Mother read to us about a woman who didn't like Christmas specially. She was going to petition Congress to have the Christ Child born in leap-year so that Christmas couldn't come oftener than once in four years. It worried us a little. Father laughed. Mother had only one worry in the world. She had it every year.

"Oh, my darling, darling Winter garden!" worried my mother. "Wouldn't it be *awful* if I ever had to die just as my best Christmas tree was coming into bloom?"

It frightened us a little. But not too much. Father had the same worry every Spring about his Spring garden. Every Maytime when the tulip-buds were so fat and tight you could fairly hear them splitting, father worried.

"Oh, wouldn't it be perfectly *terrible* if I should die before I find out whether those new 'Rembrandts' are everything that the catalogue promised? Or whether the 'Bizards' are really finer than the 'Byblooms'? Now, if it was in phlox-time," worried my father. "Especially if the phlox turned out magenta, one could slip away with scarcely a pang. But in *tulip-time*——?"

We promised our mother she should never die at Christmas-time. We promised our father he should never die at tulip-time. We brought them rubbers. And kneeling-cushions. We carried their coats. We found their trowels. We kept them just as well as we could.

But, most of all, of course, we were busy wondering about our presents.

It hurries Christmas a lot to have a Christmas tree growing in your parlor for a whole month. Even if the parlor door is locked.

Lots of children have a Christmas tree for a whole month. But it's a *going* tree. Its going is very sad. Just one little wee day of perfect splendor it has. And then it begins to die. Every day it dies more. It tarnishes. Its presents are all gathered. Its pop-corn gets stale. The cranberries smell. It looks scragglier and scragglier. It gets brittle. Its needles begin to fall. Pretty soon it's nothing but a *clutter*. It must be dreadful to start as a Christmas tree and end by being nothing but a clutter.

But mother's Christmas tree is a *coming* tree. Every day for a month it's growing beautifuler and beautifuler! The parlor is cool. It lives in a nice box of earth. It has water every day like a dog. It never dies. It just disappears. When we come down to breakfast the day after Christmas it simply *isn't there*. That's all. It's immortal. Always when you remember it, it's absolutely perfect.

We liked very much to see the Christmas tree *come*. Every Sunday afternoon my mother unlocked the parlor door. We were not allowed to go in. But we could peep all we wanted to. It made your heart crinkle up like a handful of tinsel to watch the tin-foil buds change into presents.

Two of Carol's silver buds had bloomed. One of them had bloomed into a white-paper package that looked like a book. The otherone had strange humps. Only one of Rosalee's violet buds had bloomed. But it was a very large box tied with red ribbon. It looked like a best hat. One of father's blue buds had bloomed. One of mother's red buds. They bloomed very small. Small enough to be diamonds. Or collar-buttons. 'Way back on the further side of the tree I could see that one of my green buds had bloomed. It was a long little box. It was a narrow little box. I can most always tell when there's a doll in a box. Young Derry Willard's golden bud hadn't bloomed at all. Maybe it was a late bloomer. Some things are. The tame coon's salt fish, I've noticed, never blooms at all until just the very last moment before we go into the parlor Christmas morning. Mother says there's a reason. We didn't bother much about reasons. The parlor was very cold. It smelt very cold and mysterious. We didn't see how we could wait!

Carol helped us to wait. Not being able to talk, Carol has plenty of time to think. He can write, of course. But spelling is very hard. So he doesn't often waste his spelling on just facts. He waits till he gets enough facts to make a philosophy before he tries to spell it: He made a philosophy about Christmas coming so slow. He made it on the blackboard in the kitchen. He wrote it very tall.

"Christmas has *got* to come," he wrote. "It's part of *time*. Everything that's part of *time* has *got* to come. Nothing can stop it. It runs like a river. It runs down-hill. It can't help itself. I should worry."

Young Derry Willard never wrote at all. He telegraphed his "manners" instead. "Thank you for Thanksgiving Day," he telegraphed. "It was very wonderful." He didn't say anything else. He never even mentioned his address.

"U—m—m," said my father.

"It's because of the hundred-dollar bill," said my mother. "He doesn't want to give us any chance to return it."

"Humph!" said my father. "Do we *look* poor?"

My mother glanced at the worn spot in the dining-room rug. She glanced at my father's coat.

"We certainly do!" she laughed. "But young Derry Willard didn't leave us a hundred-dollar bill to try and make us look any richer. All young Derry Willard was trying to do was to make us look more Christmassy!"

"Well, we can't accept it!" said my father.

"Of course we can't accept it!" said my mother. "It was a mistake. But at least it was a very kind mistake."

"*Kind?*" said my father.

"*Very* kind," said my mother. "No matter how dark a young man may be or how much cane-sirup and bananas he has consumed, he can't be absolutely depraved as long as he goes about the world trying to make things look more Christmassy!"

My father looked up rather sharply.

My mother gave a funny little gasp.

"Oh, it's all right," she said. "We'll manage some way! But who ever heard of a chicken-bone hung on a Christmas tree? Or a slice of roast beef?"

"Some children don't get—anything," said my father. He looked solemn. "Money is very scarce," he said.

"It always is," said my mother. "But that's no reason why presents ought to be scarce."

My father jumped up.

My father laughed.

"Great Heavens, woman!" he said. "Can't anything dull your courage?"

"Not my—Christmas courage!" said my mother.

My father reached out suddenly and patted her hand.

"Oh, all right," he said. "I suppose we'll manage somehow."

"Of course we'll manage somehow," said my mother.

I ran back as fast as I could to Carol and Rosalee.

We thought a good deal about young Derry Willard coming. We talked about it among ourselves. We never talked about it to my father or my mother. I don't know why. I went and got my best story-book and showed the Fairy Prince to Carol. Carol stared and stared. There were palms and bananas in the picture. There was a lace-paper castle. There was a moat. There was a fiery charger. There were dragons. The Fairy Prince was all in white armor, with a white plume in his hat. It grasped your heart, it was so beautiful. I showed the picture to Rosalee. She was surprised. She turned as white as the plume in the Fairy Prince's hat. She put the book in her top bureau-drawer with her ribbons. We wondered and wondered whether young Derry Willard would come. Carol thought he wouldn't. I thought he would. Rosalee wouldn't say. Carol thought it would be too cold. Carol insisted that he was a tropic. And that tropics couldn't stand the cold. That if a single breath of cold air struck a tropic he blew up and froze. Rosalee didn't want young Derry Willard to blow up and freeze. Anybody could see that she didn't. I comforted her. I said he would come in a huge fur coat. Carol insisted that tropics didn't have huge fur coats. "All right, then," I said. "He will come in a huge *feather* coat! Blue-bird feathers it will be made of! With a soft brown breast! When he fluffs himself he will look like the god of all the birds and of next Spring! Hawks and all evil things will scuttle away!"

There certainly *was* something the matter with the Christmas tree that year.

It grew. But it didn't grow very fast.

My father said that perhaps the fertilizer hadn't been rich enough.

My mother said that maybe all Christmas trees were blooming rather late this year. Seasons changed so.

My father and mother didn't go away to town at all. Not for a single day.

Late at night after we'd gone to bed we heard them hammering things and running the sewing-machine.

Carol thought it smelt like kites.

Rosalee said it sounded to her like a blue silk waist.

It looked like a worry to me.

It got colder and colder. It snowed and snowed.

Christmas eve it snowed some more. It was beautiful. We were very much excited. We clapped our hands. We stood at the window to see how white the world was. I thought about the wise men's camels. I wondered if they could carry snow in their stomachs as well as rain. Mother said camels were tropics and didn't know anything about snow. It seemed queer.

A sleigh drove up to the door. There were three men in it. Two of them got out. The first one was young Derry Willard. It was a fur coat that he had on. He was full of bundles. My father gave one gasp.

"The—the impudent young—" gasped my father.

We ran to the door. The second man looked just exactly like young Derry Willard except that he had on a gray beard and a gray slouch hat. He looked like the picture of "a planter" in "Uncle Tom's Cabin." My father and he took just one look at each other. And then suddenly they began to pound each other on the back and to hug each other. "Hello, old top!" they shouted. "Hello—hello—*hello*!" Derry Willard's father cried a little. Everybody cried a little or shouted or pounded somebody on the back except young Derry Willard and Rosalee. Young Derry Willard and Rosalee just stood and looked at each other.

"Well—well—well!" said Derry Willard's father over and over and over. "Twenty years! *Twenty* years!" The front hall was full of bundles! We fell on them when we stepped. And we fell on new ones when we tried to get up. Whenever Derry Willard's father wasn't crying he was laughing! "So this is the wife?" he said. "And these are the children? Which is Rosalee? Ah! A very pretty girl! But not as pretty as your wife!" he laughed. "Twenty years! *Twenty* years!" he began all over again. "A bit informal, eh? Descending on you like this? But I couldn't resist the temptation after I'd seen Derry. We Southerners, you know! Our impulses are romantic! Tuck us away anywhere! Or turn us out—if you must!"

My father was like a wild man for joy! He forgot all about everything except "twenty years ago."

We had to put the two Mr. Derry Willards to bed in the parlor. There was no other room. They insisted on sleeping with the Christmas tree. They had camped under every kind of branch and twig in the world, they said. But *never* had they camped under a Christmas tree.

Father talked and talked and talked! Derry Willard's father talked and talked and talked! It was about college! It was about girls! It was about boys! It was about all sorts of pranks! Not any of it was about studies! Mother sat and laughed at them!

Rosalee and young Derry Willard sat and looked at each other. Carol and I played checkers. Everybody forgot us. I don't know who put me to bed.

When we came down-stairs the next morning and went into the parlor to see the Christmas tree we *screamed*!

Every single weeney-teeny branch of it had sprouted tinsel tassels! There were tinsel stars all over it! Red candles were blazing! Glass icicles glistened! There were candy canes! There were tin trumpets! Little white-paper presents stuck out everywhere through the branches! Big white presents piled like a snowdrift all around the base of the tree!

Young Derry Willard's father seemed to be still laughing. He rubbed his hands together.

"Excuse me, good people," he laughed, "for taking such liberties with your tree! But it's twenty years since I've had a chance to take a real whack at a Christmas tree! Palms, of course, are all right, and banana groves aren't half bad! But when it comes to real landscape effect—give me a Christmas tree in a New England parlor!"

"Palms?" we gasped. "Banana-trees?"

Young Derry Willard distributed the presents.

For my father there were boxes and boxes of cigars! And an order on some Dutch importing house for five hundred *green* tulips! Father almost sw—ooned.

For mother there was a little gold chain with a single pearl in it! And a box of oranges as big as a chicken-coop!

I got four dolls! And a paint-box! One of the dolls was jet-black. She was funny. When you squeaked her stomach she grinned her mouth and said, "Oh, lor', child!"

Rosalee had a white crêpe shawl all fringes and gay-colored birds of paradise! Rosalee had a fan made out of ivory and gold. Rosalee had a gold basket full of candied violets. Rosalee had a silver hand-mirror carved all round the edge with grasses and lilies like the edges of a little pool.

Carol had a big, big box that looked like a magic lantern. And on every branch where he had hung his seven wishes for a camel there was a white card instead with the one word "Palestine" written on it.

Everybody looked very much perplexed.

Young Derry Willard's father laughed.

"If the youngster wants camels," he said, "he must have camels! I'm going to Palestine one of these days before so very long. I'll take him with me. There must be heaps of camels still in Palestine."

"Going to Palestine before—long," gasped my mother. "How wonderful!"

Everybody turned and looked at Carol.

"Want to go, son, eh?" laughed Derry Willard's father.

Carol's mouth quivered. He looked at my mother.

My mother's mouth quivered. A little red came into her checks.

"He wants me to thank you very much, Mr. Willard," she said. "But he thinks perhaps you wouldn't want to take him to Palestine—if you knew that he can't—talk."

"Can't talk?" cried Mr. Derry Willard. "*Can't talk?*" He looked at mother! He looked at Carol! He swallowed very hard! Then suddenly he began to laugh again!

"Good enough!" he cried. "He's the very boy I'm looking for! We'll rear him for a diplomat!"

Carol got a hammer and opened his big box. It *was* a magic lantern! He was wild with joy! He beat his fists on the top of the box! He stamped his feet! He came and burrowed his head in mother's shoulder. When Carol burrows his head in my mother's shoulder it means, "Call me anything you want to!"

Mother called him anything she wanted to. Right out loud before everybody. "Shining Face!" said my mother.

There were lots of other presents besides.

My father had made a giant kite for Carol. It looked nine feet tall. My father had made the dearest little wooden work-box for my mother. There *was* a blue silk waist for Rosalee. My mother had knitted me a doll! Its body was knitted! Its cheeks were knitted! Its nose was knitted! It was wonderful!

We ate the peppermint-candy canes. All the pink stripes. All the white stripes. We sang carols. We sang,

O, the foxes have holes! And the birds build their nestsIn the crotch of the sycamore-tree!But the Little Son of God had no place for His headWhen He cameth to earth for me!

Rosalee's voice was like a lark in the sky. Carol's face looked like two larks in the sky.

The tame crow stayed in the kitchen. He was afraid of so many strangers. The tame coon wasn't afraid of anything. He crawled in and out of all the wrapping-papers, sniffing and sniffing. It made a lovely crackling sound.

Everything smelt like fir balsam. It was more beautiful every minute. Even after every last present was picked from the tree, the tree was still so fat and fluffy with tinsel and glass balls that it didn't look robbed at all.

We just sat back and stared at it.

Young Derry Willard stared only at the topmost branch.

Father looked suddenly at mother. Mother looked suddenly at Rosalee. Rosalee looked suddenly at Carol. Carol looked suddenly at me. I looked suddenly at the tame coon. The tame coon kept right on crackling through the wrapping-papers.

Young Derry Willard made a funny little face. There seemed to be dust in his throat. His voice was very dry. He laughed.

"My wish," said young Derry Willard, "seems to have been the only one that—didn't bloom."

I almost died with shame. Carol almost died with shame. In all that splendiferousness, in all that generosity, poor Derry Willard'sgold-budded wish was the only one that hadn't at least bloomed into *something*!

Rosalee jumped up very suddenly and ran into the dining-room. She looked as tho she was going to cry.

Young Derry Willard followed her. He didn't run. He walked very slowly. He looked a little troubled.

Carol and I began at once to fold the wrapping-papers very usefully.

Young Derry Willard's father looked at my father. All of a sudden he wasn't laughing at all. Or rubbing his hands.

"I'm sorry, Dick," he said. "I've always rather calculated somehow on having my boy's wishes come true."

My father spoke a little sharply.

"You must have a lot of confidence," he said, "in your boy's wishes!"

"I have!" said young Derry Willard's father, quite simply. "He's a good boy! Not only clever, I mean, but good! Never yet have I known him to wish for anything that wasn't the *best*!"

"They're too young," said my father.

"Youth," said Derry Willard's father, "is the one defect I know of that is incontestably remedial."

"How can they possibly know their own minds?" demanded my father.

"No person," said Derry Willard's father, "knows his own mind until he's ready to die. But the sooner he knows his own heart the sooner he's ready to begin to live."

My father stirred in his chair. He lit a cigar. It went out. He lit it again. It went out again. He jerked his shoulders. He looked nervous. He talked about things that nobody was talking about at all.

"The young rascal dropped a hundred-dollar bill—when he was here before!" he said. He said it as tho it was something very wicked.

Young Derry Willard's father seemed perfectly cheerful.

"Did he really?" he said.

"It's a wonder the crow didn't eat it!" snapped my father.

"But even the crow wouldn't eat it, eh?" said Derry Willard's father. Quite suddenly he began to laugh again. He looked at my mother. He stopped laughing. His voice was very gentle. "Don't be—proud," he said. "Don't ever be proud." He threw out his hand as tho he was asking something. "What difference does anything make—in the whole world," he said, "except just young love—and old friendship?"

"Oh, pshaw," said father. "Oh, pshaw!"

Rosalee came and stood in the door. She looked only at mother. She had on a red coat. And a red hat. And red mittens.

"Derry Willard wants to see the Christmas-tree garden," she said. "May I go?"

Derry Willard stood just behind her. He had on his fur coat. He looked very hard at father. When he spoke he spoke only to father.

"Is it all right?" he said. "May *I* go?"

My father looked up. And then he looked down. He looked at Derry Willard's father. He threw out his hands as tho there was no place left to look. A little smile crept into one corner of his mouth. He tried to bite it. He couldn't.

"Oh—*pshaw*!" he said.

Carol and I went out to play. We thought we'd like to see the Christmas-tree garden too. The snow was almost as deep as our heads. All the evergreen trees were weighed down with snow. Their branches dragged on the ground. It was like walking through white plumes.

We found mother's Christmas-tree garden. We found Rosalee and young Derry Willard standing right in the middle of it. It was all caves and castles! It was like a whole magic little city all made out of white plumes! The sun came out and shone on it! Blue sky opened overhead! Everything crackled! It was more beautiful even than the Christmas tree in the parlor.

They didn't hear us.

Rosalee gave a funny little cry. It was like a sob. Only happy.

"I love *Christmas*!" she said.

"I love *you*!" said Derry Willard.

He snatched her in his arms and kissed her.

A great pine-tree shivered all its snow down on them like a veil.

We heard them laugh.

We ran back to the house. We ran just as fast as we could. It almost burst our lungs. We ran into the parlor. I didn't tell. Carol couldn't tell.

My father and young Derry Willard's father were talking and talking behind great clouds of smoke. The Yule log was blazing and sputtering all sorts of fireworks and colors. Only mother was watching it. She was paring apples as she watched. A little smile was in her eyes.

"What a wonderful—wonderful day to have it happen!" she said.

I couldn't stand it any longer. I ran upstairs and got my best story-book. I brought it down and opened it at the picture of the Fairy Prince. I laid it open like that in Mr. Willard's lap. I pointed at the picture.

"*There!*" I said.

Derry Willard's father put on his glasses and looked at the picture.

"Well, upon my soul," he said, "where did you get that?"

"It's my book," I said. "It's always been my book."

My father looked at the picture.

"Why, of all things," he said.

"Why, it looks exactly like Derry!" said my mother.

"It *is* Derry!" said Derry's father. "But don't ever let Derry know that you know that it is! It seems to tease him a little. It seems to tease him a very great deal in fact. Being all rigged out like that. The illustrator is a friend of mine. He spent the Winter in Cuba three or four years ago. And he painted the picture there."

I looked at Carol. Carol looked at me. It was an absolutely perfect Christmas! If *this* were true, then everything beautiful that there was in the world was true, too! Carol nudged me to speak.

"Then Derry really *is* a Fairy Prince?" I said.

Father started to speak.

Mother stopped him.

"Yes! Rosalee's Fairy Prince!" she said.

THE GAME OF THE BE-WITCHMENTS

We like our Aunt Esta very much because she doesn't like us.

That is—she doesn't like us specially. *Toys* are what our Aunt Esta likes specially. Our Aunt Esta invents toys. She invents them for a store in New York. Our Aunt Esta is thirty years old with very serious hair. I don't know how old our other relatives are—except Rosalee! And Carol! And myself!

My sister Rosalee is seventeen years old. And a Betrothess. Her Betrother lives in Cuba. He eats bananas. My brother Carol is eleven. He has no voice in his throat. But he eats anything. I myself am only nine. But with very long legs. Our Father and Mother have no age. They are just tall.

There was a man. He was very rich. He had a little girl with sick bones. She had to sit in a wheel chair all day long and be pushed around by a Black Woman. He asked our Aunt Esta to invent a Game for her. The little girl's name was Posie.

Our Aunt Esta invented a Game. She called it the Game of the Be-Witchments. It cost two hundred dollars and forty-three cents. The Rich Man didn't seem to mind the two hundred dollars. But he couldn't bear the forty-three cents. He'd bear even that, though, he said, if it would only be sure to work!

"*Work?*" said our Aunt Esta. "Why *of course* it will work!" So just the first minute she got it invented she jammed it into her trunk and dashed up to our house to see if it would!

It worked very well. Our Aunt Esta never wastes any time. Not even kissing. Either coming or going. We went right up to her room with her. It was a big trunk. The Expressman swore a little. My Father tore his trouser-knee. My Mother began right away to re-varnish the scratches on the bureau.

It took us most all the morning to carry the Game down-stairs. We carried it to the Dining Room. It covered the table. It covered the chairs. It strewed the sideboard. It spilled over on the floor. There was a pair of white muslin angel wings all spangled over with silver and gold! There was a fairy wand! There was a shining crown! There was a blue satin clock! There was a yellow plush suit and swishy-tail all painted sideways in stripes like a tiger! There was a most furious tiger head with whisk-broom whiskers! There was a green frog's head! And a green frog's suit! There was a witch's hat and cape! And a hump on the back! There were bows and arrows! There were boxes and boxes of milliner's flowers! There were strings of beads! And yards and yards of dungeon chains made out of silver paper! And a real bugle! And red Chinese lanterns! And—and everything!

The Rich Man came in a gold-colored car to see it work. When he saw the Dining Room he sickened. He bit his cigar.

"My daughter Posie is ten years old," he said. "What I ordered for her was a Game!—not a Trousseau!"

Our Aunt Esta shivered her hands. She shrugged her shoulders.

"You don't understand," she said. "This is no paltry Toy to be exhausted and sickened of in a single hour! This is a real Game! Eth-ical! Psycho-psycho—logical! Unendingly diverting! Hour after hour! Day after day!—Once begun, you understand, it's never over!"

The Rich Man looked at his watch.

"I have to be in Chicago a week from tomorrow!" he said.

Somebody giggled. It couldn't have been Rosalee, of course. Because Rosalee is seventeen. And, of course, it wasn't Carol. So it must have been me.

The Rich Man gave an awful glare.

"Who are these children?" he demanded.

Our Aunt Esta swallowed.

"They are my—my Demonstrators," she said.

"'Demonstrators?'" sniffed the Rich Man. He glared at Carol. "Why don't you speak?" he demanded.

My mother made a rustle to the door-way.

"He can't," she said. "Our son Carol is dumb."

The Rich Man looked very queer.

"Oh, I say," he fumbled and stuttered. "Oh, I say—! After all there's no such great harm in a giggle. My little girl Posie cries all the time. *All* the time, I mean! *Cries* and *cries* and *cries*!—It's a fright!"

"She wouldn't," said our Aunt Esta, "if she had a game like this to play with."

"Eh?" said the Rich Man.

"She could wear the Witch's hideous cape!" said our Aunt Esta. "And the queer pointed black hat! And the scraggly gray wig! And the great horn-rimmed spectacles! And the hump on her back! And——"

"My daughter Posie has Ti—Titian red curls," said the Rich Man coldly. "And the most beautiful brown eyes that mortal man has ever seen! And a skin so fair that——"

"That's why I think it would rest her so," said our Aunt Esta, "to be ugly outside—instead of inside for a while."

"*Eh?*" said the Rich Man.

He glared at our Aunt Esta.

Our Aunt Esta glared at him.

Out in the kitchen suddenly the most beautiful smell happened. The smell was soup! Spiced Tomato Soup! It was as though the whole stove had bloomed! My Father came to the door. "What's it all about?" he said. He saw the Rich Man. The Rich Man saw him. "Why, how do you do?" said my Father. "Why, how do you do?" said the Rich Man. They bowed. There was no room on the Dining Room table to put the dishes. There was no room anywhere for anything. We had to eat in the kitchen. My Mother made griddle cakes. The Rich Man stirred the batter. He seemed to think it was funny. Carol had to sit on a soap-box. Our Aunt Esta sat on the edge of a barrel with her stockings swinging. It made her look not so strict. "All the same," worried the Rich Man, "I don't see just why you fixed the price at two hundred dollars and forty-three cents?—Why not two hundred dollars and forty-five cents? Or even the round sum two hundred and one dollars?"

Our Aunt Esta looked pretty mad. "I will be very glad—I'm sure," she said, "to submit an itemized bill."

"Oh, nonsense!" said the Rich Man. "It was just your mental processes I was wondering about.—The thing, of course, is worth any money—if it works!"

"If it works?" cried our Aunt Esta.

The Rich Man jumped up and strode fiercely to the Dining Room door.

Our Aunt Esta strode fiercely after him, only littler. Our Aunt Esta is *very* little.

The Rich Man waved his arms at everything,—the boxes,—the bundles,—the angel-wings,—the cloaks,—the suits,—the Chinese Lanterns.

"All the same, the thing is perfectly outrageous!—The size of it!—The extent! No house would hold it!"

"It isn't meant," said our Aunt Esta, "to be played just in the house.—It's meant to be played on a sunny porch opening out on a green lawn—so that there's plenty of room for all Posie's little playmates to go swarming in and out."

The Rich Man looked queer. He gave a little shiver.

"My little daughter Posie hasn't got any playmates," he said. "She's too cross."

Our Aunt Esta stood up very straight. Two red spots flamed in her cheeks.

"You won't be able to keep the children away from her," she said, "after they once begin to play this game!"

"You really think so?" cried the Rich Man.

Out in the kitchen my Father looked at my Mother. My Mother looked at my Father. They both looked at us. My Father made a little chuckle.

"It would seem," said my Father, "as though it was the honor of the whole family that was involved!" He made a whisper in Carol's ear. "Go to it, Son!" he whispered.

Rosalee jumped to her feet. Carol jumped to his feet. I jumped to my feet. We snatched hands. We ran right into the Dining Room. Carol's face was shining.

"Who's going to be Posie-with-the-Sick-Bones?" I cried.

"S—s—h!" said everybody except our Aunt Esta.

Our Aunt Esta suddenly seemed very much encouraged. She didn't wait a minute. She snatched a little book from her pocket. It was a little book that she had made herself all full of typewriter directions about the Game.

"*Someone*, of course," she said, "will have to be the Witch,—someone who knows the Game, I mean, so perhaps I—?"

We rushed to help her drag the old battered tricycle to the Porch! We helped her open up every porch door till all the green lawn and gay petunia blossoms came right up and fringed with the old porch rug! We helped her tie on the Witch's funny hat! And the scraggly gray wig! And the great horn-rimmed spectacles! We helped her climb into the tricycle seat! We were too excited to stay on the porch! We wheeled her right out on the green lawn itself! The green lilac hedge reared all up around her like a magic wall!

We screamed with joy! The Rich Man jumped when we screamed. The Rich Man's name was Mr. Trent.

"And Mr. Trent shall be the Black Woman who pushes you all about!" we screamed.

"I will not!" said Mr. Trent.

But Carol had already tied a black velvet ribbon on the Rich Man's leg to *show* that he was!

Our Aunt Esta seemed more encouraged every minute. She stood us all up in front of her. Even Father. She read from her book. It was a poem. The poem said:

Now come ye all to the Witch's Ball,Ye Great, ye Small,Ye Short, ye Tall,Come one, Come all!

"I will not!" said the Rich Man.

He sweated.

"Oh Shucks! Be a Sport!" said my Father.

"I will *not*!" said the Rich Man.

He glared.

Our Aunt Esta tried to read from her book and wave her wand at the same time. It waved the Rich Man in the nose.

"Foul Menial!" waved our Aunt Esta. "Bring in the Captives!"

"Who?" demanded the Rich Man.

"*You*!" said our Aunt Esta.

The Rich Man brought us in! Especially Father! He bound us all up in silver paper chains! He put a silver paper ring through my Father's beautiful nose!

"Oh, I say," protested my Father. "It was 'guests' that I understood we were to be! Not captives!"

"Ha!" sniffed the Rich Man. "Be a Sport!"

They both glared.

Our Aunt Esta had cakes in a box. They seemed to be very good cakes. "Now in about ten minutes," read our Aunt Esta from her book, "you will all begin to feel very queer."

"Oh—Lordy!" said my Father.

"I knew it!" said the Rich Man. "I knew it all the time! From the very first mouthful—my stomach——"

"Is there no antidote?" cried my Mother.

Our Aunt Esta took off her horn-rimmed spectacles. She sniffed.

"Sillies!" she said. "This is just a Game, you know!"

"Nevertheless," said the Rich Man, "I certainly feel very queer."

"When you all feel equally queer," said our Aunt Esta coldly, "we will proceed with the Game."

We all felt equally queer just as soon as we could.

Our Aunt Esta made a speech. She made it from her little book.

"Poor helpless Captives (said the Speech). You are now entirely in my power! Yet fear not! If everybody does just exactly as I say, all may yet be well!"

"Hear! Hear!" said my Father.

The Rich Man suddenly seemed to like my Father very much. He reached over and nudged him in the ribs.

"Shut up!" he whispered. "The less you say the sooner it will be over!"

My Father said less at once. He seemed very glad to know about it.

Our Aunt Esta pointed to a boxful of little envelopes.

"Foul Menial," she said. "Bring the little envelopes!"

The Rich Man brought them. But not very cheerfully.

"Oh, of course, it's all right to call *me* that," he said. "But I tell you quite frankly that my daughter Posie's maid will never stand for it! *Her* name is Elizabeth Lou!—Mrs. Jane—Frank—Elizabeth Lou—even!"

Our Aunt Esta looked at the Rich Man. Her look was scornfuller and scornfuller.

"*All* Witch's servants," she said, "are called 'Foul Menial!'—From the earliest classical records of fairy tale and legend down to——"

"Not in our times," insisted the Rich Man. "I defy you in any Intelligence Office in New York to find a—a——"

Our Aunt Esta brushed the contradiction aside. She frowned. Not just at the Rich Man. But at everybody. "We will proceed with the Rehearsal—as written!" she said. She gruffed her voice. She thumped her wand on the floor. "Each captive," she said, "will now step forward and draw a little envelope from the box."

Each captive stepped forward and drew a little envelope from the box.

Inside each envelope was a little card. Very black ink words were written on each card.

"Captives, stand up very straight!" ordered our Aunt Esta.

Every captive stood very straight.

"Knock your knees together with fear!" ordered our Aunt Esta.

Every captive knocked his knees together with fear.

"Strain at your chains!" ordered our Aunt Esta. "But not too hard! Remembering they are paper!"

Every captive strained at his chains but not too hard! Remembering they were paper!

Our Aunt Esta seemed very much pleased. She read another poem from her book. The poem said:

Imprisoned thus in my Witchy Wiles,Robbed of all hope, all food, all smiles,A Fearful Doom o'er-hangs thy Rest,Unless thou meet my Dread Behest!

"Oh, dear—oh, dear—oh, dear—oh, dear!" cried our Mother. "Can nothing save us?"

My Father burst his nose-ring!

Rosalee giggled!

Carol and I jumped up and down! We clapped our hands!

The Rich Man cocked his head on one side. He looked at our Aunt Esta. At her funny black pointed hat. At her scraggly gray wig. At her great horn-rimmed spectacles. At the hump on her back. "U-m-m," he said. "What do you mean,—'witch-y wiles?'"

"*Silence!*" said our Aunt Esta. "Read your cards!"

We read our cards.

Carol's card said "PINK BREEZE" on it. And "SLIMY FROG."

Our Aunt Esta poked Carol twice with her wand. "Pitiful Wretch!" said our Aunt Esta. "It is now two o'clock.—Unless you are back here exactly at three o'clock—bearing a *Pink Breeze* in your hands—you shall be turned for all time and eternity into a *Slimy Green Frog*!—Go hence!"

Carol went hence. He henced as far as the Mulberry Tree on the front lawn. He sat down on the grass with the card in his hand. He read the card. And read it. And read it. It puzzled him very much.

"Pitiful Wretch, go *hence*!" cried our Aunt Esta.

He henced as far as the Larch Tree this time. And sat down all over again. And puzzled. And puzzled.

"Go *hence*, I say, Pitiful Wretch!" insisted our Aunt Esta.

My Mother didn't like Carol to be called a "Pitiful Wretch."—It was because he was dumb, I suppose. When my Mother doesn't like anything it spots her cheek-bones quite red. Her cheek-bones were spotted very red.

"Stop your fussing!" said our Aunt Esta. "And attend to your own business!"

My Mother attended to her own business. The business of her card said "SILVER BIRD" and "HORSE'S HOOF."

Even our Aunt Esta looked a bit flabbergasted.

"Oh, dear—oh, dear," said our Aunt Esta. "I certainly am sorry that it was you who happened to draw that one!—And all dressed up in white too as you are! But after all—" she jerked with a great toss of her scraggly wig, "a Game is a Game! And there can be no concessions!"

"No, of course not!" said my Mother. "Lead me to the Slaughter!"

"There is not necessarily any slaughter connected with it," said our Aunt Esta very haughtily. But she hit my Mother only once with her wand.

"Frail Creature," she said. "On the topmost branch of the tallest tree in the world there is a silver bird with a song in his throat that has never been sung! Unless you bring me this bird *singing* you are hereby doomed to walk with the clatter of a Horse's Hoof!"

"Horse's Hoof?" gasped my Mother. "With the clatter of a Horse's Hoof?"

My Father was pretty mad. "Why, it's impossible!" he said. "She's as light as Thistle-Down! Even in her boots it's like a Fairy passing!"

"Nevertheless," insisted our Aunt Esta. "She shall walk with the clatter of a Horse's Hoof—unless she brings me the Silver Bird."

My Mother started at once for the Little Woods. "I can at least search the Tallest Tree in *my* world!" she said.

It made my Father nervouser and nervouser. "Now don't you *dare*," he called after her, "climb *anything* until I come!"

"Base Interloper!" said our Aunt Esta. "Keep Still!"

"Who?" said my Father.

"*You!*" said our Aunt Esta.

I giggled. Our Aunt Esta was very mad. She turned me into a White Rabbit. I was made of white canton flannel. I was very soft. I had long ears. They were lop-ears. They were lined with pink velvet. They hung way down over my shoulders so I could stroke them. I liked them very much. But my legs looked like white night-drawers. "Ruthy-the-Rabbit" was my name. Our Aunt Esta scolded it at me.

"Because of your impudence, Ruthy-the-Rabbit," she said, "you shall not be allowed to roam the woods and fields at will. But shall stay here in captivity close by my side and help the Foul Menial do the chores!"

The Rich Man seemed very much pleased. He winked an eye. He pulled one of my lop-ears. It was nice to have somebody pleased with me.

Everybody was pleased with Rosalee's bewitchment. It sounded so restful. All Rosalee had to do was to be very pretty,—justexactly as she was! And seventeen years old,—just exactly as she was! And sit on the big gray rock by the side of the brook just exactly as it was! And see whether it was a Bright Green Celluloid Fish or a Bright Red Celluloid Fish that came down the brook first! And if it was a Bright Green Celluloid Fish she was to catch it! And slit open its stomach! And take out all its Directions! And follow 'em! And if it was a Bright Red Celluloid Fish she was to catch *it*! And take out all its Directions and follow *them*!—In either case her card said she would need rubbers and a trowel.—It sounded like Buried Treasure to me! Or else Iris Roots! Our Aunt Esta is very much interested in Iris Roots.

It was my Father's Bewitchment that made the only real trouble. Nothing at all was postponed about my Father's Bewitchment. It happened all at once. It was because my Father knew too much. It was about the Alphabet that he knew too much. The words on my Father's card said "ALPHABET." And "BACKWARDS." And "PINK SILK FAIRY." And "TIN LOCOMOTIVE HEAD." And "THREE MINUTES." Our Aunt Esta turned my Father into a Pink Silk Fairy with White Tarlatan Wings because he was able to say the Alphabet backwards in three minutes! My Father refused to turn! He wouldn't! He wouldn't! He swore he wouldn't! He said it was a "cruel and unnecessary punishment!" Our Aunt Esta said it wasn't a Punishment! It was a Reward! It was the Tin Locomotive Head that was the punishment! My Father said he wouldn't have cared a rap if it had been the Tin Locomotive Head!—He could have smoked through that! But he *wouldn't* be a Pink Silk Fairy with White Tarlatan Wings!

The Rich Man began right away to untie the black velvet ribbon on his leg, and go home! He looked very cheated! He scorned my Father with ribald glances! "Work?" he gloated. "*Of course* it won't work! I knew all the time it wouldn't work!—Two hundred dollars! And forty-three cents?" he gloated. "*H-a!*"

Our Aunt Esta cried! She put her hand on my Father's arm. It was a very small hand. It didn't look a bit like a Witch's hand. Except for having no lovingness in it, it looked a good deal like my Mother's hand.

My Father consented to be turned a little! But not much! He consented to wear the white tarlatan wings! And the gold paper crown! But not the garland of roses! He would carry the pink silk dress on his arm, he said. But he would *not* wear it!

The Rich Man seemed very much encouraged. He stopped untying the black velvet ribbon from his leg. He grinned a little.

My Father told him what he thought of him. The Rich Man acknowledged that very likely it was so. But he didn't seem to mind. He kept right on grinning.

My Father stalked away in his gold paper crown with the pink dress over his arm. He looked very proud and noble. He looked as though even if dogs were sniffing at his heels he wouldn't turn. His white wings flapped as he walked. The spangles shone. It looked very holy.

The Rich Man made a funny noise. It sounded like snorting.

My Father turned round quicker than *scat*. He glared right through the Rich Man at our Aunt Esta. He told our Aunt Esta just what he thought of *her*!

The Rich Man said it wasn't so at all! That the Game undoubtedly was perfectly practical if——

"If *nothing*!" said my Father. "It's you yourself that are spoiling the whole effect by running around playing you're a Black Slave with nothing on but a velvet ribbon round one knee! The very *least* you could do," said my Father, "is to have your face blacked! And wear a plaid skirt!"

"*Eh?*" said the Rich Man.

Our Aunt Esta was perfectly delighted with the suggestion.

The Rich Man took her delight coldly.

He glared at my Father. "I don't think I need any outside help," he said, "in the management of my affairs.—As the Owner indeed of one of the largest stores in the world I——"

"That's all right," said my Father. "But you never yet have tried to manage the children's Aunt Esta.—Nothing can stop her!"

Nothing could! She pinned an old plaid shawl around the Rich Man's waist! She blacked his face! He had to kneel at her feet while it was being blacked! He seemed to sweat easily! But our Aunt Esta blacked very easily too! He looked lovely! Even my Father thought he looked lovely! When he was done he wanted to look in a mirror. My Father advised him not to. But he insisted. My Father got up from making suggestions and came and stood behind him while he looked. They looked only once. Something seemed to hit them. They doubled right up. It was laughter that hit them. They slapped each other on the back. They laughed! And laughed! And laughed! They made such a noise that my Mother came running!

It seemed to make our Aunt Esta a little bit nervous to have my Mother come running. She pointed her wand. She roared her voice.

"Where is the Silver Bird?" she roared.

My Mother looked just as swoone-y as she could. She fell on her knees. She clasped her hands.

"Oh, Cruel Witch," she said. "I *saw* the bird! But I couldn't reach him! He was in the Poplar Tree!—However in the world did you put him there?—Was that what you were bribing the Butcher's Boy about this morning? Was that——?"

"Hush!" roared our Aunt Esta. "Your Doom has overtaken you! Go hence with the clatter of a Horse's Hoof until such time as your Incompetent Head may——"

"Oh, it wasn't my head that was incompetent," said my Mother. "It was my legs. The Poplar Tree was so very tall! So very fluffy and undecided to climb! So——"

"With the clatter of a Horse's Hoof!" insisted our Aunt Esta. "There can be no mercy!"

"None?" implored my Mother.

"None!" said our Aunt Esta.

She gave my Mother two funny little wooden cups. They were something like clappers. You could hold them in your hand so they scarcely showed at all and make a noise like a horse galloping across a bridge! Or trotting! Or anything! It made quite a loud noise! It was wonderful! My Mother started right away for the village. She had on white shoes. Her feet were very small. She sounded like a great team horse stumbling up the plank of a ferry-boat. "I think I'll go get the mail!" she said.

"Like that?" screamed my Father.

My Mother turned around. Her hair was all curly. There were laughs in her eyes.

"I *have* to!" she said. "I'm bewitched!"

"I'll go with you!" said my Father.

My Mother turned around again. She looked at my Father! At his golden crown! At his white spangled wings! At the pink silk skirt over his arm!

"Like—that?" said my Mother.

My Father decided not to go.

The Rich Man said he considered the decision very wise.

They glared.

Way over on the other side of the green lilac hedge we heard my Mother trotting down the driveway. *Clack-clack—clack—*clack sounded the hoof-beats!

"My Lord—she's pacing!" groaned my Father.

"Clever work!" said the Rich Man. "Was she ever in a Band? In a Jazz Band, you know, with Bantam Rooster whistles? And drums that bark like dogs?"

"In a *what*?" cried my Father. He was awful mad.

Our Aunt Esta tried to soothe him with something worse. She turned to me.

"Now, Ruthy-the-Rabbit," she said. "Let us see what *you* can do to redeem the ignominy of your impudent giggling!" She handed me the Bright Green and the Bright Red Celluloid fishes. She poked her wand at me. "Hopping all the way," she said. "Every step of the way, you understand,—bear these two fish to the Head-Waters of the Magic Brook,—the little pool under the apple tree will do,—and start them ex—ex—peditiously down the Brook towards Rosalee!"

"Yes'm," I said.

Our Aunt Esta turned to the Rich Man.

"Foul Menial," she said. "Push my chariot a little further down the Lawn into the shade!"

The Foul Menial pushed it.

My Father pushed a little too.

I hopped along beside them flopping my long ears. Our Aunt Esta looked *ex*-actly like a Witch! The Rich Man's black face was leaking a little but not much! It would have been easier if he hadn't tripped so often on his plaid shawl skirt! My Father's white wings flapped as he pushed! He looked like an angel who wasn't quite hatched! It was handsome!

When we got to the thickest shade there was a man's black felt hat bobbing along the top of the Japonica Hedge. It was rather a soft-boiled looking hat. It was bobbing just as fast as it could towards the house.

When our Aunt Esta saw the hat she screamed! She jumped from her chariot as though it had been flames! She tore the scraggly gray wig from her head! She tore the hump from her back! She kicked off her wooden shoes! Her feet were silk! She ran like the wind for the back door!

My Father ran for the Wood-Shed!

The Rich Man dove into the Lilac Bush!

When the Rich Man was all through diving into the Lilac Bush he seemed to think that he was the only one present who hadn't done anything!

"What you so scared about, Ruthy?" he said. "What's the matter with everybody? Who's the Bloke?"

"It's the New Minister," I said.

"Has he got the Cholera or anything?" said the Rich Man.

"No, not exactly," I explained. "He's just our Aunt Esta's Suitor!"

"Your Aunt Esta's *Suitor*?" cried the Rich Man. "*Suitor*?" He clapped his hand over his mouth. He burst a safety-pin that helped lash the plaid shawl around him. "What do you mean,—'*Suitor*?'" he said.

It seemed queer he was so stupid.

"Why a Suitor," I explained, "is a Person Who Doesn't Suit—so he keeps right on coming most every day to see if he does! As soon as he suits, of course, he's your husband and doesn't come any more at all—because he's already there! The New Minister," I explained very patiently, "is a Suitor for our Aunt Esta's hand!"

We crawled through the Lilac Bush. We peeped out.

Our Aunt Esta hadn't reached the back door at all. She sat all huddled up in a little heap on the embankment trying to keep the New Minister from seeing that she was in her stocking-feet. But the New Minister didn't seem to see anything at all except her hands. Being a Suitor for her hands it was natural, I suppose, that he wasn't interested in anything except her hands. Her hands were on her hair. The scraggly gray wig had rumpled all the seriousness out of her hair. It looked quite jolly. The New Minister stared! And stared! And stared! Except for having no lovingness in them, her hands looked *very* much like my Mother's.

"Our Aunt Esta's got—nice hands," I said.

The Rich Man burst another safety pin.

"Yes, by Jove," he said. "And nice feet, too!" He seemed quite surprised. "How long's this minister fellow been coming here?" he said.

"Oh, I don't know," I said. "He comes whenever our Aunt Esta comes."

The Rich Man made a grunt. He looked at the Minister's hat.

"Think of courting a woman," he said, "in a hat like that!"

"Oh, our Aunt Esta doesn't care anything at all about hats," I said.

"It's time she did!" said the Rich Man.

"We'll go out if you say so," I suggested, "and help them have a pleasant time."

The Rich Man was awful mad. He pointed at his plaid shawl! He pointed at his black face!

"*What?*" he said. "Go out like *this*? And make a fool of myself before that Ninny-Hat?"

"Why, he'd love it!" I said.

The Rich Man choked.

"That's quite enough reason!" he said.

There was a noise in the wood-shed. We could see the noise through the window. It was my Father trying to untie his wings. He couldn't.

The Rich Man seemed to feel better suddenly. He began to mop his face.

"It's a great Game, all right," he said, "if you don't weaken!" He pulled my ears. "But why in the world, Ruthy——" he worried, "did she have to go and tuck that forty-three cents on to the end of the bill?"

"Why, that's her profit!" I explained.

"Her—profit?" gasped the Rich Man. "Her *Profit?*"

"Why, she had to have something!" I explained. "She was planning to have more, of course! She was planning to go to Atlantic City! But everything costs so big! Even toys! It's——"

"Her *Profit?*" gasped the Rich Man. "Forty-three cents on a two hundred dollar deal?" He began to laugh! And laugh! "And she calls herself a Business Woman?" he said. "Why, she ought to be in an Asylum!—All women, in fact, ought to be in Asylums—or else in homes of their own!" Quite furiously he began to pull my ears all over again. "*Business Woman*," he said. "And both her feet would go at once in the hollow of my hand! *Business Woman!*"

Out in the roadway suddenly somebody sneezed.

It made the Rich Man jump awfully.

"Ruthy, stay where you are!" he ordered.

"I can't!" I called back. "I'm already hopped out!"

From my hop-out I could see the Person Who Sneezed! Anybody would have known that it was Posie-with-the-Sick-Bones! She was sitting in an automobile peering through the hedge! There was a black woman with her!

The Rich Man crackled in the bushes. He reached out and grabbed my foot. He pulled me back. His face looked pretty queer.

"Yes, she's been there all the time," he whispered. "But not a soul knows it!—I wanted her to see it work!—I wanted to be sure that she liked it—But I was afraid to bring her in! She catches everything so! And I knew there were children here! And I was afraid there might be something contagious!"

He peered out through the Lilac Branches. There was quite a good deal to peer at.

Down in the meadow Rosalee was still running up and down the soft banks of the brook trying to catch the Celluloid Fish. She had on a green dress. It was a slim dress like a willow wand. She had her shoes and stockings in one hand. And a great bunch of wild blue Forget-me-Nots in the other. Her hair was like a gold wave across her face. She looked pretty. The Springtime looked pretty too.—Out in the wood-shed my Father was still wrestling with his wings.

Up on the green mound by the house our Aunt Esta was still patting her hair while the New Minister stared at her hands.

The Rich Man turned very suddenly and stared at me.

"*Contagious?*" he gasped out suddenly. "Why, upon my soul, Ruthie—it's just about the most contagious place that I ever was in—in my life!"

He gave a funny little laugh. He glanced back over his shoulder towards the road. He groaned.

"But I shall certainly be ruined, Ruthie," he said, "if my little daughter Posie or my little daughter Posie's Black Woman ever see me at close range—in these clothes!" He took my chin in his hands. He looked very deep into my eyes. "Ruthie," he said, "you seem to be a *very* intelligent child.—If you can think of any way—*any* way, I say—by which I can slink off undetected into the house—and be washed——"

"Oh Shucks! That's easy!" I said. "We'll *make* Posie be the Witch!"

When I hopped out this time I stayed hopped! I hopped right up on the wall! And stroked my ears!0

When Posie-with-the-Sick-Bones saw me she began to laugh! And clap her hands! And kick the Black Woman with her toes!

"Oh, I want to be the Witch!" she cried. "I want to be the Witch for ever and ever! And change everybody into everything! I'm going to wear it home in the automobile! And scare the Cook to Death! I'm going to change the Cook into a cup of Beef Tea! And throw her down the sink! I'm going to change my Poodle Dog into a New Moon!" she giggled. "I'm going to change my Doctor into a Balloon! And cut the string!"

The Rich Man seemed perfectly delighted. I could see his face in the bushes. He kept rubbing his hands! And nodding to me to go ahead!

I went ahead just as fast as I could.

The Black Woman began to giggle a little. She giggled and opened the automobile door. She giggled and lifted Posie out. She giggled and carried Posie to the Witch's chariot. She giggled and tied the Witch's hat under Posie's chin. She giggled and tied the humped-back cape around Posie's neck.

Posie never stopped clapping her hands except when the Witch's Wig itched her nose.

It was when the Witch's Wig itched her nose that the Rich Man slunk away on all fours to be washed. He giggled as he slunk. It looked friendly.

Carol came. He was pretty tired. But he had the Pink Breeze in his hands. It was Phlox! It was very pink! It was in a big flower pot! He puffed out his cheeks as he carried it and blew it into Breezes! It was pretty! It was very heavy! He knelt at the Witch's feet to offer it to her! When he looked up and saw the Strange Child in the Witch's Chair he dropped it! It broke and lay on the ground all crushed and spoiled! His mouth quivered! All the shine went out of his face!

It scared Posie to see all the shine go out of his face.

"Oh, Boy—Boy, put back your smile!" she said.

Carol just stood and shook his head.

Posie began to scream.

"Why doesn't he speak?" she screamed.

"He can't," I said. "He hasn't any speech!"

"Why doesn't he cry?" screamed Posie.

"He can't," I said. "He hasn't any cry!"

Posie stopped screaming.

"Can't he even swear?" she said.

"No, he can't," I said. "He hasn't any swear!"

Posie looked pretty surprised.

"I can speak!" she said. "I can cry! I can swear!"

"You sure can, Little Missy!" said the Black Woman.

Posie looked at Carol. She looked a long time. A little tear rolled down her cheek.

"Never mind, Boy," she said. "I will help you make a new Pink Breeze!"

"Oh Lor, Little Missy," said the Black Woman. "You never helped no one do nothin' in your life!"

"I will if I want to!" said Posie. "And we'll make a Larkspur-Colored Breeze too, if we want to!" she said. "And I'll have it on my window-sill all blue-y and frilly and fluttery when everything else in the room is horrid and hushed and smothery!—And we'll make a Green Breeze——" She gave a little cry. She looked at the Waving Meadow where all the long silver-tipped grasses ducked and dipped in the wind. She stretched out her arms. Her arms were no bigger than the handles of our croquet mallets. "We'll dig up *all* the Waving Meadow," she cried. "And pot it into Window-Sill Breezes for the hot people in the cities!"

"You can't!" I said. "It would take mor'n an hour! And you've got to be the Witch!"

"I will *not* be the Witch!" said Posie. She began to scream! "It's my Game!" she screamed. "And I'll do anything I like with it!" She tore off her black pointed hat! She kicked off her stubby wooden shoes! She screamed to the Black Woman to come and bear her away!

While the Black Woman bore her away Carol walked beside them. He seemed very much interested that any one could make so much noise.

When Posie saw how *much* interested Carol was in the noise, she stopped en—tirely screaming to the Black Woman and screamed to Carol instead.

While Carol walked beside the Noise, I saw the New Minister come down the Road and go away. His face looked red.

Our Aunt Esta came running. She was very business-like. She snatched up her wooden shoes and put them on! She crammed on the scraggly gray wig and the humped-back cape!

"Foul Menial!" she called. "Come at once and resume the Game!"

The Black Woman stepped out of the bushes. She looked very much surprised. But not half as surprised as our Aunt Esta.

Our Aunt Esta rubbed her eyes! She rubbed them again! And again! She looked at the Black Woman's face. It was a *real* black face. She looked at the Black Woman's woolly hair.—It was *real* woolly hair! Her jaw dropped!

"Ruthy-the-Rabbit, hop here!" she gasped.

I hopped.

She put her lips close to my ear.

"Ruthy-the-Rabbit," she gasped. "Do I see what I think I see?"

"Yes, you do!" I said.

She put her head down in her hands! She began to laugh! And laugh! And laugh! It was a queer laugh as though she couldn't stop! The tears ran out between her fingers!

"Well—I certainly *am* a Witch!" she laughed. Her shoulders shook like sobs.

The Rich Man came running! He had his watch in his hand! He was all clean and shining! He saw the Black Woman standing by the Witch's chair! He saw the Witch in the chair! He thought the Witch was Posie! He grabbed her right up in his arms and *hugged* her!

"Though I'm late for a dozen Directors' Meetings," he cried, "it's worth it, my Precious, to see you laugh!"

"I'm not your Precious!" cried our Aunt Esta. She bit! She tore! She scratched! She shook her scraggly gray wig-curls all over her face! It was like a mask! But all the time she kept right on laughing! She couldn't seem to stop!

The Rich Man kissed her. And kissed her! Right through her scraggly gray wig-curls he kissed her! He couldn't seem to stop!

"Now, at last, my Precious," he said. "We've learned how to live! We'll play more! We'll laugh more!"

Our Aunt Esta tore off her wig! She tore off her hump! She shook her fist at the Rich Man! But she couldn't stop laughing!

The Rich Man gave one awful gasp! He turned red! He turned white! He looked at the wood-shed window to see if my Father had seen him.

My Father had seen him!

The Rich Man said things under his breath. That is, most of them were under his breath. He stalked to his car. He ordered the Black Woman to pick up the Real Posie and stalk to his car! He looked madder than Pirates!

But when he had climbed into his car, and had started his engine, and was all ready to go, he stood up on the seat instead, and peered over the hedge-top at our Aunt Esta! And grinned!

Our Aunt Esta was standing just where he had left her. All the laughter was gone from her. But her eyes looked very astonished. Her cheeks were blazing red. Her hair was all gay and rumpled like a sky-terrier's. It seemed somehow to be rather becoming to our Aunt Esta to be kissed by mistake.

The Rich Man made a little noise in his throat. Our Aunt Esta looked up. She jumped. The Rich Man fixed his eyes right on her. His eyes were full of twinkles.

"Talk about Be-Witchments!" he said. "Talk about—*Be-Witchments*!—I'll be back on Tuesday! What for?—Great Jumping Jehosophats!" he said. "It's enough that I'll be back!"

My Father stuck his head and the tip of one battered wing out the wood-shed window. He started to say something. And cocked his ear instead.

It was towards the village that he cocked his ear.

We all stopped and cocked our ears.

It was a funny sound: Clack-Clack-*Clack*! Clack-Clack-*Clack*! Clack-Clack—*Clack*!

It was my Mother cantering home across the wooden bridge.

It sounded glad.

My Father thought of a new way suddenly to escape from his wings! And ran to meet her!

THE BLINDED LADY

The Blinded Lady lived in a little white cottage by the Mill Dam.

She had twenty-seven cats! And a braided rug! And a Chinese cabinet all full of peacock-feather fans!

Our Father and Mother took us to see them.

It smelt furry.

Carol wore his blue suit. Rosalee wore an almost grown-up dress. I wore my new middy blouse.

We looked nice.

The Blinded Lady looked nice too.

She sat in a very little chair in the middle of a very large room. Her skirts were silk and very fat. They fluffed all around her like a pen-wiper. She had on a white lace cap. There were violets in the cap. Her eyes didn't look blinded.

We sat on the edge of our chairs. And stared at her. And stared. She didn't mind.

All the cats came and purred their sides against our legs. It felt soft and sort of bubbly.

The Blinded Lady recited poetry to us. She recited "Gray's Elegy in a Country Churchyard." She recited "The Charge of the Light Brigade." She recited "Bingen on the Rhine."

When she got all through reciting poetry she asked us if we knew any.

We did.

We knew "Onward Christian Soldiers," and "Hey Diddle, Diddle, the Cat and the Fiddle." And Rosalee knew two verses about

It was many and many a year agoIn a kingdom by the sea,That a maiden lived whom you may knowBy the name of Annabel Lee.

We hoped the Blinded Lady would be pleased.

She wasn't!

The Blinded Lady said it wasn't nearly enough just to know the first two verses of anything! That you ought to know all the verses of everything! The Blinded Lady said that every baby just as soon as it was born ought to learn every poem that it possibly could so that if it ever grew up and was blinded it would have something to amuse itself with!

We promised we would!

We asked the Blinded Lady what made her blinded.

She said it was because she made all her father's shirts when she was six years old!

We promised we wouldn't!

"And now," said the Blinded Lady, "I'd like to have the Little Dumb Boy come forward and stand at my knee so I can touch his face!"

Carol didn't exactly like to be called the Little Dumb Boy, but he came forward very politely and stood at the Blinded Lady's knee. The Blinded Lady ran her fingers all up and down his face. It tickled his nose. He looked puckered.

"It's a pleasant face!" said the Blinded Lady.

"We like it!" said my Father.

"Oh *very* much!" said my Mother.

"Has he always been dumb?" said the Blinded Lady.

"Always," said my Mother. "But never deaf!"

"Oh *Tush*!" said the Blinded Lady. "Don't be stuffy! Afflictions were meant to talk about!"

"But Carol, you see," said my Mother, "can't talk about his! So *we* don't!"

"Oh—*Tush*!" said the Blinded Lady.

She pushed Carol away. She thumped her cane on the braided rug.

"There's one here, isn't there," she said, "that hasn't got anything to be sensitive about? Let the Young Lassie come forward," she said, "so I can touch her face!"

It made Rosalee very pink to have her face explored.

The Blinded Lady laughed as she explored it.

"Ha!" she said. "Age about seventeen? Gold hair? Sky-blue eyes? Complexion like peaches and cream?—Not much cause here," laughed the Blinded Lady, "for this Young Lassie ever to worry when she looks in the glass!"

"Oh but she does!" I cried. "She worries herself most to death every time she looks!—She's afraid her hair will turn gray before Derry comes!"

"S-s-h!" said everybody.

The Blinded Lady cocked her head. She ruffled herself. It looked like feathers.

"Derry?" said the Blinded Lady. "Who's Derry?—A *beau*?"

My Father gruffed his throat.

"Oh Derry's just a young friend of ours," he said.

"He lives in Cuba," said my Mother.

"Cuba's an island!" I said. "It floats in water! They eat bananas! They have fights! It's very hot! There's lots of moonlight! Derry's father says that when Rosalee's married he'll build a———."

"Hush, Ruthy!" said my Father. "You've talked quite enough already!"

The Blinded Lady patted her skirts. They billowed all around her like black silk waves. It looked funny.

"H-m-m-mmm!" she said. "Let the Child-Who's-Talked-Too-Much-Already come forward now so that I can feel her face!"

I went forward just as fast as I could.

The Blinded Lady touched my forehead.

She smoothed my nose,—my cheeks,—my chin.

"U-m-mmm," she said. "And 'Ruthy' you say is what you call her?"

My Father twinkled his eyes.

"We have to call her something!" he said politely.

"And is this bump on the forehead a natural one?" said the Blinded Lady. "Or an accidental one?"

"Both!" said my Father. "That is, it's pre-em-i-nently natural for our daughter Ruthy to have an accidental bump on her forehead."

"And there are, I infer," said the Blinded Lady, "one or two freckles on either side of the nose?"

"Your estimate," said my Father, "is conservative."

"And the hair?" said the Blinded Lady. "It hasn't exactly the texture of gold."

"'Penny-colored' we call it!" said my Mother.

"And not exactly a *new* penny at that, is it?" said the Blinded Lady.

"N—o," said my Mother. "But rather jolly0 all the same like a penny that's just bought two sticks of candy instead of one!"

"And the nose turns up a little?" said the Blinded Lady.

"Well maybe just a—trifle," admitted my Mother.

The Blinded Lady stroked my face all over again. "U-m-m-m," she said. "Well at least it's something to be thankful for that everything is perfectly normal!" She put her hands on my shoulders. She shook me a little. "Never, *never*, Ruthie," she said, "be so foolish as to complain because you're not pretty!"

"No'm!" I promised.

"Put all the Beauty you can *inside* your head!" said the Blinded Lady.

"Yes'm!" I promised. "And I've just thought of another one that I know! It's about

You must wake and call me early, call me early, mother dear,For I'm to be Queen o' the May, mother, I'm to be——"

"*Foolish!*" said the Blinded Lady. "It wasn't sounds I was thinking of this time, but *sights*!" She pushed me away. She sighed and sighed. It puffed her all out. "O—h," she sighed. "O—h! Three pairs of Young Eyes and all the World waiting to be looked at!"

She rocked her chair. She rocked it very slowly. It was like a little pain.

"I never saw *anything* after I was seventeen!" she said. "And God himself knows that I hadn't seen anywheres near enough before that! Just the little grass road to the village now and then on a Saturday afternoon to buy the rice and the meat and the matches and the soap! Just the wood-lot beyond the hill-side where the Arbutus always blossomed so early! Just old Neighbor Nora's new patch-work quilt!—Just a young man's face that looked in once at the window to ask where the trout brook was! But even these pictures," said the Blinded Lady, "They're fading! Fading! Sometimes I can't remember at all whether old Nora's quilt was patterned in diamond shapes or squares. Sometimes I'm not so powerful sure whether the young man's eye were blue or brown! After all, it's more'n fifty years ago. It's new pictures that I need now," she said. "New pictures!"

She took a peppermint from a box. She didn't pass 'em. She rocked her chair. And rocked. And rocked. She smiled a little. It wasn't a real smile. It was just a smile to save her dress. It was just a little gutter to catch her tears.

"Oh dear me—Oh dear me—Oh dear me!" said my Mother.

"Stop your babbling!" said the Blinded Lady. She sniffed. And sniffed. "But I'll tell you what I'll do," she said. "These children can come back here next Saturday afternoon and——."

"Why there's no reason in the world," said my Mother, "why they shouldn't come every day!"

The Blinded Lady stopped rocking. She almost screamed.

"Every day?" she said. "Mercy no! Their feet are muddy! And besides it's tiresome! But they can come next Saturday I tell you! And I'll give you a prize! Yes, I'll give two prizes—for the two best new pictures that they bring me to think about! And the first prize shall be a Peacock Feather Fan!" said the Blinded Lady. "And the second prize shall be a Choice of Cats!"

"A Choice of Cats?" gasped my Father.

The Blinded Lady thumped her cane. She thumped it pretty hard. It made you glad your toes weren't under it.

"Now mind you, Children!" she said.

"It's got to be a *new* picture! It's got to be something you've seen yourself! The most *beautifulest*! The most *darlingest* thing that you've ever seen! Go out in the field I say! Go out in the woods! Go up on the mountain top! And *look around*! Nobody I tell you can ever make another person see anything that he hasn't seen himself! Now be gone!" said the Blinded Lady. "I'm all tuckered out!"

"Why I'm sure," said my Father, "we never would have come at all if we hadn't supposed that——."

The Blinded Lady shook her cane right at my Father.

"Don't be stuffy!" she said. "But get out!"

We got out.

Old Mary who washed and ironed and cooked for the Blinded Lady showed us the shortest way out. The shortest way out was through the wood-shed. There were twenty-seven little white bowls of milk on the wood-shed floor. There was a cat at each bowl. It sounded lappy! Some of the cats were black. Some of the cats were gray. Some of the cats were white.

There was an old tortoise-shell cat. He had a crumpled ear. He had a great scar across his nose. He had a broken leg that had mended crooked.

Most of the cats were tortoise-shell *and* black *and* gray *and* white! It looked pretty! It looked something the way a rainbow would look if it was fur! And splashed with milk instead of water!

"How many quarts does it take?" said my Mother.

"*Quarts?*" said Old Mary. She sniffed. "*Quarts?* It takes a whole Jersey cow!"

The Blinded Lady called Rosalee to come back. I went with her. I held her hand very hard for fear we would be frightened.

There was a White Kitten in the Blinded Lady's Lap. It was a white Angora. It wasn't any bigger than a baby rabbit. It had a blue ribbon on its neck. It looked very pure. Its face said "Ruthy, I'd like very much to be your kitten!"

But the Blinded Lady's face didn't know I was there at all.

"Young Lassie," said the Blinded Lady. "What is the color of your Derry's eyes?"

"Why—why—black!" said Rosalee.

"U-m-mmm," said the Blinded Lady. "Black?" She began to munch a peppermint. "U-m-m-m," she said. She jerked her head. Her nose looked pretty sharp. "That's right, Young Lassie!" she cried. "Love *early*! Never mind what the old folks say! Sometimes there isn't any late! Love all you can! Love——!" She stopped suddenly. She sank back in her skirts again. And rocked! Her nose didn't look sharp any more. Her voice was all whispers. "Lassie," she whispered, "when you choose your Peacock Feather Fan—choose the one on the top shelf! It's the best one! It's sandal wood! It's——"

My boots made a creak.

The Blinded Lady gave an awful jump!

"There's someone else in this room besides the Young Lassie!" she cried.

I was frightened. I told a lie.

"You're en—tirely mistaken!" I said. I perked Rosalee's hand. We ran for our lives. We ran as fast as we could. It was pretty fast!

When we got out to the Road our Father and Mother were waiting for us. They looked pleasant. We liked their looks very much.

Carol was waiting too. He had his eyes shut. His mouth looked very surprised.

"Carol's trying to figure out how it would feel to be blind," said my Mother.

"Oh!" said Rosalee.

"O—h!" said I.

Carol clapped his hands.

Rosalee clapped her hands.

I clapped my hands.

It was wonderful! We all thought of it at the same moment! We shut our eyes perfectly tight and played we were blinded all the way home!

Our Father and Mother had to lead us. It was pretty bumpy! I peeped some! Rosalee walked with her hands stretched way out in front of her as though she was reaching for something. She looked like a picture. It was like a picture of something very gentle and wishful that she looked like. It made me feel queer. Carol walked with his nose all puckered up as though he was afraid something smelly was going to hit him. It didn't make me feel queer at all. It made me laugh.

It didn't make my Father laugh.

"Now see here, you young Lunatics," said my Father. "If you think your Mother and I are going to drag you up the main village street—acting like this?"

We were sorry, we explained! But it *had* to be!

When we got to the village street we bumped right into the Old Doctor. We bumped him pretty hard! He had to sit down! I climbed into his lap.

"Of course I don't know that it's *you*," I said. "But I think it is!"

The Old Doctor seemed pretty astonished. He snatched at my Father and my Mother.

"Great Zounds, Good People!" he cried. "What fearful calamity has overtaken your offspring?"

"Absolutely nothing at all," said my Father, "compared to what is *going* to overtake them as soon as I get them home!"

"We're playing *blinded*," said Rosalee.

"We've been to see the Blinded Lady!" I explained.

"We're going to get prizes," said Rosalee. "Real prizes! A Peacock Feather Fan!"

"And the Choice of Cats!" I explained.

"For telling the Blinded Lady next Saturday," cried Rosalee, "the prettiest thing that we've ever seen!"0

"Not just the prettiest!" I explained. "But the most preciousest!"

"So we thought we'd shut our eyes!" said Rosalee. "All the way home! And find out what Sight it was that we missed the most!—*Sunshine* I think it is!" said Rosalee. "*Sunshine* and all the pretty flickering little shadows! And the way the slender white church spire flares through the Poplar Trees! Oh I shall make up a picture about *sunshine*!" said Rosalee.

"Oh, Sh—h!" said my Mother. "You mustn't tell each other what you decide. That would take half the fun and the surprise out of the competition!"

"Would—it?" said Rosalee. "Would it?" She turned to the Old Doctor. She slipped into the curve of his arm. The curve of his arm seemed to be all ready for her. She reached up and patted his face. "You Old Darling," she said. "In all the world what is the most beautiful—est sight that *you* have ever seen?"

The Old Doctor gave an awful swallow.

"*Youth!*" he said.

"Oh, youth Fiddle-sticks!" said my Father. "How ever would one make a picture of *that*? All arms and legs! And wild ideas! Believe me that if I ever once get *these* wild ideas and legs and arms home to-day there will be——"

We never heard what there would be! 'Cause we bumped into the Store-Keeping Man instead! And had to tell *him* all about it!

Nobody kissed the Store-Keeping Man. He smelt of mice and crackers. We talked to him just as we would have talked to Sugar or Potatoes.

"Mr. Store-Keeping Man," we said. "You are very wise! You have a store! And a wagon! And a big iron safe! And fly-papers besides!—In all the world—what is the most beautifulest thing that you have ever seen?"

The Store-Keeping Man didn't have to worry about it at all. He never even swallowed. The instant he crossed his hands on his white linen stomach he *knew*!

"My Bank Book!" he said.

My Father laughed. "*Now* you naughty children," said my Father, "I trust you'll be satisfied to proceed home with your eyes open!"

But my Mother said no matter how naughty we were we couldn't go home without buying pop-corn at the pop-corn stand!

So we had to tell the Pop-Corn Man all about it too! The Pop-Corn Man was very little. He looked like a Pirate. He had black eyes. He had gold rings through his ears. We loved him a good deal!

"In all the world—" we asked the Pop-Corn Man, "what is the most beautiful—est sight that you have ever seen?"

It took the Pop-Corn Man an awful long time to think! It took him so long that while he was thinking he filled our paper bags till they busted! It was a nice bustedness!

"The most beautifulest thing—in all zee world?" said the Pop-Corn Man. "In all zee world? It was in my Italy! In such time as I was no more than one bambino I did see zee peacock, zee great blue peacock stride out through zee snow-storm of apple-blossoms! And dance to zee sun!"

"O—h," said Rosalee. "How pretty!"

"Pretty?" said the Pop-Corn Man. "It was to zee eyes one miracle of remembrances! Zee blue! Zee gold! Zee dazzle! Zee soft fall of zee apple-blossoms!—Though I live to be zee hundred! Though I go blind! Though I go prison! Though my pop-corn all burn up! It fade not! Not never! That peacock! That apple-blossom! That shiver!"

"Our supper will all burn up," said my Mother, "if you children don't open your eyes and run home! Already I *think* I can smell scorched Ginger-bread!"

We children all opened our eyes and ran home!

My Mother laughed to see us fly!

My Father laughed a little!

We thought about the Peacock as we ran! We thought quite a little about the Ginger-bread! We wished we had a Peacock! We hoped we had a Ginger-bread!

Our Home looked nice. It was as though we hadn't seen it for a long while. It was as though we hadn't seen anything for a long while! The Garden didn't look like Just a Garden any more! It looked like a *Bower*! Carol's tame crow came hopping up the gravel walk! We hadn't remembered that he was so black! The sun through the kitchen window was real gold! There *was* Ginger-bread!

"Oh dear—Oh dear—Oh *dear*!" said Rosalee. "In a world so full of beautiful things—however shall we choose what to tell the Blinded Lady?"

Carol ran to the desk. He took a pencil. He took a paper. He slashed the words down. He held it out for us to see.

"I know what I'm going to choose," said the words.

He took his pencil. He ran away.

Rosalee took her pencil. She ran away. Over her shoulder she called back something. What she called back was "Oh Goody! I know what *I'm* going to choose!"

I took my Father's pencil. I ran away. I didn't run very far. I found a basket instead. It was a pretty basket. I made a nest for the White Kitten in case I should win it! I lined the nest with green moss. There was a lot of sunshine in the moss. And little blue flowers. I forgot to come home for supper. That's how I chose what I was going to write!

When we woke up the next morning we all felt very busy. It made the day seem funny.

It made every day that happened seem funny.

Every day somebody took somebody's pencil and ran away! My Mother couldn't find anything! Not children! Not pencils!

Rosalee took the Dictionary Book besides.

"Anybody'd think," said my Father, "that this was a Graduation Essay you were making instead of just a simple little word-picture for a Blinded Lady!"

"Word-picture?" said Rosalee. "What I'm trying to make is a Peacock Feather Fan!"

"I wish there were three prizes instead of two!" said my Mother.

"Why?" said my Father.

Carol came and kicked his feet on the door. His hands were full of stones. He wanted a drink of water. All day long when he wasn't sitting under the old Larch Tree with a pencil in his mouth he was carrying stones! And kicking his feet on the door! And asking for a drink of water!

"Whatever in the world," said my Mother, "are you doing with all those stones?"

Carol nodded his head that I could tell.

"He's building something," I said. "Out behind the barn!—I don't know what it is!"

Carol dropped his stones. He took a piece of chalk. He knelt down on the kitchen floor. He wrote big white letters on the floor.

"It's an Ar—Rena," is what he wrote.

"An Arena?" said my Mother. "An *Arena*?" She looked quite sorry. "Oh Laddie!" she said. "I did so want you to win a prize!—*Couldn't* you have kept your mind on it just a day or two longer?"

It was the longest week I ever knew! It got longer every day! Thursday was twice as long as Wednesday! I don't seem to remember about Friday! But Saturday came so early in the morning I wasn't even awake when my Mother called me!

We went to the Blinded Lady's house right after dinner. We couldn't wait any longer.

The Blinded Lady pretended she was surprised to see us.

"Mercy me!" she said. "What? Have these children come again? Muddy feet? Chatter? And all?" She thumped her cane! She rocked her chair! She billowed her skirts!

We weren't frightened a bit! We sat on the edge of our chairs and laughed! And laughed!

There was a little white table spread with pink-frosted cookies! There were great crackly glasses of raspberry vinegar and ice! Old Mary had on a white apron!—That's why we laughed! We *knew* we were expected!

My Father explained it to everybody.

"As long as Carol couldn't speak his piece," he said, "It didn't seem fair that any of the children should speak 'em! So the children have all written their pieces to read aloud and——"

"But as long as Carol wasn't able to read his aloud," cried my Mother, "it didn't seem fair that any of 'em should read theirs aloud! So the children's father is going to read 'em. And——"

"Without giving any clue of course," said my Father, "as to which child wrote which. So that you won't be unduly influenced at all—in any way by—gold-colored hair, for instance or—freckles——"

"Or *anything*!" said my Mother.

"U-m-m-m," said the Blinded Lady.

"Understanding of course," said my Father, "that we ourselves have not seen the papers yet!"

"Nor assisted in any way with the choice0 of subject," said my Mother. "Nor with the treatment of it!"

"U-m-m," said the Blinded Lady.

"I will now proceed to read," said my Father.

"So do," said the Blinded Lady.

My Father so did.

He took a paper from his pocket. He cleared his throat. He put on his eye-glasses. He looked a little surprised.

"The first one," he said, "seems to be about 'Ginger-bread'!"

"*Ginger-bread?*" said the Blinded Lady.

"Ginger-bread!" said my Father.

"Read it!" said the Blinded Lady.

"I will!" said my Father.

Ginger-bread is very handsome! It's so brown! And every time you eat a piece you have to have another! That shows its worth as well as its handsomeness! And besides you can smell it a long way off when you're coming home! Especially when you're coming home from school! It has molasses in it too. And that's very instructive! As well as ginger! And other spices! The Geography is full of them! Molasses comes from New Orleans! Spices come from Asia! Except Jamaica Ginger comes from Drug Stores! There are eggs in ginger-bread too! And that's Natural History and very important! They have to be hen's eggs I think! I had some guineas once and they looked like chipmunks when they hatched. You can't make ginger-bread out of anything that looks like chipmunks! It takes three eggs to make ginger-bread! And one cupful of sugar! And some baking soda! And——

"Oh Tush!" said the Blinded Lady. "That isn't a picture! It's a recipe!—Read another!"

"Dear me! Dear me!" said my Mother. "Now some child is suffering!" She looked all around to see which child it was.

Carol kicked Rosalee. Rosalee kicked me. I kicked Carol. We all looked just as queer as we could outside.

"Read *on*!" thumped the Blinded Lady.

My Father read on.

"This next one," he said, "seems to be about Soldiers!"

"Soldiers?" said the Blinded Lady. "Soldiers?" She sat up very straight. She cocked her head on one side. "Read it!" she said.

"I'm reading it!" said my Father.

The most scrumptious sight I've ever seen in my life is Soldiers Marching! I saw them once in New York! It was *glorious*! All the reds and the blues and the browns of the Uniforms! And when the Band played all the different instruments it seemed as though it was really *gold* and *silver* music they were playing! It makes you feel so brave! And so unselfish! But most of all it makes you wish you were a milk-white pony with diamond hoofs! So that you could *sparkle*! And *prance*! And *rear*! And *run away* just for fun! And *run* and *run* and *run* down clattery streets and through black woods and across green pastures *snorting fire*—till you met more Soldiers and more Bands and more Gold and Silver Music! So that you could *prance* and *sparkle* and *rear* and *run away* all over again,—with *flags flying*!

"U-m-m," said the Blinded Lady. "That *is* pretty! And spirited too!—But—But it doesn't exactly warm the heart.—And no one but a boy, anyway, would *want* to think about soldiers every day.—Read the next one!" said the Blinded Lady.

"Oh all right," said my Father. "Here's the last one."

"Read it!" said the Blinded Lady.

"I'm trying to!" said my Father. He cleared his throat and put on his eye-glasses all over again. "Ahem!" he said.

"The most beautifulest thing I've ever seen in all my life is my Mother's face. It's so——"

"*What?*" cried my Mother.

My Father looked at her across the top of his glasses. He smiled. "*Your face!*" he said.

"W—what?" stammered my Mother.

My Father cleared his throat and began all over again.

The most beautifulest thing I've ever seen in all my life is my Mother's face! It's so pleasant! It tries to make everything so pleasant! When you go away it smiles you away! When you come home it smiles you home! When you're sick it smiles you well! When you're bad it smiles you good! It's so pretty too! It has soft hair all full of little curls! It has brown eyes! It has the *sweetest* ears!—It has a little hat! The jolliest little hat! All trimmed with do-dabs! And teeny pink roses! And there's a silver ribbon on it! And——

"My Mother had a hat like that!" cried the Blinded Lady.

"*Did* she?" said my Mother. Her face still looked pretty queer and surprised.

The Blinded Lady perked way forward in her chair. She seemed all out of breath. She talked so fast it almost choked her!

"Yes! Just *exactly* like that!" cried the Blinded Lady. "My Mother bought it in Boston! It cost three dollars! My Father thought it was an awful price!—She wore it with a lavender dress all sprigged with yellow leaves! She looked like an angel in it! She *was* an angel! *Her* hair was brown too!—I haven't thought of it for ages!—And all full of little curls! She had the kindest smile! The minister said it was worth any two of his sermons! And when folks were sick she went anywhere to help them! *Anywhere!*—She went twenty miles once! We drove the old white horse! I can see it all! My brothers' and sisters' faces at the window waving good-bye! My father cautioning us through his long gray beard not to drive too fast!—The dark shady wood's road! The little bright meadows!—A blue bird that flashed across our heads at the watering trough! The gay village streets! A red plaid ribbon in a shop window! The patch on a peddler's shoe! The great hills over beyond!—There was hills all around us!—My sister Amy married a man from way over beyond! He was different from us! His father sailed the seas! He brought us dishes and fans from China! When my sister Amy was married she wore a white crêpe shawl. There was a peacock embroidered in one corner of it! It was pretty! We curled her hair! There were yellow roses in bloom! There was a blue larkspur!——-"

The Blinded Lady sank back in her chair. She gave a funny little gasp.

"I *remember*!" she gasped. "The Young Man's eyes were *blue*! His teeth were like pearls! When he asked the way to the trout brook he laughed and said——"

The Blinded Lady's cheeks got all pink. She clapped her hands. She sank back into her Skirts. Her eyes looked awful queer.

"I see *everything*!" she cried. "*Everything!*—Give the Peacock Feather Fan to the Magician!"

Rosalee looked at Carol. Carol looked at me. I looked at Rosalee.

"To the Magician?" said my Father.

"To the Magician?" said my Mother.

"To the Young Darling who wrote about her Mother's Face!" thumped the Blinded Lady.

My Father twisted his mouth.

"Will the 'Young Darling' who wrote about her Mother's Face please come forward—and get the Peacock Feather Fan!" said my Father.

Carol came forward. He looked very ashamed. He stubbed his toe on the braided rug.

"It seems to be our son Carol," said my Father, "who conjured up the picture of—of the blue larkspur!"

"What?" said the Blinded Lady. "*What?*"

She tapped her foot on the floor. She frowned her brows. "Well—well—well," she said. "It wasn't at all what I intended! Not at *all*!—Well—well—well!" She began to rock her chair. "But after all," she said, "an agreement is an agreement! And the First Prize is the First Prize!—Let the Little Dumb Boy step forward to the Chinese Cabinet and choose his Peacock Feather Fan!"

Rosalee gave a little cry. It sounded almost like tears. She ran forward. She whispered in Carol's ear.

Carol opened his eyes. He took a chair. He pushed it against the cabinet. He climbed up to the highest shelf. There was a fan as big as the moon! It was sandalwood! It was carved! It was all peacock feathers! Blue! Bronze! It was *beautiful*! He took it! He went back to his seat! His mouth smiled a little! But he carried the Fan as though it was hot!

"The second prize of course," said the Blinded Lady, "goes to the child who wrote about the soldiers!"

Rosalee stepped forward.

The Blinded Lady took her hand. "It is not exactly as I had wished," said the Blinded Lady. "But a Choice of Cats is a Choice of Cats!—You will find them all in the wood-shed Young Lassie—awaiting your decision! Choose wisely! A good cat is a great comfort!"

We went to the wood-shed to help Rosalee choose her cat.0

All the cats purred to be chosen. It was sad. My Father said it wasn't. My Father said one cat was plenty.

The White Persian Kitten lay on a soap box. It looked like Easter Lilies. Rosalee saw it. She forgot all about the fan.

Carol didn't forget about the fan. He stamped his foot. He shook his head. He took Rosalee's hand and led her to the old Tortoise Shell Cat. He put the old Tortoise Shell cat in Rosalee's arms. Rosalee looked pretty surprised. So did the cat.

My sorrow made tears in my eyes. My Mother came running.

"Bless your heart, Ruthy-Girl," she said. "You shall have a Ginger-bread to-night that *is* a Picture!" She put a little box in my hand. There was a little gold pencil in the box. It was my Mother's best little gold pencil with the agate stone in the end. "Here's Mother's prize, Darling," she said. "The Prize Mother brought for *whichever* child didn't win the Blinded Lady's prizes! Don't you worry! Mother'll always have a prize for whichever child doesn't win the other prizes!"

My sorrow went away.

We all ran back to the Blinded Lady to thank her for our Beautiful Party. And for the prizes.

My Father made a speech to the Blinded Lady.

"But after all, my dear Madam," he said, "I am afraid you have been cheated!—It was '*new*' pictures that you wanted, not old ones!"

The Blinded Lady whacked at him with her cane. She was awful mad.

"How do *you* know what I want?" she said. "How do *you* know what I want?"

My Father and my Mother looked at each other. They made little laughs with their eyes.

The Blinded Lady smoothed herself.

"But I certainly am flabbergasted," she said, "about the Old Tom Cat! Whatever in the world made the Young Lassie choose the old battle-scarred Tom?"

Rosalee looked at Carol. Carol looked at me. I looked at the Old Tom.

"Maybe she chose him for—for his historicalness," said my Mother.

"——Maybe," said my Father.

We started for the door. We got as far as the Garden. I remembered something suddenly. I clapped my hands. I laughed right out! "No! She didn't either!" I said. "She chose him for Carol's Ar—Rena—I bet'cher! Carol's going to have him for a Cham—peen! We'll fight him every afternoon! Maybe there'll be tickets!"

"Tickets?" said my Father.

"Oh my dears," said my Mother. "A cat-fight is a dreadful thing!"

My Father looked at the Old Tom! At his battered ears! At his scarred nose! At his twisted eye! The Old Tom looked at my Father! They both smiled!

"Infamous!" said my Father. "How much will the tickets be?"

We went home. We went home through the fields instead of through the village.

Carol held the Peacock Feather Fan as though he was afraid it would bite him.

Rosalee carried the Old Tom as though she *knew* it would bite her.

When we got to the Willow Tree they changed prizes. It made a difference.

Rosalee carried the Peacock Feather as though it was a magic sail. She tipped it to the breeze. She pranced it. And danced it. It looked fluffy.

Carol carried the Old Tom hugged tight to his breast. The Old Tom looked *very* historical. Carol looked very shining and pure. He looked like a choir-boy carrying his singing book. He looked as though his voice would be very high.

My Father and Mother carried each other's hands. They laughed very softly to themselves as though they knew pleasant things that no one else knew.

My hand would have felt pretty lonely if I hadn't had the little gold pencil to carry.

I felt pretty tired. I walked pretty far behind.

I decided that when I grew up I'd be a Writer! So that no matter what happened I'd always have a gold pencil in my hand and *couldn't* be lonely!

THE GIFT OF THE PROBABLE PLACES

My Mother says that everybody in the world has got some special Gift. Some people have one kind and some have another.

I got my skates and dictionary-book last Spring when I was nine. I've always had my freckles.

My brother Carol's Gift is Being Dumb. No matter what anybody says to him he doesn't have to answer 'em.

There was an old man in our town named Old Man Smith.

Old Man Smith had a wonderful Gift.

It wasn't a Christmas Gift like toys and games. It wasn't a Birthday Gift all stockings and handkerchiefs.

It was the *Gift of Finding Things*!

He called it "The Gift of the Probable Places."

Most any time when you lost anything he could find it for you. He didn't find it by floating a few tea-leaves in a cup. Or by trying to match cards. Or by fooling with silly things like ghosts. He didn't even find it with his legs. He found it with his head. He found it by thinking very hard with his head.

People came from miles around to borrow his head. He always charged everybody just the same no matter what it was that they'd lost. One dollar was what he charged. It was just as much trouble to him he said to think about a thimble that was lost as it was to think about an elephant that was lost.—I never knew anybody who lost an elephant.

When the Post Master's Wife lost her diamond ring she hunted more than a hundred places for it! She was most distracted! She thought somebody had stolen it from her! She hunted it in all the Newspapers! She hunted it in all the stores! She hunted it all up and down the Village streets! She hunted it in the Depot carriage! She hunted it in the Hired Girl's trunk! Miles and miles and miles she must have hunted it with her hands and with her feet!

But Old Man Smith found it for her without budging an inch from his wheel-chair! Just with his head alone he found it! Just by asking her a question that made her mad he found it! The question that made her mad was about her Baptismal name.—Her Baptismal name was Mehetabelle Euphemia.

"However in the world," said Old Man Smith, "did you get such a perfectly hideous name as Mehetabelle Euphemia?"

The Post Master's wife was madder than Scat! She wrung her hands. She snapped her thumbs! She crackled her finger-joints!

"Never—*Never*," she said had she been "so insulted!"

"U-m-m-m—exactly what I thought," said Old Man Smith. "Now just when—if you0 can remember, was the last time that you felt you'd never been so insulted before?"

"Insulted?" screamed the Post Master's Wife. "Why, I haven't been so insulted as this since two weeks ago last Saturday when I was out in my back yard under the Mulberry Tree dyeing my old white dress peach-pink! And the Druggist's Wife came along and asked me if I didn't think I was just a little bit too old to be wearing peach-pink?—*Me—Too Old? Me?*" screamed the Post Master's Wife.

"U-m-m," said Old Man Smith. "Pink, you say? Pink?—A little powdered Cochineal, I suppose? And a bit of Cream o' Tartar? And more than a bit of Alum? It's a pretty likely combination to make the fingers slippery.—And a lady what crackles her finger-joints so every time she's mad,—and snaps her thumbs—and?—Yes! Under the Mulberry Tree is a *very Probable Place*!—One dollar, please!" said Old Man Smith.

And when the Grocer's Nephew got suspended from college for sitting up too late at night and getting headaches, and came to spend a month with his Uncle and couldn't find his green plaid overcoat when it was time to go home he was perfectly positive that somebody had borrowed it from the store! Or that he'd dropped it out of the delivery wagon working over-time! Or that he'd left it at the High School Social!

But Old Man Smith found it for him just by glancing at his purple socks! And his plaid necktie. And his plush waistcoat.

"Oh, yes, of course, it's perfectly possible," said Old Man Smith, "that you dropped it from the basket of a balloon on your way to a Missionary Meeting.—But have you looked in the Young Widow Gayette's back hall? 'Bout three pegs from the door?—Where the shadows are fairly private?—One dollar, please!" said Old Man Smith.

And when the Old Preacher lost the Hymn Book that George Washington had given his grandfather, everybody started to take up the floor of the church to see if it had fallen down through a crack in the pulpit!

But Old Man Smith sent a boy running to beg 'em not to tear down the church till they'd looked in the Old Lawyer's pantry,—'bout the second shelf between the ice chest and the cheese crock. Sunday evening after meeting was rather a lean time with Old Preachers he said he'd always noticed.—And Old Lawyers was noted for their fat larders.—And there were certain things about cheese somehow that seemed to be soothin' to the memory.

"Why, how perfectly extraordinary!" said everybody.

"One dollar, please!" said Old Man Smith again.

And when Little Tommy Bent ran away to the city his Mother hunted all the hospitals for him! And made 'em drag the river! And wore a long black veil all the time! And howled!

But Old Man Smith said, "Oh Shucks! It ain't at all probable, is it, that he was aimin' at hospitals or rivers when he went away?—What's the use of worryin' over the things he *weren't* aimin' at till you've investigated the things he *was*?"

"Aimin' at?" sobbed Mrs. Bent. "Aimin' at?—Who in the world could ever tell what any little boy was aimin' at?"

"And there's something in that, too!" said Old Man Smith. "What did he look like?"

"Like his father," said Mrs. Bent.

"U-m-m. Plain, you mean?" said Old Man Smith.

"He was only nine years old," sobbed Mrs. Bent. "But he did love Meetings so! No matter what they was about he was always hunting for some new Meetings to go to! He just seemed naturally to dote hisself on any crowd of people that was all facing the other way looking at somebody else! He had a little cowlick at the back of his neck!" sobbed Mrs. Bent. "It was a comical little cowlick! People used to laugh at it! He never liked to sit any place where there was anybody sitting behind him!"

"Now you're talking!" said Old Man Smith. "Will he answer to the name of 'Little Tommy Bent?'"

"He will not!" said Mrs. Bent "He's that stubborn! He's exactly like his Father!"

Old Man Smith wrote an entirely new advertisement to put in the papers. It didn't say anything about Rivers! Or Hospitals! Or 'Dead or Alive!' It just said:

LOST: In the back seat of Most Any Meeting, a Very Plain Little Boy. Will *not* answer to the name of "Little Tommy Bent." Stubborn, like his Father.

"We'll put that in about being 'stubborn,'" said Old Man Smith, "because it sounds quaint and will interest people."

"It won't interest Mr. Bent!" sobbed Mrs. Bent. "And it seems awful cruel to make it so public about the child's being plain!"

Old Man Smith spoke coldly to her.

"Would you rather lose him—handsome," he said. "Or find him—*plain*?"

Mrs. Bent seemed to think that she'd rather find him plain.

She found him within two days! He was awful plain. His shoes were all worn out. And his stomach was flat. He was at a meeting of men who sell bicycles to China. The men were feeling pretty sick. They'd sent hundreds and hundreds of he-bicycles to China and the Chinamen couldn't ride 'em on account of their skirts!—It was the smell of an apple in a man's pocket that made Tommy Bent follow the man to the meeting.—And he answered to every name except 'Tommy Bent' so they knew it was he!

"Mercy! What this experience has cost me!" sobbed Mrs. Bent.

"One dollar, please!" said Old Man Smith.

"It's a perfect miracle!" said everybody.

"It 'tain't neither!" said Old Man Smith. "It's plain Hoss Sense! There's laws about findin' things same as there is about losin' 'em! Things has got regular habits and haunts same as Folks! And Folks has got regular haunts and habits same as birds and beasts! It ain't the Possible Places that I'm arguin' about!—The world is full of 'em! But the *Probable Places* can be reckoned most any time on the fingers of one hand!—That's the trouble with folks! They're always wearin' themselves out on the Possible Places and never gettin' round at all to the *Probable* ones!—Now, it's perfectly possible, of course," said Old Man Smith, "that you might find a trout in a dust-pan or a hummin' bird in an Aquarium—or meet a panther in your Mother's parlor!—But the chances are," said Old Man Smith, "that if you really set out to organize a troutin' expedition or a hummin' bird collection or a panther hunt—you wouldn't look in the dust pan or the Aquarium or your Mother's parlor *first*!—When you lose something that *ain't got* no *Probable Place*—then I sure *am* stumped!" said Old Man Smith.

But when Annie Halliway lost her *mind*, everybody in the village was stumped about it. And everything was all mixed up. It was Annie Halliway's mother and Annie Halliway's father and Annie Halliway's uncles and aunts and cousins and friends who did all the worrying about it! While Annie Halliway herself didn't seem to care at all! But just sat braiding things into her hair!

Some people said it was a railroad accident that she lost her mind in. Some said it was because she'd studied too hard in Europe. Some said it was an earthquake. Everybody said something.

Annie Halliway's father and mother were awful rich. They brought her home in a great big ship! And gave her twelve new dresses and the front parlor and a brown piano! But she wouldn't stay in any of them! All she'd stay in was a little old blue silk dress she'd had before she went away!

Carol and I got excused from school one day because we were afraid our heads might ache, and went to see what it was all about.

It seemed to be about a great many things.

But after we'd walked all around Annie Halliway twice and looked at her all we could and asked how old she was and found out that she was nineteen, we felt suddenly very glad about something.—We felt suddenly very glad that if she really was obliged to lose anything out of her face, it was her *mind* that she lost! Instead of her eyes! Or her nose! Or her red, red mouth! Or her cunning little ears! *She was so pretty!*

She seemed to like us very much too. She asked us to come again.

We said we would.

We did.

We went every Saturday afternoon.

They let us take her to walk if we were careful. We didn't walk her in the village because her hair looked so funny. We walked her in the pleasant fields. We gathered flowers. We gathered ferns. We explored birds. We built little gurgling harbors in the corners of the brook. Sometimes we climbed hills and looked off. Annie Halliway seemed to like to climb hills and look off.

It was the day we climbed the Sumac Hill that we got our Idea!

It was a nice day!

Annie Halliway wore her blue dress! And her blue scarf! Her hair hung down like two long, loose black ropes across her shoulders! Blue Larkspur was braided into her hair! And a little tin trumpet tied with blue ribbon! And a blue Japanese fan! And a blue lead pencil! And a blue silk stocking!0 And a blue-handled basket! She looked like a Summer Christmas Tree. It was pretty.

There were lots of clouds in the sky. They seemed very near. It sort of puckered your nose.

"Smell the clouds!" said Annie Halliway.

Somebody had cut down a tree that used to be there. It made a lonely hole in the edge of the hill and the sky. Through the lonely hole in the edge of the hill and the sky you could see miles and miles. Way down in the valley a bright light glinted. It was as though the whole sun was trying to bore a hole in a tiny bit of glass and couldn't do it.

Annie Halliway stretched out her arms towards the glint. And started for it.

I looked at Carol. Carol looked at me. We knew where the glint was. It was Old Man Smith's house. Old Man Smith's house was built of tea cups! And broken tumblers! And bits of plates! First of all, of course, it was built of clay or mud or something soft and loose like that! And while it was still soft he had stuck it all full of people's broken dishes! So that wherever you went most all day long the sun was trying to bore a hole in it!—And couldn't do it!

It seemed to be the glint that Annie Halliway wanted. She thought it was something new to braid in her hair, I guess. She kept right on walking towards it with her arms stretched out.

Carol kept right on looking at me. His mouth was all turned white. Sometimes when people *talk* to me I can't understand at all what they mean. But when Carol looks at me with his mouth all turned white, I always know just exactly what he means! It made my own mouth feel pretty white!

"We shall be punished!" I said. "We'll surely be punished if we do it!"

My brother Carol smiled. It was quite a white smile. He put out his hand. I took it. We ran down the hill after young Annie Halliway! And led her to the glint!

Old Man Smith was pretty surprised to see us. He was riding round the door-yard in his wheel chair. He rolled his chair to the gate to meet us. The chair squeaked a good deal. But even if he'd wanted to walk he couldn't. The reason why he couldn't is because he's dumb in his legs.

"What in the world do you want?" he asked.

I looked at Carol. Carol looked at me. He kicked me in the shins. My thoughts came very quickly.

"We've brought you a young lady that's lost her mind!" I said. "What can you do about it?"

Something happened all at once that made our legs feel queer. What happened was that Old Man Smith didn't seem pleased at all about it. He snatched his long white beard in his hands.

"Lost her mind?" he said. "Her *mind*? Her *mind*? How dar'st you mock me?" he cried.

"We *darsn't* at all!" I explained. "On account of the bears! We've read all about the mocking bears in a book!"

He seemed to feel better.

"You mean in the good book?" he said. "The Elijah bears, you mean?"

"Well, it was *quite* a good book," I admitted. "Though my Father's got lots of books on Tulips that have heap prettier covers!"

"U—m—m—m," said Old Man Smith. "U—m—m—m——. U—m——m——m."

And all the time that he was saying "U—m——m——m—U—m——m——m," young Annie Halliway was knocking down his house. With a big chunk of rock she was chipping it off. It was a piece of blue china cup with the handle still on it that she chipped off first.

When Old Man Smith saw it he screamed.

"Woman! What are you doing?" he screamed.

"Her name is Young Annie Halliway," I explained.

"Young Annie Halliway—*Come Here!*" screamed Old Man Smith.

Young Annie Halliway came here. She was perfectly gentle about it. All her ways were gentle. She sat down on the ground at Old Man Smith's feet. She lifted her eyes to Old Man Smith's eyes. She looked holy. But all the time that she looked so holy she kept right on braiding the handle of the blue china cup into her hair. It cranked against the tin trumpet. It sounded a little like the 4th of July.

Old Man Smith reached down and took her chin in his hands.

"Oh my Lord—what a beautiful face!" he said. "What a beautiful face!—And you say she's lost her mind?" he said. "You say she's lost her mind?" He turned to Carol. "And what do *you* say?" he asked.

"Oh, please, Sir, Carol doesn't say anything!" I explained. "He can't! He's dumb!"

"*Dumb?*" cried Old Man Smith. "So this is the Dumb Child, is it?" He looked at Carol. He looked at himself. He looked at my freckles. He rocked his hands on his stomach. "Merciful God!" he said. "How are we all afflicted!"

"Oh, please, Sir," I said, "my brother Carol isn't afflicted at all!—It's a great *gift* my Mother says to be born with the Gift of Silence instead of the Gift of Speech!"

He made a little chuckle in his throat. He began to look at Young Annie Halliway all over again.

"And what does your Mother say about *her*?" he pointed.

"My Mother says," I explained, "that she only hopes that the person who finds her mind will be honest enough to return it!"

"What?" said Old Man Smith. "To return it?—Honest enough to return it?"

He began to do everything all over again!—To chuckle! To rock! To take Young Annie Halliway's chin in his hand!

"And what did you say your name was, my pretty darling?" he asked.

Young Annie Halliway looked a little surprised.

"My name is Robin," she said. "Dearest—Robin—I think."

"You think wrong!" said Old Man Smith. He frowned with ferocity.

It made us pretty nervous all of a sudden.

Carol went off to look at the bee-hive to calm himself. Young Annie Halliway picked up the end of one of her long braids and looked at that. There was still about a foot of it that didn't have anything braided into it. I didn't know where to look so I looked at the house. It was very glistening. Blue it glistened. And green it glistened! And red it glistened! And pink! And purple! And yellow!

"Oh, see!" I pointed. "There's old Mrs. Beckett's rose-vase with the gold edge!—She dropped it on the brick garden-walk the day her son who'd been lost at sea for eleven years walked through the gate all alive and perfectly dry!—And that chunky white nozzle with the blue stripe on it?—I know what that is!—It's the nose of Deacon Perry's first wife's best tea pot!—I've seen it there! In a glass cupboard! On the top shelf!—She never used it 'cept when the Preacher came!"

"The Deacon's second wife broke it—feeding chickens out of it," said Old Man Smith.

"And that little scrap of saucer," I cried, "with the pansy petal on it?—Why—Why *that's* little Hallie Bent's doll-dishes!—We played with 'em down in the orchard! She died!" I cried. "She had the whooping-measles!"

"That little scrap of saucer," said Old Man Smith, "was the only thing they found in Mr. Bent's bank box.—What the widow was lookin' for was gold!"

"And that green glass stopper!" I cried. "Oh, Goodie——Goodie——*Goodie*!—Why, that——"

"Hush your noise!" said Old Man Smith. "History is solemn!—The whole history of the village is written on the outer walls of my house!—When the Sun strikes here,—strikes there,—on that bit of glass,—on this bit of crockles—the edge of a plate,—the rim of a tumbler,—I read about folk's minds!—What they loved!—What they hated!—What they was thinking of instead when it broke!—" He snatched his long white beard in his hands. He wagged his head at me. "There's a law about breakin' things," he said, "same as there's a law about losin' them! My house is a sample-book," he said. "On them there walls—all stuck up like that—I've got a sample of most every mind in the village!—People give 'em to me themselves," he said. "They let me rake out their trash barrels every now and then. They don't know what they're givin.'—Now, that little pewter rosette there——"

"It would be nice—wouldn't it," I said, "if you could find a sample of Young Annie Halliway's mind? Then maybe you could match it!"

"*Eh?*" said Old Man Smith. "A sample of her mind?" He looked jerky. He growled in his throat. "A—hem——A—hem," he said. He closed his eyes. I thought he'd decided to die. I screamed for Carol. He came running. He'd only been bee-stung twice. Old Man Smith opened his eyes. His voice sounded queer. "Where do they *think* she lost her mind?" he whispered.0

"In Europe," I said. "Maybe in a train! Maybe on a boat! They don't know! She can't remember anything about it."

"U—m—m," said Old Man Smith. He looked at Young Annie Halliway. "And where do *you* think you lost it?" he said.

Young Annie Halliway seemed very much pleased to be asked. She laughed right out.

"In a March wind!" she said.

"*Eh?*" said Old Man Smith. He turned to me again. "What did you say her name was?" he asked.

I felt a little cross.

"Halliway!" I said. "Halliway—Halliway—*Halliway*! They live in the big house out by the Chestnut Trees! They only come here in the Summers! Except now! The Doctors say it's Mysteria!"

"The Doctors say *what* is Mysteria?" said Old Man Smith.

"What Annie's got!" I explained. "What made her lose her mind! Mysteria is what they call it."

"U—m—m," said Old Man Smith. He reached way down into his pocket. He pulled out a box. He opened the box. It was full of pieces of colored glass! And of china! He juggled them in his hands. They looked gay. Red they were! And green! And white! And yellow! And blue! He snatched out all the blue ones and hid 'em quick in his pocket. "She seems sort of partial to blue," he said.

There was one funny big piece of glass that was awful shiny. When he held it up to the light it glinted and glowed all sorts of colors. It made your eyes feel very calm.

Annie Halliway reached out her hand for it. She didn't say a word. She just stared at it with her hand all reached out.

But Old Man Smith didn't give it to her. He just sat and stared at her eyes.

Her eyes never moved from the shining bit of glass. They looked awful funny. Bigger and bigger they got! And rounder and rounder! And stiller and stiller!

It was like a puppy-dog pointing a little bird in the grass. It made you feel queer. It made you feel all sort of hollow inside. It made your legs wobble.

Carol's mouth was wide open.

So was Old Man Smith's.

Old Man Smith reached out suddenly and put the shining bit of glass right into Annie Halliway's hand. It fell through her fingers. But her hand stayed just where it was, reaching out into the air.

"Put down your arm!" said Old Man Smith.

Annie Halliway put it down. Her eyes were still staring very wide.

"Look!" said Old Man Smith. "Look!" He dropped several pieces of colored glass china into her lap.

She chose the handle of a red tea cup and a little chunk of yellow crockery. She stared and stared at them. But all the time it was as though her eyes didn't see them. All the time it was as though she was looking at something very far away. Then all of a sudden she began to jingle them together in her hand,—the little piece of red china and the chunk of yellow bowl! And swing her shoulders! And stamp her foot! It looked like dancing. It sounded like clappers.

"Oh, Ho! *This* is Spain!" she laughed.

Old Man Smith snatched all the blue pieces of china and glass out of his pocket again and tossed them into her lap. He looked sort of mad.

"Spain?" he said. "Spain? What in the Old Harry has a handful of glass and china got to do with Spain?"

"Harry?" said Annie Halliway. "Old—Harry?" Her eyes looked wider and blinder every minute. It was as though everything in her was wide awake except the thing she was thinking about. "Har—ry?" she puzzled. "Harry?" she dropped the red and yellow china from her hand and picked up a piece of blue glass and offered it to Old Man Smith. "Why, *that* is Harry!" she said. She reached for the pig-tail that had the blue Larkspur braided into it. She pointed to the pig-tail that had the blue fan braided into it. "Why, *that* is Harry!" she said. She made a little sob in her throat.

Old Man Smith jingled his hands at her.

"There—There—There, my Pretty!" he said. "Never mind—Never mind!"

He opened his hands. There were some little teeny-tiny pieces of plain glass in his hands. Little round knobs like beads they were. Very shining. They made a nice jingle.

When Annie Halliway saw them she screamed! And snatched them in her hand! And threw them away just as far as she could! All over the grass she threw them!

"I will not!" she screamed. "*I will not! I will not!*" Her tears were awful.

When she got through screaming her face looked like a wet cloth that had everything else wrung out of it except shadows.

"Where—is—Harry?" said Old Man Smith. He said it very slowly. And then all over again. "Where—is—Harry?—You wouldn't have dar'st not tell him if you'd known."

Annie Halliway started to pick up some blue glass again. Then she stopped and looked all around her. It was a jerky stop. Her jaw sort of dropped.

"Harry—is—in—prison!" she said. Even though she'd said it herself she seemed to be awfully surprised at the news. She shook and shook her head as though she was trying to wake up the idea that was asleep. Her eyes were all scrunched up now with trying to remember about it. She dragged the back of her hands across her forehead. First one hand and then the other. She opened her eyes very wide again and looked at Old Man Smith.

"Where—is—Harry?" said Old Man Smith.

Annie Halliway never took her eyes from Old Man Smith's face.

"It—It was the night we crossed the border from France to Spain," she said. Her voice sounded very funny and far away. It sounded like reciting a lesson too. "There were seven of us and a teacher from the Paris art school," she recited. "It—It was the March holiday.——There—There—was a woman——a strange woman in the next compartment who made friends with me.—She seemed to be crazy over my hair.—She asked if she might braid it for the night."

Without any tears at all Annie Halliway began to sob again.

"When they waked us up at the Customs," she sobbed, "Harry came running! His face was awful! 'She's braided diamonds in your hair!' he cried. 'I heard her talking with her accomplice! A hundred thousand dollars' worth of diamonds! Smugglers and murderers both they are!—Everybody will be searched!'—He tore at my braids! I tore at my braids! The diamonds rattled out! Harry tried to catch them!—He pushed me back into the train! I saw soldiers running!—I thought they were going to shoot him! He thought they were going to shoot him!—I saw his eyes!—He looked so—so surprised!—I'd never noticed before how blue his eyes were!—I tell you I saw his eyes!—I couldn't speak!—There wasn't anybody to explain just why he had his hands full of diamonds!—I *saw* his eyes! I tell you I couldn't speak!—I tell you I *never* spoke!—My tongue went dead in my mouth! For months I never spoke!—I've only just begun to speak again!—I've only just——"

She started to jump up from the ground where she was sitting! She couldn't!—She had braided Old Man Smith and his wheel chair into her hair! When she saw what she had done she toppled right over on her face! And fainted all out!

Over behind the lilac bush somebody screamed.

It was Annie Halliway's Mother! With her was a strange gentleman who had come all the way from New York to try and cure Annie Halliway. The strange gentleman was some special kind of a doctor.

"Hush—Hush!" the Special Doctor kept saying to everybody. "This is a very crucial moment! Can't you see that this a very crucial moment?" He pointed to Annie Halliway on the grass. Her Mother knelt beside her trying very hard to comb Old Man Smith and his wheel-chair out of her pig-tail. "Speak to her!" said the Doctor. "Speak to her very gently!"

"Annie?" cried her Mother. "Annie?—Annie—*Annie?*"

Annie Halliway opened her eyes very slowly and looked up. It was a brand new kind of a look. It had a bottom to it instead of being just through and through and through. There was a little smile in it too. It was a pretty look.

"Why, Mother," said Annie Halliway. "Where am I?"

The Special Man from New York made a queer little sound in his throat.

"Thank God!" he said. "She's all right *now*!"

It seemed pretty quick to me.

"You mean—" I said, "that her Mysteria is all cured—now?"

"Not *My*steria," said the Special Man from New York, *"Hy*steria!"

"No!—*Her*steria!" corrected Old Man Smith.0

The Special Man from New York began to laugh.

But Annie Halliway's Mother began to cry.

"Oh, just suppose we'd never found her?" she cried. She looked at Carol. She looked at me. She glared a little. But not so awfully much. "When you naughty children ran away with her?" she cried. "And we couldn't find her anywhere?—And the Doctor came? And there was only an hour to spare?—And we got a horse and drove round anywhere? And—And——"

"I wouldn't have missed it for anything!" said the Special Man from New York.

"And all your appointments waiting?" cried Annie Halliway's Mother.

"Darn the appointments!" said the Special Man from New York. He slanted his head and looked at Old Man Smith. "We arrived," he said, "just at the moment when the young lady was gazing so—so intently at the piece of shiny glass." He made a funny grunt in his throat. "Let me congratulate you, Mr.—Mr. Smith!" he said. "Your treatment was most efficient!—Your hypnosis was perfect! Your——"

"Hip *nothing*!" said Old Man Smith.

"Of course, in a case like this," said the Special Man from New York, "the Power of Suggestion is always——"

"All young folks," said Old Man Smith, "are cases of one kind or another—and the most powerful suggestion that I can make is that somebody find 'Harry!'"

"'Harry?'" said Annie Halliway's Mother. "'*Harry?*'—Why, I've got four letters at home for Annie in my desk now—from some im—impetuous young man who signs himself 'Harry!'—He seems to be in an Architect's office in Paris! 'Robin' is what he calls Annie!—'*Dearest* Robin'——"

"Eh?" said Annie Halliway. "What? *Where?*" She sat bolt upright! She scrambled to her feet! She started for the carriage!

55

Her Mother had to run to catch her.

The Special Man from New York followed them just as fast as he could.

Old Man Smith wheeled his chair to the gate to say "Good-bye."

Everything seemed all mixed up.

Annie Halliway's Mother never stopped talking a single second.

"Oh, my Pet!" she cried. "My Precious. My Treasure!"

With one foot on the carriage step the Special Man from New York turned round and looked at Old Man Smith. He smiled a funny little smile.

"Seek—and ye shall find!" he said. "That is—if you only know *How* and *Where* to seek."

Old Man Smith began to chuckle in his beard.

"Yes, I admit that's quite a help," he said, "the knowing *How* and *Where!*—But before you set out seekin' very hard for anything that's lost it's a pretty good idea to find out first just exactly what it is that you're seekin' for!—When a young lady's lost her *mind,* for instance, that's one thing!—But if it's her *heart* that's lost, why, that, of course, is quite another!"

Annie Halliway's face wasn't white any more. It was as red as roses. She had it in her Mother's shoulder.

The horses began to prance. The carriage began to creak.

Annie Halliway's Mother looked all around.

"Oh, dear—oh, dear—oh, dear, Mr.—Mr. Smith," she said. "How shall I ever repay you?"

Old Man Smith reached out his hand across the fence. There was sort of a twinkle in his eye.

"One dollar, please," said Old Man Smith.

THE BOOK OF THE FUNNY SMELLS—AND EVERYTHING

It was Carol who invented the Book. He didn't mean any harm.

I helped him.

We called it "The Book of the Funny Smells—and Everything."

It was one Tuesday noon coming home from school that we stopped the Lady on the street.

She was a very interesting looking lady. She looked like all sorts of different-colored silk roses. And a diamond brooch.

"Excuse us, Madam," I said. "But we are making a book! And we have decided to begin it with you! If you were a Beautiful Smell instead of a Beautiful Lady,—what Beautiful Smell in the Whole Wide World would you choose to be?"

The lady reeled back against the wall of the Post Office. And put on a gold eyeglass to support her.

"Merciful Impudences!" she said. "What new kind of census is this?"

We knew what a "census" was.

"No! It isn't that at all!" I explained. "This is something important."

Carol showed her the book. He showed her the pencil he was going to write the book with.

"When it's all done," I explained, "everybody will want to read it!"

"I can well believe it," said the Lady. She looked at Carol. Everybody looks at Carol.

"Who are you children, anyway?" she said.

"My name is Ruthy," I explained. "And this is my brother Carol."

She began to look at Carol all over again. She reached out and shook him by the shoulder.

"Dumbness!" she said. "Why let Sister do all the talking?"

My stomach felt pretty queer.

"My brother Carol *can't* talk," I explained. "He *is* dumb!"

The Lady turned very red.

"Oh dear—Oh dear—Oh dear," she said. She opened her purse. She took out a dollar bill. "Surely something could be done about it!" she said.

"We are not looking for money," I explained. "We are perfectly rich. We have warm underalls. And two parents. And an older sister. We have a tame coon. And a tame crow. Our Father could paint the house any Autumn he wanted to if he'd rather do it than plant Tulips."

The Lady looked at her watch. It was a bright blue watch no bigger than a violet is.

"This is all very interesting," she said. "But at the obnoxious hotel which you run0 in this village dinner is at twelve o'clock and if I'm not there at exactly that moment there will not be another dinner, I suppose, until twelve o'clock the next day. So——"

"Probably not," I said. "So if you don't feel timid at all about walking out with strangers, my brother Carol and I will walk home to the Hotel with you and write our book as we go."

The Lady bit herself. She bit herself in the lip. She began to walk very fast.

Carol walked very fast on one side of her. I walked very fast on the other. Carol carried the book. He carried it wide open so as to be all ready any moment. I carried the pencil.

"Can you tell me," said the Lady, "just why you and your brother have picked upon me as the first victim of your most astonishing interrogations?"

"Because you are the only Lady we ever saw in our lives that we didn't know who she was!" I explained. "And that makes it more interesting!"

"O——h," said the Lady. She gave a queer little gasp. It was the Hotel happening! She ran up the hotel steps. There was a Gentleman waiting for her at the top of the steps. He was a tall Gentleman with a very cross mustache. The Lady whispered something to him. He shook his mustache at us.

"Get out of here, you Young Scamps!" he cried. "Get out of here, I say! *Get out!*"

No one had ever shaken his mustache at us before. We sat down on the step to think about it.

The Gentleman ran off to call the Hotel Proprietor.

The Lady looked a little sorry. She came running back. She stooped down. She took the book from Carol. And the pencil from me. She laughed a little.

"You funny—funny children," she said. "What is it you want to know? The Most Beautiful Smell in the whole wide world,—is that it?—The Most Beautiful Smell in the whole wide world?" She looked back over her shoulder. She wrote very fast. Her cheeks looked pink. She banged the book together just the first second she had finished. She pulled my ear. "I'm——I'm sorry," she said.

"Oh, that's all right," I assured her. "We'll be round and write the rest of the book some other day!"

The Man with the Cross Mustache kept right on hunting all around.

When the Hotel Proprietor came running and saw who we were he gave us two oranges instead, and a left-over roll of wall-paper with parrots on it, and all the old calendars that were in his desk.

We had to race home across the railroad trestle to get there in time. It wasn't till we reached the Blacksmith Shop that we had achance to stop and see what the Lady had written in our book. There was a Smoke Tree just outside the Blacksmith Shop. It was all in smoke. We sat down under it and opened our book.

This is what the Lady had written in our book.

The most beautiful smell in the world is the smell of an old tattered baseball glove—that's been lying in the damp grass—by the side of a brook—in June Time.

I looked at Carol. Carol looked at me. We felt surprised. It wasn't exactly what you would have expected. Carol rolled over on his stomach. He clapped his heels in the air. He pounded his fists in the grass.

We forgot all about going home. We went into the Blacksmith's Shop instead. It was a very earthy place. But nothing grew there. Not grass. Not flowers. Not even vines. Just Junk!

The Blacksmith's name was Jason. He looked something like a Stove that could be doubled up in its stomach and carried round to all four corners of a horse for the horse to put his foot on. He was making shoes for a very stout black horse. The horse's name was Ezra. There were a great many sparks around! And iron noises! And flames! And smouches! Ezra's hoofs seemed to be burning! It smelt so funny we didn't think it would be polite to ask Jason what he'd rather smell like instead! So we decided to begin the other way about. But whatever way you decided you had to scream it.

"Jason," I screamed. "If you were a Beautiful Sound instead of a Beautiful Blacksmith, what Beautiful Sound in the whole wide world would you choose to be?"

"*Eh?*" screamed Jason. He stopped hammering. He stopped thumping. He stopped boiling poor Ezra's hoof with a red hot poker. "*Eh?*" he said all over again. "Well, that's a new one on me! What's the Big Idea?"

"Well—I want to know," said Jason. He sat down on a great block of wood. He wiped his sleeve on his face. It made his sleeve all black. "If I was a Sound—?" he said. "Instead of a Man?—Instead of a man?" It seemed to puzzle him a good deal. "Not to be a man—any more you mean? No arms? Legs? Stomach? Eyes?—To get all worn out and busted stayin' on forever in one place? And then thrung away?—But to be just a—just a Sound?—Just a Sound? Well, of all the comical ideas! Of all the——" Then quite suddenly he whacked his hand down in a great black smouch on his knee and clanged his feet like dungeon chains across a clutter of horseshoes. "I've got it!" he cried. "I've got it!—If I was a Sound instead of a man I'd choose to be a Song!—Not great loud band-tunes, I mean, that nobody could play unless he was hired! And charged tickets! But some nice—pretty little Song—floatin' round all soft and easy on ladies' lips and in men's hearts. Or tinklin' out as pleasant as you please on moonlight nights from mandolin strings and young folks sparkin'. Or turnin' up just as likely as not in some old guy's whistle on the top of one of these 'ere omnibuses in London Town. Or travellin' even in a phonograph through the wonders of the great Sahara Desert. Something all simple—I mean that you could hum without even botherin' with the words. Something people would know who you was even if there *wasn't* any words!—Something all sweet and low——'Sweet and Low,' that's it! My Mother used to sing it! I hain't thought of it for forty years!*That's* the one I mean!"

"Sweet and Low"—he began to sing.

Sweet and low—Sweet and low—Wind of the Western Sea———

His voice was all deep and full of sand like the way a bass drum makes you feel in your stomach. I looked at Carol. Carol looked at me. We felt pretty surprised. Jason the Blacksmith looked more surprised than anyone! But he kept right on singing!

Over the rolling waters go—Come from the—the something—moon and blow—While my little one—while my pretty one—sleeps.Father will come to his babe in the nest—S-silvery—something—all out of the West—Silvery———

We ran!
When we got to the Smoke Tree and looked back there was no sound at all in the Blacksmith Shop except the sound of Ezra thumping his hoofs. And Jason being a Song instead of a man!
The faster we ran the more surprised we felt.
When you *read* a book, of course, you expect to be surprised. If you didn't think the person who made the book was going to tell you something that you didn't know before you wouldn't bother to read it. But when you're *writing* a book it doesn't seem exactly as though so many unexpected things ought to happen to you!
We were pretty glad when we ran right into the Old Minister who preaches sometimes when all the young ministers can't think of anything more to preach about.
The Old Minister was leaning against the Bridge. The Old Lawyer was leaning against the Bridge with him. They were waving their canes. And their long white beards. And arguing about the "Thirty-Nine Articles."—Carol thinks it was the "Fifty-Seven Varieties" they were arguing about. But the "Fifty-Seven Varieties" I'm almost sure is Pickles. It's the "Thirty-Nine Articles" that is Arguments!
The Old Minister laughed when he saw us coming. "Well—Well—Well!" he cried. "See who's here! And carrying such a big book too! And all out of breath!" He put his arm round Carol. I thought he was going to ask us our Catechisms. And there wasn't any breath left in our catechisms.
"Oh, if you were a Beautiful Sound," I gasped, "instead of a Beautiful Preacher—what Beautiful Sound in the whole wide world—would you—would you choose to be?"
"Eh?" said the Old Minister. "Eh?—What's—that? A—A—Sound instead of a Preacher? Well, upon my word!—This minute, you mean? Or any minute? If I was a Beautiful Sound instead of——?" He mopped his forehead. He looked pretty hot. He twinkled his eyes at the Old Lawyer. "Well—just *this* minute," he said, "I'd rather be the Sound of Foaming Beer than anything else in the world that I can think of!" He thumped his cane on the ground. The Old Lawyer thumped his cane on the ground. They both started off down the road thumping0 as they walked. We heard them chuckling as they thumped. They weren't arguing any more about the "Thirty-Nine Articles." They were arguing about Cheese.
And that was surprising too!
There wasn't any dinner left when we got home except just knives and forks and spoons. My Mother found us two bowls to go with the spoons. And some milk to go with the bowls. And some crackers to go with the milk. Everything went very well.
We told my Mother we were sorry to be late but that we were writing a book and it was very important.
My Mother said yes,—she knew that writing books was very important and had always noticed that people who wrote 'em were very apt to be late to things. Her only regret, she said, was that Carol and I hadn't had a little more time in which to form habits of promptness before we began on such a chronic career as Literature.
My Father said "Stuff and Nonsense!" My Father said that if we'd kindly condescend to tear ourselves away from the Charms of Literature for one brief afternoon he'd like to have us weed the Tulip Bed.
We said we would.

We forgot all about our book. It isn't that pulling up weeds is any special fun. It's the putting flowers back that you've pulled up by mistake that is such a Game in itself. You have to make little splints for them out of Forsythia twigs. You have to build little collars of pebble-stone all around them to keep marauding beetles from eating up their wiltedness. You have to bring them medicine-water from the brook instead of from the kitchen—so that nobody will scream and say, "Oh, what have you done now?—Oh, what have you done *now*?"

It was Supper Time before we knew it. There was creamed chicken for supper. And wild strawberry preserve. And a letter from our sister Rosalee. Our sister Rosalee is in Cuba visiting her Betrother. She wrote seven pages about it. She seemed to like her Betrother very much.

My Mother cried a little. My Father said "Oh, Pshaw! Oh, Pshaw! You can't keep 'em babies forever!" My Mother tried not to look at my Father's eyes. She looked at his feet instead. When she looked at his feet instead she saw that there were holes in his slippers. She seemed very glad. She ran and got a big needle. And a big thread. My Father had to sit very still.

It seemed a very good time to remember about the Book.

Carol went and got the Book. He put it down on the Dining Room table. It was a gray book with a red back to it. It said "Lanos Bryant" across the back of it. It was Lanos Bryant who had given us the book. Lanos Bryant was the Butcher. It was an old Account Book. The front of it was all mixed up with figurings. It was in the back of it that we were making Our Book.

My Mother looked up. She smiled at us.

"Why, bless my heart," she said, "we mustn't forget about the children's Book!"

"No such luck," said my Father.

Everybody smiled a little.

"What's the Book about?" said my Mother.

I looked at Carol. Carol looked at me. He nudged me to go on.

"It's about You!" I said. "And about Father! And about Jason the Blacksmith! And about the Old Preacher. And about most anybody I guess that would like to be About-ed!"

"Well—Well—Well," said my Mother. "And what is it for?"

"Oh, it's just for fun," I said. "But it's very important.—Just the first instant anybody reads it he'll know all there is to know about everybody without ever having to go and make calls on them! Everything interesting about them I mean! Everything that really matters! Lots of things that nobody would have guessed!"

"Mercy!" said my Mother. She stopped mending my Father and jumped right up.

My Father jumped right up too!

"Oh, it isn't written yet!" I said. "It's only just begun!"

"O—h," said my Mother. And sat down again.

"We though maybe you and Father would help us," I said.

"O—h," said my Father. And sat down again too.

Carol began to laugh. I don't know why he laughed.

"It's—it's just a set of questions," I explained.

Carol opened the Book and found the questions.

"Just five or six questions," I explained. "All you have to do is to answer the questions—and tell us how to spell it perhaps.—And then that makes the Book!"

"It certainly sounds simple," said my Mother. She began mending my Father very hard. "And what are some of the questions?" she asked.

"Well—the first question," I explained, "is 'What is your name?'"

My Mother gave a little giggle. She hushed my Father with her hand.

"Oh surely," she said, "there couldn't be any objection to telling these pleasant children our names?"

"No—o," admitted my Father.

My Mother looked up. She twinkled her eyes a little as well as her mouth.

"Our names are 'Father' and 'Mother'," she said.

Carol wrote the names in the Book. He wrote them very black and literary looking. "Father" at the top of one page. And "Mother" at the top of the other. They looked nice.

"All right then," said my Father. "Fire away!"

I looked at my Father. I looked at my Mother. I didn't know just which one to begin with. Carol kicked me in the shins for encouragement. I decided to begin with my Mother.

"Oh Mother," I said. "If you were a Beautiful Smell instead of a Beautiful Mother,—what Beautiful Smell in the whole wide world—would you choose to be?"

"Eh? What's that? *What?*" said my Father. "Well, of all the idiotic foolishness! Of all the—"

59

"Why no—not at all," said my Mother. "Why—Why I think it's rather interesting! Why—Why—Though I must admit," she laughed out suddenly, "that I never quite thought of things in just that way before!" She looked out the window. She looked in the fire-place. She looked at my Father. She looked at Carol. She looked at me. She began to clap her hands. "I've got it!" she said. "I know what I'd choose! A White Iris! In all the world there's no perfume that can compare with the perfume of a White Iris!—Orris root they call it. Orris—"

"Humph! What's the matter with Tulips?" said my Father.

"Oh but Tulips don't have any smell at all," said my Mother. "Except just the nice earthy smell of Spring winds and Spring rains and Spring sunbeams!—Oh of course they *look* as though they were going to smell tremendously sweet!" she acknowledged very politely. "But they're just so busy being *gay* I suppose that—"

"The Tulip Goldfinch," said my Father coldly, "is noted for its fragrance."

"Oh dear—Oh dear—Oh dear," said my Mother. She seemed very sorry. She folded her hands. "Oh very well," she said. "Mondays,—Wednesdays,—Fridays,—and Sundays,—I will be the fragrance of the Tulip Goldfinch. But Tuesdays,—Thursdays and Saturdays I really must insist on being the fragrance of a White Iris!"

"Humph!" said my Father. "There aren't any of them that are worth the nice inky lithograph smell of the first Garden Catalogues that come off the presses 'long about February!"

My Mother clapped her hands again.

"Oh Goodie!" she said. "Write Father down as choosing to smell like 'the nice inky lithograph smell of the first Garden Catalogues that come off the presses 'long about February'!"

My Father had to tell us how to spell "Lithograph." Carol wrote it very carefully. My Mother laughed.

"Well really," said my Mother, "I'm beginning to have a very good time.—What is Question No. 2?"

"Question No. 2," I said, "is:—If you were a Beautiful Sound instead of a Beautiful Father and Mother,—what Beautiful Sound in the whole wide world would you choose to be?"

My Father felt better almost at once.

"Oh Pshaw!" he said. "That's easy. I'd be the Sound of Gold Pieces jingling in the pocket of a man—of a man—" He looked at my Mother. "—Of a man who had a Brown-Eyed Wife who looked something like my Brown-Eyed Wife—and three children whose names—when you spoke 'em quickly sounded very similar—yes, very similar indeed to 'Ruthy' and 'Carol' and 'Rosalee'!"

"Oh what nonsense!" said my Mother.

"What does the jingle of Gold Pieces amount to?—Now if I could be any Sound I wanted to—I'd choose to be the sweet—soft—breathy0 little *stir* that a nice little family makes when it wakes up in the morning—so that no matter how much you've worried during the long black night you can feel at once that everything's all right! And that everybody's all there!—In all the world," cried my Mother, "I know of no sweeter sound than the sound of a nice little family—waking up in the morning!"

I turned to Carol's page. I laughed and laughed. "Bubbling Fat is what Carol would like to sound like!" I cried. "The noise that Bubbling Fat makes when you drop doughnuts into it!—But I?—If I could be any lovely Sound I wanted to,—I'd like to be the Sound of Rain on a Tin Roof—at night! All over the world people would be lying awake listening to you! And even if they didn't want to listen they'd have to! Till you were good and ready to stop!"

It took Carol a good while to write down everything about "Gold Pieces" and a "Nice Little Family waking up in the Morning" and "Rain on a Tin Roof."

"The next question is pretty hard," I explained. "Maybe you'd like to be thinking about it.—If you were a Beautiful Sight—that people came miles to see,—what Beautiful Sight in the whole wide world would you choose to be?"

My Father didn't wait a minute. "A Field of Tulips!" he said.

Carol pounded the table with his fists. His face was like an explosion of smiles. He pointed to my Father's page in the Book.

"It's already written!" I said. "We guessed it all the time!"

We turned to my Mother. We saw a little quiver go through my Mother's shoulders.

"I'd choose to be a Storm at Sea!" said my Mother.

"*What?*" cried my Father.

"A Storm at Sea!" said my Mother.

My Father stopped saying "What?" And made a little gasping sound instead. "*You?—You?*" he said. "The gentlest soul that ever breathed?—Would like to be a 'Storm at Sea'?"

"It's only the 'mother' side of me that is gentle!" laughed my Mother. She threw back her head suddenly. She thrust out her hands. It jerked her soft, calm hair all fluffy and wild across her forehead. Her eyes danced! Her cheeks turned all pink! "Oh *wouldn't* it be fun?" she cried. "All the roaring! And the ranting! And the foaming! And the *Furying*!—Racing up the beaches in great waves! And splashes! *Banging* against the rocks! Scaring the fishes almost to pieces! Rocking the boats till people fell *Bump* right out of their berths onto the floor! Ruffling the gulls till——"

"You wouldn't actually—wreck a boat would you?" said my Father.

My Mother stopped tossing her head. And waving her hands. She gave a little sigh. She began mending my Father again very hard.

"Just——pirates," she said.

"O—h," said my Father.

"We intended to make the next one about 'Motions,'" I explained. "But it was too hard. Carol wanted to be an Elevator!—Carol says an Elevator is like quick-silver in a giant thermometer that's gone mad!—He wanted to be the motion it makes when the Elevator's going down and the floor's coming up! But it made me feel queer in my stomach!"

"Merciful Heavens!" said my Father. "What kind of a family have I drawn?—My Wife wants to be a 'Storm at Sea' and my Son aspires to feel like an 'Elevator Gone Mad'!"

Carol looked at my Mother. My Mother looked at Carol. They laughed their eyes together.

"So we made it 'Money' and 'Memory' instead," I explained.

"Made what 'Money' and 'Memory' instead?" said my Father.

"The next two questions," I explained.

"O—h," said my Mother.

"Fire away!" said my Father.

"Question No. 4," I said. "Which do you like best? *Times?* or *Things?*"

"Times or Things?" said my Father. "Whatever in the world do you mean?" His eyebrows looked pretty puzzled.

"Why, we mean," I explained, "if somebody gave you five whole dollars for your birthday—how would you rather spend it?—What would you get most fun out of, we mean?—*Times?* Or *Things?*—Would you be most apt to spend it for Rabbits, we mean? Or going to a Fair?"

"Oh," said my Father, "I see!—Times or Things?—Times—or things?—Why *Things*!" he decided almost at once. "*Things* of course!—When you buy a *Thing* you've got something really tangible for your money! Something definite! Something really to show!—'Rabbits' I admit would probably not be my choice.—But a book, now! A set of garden tools?—A pair of rubber boots even?"

"N—o," said my Mother very softly, "I'm almost sure I'd rather 'go to the Fair'!—'*Times*' or '*Things*'?—Yes I'm perfectly positive," she cried out, "that *Times* give me more pleasure than *Things* do!—Now that I think of it I can see quite plainly that always—always I've preferred to spend my money 'going to the Fair'!"

"Yes, but how foolish," said my Father. "When the Fair's over it's over!—Nothing left to show for it but just a memory."

My Mother laughed right out loud. It was the prettiest laugh.

"Now that's where you're mistaken!" she laughed. "When the Fair's what you call 'over,'—that's the time it's really *just begun*!—Books get lost—or puppies chew them! Garden tools rust! Even the best rubber boots in the world get the most awful holes poked through their toes!—But a Happy Memory?—A Happy Memory—?" She jumped up suddenly and crept into my Father's arms.

My Father stroked her hair. And stroked it.

Carol kicked me in the shins.

"There's only one more question!" I cried out pretty loud.

"What is it?" said my Mother. It sounded pretty mumbly through my Father's shoulder.

"Oh this one is very important," I said. "It's about *colors*."

"Colors?" said my Father. He didn't seem to care nearly as much as you'd have thought he would.

"C—Colors," mumbled my Mother.

"Somewhere in a book," I explained, "we read about a man who wanted his memory 'kept green?'—Why *green?* Why not pink?—Why not blue?—Or even red with a cunning little white line in it?"

"*Eh?*" said my Father.

"If you were going away," I explained.

My Mother's hands clutched at his coat. She gave a queer little shiver. "Oh not—'away'!" she protested.

"For ever and ever," I explained.

My Mother's face came peering out from the shadow of my Father's shoulder. She started to laugh. And made a little sob instead. "Oh not for——ever——and *ever*?" she said.

We all sat and looked at each other. I felt awful queer in my stomach.

Carol kicked me in the shins. He wrote something quick on a piece of paper and shoved it across the table at me.

61

"*China* was the place that Carol meant!" I explained. "Oh he didn't mean—at all—what you thought he meant!—If you were going away to—to *China*—for ever and ever—and ever—and gave your Best Friend a whole lot of money like twenty-five dollars to remember you by—what color do you *hope* he'd keep your memory?"

"Oh—yes—why of course!" said my Father quite quickly. "It's a jolly one after all, isn't it!—Color—Color?—Let me see!—For twenty-five dollars you say? Yes Yes!—The very thing! *Yellow* of course! I hope my Best Friend would have wit enough to buy a *Lamp*!—Nothing fancy you know but something absolutely reliable.—Daytimes to be sure your memory wouldn't be much use to him. But nights—the time everybody needs everybody the most,—Nights I say,—looking back from—from *China*, was it that you designated?—Nights it would be rather pleasant I think to feel that one lived on and on—as a yellow glow in his friend's life."

My Father reached out and pinched my ear.

"How about it, Ruthy?" he asked.

"Oh that's all right," I admitted. "But if *I* gave my Best Friend twenty-five dollars to remember me by—I hope he'd buy a Blueberry Bush!—Just *think* of all the colors it would keep your memory!—White in blossom-time! And blue in fruit-season! And red as blood all the Autumn! With brown rabbits hopping through you!—And speckled birds laying—goodness knows *what* colored eggs! And—"

Somebody banged the front door. Somebody scuffled on the threshold. Somebody shouted "Hello—Hello—Hello—!" It was the Old Doctor.

We ran to see if he had peppermints in his pocket.

He had!

After the Old Doctor had given us all the peppermints he thought we ought to have—and seven more besides, he sat down in the big cretonne chair by the window, and fanned0 his neck with a newspaper. He seemed to be pretty mad at the people who had made his collars.

"W-hew!" he said. "The man who invented a 21-inch collar ought to be forced to suck boiling starch through the neck of a Blueing Bottle!"

We didn't see just why.

The Old Doctor said he didn't care to discuss it.

"Any news to-day?" asked my Father.

"News enough!" said the Old Doctor. He seemed pretty mad about that too!

"Such as what?" asked my Father.

"There's a Prince and Princess in town!" said the Old Doctor. "Or a Duch and Duchess!—Or a Fool and Fooless!—I don't care what you call 'em!—They've got some sort of a claim on the old Dun Voolees estate. Brook,—meadow,—blueberry——hillside,—popple grove,—everything! They've come way from Austria to prove it! Going to build a Tannery! Or a Fertilizer Factory! Or some other equally odoriferous industry! Fill the town with foreign laborers!—String a line of lowsy shacks clear from the Blacksmith Shop to the river!—Hope they *choke*!"

"Oh my dear—my dear!" said my Mother.

The Old Doctor looked a little funny.

"Oh I admit it's worth something," he said, "to have you call me your 'dear.'—But I'm mad I tell you clear through. And when you've got as much '*through*' to you as I have, that's *some mad*!—W-hew!" he said. "When I think of our village,—our precious, clean, decent, simple little All-American village—turned into a cheap—racketty—crowd-you-off-the-sidewalk Saturday Night Hell Hole...?"

"Oh—Oh—OH!" cried my Mother.

"Quick! Get him some raspberry shrub," cried my Father.

"Maybe he'd like to play the Children's new Game!" cried my Mother.

"It isn't a Game," I explained. "It's a Book!"

My Mother ran to get the Raspberry Shrub. She brought a whole pitcher. It tinkled with ice. It sounded nice. When the Old Doctor had drunken it he seemed cooled quite a little. He put the glass down on the table. He saw the Book. He looked surprised.

"Lanos—Bryant? Accounts?" he read. He looked at the date. He looked at my Father. "What you trying to do, Man?" he said. "Reconstruct a financial picture of our village as it was a generation ago? Or trace your son Carol's very palpable distaste for a brush, back to his grandfather's somewhat avid devotion to pork chops?" He picked up the book. He opened the first pages. He read the names written at the tops of the pages. Some of the names were pretty faded.—"Alden, Hoppin, Weymoth, Dun Vorlees," he read. He put on his glasses. He scrunched his eyes. He grunted his throat. "W-hew!" he said. "A hundred pounds of beans in one month?—Is it any wonder that young Alden ran away to sea—and sunk clear to the bottom in his first shipwreck?—'Roast Beef'?—'Roast Beef'?—'Malt and Hops'?—'Malt and Hops'?—'Roast Beef'?—'Malt and Hops'?—Is *that* where Old Man Weymoth got his rheumatism?—And Young Weymoth—his blood pressure?—Dun Vorlees?—Dun Vorlees?—*What?* No meat at all from November to February?—No fruit?—Only three pounds of sugar?—Great Gastronomics! Back of all that arrogance,—that insulting aloofness,—was *real* Hunger gnawing at the Dun Vorlees vitals?—Was *that* the reason why—?—Merciful Heavens!" cried the Old Doctor. "This book is worth twenty dollars to me—this very minute in my Practice! The light it sheds on the Village Stomach,—the Village Nerves,—the—"

"Please, Sir," I said. "The Book is Carol's. Mr. Lanos Bryant gave it to him.—And we're planning to get a great deal more than twenty dollars for it when we sell it!"

"*Eh?*" said the Old Doctor. "*What?*"

He jerked round in his chair and *glared* at Carol.

"*This* I'll have you understand, my Young Man," he said, "is in the cause of Science!"

Carol looked pretty nervous. He began to smooth his hair as well as he could without bristles. It didn't smooth much.

"Oh please, Sir," I explained, "people who write books *never* have smooth hair!"

"Who's talking about writing books?" roared the Old Doctor.

"Please, Sir, *we're* trying to talk about it," I said. My voice sounded pretty little. "It's the *back* part of the book that's the important part," I explained. "It's the back part of the book that we're writing!"

"*Eh?*" said the Old Doctor.

He slammed the book together. He stood up and began to look for his hat.

There didn't seem a moment to lose if we we're going to get him into our book. I ran and caught him by the hand. Even if his face was busy his hands always had time to be friends with Carol and me.

"Oh please—please—*please*," I besought him. "If you were a Beautiful Smell instead of a Beautiful Doctor,—what Beautiful Smell in the whole wide world would you choose to be?"

"What?" said the old Doctor. "*What? W-h-a-t?*" he kept saying over and over. He looked at my Father. He looked at my Mother. My Mother told him about our Book. He made a loud Guffaw. "Guffaw" I *think* is the noise he made. Carol is *sure* that it is! He looked at Carol. He looked at me. He began to Guffaw all over again.

"Well really, Young Authorettes," he said, "I hardly know how to answer you or how to choose. Ether or Chloroform and general Disinfectants being the most familiar savors of my daily life,—the only savors indeed that I ever expect to suggest to anybody—" He looked out the window. There was an apple-blossom tree. It made the window look very full of June. His collar seemed to hurt him. It made him pretty serious. It made his voice all solemn.

"But I'll tell you, Kiddies," he said quite suddenly. "I'll tell you the Sweetest Thing that I ever smelled in my life!—It was the first Summer I was back from College.—I was out on the Common playing ball. Somebody brought me word that my Father was dead.—I didn't go home.—I slunk off instead to my favorite trout-brook—and sat down under a big white birch tree—and *cursed*!—I was very bitter. I needed my Father very much that year. And my step-mother was a harsh woman.—Late that night when I got home,—ugly with sorrow,—I found that I'd left my Catcher's glove. It happened to be one that my Father had given me.—With matches and a tin-can lantern I fumbled my way back to the brook. The old glove lay palm-upward in the moss and leaves. Somebody had filled the palm with wild violets.—I put my face down in it—like a kid—and bawled my heart out.—It was little Annie Dun Vorlees it seemed who had put the violets there. Trailed me clear from the Ball Field. Little kid too. Only fourteen years to my twenty. Why her Mother wouldn't even let me come to the house. Had made Annie promise even not to speak to me.—But when Trouble hit me, little Annie—?" The Old Doctor frowned his eyebrows. "Words!" he said. "It's *words* after all that have the real fragrance to 'em!—Now take that word 'Loyalty' for instance. I can't even see it in a Newspaper without—" He put back his head suddenly. He gave a queer little chuckle. "Sounds funny, doesn't it, Kiddies," he laughed, "to say that the sweetest thing you ever smelled in your life was an old baseball glove thrown down on the mossy bank of a brook?"

I looked at Carol. Carol looked at me. His eyes were popping. We ran to the Book. We snatched it open. It bumped our heads. We pointed to the writing. I read it out loud.

The most beautiful smell in the world is the smell of an old tattered baseball glove that's been lying in the damp grass—by the side of a brook—in June Time.

My Mother looked funny.

"Good Gracious," she said. "Are my children developing 'Second Sight'?—First it was the 'Field of Tulips' already written down as their Father's choice before he could even get the words out of his mouth!—And now, hours before the Old Doctor ever even dreamed of the Book's existence they've got his distinctly unique taste in perfumes all—"

"But this isn't the Old Doctor!" I cried out. "She wrote it herself. It's the Lady down at the hotel. It's the—the Empress that the Old Doctor was talking about!"

"The—Empress?" gasped the Old Doctor.

"Well maybe you said 'Princess,'" I admitted. "It was some one from Austria anyway—come to fuss about the old Dun Vorlees place! You said it was! You said that's who it was!—It's the only Strange Lady in the village!"

"What?" gasped the Old Doctor. "*What?*" He looked at the book. He read the Lady's writing. Anybody could have seen that it wasn't our writing. It was too dressy. He put on his glasses. He read it again.

—the smell of an old tattered baseball glove—that's been lying in the damp grass—side of a brook—June Time.

"Good Lord!" he cried out. "Good Lord!"—He couldn't seem to swallow through his collar. "Not anyone else!" he0 gasped. "In all the world!—There couldn't possibly be anyone else! It must—It *must* be little Annie Dun Vorlees herself!"

He rushed to the window. There was a grocery boy driving by.

"Hi! Hi there!" he called out. "Don't mind anybody's orders just now! Take me quick to the Hotel!—It's an Emergency I tell you! She may be gone before I get there!"

We sat down on the sofa and curled up our legs. Our legs felt queer.

My Mother and Father sat down on the other sofa. They looked queer all over. They began to talk about the Village. It wasn't exactly the Village that we knew. It was as though they talked about the Village when it was a *child*. They talked about when the Bridge was first built. They talked about the Spring when the Big Freshet swept the meadow. They talked about the funny color of Jason the Blacksmith's first long trousers. They talked about a tiny mottled Fawn that they had caught once with their own hands at a Sunday School picnic in the Arbutus Woods. They talked about the choir rehearsals in the old white church. They talked about my Father's Graduation Essay in the High School. It was like History that was sweet instead of just true. It made you feel a little lonely in your throat. Our Tame Coon came and curled up on our legs. It made our legs feel better. The clock struck nine. Our Father and Mother forgot all about us. Pretty soon we forgot all about ourselves. When we woke up the Old Doctor had come back. He was standing by the table in the lamplight talking to my Father and my Mother.

He looked just the same—only different—like a portrait in a newspaper that somebody had tried to copy. All around the inner edges of his bigness it was as though someone had sketched the outline of a slimmer man.—It looked nice.

"Well it *was* little Annie Dun Vorlees!" he said.

"Was it indeed?" said my Father.

"Hasn't changed a mite!" said the Old Doctor. "Not a mite!—Oh of course she's wearing silks now instead of gingham.—And her hair?—Well perhaps it's just a little bit gray but———"

"Gray hair's very pretty," said my Mother.

"Humph!" said the Old Doctor. "I expected of course that she'd think me changed a good deal. I've grown stout. 'Healthy' she called it.—She thought I looked 'very healthy'!" The Old Doctor shifted his feet. He twitched at a newspaper on the table. "That Austrian gentlemen with her isn't her Husband," he said. "She's a—she's a widow now.—It's her Husband's brother."

"Really?" said my Father.

"Oh *Thunder*!" said the Old Doctor. "I guess perhaps I spoke a little bit hastily when I was here before—about their ruining the Village!—I've been talking a bit with Annie and—" His face turned quite red suddenly. He laughed a little. "There won't be any changes made at present in the old Dun Vorlees place—I imagine.—Not at present anyhow."

He looked over at us. We scrunched our eyes perfectly tight.

"Asleep," he said. He picked up our Book. He tucked it under his arm. He looked at my Father and Mother. "It's quite time," he said, "that you started a Bank Account for these children's college education.—It costs a great deal to send children to college nowadays. Carol will surely want a lot of baseball bats.—And girls I know are forever needing bonnets!" He took two Big Gold Pieces from his pocket and put them down on the table where our Book had been. They looked very shining.

My Father gave a little gasp. He jumped up! He started to argue!

My Mother hushed him with her hand. "S—sh———not to-night!" she whispered. "Not to-night!"

She looked at the Old Doctor. She looked at our Book all hugged up tight under his arm. Her eyes looked as though they were going to cry. But her mouth looked as though it was going to laugh.

"Oh of course—if it's in the Cause of Science," she said. "If it's in the Cause of Science."

THE LITTLE DOG WHO COULDN'T SLEEP

It was our Uncle Peter who sent us the little piece of paper.

It was a piece of paper torn out of that part of a newspaper where people tell what they want if they've got money enough to pay for it.

This is what it said:

"WANTED a little dog who can't sleep to be night companion for a little boy who can't sleep. Will pay fifty dollars."

Our Uncle Peter sent it to my Father and told him to give it to us.

"Your children know so many dogs," he said.

"Not—fifty dollars' worth," said my Father. He said it with points in his eyes.

"Oh—I'm not so sure," said my Mother. She said it with just a little smile in her voice.

It was my Mother who gave us the big sheet of brown paper to make our sign. My brother Carol mixed the paint. I mixed the letters. It was a nice sign. We nailed it on the barn where everybody who went by could see it. It said:

"Carol and Ruthy. Dealers in Dogs who Can't Sleep."

Nobody dealt with us. We were pretty discouraged.

We asked the Grocer if he had a little dog who couldn't sleep. We asked the Postman. We asked the Butcher. They hadn't.

We asked the old whiskery man who came every Spring to buy old bottles and papers. HE HAD!

He brought the dog on a dungeon chain. He said if we'd give him fifty cents for the dungeon chain we could have the dog for nothing.

It seemed like a very good bargain.

Our Father lent us the fifty cents.

He was a nice dog. We named him Tiger Lily. His hair was red and smooth as Sunday all except his paws and ears. His paws and ears were sort of rumpled. His eyes were gold and very sweet like keepsakes you must never spend. He had a sad tail. He was a setter dog. He was meant to hunt. But he couldn't hunt because he was so shy. It was guns that he was so shy about.

Our Mother invited us to wash him. He washed very nicely.

We wrote our triumph to our Uncle Peter and asked him to send us the fifty dollars.

Our Uncle Peter came instead in an automobile and took Tiger Lily and Carol and me to the city.

"Of course he isn't exactly a 'little dog,'"0 we admitted. "But at least he's a dog! And at least he 'can't sleep'!"

"Well—I wonder," said our Uncle Peter. He seemed very pleased to wonder about it. He twisted his head on one side and looked at Tiger Lily. "What do you mean,—'doesn't sleep'?" he said.

Because my brother Carol is dumb and never talks I always have to do the explaining. It was easy to explain about Tiger Lily.

"Why when you're in bed and fast asleep," I explained, "he comes and puts his nose in your neck! It feels wet! It's full of sighs and a cool breeze! It makes you jump and want your Mother!—All the rest of the time at night he's roaming! And prowling! And s'ploring!—Up the front stairs and down the back—and up the front and down the back!—Every window he comes to he stops and listens! And listens!—His toe-nails have never been cut!—It sounds lonely!"

"What does he seem to be listening for?" said our Uncle Peter.

"Listening for gun-bangs," I explained.

"O—h," said our Uncle Peter.

The city was full of noises like gun-bangs. It made Tiger Lily very nervous. He tried to get under everything. It took us most all the afternoon to get him out.

The little boy's name was Dicky. He wasn't at home. "Come again," said the man at the door. We came again about eight o'clock at night. It seemed as late as Christmas Eve and sort of lonely without our Parents or any other presents. We had to climb a lot of stairs. It made Tiger Lily puff a little and look very glad. It made our Uncle Peter puff some too. It made the little boy's Mother puff a good deal. There wasn't any Father. The Mother was all in black about it. Her clothes looked very sorrowful. But her face was just sort of surprised. She had white hands. She carried them all curved up like pond-lilies. She was pretty. Even if you'd never seen her but once in a train window you'd always have remembered.

The little boy's room was very large and full of lights. There were tinkly glass things hanging everywhere. There was a music-box playing. There was a tin railroad train running round and round the room all by itself making a bangy noise. There was a wound-up bird in a toy cage crying "Hi! Hi!" There was a crackling fire. Everything was tinkling or playing or singing or banging or crackling. It sounded busy. You had to talk very loud to make any one hear you.

The little boy sat on top of a table in a big bay window looking out at the night. His knees were all cuddled up into the curve of his arms. He had on a little red wrapper and bare legs and fur slippers. He was lots littler than us. He looked cunning.

We stamped our feet on the rug.

"Here's your dog!" I said.

When the little boy saw Tiger Lilly he jumped right down from the table and screamed. It was with joy that he screamed. He threw his arms right around Tiger Lily's neck and screamed all over again. Tiger Lily liked it very much.

"What makes his paws so fluffy?" he screamed. "How soft his face is! He's got sweet eyes! He's got a sad tail! What's his name? Where did you get him? Is he for me? Do I have to pay money for him? What does he eat? Will he drink coffee?" Just as though he was mad about something he began suddenly to jump up and down and cry tears. "Why doesn't somebody answer me?" he screamed. "Why doesn't somebody tell me?"

He got so excited about it that he hit Carol on the nose and blooded him quite a good deal.

The little boy's mother came running.

"Oh hush—hush, Dicky!" she cried. "Don't be in such a hurry! The boy will tell you all about it in time! Give him time I say! Give him time!"

"No he won't," I explained. "My brother Carol never tells anything. He can't."

"He's—dumb," said our Uncle Peter.

The Lady looked sort of queer.

"Oh dear—Oh dear—Oh dear," she said. "What a misfortune!"

Our Uncle Peter sort of sniffed his expression.

"Misfortune?" he said. "I call it the greatest blessing in the world!" He glared at little Dicky. "Yes the greatest blessing in the world!" he said. "A child who doesn't babble or fuss!—Or SCREAM!"

The Lady looked more and more surprised. She turned to the little boy.

"'Dumb,' Dicky," she said. "You understand? Doesn't speak?"

Dicky looked at his Mother. He looked at Carol. A little pucker came and blacked itself between his eyebrows. As though to toss the pucker away he tossed back his whole head and ran to Tiger Lily and threw his arms around Tiger Lily's neck.

"Doesn't——EVER?" he said.

"Doesn't ever—what?" said our Uncle Peter.

"Sleep?" said Dicky.

"It was the boy we were talking about," laughed his Mother. "Not the doggie." She tried to put her arms around him.

He wiggled right out of them and ran back to Tiger Lily.

"Is it his adenoids?" he cried. "Have you had his eyes tested? How do you know but what it's his teeth?"

"Whose teeth?" frowned our Uncle Peter.

"Tiger Lily's!" cried Dicky.

His Mother made a sorry sound in her throat.

"Poor Dicky," she said. "He's had most everything done to him!—Tonsils,—spine,—eyes,—ears,—teeth!— Why the last Doctor I saw was almost positive that the Insomnia was due entirely to—" In the very middle of what it was due to she turned to our Uncle Peter. Her voice got very private. Our Uncle Peter had to stoop his head to hear it. He had a proud head. It didn't stoop very easily.

"He isn't my own little boy," she whispered.

As though his ears were magic the little boy looked up and grinned. His eyes looked naughty.

"Nobody's own little boy," he said. "Nobody's own little boy!" As though it was a song without any tune he began to sing it. "Nobody's—Nobody's own little boy!"

The Lady tried to stop him. He struck at her with his feet. It made a hurt on her arm. He snatched Tiger Lily by the collar and started for the door.

"Going to find Cook and get a bone!" he said. He said it like a boast. He slammed the door behind him. It made a rude noise. He came running back and looked a little sorry, but mostly bashful. He pointed at Tiger Lily. "What— What's HE afraid of?" he said.

"Noises," I explained.

"Noises?" cried the little boy. He cried it with a sort of a hoot. It sounded scornful.

"Oh pshaw!" he said. "There isn't a noise in the world that I'm afraid of! Not thunder! Not guns! Not ANYTHING! Noises are my friends! In the night I take torpedoes and crack 'em on the hearth just to hear them sputter! I've got three tin pans tied on a string! I've got a pop-gun!"

He ran back to the table to get the gun. It was a nice gun. It was painted bright blue. It looked loud.

When Tiger Lily saw it he dove under the bed. It was hard to get him out. The little boy looked very astonished.

"It's gun-bangs—specially—that Tiger Lily is afraid of," I explained.

"Gun-bangs?" said the little boy.

"That's why he can't ever hunt," I explained.

"Hunt?" said the little boy. "Not—ever you mean?" He looked at Tiger Lily. He looked at the blue pop-gun. "Not ever? Ever? Ever?" Way down in his little fur slippers it was as though a little sigh started and shivered itself up-up-up—up till it reached his smile. It made his smile sort of wobbly. "Oh all right!" he said and ran away as fast as he could to hide the blue pop-gun in the bottom of the closet. A velocipede he piled on top of it and two pillows and a Noah's Ark and a stuffed squirrel. When the piling was all done he looked back at our Uncle Peter. It was across one shoulder that he looked back. It made his little smile look twisty as well as wobbly. One of his eyebrows had crooked itself. "It's—It's SILENCES that I'm afraid of," he said.

He grabbed Tiger Lily by the collar again and started for the door. As though he was playing a Game he reached out one finger and tagged everybody as he passed them. Everybody except Carol. When he started to tag Carol he snatched back his finger and screamed instead. "He's a Silence!" he screamed. "He's a Silence!" Still holding tight to Tiger Lily's collar he ran for the stairs.

Flop-Flop-Flop his little fur slippers thudded on the hard wood floor. Tick-Tick-Tick Lily's toe-nails clicked along beside him. It sounded cool. And slippery.

His Mother wrung her hands. It seemed to be with despair that she wrung them.

"Yes that's just it," she despaired. "It's 'Silences' that he's afraid of! That's what keeps him awake all night banging at things! That's what worries him so!"

"But he gave up the noisy pop-gun," said our Uncle Peter. "Gave it up of his own0 accord when he saw that it frightened the dog."

"Why so he did!" said the Mother. She seemed very much surprised. "Why so he did!—Why I don't know that I ever knew him to give up anything before. He's been so delicate—and—and the only child and everything—I'm afraid we've spoiled him."

"U—m—m," said our Uncle Peter.

"And all the circumstances of the case are so bewildering," despaired the lady.

Like white pond-lilies floating in a black gloom her sad hands curled in her lap. It seemed to be at our Uncle Peter that they curled.

"Are they indeed?" said our Uncle Peter. It was the "circumstances" that he meant.

"Very bewildering," said the Lady. Her cheeks got a little pink. She jumped up and went to the door and listened a minute at the head of the stairs. When she came back to her chair she shut the door behind her.

"As I told you," she whispered, "the little boy isn't my own little boy."

"So I understood," said our Uncle Peter.

"His Mother died when he was born," said the Lady.

"Very sad indeed," said our Uncle Peter.

"Dicky is six years old," said the Lady. "I married his Father a year and a half ago. His Father was killed in an accident a year ago—"

"Oh dear—Oh dear," said our Uncle Peter.

The Lady began all over again as though it was a lesson.

"Dicky is six years old," she said. "I married his Father a year and a half ago. He was killed in an accident a year ago. It was all so sudden,—the marriage,—the accident,—everything—!" She began to cry a little. It made her clothes look sorrowfuller and sorrowfuller and her face more and more surprised. Once again she curled up her white pond-lily hands at our Uncle Peter. It was as though she thought that our Uncle Peter could help her perhaps with some of her surprises. "I—I didn't know his Father very long," she cried. "I never knew his Mother at all!—--It's—It's pretty bewildering," she said, "to be left all alone—for life—with a perfectly, strange little boy—who isn't any relation at all!—All his funny little suits to worry about—and his mumps and his measles—and—and whether he ought to play marbles 'for keeps'—and shall I send him to college or not? And suppose he turns out a burglar or something dreadful like that?—And how in the world am I going to tackle his first love affair? Or his choice of a profession?—Merciful Heavens!—Perhaps he'll want to fly!"

"Why—you're just like a Hen," said our Uncle Peter.

The Lady didn't like to be called a Hen.

It ruffled her all up.

Our Uncle Peter had to talk about Base Ball to soothe her.

The Lady didn't know anything about Base Ball but it seemed to soothe her considerably to hear about it.

When our Uncle Peter was all through soothing her she looked up as pleasant as pleasant could be.

"WHY?" she said.

"Why—what?" said our Uncle Peter. He seemed a little perplexed.

"Why—am I like a Hen?" said the Lady.

"O—h," said our Uncle Peter. He acted very much relieved. "O—h," he said. "I was afraid it was something you were going to ask me about Base Ball. But a Hen——?" He looked with smiles at the Lady. "Oh but a Hen—?—Why even a Hen, my dear Madam," he smiled, "a real professional true-enough hen doesn't take any too easily to the actual chick itself until she's served a certain sit-tightly, go-lightly, egg-shell sort of apprenticeship as it were to the IDEA.—Thrust a bunch of chicks under her before she's served this apprenticeship and——"

I jumped up and down and clapped my hands. I just couldn't help it.

"Oh, I know what happens!" I cried. "She sits too heavy! And squashes 'em perfectly flat!—There was a hen," I cried. "Her name was Lizzie! She was a good hen! But childless! The Grocer gave us some day-old chicks to put under her! But when we went out to the nest the next morning to see 'em—they couldn't have been flatter if they'd been pressed in the Bible!—My Brother Carol cried,—I cried,—my Mother——"

"I don't care at all who cried," said the Lady. It was true. She didn't. All she cared was to look at our Uncle Peter. The look was a stern look.

"And are you trying to imply, Mr.—Mr.—?"

"Merredith," said our Uncle Peter. "Percival Merredith.—'Uncle Peter' for short."

"Mr. Merredith," repeated the Lady coldly. "Are you trying to imply that my——step-son looks as though he had been pressed in a—a—Bible?"

I shook in my boots. Carol shook in his boots. You could hear us.

Our Uncle Peter never shook a bit. He just twinkled.

"Well—hardly," he said.

The Lady looked pretty surprised. When she wasn't looking surprised she looked thoughtful.

Her voice sounded little when she got it started again.

"Maybe—Maybe I DO take my responsibilities too heavily," she said. "But it's this—this sleeping business that worries me so."

"I should think it would," said our Uncle Peter.

"No Nurse Maid will stay with me," said the Lady. "They say it gives them the creeps.—It's enough to give anyone the creeps.—Agrown person of course expects a certain amount of wakefulness, but a child,—a little care-free—heedless child—? Just when you think you've got him safely to sleep—all cuddled up in your own bed or even in his own bed—and are just drowsing off into the first real sleep you've had for a week—?—Patter—Patter—Patter in the hall! Creak—Creak—Creak on the stairs! A chair bumped over in the Library!—Bumped over on purpose you understand! Just to make a noise! 'Noises are his friends,' he says. Why once—once—" The Lady's mouth smiled a little. "Once when I woke and missed him and hunted everywhere—I found him at last in the Pantry—on the floor—with his ear cuddled close up to a mouse-hole! Mouse-Nibble Noises he says are his special friends in the middle of the night when there isn't anything else.—ANYTHING to break the silence it seems to be!—Why in the world should he be afraid of a Silence? Nobody can account for it!"

"Possibly not," said our Uncle Peter. "Yet the fact remains that either within or just outside the borders of his consciousness the only two people responsible for his Being have disappeared unaccountably into a Silence——from which they have not returned."

"Oh dear," said the Lady. "I never thought of that! You mean—You mean—that perhaps he thinks that a Silence is a Hole that you might fall into if you don't fill it up with a Noise? Why the poor little fellow!—How in the world is one ever to tell?—Oh dear—Oh dear——" She sank back in her chair and floated her hands in her lap. Her eyes looked as though she was going to cry again. But she didn't cry. That is, not much. Mostly she just sighed. "It isn't as though he was an easy child to understand," she sighed. "He catches cold so easily, and mumps and everything.—And he's so irritable.—He kicks,—he bites,—he scratches!"

"So I have seen demonstrated," said our Uncle Peter.

"Oh, it's quite evident," cried the Lady, "that you think I'm harsh with him!—But whatever in the world would YOU do?" She threw out her hands toward the pretty room,—the rugs,—the pictures,—the fire,—the toys. "Perhaps you can tell me what he NEEDS?" she said.

"A good spanking," said our Uncle Peter.

The Lady gave a little gasp.

"Oh, not for punishment," said our Uncle Peter. "But just for exercise.—It's the only exercise that a lot of pampered, sedentary children ever get!"

"P—Pampered?" gasped the Lady. "S—Sed—entary?" As though her head was bursting with the noises all around the room she clapped her hands over her ears.

Our Uncle Peter jumped up from his chair and began to chase the little tin railroad train. It looked funny to see so large a man running after so small a train. When he caught it it was having a railroad accident in the tunnel under the table where a book had fallen on the track. Like a beetle with no paint on its stomach he left it lying on its back with its little wheels kicking in the air.

"If only all the racket was as easily disposed of!" said the Lady.

"It IS!" said our Uncle Peter.

Like turning off faucets of water he turned off the noises one by one,—the window-breeze that made the glass dangles tinkle,—the funny jiggly spring that kept the toy bird screaming "Hi-Hi" in its wicker cake,—the music box that tooted horns and beat drums right in the middle of its best tunes! He looked like a giant stalking through the Noah's Ark animals! His foot was longer than the village store!

"If only I figured as largely in a less miniature world!" he said.

He looked at the Lady very hard when he0 said it as though he was saying something very important.

The Lady didn't seem to consider it important at all. She looked at her skirts instead and smoothed them very tidily.

"It's a—It's a pleasant day—isn't it?" said our Uncle Peter.

"V—very," said the Lady. Quite suddenly she looked up at him. Her cheeks were pink. She seemed to want to speak but didn't know quite how. She looked more surprised than ever. She bent forward very suddenly and stared and stared at him.

"Why—Why you're the gentleman," she said, "who was in the Fruit Store the day I bought the Alligator pears and dropped my pocket-book down behind the trash-barrel?"

"Also the day you bought the Red Mackintosh Apples," said our Uncle Peter. "The Grocer cheated you outrageously on them.—Also the day you wore the bunch of white violets and pricked your finger so brutally,—also the day on the ferry when there was a slight collision with a tug-boat and I had the privilege of—of——."

The Lady looked very haughty.

"It was the day of the Alligator Pears—that I referred to," she said. "The only day in my recollection!" Very positively she said it,—"the only day in my recollection." But all the time that she said it her cheeks got pinker and pinker. It was when she looked in the glass and saw how mistaken her positiveness looked that her cheeks got so pink. Tap—Tap—Tap her foot stamped on the rug. "Did—Did you know who it was going to be——when you brought the dog?" she said. "That is,—did you know when you first saw the advertisement in the paper." Her white forehead got all black and frowny. "How in the world did you know—my name?" she said.

Our Uncle Peter made an expression on his face. It was the expression that our Mother calls his "Third-Helping-of-Apple-Pie Expression,"—bold and unashamed.

"I asked the Grocer," he said.

"It was a—a great liberty," said the Lady.

"Was it?" said our Uncle Peter. He didn't seem as sorry as you'd have expected.

The Lady looked at Carol. The Lady looked at me.

"How many children have you?" she said.

"None of my own," said our Uncle Peter. "But three of my brother Philip's,—Carol and Ruthy as here observed, and Rosalee aet. eighteen who is at present in Cuba engaging herself to be married."

"O—h," said the Lady.

"I am in short," said our Uncle Peter, "that object of Romance and Pity popularly known as a 'Bachelor Uncle.'"

"O—h," said the Lady. She seemed more relieved than you'd have supposed.

"But in my own case, of course—" said our Uncle Peter.

In the very midst of his own case he stopped right off short to look all around the room again as though he was counting how heavy the toys were and how heavy the money was that had bought the toys. All the twinkle came back to his eyes.

"But in my own case," he said, "I've always known ahead—of course—for a very long time—that I was going to have 'em.—Learned to sit lightly on the idea,—re-balance my prejudices,—re-adjust my—"

"Have—what?" gasped the Lady.

"Nephews and nieces," said our Uncle Peter.

"O—h," said the Lady.

"Had their names all selected I mean," explained our Uncle Peter. "Their virtues, their vices, their avocations, all decided upon.——Ruthy of course might have done with less freckles, and Carol here doesn't quite come up to specifications yet concerning muscle and brawn—and it was never my original intention of course that any young whipper-snapper niece of mine should engage herself to the first boy she fell in love with.—But taken all in all,—all in all I say—"

"I think," frowned the Lady, "you are perfectly——absurd."

The word "absurd" didn't seem to be at all the word she meant to say. She tried to bite it back but got it all mixed up with a little giggle. She bit the giggle instead. It twisted her mouth like a bitter taste.

Our Uncle Peter looked very sympathetic.

"You ought to get away somewhere on a journey," he said. "There's nothing like it as a tonic for the mind. Even if it's a place you don't like very much it clarifies the vision so,—dissipates all one's minor worries."

"—Minor worries?" said the Lady.

"Travel! Yes that's the thing!" said our Uncle Peter quite positively. All in a minute he seemed to rustle with time tables and mapsand smell of cinders and railroad tickets. "Now there's Bermuda for instance!" he suggested. "Just a month of blue waters and white sand would put the roses back in your cheeks.—And Dicky—"

"Impossible," said the Lady.

"Or if Bermuda's too far," insisted our Uncle Peter. "What about Atlantic City? Think how Dicky would enjoy romping on the board walk—while you followed more sedately of course in a luxurious wheel chair!—The most diverting place in the world!—Yes quite surely you must go to Atlantic City!"

The Lady made a little gasp as though her Patience was bursted.

"You don't seem to understand," she said. "I tell you it's quite impossible!"

"W-H-Y?" said our Uncle Peter. He said it sharply like a Teacher. It HAD to be answered.

The Lady looked up. She looked down. She looked sideways. She wrung her hands in her lap. Her face got sort of white.

"It isn't very kind of you," she said, "to force me so to a confession of poverty."

"'Poverty'?" laughed our Uncle Peter. He looked around at the furniture,—at the toys,—at the pictures. It was at most everything that he looked around. He seemed to be very cheerful about it.

The Lady didn't like his cheerfulness.

"Oh I've always had a little for myself," she explained. "Enough for one person to live very simply on. But NOW——? With this strange little boy on my hands,—I—I intend to go to work!"

"Go to——work?" said our Uncle Peter. "WORK?" He said it with a sort of a hoot. "Work? Work? Why, what in the world could YOU do?"

"I can crochet," said the Lady proudly. "And embroider. I can mend. I can play the piano. And really you know I can make the most beautiful pies."

"Apple pies," said our Uncle Peter.

"Apple pies," said the Lady. Like a handful of black tissue paper she crumpled up suddenly in her chair. Her shoulders shook and shook. The sound she made was like a sob going down and a laugh coming up. "I'm not crying," she said, "because it's so hard—but b—because the idea is so f—funny."

"F—F—Funny?" said our Uncle Peter. "It's preposterous! It's gro—tesque! It's—it's fantastic!"

He began to walk very fast from the book-case to the window and from the window back to the book-case again. It wasn't till he'd stubbed his toe twice on a toy Ferris Wheel that the twinkle came back to his eyes.

"Carol!" he said. "Ruthy!—In consideration of the reduced circumstances in which this very pleasant Lady finds herself don't you think that you could afford to offer her a reduced price on the dog,—your original profit on the deal being as noted $49.50?"

The Lady jumped to her feet.

"Oh no—no—no!" she said. "Not for a moment! Fifty dollars is what I offered! And fifty dollars it shall be! All dogs I'm sure are worth fifty dollars. Especially if they don't sleep! Why all the other dogs that people brought me did nothing except sleep! On my sofas! In my chairs! Under my tables! Night or day you couldn't drop even so much as a handkerchief on the floor that one or the other of them didn't camp right down and go to sleep on it! Oh, no—no—no," protested the Lady, "whatever my faults, a bargain is a bargain and——"

"Whatever your faults, my dear Madam," said our Uncle Peter, "they are essentially feminine and therefore enchanting! It is only when ladies ape the faults of men that men resent the same!—Your extravagant indulgency—" he bowed towards the toys—"yourabsolute innocence of all business guile—" he bowed towards Tiger Lily—"nerves strung so exquisitely that the slightest—the slightest—"

The Lady shivered her clothes like a black frost.

"It was advice that I was looking for, not compliments," she said.

"Oh ho!" said Uncle Peter. "I'm infinitely more adept with advice than I am with compliments!"

The Lady looked a little bit surprised. She frowned.

"It's my little boy that I want advice about," she said. "What IS the best thing I can do for him?"

Our Uncle Peter looked at the ceiling. He looked at the rug. He looked at the pictures on the wall. But it seemed to satisfy him most to look at the Lady's face.

"U—m—m," he said. "U—m—mmmm.—That isn't an easy question to answer unless0 you're willing first to answer a question of mine."

"Ask any question you want to," said the Lady.

"U—m—m," said our Uncle Peter all over again. "U—m—m—Um—m—m—U—m—m. It takes a great deal of patience," said our Uncle Peter, "to bring up a little boy.—Unless every time he's naughty you can say to yourself 'Well, even so—think what a good man his Father grew to be!'——Or every time he's good you're fair enough to admit that 'Even his naughty Father was once as nice as this!'"——All the twinkle went suddenly out of our Uncle Peter's eyes. It left them looking narrow. He made a quick glance at Carol. He made a quick glance at me. He seemed very pleased that we were so busy looking at a map of Bermuda. He stepped a little nearer to the Lady. His voice sounded funny. "Were you—were you very fond of the little boy's Father?" he said.

The Lady's face went blazing like a flame out of her black clothes. It was like a white flame that it went blazing. Her eyes looked screaming.

"How dare you?" she said. "You have no business!—What if I was?—What if I wasn't?" All the scream in her eyes fell down her throat into a whisper. "Suppose—Suppose—I—WASN'T?" she whispered.

"Then indeed I CAN give you advice," said our Uncle Peter.

The Lady reached out a hand to the book-case to make herself more steady.

"What—what is it?" she said.

Our Uncle Peter looked funnier and funnier. It wasn't like Christmas that he looked. Nor Fourth of July. Nor even like when we've got the mumps or the measles. It was like Easter Sunday that he looked! There was no twinkle in it. Nor any smoke. Nor even paper dolls. But just SHININGNESS! His voice was all SHININGNESS too!—If it hadn't been you never could have heard it 'cause he made his words so little.

"It's almost a year now," he said, "since our eyes first met.—You've tried your best to hide from me—but you couldn't do it.—Fate had other ideas in mind.—A chance encounter on the street,—that day on the ferry boat,—your funny little dog-advertisement in the paper?"

Quite suddenly our Uncle Peter straightened up like a soldier and spoke right out loud again.

"About your little boy," he said, "my advice about your little boy?—It being indeed so well-nigh impossible, Madam, for a woman to bring up a little boy very successfully unless—she did love his Father,—my advice to you is that without the slightest unnecessary delay you proceed to get him a Father whom you COULD love!"

Whereupon, as people always say in books, our Uncle Peter turned upon his heel and started for the door.

The Lady swooned into her chair.

Our Uncle Peter had to get a glass of water to un-swoon her.

I ran for a fan. It bursted my garter. When our Uncle Peter tried to mend it he swore instead.

The Lady came out of her swoon without an instant's hesitation.

"Here at least," she said, "is something that I know enough to do."

Her mouth was full of scorn and pins. It was with pins that she knew enough to do it.

Our Uncle Peter looked very humble.

The Lady patted my knees.

"Little girls are so much easier to manage than little boys," she said. "I don't seem to understand little boys."

"Nor big boys either!" said our Uncle Peter. He said it with gruffness. It sounded cross.

"Perhaps I—don't want to understand them," said the Lady.

Our Uncle Peter's cheeks got sort of red.

"Suit yourself, my dear Madam," he said and started for the door. He picked up my hat and put it on Carol's head.—Carol's head looked pretty astonished. He took Carol's cap and put it on my head. He handed us our coats upside down.—All our pennies and treasures fell out on the floor. He snatched up the little boy's gloves by mistake and thrust them into his own pockets.

The Lady collected everything again and re-distributed them. She seemed to think it was funny. Not very funny but just a little. She looked at Carol sort of specially.

"Oh my dear Child," she said. "I hope you didn't mind because Dicky called you a 'Silence'?"

Carol did mind. He minded very much. I could tell by the way he carried his ears. They looked very stately. Our Uncle Peter whirled round in the door-way. His ears looked pretty stately too.

"All the men in our family," he said, "aim to meet the exigencies of life—sensibly."

The Lady seemed to consider the fact quite a long time before she smiled again.

"Oh very well," she said. "If the Uncle really is as sensible as the nephew perhaps he will consent to leave the children here with me to-night—instead of bearing them off to the confusion and general mis-button-ness of hotels."

Our Uncle Peter's face fairly burst into relief.

"Oh, do you really mean that?" he cried. "It IS their infernal buttons that makes most of the worry!—And their prayers?—What IS the difference anyway between a morning and an evening prayer?—And this awful responsibility about cereals? And how in the world do you make sure about their necks?"

"Oh those are the things I know perfectly," said the Lady. "All the nice gentle in-door things."

Our Uncle Peter began to strut again.

"Oh pshaw!" he said. "It's only the outdoor things that are really important,—how to climb mountains, how to stop a runaway horse,—how to smother a grass fire!"

It put the Lady all in a flutter.

"Oh pshaw!" said our Uncle Peter. "That's nothing!—The very first instant you hear the maddened hoofs on the pavement you place yourself thus! And THUS!—And——"

The Lady tried to explain to him the difference between a morning and an evening prayer. "Now at night, of course," she explained, "everything is so very lonely that—"

Our Uncle Peter didn't seem to care at all how lonely it was.

"The instant you see the horses's blood-red nostrils,—JUMP!" cried our Uncle Peter.

It sounded pretty muddled to me.

"Personally," insisted the Lady, "I consider a rather soft sponge best for the neck."

"So that with your hands clutched like a vise on either side of the mouth," cried our Uncle Peter, "you can saw up and down with all the violence at your command! Now in fighting a grass fire, it's craft, not might, that you need. In that case of course—"

"Two hours if you're using a double boiler," explained the Lady, "but many people consider a rapider action more digestible, I suppose."

"My dear Lady——let me finish my explanation!" said our Uncle Peter.

"But I want to finish mine!" said the Lady.

Our legs got pretty tired waiting for all the explanations to get un-mixed up again.

It was nine o'clock before the Lady gave our Uncle Peter a cup of hot chocolate and turned him out doors.

"Just like a dog," said our Uncle Peter. We heard him say it across his shoulder as he went down the steps.

It made the Lady laugh a little.

It was warm milk in two great blue bowls that she gave us. "Just like kittens," we thought it was!

We heard the little boy's feet come thud-thud-thudding up the stairs. We heard Tiger Lily's toe-nails click-click-click along behind him.

The little boy looked very full of chicken and joyfulness. So did Tiger Lily.

"Cook says I've got to romp him!" he said. "Every day!—Twice every day!—More'n a hundred times some days! Out doors too! Not just in parks,—parks are good enough for cats,—but in real fields! Else he'll DIE!" Almost as though he was frightened he stooped down suddenly and laid his little ear on Tiger Lily's soft breast. "He's alive now!" he boasted. "You can hear his heart nibbling!" He threw back his little head and laughed and laughed and clapped his hands. He took Tiger Lily by the collar and led him over to the table by the window. He climbed up on the table and pulled Tiger Lily after him.

Tiger Lily was frightened, but not too much. He felt proud. His ears looked fluffy. His back was shining silk. His tail hung down across the edge of the table like a plume.

Far off in the city streets somewhere there was a noise that trolly cars make when they're climbing up a hill and the switch is too hard for them. It was a sour sound.

Tiger Lily started to make a little quiver in his back. The little boy threw his arm around him. A mouse nibbled in the wall. Tiger Lily cocked his head to listen but kissed the little boy's cheek instead. It was a nice kiss. But wet. The little boy laughed right out loud. Way down on the very tip end of Tiger Lily's plumey tail about two hairs wagged. When the little boy saw it his face went all shining. He threw both arms around Tiger Lily's neck. "T—Tiger Lily's—little boy!" he said. "T—T—" Something funny happened0to his mouth. It was a teeny-weeny yawn that didn't seem to know just what to do about it. Nothing in all the world felt lonely any more.

Except me.

The Lady put me to bed.

Carol put himself to bed all except the knots in his shoestrings.

We went to sleep.

Pretty soon it was morning. And we went home.

Our Uncle Peter changed a lot of our dog-money into nickles so it would jingle. We sounded like cow-bells. It felt rich. Our Uncle Peter held us very tight by the hands all the way. He said he was afraid we might step into something wet and sink.

It had been Wednesday when we went away. It was only Thursday when we got home. It seemed later than that.

Our Mother was very glad to see us. So was our Father.

The Tame Crow flew down out of the Maple Tree and sat on Carol's head.

Our Tame Coon came out of the hole under the piazza and sniffed at our heels.

The posie bed in front of the house was blue with violets. The white Spirea bush foamed like a wave against the wood-shed window.

In spite of our absence nothing seemed changed.

We gave our Father a dollar of our money to buy some Tulips. We gave our Mother a dollar to spend any way she wanted to. We put the rest of it in a book. It was a Savings Bank Book that we put it into.

"For your old age," our Father said.

Our Father's eyes had twinkles in them.

"I hope you've thanked your Uncle Peter properly!" he said.

"For what?" said our Uncle Peter.

Our Father jingled the twenty nickles in his hand. "For all favors," he said.

Our Uncle Peter said he was perfectly repaid. He made a frown at my Father.

When bed-time came I climbed up into my Mother's lap and told her all about it,—the house,—the cocoa,—the toy Ferris Wheel,—the blue daisies on the stair carpet,—the pigeon that lit on my window-sill in the morning,—the splashy way Tiger Lily lapped his milk.

"It will be interesting," said my Mother, "to see what we hear from Tiger Lily as Time goes on."

Time went on pretty quickly. Pansies happened and yellow poppies and ducks and two kittens and August.

It wasn't till almost Autumn that we ever heard from Tiger Lily or the little boy again.

When the letter came it was from the little boy. But it was the Lady who wrote it.

We thought her writing would be all black and sorrowful. But it was violet-colored instead, with all the ends of her letters quirked up with surprise like her face, only prancier.

"My dear little friends," wrote the Lady, "Dicky wishes me to tell you how much we enjoyed your delightful visit, and to say that Tiger Lily is a sweet dog. He thinks you are mistaken about Tiger Lily not hunting. Tiger Lily hunts very well he says,—'only different.' It's mice, he wants me to tell you, that Tiger Lily is very fierce about. And bugs of any sort. All in-door hunting in fact. Certainly our wood-boxes and our fire-places have been kept absolutely free of mice this entire season. And Cook says that not a June Bug has survived. Truly it's very gratifying. Also Dicky wants me to tell you that there's a field. It's got a brook in it where you can sail boats and everything. It's most a mile. This is all for this time Dicky says.

"With affectionate regards, I am, etc.——"

Our Mother looked up across the top of the letter. It was at my Father that she looked.

"Poor dear Lady," she said. "I hope she's happier now. It's that Mrs. Harnon, you know. Her marriage was so unfortunate to that dreadful Harnon man."

"U—m—m," said my Father.

We read the letter over and over waiting for the next one and wondering about Tiger Lily.

There wasn't any next one till most Thanksgiving. When it came at last it was Dicky's letter just the same, but it was written in our Uncle Peter's handwriting this time. It seemed funny. But perhaps the Lady's hand was lame and she advertised for help.—Our Uncle Peter reads all the newspapers.

The letter was awful short. And there weren't any quirks in it or anything. Just ink. This is what it said:

"Mutts:

Tiger Lily's got nine puppies. We're sleeping fine.

Dicky."

Our Mother looked at our Father. Our Father looked at our Mother. They both looked at the letter again.

"My brother Peter's handwriting just as sure as you're born!" said my Father.

"Of course it's Peter's writing," said our Mother. Her cheeks were quite pink. "Well of all the unexpected romances—" she said.

"Whose?" I said.

"Tiger Lily's," said my Father. He seemed to be in an awful hurry to say it.

I looked at my Mother. Her eyes were shining.

"Is a—Is a 'Romance' a something that you make a story out of?" I said.

"Yes it is," said my Mother.

I thought of my gold pencil.

"Oh, all right," I said, "when I get tall enough and more spelly I'll make a little story about it."

"You already have!" said my Mother.

73

The Indiscreet Letter

The Railroad Journey was very long and slow. The Traveling Salesman was rather short and quick. And the Young Electrician who lolled across the car aisle was neither one length nor another, but most inordinately flexible, like a suit of chain armor.

More than being short and quick, the Traveling Salesman was distinctly fat and unmistakably dressy in an ostentatiously new and pure-looking buff-colored suit, and across the top of the shiny black sample-case that spanned his knees he sorted and re-sorted with infinite earnestness a large and varied consignment of "Ladies' Pink and Blue Ribbed Undervests." Surely no other man in the whole southward-bound Canadian train could have been at once so ingenuous and so nonchalant.

There was nothing dressy, however, about the Young Electrician. From his huge cowhide boots to the lead smouch that ran from his rough, square chin to the very edge of his astonishingly blond curls, he was one delicious mess of toil and old clothes and smiling, blue-eyed indifference. And every time that he shrugged his shoulders or crossed his knees he jingled and jangled incongruously among his coil-boxes and insulators, like some splendid young Viking of old, half blacked up for a modern minstrel show.

More than being absurdly blond and absurdly messy, the Young Electrician had one of those extraordinarily sweet, extraordinarily vital, strangely mysterious, utterly unexplainable masculine faces that fill your senses with an odd, impersonal disquietude, an itching unrest, like the hazy, teasing reminder of some previous existence in a prehistoric cave, or, more tormenting still, with the tingling, psychic prophecy of some amazing emotional experience yet to come. The sort of face, in fact, that almost inevitably flares up into a woman's startled vision at the one crucial moment in her life when she is not supposed to be considering alien features.

Out from the servient shoulders of some smooth-tongued Waiter it stares, into the scared dilating pupils of the White Satin Bride with her pledged hand clutching her Bridegroom's sleeve. Up from the gravelly, pick-and-shovel labor of the new-made grave it lifts its weirdly magnetic eyes to the Widow's tears. Down from some petted Princeling's silver-trimmed saddle horse it smiles its electrifying, wistful smile into the Peasant's sodden weariness. Across the slender white rail of an always *out-going* steamer it stings back into your gray, land-locked consciousness like the tang of a scarlet spray. And the secret of the face, of course, is "Lure"; but to save your soul you could not decide in any specific case whether the lure is the lure of personality, or the lure of physiognomy—a mere accidental, coincidental, haphazard harmony of forehead and cheek-bone and twittering facial muscles.

Something, indeed, in the peculiar set of the Young Electrician's jaw warned you quite definitely that if you should ever even so much as hint the small, sentimental word "lure" to him he would most certainly "swat" you on firstimpulse for a maniac, and on second impulse for a liar—smiling at you all the while in the strange little wrinkly tissue round his eyes.

The voice of the Railroad Journey was a dull, vague, conglomerate, cinder-scented babble of grinding wheels and shuddering window frames; but the voices of the Traveling Salesman and the Young Electrician were shrill, gruff, poignant, inert, eternally variant, after the manner of human voices which are discussing the affairs of the universe.

"Every man," affirmed the Traveling Salesman sententiously—"every man has written one indiscreet letter during his lifetime!"

"Only one?" scoffed the Young Electrician with startling distinctness above even the loudest roar and rumble of the train.

With a rather faint, rather gaspy chuckle of amusement the Youngish Girl in the seat just behind the Traveling Salesman reached forward then and touched him very gently on the shoulder.

"Oh, please, may I listen?" she asked quite frankly.

With a smile as benevolent as it was surprised, the Traveling Salesman turned half-way around in his seat and eyed her quizzically across the gold rim of his spectacles.

"Why, sure you can listen!" he said.

The Traveling Salesman was no fool. People as well as lisle thread were a specialty of his. Even in his very first smiling estimate of the Youngish Girl's face, neither vivid blond hair nor luxuriantly ornate furs misled him for an instant. Just as a Preacher's high waistcoat passes him, like an official badge of dignity and honor, into any conceivable kind of a situation, so also does a woman's high forehead usher her with delicious impunity into many conversational experiences that would hardly be wise for her lower-browed sister.

With an extra touch of manners the Salesman took off his neat brown derby hat and placed it carefully on the vacant seat in front of him. Then, shifting his sample-case adroitly to suit his new twisted position, he began to stick cruel little prickly price marks through alternate meshes of pink and blue lisle.

"Why, sure you can listen!" he repeated benignly. "Traveling alone's awful stupid, ain't it? I reckon you were glad when the busted heating apparatus in the sleeper gave you a chance to come in here and size up a few new faces. Sure you can listen! Though, bless your heart, we weren't talking about anything so very specially interesting," he explained conscientiously. "You see, I was merely arguing with my young friend here that if a woman really loves you, she'll follow you through any kind of blame or disgrace—follow you anywheres, I said—anywheres!"

"Not anywheres," protested the Young Electrician with a grin. "'Not up a telegraph pole!'" he requoted sheepishly.

"Y-e-s—I heard that," acknowledged the Youngish Girl with blithe shamelessness.

"Follow you '*anywheres*,' was what I said," persisted the Traveling Salesman almost irritably. "Follow you '*anywheres*'! Run! Walk! Crawl on her hands and knees if it's really necessary. And yet—" Like a shaggy brown line drawn across the bottom of a column of figures, his eyebrows narrowed to their final calculation. "And yet—" he estimated cautiously, "and yet—there's times when I ain't so almighty sure that her following you is any more specially flattering to you than if you was a burglar. She don't follow you so much, I reckon, because you *are* her love as because you've *got* her love. God knows it ain't just you, yourself, she's afraid of losing. It's what she's already invested in you that's worrying her! All her pinky-posy, cunning kid-dreams about loving and marrying, maybe; and the pretty-much grown-up winter she fought out the whisky question with you, perhaps; and the summer you had the typhoid, likelier than not; and the spring the youngster was born—oh, sure, the spring the youngster was born! Gee! If by swallowing just one more yarn you tell her, she can only keep on holding down all the old yarns you ever told her—if, by forgiving you just one more forgive-you, she can only hang on, as it were, to the original worth-whileness of the whole darned business—if by—"

"Oh, that's what you meant by the 'whole darned business,' was it?" cried the Youngish Girl suddenly, edging away out to the front of her seat. Along the curve of her cheeks an almost mischievous smile began to quicken. "Oh, yes! I heard that, too!" she confessed cheerfully. "But what was the beginning of it all? The very beginning? What was the first thing you said? What started you talking about it? Oh, please, excuse me for hearing anything at all," she finished abruptly; "but I've been traveling alone now for five dreadful days, all the way down from British Columbia, and—if—you—will—persist—in—saying interesting things—in trains—you must take the consequences!"

There was no possible tinge of patronage or condescension in her voice, but rather, instead, a bumpy, naive sort of friendliness, as lonesome Royalty sliding temporarily down from its throne might reasonably contend with each bump, "A King may look at a cat! He may! He may!"

Along the edge of the Young Electrician's cheek-bones the red began to flush furiously. He seemed to have a funny little way of blushing just before he spoke, and the physical mannerism gave an absurdly italicized sort of emphasis to even the most trivial thing that he said.

"I guess you'll have to go ahead and tell her about 'Rosie,'" he suggested grinningly to the Traveling Salesman.

"Yes! Oh, do tell me about 'Rosie,'" begged the Youngish Girl with whimsical eagerness. "Who in creation was 'Rosie'?" she persisted laughingly. "I've been utterly mad about 'Rosie' for the last half-hour!"

"Why, 'Rosie' is nobody at all—probably," said the Traveling Salesman a trifle wryly.

"Oh, pshaw!" flushed the Young Electrician, crinkling up all the little smile-tissue around his blue eyes. "Oh, pshaw! Go ahead and tell her about 'Rosie.'"

"Why, I tell you it wasn't anything so specially interesting," protested the Traveling Salesman diffidently. "We simply got jollying a bit in the first place about the amount of perfectly senseless, no-account truck that'll collect in a fellow's pockets; and then some sort of a scorched piece of paper he had, or something, got him telling me about a nasty, sizzling close call he had to-day with a live wire; and then I got telling him here about a friend of mine—and a mighty good fellow, too—who dropped dead on the street one day last summer with an unaddressed, typewritten letter in his pocket that began 'Dearest Little Rosie,' called her a 'Honey' and a 'Dolly Girl' and a 'Pink-Fingered Precious,' made a rather foolish dinner appointment for Thursday in New Haven, and was signed—in the Lord's own time—at the end of four pages, 'Yours forever, and then some. TOM.'—Now the wife of the deceased was named—Martha."

Quite against all intention, the Youngish Girl's laughter rippled out explosively and caught up the latent amusement in the Young Electrician's face. Then, just as unexpectedly, she wilted back a little into her seat.

"I don't call that an 'indiscreet letter'!" she protested almost resentfully. "You might call it a knavish letter. Or a foolish letter. Because either a knave or a fool surely wrote it! But 'indiscreet'? U-m-m, No!"

"Well, for heaven's sake!" said the Traveling Salesman. "If—you—don't—call—that—an—indiscreet letter, what would you call one?"

"Yes, sure," gasped the Young Electrician, "what would you call one?" The way his lips mouthed the question gave an almost tragical purport to it.

"What would I call an 'indiscreet letter'?" mused the Youngish Girl slowly. "Why—why—I think I'd call an 'indiscreet letter' a letter that was pretty much—of a gamble perhaps, but a letter that was perfectly, absolutely legitimate for you to send, because it would be your own interests and your own life that you were gambling with, not the happiness of your wife or the honor of your husband. A letter, perhaps, that might be a trifle risky—but a letter, I mean, that is absolutely on the square!"

"But if it's absolutely 'on the square,'" protested the Traveling Salesman, worriedly, "then where in creation does the 'indiscreet' come in?"

The Youngish Girl's jaw dropped. "Why, the 'indiscreet' part comes in," she argued, "because you're not able to prove in advance, you know, that the stakes you're gambling for are absolutely 'on the square.' I don't know exactly how to express it, but it seems somehow as though only the very little things of Life are offered in open packages—that all the big things come sealed very tight. You can poke them a little and make a guess at the shape, and you can rattle them a little and make a guess at the size, but you can't ever open them and prove them—until the money is paid down and gone forever from your hands. But goodness me!" she cried, brightening perceptibly; "if you were to put an advertisement in the biggest newspaper in the biggest city in the world, saying: 'Every person who has ever written an indiscreet letter in his life is hereby invited to attend a mass-meeting'—and if people would really go—you'd see the most distinguished public gathering that you ever saw in your life! Bishops and Judges and Statesmen and Beautiful Society Women and Little Old White-Haired Mothers—everybody, in fact, who had ever had red blood enough at least once in his life to write down in cold black and white the one vital, quivering, questioning fact that happened to mean the most to him at that moment! But your 'Honey' and your 'Dolly Girl' and your 'Pink-Fingered Precious' nonsense! Why, it isn't real! Why, it doesn't even *make sense*!"

Again the Youngish Girl's laughter rang out in light, joyous, utterly superficial appreciation.

Even the serious Traveling Salesman succumbed at last.

"Oh, yes, I know it sounds comic," he acknowledged wryly. "Sounds like something out of a summer vaudeville show or a cheap Sunday supplement. But I don't suppose it sounded so specially blamed comic to the widow. I reckon she found it plenty-heap indiscreet enough to suit her. Oh, of course," he added hastily, "I know, and Martha knows that Thomkins wasn't at all that kind of a fool. And yet, after all—when you really settle right down to think about it, Thomkins' name was easily 'Tommy,' and Thursday sure enough was his day in New Haven, and it was a yard of red flannel that Martha had asked him to bring home to her—not the scarlet automobile veil that they found in his pocket. But 'Martha,' I says, of course, 'Martha, it sure does beat all how we fellows that travel round so much in cars and trains are always and forever picking up automobile veils—dozens of them, *dozens*—red, blue, pink, yellow—why, I wouldn't wonder if my wife had as many as thirty-four tucked away in her top bureau drawer!'—'I wouldn't wonder,' says Martha, stooping lower and lower over Thomkins's blue cotton shirt that she's trying to cut down into rompers for the baby. 'And, Martha,' I says, 'that letter is just a joke. One of the boys sure put it up on him!'—'Why, of course,' says Martha, with her mouth all puckered up crooked, as though a kid had stitched it on the machine. 'Why, of course! How dared you think—'"

Forking one bushy eyebrow, the Salesman turned and stared quizzically off into space.

"But all the samey, just between you and I," he continued judicially, "all the samey, I'll wager you anything you name that it ain't just death that's pulling Martha down day by day, and night by night, limper and lanker and clumsier-footed. Martha's got a sore thought. That's what ails her. And God help the crittur with a sore thought! God help anybody who's got any one single, solitary sick idea that keeps thinking on top of itself, over and over and over, boring into the past, bumping into the future, fussing, fretting, eternally festering. Gee! Compared to it, a tight shoe is easy slippers, and water dropping on your head is perfect peace!—Look close at Martha, I say. Every night when the blowsy old moon shines like courting time, every day when the butcher's bill comes home as big as a swollen elephant, when the crippled stepson tries to cut his throat again, when the youngest kid sneezes funny like his father—'WHO WAS ROSIE? WHO WAS ROSIE?'"

"Well, who was Rosie?" persisted the Youngish Girl absent-mindedly.

"Why, Rosie was *nothing*!" snapped the Traveling Salesman; "nothing at all—probably." Altogether in spite of himself, his voice trailed off into a suspiciously minor key. "But all the same," he continued more vehemently, "all the same—it's just that little darned word 'probably' that's making all the mess and bother of it—because, as far as I can reckon, a woman can stand absolutely anything under God's heaven that she knows; but she just up and can't stand the littlest, teeniest, no-account sort of thing that she ain't sure of. Answers may kill 'em dead enough, but it's questions that eats 'em alive."

For a long, speculative moment the Salesman's gold-rimmed eyes went frowning off across the snow-covered landscape. Then he ripped off his glasses and fogged them very gently with his breath.

"Now—I—ain't—any—saint," mused the Traveling Salesman meditatively, "and I—ain't very much to look at, and being on the road ain't a business that would exactly enhance my valuation in the eyes of a lady who was actually looking out for some safe place to bank her affections; but I've never yet reckoned on running with any firm that didn't keep up to its advertising promises, and if a man's courtship ain't his own particular, personal advertisingproposition—then I don't know anything about—*anything*! So if I should croak sudden any time in a railroad accident or a hotel fire or a scrap in a saloon, I ain't calculating on leaving my wife any very large amount of 'sore thoughts.' When a man wants his memory kept green, he don't mean—gangrene!

"Oh, of course," the Salesman continued more cheerfully, "a sudden croaking leaves any fellow's affairs at pretty raw ends—lots of queer, bitter-tasting things that would probably have been all right enough if they'd only had time to get ripe. Lots of things, I haven't a doubt, that would make my wife kind of mad, but nothing, I'm calculating, that she wouldn't understand. There'd be no questions coming in from the office, I mean, and no fresh talk from the road that she ain't got the information on hand to meet. Life insurance ain't by any means, in my mind, the only kind of protection that a man owes his widow. Provide for her Future—if you can!—That's my motto!—But a man's just a plain bum who don't provide for his own Past! She may have plenty of trouble in the years to come settling her own bills, but she ain't going to have any worry settling any of mine. I tell you, there'll be no ladies swelling round in crape at my funeral that my wife don't know by their first names!"

With a sudden startling guffaw the Traveling Salesman's mirth rang joyously out above the roar of the car.

"Tell me about your wife," said the Youngish Girl a little wistfully.

Around the Traveling Salesman's generous mouth the loud laugh flickered down to a schoolboy's bashful grin.

"My wife?" he repeated. "Tell you about my wife? Why, there isn't much to tell. She's little. And young. And was a school-teacher. And I married her four years ago."

"And were happy—ever—after," mused the Youngish Girl teasingly.

"No!" contradicted the Traveling Salesman quite frankly. "No! We didn't find out how to be happy at all until the last three years!"

Again his laughter rang out through the car.

"Heavens! Look at me!" he said at last. "And then think of her!—Little, young, a school-teacher, too, and taking poetry to read on the train same as you or I would take a newspaper! Gee! What would you expect?" Again his mouth began to twitch a little. "And I thought it was her fault—'most all of the first year," he confessed delightedly. "And then, all of a sudden," he continued eagerly, "all of a sudden, one day, more mischievous-spiteful than anything else, I says to her, 'We don't seem to be getting on so very well, do we?' And she shakes her head kind of slow. 'No, we don't!' she says.—'Maybe you think I don't treat you quite right?' I quizzed, just a bit mad.—'No, you don't! That is, not—exactly right,' she says, and came burrowing her head in my shoulder as cozy as could be.—'Maybe you could show me how to treat you—righter,' I says, a little bit pleasanter.—'I'm perfectly sure I could!' she says, half laughing and half crying. 'All you'll have to do,' she says, 'is just to watch me!'—'Just watch what *you*do?' I said, bristling just a bit again.—'No,' she says, all pretty and soft-like; 'all I want you to do is to watch what I*don't* do!'"

With slightly nervous fingers the Traveling Salesman reached up and tugged at his necktie as though his collar were choking him suddenly.

"So that's how I learned my table manners," he grinned, "and that's how I learned to quit cussing when I was mad round the house, and that's how I learned—oh, a great many things—and that's how I learned—" grinning broader and broader—"that's how I learned not to come home and talk all the time about the 'peach' whom I saw on the train or the street. My wife, you see, she's got a little scar on her face—it don't show any, but she's awful sensitive about it, and 'Johnny,' she says, 'don't you never notice that I don't ever rush home and tell *you* about the wonderful*slim* fellow who sat next to me at the theater, or the simply elegant *grammar* that I heard at the lecture? I can recognize a slim fellow when I see him, Johnny,' she says, 'and I like nice grammar as well as the next one, but praising 'em to you, dear, don't seem to me so awfully polite. Bragging about handsome women to a plain wife, Johnny,' she says, 'is just about as raw as bragging about rich men to a husband who's broke.'

"Oh, I tell you a fellow's a fool," mused the Traveling Salesman judicially, "a fellow's a fool when he marries who don't go to work deliberately to study and understand his wife. Women are awfully understandable if you only go at it right. Why, the only thing that riles them in the whole wide world is the fear that the man they've married ain't quite bright. Why, when I was first married I used to think that my wife was awful snippety about other women. But, Lord! when you point a girl out in the car and say, 'Well, ain't that girl got the most gorgeous head of hair you ever saw in your life?' and your wife says: 'Yes—Jordan is selling them puffs six for a dollar seventy-five this winter,' she ain't intending to be snippety at all. No!—It's only, I tell you, that it makes a woman feel just plain silly to think that her husband don't even know as much as she does. Why, Lord! she don't care how much you praise the grocer's daughter's style, or your stenographer's spelling, as long as you'll only show that you're *equally wise* to the fact that the grocer's daughter sure has a nasty temper, and that the stenographer's spelling is mighty near the best thing about her.

"Why, a man will go out and pay every cent he's got for a good hunting dog—and then snub his wife for being the finest untrained retriever in the world. Yes, sir, that's what she is—a retriever; faithful, clever, absolutely unscarable, with no other object in life except to track down and fetch to her husband every possible interesting fact in the world that he don't already know. And then she's so excited and pleased with what she's got in her mouth that it 'most breaks her heart if her man don't seem to care about it. Now, the secret of training her lies in the fact that she won't never trouble to hunt out and fetch you any news that she sees you already know. And just as soon as a man once appreciates all this—then Joy is come to the Home!

"Now there's Ella, for instance," continued the Traveling Salesman thoughtfully. "Ella's a traveling man, too. Sells shotguns up through the Aroostook. Yes, shotguns! Funny, ain't it, and me selling undervests? Ella's an awful smart girl. Good as gold. But cheeky? Oh, my!—Well, once I would have brought her down to the house for Sunday, and advertised her as a 'peach,' and a 'dandy good fellow,' and praised her eyes, and bragged about her cleverness, and generally done my best to smooth over all her little deficiencies with as much palaver as I could. And that little retriever of mine would have gone straight to work and ferreted out every single, solitary, uncomplimentary thing about Ella that she could find, and 'a' fetched 'em to me as pleased and proud as a puppy, expecting, for all the world, to be petted and patted for her astonishing shrewdness. And there would sure have been gloom in the Sabbath.

"But now—now—what I say now is: 'Wife, I'm going to bring Ella down for Sunday. You've never seen her, and you sure will hate her. She's big, and showy, and just a little bit rough sometimes, and she rouges her cheeks too much, and she's likelier than not to chuck me under the chin. But it would help your old man a lot in a business way if you'd be pretty nice to her. And I'm going to send her down here Friday, a day ahead of me.'—And oh, gee!—I ain't any more than jumped off the car Saturday night when there's my little wife out on the street corner with her sweater tied over her head, prancing up and down first on one foot and then on the other—she's so excited, to slip her hand in mine and tell me all about it. 'And Johnny,' she says—even before I've got my glove off—'Johnny,' she says, 'really, do you know, I think you've done Ella an injustice. Yes, truly I do. Why, she's *just as kind*! And she's shown me how to cut my last year's coat over into the nicest sort of a little spring jacket! And she's made us a chocolate cake as big as a dish-pan. Yes, she has! And Johnny, don't you dare tell her that I told you—but do you know she's putting her brother's boy through Dartmouth? And you old Johnny Clifford, I don't care a darn whether she rouges a little bit or not—and you oughtn't to care—either! So there!'"

With sudden tardy contrition the Salesman's amused eyes wandered to the open book on the Youngish Girl's lap.

"I sure talk too much," he muttered. "I guess maybe you'd like half a chance to read your story."

The expression on the Youngish Girl's face was a curious mixture of humor and seriousness. "There's no special object in reading," she said, "when you can hear a bright man talk!"

As unappreciatingly as a duck might shake champagne from its back, the Traveling Salesman shrugged the compliment from his shoulders.

"Oh, I'm bright enough," he grumbled, "but I ain't refined." Slowly to the tips of his ears mounted a dark red flush of real mortification.

"Now, there's some traveling men," he mourned, "who are as slick and fine as any college president you ever saw. But me? I'd look coarse sipping warm milk out of a gold-lined spoon. I haven't had any education. And I'm fat, besides!" Almost plaintively he turned and stared for a second from the Young Electrician's embarrassed grin to the Youngish Girl's more subtle smile. "Why, I'm nearly fifty years old," he said, "and since I was fifteen the only learning I've ever got was what I picked up in trains talking to whoever sits nearest to me. Sometimes it's hens I learn about. Sometimes it's national politics. Once a young Canuck farmer sitting up all night with me coming down from St. John learned me all about the French Revolution. And now and then high school kids will give me a point or two on astronomy. And in this very seat I'm sitting in now, I guess, a red-kerchiefed Dago woman, who worked on a pansy farm just outside of Boston, used to ride in town with me every night for a month, and she coached me quite a bit on Dago talk, and I paid her five dollars for that."

"Oh, dear me!" said the Youngish Girl, with unmistakable sincerity. "I'm afraid you haven't learned anything at all from me!"

"Oh, yes, I have too!" cried the Traveling Salesman, his whole round face lighting up suddenly with real pleasure. "I've learned about an entirely new kind of lady to go home and tell my wife about. And I'll bet you a hundred dollars that you're a good deal more of a 'lady' than you'd even be willing to tell us. There ain't any provincial— 'Don't-you-dare-speak-to-me—this-is-the-first-time-I-ever-was-on-a-train air about you! I'll bet you've traveled a lot—all round the world—froze your eyes on icebergs and scorched 'em some on tropics."

"Y-e-s," laughed the Youngish Girl.

"And I'll bet you've met the Governor-General at least once in your life."

"Yes," said the Girl, still laughing. "He dined at my house with me a week ago yesterday."

"And I'll bet you, most of anything," said the Traveling Salesman shrewdly, "that you're haughtier than haughty with folks of your own kind. But with people like us—me and the Electrician, or the soldier's widow from South Africa who does your washing, or the Eskimo man at the circus—you're as simple as a kitten. All your own kind of folks are nothing but grown-up people to you, and you treat 'em like grown-ups all right—a hundred cents to the dollar—but all our kind of folks are *playmates* to you, and you take us as easy and pleasant as you'd slide down on the floor and play with any other kind of a kid. Oh, you can tackle the other proposition all right—dances and balls and general gold lace glories; but it ain't fine loafers sitting round in parlors talking about the weather that's going to hold you very long, when all the time your heart's up and over the back fence with the kids who are playing the games. And, oh, say!" he broke off abruptly—"would you think it awfully impertinent of me if I asked you how you do your hair like that? 'Cause, surer than smoke, after I get home and supper is over and the dishes are washed and I've just got to sleep, that little wife of mine will wake me up and say: 'Oh, just one thing more. How did that lady in the train do her hair?'"

With her chin lifting suddenly in a burst of softly uproarious delight, the Youngish Girl turned her head half-way around and raised her narrow, black-gloved hands to push a tortoise-shell pin into place.

"Why, it's perfectly simple," she explained. "It's just three puffs, and two curls, and then a twist."

"And then a twist?" quizzed the Traveling Salesman earnestly, jotting down the memorandum very carefully on the shiny black surface of his sample-case. "Oh, I hope I ain't been too familiar," he added, with sudden contriteness. "Maybe I ought to have introduced myself first. My name's Clifford. I'm a drummer for Sayles & Sayles. Maine and the Maritime Provinces—that's my route. Boston's the home office. Ever been in Halifax?" he quizzed a trifle proudly. "Do an awful big business in Halifax! Happen to know the Emporium store? The London, Liverpool, and Halifax Emporium?"

The Youngish Girl bit her lip for a second before she answered. Then, very quietly, "Y-e-s," she said, "I know the Emporium—slightly. That is—I—own the block that the Emporium is in."

"Gee!" said the Traveling Salesman. "Oh, gee! Now I *know* I talk too much!"

In nervously apologetic acquiescence the Young Electrician reached up a lean, clever, mechanical hand and smouched one more streak of black across his forehead in a desperate effort to reduce his tousled yellow hair to the particular smoothness that befitted the presence of a lady who owned a business block in any city whatsoever.

"My father owned a store in Malden, once," he stammered, just a trifle wistfully, "but it burnt down, and there wasn't any insurance. We always were a powerfully unlucky family. Nothing much ever came our way!"

Even as he spoke, a toddling youngster from an overcrowded seat at the front end of the car came adventuring along the aisle after the swaying, clutching manner of tired, fretty children on trains. Hesitating a moment, she stared up utterly unsmilingly into the Salesman's beaming face, ignored the Youngish Girl's inviting hand, and with a sudden little chuckling sigh of contentment, climbed up clumsily into the empty place beside the Young Electrician, rummaged bustlingly around with its hands and feet for an instant, in a petulant effort to make acomfortable nest for itself, and then snuggled down at last, lolling half-way across the Young Electrician's perfectly strange knees, and drowsed off to sleep with all the delicious, friendly, unconcerned sang-froid of a tired puppy. Almost unconsciously the Young Electrician reached out and unfastened the choky collar of the heavy, sweltering little overcoat; yet not a glance from his face had either lured or caressed the strange child for a single second. Just for a moment, then, his smiling eyes reassured the jaded, jabbering French-Canadian mother, who turned round with craning neck from the front of the car.

"She's all right here. Let her alone!" he signaled gesticulatingly from child to mother.

Then, turning to the Traveling Salesman, he mused reminiscently: "Talking's—all—right. But where in creation do you get the time to *think*? Got any kids?" he asked abruptly.

"N-o," said the Traveling Salesman. "My wife, I guess, is kid enough for me."

Around the Young Electrician's eyes the whimsical smile-wrinkles deepened with amazing vividness. "Huh!" he said. "I've got six."

"Gee!" chuckled the Salesman. "Boys?"

The Young Electrician's eyebrows lifted in astonishment. "Sure they're boys!" he said. "Why, of course!"

The Traveling Salesman looked out far away through the window and whistled a long, breathy whistle. "How in the deuce are you ever going to take care of 'em?" he asked. Then his face sobered suddenly. "There was only two of us fellows at home—just Daniel and me—and even so—there weren't ever quite enough of anything to go all the way round."

For just an instant the Youngish Girl gazed a bit skeptically at the Traveling Salesman's general rotund air of prosperity.

"You don't look—exactly like a man who's never had enough," she said smilingly.

"Food?" said the Traveling Salesman. "Oh, shucks! It wasn't food I was thinking of. It was education. Oh, of course," he added conscientiously, "of course, when the crops weren't either too heavy or too blooming light, Pa usually managed some way or other to get Daniel and me to school. And schooling was just nuts to me, and not a single nut so hard or so green that I wouldn't have chawed and bitten my way clear into it. But Daniel—Daniel somehow couldn't seem to see just how to enter a mushy Bartlett pear without a knife or a fork—in some other person's fingers. He was all right, you know—but he just couldn't seem to find his own way alone into anything. So when the time came—" the grin on the Traveling Salesman's mouth grew just a little bit wry at one corner—"and so when the time came—it was an awful nice, sweet-smelling June night, I remember, and I'd come home early—I walked into the kitchen as nice as pie, where Pa was sitting dozing in the cat's rocking-chair, in his gray stocking feet, and I threw down before him my full year's school report. It was pink, I remember, which was supposed to be the rosy color of success in our school; and I says: 'Pa! There's my report! And Pa,' I says, as bold and stuck-up as a brass weathercock on a new church, 'Pa! Teacher says that one of your boys has got to go to college!' And I was grinning all the while, I remember, worse than any Chessy cat.

"And Pa he took my report in both his horny old hands and he spelt it all out real careful and slow and respectful, like as though it had been a lace valentine, and 'Good boy!' he says, and 'Bully boy!' and 'So Teacher says that one of my boys has got to go to college? One of my boys? Well, which one? Go fetch me Daniel's report.' So I went and fetched him Daniel's report. It was gray, I remember—the supposed color of failure in our school—and I stood with the grin still half frozen on my face while Pa spelt out the dingy record of poor Daniel's year. And then, 'Oh, gorry!' says Pa. 'Run away and g'long to bed. I've got to think. But first,' he says, all suddenly cautious and thrifty, 'how much does it cost to go to college?' And just about as delicate and casual as a missionary hinting for a new chapel, I blurted out loud as a bull: 'Well, if I go up state to our own college, and get a chance to work for part of my board, it will cost me just $255 a year, or maybe—maybe,' I stammered, 'maybe, if I'm extra careful, only $245.50, say. For four years that's only $982,' I finished triumphantly.

"'*G-a-w-d!*' says Pa. Nothing at all except just, '*G-a-w-d!*'

"When I came down to breakfast the next morning, he was still sitting there in the cat's rocking-chair, with his face as gray as his socks, and all the rest of him—blue jeans. And my pink school report, I remember, had slipped down under the stove, and the tortoise-shell cat was lashing it with her tail; but Daniel's report, gray as his face, was still clutched up in Pa's horny old hand. For just a second we eyed each other sort of dumb-like, and then for the first time, I tell you, I seen tears in his eyes.

"'Johnny,' he says, 'it's Daniel that'll have to go to college. Bright men,' he says, 'don't need no education.'"

Even after thirty years the Traveling Salesman's hand shook slightly with the memory, and his joggled mind drove him with unwonted carelessness to pin price mark after price mark in the same soft, flimsy mesh of pink lisle. But the grin on his lips did not altogether falter.

"I'd had pains before in my stomach," he acknowledged good-naturedly, "but that morning with Pa was the first time in my life that I ever had any pain in my plans!—So we mortgaged the house and the cow-barn and the maple-sugar trees," he continued, more and more cheerfully, "and Daniel finished his schooling—in the Lord's own time—and went to college."

With another sudden, loud guffaw of mirth all the color came flushing back again into his heavy face.

"Well, Daniel has sure needed all the education he could get," he affirmed heartily. "He's a Methodist minister now somewhere down in Georgia—and, educated 'way up to the top notch, he don't make no more than $650 a year. $650!—oh, glory! Why, Daniel's piazza on his new house cost him $175, and his wife's last hospital bill was $250, and just one dentist alone gaffed him sixty-five dollars for straightening his oldest girl's teeth!"

"Not sixty-five?" gasped the Young Electrician in acute dismay. "Why, two of my kids have got to have it done! Oh, come now—you're joshing!"

"I'm not either joshing," cried the Traveling Salesman. "Sure it was sixty-five dollars. Here's the receipted bill for it right here in my pocket." Brusquely he reached out and snatched the paper back again. "Oh, no, I beg your pardon. That's the receipt for the piazza.—What? It isn't? For the hospital bill then?—Oh, hang! Well, never mind. It *was* sixty-five dollars. I tell you I've got it somewhere."

"Oh—you—paid—for—them—all, did you?" quizzed the Youngish Girl before she had time to think.

"No, indeed!" lied the Traveling Salesman loyally. "But $650 a year? What can a family man do with that? Why, I earned that much before I was twenty-one! Why, there wasn't a moment after I quit school and went to work that I wasn't earning real money! From the first night I stood on a street corner with a gasoline torch, hawking rasin-seeders, up to last night when I got an eight-hundred-dollar raise in my salary, there ain't been a single moment in my life when I couldn't have sold you my boots; and if you'd buncoed my boots away from me I'd have sold you my stockings; and if you'd buncoed my stockings away from me I'd have rented you the privilege of jumping on my bare toes. And I ain't never missed a meal yet—though once in my life I was forty-eight hours late for one!— Oh, I'm bright enough," he mourned, "but I tell you I ain't refined."

With the sudden stopping of the train the little child in the Young Electrician's lap woke fretfully. Then, as the bumpy cars switched laboriously into a siding, and the engine went puffing off alone on some noncommittal errand of its own, the Young Electrician rose and stretched himself and peered out of the window into the acres and acres of snow, and bent down suddenly and swung the child to his shoulder, then, sauntering down the aisle to the door, jumped off into the snow and started to explore the edge of a little, snow-smothered pond which a score of redmittened children were trying frantically to clear with huge yellow brooms. Out from the crowd of loafers that hung about the station a lean yellow hound came nosing aimlessly forward, and then suddenly, with much fawning and many capers, annexed itself to the Young Electrician's heels like a dog that has just rediscovered its long-lost master. Halfway up the car the French Canadian mother and her brood of children crowded their faces close to the window—and thought they were watching the snow.

And suddenly the car seemed very empty. The Youngish Girl thought it was her book that had grown so astonishingly devoid of interest. Only the Traveling Salesman seemed to know just exactly what was the matter. Craning his neck till his ears reddened, he surveyed and resurveyed the car, complaining: "What's become of all the folks?"

A little nervously the Youngish Girl began to laugh. "Nobody has gone," she said, "except—the Young Electrician."

With a grunt of disbelief the Traveling Salesman edged over to the window and peered out through the deepening frost on the pane. Inquisitively the Youngish Girl followed his gaze. Already across the cold, white, monotonous, snow-smothered landscape the pale afternoon light was beginning to wane, and against the lowering red and purple streaks of the wintry sunset the Young Electrician's figure, with the little huddling pack on its shoulder, was silhouetted vaguely, with an almost startling mysticism, like the figure of an unearthly Traveler starting forth upon an unearthly journey into an unearthly West.

"Ain't he the nice boy!" exclaimed the Traveling Salesman with almost passionate vehemence.

"Why, I'm sure I don't know!" said the Youngish Girl a trifle coldly. "Why—it would take me quite a long time—to decide just how—nice he was. But—" with a quick softening of her voice—"but he certainly makes one think of—nice things—Blue Mountains, and Green Forests, and Brown Pine Needles, and a Long, Hard Trail, shoulder to shoulder—with a chance to warm one's heart at last at a hearth-fire—bigger than a sunset!"

Altogether unconsciously her small hands went gripping out to the edge of her seat, as though just a grip on plush could hold her imagination back from soaring into a miraculous, unfamiliar world where women did not idle all day long on carpets waiting for men who came on—pavements.

"Oh, my God!" she cried out with sudden passion. "I wish I could have lived just one day when the world was new. I wish—I wish I could have reaped just one single, solitary, big Emotion before the world had caught it and—appraised it—and taxed it—and licensed it—and *staled* it!"

"Oh-ho!" said the Traveling Salesman with a little sharp indrawing of his breath. "Oh-ho!—So that's what the—Young Electrician makes you think of, is it?"

For just an instant the Traveling Salesman thought that the Youngish Girl was going to strike him.

"I wasn't thinking of the Young Electrician at all!" she asserted angrily. "I was thinking of something altogether—different."

"Yes. That's just it," murmured the Traveling Salesman placidly. "Something—altogether—different. Every time I look at him it's the darnedest thing! Every time I look at him I—forget all about him. My head begins to wag and my foot begins to tap—and I find myself trying to—*hum* him—as though he was the words of a tune I used to know."

When the Traveling Salesman looked round again, there were tears in the Youngish Girl's eyes, and an instant after that her shoulders went plunging forward till her forehead rested on the back of the Traveling Salesman's seat.

But it was not until the Young Electrician had come striding back to his seat, and wrapped himself up in the fold of a big newspaper, and not until the train had started on again and had ground out another noisy mile or so, that the Traveling Salesman spoke again—and this time it was just a little bit surreptitiously.

"What—you—crying—for?" he asked with incredible gentleness.

"I don't know, I'm sure," confessed the Youngish Girl, snuffingly. "I guess I must be tired."

"U-m-m," said the Traveling Salesman.

After a moment or two he heard the sharp little click of a watch.

"Oh, dear me!" fretted the Youngish Girl's somewhat smothered voice. "I didn't realize we were almost two hours late. Why, it will be dark, won't it, when we get into Boston?"

"Yes, sure it will be dark," said the Traveling Salesman.

After another moment the Youngish Girl raised her forehead just the merest trifle from the back of the Traveling Salesman's seat, so that her voice sounded distinctly more definite and cheerful. "I've—never—been—to—Boston—before," she drawled a little casually.

"What!" exclaimed the Traveling Salesman. "Been all around the world—and never been to Boston?—Oh, I see," he added hurriedly, "you're afraid your friends won't meet you!"

Out of the Youngish Girl's erstwhile disconsolate mouth a most surprising laugh issued. "No! I'm afraid they *will* meet me," she said dryly.

Just as a soldier's foot turns from his heel alone, so the Traveling Salesman's whole face seemed to swing out suddenly from his chin, till his surprised eyes stared direct into the Girl's surprised eyes.

"My heavens!" he said. "You don't mean that *you've*—been writing an—'indiscreet letter'?"

"Y-e-s—I'm afraid that I have," said the Youngish Girl quite blandly. She sat up very straight now and narrowed her eyes just a trifle stubbornly toward the Traveling Salesman's very visible astonishment. "And what's more," she continued, clicking at her watch-case again—"and what's more, I'm on my way now to meet the consequences of said indiscreet letter.'"

"Alone?" gasped the Traveling Salesman.

The twinkle in the Youngish Girl's eyes brightened perceptibly, but the firmness did not falter from her mouth.

"Are people apt to go in—crowds to—meet consequences?" she asked, perfectly pleasantly.

"Oh—come, now!" said the Traveling Salesman's most persuasive voice. "You don't want to go and get mixed up in any sensational nonsense and have your picture stuck in the Sunday paper, do you?"

The Youngish Girl's manner stiffened a little. "Do I look like a person who gets mixed up in sensational nonsense?" she demanded rather sternly.

"N-o-o," acknowledged the Traveling Salesman conscientiously. "N-o-o; but then there's never any telling what you calm, quiet-looking, still-waters sort of people will go ahead and do—once you get started." Anxiously he took out his watch, and then began hurriedly to pack his samples back into his case. "It's only twenty-five minutes more," he argued earnestly. "Oh, I say now, don't you go off and do anything foolish! My wife will be down at the station to meet me. You'd like my wife. You'd like her fine!—Oh, I say now, you come home with us for Sunday, and think things over a bit."

As delightedly as when the Traveling Salesman had asked her how she fixed her hair, the Youngish Girl's hectic nervousness broke into genuine laughter. "Yes," she teased, "I can see just how pleased your wife would be to have you bring home a perfectly strange lady for Sunday!"

"My wife is only a kid," said the Traveling Salesman gravely, "but she likes what I like—all right—and she'd give you the shrewdest, eagerest little 'helping hand' that you ever got in your life—if you'd only give her a chance to help you out—with whatever your trouble is."

"But I haven't any 'trouble,'" persisted the Youngish Girl with brisk cheerfulness. "Why, I haven't any trouble at all! Why, I don't know but what I'd just as soon tell you all about it. Maybe I really ought to tell somebody about it. Maybe—anyway, it's a good deal easier to tell a stranger than a friend. Maybe it would really do me good to hear how it sounds out loud. You see, I've never done anything but whisper it—just to myself—before. Do you remember the wreck on the Canadian Pacific Road last year? Do you? Well—I was in it!"

"Gee!" said the Traveling Salesman. "'Twas up on just the edge of Canada, wasn't it? And three of the passenger coaches went off the track? And the sleeper went clear over the bridge? And fell into an awful gully? And caught fire besides?"

"Yes," said the Youngish Girl. "I was in the sleeper."

Even without seeming to look at her at all, the Traveling Salesman could see quite distinctly that the Youngish Girl's knees were fairly knocking together and that the flesh around her mouth was suddenly gray and drawn, like an old person's. But the little persistent desire to laugh off everything still flickered about the corners of her lips.

"Yes," she said, "I was in the sleeper, and the two people right in front of me were killed; and it took almost three hours, I think, before they got any of us out. And while I was lying there in the darkness and mess and everything, I cried—and cried—and cried. It wasn't nice of me, I know, nor brave, nor anything, but I couldn't seem to help it—underneath all that pile of broken seats and racks and beams and things.

"And pretty soon a man's voice—just a voice, no face or anything, you know, but just a voice from somewhere quite near me, spoke right out and said: 'What in creation are you crying so about? Are you awfully hurt?' And I said—though I didn't mean to say it at all, but it came right out—'N-o, I don't think I'm hurt, but I don't like having all these seats and windows piled on top of me,' and I began crying all over again. 'But no one else is crying,' reproached the Voice.—'And there's a perfectly good reason why not,' I said. 'They're all dead!'—'O—h,' said the Voice, and then I began to cry harder than ever, and principally this time, I think, I cried because the horrid, old red plush cushions smelt so stale and dusty, jammed against my nose.

"And then after a long time the Voice spoke again and it said, 'If I'll sing you a little song, will you stop crying?' And I said, 'N-o, I don't think I could!' And after a long time the Voice spoke again, and it said, 'Well, if I'll tell you a story will you stop crying?' And I considered it a long time, and finally I said, 'Well, if you'll tell me a perfectly true story—a story that's never, never been told to any one before—*I'll try and stop!*'

"So the Voice gave a funny little laugh almost like a woman's hysterics, and I stopped crying right off short, and the Voice said, just a little bit mockingly: 'But the only perfectly true story that I know—the only story that's never—never been told to anybody before is the story of my life.' 'Very well, then,' I said, 'tell me that! Of course I was planning to live to be very old and learn a little about a great many things; but as long as apparently I'm not going to live to even reach my twenty-ninth birthday—to-morrow—you don't know how unutterably it would comfort me to think that at least I knew *everything* about some one thing!'

"And then the Voice choked again, just a little bit, and said: 'Well—here goes, then. Once upon a time—but first, can you move your right hand? Turn it just a little bit more this way. There! Cuddle it down! Now, you see, I've made a little home for it in mine. Ouch! Don't press down too hard! I think my wrist is broken. All ready, then? You won't cry another cry? Promise? All right then. Here goes. Once upon a time—'

"Never mind about the story," said the Youngish Girl tersely. "It began about the first thing in all his life that he remembered seeing—something funny about a grandmother's brown wig hung over the edge of a white piazza railing—and he told me his name and address, and all about his people, and all about his business, and what banks his money was in, and something about some land down in the Panhandle, and all the bad things that he'd ever done in his life, and all the good things, that he wished there'd been more of, and all the things that no one would dream of telling you if he ever, ever expected to see Daylight again—things so intimate—things so—

"But it wasn't, of course, about his story that I wanted to tell you. It was about the 'home,' as he called it, that his broken hand made for my—frightened one. I don't know how to express it; I can't exactly think, even, of any words to explain it. Why, I've been all over the world, I tell you, and fairly loafed and lolled in every conceivable sort of ease and luxury, but the Soul of me—the wild, restless, breathless, discontented *soul* of me—*never sat down before in all its life*—I say, until my frightened hand cuddled into his broken one. I tell you I don't pretend to explain it, I don't pretend to account for it; all I know is—that smothering there under all that horrible wreckage and everything—the instant my hand went home to his, the most absolute sense of serenity and contentment went over me. Did you ever see young white horses straying through a white-birch wood in the springtime? Well, it felt the way that *looks*!—Did you ever hear an alto voice singing in the candle-light? Well, it felt the way that *sounds*! The last vision you would like to glut your eyes on before blindness smote you! The last sound you would like to glut your ears on before deafness dulled you! The last touch—before Intangibility! Something final, complete, supreme—ineffably satisfying!

"And then people came along and rescued us, and I was sick in the hospital for several weeks. And then after that I went to Persia. I know it sounds silly, but it seemed to me as though just the smell of Persia would be able to drive away even the memory of red plush dust and scorching woodwork. And there was a man on the steamer whom I used to know at home—a man who's almost always wanted to marry me. And there was a man who joined our party at Teheran—who liked me a little. And the land was like silk and silver and attar of roses. But all the time I couldn't seem to think about anything except how perfectly awful it was that a *stranger* like me should be running round loose in the world, carrying all the big, scary secrets of a man who didn't even know where I was. And then it came to me all of a sudden, one rather worrisome day, that no woman who knew as much about a man as I did was exactly a 'stranger' to him. And then, twice as suddenly, to great, grown-up, cool-blooded, money-staled, book-tamed *me*—it swept over me like a cyclone that I should never be able to decide anything more in all my life—not the width of a tinsel ribbon, not the goal of a journey, not the worth of a lover—until I'd seen the Face that belonged to the Voice in the railroad wreck.

"And I sat down—and wrote the man a letter—I had his name and address, you know. And there—in a rather maddening moonlight night on the Caspian Sea—all the horrors and terrors of that other—Canadian night came back to me and swamped completely all the arid timidity and sleek conventionality that women like me are hidebound with all their lives, and I wrote him—that unknown, unvisualized, unimagined—MAN—the utterly free, utterly frank, utterly honest sort of letter that any brave soul would write any other brave soul—every day of the world—if there wasn't any flesh. It wasn't a love letter. It wasn't even a sentimental letter. Never mind what I told him. Never mind anything except that there, in that tropical night on a moonlit sea, I asked him to meet me here, in Boston, eight months afterward—on the same Boston-bound Canadian train—on this—the anniversary of our other tragic meeting."

"And you think he'll be at the station?" gasped the Traveling Salesman.

The Youngish Girl's answer was astonishingly tranquil. "I don't know, I'm sure," she said. "That part of it isn't my business. All I know is that I wrote the letter—and mailed it. It's Fate's move next."

"But maybe he never got the letter!" protested the Traveling Salesman, buckling frantically at the straps of his sample-case.

"Very likely," the Youngish Girl answered calmly. "And if he never got it, then Fate has surely settled everything perfectly definitely for me—that way. The only trouble with that would be," she added whimsically, "that an unanswered letter is always pretty much like an unhooked hook. Any kind of a gap is apt to be awkward, and the hook that doesn't catch in its own intended tissue is mighty apt to tear later at something you didn't want torn."

"I don't know anything about that," persisted the Traveling Salesman, brushing nervously at the cinders on his hat. "All I say is—maybe he's married."

"Well, that's all right," smiled the Youngish Girl. "Then Fate would have settled it all for me perfectly satisfactorily—*that* way. I wouldn't mind at all his not being at the station. And I wouldn't mind at all his being married. And I wouldn't mind at all his turning out to be very, very old. None of those things, you see, would interfere in the slightest with the memory of the—Voice or the—chivalry of the broken hand. THE ONLY THING I'D MIND, I TELL YOU, WOULD BE TO THINK THAT HE REALLY AND TRULY WAS THE MAN WHO WAS MADE FOR ME—AND I MISSED FINDING IT OUT!—Oh, of course, I've worried myself sick these past few months thinking of the audacity of what I've done. I've got such a 'Sore Thought,' as you call it, that I'm almost ready to scream if anybody mentions the word 'indiscreet' in my presence. And yet, and yet—after all, it isn't as though I were reaching out into the darkness after an indefinite object. What I'm reaching out for is a *light*, so that I can tell exactly just what object is there. And, anyway," she quoted a little waveringly:

"He either fears his fate too much,Or his, deserts are small,Who dares not put it to the touchTo gain or lose it all!"

"Ain't you scared just a little bit?" probed the Traveling Salesman.

All around them the people began bustling suddenly with their coats and bags. With a gesture of impatience the Youngish Girl jumped up and started to fasten her furs. The eyes that turned to answer the Traveling Salesman's question were brimming wet with tears.

"Yes—I'm—scared to death!" she smiled incongruously.

Almost authoritatively the Salesman reached out his empty hand for her traveling-bag. "What you going to do if he ain't there?" he asked.

The Girl's eyebrows lifted. "Why, just what I'm going to do if he *is* there," she answered quite definitely. "I'm going right back to Montreal to-night. There's a train out again, I think, at eight-thirty. Even late as we are, that will give me an hour and a half at the station."

"Gee!" said the Traveling Salesman. "And you've traveled five days just to see what a man looks like—for an hour and a half?"

"I'd have traveled twice five days," she whispered, "just to see what he looked like—for a—second and a half!"

"But how in thunder are you going to recognize him?" fussed the Traveling Salesman. "And how in thunder is he going to recognize you?"

"Maybe I won't recognize him," acknowledged the Youngish Girl, "and likelier than not he won't recognize me; but don't you see?—can't you understand?—that all the audacity of it, all the worry of it—is absolutely nothing compared to the one little chance in ten thousand that we *will* recognize each other?"

"Well, anyway," said the Traveling Salesman stubbornly, "I'm going to walk out slow behind you and see you through this thing all right."

"Oh, no, you're not!" exclaimed the Youngish Girl. "Oh, no, you're not! Can't you see that if he's there, I wouldn't mind you so much; but if he doesn't come, can't you understand that maybe I'd just as soon you didn't know about it?"

"O-h," said the Traveling Salesman.

A little impatiently he turned and routed the Young Electrician out of his sprawling nap. "Don't you know Boston when you see it?" he cried a trifle testily.

For an instant the Young Electrician's sleepy eyes stared dully into the Girl's excited face. Then he stumbled up a bit awkwardly and reached out for all his coil-boxes and insulators.

"Good-night to you. Much obliged to you," he nodded amiably.

A moment later he and the Traveling Salesman were forging their way ahead through the crowded aisle. Like the transient, impersonal, altogether mysterious stimulant of a strain of martial music, the Young Electrician vanished into space. But just at the edge of the car steps the Traveling Salesman dallied a second to wait for the Youngish Girl.

"Say," he said, "say, can I tell my wife what you've told me?"

"Y-e-s," nodded the Youngish Girl soberly.

"And say," said the Traveling Salesman, "say, I don't exactly like to go off this way and never know at all how it all came out." Casually his eyes fell on the big lynx muff in the Youngish Girl's hand. "Say," he said, "if I promise, honest-Injun, to go 'way off to the other end of the station, couldn't you just lift your muff up high, once, if everything comes out the way you want it?"

"Y-e-s," whispered the Youngish Girl almost inaudibly.

Then the Traveling Salesman went hurrying on to join the Young Electrician, and the Youngish Girl lagged along on the rear edge of the crowd like a bashful child dragging on the skirts of its mother.

Out of the groups of impatient people that flanked the track she saw a dozen little pecking reunions, where some one dashed wildly into the long, narrow stream of travelers and yanked out his special friend or relative, like a good-natured bird of prey. She saw a tired, worn, patient-looking woman step forward with four noisy little boys, and then stand dully waiting while the Young Electrician gathered his riotous offspring to his breast. She saw the Traveling Salesman grin like a bashful school-boy, just as a red-cloaked girl came running to him and bore him off triumphantly toward the street.

And then suddenly, out of the blur, and the dust, and the dizziness, and the half-blinding glare of lights, the figure of a Man loomed up directly and indomitably across the Youngish Girl's path—a Man standing bare-headed andfaintly smiling as one who welcomes a much-reverenced guest—a Man tall, stalwart, sober-eyed, with a touch of gray at his temples, a Man whom any woman would be proud to have waiting for her at the end of any journey. And right there before all that hurrying, scurrying, self-centered, unseeing crowd, he reached out his hands to her and gathered her frightened fingers close into his.

"You've—kept—me—waiting—a—long—time," he reproached her.

"Yes!" she stammered. "Yes! Yes! The train was two hours late!"

"It wasn't the hours that I was thinking about," said the Man very quietly. "It was the—*year*!"

And then, just as suddenly, the Youngish Girl felt a tug at her coat, and, turning round quickly, found herself staring with dazed eyes into the eager, childish face of the Traveling Salesman's red-cloaked wife. Not thirty feet away from her the Traveling Salesman's shameless, stolid-looking back seemed to be blocking up the main exit to the street.

"Oh, are you the lady from British Columbia?" queried the excited little voice. Perplexity, amusement, yet a divine sort of marital confidence were in the question.

"Yes, surely I am," said the Youngish Girl softly.

Across the little wife's face a great rushing, flushing wave of tenderness blocked out for a second all trace of the cruel, slim scar that marred the perfect contour of one cheek.

"Oh, I don't know at all what it's all about," laughed the little wife, "but my husband asked me to come back and kiss you!"

Molly Make-Believe

I

The morning was as dark and cold as city snow could make it—a dingy whirl at the window; a smoky gust through the fireplace; a shadow black as a bear's cave under the table. Nothing in all the cavernous room, loomed really warm or familiar except a glass of stale water, and a vapid, half-eaten grape-fruit.

Packed into his pudgy pillows like a fragile piece of china instead of a human being Carl Stanton lay and cursed the brutal Northern winter.

Between his sturdy, restive shoulders the rheumatism snarled and clawed like some utterly frenzied animal trying to gnaw-gnaw-gnaw its way out. Along the tortured hollow of his back a red-hot plaster fumed and mulled and sucked at the pain like a hideously poisoned fang trying to gnaw-gnaw-gnaw its way in. Worse than this; every four or five minutes an agony as miserably comic as a crashing blow on one's crazy bone went jarring and shuddering through his whole abnormally vibrant system.

In Stanton's swollen fingers Cornelia's large, crisp letter rustled not softly like a lady's skirts but bleakly as an ice-storm in December woods.

Cornelia's whole angular handwriting, in fact, was not at all unlike a thicket of twigs stripped from root to branch of every possible softening leaf.

"DEAR CARL" crackled the letter, "In spite of your unpleasant tantrum yesterday, because I would not kiss you good-by in the presence of my mother, I am good-natured enough you see to write you a good-by letter after all. But I certainly will not promise to write you daily, so kindly do not tease me any more about it. In the first place, you understand that I greatly dislike letter-writing. In the second place you know Jacksonville quite as well as I do, so there is no use whatsoever in wasting either my time or yours in purely geographical descriptions. And in the third place, you ought to be bright enough to comprehend by this time just what I think about 'love-letters' anyway. I have told you once that I love you, and that ought to be enough. People like myself do not change. I may not talk quite as much as other people, but when I once say a thing I mean it! You will never have cause, I assure you, to worry about my fidelity.

"I will honestly try to write you every Sunday these next six weeks, but I am not willing to literally promise even that. Mother indeed thinks that we ought not to write very much at all until our engagement is formally announced.

"Trusting that your rheumatism is very much better this morning, I am

"Hastily yours,

"CORNELIA.

"P. S. Apropos of your sentimental passion for letters, I enclose a ridiculous circular which was handed to me yesterday at the Woman's Exchange. You had better investigate it. It seems to be rather your kind."

As the letter fluttered out of his hand Stanton closed his eyes with a twitch of physical suffering. Then he picked up the letter again and scrutinized it very carefully from the severe silver monogram to the huge gothic signature, but he could not find one single thing that he was looking for;—not a nourishing paragraph; not a stimulating sentence; not even so much as one small sweet-flavored word that was worth filching out of the prosy text to tuck away in the pockets of his mind for his memory to munch on in its hungry hours. Now everybody who knows anything at all knows perfectly well that even a business letter does not deserve the paper which it is written on unless it contains at least one significant phrase that is worth waking up in the night to remember and think about. And as to the Lover who does not write significant phrases—Heaven help the young mate who finds himself thus mismated to so spiritually commonplace a nature! Baffled, perplexed, strangely uneasy, Stanton lay and studied the barren page before him. Then suddenly his poor heart puckered up like a persimmon with the ghastly, grim shock which a man experiences when he realizes for the first time that the woman whom he loves is not shy, but—*stingy*.

With snow and gloom and pain and loneliness the rest of the day dragged by. Hour after hour, helpless, hopeless, utterly impotent as though Time itself were bleeding to death, the minutes bubbled and dripped from the old wooden clock. By noon the room was as murky as dish-water, and Stanton lay and fretted in the messy, sudsy snow-light like a forgotten knife or spoon until the janitor wandered casually in about three o'clock and wrung a piercing little wisp of flame out of the electric-light bulb over the sick man's head, and raised him clumsily out of his soggy pillows and fed him indolently with a sad, thin soup. Worst of all, four times in the dreadful interim between breakfast and supper the postman's thrilly footsteps soared up the long metallic stairway like an ecstatically towering high-note, only to flat off discordantly at Stanton's door without even so much as a one-cent advertisement issuing from the letter-slide.—And there would be thirty or forty more days just like this the doctor had assured him; and Cornelia had said that—perhaps, if she felt like it—she would write—six—times.

Then Night came down like the feathery soot of a smoky lamp, and smutted first the bedquilt, then the hearth-rug, then the window-seat, and then at last the great, stormy, faraway outside world. But sleep did not come. Oh, no! Nothing new came at all except that particularly wretched, itching type of insomnia which seems to rip away from one's body the whole kind, protecting skin and expose all the raw, ticklish fretwork of nerves to the mercy of a gritty blanket or a wrinkled sheet. Pain came too, in its most brutally high night-tide; and sweat, like the smother of furs in summer; and thirst like the scrape of hot sand-paper; and chill like the clammy horror of raw fish. Then, just as the mawkish cold, gray dawn came nosing over the house-tops, and the poor fellow's mind had reached the point where the slam of a window or the ripping creak of a floorboard would have shattered his brittle nerves into a thousand cursing tortures—then that teasing, tantalizing little friend of all rheumatic invalids—the Morning Nap—came swooping down upon him like a sponge and wiped out of his face every single bit of the sharp, precious evidence of pain which he had been accumulating so laboriously all night long to present to the Doctor as an incontestable argument in favor of an opiate.

Whiter than his rumpled bed, but freshened and brightened and deceptively free from pain, he woke at last to find the pleasant yellow sunshine mottling his dingy carpet like a tortoise-shell cat. Instinctively with his first yawny return to consciousness he reached back under his pillow for Cornelia's letter.

Out of the stiff envelope fluttered instead the tiny circular to which Cornelia had referred so scathingly.

It was a dainty bit of gray Japanese tissue with the crimson-inked text glowing gaily across it. Something in the whole color scheme and the riotously quirky typography suggested at once the audaciously original work of some young art student who was fairly splashing her way along the road to financial independence, if not to fame. And this is what the little circular said, flushing redder and redder and redder with each ingenuous statement:

THE SERIAL-LETTER COMPANY.
Comfort and entertainment Furnished for Invalids,
Travelers, and all Lonely People.
Real Letters
from
Imaginary Persons.

Reliable as your Daily Paper. Fanciful as your Favorite Story Magazine. Personal as a Message from your Best Friend. Offering all the Satisfaction of *receiving* Letters with no Possible Obligation or even Opportunity of Answering Them.

SAMPLE LIST.

Letters from a Japanese Fairy. Bi-weekly.	(Especially acceptable to a Sick Child. Fragrant with Incense and Sandal Wood. Vivid with purple and orange and scarlet Lavishly interspersed with the most adorable Japanese toys that you ever saw in your life.)
Letters from a little Son. Weekly.	(Very sturdy. Very spunky. Slightly profane.)
Letters from a Little Daughter. Weekly.	(Quaint. Old-Fashioned. Daintily Dreamy. Mostly about Dolls.)

Letters from a Banda-Sea Pirate. Monthly.	(Luxuriantly tropical. Salter than the Sea. Sharper than Coral. Unmitigatedly murderous. Altogether blood-curdling.)
Letters from a Gray-Plush Squirrel. Irregular.	(Sure to please Nature Lovers of Either Sex. Pungent with wood-lore. Prowly. Scampery. Deliciously wild. Apt to be just a little bit messy perhaps with roots and leaves and nuts.)
Letters from Your Favorite Historical Character. Fortnightly.	(Biographically consistent. Historically reasonable. Most vivaciously human. Really unique.)
Love Letters. Daily.	(Three grades: Shy. Medium. Very Intense.)

In ordering letters kindly state approximate age, prevalent tastes,—and in case of invalidism, the presumable severity of illness. For price list, etc., refer to opposite page. Address all communications to Serial Letter Co. Box, etc., etc.

As Stanton finished reading the last solemn business detail he crumpled up the circular into a little gray wad, and pressed his blond head back into the pillows and grinned and grinned.

"Good enough!" he chuckled. "If Cornelia won't write to me there seem to be lots of other congenial souls who will—cannibals and rodents and kiddies. All the same—" he ruminated suddenly: "All the same I'll wager that there's an awfully decent little brain working away behind all that red ink and nonsense."

"Good enough!" he chuckled

Still grinning he conjured up the vision of some grim-faced spinster-subscriber in a desolate country town starting out at last for the first time in her life, with real, cheery self-importance, rain or shine, to join the laughing, jostling, deliriously human Saturday night crowd at the village post-office—herself the only person whose expected letter never failed to come! From Squirrel or Pirate or Hopping Hottentot—what did it matter to her? Just the envelope alone was worth the price of the subscription. How the pink-cheeked high school girls elbowed each other to get a peep at the post-mark! How the—. Better still, perhaps some hopelessly unpopular man in a dingy city office would go running up the last steps just a little, wee bit faster—say the second and fourth Mondays in the month—because of even a bought, made-up letter from Mary Queen of Scots that he knew absolutely without slip or blunder would be waiting there for him on his dusty, ink-stained desk among all the litter of bills and invoices concerning—shoe leather. Whether 'Mary Queen of Scots' prattled pertly of ancient English politics, or whimpered piteously about dull-colored modern fashions—what did it matter so long as the letter came, and smelled of faded fleur-de-lis—or of Darnley's tobacco smoke? Altogether pleased by the vividness of both these pictures Stanton turned quite amiably to his breakfast and gulped down a lukewarm bowl of milk without half his usual complaint.

It was almost noon before his troubles commenced again. Then like a raging hot tide, the pain began in the soft, fleshy soles of his feet and mounted up inch by inch through the calves of his legs, through his aching thighs, through his tortured back, through his cringing neck, till the whole reeking misery seemed to foam and froth in his brain in an utter frenzy of furious resentment. Again the day dragged by with maddening monotony and loneliness. Again the clock mocked him, and the postman shirked him, and the janitor forgot him. Again the big, black night came crowding down and stung him and smothered him into a countless number of new torments.

Again the treacherous Morning Nap wiped out all traces of the pain and left the doctor still mercilessly obdurate on the subject of an opiate.

And Cornelia did not write.

Not till the fifth day did a brief little Southern note arrive informing him of the ordinary vital truths concerning a comfortable journey, and expressing a chaste hope that he would not forget her. Not even surprise, not even curiosity, tempted Stanton to wade twice through the fashionable, angular handwriting. Dully impersonal, bleak as the shadow of a brown leaf across a block of gray granite, plainly—unforgivably—written with ink and ink only, the stupid, loveless page slipped through his fingers to the floor.

After the long waiting and the fretful impatience of the past few days there were only two plausible ways in which to treat such a letter. One way was with anger. One way was with amusement. With conscientious effort Stanton finally summoned a real smile to his lips.

Stretching out perilously from his snug bed he gathered the waste-basket into his arms and commenced to dig in it like a sportive terrier. After a messy minute or two he successfully excavated the crumpled little gray tissue circular and smoothed it out carefully on his humped-up knees. The expression in his eyes all the time was quite a curious mixture of mischief and malice and rheumatism.

"After all" he reasoned, out of one corner of his mouth, "After all, perhaps I have misjudged Cornelia. Maybe it's only that she really doesn't know just what a love-letter OUGHT to be like."

Then with a slobbering fountain-pen and a few exclamations he proceeded to write out a rather large check and a very small note.

"TO THE SERIAL-LETTER CO." he addressed himself brazenly. "For the enclosed check—which you will notice doubles the amount of your advertised price—kindly enter my name for a six weeks' special 'edition de luxe' subscription to one of your love-letter serials. (Any old ardor that comes most convenient) Approximate age of victim: 32. Business status: rubber broker. Prevalent tastes: To be able to sit up and eat and drink and smoke and go to the office the way other fellows do. Nature of illness: The meanest kind of rheumatism. Kindly deliver said letters as early and often as possible!

"Very truly yours, etc."

Sorrowfully then for a moment he studied the depleted balance in his check-book. "Of course" he argued, not unguiltily, "Of course that check was just the amount that I was planning to spend on a turquoise-studded belt for Cornelia's birthday; but if Cornelia's brains really need more adorning than does her body—if this special investment, in fact, will mean more to both of us in the long run than a dozen turquoise belts—."

Big and bland and blond and beautiful, Cornelia's physical personality loomed up suddenly in his memory—so big, in fact, so bland, so blond, so splendidly beautiful, that he realized abruptly with a strange little tucked feeling in his heart that the question of Cornelia's "brains" had never yet occurred to him. Pushing the thought impatiently aside he sank back luxuriantly again into his pillows, and grinned without any perceptible effort at all as he planned adroitly how he would paste the Serial Love Letters one by one into the gaudiest looking scrap-book that he could find and present it to Cornelia on her birthday as a text-book for the "newly engaged" girl. And he hoped and prayed with all his heart that every individual letter would be printed with crimson ink on a violet-scented page and would fairly reek from date to signature with all the joyous, ecstatic silliness that graces either an old-fashioned novel or a modern breach-of-promise suit.

So, quite worn out at last with all this unwonted excitement, he drowsed off to sleep for as long as ten minutes and dreamed that he was a—bigamist.

The next day and the next night were stale and mean and musty with a drizzling winter rain. But the following morning crashed inconsiderately into the world's limp face like a snowball spiked with icicles. Gasping for breath and crunching for foothold the sidewalk people breasted the gritty cold. Puckered with chills and goose-flesh, the fireside people huddled and sneezed around their respective hearths. Shivering like the ague between his cotton-flannel blankets, Stanton's courage fairly raced the mercury in its downward course. By noon his teeth were chattering like a mouthful of cracked ice. By night the sob in his thirsty throat was like a lump of salt and snow. But nothing outdoors or in, from morning till night, was half as wretchedly cold and clammy as the rapidly congealing hot-water bottle that slopped and gurgled between his aching shoulders.

It was just after supper when a messenger boy blurted in from the frigid hall with a great gust of cold and a long pasteboard box and a letter.

Frowning with perplexity Stanton's clumsy fingers finally dislodged from the box a big, soft blanket-wrapper with an astonishingly strange, blurry pattern of green and red against a somber background of rusty black. With increasing amazement he picked up the accompanying letter and scanned it hastily.

"Dear Lad," the letter began quite intimately. But it was not signed "Cornelia". It was signed "Molly"!

II

Turning nervously back to the box's wrapping-paper Stanton read once more the perfectly plain, perfectly unmistakable name and address,—his own, repeated in absolute duplicate on the envelope. Quicker than his mental comprehension mere physical embarrassment began to flush across his cheek-bones. Then suddenly the whole truth dawned on him: The first installment of his Serial-Love-Letter had arrived.

"But I thought—thought it would be type-written," he stammered miserably to himself. "I thought it would be a—be a—hectographed kind of a thing. Why, hang it all, it's a real letter! And when I doubled my check and called for a special edition de luxe—I wasn't sitting up on my hind legs begging for real presents!"

But "Dear Lad" persisted the pleasant, round, almost childish handwriting:

"DEAR LAD,

"I could have *cried* yesterday when I got your letter telling me how sick you were. Yes!—But crying wouldn't 'comfy' you any, would it? So just to send you right-off-quick something to prove that I'm thinking of you, here's a great, rollicking woolly wrapper to keep you snug and warm this very night. I wonder if it would interest you any at all to know that it is made out of a most larksome Outlaw up on my grandfather's sweet-meadowed farm,—a really, truly Black Sheep that I've raised all my own sweaters and mittens on for the past five years. Only it takes two whole seasons to raise a blanket-wrapper, so please be awfully much delighted with it. And oh, Mr. Sick Boy, when you look at the funny, blurry colors, couldn't you just please pretend that the tinge of green is the flavor of pleasant pastures, and that the streak of red is the Cardinal Flower that blazed along the edge of the noisy brook?

"Goodby till to-morrow,

"MOLLY."

With a face so altogether crowded with astonishment that there was no room left in it for pain, Stanton's lame fingers reached out inquisitively and patted the warm, woolly fabric.

"Nice old Lamb—y" he acknowledged judicially.

Then suddenly around the corners of his under lip a little balky smile began to flicker.

"Of course I'll save the letter for Cornelia," he protested, "but no one could really expect me to paste such a scrumptious blanket-wrapper into a scrap-book."

Laboriously wriggling his thinness and his coldness into the black sheep's luxuriant, irresponsible fleece, a bulging side-pocket in the wrapper bruised his hip. Reaching down very temperishly to the pocket he drew forth a small lace-trimmed handkerchief knotted pudgily across a brimming handful of fir-balsam needles. Like a scorching hot August breeze the magic, woodsy fragrance crinkled through his nostrils.

"These people certainly know how to play the game all right," he reasoned whimsically, noting even the consistent little letter "M" embroidered in one corner of the handkerchief.

Then, because he was really very sick and really very tired, he snuggled down into the new blessed warmth and turned his gaunt cheek to the pillow and cupped his hand for sleep like a drowsy child with its nose and mouth burrowed eagerly down into the expectant draught. But the cup did not fill.—Yet scented deep in his curved, empty, balsam-scented fingers lurked—somehow—somewhere—the dregs of a wonderful dream: Boyhood, with the hot, sweet flutter of summer woods, and the pillowing warmth of the soft, sunbaked earth, and the crackle of a twig, and the call of a bird, and the drone of a bee, and the great blue, blue mystery of the sky glinting down through a green-latticed canopy overhead.

For the first time in a whole, cruel tortuous week he actually smiled his way into his morning nap.

When he woke again both the sun and the Doctor were staring pleasantly into his face.

"You look better!" said the Doctor. "And more than that you don't look half so 'cussed cross'."

"Sure," grinned Stanton, with all the deceptive, undauntable optimism of the Just-Awakened.

"Nevertheless," continued the Doctor more soberly, "there ought to be somebody a trifle more interested in you than the janitor to look after your food and your medicine and all that. I'm going to send you a nurse."

"Oh, no!" gasped Stanton. "I don't need one! And frankly—I can't afford one." Shy as a girl, his eyes eluded the doctor's frank stare. "You see," he explained diffidently; "you see, I'm just engaged to be married—and though business is fairly good and all that—my being away from the office six or eight weeks is going to cut like the deuce into my commissions—and roses cost such a horrid price last Fall—and there seems to be a game law on diamonds this year; they practically fine you for buying them, and—"

The Doctor's face brightened irrelevantly. "Is she a Boston young lady?" he queried.

"Oh, yes," beamed Stanton.

"Good!" said the Doctor. "Then of course she can keep some sort of an eye on you. I'd like to see her. I'd like to talk with her—give her just a few general directions as it were."

A flush deeper than any mere love-embarrassment spread suddenly over Stanton's face.

"She isn't here," he acknowledged with barely analyzable mortification. "She's just gone south."

"*Just* gone south?" repeated the Doctor. "You don't mean—since you've been sick?"

Stanton nodded with a rather wobbly grin, and the Doctor changed the subject abruptly, and busied himself quickly with the least bad-tasting medicine that he could concoct.

Then left alone once more with a short breakfast and a long morning, Stanton sank back gradually into a depression infinitely deeper than his pillows, in which he seemed to realize with bitter contrition that in some strange, unintentional manner his purely innocent, matter-of-fact statement that Cornelia "had just gone south" had assumed the gigantic disloyalty of a public proclamation that the lady of his choice was not quite up to the accepted standard of feminine intelligence or affections, though to save his life he could not recall any single glum word or gloomy gesture that could possibly have conveyed any such erroneous impression to the Doctor.

Every girl like Cornelia had to go South sometime between November and March

"Why Cornelia *had* to go South," he reasoned conscientiously. "Every girl like Cornelia *had* to go South sometime between November and March. How could any mere man even hope to keep rare, choice, exquisite creatures like that cooped up in a slushy, snowy New England city—when all the bright, gorgeous, rose-blooming South was waiting for them with open arms? 'Open arms'! Apparently it was only 'climates' that were allowed any such privileges with girls like Cornelia. Yet, after all, wasn't it just exactly that very quality of serene, dignified aloofness that had attracted him first to Cornelia among the score of freer-mannered girls of his acquaintance?"

Glumly reverting to his morning paper, he began to read and reread with dogged persistence each item of politics and foreign news—each gibbering advertisement.

At noon the postman dropped some kind of a message through the slit in the door, but the plainly discernible green one-cent stamp forbade any possible hope that it was a letter from the South. At four o'clock again someone thrust an offensive pink gas bill through the letter-slide. At six o'clock Stanton stubbornly shut his eyes up perfectly tight and muffled his ears in the pillow so that he would not even know whether the postman came or not. The only thing that finally roused him to plain, grown-up sense again was the joggle of the janitor's foot kicking mercilessly against the bed.

"Here's your supper," growled the janitor.

On the bare tin tray, tucked in between the cup of gruel and the slice of toast loomed an envelope—a real, rather fat-looking envelope. Instantly from Stanton's mind vanished every conceivable sad thought concerning Cornelia. With his heart thumping like the heart of any love-sick school girl, he reached out and grabbed what he supposed was Cornelia's letter.

But it was post-marked, "Boston"; and the handwriting was quite plainly the handwriting of The Serial-Letter Co.

Muttering an exclamation that was not altogether pretty he threw the letter as far as he could throw it out into the middle of the floor, and turning back to his supper began to crunch his toast furiously like a dragon crunching bones.

At nine o'clock he was still awake. At ten o'clock he was still awake. At eleven o'clock he was still awake. At twelve o'clock he was still awake.... At one o'clock he was almost crazy. By quarter past one, as though fairly hypnotized, his eyes began to rivet themselves on the little bright spot in the rug where the "serial-letter" lay gleaming whitely in a beam of electric light from the street. Finally, in one supreme, childish impulse of petulant curiosity, he scrambled shiveringly out of his blankets with many "O—h's" and "O-u-c-h-'s," recaptured the letter, and took it growlingly back to his warm bed.

Worn out quite as much with the grinding monotony of his rheumatic pains as with their actual acuteness, the new discomfort of straining his eyes under the feeble rays of his night-light seemed almost a pleasant diversion.

The envelope was certainly fat. As he ripped it open, three or four folded papers like sleeping-powders, all duly numbered, "1 A. M.," "2 A. M.," "3 A. M.," "4 A. M." fell out of it. With increasing inquisitiveness he drew forth the letter itself.

"Dear Honey," said the letter quite boldly. Absurd as it was, the phrase crinkled Stanton's heart just the merest trifle.

"DEAR HONEY:

"There are so many things about your sickness that worry me. Yes there are! I worry about your pain. I worry about the horrid food that you're probably getting. I worry about the coldness of your room. But most of anything in the world I worry about your *sleeplessness*. Of course you *don't* sleep! That's the trouble with rheumatism. It's such an old Night-Nagger. Now do you know what I'm going to do to you? I'm going to evolve myself into a sort of a Rheumatic Nights Entertainment—for the sole and explicit purpose of trying to while away some of your long, dark hours. Because if you've simply *got* to stay awake all night long and think—you might just as well be thinking about ME, Carl Stanton. What? Do you dare smile and suggest for a moment that just because of the Absence between us I cannot make myself vivid to you? Ho! Silly boy! Don't you know that the plainest sort of black ink throbs more than some blood—and the touch of the softest hand is a harsh caress compared to the touch of a reasonably shrewd pen? Here—now, I say—this very moment: Lift this letter of mine to your face, and swear—if you're honestly able to—that you can't smell the rose in my hair! A cinnamon rose, would you say—a yellow, flat-faced cinnamon rose? Not quite so lusciously fragrant as those in your grandmother's July garden? A trifle paler? Perceptibly cooler? Something forced into blossom, perhaps, behind brittle glass, under barren winter moonshine? And yet—A-h-h! Hear me laugh! You didn't really mean to let yourself lift the page and smell it, did you? But what did I tell you?

"I mustn't waste too much time, though, on this nonsense. What I really wanted to say to you was: Here are four—not 'sleeping potions', but waking potions—just four silly little bits of news for you to think about at one o'clock, and two, and three—and four, if you happen to be so miserable to-night as to be awake even then.

"With my love,

"MOLLY."

Whimsically, Stanton rummaged around in the creases of the bed-spread and extricated the little folded paper marked, "No. 1 o'clock." The news in it was utterly brief.

"My hair is red," was all that it announced.

With a sniff of amusement Stanton collapsed again into his pillows. For almost an hour then he lay considering solemnly whether a red-headed girl could possibly be pretty. By two o'clock he had finally visualized quite a striking, Juno-esque type of beauty with a figure about the regal height of Cornelia's, and blue eyes perhaps just a trifle hazier and more mischievous.

But the little folded paper marked, "No. 2 o'clock," announced destructively: "My eyes are brown. And I am *very* little."

With an absurdly resolute intention to "play the game" every bit as genuinely as Miss Serial-Letter Co. was playing it, Stanton refrained quite heroically from opening the third dose of news until at least two big, resonant city clocks had insisted that the hour was ripe. By that time the grin in his face was almost bright enough of itself to illuminate any ordinary page.

"I am lame," confided the third message somewhat depressingly. Then snugglingly in parenthesis like the tickle of lips against his ear whispered the one phrase: "My picture is in the fourth paper,—if you should happen still to be awake at four o'clock."

An elderly dame

Where now was Stanton's boasted sense of honor concerning the ethics of playing the game according to directions? "Wait a whole hour to see what Molly looked like? Well he guessed not!" Fumbling frantically under his pillow and across the medicine stand he began to search for the missing "No. 4 o'clock." Quite out of breath, at last he discovered it lying on the floor a whole arm's length away from the bed. Only with a really acute stab of pain did he finally succeed in reaching it. Then with fingers fairly trembling with effort, he opened forth and disclosed a tiny snap-shot photograph of a grim-jawed, scrawny-necked, much be-spectacled elderly dame with a huge gray pompadour.

"Stung!" said Stanton.

Rheumatism or anger, or something, buzzed in his heart like a bee the rest of the night.

Fortunately in the very first mail the next morning a postal-card came from Cornelia—such a pretty postal-card too, with a bright-colored picture of an inordinately "riggy" looking ostrich staring over a neat wire fence at an eager group of unmistakably Northern tourists. Underneath the picture was written in Cornelia's own precious hand the heart-thrilling information:

"We went to see the Ostrich Farm yesterday. It was really very interesting. C."

III

For quite a long time Stanton lay and considered the matter judicially from every possible point of view. "It would have been rather pleasant," he mused "to know who 'we' were." Almost childishly his face cuddled into the pillow. "She might at least have told me the name of the ostrich!" he smiled grimly.

Thus quite utterly denied any nourishing Cornelia-flavored food for his thoughts, his hungry mind reverted very naturally to the tantalizing, evasive, sweetly spicy fragrance of the 'Molly' episode—before the really dreadful photograph of the unhappy spinster-lady had burst upon his blinking vision.

Scowlingly he picked up the picture and stared and stared at it. Certainly it was grim. But even from its grimness emanated the same faint, mysterious odor of cinnamon roses that lurked in the accompanying letter. "There's some dreadful mistake somewhere," he insisted. Then suddenly he began to laugh, and reaching out once more for pen and paper, inscribed his second letter and his first complaint to the Serial-Letter Co.

"To the Serial-Letter Co.," he wrote sternly, with many ferocious tremors of dignity and rheumatism.

"Kindly allow me to call attention to the fact that in my recent order of the 18th inst., the specifications distinctly stated 'love-letters', and *not* any correspondence whatsoever,—no matter how exhilarating from either a 'Gray-Plush Squirrel' or a 'Banda Sea Pirate' as evidenced by enclosed photograph which I am hereby returning. Please refund money at once or forward me without delay a consistent photograph of a 'special edition de luxe' girl.

"Very truly yours."

The letter was mailed by the janitor long before noon. Even as late as eleven o'clock that night Stanton was still hopefully expecting an answer. Nor was he altogether disappointed. Just before midnight a messenger boy appeared with a fair-sized manilla envelope, quite stiff and important looking.

"Oh, please, Sir," said the enclosed letter, "Oh, please, Sir, we cannot refund your subscription money because—we have spent it. But if you will only be patient, we feel quite certain that you will be altogether satisfied in the long run with the material offered you. As for the photograph recently forwarded to you, kindly accept our apologies for a very clumsy mistake made here in the office. Do any of these other types suit you better? Kindly mark selection and return all pictures at your earliest convenience."

Before the messenger boy's astonished interest Stanton spread out on the bed all around him a dozen soft sepia-colored photographs of a dozen different girls. Stately in satin, or simple in gingham, or deliciously hoydenish in fishing-clothes, they challenged his surprised attention. Blonde, brunette, tall, short, posing with wistful tenderness in the flickering glow of an open fire, or smiling frankly out of a purely conventional vignette—they one and all defied him to choose between them.

"Oh! Oh!" laughed Stanton to himself. "Am I to try and separate her picture from eleven pictures of her friends! So that's the game, is it? Well, I guess not! Does she think I'm going to risk choosing a tom-boy girl if the gentle little creature with the pansies is really herself? Or suppose she truly is the enchanting little tom-boy, would she probably write me any more nice funny letters if I solemnly selected her sentimental, moony-looking friend at the heavily draped window?"

Craftily he returned all the pictures unmarked to the envelope, and changing the address hurried the messenger boy off to remail it. Just this little note, hastily scribbled in pencil went with the envelope:

"Dear Serial-Letter Co.:

"The pictures are not altogether satisfactory. It isn't a 'type' that I am looking for, but a definite likeness of 'Molly' herself. Kindly rectify the mistake without further delay! or REFUND THE MONEY."

Almost all the rest of the night he amused himself chuckling to think how the terrible threat about refunding the money would confuse and conquer the extravagant little Art Student.

But it was his own hands that did the nervous trembling when he opened the big express package that arrived the next evening, just as his tiresome porridge supper was finished.

"Ah, Sweetheart—" said the dainty note tucked inside the package—"Ah, Sweetheart, the little god of love be praised for one true lover—Yourself! So it is a picture of *me* that you want? The *real me*! The *truly me*! No mere pink and white likeness? No actual proof even of 'seared and yellow age'? No curly-haired, coquettish attractiveness that the shampoo-lady and the photograph-man trapped me into for that one single second? No deceptive profile of the best side of my face—and I, perhaps, blind in the other eye? Not even a fair, honest, every-day portrait of my father's and mother's composite features—but a picture of *myself*! Hooray for you! A picture, then, not of my physiognomy, but of my *personality*. Very well, sir. Here is the portrait—true to the life—in this great, clumsy, conglomerate package of articles that represent—perhaps—not even so much the prosy, literal things that I am, as the much more illuminating and significant things that *I would like to be*. It's what we would 'like to be' that really tells most about us, isn't it, Carl Stanton? The brown that I have to wear talks loudly enough, for instance, about the color of my complexion, but the forbidden pink that I most crave whispers infinitely more intimately concerning the color of my spirit. And as to my Face—*am I really obliged to have a face*? Oh, no—o! 'Songs without words' are surely the only songs in the world that are packed to the last lilting note with utterly limitless meanings. So in these 'letters without faces' I cast myself quite serenely upon the mercy of your imagination.

"What's that you say? That I've simply *got* to have a face? Oh, darn!—well, do your worst. Conjure up for me then, here and now, any sort of features whatsoever that please your fancy. Only, Man of Mine, just remember this in your imaginings: Gift me with Beauty if you like, or gift me with Brains, but do not make the crude masculine mistake of gifting me with both. Thought furrows faces you know, and after Adolescence only Inanity retains its heavenly smoothness. Beauty even at its worst is a gorgeously perfect, flower-sprinkled lawn over which the most ordinary, every-day errands of life cannot cross without scarring. And brains at their best are only a ploughed field teeming always and forever with the worries of incalculable harvests. Make me a little pretty, if you like, and a little wise, but not too much of either, if you value the verities of your Vision. There! I say: do your worst! Make me that face, and that face only, that you *need the most* in all this big, lonesome world: food for your heart, or fragrance for your nostrils. Only, one face or another—I insist upon having *red hair*!

"MOLLY."

With his lower lip twisted oddly under the bite of his strong white teeth, Stanton began to unwrap the various packages that comprised the large bundle. If it was a "portrait" it certainly represented a puzzle-picture.

First there was a small, flat-footed scarlet slipper with a fluffy gold toe to it. Definitely feminine. Definitely small. So much for that! Then there was a sling-shot, ferociously stubby, and rather confusingly boyish. After that, round and flat and tantalizing as an empty plate, the phonograph disc of a totally unfamiliar song—"The Sea Gull's Cry": a clue surely to neither age nor sex, but indicative possibly of musical preference or mere individual temperament. After that, a tiny geographical globe, with Kipling's phrase—

"For to admire an' for to see,For to be'old this world so wide—It never done no good to me,But I can't drop it if I tried!"—

written slantingly in very black ink across both hemispheres. Then an empty purse—with a hole in it; a silver-embroidered gauntlet such as horsemen wear on the Mexican frontier; a white table-doily partly embroidered with silky blue forget-me-nots—the threaded needle still jabbed in the work—and the small thimble, Stanton could have sworn, still warm from the snuggle of somebody's finger. Last of all, a fat and formidable edition of Robert Browning's poems; a tiny black domino-mask, such as masqueraders wear, and a shimmering gilt picture frame inclosing a pert yet not irreverent handmade adaptation of a certain portion of St. Paul's epistle to the Corinthians:

"Though I speak with the tongues of men and of angels and have not a Sense of Humor, I am become as sounding brass, or a tinkling symbol. And though I have the gift of Prophecy—and all knowledge—so that I could remove Mountains, and have not a Sense of Humor, I am nothing. And though I bestow all my Goods to feed the poor, and though I give my body to be burned, and have not a Sense of Humor it profiteth me nothing.

"A sense of Humor suffereth long, and is kind. A Sense of Humor envieth not. A Sense of Humor vaunteth not itself—is not puffed up. Doth not behave itself Unseemly, seeketh not its own, is not easily provoked, thinketh no evil—Beareth all things, believeth all things, hopeth all things, endureth all things. A Sense of Humor never faileth. But whether there be unpleasant prophecies they shall fail, whether there be scolding tongues they shall cease, whether there be unfortunate knowledge it shall vanish away. When I was a fault-finding child I spake as a fault-finding child, I understood as a fault-finding child,—but when I became a woman I put away fault-finding things.

"And now abideth faith, hope, charity, these three. *But the greatest of these is a sense of humor!*"

With a little chuckle of amusement not altogether devoid of a very definite consciousness of being *teased*, Stanton spread all the articles out on the bed-spread before him and tried to piece them together like the fragments of any other jig-saw puzzle. Was the young lady as intellectual as the Robert Browning poems suggested, or did she mean simply to imply that she *wished* she were? And did the tom-boyish sling-shot fit by any possible chance with the dainty, feminine scrap of domestic embroidery? And was the empty purse supposed to be especially significant of an inordinate fondness for phonograph music—or what?

Pondering, puzzling, fretting, fussing, he dozed off to sleep at last before he even knew that it was almost morning. And when he finally woke again he found the Doctor laughing at him because he lay holding a scarlet slipper in his hand.

IV

The next night, very, very late, in a furious riot of wind and snow and sleet, a clerk from the drug-store just around the corner appeared with a perfectly huge hot-water bottle fairly sizzling and bubbling with warmth and relief for aching rheumatic backs.

"Well, where in thunder—?" groaned Stanton out of his cold and pain and misery.

"Search me!" said the drug clerk. "The order and the money for it came in the last mail this evening. 'Kindly deliver largest-sized hot-water bottle, boiling hot, to Mr. Carl Stanton,... 11.30 to-night.'"

"OO-w!" gasped Stanton. "O-u-c-h! G-e-e!" then, "Oh, I wish I could purr!" as he settled cautiously back at last to toast his pains against the blessed, scorching heat. "Most girls," he reasoned with surprising interest, "would have sent ice cold violets shrouded in tissue paper. Now, how does this special girl know—Oh, Ouch! O-u-c-h! O-u-c-h—i—t—y!" he crooned himself to sleep.

The next night just at supper-time a much-freckled messenger-boy appeared dragging an exceedingly obstreperous fox-terrier on the end of a dangerously frayed leash. Planting himself firmly on the rug in the middle of the room, with the faintest gleam of saucy pink tongue showing between his teeth, the little beast sat and defied the entire situation. Nothing apparently but the correspondence concerning the situation was actually transferable from the freckled messenger boy to Stanton himself.

"Oh, dear Lad," said the tiny note, "I forgot to tell you my real name, didn't I!—Well, my last name and the dog's first name are just the same. Funny, isn't it? (You'll find it in the back of almost any dictionary.)

"With love,

"MOLLY.

"P. S. Just turn the puppy out in the morning and he'll go home all right of his own accord."

A much-freckled messenger-boy appeared dragging an exceedingly obstreperous fox-terrier

With his own pink tongue showing just a trifle between his teeth, Stanton lay for a moment and watched the dog on the rug. Cocking his small, keen, white head from one tippy angle to another, the little terrier returned the stare with an expression that was altogether and unmistakably mirthful. "Oh, it's a jolly little beggar, isn't it?" said Stanton. "Come here, sir!" Only a suddenly pointed ear acknowledged the summons. The dog himself did not budge. "Come here, I say!" Stanton repeated with harshperemptoriness. Palpably the little dog winked at him. Then in succession the little dog dodged adroitly a knife, a spoon, a copy of Browning's poems, and several other sizable articles from the table close to Stanton's elbow. Nothing but the dictionary seemed too big to throw. Finally with a grin that could not be disguised even from the dog, Stanton began to rummage with eye and hand through the intricate back pages of the dictionary.

"You silly little fool," he said. "Won't you mind unless you are spoken to by name?"

"Aaron—Abidel—Abel—Abiathar—" he began to read out with petulant curiosity, "Baldwin—Barachias—Bruno (Oh, hang!) Cadwallader—Cæsar—Caleb (What nonsense!) Ephraim—Erasmus (How could a girl be named anything like that!) Gabriel—Gerard—Gershom (Imagine whistling a dog to the name of Gershom!) Hannibal—Hezekiah—Hosea (Oh, Hell!)" Stolidly with unheedful, drooping ears the little fox-terrier resumed his seat on the rug. "Ichabod—Jabez—Joab," Stanton's voice persisted, experimentally. By nine o'clock, in all possible variations of accent and intonation, he had quite completely exhausted the alphabetical list as far as "K." and the little dog was blinking himself to sleep on the far side of the room. Something about the dog's nodding contentment started Stanton's mouth to yawning and for almost an hour he lay in the lovely, restful consciousness of being at least half asleep. But at ten o'clock he roused up sharply and resumed the task at hand, which seemed suddenly to have assumed really vital importance. "Laban—Lorenzo—Marcellus," he began again in a loud, clear, compelling voice. "Meredith—" (Did the little dog stir? Did he sit up?) "Meredith? Meredith?" The little dog barked. Something in Stanton's brain flashed. "It is 'Merry' for the dog?" he quizzed. "Here, MERRY!" In another instant the little creature had leaped upon the foot of his bed, and was talking away at a great rate with all sorts of ecstatic grunts and growls. Stanton's hand went out almost shyly to the dog's head. "So it's 'Molly Meredith'," he mused. But after all there was no reason to be shy about it. It was the *dog's* head he was stroking.

Tied to the little dog's collar when he went home the next morning was a tiny, inconspicuous tag that said "That was easy! The pup's name—and yours—is 'Meredith.' Funny name for a dog but nice for a girl."

The Serial-Letter Co.'s answers were always prompt, even though perplexing.

"DEAR LAD," came this special answer. "You are quite right about the dog. And I compliment you heartily on your shrewdness. But I must confess,—even though it makes you very angry with me, that I have deceived you absolutely concerning my own name. Will you forgive me utterly if I hereby promise never to deceive you again? Why what could I possibly, possibly do with a great solemn name like 'Meredith'? My truly name, Sir, my really, truly, honest-injun name is 'Molly Make-Believe'. Don't you know the funny little old song about 'Molly Make-Believe'? Oh, surely you do:

"'Molly, Molly Make-Believe,Keep to your play if you would not grieve!For Molly-Mine here's a hint for you,Things that are true are apt to be blue!'

"Now you remember it, don't you? Then there's something about

"'Molly, Molly Make-a-Smile,Wear it, swear it all the while.Long as your lips are framed for a joke,Who can prove that your heart is broke?'

"Don't you love that 'is broke'! Then there's the last verse—my favorite:

"'Molly, Molly Make-a-Beau,Make him of mist or make him of snow,Long as your DREAM stays fine and fair,*Molly, Molly what do you care!*'"

"Well, I'll wager that her name *is* 'Meredith' just the same," vowed Stanton, "and she's probably madder than scat to think that I hit it right."

Whether the daily overtures from the Serial-Letter Co. proved to be dogs or love-letters or hot-water bottles or funny old songs, it was reasonably evident that something unique was practically guaranteed to happen every single, individual night of the six weeks' subscription contract. Like a youngster's joyous dream of chronic Christmas Eves, this realization alone was enough to put an absurdly delicious thrill of expectancy into any invalid's otherwise prosy thoughts.

Yet the next bit of attention from the Serial-Letter Co. did not please Stanton one half as much as it embarrassed him.

Wandering socially into the room from his own apartments below, a young lawyer friend of Stanton's had only just seated himself on the foot of Stanton's bed when an expressman also arrived with two large pasteboard hat-boxes which he straightway dumped on the bed between the two men with the laconic message that he would call for them again in the morning.

"Heaven preserve me!" gasped Stanton. "What is this?"

Fearsomely out of the smaller of the two boxes he lifted with much rustling snarl of tissue paper a woman's brown fur-hat,—very soft, very fluffy, inordinately jaunty with a blush-pink rose nestling deep in the fur. Out of the other box, twice as large, twice as rustly, flaunted a green velvet cavalier's hat, with a green ostrich feather as long as a man's arm drooping languidly off the brim.

"Holy Cat!" said Stanton.

Pinned to the green hat's crown was a tiny note. The handwriting at least was pleasantly familiar by this time.

"Oh, I say!" cried the lawyer delightedly.

With a desperately painful effort at nonchalance, Stanton shoved his right fist into the brown hat and his left fist into the green one, and raised them quizzically from the bed.

"Darned—good-looking—hats," he stammered.

"Oh, I say!" repeated the lawyer with accumulative delight.

Crimson to the tip of his ears, Stanton rolled his eyes frantically towards the little note.

"She sent 'em up just to show 'em to me," he quoted wildly. "Just 'cause I'm laid up so and can't get out on the streets to see the styles for myself.—And I've got to choose between them for her!" he ejaculated. "She says she can't decide alone which one to keep!"

"Bully for her!" cried the lawyer, surprisingly, slapping his knee. "The cunning little girl!"

Speechless with astonishment, Stanton lay and watched his visitor, then "Well, which one would you choose?" he asked with unmistakable relief.

The lawyer took the hats and scanned them carefully. "Let—me—see" he considered. "Her hair is so blond—"

"No, it's red!" snapped Stanton.

With perfect courtesy the lawyer swallowed his mistake. "Oh, excuse me," he said. "I forgot. But with her height—"

"She hasn't any height," groaned Stanton. "I tell you she's little."

"Choose to suit yourself," said the lawyer coolly. He himself had admired Cornelia from afar off.

The next night, to Stanton's mixed feelings of relief and disappointment the "surprise" seemed to consist in the fact that nothing happened at all. Fully until midnight the sense of relief comforted him utterly. But some time after midnight, his hungry mind, like a house-pet robbed of an accustomed meal, began to wake and fret and stalk around ferociously through all the long, empty, aching, early morning hours, searching for something novel to think about.

By supper-time the next evening he was in an irritable mood that made him fairly clutch the special delivery letter out of the postman's hand. It was rather a thin, tantalizing little letter, too. All it said was,

"To-night, Dearest, until one o'clock, in a cabbage-colored gown all shimmery with green and blue and September frost-lights, I'm going to sit up by my white birch-wood fire and read aloud to you. Yes! Honest-Injun! And out of Browning, too. Did you notice your copy was marked? What shall I read to you? Shall it be

"'If I could have that little head of hersPainted upon a background of pale gold.'

"or

'Shall I sonnet-sing you about myself?Do I live in a house you would like to see?'

"or

'I am a Painter who cannot paint,——No end to all I cannot do.*Yet do one thing at least I can,Love a man, or hate a man!*'

"or just

'Escape me?Never,Beloved!While I am I, and you are you!'

"Oh, Honey! Won't it be fun? Just you and I, perhaps, in all this Big City, sitting up and thinking about each other. Can you smell the white birch smoke in this letter?"

"Well I'll be hanged," growled Stanton, "if I'm going to be strung by any boy!"

Almost unconsciously Stanton raised the page to his face. Unmistakably, up from the paper rose the strong, vivid scent—of a briar-wood pipe.

"Well I'll be hanged," growled Stanton, "if I'm going to be strung by any boy!" Out of all proportion the incident irritated him.

But when, the next evening, a perfectly tremendous bunch of yellow jonquils arrived with a penciled line suggesting, "If you'll put these solid gold posies in your window to-morrow morning at eight o'clock, so I'll surely know just which window is yours, I'll look up—when I go past," Stanton most peremptorily ordered the janitor to display the bouquet as ornately as possible along the narrow window-sill of the biggest window that faced the street. Then all through the night he lay dozing and waking intermittently, with a lovely, scared feeling in the pit of his stomach that something really rather exciting was about to happen. By surely half-past seven he rose laboriously from his bed, huddled himself into his black-sheep wrapper and settled himself down as warmly as could be expected, close to the draughty edge of the window.

V

"Little and lame and red-haired and brown-eyed," he kept repeating to himself.

Old people and young people, cab-drivers and jaunty young girls, and fat blue policeman, looked up, one and all with quick-brightening faces at the really gorgeous Spring-like flame of jonquils, but in a whole chilly, wearisome hour the only red-haired person that passed was an Irish setter puppy, and the only lame person was a wooden-legged beggar.

Cold and disgusted as he was, Stanton could not altogether help laughing at his own discomfiture.

"Why—hang that little girl! She ought to be s-p-a-n-k-e-d," he chuckled as he climbed back into his tiresome bed.

Then as though to reward his ultimate good-nature the very next mail brought him a letter from Cornelia, and rather a remarkable letter too, as in addition to the usual impersonal comments on the weather and the tennis and the annual orange crop, there was actually one whole, individual, intimate sentence that distinguished the letter as having been intended solely for him rather than for Cornelia's dressmaker or her coachman's invalid daughter, or her own youngest brother. This was the sentence:

"Really, Carl, you don't know how glad I am that in spite of all your foolish objections, I kept to my original purpose of not announcing my engagement until after my Southern trip. You've no idea what a big difference it makes in a girl's good time at a great hotel like this."

This sentence surely gave Stanton a good deal of food for his day's thoughts, but the mental indigestion that ensued was not altogether pleasant.

Not until evening did his mood brighten again. Then—

"Lad of Mine," whispered Molly's gentler letter. "Lad of Mine, *how blond your hair is!*—Even across the chin-tickling tops of those yellow jonquils this morning, I almost laughed to see the blond, blond shine of you.—Some day I'm going to stroke that hair." (Yes!)

"P. S. The Little Dog came home all right."

With a gasp of dismay Stanton sat up abruptly in bed and tried to revisualize every single, individual pedestrian who had passed his window in the vicinity of eight o'clock that morning. "She evidently isn't lame at all," he argued, "or little, or red-haired, or anything. Probably her name isn't Molly, and presumably it isn't even 'Meredith.' But at least she did go by: And is my hair so very blond?" he asked himself suddenly. Against all intention his mouth began to prance a little at the corners.

As soon as he could possibly summon the janitor, he despatched his third note to the Serial-Letter Co., but this one bore a distinctly sealed inner envelope, directed, "For Molly. Personal." And the message in it, though brief was utterly to the point. "Couldn't you *please* tell a fellow who you are?"

But by the conventional bed-time hour the next night he wished most heartily that he had not been so inquisitive, for the only entertainment that came to him at all was a jonquil-colored telegram warning him—

"Where the apple reddens do not pry,Lest we lose our Eden—you and I."

The couplet was quite unfamiliar to Stanton, but it rhymed sickeningly through his brain all night long like the consciousness of an over-drawn bank account.

It was the very next morning after this that all the Boston papers flaunted Cornelia's aristocratic young portrait on their front pages with the striking, large-type announcement that "One of Boston's Fairest Debutantes Makes a Daring Rescue in Florida waters. Hotel Cook Capsized from Row Boat Owes His Life to the Pluck and Endurance—etc., etc."

With a great sob in his throat and every pulse pounding, Stanton lay and read the infinite details of the really splendid story; a group of young girls dallying on the Pier; a shrill cry from the bay; the sudden panic-stricken helplessness of the spectators, and then with equal suddenness the plunge of a single, feminine figure into the water; the long hard swim; the furious struggle; the final victory. Stingingly, as though it had been fairly branded into his eyes, he saw the vision of Cornelia's heroic young face battling above the horrible, dragging-down depths of the bay. The bravery, the risk, the ghastly chances of a less fortunate ending, sent shiver after shiver through his already tortured senses. All the loving thoughts in his nature fairly leaped to do tribute to Cornelia. "Yes!" he reasoned, "Cornelia was made like that! No matter what the cost to herself—no matter what was the price—Cornelia would never, never fail to do her *duty*!" When he thought of the weary, lagging, riskful weeks that were still to ensue before he should actually see Cornelia again, he felt as though he should go utterly mad. The letter that he wrote to Cornelia that night was like a letter written in a man's own heart-blood. His hand trembled so that he could scarcely hold the pen.

Cornelia did not like the letter. She said so frankly. The letter did not seem to her quite "nice." "Certainly," she attested, "it was not exactly the sort of letter that one would like to show one's mother." Then, in a palpably conscientious effort to be kind as well as just, she began to prattle inkily again about the pleasant, warm, sunny weather. Her only comment on saving the drowning man was the mere phrase that she was very glad that she had learned to be a good swimmer. Never indeed since her absence had she spoken of missing Stanton. Not even now, after what was inevitably a heart-racking adventure, did she yield her lover one single iota of the information which he had a lover's right to claim. Had she been frightened, for instance—way down in the bottom of that serene heart of hers had she been frightened? In the ensuing desperate struggle for life had she struggled just one little tiny bit harder because Stanton was in that life? Now, in the dreadful, unstrung reaction of the adventure, did her whole nature waken and yearn and cry out for that one heart in all the world that belonged to her? Plainly, by her silence in the matter, she did not intend to share anything as intimate even as her fear of death with the man whom she claimed to love.

It was just this last touch of deliberate, selfish aloofness that startled Stanton's thoughts with the one persistent, brutally nagging question: After all, was a woman's undeniably glorious ability to save a drowning man the supreme, requisite of a happy marriage?

Day by day, night by night, hour by hour, minute by minute, the question began to dig into Stanton's brain, throwing much dust and confusion into brain-corners otherwise perfectly orderly and sweet and clean.

Week by week, grown suddenly and morbidly analytical, he watched for Cornelia's letters with increasingly passionate hopefulness, and met each fresh disappointment with increasingly passionate resentment. Except for the Serial-Letter Co.'s ingeniously varied attentions there was practically nothing to help him make either day or night bearable. More and more Cornelia's infrequent letters suggested exquisitely painted empty dishes offered to a starving person. More and more "Molly's" whimsical messages fed him and nourished him and joyously pleased him like some nonsensically fashioned candy-box that yet proved brimming full of real food for a real man. Fight as he would against it, he began to cherish a sense of furious annoyance that Cornelia's failure to provide for him had so thrust him out, as it were, to feed among strangers. With frowning perplexity and real worry he felt the tingling, vivid consciousness of Molly's personality begin to permeate and impregnate his whole nature. Yet when he tried to acknowledge and thereby cancel his personal sense of obligation to this "Molly" by writing an exceptionally civil note of appreciation to the Serial-Letter Co., the Serial-Letter Co. answered him tersely—

"Pray do not thank us for the jonquils,—blanket-wrapper, etc., etc. Surely they are merely presents from yourself to yourself. It is your money that bought them."

And when he had replied briefly, "Well, thank you for your brains, then!" the "company" had persisted with undue sharpness, "Don't thank us for our brains. Brains are our business."

VI

It was one day just about the end of the fifth week that poor Stanton's long-accumulated, long-suppressed perplexity blew up noisily just like any other kind of steam.

It was the first day, too, throughout all his illness that he had made even the slightest pretext of being up and about. Slippered if not booted, blanket-wrapped if not coated, shaven at least, if not shorn, he had established himself fairly comfortably, late in the afternoon, at his big study-table close to the fire, where, in his low Morris chair, with his books and his papers and his lamp close at hand, he had started out once more to try and solve the absurd little problem that confronted him. Only an occasional twitch of pain in his shoulder-blade, or an intermittent shudder of nerves along his spine had interrupted in any possible way his almost frenzied absorption in his subject.

Here at the desk very soon after supper-time the Doctor had joined him, and with an unusual expression of leisure and friendliness had settled down lollingly on the other side of the fireplace with his great square-toed shoes nudging the bright, brassy edge of the fender, and his big meerschaum pipe puffing the whole bleak room most deliciously, tantalizingly full of forbidden tobacco smoke. It was a comfortable, warm place to chat. The talk had begun with politics, drifted a little way toward the architecture of several new city buildings, hovered a moment over the marriage of some mutual friend, and then languished utterly.

With a sudden narrowing-eyed shrewdness the Doctor turned and watched an unwonted flicker of worry on Stanton's forehead.

"What's bothering you, Stanton?" he asked, quickly. "Surely you're not worrying any more about your rheumatism?"

"No," said Stanton. "It—isn't—rheumatism."

For an instant the two men's eyes held each other, and then Stanton began to laugh a trifle uneasily.

"Doctor," he asked quite abruptly, "Doctor, do you believe that any possible conditions could exist—that would make it justifiable for a man to show a woman's love-letter to another man?"

"Why—y-e-s," said the Doctor cautiously, "I think so. There might be—circumstances—"

Still without any perceptible cause, Stanton laughed again, and reaching out, picked up a folded sheet of paper from the table and handed it to the Doctor.

"Read that, will you?" he asked. "And read it out loud."

With a slight protest of diffidence, the Doctor unfolded the paper, scanned the page for an instant, and began slowly.

"Carl of Mine.

"There's one thing I forgot to tell you. When you go to buy my engagement ring—I don't want any! No! I'd rather have two wedding-rings instead—two perfectly plain gold wedding-rings. And the ring for my passive left hand I want inscribed, 'To Be a Sweetness More Desired than Spring!' and the ring for my active right hand I want inscribed, 'His Soul to Keep!' Just that.

"And you needn't bother to write me that you don't understand, because you are not expected to understand. It is not Man's prerogative to understand. But you are perfectly welcome if you want, to call me crazy, because I am—utterly crazy on just one subject, and *that's you*. Why, Beloved, if—"

"Here!" cried Stanton suddenly reaching out and grabbing the letter. "Here! You needn't read any more!" His cheeks were crimson.

The Doctor's eyes focused sharply on his face. "That girl loves you," said the Doctor tersely. For a moment then the Doctor's lips puffed silently at his pipe, until at last with an almost bashful gesture, he cried out abruptly: "Stanton, somehow I feel as though I owed you an apology, or rather, owed your fiancée one. Somehow when you told me that day that your young lady had gone gadding off to Florida and—left you alone with your sickness, why I thought—well, most evidently I have misjudged her."

Stanton's throat gave a little gasp, then silenced again. He bit his lips furiously as though to hold back an exclamation. Then suddenly the whole perplexing truth burst forth from him.

"That isn't from my fiancée!" he cried out. "That's just a professional love-letter. I buy them by the dozen,—so much a week." Reaching back under his pillow he extricated another letter. "*This* is from my fiancée," he said. "Read it. Yes, do."

"Aloud?" gasped the Doctor.

Stanton nodded. His forehead was wet with sweat.

"DEAR CARL,

"The weather is still very warm. I am riding horseback almost every morning, however, and playing tennis almost every afternoon. There seem to be an exceptionally large number of interesting people here this winter. In regard to the list of names you sent me for the wedding, really, Carl, I do not see how I can possibly accommodate so many of your friends without seriously curtailing my own list. After all you must remember that it is the bride's day, not the groom's. And in regard to your question as to whether we expect to be home for Christmas and could I possibly arrange to spend Christmas Day with you—why, Carl, you are perfectly preposterous! Of course it is very kind of you to invite me and all that, but how could mother and I possibly come to your rooms when our engagement is not even announced? And besides there is going to be a very smart dance here Christmas Eve that I particularly wish to attend. And there are plenty of Christmases coming for you and me.

"Cordially yours,

"CORNELIA.

"P. S. Mother and I hope that your rheumatism is much better."

"That's the girl who loves me," said Stanton not unhumorously. Then suddenly all the muscles around his mouth tightened like the facial muscles of a man who is hammering something. "I mean it!" he insisted. "I mean it—absolutely. That's the—girl—who—loves—me!"

Silently the two men looked at each other for a second. Then they both burst out laughing.

"Oh, yes," said Stanton at last, "I know it's funny. That's just the trouble with it. It's altogether too funny."

Out of a book on the table beside him he drew the thin gray and crimson circular of The Serial-Letter Co. and handed it to the Doctor. Then after a moment's rummaging around on the floor beside him, he produced with some difficulty a long, pasteboard box fairly bulging with papers and things.

"These are the—communications from my make-believe girl," he confessed grinningly. "Oh, of course they're not all letters," he hurried to explain. "Here's a book on South America.—I'm a rubber broker, you know, and of course I've always been keen enough about the New England end of my job, but I've never thought anything so very special about the South American end of it. But that girl—that make-believe girl, I mean—insists that I ought to know all about South America, so she sent me this book; and it's corking reading, too—all about funny things like eating monkeys and parrots and toasted guinea-pigs—and sleeping outdoors in black jungle-nights under mosquito netting, mind you, as a protection against prowling panthers.—And here's a queer little newspaper cutting that she sent me one blizzardy Sunday telling all about some big violin maker who always went out into the forests himself and chose his violin woods from the *north* side of the trees. Casual little item. You don't think anything about it at the moment. It probably isn't true. And to save your soul you couldn't tell what kind of trees violins are made out of, anyway. But I'll wager that never again will you wake in the night to listen to the wind without thinking of the great storm-tossed, moaning, groaning, slow-toughening forest trees—learning to be violins!... And here's a funny little old silver porringer that she gave me, she says, to make my 'old gray gruel taste shinier.' And down at the bottom of the bowl—the ruthless little pirate—she's taken a knife or a pin or something and scratched the words, 'Excellent Child!'—But you know I never noticed that part of it at all till last week. You see I've only been eating down to the bottom of the bowl just about a week.—And here's a catalogue of a boy's school, four or five catalogues in fact that she sent me one evening and asked me if I please wouldn't look them over right away and help her decide where to send her little brother. Why, man, it took me almost all night! If you get the athletics you want in one school, then likelier than not you slip up on the manual training, and if they're going to schedule eight hours a week for Latin, why where in Creation—?"

Shrugging his shoulders as though to shrug aside absolutely any possible further responsibility concerning, "little brother," Stanton began to dig down deeper into the box. Then suddenly all the grin came back to his face.

"And here are some sample wall papers that she sent me for 'our house'," he confided, flushing. "What do you think of that bronze one there with the peacock feathers?—say, old man, think of a library—and a cannel coal fire—and a big mahogany desk—and a red-haired girl sitting against that paper! And this sun-shiny tint for a breakfast-room isn't half bad, is it?—Oh yes, and here are the time-tables, and all the pink and blue maps about Colorado and Arizona and the 'Painted Desert'. If we can 'afford it,' she writes, she 'wishes we could go to the Painted Desert on our wedding trip.'—But really, old man, you know it isn't such a frightfully expensive journey. Why if you leave New York on Wednesday—Oh, hang it all! What's the use of showing you any more of this nonsense?" he finished abruptly.

With brutal haste he started cramming everything back into place. "It is nothing but nonsense!" he acknowledged conscientiously; "nothing in the world except a boxful of make-believe thoughts from a make-believe girl. And here," he finished resolutely, "are my own fiancée's thoughts—concerning me."

Out of his blanket-wrapper pocket he produced and spread out before the Doctor's eyes five thin letters and a postal-card.

"Not exactly thoughts concerning *you*, even so, are they?" quizzed the Doctor.

Stanton began to grin again. "Well, thoughts concerning the weather, then—if that suits you any better."

Twice the Doctor swallowed audibly. Then, "But it's hardly fair—is it—to weigh a boxful of even the prettiest lies against five of even the slimmest real, true letters?" he asked drily.

"But they're not lies!" snapped Stanton. "Surely you don't call anything a lie unless not only the fact is false, but the fancy, also, is maliciously distorted! Now take this case right before us. Suppose there isn't any 'little brother' at all; suppose there isn't any 'Painted Desert', suppose there isn't any 'black sheep up on a grandfather's farm', suppose there isn't *anything*; suppose, I say, that every single, individual fact stated is *false*—what earthly difference does it make so long as the *fancy* still remains the truest, realest,0 dearest, funniest thing that ever happened to a fellow in his life?"

"Oh, ho!" said the Doctor. "So that's the trouble is it! It isn't just rheumatism that's keeping you thin and worried looking, eh? It's only that you find yourself suddenly in the embarrassing predicament of being engaged to one girl and—in love with another?"

Some poor old worn-out story-writer

"N—o!" cried Stanton frantically. "N—O! That's the mischief of it—the very mischief! I don't even know that the Serial-Letter Co.*is* a girl. Why it might be an old lady, rather whimsically inclined. Even the oldest lady, I presume, might very reasonably perfume her note-paper with cinnamon roses. It might even be a boy. One letter indeed smelt very strongly of being a boy—and mighty good tobacco, too! And great heavens! what have I got to prove that it isn't even an old man—some poor old worn out story-writer trying to ease out the ragged end of his years?"

"Have you told your fiancée about it?" asked the Doctor.

Stanton's jaw dropped. "Have I told my fiancée about it?" he mocked. "Why it was she who sent me the circular in the first place! But, 'tell her about it'? Why, man, in ten thousand years, and then some, how could I make any sane person understand?"

"You're beginning to make me understand," confessed the Doctor.

"Then you're no longer sane," scoffed Stanton. "The crazy magic of it has surely then taken possession of you too. Why how could I go to any sane person like Cornelia—and Cornelia is the most absolutely, hopelessly sane person you ever saw in your life—how could I go to anyone like that, and announce: 'Cornelia, if you find any perplexing change in me during your absence—and your unconscious neglect—it is only that I have fallen quite madly in love with a person'—would you call it a person?—who doesn't even exist. Therefore for the sake of this 'person who doesn't exist', I ask to be released."

"Oh! So you do ask to be released?" interrupted the Doctor.

"Why, no! Certainly not!" insisted Stanton. "Suppose the girl you love does hurt your feelings a little bit now and then, would any man go ahead and give up a real flesh-and-blood sweetheart for the sake of even the most wonderful paper-and-ink girl whom he was reading about in an unfinished serial story? Would he, I say—would he?"

"Y-e-s," said the Doctor soberly. "Y-e-s, I think he would, if what you call the 'paper-and-ink girl' suggested suddenly an entirely new, undreamed-of vista of emotional and spiritual satisfaction."

"But I tell you 'she's' probably a BOY!" persisted Stanton doggedly.

"Well, why don't you go ahead and find out?" quizzed the Doctor.

"Find out?" cried Stanton hotly. "Find out? I'd like to know how anybody is going to find out, when the only given address is a private post-office box, and as far as I know there's no sex to a post-office box. Find out? Why, man, that basket over there is full of my letters returned to me because I tried to 'find out'. The first time I asked, they answered me with just a teasing, snubbing telegram, but ever since then they've simply sent back my questions with a stern printed slip announcing, "Your letter of —— is hereby returned to you. Kindly allow us to call your attention to the fact that we are not running a correspondence bureau. Our circular distinctly states, etc."

"Sent you a printed slip?" cried the Doctor scoffingly. "The love-letter business must be thriving. Very evidently you are by no means the only importunate subscriber."

"Oh, Thunder!" growled Stanton. The idea seemed to be new to him and not altogether to his taste. Then suddenly his face began to brighten. "No, I'm lying," he said. "No, they haven't always sent me a printed slip. It was only yesterday that they sent me a rather real sort of letter. You see," he explained, "I got pretty mad at last and I wrote them frankly and told them that I didn't give a darn who 'Molly' was, but simply wanted to know *what* she was. I told them that it was just gratitude on my part, the most formal, impersonal sort of gratitude—a perfectly plausible desire to say 'thank you' to some one who had been awfully decent to me these past few weeks. I said right out that if 'she' was a boy, why we'd surely have to go fishing together in the spring, and if 'she' was an old man, the very least I could do would be to endow her with tobacco, and if 'she' was an old lady, why I'd simply be obliged to drop in now and then of a rainy evening and hold her knitting for her."

"And if 'she' were a girl?" probed the Doctor.

Stanton's mouth began to twitch. "Then Heaven help me!" he laughed.

"Well, what answer did you get?" persisted the Doctor. "What do you call a realish sort of letter?"

With palpable reluctance Stanton drew a gray envelope out of the cuff of his wrapper.

"I suppose you might as well see the whole business," he admitted consciously.

There was no special diffidence in the Doctor's manner this time. His clutch on the letter was distinctly inquisitive, and he read out the opening sentences with almost rhetorical effect.

"Oh, Carl dear, you silly boy, WHY do you persist in hectoring me so? Don't you understand that I've got only a certain amount of ingenuity anyway, and if you force me to use it all in trying to conceal my identity from you, how much shall I possibly have left to devise schemes for your amusement? Why do you persist, for instance, in wanting to see my face? Maybe I haven't got any face! Maybe I lost my face in a railroad accident. How do you suppose it would make me feel, then, to have you keep teasing and teasing.—Oh, Carl!

"Isn't it enough for me just to tell you once for all that there is an insuperable obstacle in the way of our ever meeting. Maybe I've got a husband who is cruel to me. Maybe, biggest obstacle of all, I've got a husband whom I am utterly devoted to. Maybe, instead of any of these things, I'm a poor, old wizened-up, Shut-In, tossing day and night on a very small bed of very big pain. Maybe worse than being sick I'm starving poor, and maybe, worse than being sick or poor, I am most horribly tired of myself. Of course if you are very young and very prancy and reasonably good-looking, and still are tired of yourself, you can almost always rest yourself by going on the stage where—with a little rouge and a different colored wig, and a new nose, and skirts instead of trousers, or trousers instead of skirts, and age instead of youth, and badness instead of goodness—you can give your ego a perfectly limitless number of happy holidays. But if you were oldish, I say, and pitifully 'shut in', just how would you go to work, I wonder, to rest your personality? How for instance could you take your biggest, grayest, oldest worry about your doctor's bill, and rouge it up into a radiant, young joke? And how, for instance, out of your lonely, dreary, middle-aged orphanhood are you going to find a way to short-skirt your rheumatic pains, and braid into two perfectly huge pink-bowed pigtails the hair that you *haven't got*, and caper round so ecstatically before the footlights that the old gentleman and lady in the front seat absolutely swear you to be the living image of their 'long lost Amy'? And how, if the farthest journey you ever will take again is the monotonous hand-journey from your pillow to your medicine bottle, then how, for instance, with map or tinsel or attar of roses, can you go to work to solve even just for your own satisfaction the romantic, shimmering secrets of—Morocco?

"Ah! You've got me now, you think? All decided in your mind that I am an aged invalid? I didn't say so. I just said 'maybe'. Likelier than not I've saved my climax for its proper place. How do you know,—for instance, that I'm not a—'Cullud Pusson'?—So many people are."

Without signature of any sort, the letter ended abruptly then and there, and as though to satisfy his sense of something left unfinished, the Doctor began at the beginning and read it all over again in a mumbling, husky whisper.

"Maybe she is—'colored'," he volunteered at last.

"Very likely," said Stanton perfectly cheerfully. "It's just those occasional humorous suggestions that keep me keyed so heroically up to the point where I'm actually infuriated if you even suggest that I might be getting really interested in this mysterious Miss Molly! You haven't said a single sentimental thing about her that I haven't scoffed at—now have you?"

"N—o," acknowledged the Doctor. "I can see that you've covered your retreat all right. Even if the author of these letters should turn out to be a one-legged veteran of the War of 1812, you still could say, 'I told you so'. But all the same, I'll wager that you'd gladly give a hundred dollars, cash down, if you could only go ahead and prove the little girl's actual existence."

Stanton's shoulders squared suddenly but his mouth retained at least a faint vestige of its original smile.

"You mistake the situation entirely," he said. "It's the little girl's non-existence that I am most anxious to prove."

Then utterly without reproach or interference, he reached over and grabbed a forbidden cigar from the Doctor's cigar case, and lighted it, and retreated as far as possible into the gray film of smoke.

"Maybe she is—'colored,'" he volunteered at last

It was minutes and minutes before either man spoke again. Then at last after much crossing and re-crossing of his knees the Doctor asked drawlingly, "And when is it that you and Cornelia are planning to be married?"

"Next April," said Stanton briefly.

"U—m—m," said the Doctor. After a few more minutes he said, "U—m—m," again.

The second "U—m—m" seemed to irritate Stanton unduly. "Is it your head that's spinning round?" he asked tersely. "You sound like a Dutch top!"

The Doctor raised his hands cautiously to his forehead. "Your story does make me feel a little bit giddy," he acknowledged. Then with sudden intensity, "Stanton, you're playing a dangerous game for an engaged man. Cut it out, I say!"

"Cut what out?" said Stanton stubbornly.

The Doctor pointed exasperatedly towards the big box of letters. "Cut those out," he said. "A sentimental correspondence with a girl who's—more interesting than your fiancée!"

"W-h-e-w!" growled Stanton, "I'll hardly stand for that statement."

"Well, then lie down for it," taunted the Doctor. "Keep right on being sick and worried and—." Peremptorily he reached out both hands towards the box. "Here!" he insisted. "Let's dump the whole mischievous nonsense into the fire and burn it up!"

With an "Ouch," of pain Stanton knocked the Doctor's hands away. "Burn up my letters?" he laughed. "Well, I guess not! I wouldn't even burn up the wall papers. I've had altogether too much fun out of them. And as for the books, the Browning, etc.—why hang it all, I've gotten awfully fond of those books!" Idly he picked up the South American volume and opened the fly-leaf for the Doctor to see. "Carl from his Molly," it said quite distinctly.

"Oh, yes," mumbled the Doctor. "It looks very pleasant. There's absolutely no denying that it looks very pleasant. And some day—out of an old trunk, or tucked down behind your library encyclopedias—your wife will discover the book and ask blandly, 'Who was Molly? I don't remember your ever saying anything about a "Molly".—Just someone you used to know?' And your answer will be innocent enough: 'No, dear, *someone whom I never knew*!' But how about the pucker along your spine, and the awfully foolish, grinny feeling around your cheek-bones? And on the street and in the cars and at the theaters you'll always and forever be looking and searching, and asking yourself, 'Is it by any chance possible that this girl sitting next to me now—?' And your wife will keep saying, with just a barely perceptible edge in her voice, 'Carl, do you know that red-haired girl whom we just passed? You stared at her so!' And you'll say, 'Oh, no! I was merely wondering if—' Oh yes, you'll always and forever be 'wondering if'. And mark my words, Stanton, people who go about the world with even the most innocent chronic question in their eyes, are pretty apt to run up against an unfortunately large number of wrong answers."

"But you take it all so horribly seriously," protested Stanton. "Why you rave and rant about it as though it was actually my affections that were involved!"

"Your affections?" cried the Doctor in great exasperation. "Your affections? Why, man, if it was only your affections, do you suppose I'd be wasting even so much as half a minute's worry on you? But it's your *imagination* that's involved. That's where the blooming mischief lies. Affection is all right. Affection is nothing but a nice, safe flame that feeds only on one special kind of fuel,—its own particular object. You've got an 'affection' for Cornelia, and wherever Cornelia fails to feed that affection it is mercifully ordained that the starved flame shall go out into cold gray ashes without making any further trouble whatsoever. But you've got an 'imagination' for this make-believe girl—heaven help you!—and an 'imagination' is a great, wild, seething, insatiate tongue of fire that, thwarted once and for all in its original desire to gorge itself with realities, will turn upon you body and soul, and lick up your crackling fancy like so much kindling wood—and sear your common sense, and scorch your young wife's happiness. Nothing but Cornelia herself will ever make you want—Cornelia. But the other girl, the unknown girl—why she's the face in the clouds, she's the voice in the sea; she's the glow of the sunset; she's the hush of the June twilight! Every0 summer breeze, every winter gale, will fan the embers! Every thumping, twittering, twanging pulse of an orchestra, every—. Oh, Stanton, I say, it isn't the ghost of the things that are dead that will ever come between you and Cornelia. There never yet was the ghost of any lost thing that couldn't be tamed into a purring household pet. But—the—ghost—of—a—thing—that—you've—never—yet—found? *That*, I tell you, is a very different matter!"

Pounding at his heart, and blazing in his cheeks, the insidious argument, the subtle justification, that had been teeming in Stanton's veins all the week, burst suddenly into speech.

"But I gave Cornelia the *chance* to be 'all the world' to me," he protested doggedly, "and she didn't seem to care a hang about it! Great Scott, man! Are you going to call a fellow unfaithful because he hikes off into a corner now and then and reads a bit of Browning, for instance, all to himself—or wanders out on the piazza some night all sole alone to stare at the stars that happen to bore his wife to extinction?"

"But you'll never be able to read Browning again 'all by yourself'," taunted the Doctor. "Whether you buy it fresh from the presses or borrow it stale and old from a public library, you'll never find another copy as long as you live that doesn't smell of cinnamon roses. And as to 'star-gazing' or any other weird thing that your wife doesn't care for—you'll never go out alone any more into dawns or darknesses without the very tingling conscious presence of a wonder whether the 'other girl' *would* have cared for it!"

"Oh, shucks!" said Stanton. Then, suddenly his forehead puckered up. "Of course I've got a worry," he acknowledged frankly. "Any fellow's got a worry who finds himself engaged to be married to a girl who isn't keen enough about it to want to be all the world to him. But I don't know that even the most worried fellow has any real cause to be scared, as long as the girl in question still remains the only flesh-and-blood girl on the face of the earth whom he wishes *did* like him well enough to want to be 'all the world' to him."

"The only 'flesh-and-blood' girl?" scoffed the Doctor. "Oh, you're all right, Stanton. I like you and all that. But I'm mighty glad just the same that it isn't my daughter whom you're going to marry, with all this 'Molly Make-Believe' nonsense lurking in the background. Cut it out, Stanton, I say. Cut it out!"

"Cut it out?" mused Stanton somewhat distrait. "Cut it out? What! Molly Make-Believe?"

Under the quick jerk of his knees the big box of letters and papers and things brimmed over in rustling froth across the whole surface of the table. Just for a second the muscles in his throat tightened a trifle. Then, suddenly he burst out laughing—wildly, uproariously, like an excited boy.

"Cut it out?" he cried. "But it's such a joke! Can't you see that it's nothing in the world except a perfectly delicious, perfectly intangible joke?"

"U—m—m," reiterated the Doctor.

In the very midst of his reiteration, there came a sharp rap at the door, and in answer to Stanton's cheerful permission to enter, the so-called "delicious, intangible joke" manifested itself abruptly in the person of a rather small feminine figure very heavily muffled up in a great black cloak, and a rose-colored veil that shrouded her nose and chin bluntly like the nose and chin of a face only half hewed out as yet from a block of pink granite.

"It's only Molly," explained an undeniably sweet little alto voice. "Am I interrupting you?"

VII

Jumping to his feet, the Doctor stood staring wildly from Stanton's amazed face to the perfectly calm, perfectly accustomed air of poise that characterized every movement of the pink-shrouded visitor. The amazement in fact never wavered for a second from Stanton's blush-red visage, nor the supreme serenity from the lady's whole attitude. But across the Doctor's startled features a fearful, outraged consciousness of having been deceived, warred mightily with a consciousness of unutterable mirth.

Advancing toward the fireplace with a rather slow-footed, hesitating gait, the little visitor's attention focused suddenly on the cluttered table and she cried out with unmistakable delight. "Why, what are you people doing with all my letters and things?"

Then climbing up on the sturdy brass fender, she thrust her pink, impenetrable features right into the scared, pallid face of the shabby old clock and announced pointedly, "It's almost half-past seven. And I can stay till just eight o'clock!"

When she turned around again the Doctor was gone.

With a tiny shrug of her shoulders, she settled herself down then in a big, high-backed chair before the fire and stretched out her overshoed toes to the shining edge of the fender. As far as any apparent self-consciousness was concerned, she might just as well have been all alone in the room.

Convulsed with amusement, yet almost paralyzed by a certain stubborn, dumb sort of embarrassment, nothing on earth could have forced Stanton into making even an indefinite speech to the girl until she had made at least one perfectly definite and reasonably illuminating sort of speech to him. Biting his grinning lips into as straight a line as possible, he gathered up the scattered pages of the evening paper and attacked them furiously with scowling eyes.

After a really dreadful interim of silence, the mysterious little visitor rose in a gloomy, discouraged kind of way, and climbing up again on the narrow brass fender, peered once more into the face of the clock.

"It's twenty minutes of eight, now," she announced. Into her voice crept for the first time the faintest perceptible suggestion of a tremor. "It's twenty minutes of eight—now—and I've got to leave here exactly at eight. Twenty minutes is a rather—a rather stingy little bit out of a whole—lifetime," she added falteringly.

Then, and then only did Stanton's nervousness break forth suddenly into one wild, uproarious laugh that seemed to light up the whole dark, ominous room as though the gray, sulky, smoldering hearth-fire itself had exploded into iridescent flame. Chasing close behind the musical contagion of his deep guffaws followed the softer, gentler giggle of the dainty pink-veiled lady.

By the time they had both finished laughing it was fully quarter of eight.

"But you see it was just this way," explained the pleasant little voice—all alto notes again. Cautiously a slim, unringed hand burrowed out from the somber folds of the big cloak, and raised the pink mouth-mumbling veil as much as half an inch above the red-lipped speech line. "You see it was just this way. You paid me a lot of money—all in advance—for a six weeks' special edition de luxe Love-Letter Serial. And I spent your money the day I got it; and worse than that I owed it—long before I even got it! And worst of all, I've got a chance now to go home to-morrow for all the rest of the winter. No, I don't mean that exactly. I mean I've found a chance to go up to Vermont and have all my expenses paid—just for reading aloud every day to a lady who isn't so awfully deaf. But you see I still owe you a week's subscription—and I can't refund you the money because I haven't got it. And it happens that I can't run a fancy love-letter business from the special house that I'm going to. There aren't enough resources there—and all that. So I thought that perhaps—perhaps—considering how much you've been teasing and teasing to know who I was—I thought that perhaps if I came here this0 evening and let you really see me—that maybe, you know—maybe, not positively, but just *maybe*—you'd be willing to call that equivalent to one week's subscription. *Would you?*"

In the sharp eagerness of her question she turned her shrouded face full-view to Stanton's curious gaze, and he saw the little nervous, mischievous twitch of her lips at the edge of her masking pink veil resolve itself suddenly into a whimper of real pain. Yet so vivid were the lips, so blissfully, youthfully, lusciously carmine, that every single, individual statement she made seemed only like a festive little announcement printed in red ink.

"I guess I'm not a very—good business manager," faltered the red-lipped voice with incongruous pathos. "Indeed I know I'm not because—well because—the Serial-Letter Co. has 'gone broke! Bankrupt', is it, that you really say?"

With a little mockingly playful imitation of a stride she walked the first two fingers of her right hand across the surface of the table to Stanton's discarded supper dishes.

"Oh, please may I have that piece of cold toast?" she asked plaintively. No professional actress on the stage could have spoken the words more deliciously. Even to the actual crunching of the toast in her little shining white teeth, she sought to illustrate as fantastically as possible the ultimate misery of a bankrupt person starving for cold toast.

Stanton's spontaneous laughter attested his full appreciation of her mimicry.

"But I tell you the Serial-Letter Co. *has* 'gone broke'!" she persisted a trifle wistfully. "I guess—I guess it takes a man to really run a business with any sort of financial success, 'cause you see a man never puts anything except his head into his business. And of course if you only put your head into it, then you go right along giving always just a little wee bit less than 'value received'—and so you can't help, sir, making a profit. Why people would think you were plain, stark crazy if you gave them even one more pair of poor rubber boots than they'd paid for. But a woman! Well, you see my little business was a sort of a scheme to sell sympathy—perfectly good sympathy, you know—but to sell it to people who really needed it, instead of giving it away to people who didn't care anything about it at all. And you have to run that sort of business almost entirely with your heart—and you wouldn't feel decent at all, unless you delivered to everybody just a little tiny bit more sympathy than he paid for. Otherwise, you see you wouldn't be delivering perfectly good sympathy. So that's why—you understand now—that's why I had to send you my very own woolly blanket-wrapper, and my very own silver porringer, and my very own sling-shot that I fight city cats with,—because, you see, I had to use every single cent of your money right away to pay for the things that I'd already bought for other people."

"For other people?" quizzed Stanton a bit resentfully.

"Oh, yes," acknowledged the girl; "for several other people." Then, "Did you like the idea of the 'Rheumatic Nights Entertainment'?" she asked quite abruptly.

"Did I like it?" cried Stanton. "Did I *like* it?"

With a little shrugging air of apology the girl straightened up very stiffly in her chair.

"Of course it wasn't exactly an original idea," she explained contritely. "That is, I mean not original for you. You see, it's really a little club of mine—a little subscription club of rheumatic people who can't sleep; and I go every night in the week, an hour to each one of them. There are only three, you know. There's a youngish lady in Boston, and a very, very old gentleman out in Brookline, and the tiniest sort of a poor little sick girl in Cambridge. Sometimes I turn up just at supper-time and jolly them along a bit with their gruels. Sometimes I don't get around till ten or eleven o'clock in the great boo-black dark. From two to three in the morning seems to be the cruelest, grayest, coldest time for the little girl in Cambridge.... And I play the banjo decently well, you know, and sing more or less—and tell stories, or read aloud; and I most always go dressed up in some sort of a fancy costume 'cause I can't seem to find any other thing to do that astonishes sick people so much and makes them sit up so bravely and look so shiny. And really, it isn't such dreadfully hard work to do, because everything fits together so well. The short skirts, for instance, that turn me into such a jolly prattling great-grandchild for the poor old gentleman, make me just a perfectly rational, contemporaneous-looking play-mate for the small Cambridge girl. I'm so very, very little!"

"Only, of course," she finished wryly; "only, of course, it costs such a horrid big lot for costumes and carriages and things. That's what's 'busted' me, as the boys say. And then, of course, I'm most dreadfully sleepy all the day times when I ought to be writing nice things for my Serial-Letter Co. business. And then one day last week—" the vivid red lips twisted oddly at one corner. "One night last week they sent me word from Cambridge that the little, little girl was going to die—and was calling and calling for the 'Gray-Plush Squirrel Lady'. So I hired a big gray squirrel coat from a furrier whom I know, and I ripped up my muff and made me the very best sort of a hot, gray, smothery face that I could—and I went out to Cambridge and sat three hours on the footboard of a bed, cracking jokes—and nuts—to beguile a little child's death-pain. And somehow it broke my heart—or my spirit—or something. Somehow I think I could have stood it better with my own skin face! Anyway the little girl doesn't need me any more. Anyway, it doesn't matter if someone did need me!... I tell you I'm 'broke'! I tell you I haven't got one single solitary more thing to give! It isn't just my pocket-book that's empty: it's my head that's spent, too! It's my heart that's altogether stripped! *And I'm going to run away! Yes, I am!*"

Jumping to her feet she stood there for an instant all out of breath, as though just the mere fancy thought of running away had almost exhausted her. Then suddenly she began to laugh.

"I'm so tired of making up things," she confessed; "why, I'm so tired of making up grandfathers, I'm so tired of making up pirates, I'm so tired of making-up lovers—that I actually cherish the bill collector as the only real, genuine acquaintance whom I have in Boston. Certainly there's no slightest trace of pretence about him!... Excuse me for being so flippant," she added soberly, "but you see I haven't got any sympathy left even for myself."

"But for heaven's sake!" cried Stanton, "why don't you let somebody help you? Why don't you let me—"

"Oh, you *can* help me!" cried the little red-lipped voice excitedly. "Oh, yes, indeed you can help me! That's why I came here this evening. You see I've settled up now with every one of my creditors except you and the youngish Boston lady, and I'm on my way to her house now. We're reading Oriental Fairy stories together. Truly I think she'll be very glad indeed to release me from my contract when I offer her my coral beads instead, because they are dreadfully nice beads, my real, unpretended grandfather carved them for me himself.... But how can I settle with you? I haven't got anything left to settle with, and it might be months and months before I could refund the actual cash money. So wouldn't you—couldn't you please call my coming here this evening an equivalent to one week's subscription?"

"Oh! Don't I look—gorgeous!" she stammered

Wriggling out of the cloak and veil that wrapped her like a chrysalis she emerged suddenly a glimmering, shimmering little oriental figure of satin and silver and haunting sandalwood—a veritable little incandescent rainbow of spangled moonlight and flaming scarlet and dark purple shadows. Great, heavy, jet-black curls caught back from her small piquant face by a blazing rhinestone fillet,—cheeks just a tiny bit over-tinted with rouge and excitement,—big, red-brown eyes packed full of high lights like a startled fawn's,—bold in the utter security of her masquerade, yet scared almost to death by the persistent underlying heart-thump of her unescapable self-consciousness,—altogether as tantalizing, altogether as unreal, as a vision out of the Arabian Nights, she stood there staring quizzically at Stanton.

"*Would* you call it—an—equivalent? *Would* you?" she asked nervously.

Then pirouetting over to the largest mirror in sight she began to smooth and twist her silken sash into place. Somewhere at wrist or ankle twittered the jingle of innumerable bangles.

"Oh! Don't I look—gorgeous!" she stammered. "O—h—h!"

VIII

Everything that was discreet and engaged-to-be-married in Stanton's conservative make-up exploded suddenly into one utterly irresponsible speech.

"You little witch!" he cried out. "You little beauty! For heaven's sake come over here and sit down in this chair where I can look at you! I want to talk to you! I—"

Pirouetting once more before the mirror, she divided one fleet glance between admiration for herself and scorn for Stanton.

"Oh, yes, I felt perfectly sure that you'd insist upon having me 'pretty'!" she announced sternly. Then courtesying low to the ground in mock humility, she began to sing-song mischievously:

"So Molly, Molly made-her-a-face,Made it of rouge and made it of lace.Long as the rouge and the lace are fair,Oh, Mr. Man, what do you care?"

"You don't need any rouge or lace to make *you* pretty!" Stanton fairly shouted in his vehemence. "Anybody might have known that that lovely, little mind of yours could only live in a—"

"Nonsense!" the girl interrupted, almost temperishly. Then with a quick, impatient sort of gesture she turned to the table, and picking up book after book, opened it and stared in it as though it had been a mirror. "Oh, maybe my mind is pretty enough," she acknowledged reluctantly. "But likelier than not, my face is not becoming—to me."

Crossing slowly over to Stanton's side she seated herself, with much jingling, rainbow-colored, sandalwood-scented dignity, in the chair that the Doctor had just vacated.

"Poor dear, you've been pretty sick, haven't you?" she mused gently. Cautiously then she reached out and touched the soft, woolly cuff of his blanket-wrapper. "Did you really like it?" she asked.

Stanton began to smile again. "Did I really like it?" he repeated joyously. "Why, don't you know that if it hadn't been for you I should have gone utterly mad these past few weeks? Don't you know that if it hadn't been for you—don't you know that if—" A little over-zealously he clutched at the tinsel fringe on the oriental lady's fan. "Don't you know—don't you know that I'm—engaged to be married?" he finished weakly.

The oriental lady shivered suddenly, as any lady might shiver on a November night in thin silken clothes. "Engaged to be married?" she stammered. "Oh, yes! Why—of course! Most men are! Really unless you catch a man very young and keep him absolutely constantly by your side you cannot hope to walk even into his friendship—except across the heart of some other woman." Again she shivered and jingled a hundred merry little bangles. "But why?" she asked abruptly, "why, if you're engaged to be married, did you come and—buy love-letters of me? My love-letters are distinctly for lonely people," she added severely.

"How dared you—How dared you go into the love-letter business in the first place?" quizzed Stanton dryly. "And when it comes to asking personal questions, how dared you send me printed slips in answer to my letters to you? Printed slips, mind you!... How many men are you writing love-letters to, anyway?"

The oriental lady threw out her small hands deprecatingly. "How many men? Only two besides yourself. There's such a fad for nature study these days that almost everybody this year has ordered the 'Gray-Plush Squirrel' series. But I'm doing one or two 'Japanese Fairies' for sick children, and a high school history class out in Omaha has ordered a weekly epistle from William of Orange."

"Hang the High School class out in Omaha!" said Stanton. "It was the love-letters that I was asking about."

"Oh, yes, I forgot," murmured the oriental lady. "Just two men besides yourself, I said, didn't I? Well one of them is a life convict out in an Illinois prison. He's subscribed for a whole year—for a fortnightly letter from a girl in Killarney who has got to be named 'Katie'. He's a very, very old man, I think, but I don't even know his name 'cause he's only a number now—'4632'—or something like that. And I have to send all my letters over to Killarney to be mailed—Oh, he's awfully particular about that. And it was pretty hard at first working up all the geography that he knew and I didn't. But—pshaw! You're not interested in Killarney. Then there's a New York boy down in Ceylon on a smelly old tea plantation. His people have dropped him, I guess, for some reason or other; so I'm just 'the girl from home' to him, and I prattle to him every month or so about the things he used to care about. It's easy enough to work that up from the social columns in the New York papers—and twice I've been over to New York to get special details for him; once to find out if his mother was really as sick as the Sunday paper said, and once—yes, really, once I butted in to a tea his sister was giving, and wrote him, yes, wrote him all about how the moths were eating up the big moose-head in his own front hall. And he sent an awfully funny, nice letter of thanks to the Serial-Letter Co.—yes, he did! And then there's a crippled French girl out in the Berkshires who is utterly crazy, it seems, about the 'Three Musketeers', so I'm d'Artagnan to her, and it's dreadfully hard work—in French—but I'm learning a lot out of that, and—"

"There. Don't tell me any more!" cried Stanton.

Then suddenly the pulses in his temples began to pound so hard and so loud that he could not seem to estimate at all just how loud he was speaking.

"Who are you?" he insisted. "Who are you? Tell me instantly, I say! *Who are you anyway?*"

The oriental lady jumped up in alarm. "I'm no one at all—to you," she said coolly, "except just—Molly Make-Believe."0

Something in her tone seemed to fairly madden Stanton.

"You shall tell me who you are!" he cried. "You shall! I say you shall!"

Plunging forward he grabbed at her little bangled wrists and held them in a vise that sent the rheumatic pains shooting up his arms to add even further frenzy to his brain.

"Tell me who you are!" he grinned. "You shan't go out of here in ten thousand years till you've told me who you are!"

Frightened, infuriated, quivering with astonishment, the girl stood trying to wrench her little wrists out of his mighty grasp, stamping in perfectly impotent rage all the while with her soft-sandalled, jingling feet.

"I won't tell you who I am! I won't! I won't!" she swore and reswore in a dozen different staccato accents. The whole daring passion of the Orient that costumed her seemed to have permeated every fiber of her small being.

Then suddenly she drew in her breath in a long quivering sigh. Staring up into her face, Stanton gave a little groan of dismay, and released her hands.

"Why, Molly! Molly! You're—crying," he whispered. "Why, little girl! Why—"

Backing slowly away from him, she made a desperate effort to smile through her tears.

"Now you've spoiled everything," she said.

"Oh no, not—everything," argued Stanton helplessly from his chair, afraid to rise to his feet, afraid even to shuffle his slippers on the floor lest the slightest suspicion of vehemence on his part should hasten that steady, backward retreat of hers towards the door.

Already she had re-acquired her cloak and overshoes and was groping out somewhat blindly for her veil in a frantic effort to avoid any possible chance of turning her back even for a second on so dangerous a person as himself.

"Yes, everything," nodded the small grieved face. Yet the tragic, snuffling little sob that accompanied the words only served to add a most entrancing, tip-nosed vivacity to the statement.

"Oh, of course I know," she added hastily. "Oh, of course I know perfectly well that I oughtn't to have come alone to your rooms like this!" Madly she began to wind the pink veil round and round and round her cheeks like a bandage. "Oh, of course I know perfectly well that it wasn't even remotely proper! But don't you think—don't you think that if you've always been awfully, awfully strict and particular with yourself about things all your life, that you might have risked—safely—just one little innocent, mischievous sort of a half hour? Especially if it was the only possible way you could think of to square up everything and add just a little wee present besides? 'Cause nothing, you know, that you can *afford* to give ever seems exactly like giving a really, truly present. It's got to hurt you somewhere to be a 'present'. So my coming here this evening—this way—was altogether the bravest, scariest, unwisest, most-like-a-present-feeling-thing that I could possibly think of to do—for you. And even if you hadn't spoiled everything, I was going away to-morrow just the same forever and ever and ever!"

Cautiously she perched herself on the edge of a chair, and thrust her narrow, gold-embroidered toes into the wide, blunt depths of her overshoes. "Forever and ever!" she insisted almost gloatingly.

"Not forever and *ever*!" protested Stanton vigorously. "You don't think for a moment, do you, that after all this wonderful, jolly friendship of ours, you're going to drop right out of sight as though the earth had opened?"

Even the little quick, forward lurch of his shoulders in the chair sent the girl scuttling to her feet again, one overshoe still in her hand.

Just at the edge of the door-mat she turned and smiled at him mockingly. Really it had been a long time since she had smiled.

"Surely you don't think that you'd be able to recognize me in my street clothes, do you?" she asked bluntly.

Stanton's answering smile was quite as mocking as hers.

"Why not?" he queried. "Didn't I have the pleasure of choosing your winter hat for you? Let me see,—it was brown, with a pink rose—wasn't it? I should know it among a million."

With a little shrug of her shoulders she leaned back against the door and stared at him suddenly out of her big red-brown eyes with singular intentness.

"Well, *will* you call it an equivalent to one week's subscription?" she asked very gravely.

Some long-sleeping devil of mischief awoke in Stanton's senses.

"Equivalent to one whole week's subscription?" he repeated with mock incredulity. "A whole week—seven days and nights? Oh, no! No! No! I don't think you've given me, yet, more than about—four days' worth to think about. Just about four days' worth, I should think."

Pushing the pink veil further and further back from her features, with plainly quivering hands, the girl's whole soul seemed to blaze out at him suddenly, and then wince back again. Then just as quickly a droll little gleam of malice glinted in her eyes.

"Oh, all right then," she smiled. "If you really think I've given you only four days' and nights' worth of thoughts—here's something for the fifth day and night."

Very casually, yet still very accurately, her right hand reached out to the knob of the door.

"To cancel my debt for the fifth day," she said, "do you really 'honest-injun' want to know who I am? I'll tell you! First, you've seen me before."

"What?" cried Stanton, plunging forward in his chair.

Something in the girl's quick clutch of the door-knob warned him quite distinctly to relax again into his cushions.

"Yes," she repeated triumphantly. "And you've talked with me too, as often as twice! And moreover you've danced with me!"

Tossing her head with sudden-born daring she reached up and snatched off her curly black wig, and shook down all around her such a great, shining, utterly glorious mass of mahogany colored hair that Stanton's astonishment turned almost into faintness.

"What?" he cried out. "What? You say I've seen you before? Talked with you? Waltzed with you, perhaps? Never! I haven't! I tell you I haven't! I never saw that hair before! If I had, I shouldn't have forgotten it to my dying day. Why—"

With a little wail of despair she leaned back against the door. "You don't even remember me *now*?" she mourned. "Oh dear, dear, dear! And I thought *you* were so beautiful!" Then, woman-like, her whole sympathy rushed to defend him from her own accusations. "Oh, well, it was at a masquerade party," she acknowledged generously, "and I suppose you go to a great many masquerades."

Heaping up her hair like so much molten copper into the hood of her cloak, and trying desperately to snare all the wild, escaping tendrils with the softer mesh of her veil, she reached out a free hand at last and opened the door just a crack.

"What?" cried Stanton, plunging forward in his chair

"And to give you something to think about for the sixth day and night," she resumed suddenly, with the same strange little glint in her eyes, "to give you something to think about the sixth day, I'll tell you that I really was hungry—when I asked you for your toast. I haven't had anything to eat to-day; and—"

Before she could finish the sentence Stanton had sprung from his chair, and stood trying to reason out madly whether one single more stride would catch her, or lose her.

"And as for something for you to think about the seventh day and night," she gasped hurriedly. Already the door had opened to her hand and her little figure stood silhouetted darkly against the bright, yellow-lighted hallway, "here's something for you to think about for *twenty*-seven days and nights!" Wildly her little hands went clutching at the woodwork. "I didn't know you were engaged to be married," she cried out passionately, "and I *loved* you—*loved* you—*loved* you!"

Then in a flash she was gone.

IX

With absolute finality the big door banged behind her. A minute later the street door, four flights down, rang out in jarring reverberation. A minute after that it seemed as though every door in every house on the street slammed shrilly. Then the charred fire-log sagged down into the ashes with a sad, puffing sigh. Then a whole row of books on a loosely packed shelf toppled over on each other with soft jocose slaps.

Crawling back into his Morris chair with every bone in his body aching like a magnetized wire-skeleton charged with pain, Stanton collapsed again into his pillows and sat staring—staring into the dying fire. Nine o'clock rang out dully from the nearest church spire; ten o'clock, eleven o'clock followed in turn with monotonous, chiming insistency. Gradually the relaxing steam-radiators began to grunt and grumble into a chill quietude. Gradually along the bare, bleak stretches of unrugged floor little cold draughts of air came creeping exploringly to his feet.

And still he sat staring—staring into the fast graying ashes.

"Oh, Glory! Glory!" he said. "Think what it would mean if all that wonderful imagination were turned loose upon just one fellow! Even if she didn't love you, think how she'd play the game! And if she did love you—Oh, lordy; Lordy! LORDY!"

Towards midnight, to ease the melancholy smell of the dying lamp, he drew reluctantly forth from his deepest blanket-wrapper pocket the little knotted handkerchief that encased the still-treasured handful of fragrant fir-balsam, and bending groaningly forward in his chair sifted the brittle, pungent needles into the face of the one glowing ember that survived. Instantly in a single dazzling flash of flame the tangible forest symbol vanished in intangible fragrance. But along the hollow of his hand,—across the edge of his sleeve,—up from the ragged pile of books and papers,—out from the farthest, remotest corners of the room, lurked the unutterable, undestroyable sweetness of all forests since the world was made.

Almost with a sob in his throat Stanton turned again to the box of letters on his table.

By dawn the feverish, excited sleeplessness in his brain had driven him on and on to one last, supremely fantastic impulse. Writing to Cornelia he told her bluntly, frankly,

"Dear Cornelia:

"When I asked you to marry me, you made me promise very solemnly at the time that if I ever changed my mind regarding you I would surely tell you. And I laughed at you. Do you remember? But you were right, it seems, and I was wrong. For I believe that I have changed my mind. That is:—I don't know how to express it exactly, but it has been made very, very plain to me lately that I do not by any manner of means love you as little as you need to be loved.

"In all sincerity,

"Carl."

To which surprising communication Cornelia answered immediately; but the 'immediately' involved a week's almost maddening interim,

"Dear Carl:

"Neither mother nor I can make any sense whatsoever out of your note. By any possible chance was it meant to be a joke? You say you do not love me 'as little' as I need to be loved. You mean 'as much', don't you? Carl, what do you mean?"

Laboriously, with the full prospect of yet another week's agonizing strain and suspense, Stanton wrote again to Cornelia.

"Dear Cornelia:

"No, I meant 'as little' as you need to be loved. I have no adequate explanation to make. I have no adequate apology to offer. I don't think anything. I don't hope anything. All I know is that I suddenly believe positively that our engagement is a mistake. Certainly I am neither giving you all that I am capable of giving you, nor yet receiving from you all that I am capable of receiving. Just this fact should decide the matter I think.

"Carl."

Cornelia did not wait to write an answer to this. She telegraphed instead. The message even in the telegraph operator's handwriting looked a little nervous.

"Do you mean that you are tired of it?" she asked quite boldly.

With miserable perplexity Stanton wired back. "No, I couldn't exactly say that I was tired of it."

Cornelia's answer to that was fluttering in his hands within twelve hours.

"Do you mean that there is someone else?" The words fairly ticked themselves off the yellow page.

It was twenty-four hours before Stanton made up his mind just what to reply. Then, "No, I couldn't exactly say there is anybody else," he confessed wretchedly.

Cornelia's mother answered this time. The telegram fairly rustled with sarcasm. "You don't seem to be very sure about anything," said Cornelia's mother.

Cornelia's mother answered this time

Somehow these words brought the first cheerful smile to his lips.

"No, you're quite right. I'm not at all sure about anything," he wired almost gleefully in return, wiping his pen with delicious joy on the edge of the clean white bed-spread.

Then because it is really very dangerous for over-wrought people to try to make any noise like laughter, a great choking, bitter sob caught him up suddenly, and sent his face burrowing down like a night-scared child into the safe, soft, feathery depths of his pillow—where, with his knuckles ground so hard into his eyes that all his tears were turned to stars, there came to him very, very slowly, so slowly in fact that it did not alarm him at all, the strange, electrifying vision of the one fact on earth that he *was* sure of: a little keen, luminous, brown-eyed face with a look in it, and a look for him only—so help him God!—such as he had never seen on the face of any other woman since the world was made. Was it possible?—was it really possible? Suddenly his whole heart seemed to irradiate light and color and music and sweet smelling things.

"Oh, Molly, Molly, Molly!" he shouted. "I want *you*! I want *you*!"

In the strange, lonesome days that followed, neither burly flesh-and-blood Doctor nor slim paper sweetheart tramped noisily over the threshold or slid thuddingly through the letter-slide.

No one apparently was ever coming to see Stanton again unless actually compelled to do so. Even the laundryman seemed to have skipped his usual day; and twice in succession the morning paper had most annoyingly failed to appear. Certainly neither the boldest private inquiry nor the most delicately worded public advertisement had proved able to discover the whereabouts of "Molly Make-Believe," much less succeeded in bringing her back. But the Doctor, at least, could be summoned by ordinary telephone, andCornelia and her mother would surely be moving North eventually, whether Stanton's last message hastened their movements or not.

In subsequent experience it seemed to take two telephone messages to produce the Doctor. A trifle coolly, a trifle distantly, more than a trifle disapprovingly, he appeared at last and stared dully at Stanton's astonishing booted-and-coated progress towards health.

"Always glad to serve you—professionally," murmured the Doctor with an undeniably definite accent on the word 'professionally'.

"Oh, cut it out!" quoted Stanton emphatically. "What in creation are you so stuffy about?"

"Well, really," growled the Doctor, "considering the deception you practised on me—"

"Considering nothing!" shouted Stanton. "On my word of honor, I tell you I never consciously, in all my life before, ever—ever—set eyes upon that wonderful little girl, until that evening! I never knew that she even existed! I never knew! I tell you I never knew—*anything*!"

As limply as any stout man could sink into a chair, the Doctor sank into the seat nearest him.

"Tell me instantly all about it," he gasped.

"There are only two things to tell," said Stanton quite blithely. "And the first thing is what I've already stated, on my honor, that the evening we speak of was actually and positively the first time I ever saw the girl; and the second thing is, that equally upon my honor, I do not intend to let it remain—the last time!"

"But Cornelia?" cried the Doctor. "What about Cornelia?"

Almost half the sparkle faded from Stanton's eyes.

"Cornelia and I have annulled our engagement," he said very quietly. Then with more vehemence, "Oh, you old dry-bones, don't you worry about Cornelia! I'll look out for Cornelia. Cornelia isn't going to get hurt. I tell you I've figured and reasoned it all out very, very carefully; and I can see now, quite plainly, that Cornelia never really loved me at all—else she wouldn't have dropped me so accidentally through her fingers. Why, there never was even the ghost of a clutch in Cornelia's fingers."

"But you loved *her*," persisted the Doctor scowlingly.

It was hard, just that second, for Stanton to lift his troubled eyes to the Doctor's face. But he did lift them and he lifted them very squarely and steadily.

"Yes, I think I did—love Cornelia," he acknowledged frankly. "The very first time that I saw her I said to myself, 'Here is the end of my journey,' but I seem to have found out suddenly that the mere fact of loving a woman does not necessarily prove her that much coveted 'journey's end.' I don't know exactly how to express it, indeed I feel beastly clumsy about expressing it, but somehow it seems as though it were Cornelia herself who had proved herself, perfectly amiably, no 'journey's end' after all, but only a way station not equipped to receive my particular kind of a permanent guest. It isn't that I wanted any grand fixings. Oh, can't you understand that I'm not finding any fault with Cornelia. There never was any slightest pretence about Cornelia. She never, never even in the first place, made any possible effort to attract me. Can't you see that Cornelia *looks* to me to-day exactly the way that she looked to me in the first place; very, amazingly, beautiful. But a traveler, you know, cannot dally indefinitely to feed his eyes on even the most wonderful view while all his precious lifelong companions,—his whims, his hobbies, his cravings, his yearnings,—are crouching starved and unwelcome outside the door.

"And I can't even flatter myself," he added wryly; "I can't even flatter myself that my—going is going to inconvenience Cornelia in the slightest; because I can't see that my coming has made even the remotest perceptible difference in her daily routine. Anyway—" he finished more lightly, "when you come right down to 'mating', or 'homing', or 'belonging', or whatever you choose to call it, it seems to be written in the stars that plans or no plans, preferences or no preferences, initiatives or no initiatives, we belong to those—and to those only, hang it all!—who happen to love *us* most!"

Fairly jumping from his chair the Doctor snatched hold of Stanton's shoulder.

"Who happen to love *us* most?" he repeated wildly. "Love *us*? *us*? For heaven's sake, who's loving you *now*?"

Utterly irrelevantly, Stanton brushed him aside, and began to rummage anxiously among the books on his table.

"Do you know much about Vermont?" he asked suddenly. "It's funny, but almost nobody seems to know anything about Vermont. It's a darned good state, too, and I can't imagine why all the geographies neglect it so." Idly his finger seemed to catch in a half open pamphlet, and he bent down casually to straighten out the page. "Area in square miles—9,565," he read aloud musingly. "Principal products—hay, oats, maple-sugar—" Suddenly he threw down the pamphlet and flung himself into the nearest chair and began to laugh. "Maple-sugar?" he ejaculated. "Maple-sugar? Oh, glory! And I suppose there are some people who think that maple-sugar is the sweetest thing that ever came out of Vermont!"

The Doctor started to give him some fresh advice—but left him a bromide instead.

X

Though the ensuing interview with Cornelia and her mother began quite as coolly as the interview with the Doctor, it did not happen to end even in hysterical laughter.

It was just two days after the Doctor's hurried exit that Stanton received a formal, starchy little note from Cornelia's mother notifying him of their return.

Except for an experimental, somewhat wobbly-kneed journey or two to the edge of the Public Garden he had made no attempts as yet to resume any outdoor life, yet for sundry personal reasons of his own he did not feel over-anxious to postpone the necessary meeting. In the immediate emergency at hand strong courage was infinitely more of an asset than0 strong knees. Filling his suitcase at once with all the explanatory evidence that he could carry, he proceeded on cab-wheels to Cornelia's grimly dignified residence. The street lamps were just beginning to be lighted when he arrived.

As the butler ushered him gravely into the beautiful drawing room he realized with a horrid sinking of the heart that Cornelia and her mother were already sitting there waiting for him with a dreadful tight lipped expression on their faces which seemed to suggest that though he was already fifteen minutes ahead of his appointment they had been waiting for him there since early dawn.

The drawing room itself was deliciously familiar to him; crimson-curtained, green carpeted, shining with heavy gilt picture frames and prismatic chandeliers. Often with posies and candies and theater-tickets he had strutted across that erstwhile magic threshold and fairly lolled in the big deep-upholstered chairs while waiting for the silk-rustling advent of the ladies. But now, with his suitcase clutched in his hand, no Armenian peddler of laces and ointments could have felt more grotesquely out of his element.

Indolently Cornelia's mother lifted her lorgnette and gazed at him skeptically from the spot just behind his left ear where the barber had clipped him too short, to the edge of his right heel that the bootblack had neglected to polish. Apparently she did not even see the suitcase but,

"Oh, are you leaving town?" she asked icily.

Only by the utmost tact on his part did he finally succeed in establishing tête-à-tête relations with Cornelia herself; and even then if the house had been a tower ten stories high, Cornelia's mother, rustling up the stairs, could not have swished her skirts any more definitely like a hissing snake.

In absolute dumbness Stanton and Cornelia sat listening until the horrid sound died away. Then, and then only, did Cornelia cross the room to Stanton's side and proffer him her hand. The hand was very cold, and the manner of offering it was very cold, but Stanton was quite man enough to realize that this special temperature was purely a matter of physical nervousness rather than of mental intention.

Slipping naturally into the most conventional groove either of word or deed, Cornelia eyed the suitcase inquisitively.

"What are you doing?" she asked thoughtlessly. "Returning my presents?"

"You never gave me any presents!" said Stanton cheerfully.

"Why, didn't I?" murmured Cornelia slowly. Around her strained mouth a smile began to flicker faintly. "Is that why you broke it off?" she asked flippantly.

"Yes, partly," laughed Stanton.

Then Cornelia laughed a little bit, too.

After this Stanton lost no possible time in getting down to facts.

Stooping over from his chair exactly after the manner of peddlers whom he had seen in other people's houses, he unbuckled the straps of his suitcase, and turned the cover backward on the floor.

Cornelia followed every movement of his hand with vaguely perplexed blue eyes.

"Surely," said Stanton, "this is the weirdest combination of circumstances that ever happened to a man and a girl—or rather, I should say, to a man and two girls." Quite accustomed as he now was to the general effect on himself of the whole unique adventure with the Serial-Letter Co. his heart could not help giving a little extra jump on this, the verge of the astonishing revelation that he was about to make to Cornelia. "Here," he stammered, a tiny bit out of breath, "here is the small, thin, tissue-paper circular that you sent me from the Serial-Letter Co. with your advice to subscribe, and there—" pointing earnestly to the teeming suitcase,—"there are the minor results of—having taken your advice."

In Cornelia's face the well-groomed expression showed sudden signs of immediate disorganization.

Snatching the circular out of his hand she read it hurriedly, once, twice, three times. Then kneeling cautiously down on the floor with all the dignity that characterized every movement of her body, she began to poke here and there into the contents of the suitcase.

He unbuckled the straps of his suitcase and turned the cover backward on the floor

"The 'minor results'?" she asked soberly.

"Why yes," said Stanton. "There were several things I didn't have room to bring. There was a blanket-wrapper. And there was a—girl, and there was a—"

Cornelia's blonde eyebrows lifted perceptibly. "A girl—whom you didn't know at all—sent you a blanket-wrapper?" she whispered.

"Yes!" smiled Stanton. "You see no girl whom I knew—very well—seemed to care a hang whether I froze to death or not."

"O—h," said Cornelia very, very slowly, "O—h." Her eyes had a strange, new puzzled expression in them like the expression of a person who was trying to look outward and think inward at the same time.

"But you mustn't be so critical and haughty about it all," protested Stanton, "when I'm really trying so hard to explain everything perfectly honestly to you—so that you'll understand exactly how it happened."

"I should like very much to be able to understand exactly how it happened," mused Cornelia.

Gingerly she approached in succession the roll of sample wall-paper, the maps, the time-tables, the books, the little silver porringer, the intimate-looking scrap of unfinished fancy-work. One by one Stanton explained them to her, visualizing by eager phrase or whimsical gesture the particularly lonesome and susceptible conditions under which each gift had happened to arrive.

At the great pile of letters Cornelia's hand faltered a trifle.

"How many did I write you?" she asked with real curiosity.

"Five thin ones, and a postal-card," said Stanton almost apologetically.

Choosing the fattest looking letter that she could find, Cornelia toyed with the envelope for a second. "Would it be all right for me to read one?" she asked doubtfully.

"Why, yes," said Stanton. "I think you might read one."

After a few minutes she laid down the letter without any comment.

"Would it be all right for me to read another?" she questioned.

"Why, yes," cried Stanton. "Let's read them all. Let's read them together. Only, of course, we must read them in order."

Almost tenderly he picked them up and sorted them out according to their dates. "Of course," he explained very earnestly, "of course I wouldn't think of showing these letters to any one ordinarily; but0 after all, these particular letters represent only a mere business proposition, and certainly this particular situation must justify one in making extraordinary exceptions."

One by one he perused the letters hastily and handed them over to Cornelia for her more careful inspection. No single associate detail of time or circumstance seemed to have eluded his astonishing memory. Letter by letter, page by page he annotated: "That was the week you didn't write at all," or "This was the stormy, agonizing, God-forsaken night when I didn't care whether I lived or died," or "It was just about that time, you know, that you snubbed me for being scared about your swimming stunt."

Breathless in the midst of her reading Cornelia looked up and faced him squarely. "How could any girl—write all that nonsense?" she gasped.

It wasn't so much what Stanton answered, as the expression in his eyes that really startled Cornelia.

"Nonsense?" he quoted deliberatingly. "But I like it," he said. "It's exactly what I like."

"But I couldn't possibly have given you anything like—that," stammered Cornelia.

"No, I know you couldn't," said Stanton very gently.

For an instant Cornelia turned and stared a bit resentfully into his face. Then suddenly the very gentleness of his smile ignited a little answering smile on her lips.

"Oh, you mean," she asked with unmistakable relief; "oh, you mean that really after all it wasn't your letter that jilted me, but my temperament that jilted you?"

"Exactly," said Stanton.

Cornelia's whole somber face flamed suddenly into unmistakable radiance.

"Oh, that puts an entirely different light upon the matter," she exclaimed. "Oh, now it doesn't hurt at all!"

Rustling to her feet, she began to smooth the scowly-looking wrinkles out of her skirt with long even strokes of her bright-jeweled hands.

"I think I'm really beginning to understand," she said pleasantly. "And truly, absurd as it sounds to say it, I honestly believe that I care more for you this moment than I ever cared before, but—" glancing with acute dismay at the cluttered suitcase on the floor, "but I wouldn't marry you now, if we could live in the finest asylum in the land!"

Shrugging his shoulders with mirthful appreciation Stanton proceeded then and there to re-pack his treasures and end the interview.

Just at the edge of the threshold Cornelia's voice called him back.

"Carl," she protested, "you are looking rather sick. I hope you are going straight home."

"No, I'm not going straight home," said Stanton bluntly. "But here's hoping that the 'longest way round' will prove even yet the very shortest possible route to the particular home that, as yet, doesn't even exist. I'm going hunting, Cornelia, hunting for Molly Make-Believe; and what's more, I'm going to find her if it takes me all the rest of my natural life!"

XI

Driving downtown again with every thought in his head, every plan, every purpose, hurtling around and around in absolute chaos, his roving eyes lit casually upon the huge sign of a detective bureau that loomed across the street. White as a sheet with the sudden new determination that came to him, and trembling miserably with the very strength of the determination warring against the weakness and fatigue of his body, he dismissed his cab and went climbing up the first narrow, dingy stairway that seemed most liable to connect with the brain behind the sign-board.

It was almost bed-time before he came down the stairs again, yet, "I think her name is Meredith, and I think she's gone to Vermont, and she has the most wonderful head of mahogany-colored hair that I ever saw in my life," were the only definite clues that he had been able to contribute to the cause.

In the slow, lagging week that followed, Stanton did not find himself at all pleased with the particular steps which he had apparently been obliged to take in order to ferret out Molly's real name and her real city address, but the actual audacity of the situation did not actually reach its climax until the gentle little quarry had been literally tracked to Vermont with detectives fairly baying on her trail like the melodramatic bloodhounds that pursue "Eliza" across the ice.

"Red-headed party found at Woodstock," the valiant sleuth had wired with unusual delicacy and caution.

"Denies acquaintance, Boston, everything, positively refuses interview, temper very bad, sure it's the party," the second message had come.

The very next northward-bound train found Stanton fretting the interminable hours away between Boston and Woodstock. Across the sparkling snow-smothered landscape his straining eyes went plowing on to their unknown destination. Sometimes the engine pounded louder than his heart. Sometimes he could not even seem to hear the grinding of the brakes above the dreadful throb-throb of his temples. Sometimes in horrid, shuddering chills he huddled into his great fur-coat and cursed the porter for having a disposition like a polar bear. Sometimes almost gasping for breath he went out and stood on the bleak rear platform of the last car and watched the pleasant, ice-cold rails go speeding back to Boston. All along the journey little absolutely unnecessary villages kept bobbing up to impede the progress of the train. All along the journey innumerable little empty railroad-stations, barren as bells robbed of their own tongues, seemed to lie waiting—waiting for the noisy engine-tongue to clang them into temporary noise and life.

Was his quest really almost at an end? Was it—was it? A thousand vague apprehensions tortured through his mind.

And then, all of a sudden, in the early, brisk winter twilight, Woodstock—happened!

Climbing out of the train Stanton stood for a second rubbing his eyes at the final abruptness and unreality of it all. Woodstock! What was it going to mean to him? Woodstock!

Everybody else on the platform seemed to be accepting the astonishing geographical fact with perfect simplicity. Already along the edge of the platform the quaint, old-fashioned yellow stage-coaches set on runners were fast filling up with utterly serene passengers.

A jog at his elbow made him turn quickly, and he found himself gazing into the detective's not ungenial face.

"Say," said the detective, "were you going up to the hotel first? Well you'd better not. You'd better not lose any time. She's leaving town in the morning." It was beyond human nature for the detective man not to nudge Stanton once in the ribs. "Say," he grinned, "you sure had better go easy, and not send in your name or anything." His grin broadened suddenly in a laugh. "Say," he confided, "once in a magazine I read something about a lady's 'piquant animosity'. That's her! And *cute*? Oh, my!"

Five minutes later, Stanton found himself lolling back in the quaintest, brightest, most pumpkin-colored coach of all, gliding with almost magical smoothness through the snow-glazed streets of the little narrow, valley-town.

"The Meredith homestead?" the driver had queried. "Oh, yes. All right; but it's quite a journey. Don't get discouraged."

A sense of discouragement regarding long distances was just at that moment the most remote sensation in Stanton's sensibilities. If the railroad journey had seemed unhappily drawn out, the sleigh-ride reversed the emotion to the point of almost telescopic calamity: a stingy, transient vista of village lights; a brief, narrow, hill-bordered road that looked for all the world like the aisle of a toy-shop, flanked on either side by high-reaching shelves where miniature house-lights twinkled cunningly; a sudden stumble of hoofs into a less-traveled snow-path, and then, absolutely unavoidable, absolutely0 unescapable, an old, white colonial house with its great solemn elm trees stretching out their long arms protectingly all around and about it after the blessed habit of a hundred years.

Nervously, and yet almost reverently, Stanton went crunching up the snowy path to the door, knocked resonantly with a slim, much worn old brass knocker, and was admitted promptly and hospitably by "Mrs. Meredith" herself—Molly's grandmother evidently, and such a darling little grandmother, small, like Molly; quick, like Molly; even young, like Molly, she appeared to be. Simple, sincere, and oh, so comfortable—like the fine old mahogany furniture and the dull-shining pewter, and the flickering firelight, that seemed to be everywhere.

"Good old stuff!" was Stanton's immediate silent comment on everything in sight.

It was perfectly evident that the little old lady knew nothing whatsoever about Stanton, but it was equally evident that she suspected him of being neither a highwayman nor a book agent, and was really sincerely sorry that Molly had "a headache" and would be unable to see him.

"But I've come so far," persisted Stanton. "All the way from Boston. Is she very ill? Has she been ill long?"

The little old lady's mind ignored the questions but clung a trifle nervously to the word Boston.

"Boston?" her sweet voice quavered. "Boston? Why you look so nice—surely you're not that mysterious man who has been annoying Mollie so dreadfully these past few days. I told her no good would ever come of her going to the city."

"Annoying Molly?" cried Stanton. "Annoying *my* Molly? I? Why, it's to prevent anybody in the whole wide world from ever annoying her again about—anything, that I've come here now!" he persisted rashly. "And don't you see—we had a little misunderstanding and—"

Into the little old lady's ivory cheek crept a small, bright, blush-spot.

"Oh, you had a little misunderstanding," she repeated softly. "A little quarrel? Oh, is that why Molly has been crying so much ever since she came home?"

Very gently she reached out her tiny, blue-veined hand, and turned Stanton's big body around so that the lamp-light smote him squarely on his face.

"Are you a good boy?" she asked. "Are you good enough for—my—little Molly?"

Impulsively Stanton grabbed her small hands in his big ones, and raised them very tenderly to his lips.

"Are you a good boy?" she asked

"Oh, little Molly's little grandmother," he said; "nobody on the face of this snow-covered earth is good enough for your Molly, but won't you give me a chance? Couldn't you please give me a chance? Now—this minute? Is she so very ill?"

"No, she's not so very ill, that is, she's not sick in bed," mused the old lady waveringly. "She's well enough to be sitting up in her big chair in front of her open fire."

"Big chair—open fire?" quizzed Stanton. "Then, are there two chairs?" he asked casually.

"Why, yes," answered the little-grandmother in surprise.

"And a mantelpiece with a clock on it?" he probed.

The little-grandmother's eyes opened wide and blue with astonishment.

"Yes," she said, "but the clock hasn't gone for forty years!"

"Oh, great!" exclaimed Stanton. "Then won't you please—please—I tell you it's a case of life or death—won't you *please* go right upstairs and sit down in that extra big chair—and not say a word or anything but just wait till I come? And of course," he said, "it wouldn't be good for you to run upstairs, but if you could hurry just a little I should be *so* much obliged."

As soon as he dared, he followed cautiously up the unfamiliar stairs, and peered inquisitively through the illuminating crack of a loosely closed door.

The grandmother as he remembered her was dressed in some funny sort of a dullish purple, but peeping out from the edge of one of the chairs he caught an unmistakable flutter of blue.

Catching his breath he tapped gently on the woodwork.

Round the big winged arm of the chair a wonderful, bright aureole of hair showed suddenly.

"Come in," faltered Molly's perplexed voice.

All muffled up in his great fur-coat he pushed the door wide open and entered boldly.

"It's only Carl," he said

"It's only Carl," he said. "Am I interrupting you?"

The really dreadful collapsed expression on Molly's face Stanton did not appear to notice at all. He merely walked over to the mantelpiece, and leaning his elbows on the little cleared space in front of the clock, stood staring fixedly at the time-piece which had not changed its quarter-of-three expression for forty years.

"It's almost half-past seven," he announced pointedly, "and I can stay till just eight o'clock."

Only the little grandmother smiled.

Almost immediately: "It's twenty minutes of eight now!" he announced severely.

"My, how time flies!" laughed the little grandmother.

When he turned around again the little grandmother had fled.

But Molly did not laugh, as he himself had laughed on that faraway, dreamlike evening in his rooms. Instead of laughter, two great tears welled up in her eyes and glistened slowly down her flushing cheeks.

"What if this old clock hasn't moved a minute in forty years?" whispered Stanton passionately, "it's such a *stingy* little time to eight o'clock—even if the hands never get there!"

Then turning suddenly to Molly he held out his great strong arms to her.

"Oh, Molly, Molly!" he cried out beseechingly, "I love you! And I'm free to love you! Won't you please come to me?"

Sliding very cautiously out of the big, deep chair, Molly came walking hesitatingly towards him. Like a little wraith miraculously tinted with bronze and blue she stopped and faced him piteously for a second.

Then suddenly she made a little wild rush into his arms and burrowed her small frightened face in his shoulder.

"Oh, Carl, Sweetheart!" she cried. "I can really love you now? Love you, Carl—love you! And not have to be just Molly Make-Believing any more!"

Little Eve Edgarton

CHAPTER I

"But you live like such a fool—of course you're bored!" drawled the Older Man, rummaging listlessly through his pockets for the ever-elusive match.

"Well, I like your nerve!" protested the Younger Man with unmistakable asperity.

"Do you—really?" mocked the Older Man, still smiling very faintly.

For a few minutes then both men resumed their cigars, staring blinkishly out all the while from their dark green piazza corner into the dazzling white tennis courts that gleamed like so many slippery pine planks in the afternoon glare and heat. The month was August, the day typically handsome, typically vivid, typically caloric.

It was the Younger Man who recovered his conversational interest first. "So you think I'm a fool?" he resumed at last quite abruptly.

"Oh, no—no! Not for a minute!" denied the Older Man. "Why, my dear sir, I never even implied that you were a fool! All I said was that you—lived like a fool!"

Starting to be angry, the Younger Man laughed instead. "You're certainly rather an amusing sort of chap," he acknowledged reluctantly.

A gleam of real pride quickened most ingenuously in the Older Man's pale blue eyes. "Why, that's just the whole point of my argument," he beamed. "Now—you look interesting. But you aren't! And I—don't look interesting. But it seems that I am!"

"You—you've got a nerve!" reverted the Younger Man.

Altogether serenely the Older Man began to rummage again through all his pockets. "Thank you for your continuous compliments," he mused. "Thank you, I say. Thank you—very much. Now for the very first time, sir, it's beginning to dawn on me just why you have honored me with so much of your company—the past three or four days. I truly believe that you like me! Eh? But up to last Monday, if I remember correctly," he added drily, "it was that showy young Philadelphia crowd that was absorbing the larger part of your—valuable attention? Eh? Wasn't it?"

"What in thunder are you driving at?" snapped the Younger Man. "What are you trying to string me about, anyway? What's the harm if I did say that I wished to glory I'd never come to this blasted hotel? Of all the stupid people! Of all the stupid places! Of all the stupid—everything!"

"The mountains here are considered quite remarkable by some," suggested the Older Man blandly.

"Mountains?" snarled the Younger Man. "Mountains? Do you think for a moment that a fellow like me comes to a God-forsaken spot like this for the sake of mountains?"

A trifle noisily the Older Man jerked his chair around and, slouching down into his shabby gray clothes, with his hands thrust deep into his pockets, his feet shoved out before him, sat staring at his companion. Furrowed abruptly from brow to chin with myriad infinitesimal wrinkles of perplexity, his lean, droll face looked suddenly almost monkeyish in its intentness.

"What does a fellow like you come to a place like this for?" he asked bluntly.

"Why—tennis," conceded the Younger Man. "A little tennis. And golf—a little golf. And—and—"

"And—girls," asserted the Older Man with precipitous conviction.

Across the Younger Man's splendidly tailored shoulders a little flicker of self-consciousness went crinkling. "Oh, of course," he grinned. "Oh, of course I've got a vacationist's usual partiality for pretty girls. But Great Heavens!" he began, all over again. "Of all the stupid—!"

"But you live like such a fool—of course you're bored," resumed the Older Man.

"There you are at it again!" stormed the Younger Man with tempestuous resentment.

"Why shouldn't I be 'at it again'?" argued the Older Man mildly. "Always and forever picking out the showiest people that you can find—and always and forever being bored to death with them eventually, but never learning anything from it—that's you! Now wouldn't that just naturally suggest to any observing stranger that there was something radically idiotic about your method of life?"

"But that Miss Von Eaton looked like such a peach!" protested the Younger Man worriedly.

"That's exactly what I say," droned the Older Man.

"Why, she's the handsomest girl here!" insisted the Younger Man arrogantly.

"That's exactly what I say," droned the Older Man.

"And the best dresser!" boasted the Younger Man stubbornly.

"That's exactly what I say," droned the Older Man.

"Why, just that pink paradise hat alone would have knocked almost any chap silly," grinned the Younger Man a bit sheepishly.

"Humph!" mused the Older Man still droningly. "Humph! When a chap falls in love with a girl's hat at a summer resort, what he ought to do is to hike back to town on the first train he can catch—and go find the milliner who made the hat!"

"Hike back to—town?" gibed the Younger Man. "Ha!" he sneered. "A chap would have to hike back a good deal farther than 'town' these days to find a girl that was worth hiking back for! What in thunder's the matter with all the girls?" he queried petulantly. "They get stupider and stupider every summer! Why, the peachiest débutante you meet the whole season can't hold your interest much beyond the stage where you once begin to call her by her first name!"

Irritably, as he spoke, he reached out for a bright-covered magazine from the great pile of books and papers that sprawled on the wicker table close at his elbow. "Where in blazes do the story-book writers find their girls?" he demanded. Noisily with his knuckles he began to knock through page after page of the magazine's big-typed advertisements concerning the year's most popular story-book heroines. "Why—here are no end of story-book girls," he complained, "that could keep a fellow guessing till his hair was nine shades of white! Look at the corking things they say! But what earthly good are any of 'em to you? They're not real! Why, there was a little girl in a magazine story last month—! Why, I could have died for her! But confound it, I say, what's the use? They're none of 'em real! Nothing but moonshine! Nothing in the world, I tell you, but just plain made-up moonshine! Absolutely improbable!"

Slowly the Older Man drew in his long, rambling legs and crossed one knee adroitly over the other.

"Improbable—your grandmother!" said the Older Man. "If there's—one person on the face of this earth who makes me sick it's the ninny who calls a thing 'improbable' because it happens to be outside his own special, puny experience of life."

Tempestuously the Younger Man slammed down his magazine to the floor.

"Great Heavens, man!" he demanded. "Where in thunder would a fellow like me start out to find a story-book girl? A real girl, I mean!"

"Almost anywhere—outside yourself," murmured the Older Man blandly.

"Eh?" jerked the Younger Man.

"That's what I said," drawled the Older Man with unruffled suavity. "But what's the use?" he added a trifle more briskly. "Though you searched a thousand years! A 'real girl'? Bah! You wouldn't know a 'real girl' if you saw her!"

"I tell you I would!" snapped the Younger Man.

"I tell you—you wouldn't!" said the Older Man.

"Prove it!" challenged the Younger Man.

"It's already proved!" confided the Older Man. "Ha! I know your type!" he persisted frankly. "You're the sort of fellow, at a party, who just out of sheer fool-instinct will go trampling down every other man in sight just for the sheer fool-joy of trying to get the first dance with the most conspicuously showy-looking, most conspicuously artificial-looking girl in the room—who always and invariably 'bores you to death' before the evening is over! And while you and the rest of your kind are battling together—year after year—for this special privilege of being 'bored to death,' the 'real girl' that you're asking about, the marvelous girl, the girl with the big, beautiful, unspoken thoughts in her head, the girl with the big, brave, undone deeds in her heart, the girl that stories are made of, the girl whom you call 'improbable'—is moping off alone in some dark, cold corner—or sitting forlornly partnerless against the bleak wall of the ballroom—or hiding shyly up in the dressing-room—waiting to be discovered! Little Miss Still-Waters, deeper than ten thousand seas! Little Miss Gunpowder, milder than the dusk before the moon ignites it! Little Miss Sleeping-Beauty, waiting for her Prince!"

"Oh, yes—I suppose so," conceded the Younger Man impatiently. "But that Miss Von Eaton—"

"Oh, it isn't that I don't know a pretty face—or hat, when I see it," interrupted the Older Man nonchalantly. "It's only that I don't put my trust in 'em." With a quick gesture, half audacious, half apologetic, he reached forward suddenly and tapped the Younger Man's coat sleeve. "Oh, I knew just as well as you," he affirmed, "oh, I knew just as well as you—at my first glance—that your gorgeous young Miss Von Eaton was excellingly handsome. But I also knew—not later certainly than my second glance—that she was presumably rather stupid. You can't be interesting, you know, my young friend, unless you do interesting things—and handsome creatures are proverbially lazy. Humph! If Beauty is excuse enough for Being, it sure takes Plainness then to feel the real necessity for—Doing.

"So, speaking of hats, if it's stimulating conversation that you're after, if you're looking for something unique, something significant, something really worth while—what you want to do, my young friend, is to find a girl with a hat you'd be ashamed to go out with—and stay home with her! That's where you'll find the brains, the originality, the vivacity, the sagacity, the real ideas!"

With his first sign of genuine amusement the Younger Man tipped back his head and laughed right up into the green-lined roof of the piazza. "Now just whom would you specially recommend for me?" he demanded mirthfully. "Among all the feminine galaxy of bores and frumps that seem to be congregated at this particular hotel—just whom would you specially recommend for me? The stoop-shouldered, school-marmy Botany dame with her incessant garden gloves? Or?—Or—?" His whole face brightened suddenly with a rather extraordinary amount of humorous malice: "Or how about that duddy-looking little Edgarton girl that I saw you talking with this morning?" he asked delightedly. "Heaven knows she's colorless enough to suit even you—with her winter-before-spring-before-summer-before-last clothes and her voice so meek you'd have to hold her in your lap to hear it. And her—"

"That 'duddy-looking' little Miss Edgarton—meek?" mused the Older Man in sincere astonishment. "Meek? Why, man alive, she was born in a snow-shack on the Yukon River! She was at Pekin in the Boxer Rebellion! She's roped steers in Oklahoma! She's matched her embroidery silks to all the sunrise tints on the Himalayas! Just why in creation should she seem meek—do you suppose—to a—to a—twenty-five-dollar-a-week clerk like yourself?"

"'A twenty-five-dollar-a-week clerk like myself?'" the Younger Man fairly gasped. "Why—why—I'm the junior partner of the firm of Barton & Barton, stock-brokers! Why, we're the biggest—"

"Is that so?" quizzed the Older Man with feigned surprise. "Well—well—well! I beg your pardon. But now doesn't it all go to prove just exactly what I said in the beginning—that it doesn't behoove a single one of us to judge too hastily by appearances?"

As if fairly overwhelmed with embarrassment he sat staring silently off into space for several seconds. Then—"Speaking of this Miss Edgarton," he resumed genially, "have you ever exactly sought her out—as it were—and actually tried to get acquainted with her?"

"No," said Barton shortly. "Why, the girl must be thirty years old!"

"S—o?" mused the Older Man. "Just about your age?"

"I'm thirty-two," growled the Younger Man.

"I'm sixty-two, thank God!" acknowledged the Older Man. "And your gorgeous Miss Von Eaton—who bores you so—all of a sudden—is about—?"

"Twenty," prompted the Younger Man.

"Poor—senile—babe," ruminated the Older Man soberly.

"Eh?" gasped the Younger Man, edging forward in his chair. "Eh? 'Senile'? Twenty?"

"Sure!" grinned the Older Man. "Twenty is nothing but the 'sere and yellow leaf' of infantile caprice! But thirty is the jocund youth of character! On land or sea the Lord Almighty never made anything as radiantly, divinely young as—thirty! Oh, but thirty's the darling age in a woman!" he added with sudden exultant positiveness. "Thirty's the birth of individuality! Thirty's the—"

"Twenty has got quite enough individuality for me, thank you!" asserted Barton with some curtness.

"But it hasn't!" cried the Older Man hotly. "You've just confessed that it hasn't!" In an amazing impulse of protest he reached out and shook his freckled fist right under the Younger Man's nose. "Twenty, I tell you, hasn't got any individuality at all!" he persisted vehemently.

"Twenty isn't anything at all except the threadbare cloak of her father's idiosyncrasies, lined with her mother's made-over tact, trimmed with her great-aunt somebody's short-lipped smile, shrouding a brand-new frame of—God knows what!"

"Eh? What?" questioned the Younger Man uneasily.

"When a girl is twenty, I tell you," persisted the Older Man—"there's not one marrying man among us—Heaven help us!—who can swear whether her charm is Love's own permanent food or just Nature's temporary bait! At twenty, I tell you, there's not one man among us who can prove whether vivacity is temperament or just plain kiddishness; whether sweetness is real disposition or just coquetry; whether tenderness is personal discrimination or just sex; whether dumbness is stupidity or just brain hoarding its immature treasure; whether indeed coldness is prudery or just conscious passion banking its fires! The dear daredevil sweetheart whom you worship at eighteen will evolve, likelier than not, into a mighty sour prig at forty; and the dove-gray lass who led you to church with her prayer-book ribbons twice every Sunday will very probably decide to go on the vaudeville stage—when her children are just in the high school; and the dull-eyed wallflower whom you dodged at all your college dances will turn out, ten chances to one, the only really wonderful woman you know! But at thirty! Oh, ye gods, Barton! If a girl interests you at thirty you'll utterly mad about her when she's forty—fifty—sixty! If she's merry at thirty, if she's ardent, if she's tender, it's her own established merriment, it's her own irreducible ardor, it's her—Why, man alive! Why—why—"

"Oh, for Heaven's sake!" gasped Barton. "Whoa there! Go slow! How in creation do you expect anybody to follow you?"

"Follow me? Follow me?" mused the Older Man perplexedly. Staring very hard at Barton, he took the opportunity to swallow rather loudly once or twice.

"Now speaking of Miss Edgarton," he resumed persistently, "now, speaking of this Miss Edgarton, I don't presume for an instant that you're looking for a wife on this trip, but are merely hankering a bit now and then for something rather specially diverting in the line of feminine companionship?"

"Well, what of it?" conceded the Younger Man.

"This of it," argued the Older Man. "If you are really craving the interesting why don't you go out and rummage around for it? Rummage around was what I said! Yes! The real hundred-cent-to-the-dollar treasures of Life, you know, aren't apt to be found labeled as such and lying round very loose on the smugly paved general highway! And astonishingly good looks and astonishingly good clothes are pretty nearly always equivalent to a sign saying, 'I've already been discovered, thank you!' But the really big sport of existence, young man, is to strike out somewhere and discover things for yourself!"

"Is—it?" scoffed Barton.

"It is!" asserted the Older Man. "The woman, I tell you, who fathoms heroism in the fellow that every one else thought was a knave—she's got something to brag about! The fellow who's shrewd enough to spy unutterable lovableness in the woman that no man yet has ever even remotely suspected of being lovable at all—God! It's like being Adam with the whole world virgin!"

"Oh, that may be all right in theory," acknowledged the Younger Man, with some reluctance. "But—"

"Now, speaking of Miss Edgarton," resumed the Older Man monotonously.

"Oh, hang Miss Edgarton!" snapped the Younger Man. "I wouldn't be seen talking to her! She hasn't any looks! She hasn't any style! She hasn't any—anything! Of all the hopelessly plain girls! Of all the—!"

"Now see here, my young friend," begged the Older Man blandly. "The fellow who goes about the world judging women by the sparkle of their eyes or the pink of their cheeks or the sheen of their hair—runs a mighty big risk of being rated as just one of two things, a sensualist or a fool."

"Are you trying to insult me?" demanded the Younger Man furiously.

Freakishly the Older Man twisted his thin-lipped mouth and one glowering eyebrow into a surprisingly sudden and irresistible smile.

"Why—no," he drawled. "Under all existing circumstances I should think I was complimenting you pretty considerably by rating you only as a fool."

"Eh?" jumped Barton again.

"U-m-m," mused the Older Man thoughtfully. "Now believe me, Barton, once and for all, there 's no such thing as a 'hopelessly plain woman'! Every woman, I tell you, is beautiful concerning the thing that she's most interested in! And a man's an everlasting dullard who can't ferret out what that interest is and summon its illuminating miracle into an otherwise indifferent face—"

"Is that so?" sniffed Barton.

Lazily the Older Man struggled to his feet and stretched his arms till his bones began to crack.

"Bah! What's beauty, anyway," he complained, "except just a question of where Nature has concentrated her supreme forces—in outgrowing energy, which is beauty; or ingrowing energy, which is brains! Now I like a little good looks as well as anybody," he confided, still yawning, "but when I see a woman living altogether on the outside of her face I don't reckon too positively on there being anything very exciting going on inside that face. So by the same token, when I see a woman who isn't squandering any centric fires at all on the contour of her nose or the arch of her eyebrows or the flesh-tints of her cheeks, it surely does pique my curiosity to know just what wonderful consuming energy she is busy about.

"A face isn't meant to be a living-room, anyway, Barton, but just a piazza where the seething, preoccupied soul can dash out now and then to bask in the breeze and refreshment of sympathy and appreciation. Surely then—it's no particular personal glory to you that your friend Miss Von Eaton's energy cavorts perpetually in the gold of her hair or the blue of her eyes, because rain or shine, congeniality or noncongeniality, her energy hasn't any other place to go. But I tell you it means some compliment to a man when in a bleak, dour, work-worn personality like the old Botany dame's for instance he finds himself able to lure out into occasional facial ecstasy the *amazing* vitality which has been slaving for Science alone these past fifty years. Mushrooms are what the old Botany dame is interested in, Barton. Really, Barton, I think you'd be surprised to see how extraordinarily beautiful the old Botany dame can be about mushrooms! Gleam of the first faint streak of dawn, freshness of the wildest woodland dell, verve of the long day's strenuous effort, flush of sunset and triumph, zeal of the student's evening lamp, puckering, daredevil smile of reckless experiment—"

"Say! Are you a preacher?" mocked the Younger Man sarcastically.

"No more than any old man," conceded the Older Man with unruffled good-nature.

"Old man?" repeated Barton, skeptically. In honest if reluctant admiration for an instant, he sat appraising his companion's extraordinary litheness and agility. "Ha!" he laughed. "It would take a good deal older head than yours to discover what that Miss Edgarton's beauty is!"

"Or a good deal younger one, perhaps," suggested the Older Man judicially. "But—but speaking of Miss Edgarton—" he began all over again.

"Oh—drat Miss Edgarton!" snarled the Younger Man viciously. "You've got Miss Edgarton on the brain! Miss Edgarton this! Miss Edgarton that! Miss Edgarton! Who in blazes is Miss Edgarton, anyway?"

"Miss Edgarton? Miss Edgarton?" mused the Older Man thoughtfully. "Who is she? Miss Edgarton? Why—no one special—except—just my daughter."

Like a fly plunged all unwittingly upon a sheet of sticky paper the Younger Man's hands and feet seemed to shoot out suddenly in every direction.

"Good Heavens!" he gasped. "Your daughter?" he mumbled. "Your daughter?" Every other word or phrase in the English language seemed to be stricken suddenly from his lips. "Your—your—daughter?" he began all over again. "Why—I—I—didn't know your name was Edgarton!" he managed finally to articulate.

An expression of ineffable triumph, and of triumph only, flickered in the Older Man's face.

"Why, that's just what I've been saying," he reiterated amiably. "You don't know anything!"

Fatuously the Younger Man rose to his feet, still struggling for speech—any old speech—a sentence, a word, a cough, anything, in fact, that would make a noise.

"Well, if little Miss Edgarton is—little Miss Edgarton," he babbled idiotically, "who in creation—are you?"

"Who am I?" stammered the Older Man perplexedly. As if the question really worried him, he sagged back a trifle against the sustaining wall of the house, and stood with his hands thrust deep in his pockets once more. "Who am I?" he repeated blandly. Again one eyebrow lifted. Again one side of his thin-lipped mouth twitched ever so slightly to the right. "Why, I'm just a man, Mr. Barton," he grinned very faintly, "who travels all over the world for the sake of whatever amusement he can get out of it. And some afternoons, of course, I get a good deal more amusement out of it—than I do others. Eh?"

Furiously the red blood mounted into the Young Man's cheeks. "Oh, I say, Edgarton!" he pleaded. Mirthlessly, wretchedly, a grin began to spread over his face. "Oh, I say!" he faltered. "I *am* a fool!"

The Older Man threw back his head and started to laugh.

'I am riding,' she murmured almost inaudibly

At the first cackling syllable of the laugh, with appalling fatefulness Eve Edgarton herself loomed suddenly on the scene, in her old slouch hat, her gray flannel shirt, her weather-beaten khaki Norfolk and riding-breeches, looking for all the world like an extraordinarily slim, extraordinarily shabby little boy just starting out to play. Up from the top of one riding-boot the butt of a revolver protruded slightly.

With her heavy black eyelashes shadowing somberly down across her olive-tinted cheeks, she passed Barton as if she did not even see him and went directly to her father.

"I am riding," she murmured almost inaudibly.

"In this heat?" groaned her father.

"In this heat," echoed Eve Edgarton.

"There will surely be a thunder-storm," protested her father.

"There will surely be a thunder-storm," acquiesced Eve Edgarton.

Without further parleying she turned and strolled off again.

Just for an instant the Older Man's glance followed her. Just for an instant with quizzically twisted eyebrows his glance flashed back sardonically to Barton's suffering face. Then very leisurely he began to laugh again.

But right in the middle of the laugh—as if something infinitely funnier than a joke had smitten him suddenly—he stopped short, with one eyebrow stranded half-way up his forehead.

"Eve!" he called sharply. "Eve! Come back here a minute!"

Very laggingly from around the piazza corner the girl reappeared.

"Eve," said her father quite abruptly, "this is Mr. Barton! Mr. Barton, this is my daughter!"

Listlessly the girl came forward and proffered her hand to the Younger Man. It was a very little hand. More than that, it was an exceedingly cold little hand.

"How do you do, sir?" she murmured almost inaudibly.

With an expression of ineffable joy the Older Man reached out and tapped his daughter on the shoulder.

"It has just transpired, my dear Eve," he beamed, "that you can do this young man here an inestimable service—tell him something—teach him something, I mean—that he very specially needs to know!"

As one fairly teeming with benevolence he stood there smiling blandly into Barton's astonished face. "Next to the pleasure of bringing together two people who like each other," he persisted, "I know of nothing more poignantly diverting than the bringing together of people who—who—" Mockingly across his daughter's unconscious head, malevolently through his mask of utter guilelessness and peace, he challenged Barton's staring helplessness. "So—taken all in all," he drawled still beamingly, "there's nothing in the world—at this particular moment, Mr. Barton—that could amuse me more than to have you join my daughter in her ride this afternoon!"

"Ride with me?" gasped little Eve Edgarton.

"This afternoon?" floundered Barton.

"Oh—why—yes—of course! I'd be delighted! I'd be—be! Only—! Only I'm afraid that—!"

Deprecatingly with uplifted hand the Older Man refuted every protest. "No, indeed, Mr. Barton," he insisted. "Oh, no—no indeed—I assure you it won't inconvenience my daughter in the slightest! My daughter is very obliging! My daughter, indeed—if I may say so in all modesty—my daughter indeed is always a good deal of a—philanthropist!"

Then very grandiloquently, like a man in an old-fashioned picture, he began to back away from them, bowing low all the time, very, very low, first to Barton, then to his daughter, then to Barton again.

"I wish you both a very good afternoon!" he said. "Really, I see no reason why either of you should expect a single dull moment!"

"I would therefore respectfully suggest as a special topic of conversation the consummate cheek of—yours truly, Paul Reymouth Edgarton"

Before the sickly grin on Barton's face his own smile deepened into actual unctuousness. But before the sudden woodeny set of his daughter's placid mouth his unctuousness twisted just a little bit wryly on his lips.

"After all, my dear young people," he asserted hurriedly, "there's just one thing in the world, you know, that makes two people congenial, and that is—that they both shall have arrived at exactly the same conclusion—by two totally different routes. It's got to be exactly the same conclusion, else there isn't any sympathy in it. But it's got to be by two totally different routes, you understand, else there isn't any talky-talk to it!"

Laboriously one eyebrow began to jerk its way up his forehead, and with a purely mechanical instinct he reached up drolly and pulled it down again. "So—as the initial test of your mutual congeniality this afternoon," he resumed, "I would therefore respectfully suggest as a special topic of conversation the consummate cheek of—yours truly, Paul Reymouth Edgarton!"

Starting to bow once more, he backed instead into the screen of the office window. Without even an expletive he turned, pushed in the screen, clambered adroitly through the aperture, and disappeared almost instantly from sight.

Very faintly from some far up-stairs region the thin, faint, single syllable of a laugh came floating down into the piazza corner.

Then just as precipitous as a man steps into any other hole, Barton stepped into the conversational topic that had just been so aptly provided for him.

"Is your father something of a—of a practical joker, Miss Edgarton?" he demanded with the slightest possible tinge of shrillness.

For the first time in Barton's knowledge of little Eve Edgarton she lifted her eyes to him—great hazel eyes, great bored, dreary, hazel eyes set broadly in a too narrow olive face.

"My father is generally conceded to be something of a joker, I believe," she said dully. "But it would never have occurred to me to call him a particularly practical one. I don't like him," she added without a flicker of expression.

"I don't either!" snapped Barton.

A trifle uneasily little Eve Edgarton went on. "Why—once when I was a tiny child—" she droned.

"I don't know anything about when you were a tiny child," affirmed Barton with some vehemence. "But just this afternoon—!"

In striking contrast to the cool placidity of her face one of Eve Edgarton's boot-toes began to tap-tap-tap against the piazza floor. When she lifted her eyes again to Barton their sleepy sullenness was shot through suddenly with an unmistakable flash of temper.

"Oh, for Heaven's sake, Mr. Barton!" she cried out. "If you insist upon riding with me, couldn't you please hurry? The afternoons are so short!"

"If I 'insist' upon riding with you?" gasped Barton.

Disconcertingly from an upper window the Older Man's face beamed suddenly down upon him. "Oh, don't mind anything she says," drawled the Older Man. "It's just her cunning, 'meek' little ways."

Precipitately Barton bolted for his room.

Once safely ensconced behind his closed door a dozen different decisions, a dozen different indecisions, rioted tempestuously through his mind. To go was just as awkward as not to go! Not to go was just as awkward as to go! Over and over and over one silly alternative chased the other through his addled senses. Then just as precipitately as he had bolted to his room he began suddenly to hurl himself into his riding-clothes, yanking out a bureau drawer here, slamming back a closet door there, rummaging through a box, tipping over a trunk, yet in all his fuming haste, his raging irritability, showing the same fastidious choice of shirt, tie, collar, that characterized his every public appearance.

Immaculate at last as a tailor's equestrian advertisement he came striding down again into the hotel office, only to plunge most inopportunely into Miss Von Eaton's languorous presence.

"Why, Jim!" gasped Miss Von Eaton. Exquisitely white and cool and fluffy and dainty, she glanced up perplexedly at him from her lazy, deep-seated chair. "Why, Jim!" she repeated, just a little bit edgily. "Riding? Riding? Well, of all things! You who wouldn't even play bridge with us this afternoon on account of the heat! Well, who in the world—who can it be that has cut us all out?"

Teasingly she jumped up and walked to the door with him, and stood there peering out beyond the cool shadow of his dark-blue shoulder into the dazzling road where, like so many figures thrust forth all unwittingly into the merciless flare of a spot-light, little shabby Eve Edgarton and three sweating horses waited squintingly in the dust.

"Oh!" cried Miss Von Eaton. "W-hy!" stammered Miss Von Eaton. "Good gracious!" giggled Miss Von Eaton. Then hysterically, with her hand clapped over her mouth, she turned and fled up the stairs to confide the absurd news to her mates.

With a face like a graven image Barton went on down the steps into the road. In one of his thirty-dollar riding-boots a disconcerting two-cent sort of squeak merely intensified his unhappy sensation of being motivated purely mechanically like a doll.

Two of the horses that whinnied cordially at his approach were rusty roans. The third was a chunky gray. Already on one of the roans Eve Edgarton sat perched with her bridle-rein oddly slashed in two, and knotted, each raw end to a stirrup, leaving her hands and arms still perfectly free to hug her mysterious books and papers to her breast.

"Good afternoon again, Miss Edgarton," smiled Barton conscientiously.

"Good afternoon again, Mr. Barton," echoed Eve Edgarton listlessly.

With frank curiosity he nodded toward her armful of papers. "Surely you're not going to carry—all that stuff with you?" he questioned.

"Yes, I am, Mr. Barton," drawled Eve Edgarton, scarcely above a whisper.

Worriedly he pointed to her stirrups. "But Great Scott, Miss Edgarton!" he protested. "Surely you're not reckless enough to ride like that? Just guiding with your feet?"

"I always—do, Mr. Barton," singsonged the girl monotonously.

"But the extra horse?" cried Barton. With a sudden little chuckle of relief he pointed to the chunky gray. There was a side-saddle on the chunky gray. "Who's going with us?"

Almost insolently little Eve Edgarton narrowed her sleepy eyes.

"I always taken an extra horse with me, Mr. Barton—Thank you!" she yawned, with the very faintest possible tinge of asperity.

"Oh!" stammered Barton quite helplessly. "O—h!" Heavily, as he spoke, he lifted one foot to his stirrup and swung up into his saddle. Through all his mental misery, through all his physical discomfort, a single lovely thought sustained him. There was only one really good riding road in that vicinity! And it was shady! And, thank Heaven, it was most inordinately short!

But Eve Edgarton falsified the thought before he was half through thinking it.

She swung her horse around, reared him to almost a perpendicular height, merged herself like so much fluid khaki into his great, towering, threatening neck, reacted almost instantly to her own balance again, and went plunging off toward the wild, rough, untraveled foot-hills and—certain destruction, any unbiased onlooker would have been free to affirm!

Snortingly the chunky gray went tearing after her. A trifle sulkily Barton's roan took up the chase.

Shade? Oh, ye gods! If Eve Edgarton knew shade when she saw it she certainly gave no possible sign of such intelligence. Wherever the galloping, grass-grown road hesitated between green-roofed forest and devastated wood-lot, she chose the devastated wood-lot! Wherever the trotting, treacherous pasture faltered between hobbly, rock-strewn glare and soft, lush-carpeted spots of shade, she chose the hobbly, rock-strewn glare! On and on and on! Till dust turned sweat! And sweat turned dust again! On and on and on! With the riderless gray thudding madly after her! And Barton's sulky roan balking frenziedly at each new swerve and turn!

It must have been almost three miles before Barton quite overtook her. Then in the scudding, transitory shadow of a growly thunder-cloud she reined in suddenly, waited patiently till Barton's panting horse was nose and nose with hers, and then, pushing her slouch hat back from her low, curl-fringed forehead, jogged listlessly along beside him with her pale olive face turned inquiringly to his drenched, beet-colored visage.

"What was it that you wanted me to do for you, Mr. Barton?" she asked with a laborious sort of courtesy. "Are you writing a book or something that you wanted me to help you about? Is that it? Is that what Father meant?"

"Am I writing a—book?" gasped Barton. Desperately he began to mop his forehead. "Writing a book? Am—I—writing—a—book? Heaven forbid!"

"What are you doing?" persisted the girl bluntly.

"What am I doing?" repeated Barton. "Why, riding with you! Trying to ride with you!" he called out grimly as, taking the lead impetuously again, Eve Edgarton's horse shied off at a rabbit and went sidling down a sand-bank into a brand-new area of rocks and stubble and breast-high blueberry bushes.

Barton liked to ride and he rode fairly well, but he was by no means an equestrian acrobat, and, quite apart from the girl's unquestionably disconcerting mannerisms, the foolish floppity presence of the riderless gray rattled him more than he could possibly account for. Yet to save his life he could not have told which would seem more childish—to turn back in temper, or to follow on—in the same.

More in helplessness than anything else he decided to follow on.

"On and on and on," would have described it more adequately.

Blacker and blacker the huddling thunder-caps spotted across the brilliant, sunny sky. Gaspier and gaspier in each lulling tree-top, in each hushing bird-song, in each drooping grass-blade, the whole torrid earth seemed to be sucking in its breath as if it meant never, never to exhale it again.

Once more in the midst of a particularly hideous glare the girl took occasion to rein in and wait for him, turning once more to his flushed, miserable countenance a little face inordinately pale and serene.

"If you're not writing a book, what would you like to talk about, Mr. Barton?" she asked conscientiously. "Would you like to talk about peat-bog fossils?"

"What?" gasped Barton.

"Peat-bog fossils," repeated the mild little voice. "Are you interested in peat-bog fossils? Or would you rather talk about the Mississippi River pearl fisheries? Or do you care more perhaps for politics? Would you like to discuss the relative financial conditions of the South American republics?"

Before the expression of blank despair in Barton's face, her own face fell a trifle. "No?" she ventured worriedly. "No? Oh, I'm sorry, Mr. Barton, but you see—you see—I've never been out before with anybody—my own age. So I don't know at all what you would be interested in!"

"Never been out before with any one her own age?" gasped Barton to himself. Merciful Heavens! what was her "own age"? There in her little khaki Norfolk and old slouch hat she looked about fifteen years old—and a boy, at that. Altogether wretchedly he turned and grinned at her.

"Miss Edgarton," he said, "believe me, there's not one thing to-day under God's heaven that does interest me—except the weather!"

"The weather?" mused little Eve Edgarton thoughtfully. Casually, as she spoke, she glanced down across the horses' lathered sides and up into Barton's crimson face. "The weather? Oh!" she hastened anxiously to affirm. "Oh, yes! The meteorological conditions certainly are interesting this summer. Do you yourself think that it's a shifting of the Gulf Stream? Or just a—just a change in the paths of the cyclonic areas of low pressure?" she persisted drearily.

"Eh?" gasped Barton. "The weather? Heat was what I meant, Miss Edgarton! Just plain heat!—DAMNED HEAT—was what I meant—if I may be so explicit, Miss Edgarton."

"It is hot," conceded Eve apologetically.

"In fact," snapped Barton, "I think it's the hottest day I ever knew!"

"Really?" droned Eve Edgarton.

"Really!" snapped Barton.

It must have been almost half an hour before anybody spoke again. Then, "Pretty hot, isn't it?" Barton began all over again.

"Yes," said Eve Edgarton.

"In fact," hissed Barton through clenched teeth, "in fact I know it's the hottest day I ever knew!"

"Really?" droned Eve Edgarton.

"Really!" choked Barton.

Creakily under their hot, chafing saddles the sweltering roans lurched off suddenly through a great snarl of bushes into a fern-shaded spring-hole and stood ankle-deep in the boggy grass, guzzling noisily at food and drink, with the chunky gray crowding greedily against first one rider and then the other.

Quite against all intention Barton groaned aloud. His sun-scorched eyes seemed fairly shriveling with the glare. His wilted linen collar slopped like a stale poultice around his tortured neck. In his sticky fingers the bridle-rein itched like so much poisoned ribbon.

Reaching up one small hand to drag the soft flannel collar of her shirt a little farther down from her slim throat, Eve Edgarton rested her chin on her knuckles for an instant and surveyed him plaintively. "Aren't—we—having—an—awful time?" she whispered.

Even then if she had looked woman-y, girl-y, even remotely, affectedly feminine, Barton would doubtless have floundered heroically through some protesting lie. But to the frank, blunt, little-boyishness of her he succumbed suddenly with a beatific grin of relief. "Yes, we certainly are!" he acknowledged ruthlessly.

"And what good is it?" questioned the girl most unexpectedly.

"Not any good!" grunted Barton.

"To any one?" persisted the girl.

"Not to any one!" exploded Barton.

With an odd little gasp of joy the girl reached out dartingly and touched Barton on his sleeve. Her face was suddenly eager, active, transcendently vital.

"Then oh—won't you please—please—turn round—and go home—and leave me alone?" she pleaded astonishingly.

"Turn round and go home?" stammered Barton.

The touch on his sleeve quickened a little. "Oh, yes—please, Mr. Barton!" insisted the tremulous voice.

"You—you mean I'm in your way?" stammered Barton.

Very gravely the girl nodded her head. "Oh, yes, Mr. Barton—you're terribly in my way," she acknowledged quite frankly.

"Good Heavens," thought Barton, "is there a man in this? Is it a tryst? Well, of all things!"

Jerkily he began to back his horse out of the spring-hole, back—back—back through the intricate, overgrown pathway of flapping leaves and sharp, scratchy twigs.

"I am very sorry, Miss Edgarton, to have forced my presence on you so!" he murmured ironically.

"Oh, it isn't just you!" said little Eve Edgarton quite frankly. "It's all Father's friends." Almost threateningly as she spoke she jerked up her own horse's drizzling mouth and rode right at Barton as if to force him back even faster through the great snarl of underbrush. "I hate clever people!" she asserted passionately. "I hate them—hate them—hate them! I hate all Father's clever friends! I hate—"

"But you see I'm not clever," grinned Barton in spite of himself. "Oh, not clever at all," he reiterated with some grimness as an alder branch slapped him stingingly across one eye. "Indeed—" he dodged and ducked and floundered, still backing, backing, everlastingly backing—"indeed, your father has spent quite a lot of his valuable time this afternoon assuring me—and reassuring me—that—that I'm altogether a fool!"

Unrelentingly little Eve Edgarton's horse kept right on forcing him back—back—back.

"But if you're not one of Father's clever friends—who are you?" she demanded perplexedly. "And why did you insist so on riding with me this afternoon?" she cried accusingly.

"I didn't exactly—insist," grinned Barton with a flush of guilt. The flush of guilt added to the flush of heat made him look suddenly very confused.

Across Eve Edgarton's thin little face the flash of temper faded instantly into mere sulky ennui again.

"Oh, dear—oh, dear," she droned. "You—you didn't want to marry me, did you?"

Just for one mad, panic-stricken second the whole world seemed to turn black before Barton's eyes. His heart stopped beating. His ear-drums cracked. Then suddenly, astonishingly, he found himself grinning into that honest little face, and answering comfortably:

"Why, no, Miss Edgarton, I hadn't the slightest idea in the world of wanting to marry you."

"Thank God for that!" gasped little Eve Edgarton. "So many of Father's friends do want to marry me," she confided plaintively, still driving Barton back through that horrid scratchy thicket. "I'm so rich, you see," she confided with equal simplicity, "and I know so much—there's almost always somebody in Petrozavodsk or Broken Hill or Bashukulumbwe who wants to marry me."

"In—where?" stammered Barton.

"Why—in Russia!" said little Eve Edgarton with some surprise. "And Australia! And Africa! Were you never there?"

"I've been in Jersey City," babbled Barton with a desperate attempt at facetiousness.

"I was never there!" admitted little Eve Edgarton regretfully.

Vehemently with one hand she lunged forward and tried with her tiny open palm to push Barton's horse a trifle faster back through the intricate thicket. Then once in the open again she drew herself up with an absurd air of dignity and finality and bowed him from her presence.

"Good-by, Mr. Barton," she said. "Good-by, Mr. Barton."

"But Miss Edgarton—" stammered Barton perplexedly. Whatever his own personal joy and relief might be, the surrounding country nevertheless was exceedingly wild, and the girl an extravagantly long distance from home. "But Miss Edgarton—" he began all over again.

"Good-by, Mr. Barton! And thank you for going home!" she added conscientiously.

"But what will I tell your father?" worried Barton.

"Oh—hang Father," drawled the indifferent little voice.

"But the extra horse?" argued Barton with increasing perplexity. "The gray? If you've got some date up your sleeve, don't you want me to take the gray home with me, and get him out of your way?"

With sluggish resentment little Eve Edgarton lifted her eyes to his. "What would the gray go home with you for?" she asked tersely. "Why, how silly! Why, it's my—mother's horse! That is, we call it my mother's horse," she hastened to explain. "My mother's dead, you know. She's almost always been dead, I mean. So Father always makes me buy an extra place for my mother. It's just a trick of ours, a sort of a custom. I play around alone so much you know. And we live in such wild places!"

Casually she bent over and pushed the protruding butt of her revolver a trifle farther down into her riding boot. "S'long—Mr. Barton!" she called listlessly over the other, and started on, stumblingly, clatteringly, up the abruptly steep and precipitous mountain trail—a little dust-colored gnome on a dust-colored horse, with the dutiful gray pinking cautiously along behind her.

By some odd twist of his bridle-rein the gray's chunky neck arched slightly askew, and he pranced now and then from side to side of the trail as if guided thus by an invisible hand.

With an uncanny pucker along his spine as if he found himself suddenly deserting two women instead of one, Barton went fumbling and squinting out through the dusty green shade into the expected glare of the open pasture, and discovered, to his further disconcerting, that there was no glare left.

Before his astonished eyes he saw sun-scorched mountain-top, sun-scorched granite, sun-scorched field stubble turned suddenly to shade—no cool, translucent miracle of fluctuant greens, but a horrid, plushy, purple dusk under a horrid, plushy, purple sky, with a rip of lightning along the horizon, a galloping gasp of furiously oncoming wind, an almost strangling stench of dust-scented rain.

But before he could whirl his horse about, the storm broke! Heaven fell! Hell rose! The sides of the earth caved in! Chaos unspeakable tore north, east, south, west!

Snortingly for one single instant the roan's panic-stricken nostrils went blooming up into the cloud-burst like two parched scarlet poinsettias. Then man and beast as one flesh, as one mind, went bolting back through the rain-drenched, wind-ravished thicket to find their mates.

Up, up, up, everlastingly up, the mountain trail twisted and scrambled through the unholy darkness. Now and again a slippery stone tripped the roan's fumbling feet. Now and again a swaying branch slapped Barton stingingly across his straining eyes. All around and about them tortured forest trees moaned and writhed in the gale. Through every cavernous vista gray sheets of rain went flapping madly by them. The lightning was incredible. The thunder like the snarl of a glass sky shivering into inestimable fragments.

With every gasping breath beginning to rip from his poor lungs like a knifed stitch, the roan still faltered on each new ledge to whinny desperately to his mate. Equally futilely from time to time, Barton, with his hands cupped to his mouth, holloed—holloed—holloed—into the thunderous darkness.

Then at a sharp turn in the trail, magically, in a pale, transient flicker of light, loomed little Eve Edgarton's boyish figure, drenched to the skin apparently, wind-driven, rain-battered, but with hands in her pockets, slouch hat rakishly askew, strolling as nonchalantly down that ghastly trail as a child might come strolling down a stained-glassed, Persian-carpeted stairway to meet an expected guest.

In vaguely silhouetted greeting for one fleet instant a little khaki arm lifted itself full length into the air.

Then more precipitately than any rational thing could happen, more precipitately than any rational thing could even begin to happen, could even begin to begin to happen, without shock, without noise, without pain, without terror or turmoil, or any time at all to fight or pray—a slice of living flame came scaling through the darkness—and cut Barton's consciousness clean in two!

CHAPTER II

When Barton recovered the severed parts of his consciousness again and tried to pull them together, he found that the Present was strangely missing.

The Past and the Future, however, were perfectly plain to him. He was a young stock-broker. He remembered that quite distinctly! And just as soon as the immediate dizzy mystery had been cleared up he would, of course, be a young stock-broker again! But between this snug conviction as to the Past, this smug assurance as to the Future, his mind lay tugging and shivering like a man under a split blanket. Where in creation was the Present? Alternately he tried to yank both Past and Future across the chilly interim.

"There was—a—green and white piazza corner," vaguely his memory reminded him. "Never again!" some latent determination leaped to mock him. And there had been—some sort of an argument—with a drollish old man—concerning all homely girls in general and one very specially homely little girl in particular. And the—very specially homely little girl in particular had turned out to be the old man's—daughter!—"Never again!" his original impulse hastened to reassure him. And there had been a horseback ride—with the girl. Oh, yes—out of some strained sense of—of parental humor—there had been a forced horseback ride. And the weather had been—hot—and black—and then suddenly very yellow. Yellow? Yellow? Dizzily the world began to whir through his senses—a prism of light, a fume of sulphur! Yellow? Yellow? What was yellow? What was anything? What was anything? Yes! That was just it! Where was anything?

Whimperingly, like a dream-dazed dog, the soul of him began to shiver with fear. Oh, ye gods! If returning consciousness would only manifest itself first by some one indisputable proof of a still undisintegrated body, some crisp, reassuring method of outlining one's corporeal edges, some sensory roll-call, as it were of—head, hands, feet, sides! But out of oblivion, out of space abysmal, out of sensory annihilation, to come vaporing back, back, back,—headless, armless, legless, trunkless, conscious only of consciousness, uncertain yet whether the full awakening prove itself—this world or the next! As sacred of Heaven—as—of hell! As—!

Then very, very slowly, with no realization of eyelids, with no realization of lifting his eyelids, Barton began to see things. And he thought he was lying on the soft outer edges of a gigantic black pansy, staring blankly through its glowing golden center into the droll, sketchy little face of the pansy.

And then suddenly, with a jerk that seemed almost to crack his spine, he sensed that the blackness wasn't a pansy at all, but just a round, earthy sort of blackness in which he himself lay mysteriously prone. And he heard the wind still roaring furiously away off somewhere. And he heard the rain still drenching and sousing away off somewhere. But no wind seemed to be tugging directly at him, and no rain seemed to be splashing directly on him. And instead of the cavernous golden crater of a supernatural pansy there was just a perfectly tame yellow farm-lantern balanced adroitly on a low stone in the middle of the mysterious round blackness.

And in the sallow glow of that pleasant lantern-light little Eve Edgarton sat cross-legged on the ground with a great pulpy clutter of rain-soaked magazines spread out all around her like a giant's pack of cards. And diagonally across her breast from shoulder to waistline her little gray flannel shirt hung gashed into innumerable ribbons.

To Barton's blinking eyes she looked exceedingly strange and untidy. But nothing seemed to concern little Eve Edgarton except that spreading circle of half-drowned papers.

"For Heaven's sake—wha—ght are you—do'?" mumbled Barton.

Out from her flickering aura of yellow lantern-light little Eve Edgarton peered forth quizzically into Barton's darkness. "Why—I'm trying to save—my poor dear—books," she drawled.

"Wha—ght?" struggled Barton. The word dragged on his tongue like a weight of lead. "Wha—ght?" he persisted desperately. "Wh—ere?—For—Heaven's sake—wha—ght's the matter—with us?"

Solicitously little Eve Edgarton lifted a soggy magazine-page to the lantern's warm, curving cheek.

"Why—we're in my cave," she confided. "In my very own—cave—you know—that I was headed for—all the time. We got—sort of—struck by lightning," she started to explain. "We—"

"Struck by—lightning?" gasped Barton. Mentally he started to jump up. But physically nothing moved. "My God! I'm paralyzed!" he screamed.

"Oh, no—really—I don't think so," crooned little Eve Edgarton.

With the faintest possible tinge of reluctance she put down her papers, picked up the lantern, and, crawling over to where Barton lay, sat down cross-legged again on the ground beside him, and began with mechanically alternate fist and palm to rubadubdub and thump-thump-thump and stroke-stroke-stroke his utterly helpless body.

"Oh—of—course—you've had—an awfully close call!" she drummed resonantly upon his apathetic chest. "But I've seen—three lightning people—a lot worse off than you!" she kneaded reassuringly into his insensate neck-muscles. "And—they—came out of it—all right—after a few days!" she slapped mercilessly into his faintly conscious sides.

Very slowly, very sluggishly, as his circulation quickened again, a horrid suspicion began to stir in Barton's mind; but it took him a long time to voice the suspicion in anything as loud and public as words.

"Miss—Edgarton!" he plunged at last quite precipitately. "Miss Edgarton! Do I seem to have—any shirt on?"

"No, you don't seem to, exactly, Mr. Barton," conceded little Eve Edgarton. "And your skin—"

From head to foot Barton's whole body strained and twisted in a futile effort to raise himself to at least one elbow. "Why, I'm stripped to my waist!" he stammered in real horror.

"Why, yes—of course," drawled little Eve Edgarton. "And your skin—" Imperturbably as she spoke she pushed him down flat on the ground again and began, with her hands edged vertically like two slim boards, to slash little blissful gashes of consciousness and pain into his frigid right arm. "You see—I had to take both your shirts," she explained, "and what was left of your coat—and all of my coat—to make a soft, strong rope to tie round under your arms so the horse could drag you."

"Did the roan drag me—'way up here?" groaned Barton a bit hazily.

With the faintest possible gasp of surprise little Eve Edgarton stopped slashing his arm and, picking up the lantern, flashed it disconcertingly across his blinking eyes and naked shoulders. "The roans are in heaven," she said quite simply. "It was Mother's horse that dragged you up here." As casually as if he had been a big doll she reached out one slim brown finger and drew his under lip a little bit down from his teeth. "My! But you're still blue!" she confided frankly. "I guess perhaps you'd better have a little more vodka."

Again Barton struggled vainly to raise himself on one elbow. "Vodka?" he stammered.

Again the lifted lantern light flashed disconcertingly across his face and shoulders. "Why, don't you remember—anything?" drawled little Eve Edgarton. "Not anything at all? Why, I must have worked over you two hours—artificial respiration, you know, and all that sort of thing—before I even got you up here! My! But you're heavy!" she reproached him frowningly. "Men ought to stay just as light as they possibly can, so when they get into trouble and things—it would be easier for women to help them. Why, last year in the China Sea—with Father and five of his friends—!"

A trifle shiveringly she shrugged her shoulders. "Oh, well, never mind about Father and the China Sea," she retracted soberly. "It's only that I'm so small, you see, and so flexible—I can crawl 'round most anywhere through port-holes and things—even if they're capsized. So we only lost one of them—one of Father's friends, I mean; and I never would have lost him if he hadn't been so heavy."

"Hours?" gasped Barton irrelevantly. With a wry twist of his neck he peered out through the darkness to where the freshening air, the steady, monotonous slosh-slosh-slosh of rain, the pale intermittent flare of stale lightning, proclaimed the opening of the cave.

"For Heaven's sake, wh-at—what time is it?" he faltered.

"Why, I'm sure I don't know," said little Eve Edgarton. "But I should guess it might be about eight or nine o'clock. Are you hungry?"

With infinite agility she scrambled to her knees and went darting off on all fours like a squirrel into some mysterious, clattery corner of the darkness from which she emerged at last with one little gray flannel arm crooked inclusively around a whole elbowful of treasure.

"There," she drawled. "There. There. There."

Only the soft earthy thud that accompanied each "There" pointed the slightest significance to the word. The first thud was a slim, queer, stone flagon of vodka. Wanly, like some far pinnacle on some far Russian fortress, its grim shape loomed in the sallow lantern light. The second thud was a dust-colored basket of dates from some green-spotted Arabian desert. Vaguely its soft curving outline merged into shadow and turf. The third thud was a battered old drinking-cup—dully silver, mysteriously Chinese. The fourth thud was a big glass jar of frankly American beef. Familiarly, reassuringly, its sleek sides glinted in the flickering flame.

"Supper," announced little Eve Edgarton.

As tomboyishly as a miniature brigand she crawled forward again into the meager square of lantern-tinted earth and, yanking a revolver out of one boot-leg and a pair of scissors from the other, settled herself with unassailable girlishness to jab the delicate scissors-points into the stubborn tin top of the meat jar.

As though the tin had been his own flesh the act goaded Barton half upright into the light—a brightly naked young Viking to the waist, a vaguely shadowed equestrian Fashion Plate to the feet.

"Well—I certainly never saw anybody like you before!" he glowered at her.

With equal gravity but infinitely more deliberation little Eve Edgarton returned the stare. "I never saw anybody like you before, either," she said enigmatically.

Barton winced back into the darkness. "Oh, I say," he stammered. "I wish I had a coat! I feel like a—like a—"

"Why—why?" droned little Eve Edgarton perplexedly. Out from the yellow heart of the pansy-blackness her small, grave, gnomish face peered after him with pristine frankness. "Why—why—I think you look—nice," said little Eve Edgarton.

With a really desperate effort Barton tried to clothe himself in facetiousness, if in nothing else. "Oh, very well," he grinned feebly. "If you don't mind—there's no special reason, I suppose, why I should."

Vaguely, blurrishly, like a figure on the wrong side of a stained-glass window, he began to loom up again into the lantern light. There was no embarrassment certainly about his hunger, nor any affectation at all connected with his thirst. Chokingly from the battered silver cup he gulped down the scorching vodka. Ravenously he attacked the salty meat, the sweet, cloying dates.

Watching him solemn-eyed above her own intermittent nibbles, the girl spoke out quite simply the thought that was uppermost in her mind. "This supper'll come in mighty handy, won't it, if we have to be out here all night, Mr. Barton?"

"If we have to be out here—all night?" faltered Barton.

Oh, ye gods! If just their afternoon ride together had been hotel talk—as of course it was within five minutes after their departure—what would their midnight return be? Or rather their non-return? Already through his addled brain he heard the monotonous creak-creak of rocking-chair gossip, the sly jest of the smoking-room, the whispered excitement of the kitchen—all the sophisticated old worldlings hoping indifferently for the best, all the unsophisticated old prudes yearning ecstatically for the worst!

"If we have to stay out here all night?" he repeated wildly. "Oh, what—oh, what will your father say, Miss Edgarton?"

"What will Father say?" drawled little Eve Edgarton. Thuddingly she set down the empty beef-jar. "Oh, Father'll say: What in creation is Eve out trying to save to-night? A dog? A cat? A three-legged deer?"

"Well, what do you expect to save?" quizzed Barton a bit tartly.

"Just—you," acknowledged little Eve Edgarton without enthusiasm. "And isn't it funny," she confided placidly, "that I've never yet succeeded in saving anything that I could take home with me—and keep! That's the trouble with boarding!"

In a vague, gold-colored flicker of appeal her lifted face flared out again into Barton's darkness. Too fugitive to be called a smile, a tremor of reminiscence went scudding across her mouth before the brooding shadow of her old slouch hat blotted out her features again.

"In India once," persisted the dreary little voice, "in India once, when Father and I were going into the mountains for the summer, there was a—there was a sort of fakir at one of the railway stations doing tricks with a crippled tiger-cub—a tiger-cub with a shot-off paw. And when Father wasn't looking I got off the train and went back—and I followed that fakir two days till he just naturally had to sell me the tiger-cub; he couldn't exactly have an Englishwoman following him indefinitely, you know. And I took the tiger-cub back with me to Father and he was very cunning—but—" Languorously the speech trailed off into indistinctness. "But the people at the hotel were—were indifferent to him," she rallied whisperingly. "And I had to let him go."

"You got off a train? In India? Alone?" snapped Barton. "And went following a dirty, sneaking fakir for two days? Well, of all the crazy—indiscreet—"

"Indiscreet?" mused little Eve Edgarton. Again out of the murky blackness her tilted chin caught up the flare of yellow lantern-light. "Indiscreet?" she repeated monotonously. "Who? I?"

"Yes—you," grunted Barton. "Traipsing 'round all alone—after—"

"But I never am alone, Mr. Barton," protested the mild little voice. "You see I always have the extra saddle, the extra railway ticket, the extra what-ever-it-is. And—and—" Caressingly a little gold-tipped hand reached out through the shadows and patted something indistinctly metallic. "My mother's memory? My father's revolver?" she drawled. "Why, what better company could any girl have? Indiscreet?" Slowly the tip of her little nose tilted up into the light. "Why, down in the Transvaal—two years ago," she explained painstakingly, "why, down in the Transvaal—two years ago—they called me the best-chaperoned girl in Africa. Indiscreet? Why, Mr. Barton, I never even saw an indiscreet woman in all my life. Men, of course, are indiscreet sometimes," she conceded conscientiously. "Down in the Transvaal two years ago, I had to shoot up a couple of men for being a little bit indiscreet, but—"

In one jerk Barton raised himself to a sitting posture.

"You 'shot up' a couple of men?" he demanded peremptorily.

Through the crook of a mud-smeared elbow shoving back the sodden brim of her hat, the girl glanced toward him like a vaguely perplexed little ragamuffin. "It was—messy," she admitted softly. Out from her snarl of storm-blown hair, tattered, battered by wind and rain, she peered up suddenly with her first frowning sign of self-consciousness. "If there's one thing in the world that I regret," she faltered deprecatingly, "it's a—it's—an untidy fight."

Altogether violently Barton burst out laughing. There was no mirth in the laugh, but just noise. "Oh, let's go home!" he suggested hysterically.

"Home?" faltered little Eve Edgarton. With a sluggish sort of defiance she reached out and gathered the big wet scrap-book to her breast. "Why, Mr. Barton," she said, "we couldn't get home now in all this storm and darkness and wash-out—to save our lives. But even if it were moonlight," she singsonged, "and starlight—and high-noon; even if there were—chariots—at the door, I'm not going home—now—till I've finished my scrap-book—if it takes a week."

"Eh?" jerked Barton. "What?" Laboriously he edged himself forward. For five hours now of reckless riding, of storm and privation, through death and disaster, the girl had clung tenaciously to her books and papers. What in creation was in them? "For Heaven's sake—Miss Edgarton—" he began.

"Oh, don't fuss—so," said little Eve Edgarton. "It's nothing but my paper-doll book."

"Your PAPER-DOLL BOOK?" stammered Barton. With another racking effort he edged himself even farther forward. "Miss Edgarton!" he asked quite frankly, "are you—crazy?"

"Your paper-doll book?" stammered Barton

"N—o! But—very determined," drawled little Eve Edgarton. With unruffled serenity she picked up a pulpy magazine-page from the ground in front of her and handed it to him. "And it—would greatly facilitate matters, Mr. Barton," she confided, "if you would kindly begin drying out some papers against your side of the lantern."

"What?" gasped Barton.

Very gingerly he took the pulpy sheet between his thumb and forefinger. It was a full-page picture of a big gas-range, and slowly, as he scanned it for some hidden charm or value, it split in two and fell soggily back to its mates. Once again for sheer nervous relief he burst out laughing.

Out of her diminutiveness, out of her leanness, out of her extraordinary litheness, little Eve Edgarton stared up speculatively at Barton's great hulking helplessness. Her hat looked humorous. Her hair looked humorous. Her tattered flannel shirt was distinctly humorous. But there was nothing humorous about her set little mouth.

"If you—laugh," she threatened, "I'll tip you over backward again—and—trample on you."

"I believe you would!" said Barton with a sudden sobriety more packed with mirth than any laugh he had ever laughed.

"Well, I don't care," conceded the girl a bit sheepishly. "Everybody laughs at my paper-doll book! Father does! Everybody does! When I'm rearranging their old mummy collections—and cataloguing their old South American birds—or shining up their old geological specimens—they think I'm wonderful. But when I try to do the teeniest—tiniest thing that happens to interest me—they call me 'crazy'! So that's why I come 'way out here to this cave—to play," she whispered with a flicker of real shyness. "In all the world," she confided, "this cave is the only place I've ever found where there wasn't anybody to laugh at me."

Between her placid brows a vindictive little frown blackened suddenly. "That's why it wasn't specially convenient, Mr. Barton—to have you ride with me this afternoon," she affirmed. "That's why it wasn't specially convenient to—to have you struck by lightning this afternoon!" Tragically, with one small brown hand, she pointed toward the great water-soaked mess of magazines that surrounded her. "You see," she mourned, "I've been saving them up all summer—to cut out—to-day! And now?—Now—? We're sailing for Melbourne Saturday!" she added conclusively.

"Well—really!" stammered Barton. "Well—truly!—Well, of all—damned things! Why—what do you want me to do? Apologize to you for having been struck by lightning?" His voice was fairly riotous with astonishment and indignation. Then quite unexpectedly one side of his mouth began to twist upward in the faintest perceptible sort of a real grin.

"When you smile like that you're—quite pleasant," murmured little Eve Edgarton.

"Is that so?" grinned Barton. "Well, it wouldn't hurt you to smile just a tiny bit now and then!"

"Wouldn't it?" said little Eve Edgarton. Thoughtfully for a moment, with her scissors poised high in the air, she seemed to be considering the suggestion. Then quite abruptly again she resumed her task of prying some pasted object out of her scrap-book. "Oh, no, thank you, Mr. Barton," she decided. "I'm much too bored—all the while—to do any smiling."

"Bored?" snapped Barton. Staring perplexedly into her dreary, meek little face, something deeper, something infinitely subtler than mere curiosity, wakened precipitately in his consciousness. "For Heaven's sake, Miss Edgarton!" he stammered. "From the Arctic Ocean to the South Seas, if you've seen all the things that you must have seen, if you've done all the things that you must have done—WHY SHOULD YOU LOOK SO BORED?"

Flutteringly the girl's eyes lifted and fell. "Why, I'm bored, Mr. Barton," drawled little Eve Edgarton, "I'm bored because—I'm sick to death—of seeing all the things I've seen. I'm sick to death of—doing all the things I've done." With little metallic snips of sound she concentrated herself and her scissors suddenly upon the mahogany-colored picture of a pianola.

"Well, what do you want?" quizzed Barton.

In a sullen, turgid sort of defiance the girl lifted her somber eyes to his. "I want to stay home—like other people—and have a house," she wailed. "I want a house—and—the things that go with a house: a cat, and the things that go with a cat; kittens, and the things that go with kittens; saucers of cream, and the things that go with saucers of cream; ice-chests, and—and—" Surprisingly into her languid, sing-song tone broke a sudden note of passion. "Bah!" she snapped. "Think of going all the way to India just to plunge your arms into the spooky, foamy Ganges and 'make a wish'! 'What do you wish?' asks Father, pleased-as a Chessy-puss. Humph! I wish it was the soap-suds in my own wash-tub!—Or gallivanting down to British Guiana just to smell the great blowsy water-lilies in the canals! I'd rather smell burned crackers in my own cook stove!"

"But you'll surely have a house—some time," argued Barton with real sympathy. Quite against all intention the girl's unexpected emotion disturbed him a little. "Every girl gets a house—some time!" he insisted resolutely.

"N—o, I don't—think so," mused Eve Edgarton judicially. "You see," she explained with soft, slow deliberation, "you see, Mr. Barton, only people who live in houses know people who live in houses! If you're a nomad you meet—only nomads! Campers mate just naturally with campers, and ocean-travelers with ocean-travelers—and red-velvet hotel-dwellers with red-velvet hotel-dwellers. Oh, of course, if Mother had lived it might have been different," she added a trifle more cheerfully. "For, of course, if Mother had lived I should have been—pretty," she asserted calmly, "or interesting-looking, anyway. Mother would surely have managed it—somehow; and I should have had a lot of beaux—young men beaux I mean, like you. Father's friends are all so gray!—Oh, of course, I shall marry—some time," she continued evenly. "Probably I'm going to marry the British consul at Nunko-Nono. He's a great friend of Father's—and he wants me to help him write a book on 'The Geologic Relationship of Melanesia to the Australian Continent'!"

Dully her voice rose to its monotone: "But I don't suppose—we shall live in a—house," she moaned apathetically. "At the best it will probably be only a musty room or two up over the consulate—and more likely than not it won't be anything at all except a nipa hut and a typewriter-table."

As if some mote of dust disturbed her, suddenly she rubbed the knuckles of one hand across her eyes. "But maybe we'll have—daughters," she persisted undauntedly. "And maybe they'll have houses!"

"Oh, shucks!" said Barton uneasily. "A—a house isn't so much!"

"It—isn't?" asked little Eve Edgarton incredulously. "Why—why—you don't mean—"

"Don't mean—what?" puzzled Barton.

"Do—you—live—in—a—house?" asked little Eve Edgarton abruptly. Her hands were suddenly quiet in her lap, her tousled head cocked ever so slightly to one side, her sluggish eyes incredibly dilated.

"Why, of course I live in a house," laughed Barton.

"O—h," breathed little Eve Edgarton. "Re—ally? It must be wonderful." Wiltingly her eyes, her hands, drooped back to her scrap-book again. "In—all—my—life," she resumed monotonously, "I've never spent a single night—in a real house."

"What?" questioned Barton.

"Oh, of course," explained the girl dully, "of course I've spent no end of nights in hotels and camps and huts and trains and steamers and—But—What color is your house?" she asked casually.

"Why, brown, I guess," said Barton.

"Brown, you 'guess'?" whispered the girl pitifully. "Don't you—know?"

"No, I wouldn't exactly like to swear to it," grinned Barton a bit sheepishly.

Again the girl's eyes lifted just a bit over-intently from the work in her lap.

"What color is the wall-paper—in your own room?" she asked casually. "Is it—is it a—dear pinkie-posie sort of effect? Or just plain—shaded stripes?"

"Why, I'm sure I don't remember," acknowledged Barton worriedly. "Why, it's just paper, you know—paper," he floundered helplessly. "Red, green, brown, white—maybe it's white," he asserted experimentally. "Oh, for goodness' sake—how should I know!" he collapsed at last. "When my sisters were home from Europe last year, they fixed the whole blooming place over for—some kind of a party. But I don't know that I ever specially noticed just what it was that they did to it. Oh, it's all right, you know!" he attested with some emphasis. "Oh, it's all right enough—early Jacobean, or something like that—'perfectly corking,' everybody calls it! But it's so everlasting big, and it costs so much to run it, and I've lost such a wicked lot of money this year, that I'm not going to keep it after this autumn—if my sisters ever send me their Paris address so I'll know what to do with their things."

Frowningly little Eve Edgarton bent forward.

"'Some kind of a party?'" she repeated in unconscious mimicry. "You mean you gave a party? A real Christian party? As recently as last winter? And you can't even remember what kind of a party it was?" Something in her slender brown throat fluttered ever so slightly. "Why, I've never even been to a Christian party—in all my life!" she said. "Though I can dance in every language of Asia!

"And you've got sisters?" she stammered. "Live silk-and-muslin sisters? And you don't even know where they are? Why, I've never even had a girl friend in all my life!"

Incredulously she lifted her puzzled eyes to his. "And you've got a house?" she faltered. "And you're not going to keep it? A real—truly house? And you don't even know what color it is? You don't even know what color your own room is? And I know the name of every house-paint there is in the world," she muttered, "and the name of every wall-paper there is in the world, and the name of every carpet, and the name of every curtain, and the name of—everything. And I haven't got any house at all—"

Then startlingly, without the slightest warning, she pitched forward suddenly on her face and lay clutching into the turf—a little dust-colored wisp of a boyish figure sobbing its starved heart out against a dust-colored earth.

"Why—what's the matter!" gasped Barton. "Why!—Why—Kid!" Very laboriously with his numbed hands, with his strange, unresponsive legs, he edged himself forward a little till he could just reach her shoulder. "Why—Kid!" he patted her rather clumsily. "Why, Kid—do you mean—"

Slowly through the darkness Eve Edgarton came crawling to his side. Solemnly she lifted her eyes to Barton's. "I'll tell you something that Mother told me," she murmured. "This is it: 'Your father is the most wonderful man that ever lived,' my mother whispered to me quite distinctly. 'But he'll never make any home for you—except in his arms; and that is plenty Home-Enough for a wife—but not nearly Home-Enough for a daughter! And—and—"

"Why, you say it as if you knew it by heart," interrupted Barton.

"Why, of course I know it by heart!" cried little Eve Edgarton almost eagerly. "My mother whispered it to me, I tell you! The things that people shout at you—you forget in half a night. But the things that people whisper to you, you remember to your dying day!"

"If I whisper something to you," said Barton quite impulsively, "will you promise to remember it to your dying day?"

"Oh, yes, Mr. Barton," droned little Eve Edgarton.

Abruptly Barton reached out and tilted her chin up whitely toward him. "In this light," he whispered, "with your hat pushed back like—that!—and your hair fluffed up like—that!—and the little laugh in your eyes!—and the flush!—and the quiver!—you look like an—elf! A bronze and gold elf! You're wonderful! You're magical! You ought always to dress like that! Somebody ought to tell you about it! Woodsy, storm-colored clothes with little quick glints of light in them! Paquin or some of those people could make you famous!"

As spontaneously as he had touched her he jerked his hand away, and, snatching up the lantern, flashed it bluntly on her astonished face.

For one brief instant her hand went creeping up to the tip of her chin. Then very soberly, like a child with a lesson, she began to repeat Barton's impulsive phrases.

"'In this light,'" she droned, "'with your hat pushed back like that—and your hair fluffed up like that—and the—the—'" More unexpectedly then than anything that could possibly have happened she burst out laughing—a little low, giggly, school-girlish sort of laugh. "Oh, that's easy to remember!" she announced. Then, all one narrow black silhouette again, she crouched down into the semi-darkness.

"For a lady," she resumed listlessly, "who rode side-saddle and really enjoyed hiking 'round all over the sticky face of the globe, my mother certainly did guess pretty keenly just how things were going to be with me. I'll tell you what she said to sustain me," she repeated dreamily, "'Any foolish woman can keep house, but the woman who travels with your father has got to be able to keep the whole wide world for him! It's nations that you'll have to put to bed! And suns and moons and stars that you'll have to keep scoured and bright! But with the whole green earth for your carpet, and shining heaven for your roof-tree, and God Himself for your landlord, now wouldn't you be a fool, if you weren't quite satisfied?'"

"'If—you—weren't—quite satisfied,'" finished Barton mumblingly.

Little Eve Edgarton lifted her great eyes, soft with sorrow, sharp with tears, almost defiantly to Barton's.

"That's—what—Mother said," she faltered. "But all the same—I'd RATHER HAVE A HOUSE!"

"Why, you poor kid!" said Barton. "You ought to have a house! It's a shame! It's a beastly shame! It's a—"

Very softly in the darkness his hand grazed hers.

"Did you touch my hand on purpose, or just accidentally?" asked Eve Edgarton, without a flicker of expression on her upturned, gold-colored face.

"Why, I'm sure I don't know," laughed Barton. "Maybe—maybe it was a little of each."

With absolute gravity little Eve Edgarton kept right on staring at him. "I don't know whether I should ever specially like you—or not, Mr. Barton," she drawled. "But you are certainly very beautiful!"

"Oh, I say!" cried Barton wretchedly. With a really desperate effort he struggled almost to his feet, tottered for an instant, and then came sagging down to the soft earth again—a great, sprawling, spineless heap, at little Eve Edgarton's feet.

Unflinchingly, as if her wrists were built of steel wires, the girl jumped up and pulled and tugged and yanked his almost dead weight into a sitting posture again.

"My! But you're chock-full of lightning!" she commiserated with him.

Out of the utter rage and mortification of his helplessness Barton could almost have cursed her for her sympathy. Then suddenly, without warning, a little gasp of sheer tenderness escaped him.

"Eve Edgarton," he stammered, "you're—a—brick! You—you must have been invented just for the sole purpose of saving people's lives. Oh, you've saved mine all right!" he acknowledged soberly. "And all this black, blasted night you've nursed me—and fed me—and jollied me—without a whimper about yourself—without—a—" Impulsively he reached out his numb-palmed hand to her, and her own hand came so cold to it that it might have been the caress of one ghost to another. "Eve Edgarton," he reiterated, "I tell you—you're a brick! And I'm a fool—and a slob—and a mutt-head—even when I'm not chock-full of lightning, as you call it! But if there's ever anything I can do for you!"

"What did you say?" muttered little Eve Edgarton.

"I said you were a brick!" repeated Barton a bit irritably.

"Oh, no, I didn't mean—that," mused the girl. "But what was the—last thing you said?"

"Oh!" grinned Barton more cheerfully. "I said—if there was ever anything that I could do for you, anything—"

"Would you rent me your attic?" asked little Eve Edgarton.

"Would I rent you my attic?" stammered Barton. "Why in the world should you want to hire my attic?"

"So I could buy pretty things in Siam—or Ceylon—or any other queer country—and have some place to send them," said little Eve Edgarton. "Oh, I'd pay the express, Mr. Barton," she hastened to assure him. "Oh, I promise you there never would be any trouble about the express! Or about the rent!" Expeditiously as she spoke she reached for her hip pocket and brought out a roll of bills that fairly took Barton's breath away. "If there's one thing in the world, you know, that I've got, it's money," she confided perfectly simply. "So you see, Mr. Barton," she added with sudden wistfulness, "there's almost nothing on the face of the globe that I couldn't have—if I only had some place to put it." Without further parleying she proffered the roll of bills to him.

"Miss Edgarton! Are you crazy?" Barton asked again quite precipitously.

Again the girl answered his question equally frankly, and without offense. "Oh, no," she said. "Only very determined."

"Determined about what?" grinned Barton in spite of himself.

"Determined about an attic," drawled little Eve Edgarton.

With an unwonted touch of vivacity she threw out one hand in a little, sharp gesture of appeal; but not a tone of her voice either quickened or deepened.

"Why, Mr. Barton," she droned, "I'm thirty years old—and ever since I was born I've been traveling all over the world—in a steamer trunk. In a steamer trunk, mind you. With Father always standing over every packing to make sure that we never carry anything that—isn't necessary. With Father, I said," she re-emphasized by a sudden distinctness. "You know Father!" she added significantly.

"Yes—I know 'Father,'" assented Barton with astonishing glibness.

Once again the girl threw out her hand in an incongruous gesture of appeal.

"The things that Father thinks are necessary!" she exclaimed softly. Noiselessly as a shadow she edged herself forward into the light till she faced Barton almost squarely. "Maybe you think it's fun, Mr. Barton," she whispered. "Maybe you think it's fun—at thirty years of age—with all your faculties intact—to own nothing in the world except—except a steamer trunkful of the things that Father thinks are necessary!"

Very painstakingly on the fingers of one hand she began to enumerate the articles in question. "Just your riding togs," she said, "and six suits of underwear—and all the United States consular reports—and two or three wash dresses and two 'good enough' dresses—and a lot of quinine—and—a squashed hat—and—and—" Very faintly the ghost of a smile went flickering over her lips—"and whatever microscopes and specimen-cases get crowded out of Father's trunk. What's the use, Mr. Barton," she questioned, "of spending a whole year investigating the silk industry of China—if you can't take any of the silks home? What's the use, Mr. Barton, of rolling up your sleeves and working six months in a heathen porcelain factory—just to study glaze—if you don't own a china-closet in any city on the face of the earth? Why—sometimes, Mr. Barton," she confided, "it seems as if I'd die a horrible death if I couldn't buy things the way other people do—and send them somewhere—even if it wasn't 'home'! The world is so full of beautiful things," she mused. "White enamel bath-tubs—and Persian rugs—and the most ingenious little egg-beaters—and—"

"Eh?" stammered Barton. Quite desperately he rummaged his brain for some sane-sounding expression of understanding and sympathy.

"You could, I suppose," he ventured, not too intelligently, "buy the things and give them to other people."

"Oh, yes, of course," conceded little Eve Edgarton without enthusiasm. "Oh, yes, of course, you can always buy people the things they want. But understand," she said, "there's very little satisfaction in buying the things you want to give to people who don't want them. I tried it once," she confided, "and it didn't work.

"The winter we were in Paraguay," she went on, "in some stale old English newspaper I saw an advertisement of a white bedroom set. There were eleven pieces, and it was adorable, and it cost eighty-two pounds—and I thought after I'd had the fun of unpacking it, I could give it to a woman I knew who had a tea plantation. But the instant she got it—she painted it—green! Now when you send to England for eleven pieces of furniture because they are white," sighed little Eve Edgarton, "and have them crated—because they're white—and sent to sea because they're white—and then carried overland—miles and miles and miles—on Indians' heads—because they're white, you sort of want 'em to stay white. Oh, of course it's all right," she acknowledged patiently. "The Tea Woman was nice, and the green paint by no means—altogether bad. Only, looking back now on our winter in Paraguay, I seem to have missed somehow the particular thrill that I paid eighty-two pounds and all that freightage for."

"Yes, of course," agreed Barton. He could see that.

"So if you could rent me your attic—" she resumed almost blithely.

"But my dear child," interrupted Barton, "what possible—"

"Why—I'd have a place then to send things to," argued little Eve Edgarton.

"But you're off on the high seas Saturday, you say," laughed Barton.

"Yes, I know," explained little Eve Edgarton just a bit impatiently. "But the high seas are so dull, Mr. Barton. And then we sail so long!" she complained. "And so far!—via this, via that, via every other stupid old port in the world! Why, it will be months and months before we ever reach Melbourne! And of course on every steamer," she began to monotone, "of course on every steamer there'll be some one with a mixed-up collection of shells or coins—and that will take all my mornings. And of course on every steamer there'll be somebody struggling with the Chinese alphabet or the Burmese accents—and that will take all my afternoons. But in the evenings when people are just having fun," she kindled again, "and nobody wants me for anything, why, then you see I could steal 'way up in the bow—where you're not allowed to go—and think about my beautiful attic. It's pretty lonesome," she whispered, "all snuggled up there alone with the night, and the spray and the sailors' shouts, if you haven't got anything at all to think about except just 'What's ahead?—What's ahead?—What's ahead?' And even that belongs to God," she sighed a bit ruefully.

With a quick jerk she edged herself even closer to Barton and sat staring up at him with her tousled head cocked on one side like an eager terrier.

"So if you just—could, Mr. Barton!" she began all over again. "And oh, I know it couldn't be any real bother to you!" she hastened to reassure him. "Because after Saturday, you know, I'll probably never—never be in America again!"

"Then what satisfaction," laughed Barton, "could you possibly get in filling up an attic with things that you will never see again?"

"What satisfaction?" repeated little Eve Edgarton perplexedly. "What satisfaction?" Between her placid brows a very black frown deepened. "Why, just the satisfaction," she said, "of knowing before you die, that you had definitely diverted to your own personality that much specific treasure out of the—out of the—world's chaotic maelstrom of generalities."

"Eh?" said Barton. "What? For Heaven's sake say it again!"

"Why—just the satisfaction—" began Eve Edgarton. Then abruptly the sullen lines grayed down again around her mouth.

"It seems funny to me, Mr. Barton," she almost whined, "that anybody as big as you are—shouldn't be able to understand anybody as little as—I am. But if I only had an attic!" she cried out with apparent irrelevance. "Oh, if just once in my whole life I could have even so much as an atticful of home! Oh, please—please—please, Mr. Barton!" she pleaded. "Oh, please!"

Precipitously she lifted her small brown face to his, and in her eyes he saw the strangest little unfinished expression flame up suddenly and go out again, a little fleeting expression so sweet, so shy, so transcendently lovely, that if it had ever lived to reach her frowning brow, her sulky little mouth, her—!

Then startlingly into his stare, into his amazement, broke a great white glare through the opening of the cave.

"My God!" he winced, with his elbow across his eyes.

"Why, it isn't lightning!" laughed little Eve Edgarton. "It's the moon!" Quick as a sprite she flashed to her feet and ran out into the moonlight. "We can go home now!" she called back triumphantly over her shoulder.

"Oh, we can, can we?" snapped Barton. His nerves were strangely raw. He struggled to his knees, and tottered there watching the cheeky little moonbeams lap up the mystery of the cave, and scare the yellow lantern-flame into a mere sallow glow.

Poignantly from the forest he heard Eve Edgarton's voice calling out into the night. "Come—Mother's—horse! Come—Mother's—horse H—o—o, hoo! Come—come—come!" Softly above the crackle of twigs, the thud of a hoof, the creak of a saddle, he sensed the long, tremulous, answering whinny. Then almost like a silver apparition the girl's figure and the horse's seemed to merge together before him in the moonlight.

"Well—of—all—things!" stammered Barton.

"Oh, the horse is all right. I thought he'd stay 'round," called the girl. "But he's wild as a hawk—and it's going to be the dickens of a job, I'm afraid, to get you up."

Half walking, half crawling, Barton emerged from the cave. "To get me up?" he scoffed. "Well, what do you think you're going to do?" Limply as he asked he sank back against the support of a tree.

"Why, I think," drawled Eve Edgarton, "I think—very naturally—that you're going to ride—and I'm going to walk—back to the hotel."

"Well, I am not!" snapped Barton. "Well, you are not!" he protested vehemently. "For Heaven's sake, Miss Edgarton, why don't you go scooting back on the gray and send a wagon or something for me?"

"Why, because it would make—such a fuss," droned little Eve Edgarton drearily. "Doors would bang—and lights would blaze—and somebody'd scream—and—and—you make so much fuss when you're born," she said, "and so much fuss when you die—don't you think it's sort of nice to keep things as quietly to yourself as you can all the rest of your days?"

"Yes, of course," acknowledged Barton. "But—"

"But NOTHING!" stamped little Eve Edgarton with sudden passion. "Oh, Mr. Barton—won't you please hurry! It's almost dawn now! And the nice hotel cook is very sick in a cot bed. And I promised her faithfully this noon that I'd make four hundred muffins for breakfast!"

"Oh, confound it!" said Barton.

Stumblingly he reached the big gray's side.

"But it's miles!" he protested in common decency. "Miles!—and miles! Rough walking, too, darned rough! And your poor little feet—"

"I don't walk particularly with my 'poor little feet,'" gibed Eve Edgarton. "Most especially, thank you, Mr. Barton, I walk with my big wanting-to-walk!"

"Oh," said Barton. "O—h." The bones in his knees began suddenly to slump like so many knots of tissue-paper. "Oh—all right—Eve!" he called out a bit hazily.

Then slowly and laboriously, with a very good imitation of meekness, he allowed himself to be pulled and pushed and jerked to the top of an old tree-stump, and from there at last, with many tricks and tugs and subterfuges, to the cramping side-saddle of the restive, rearing gray. Helplessly in the clear white moonlight he watched the girl's neck muscles cord and strain. Helplessly in the clear white moonlight he heard the girl's breath rip and tear like a dry sob out of her gasping lungs. And then at last, blinded with sweat, dizzy with weakness, as breathless as herself, as wrenched, as triumphant, he found himself clinging fast to a worn suede pommel, jogging jerkily down the mountainside with Eve Edgarton's doll-sized hand dragging hard on the big gray's curb and her whole tiny weight shoved back aslant and astrain against the big gray's too eager shoulder—little droll, colorless, "meek" Eve Edgarton, after her night of stress and terror, with her precious scrap-book still hugged tight under one arm striding stanchly home through the rough-footed, woodsy night to "make four hundred muffins for breakfast!"

At the first crook in the trail she glanced back hastily over her shoulder into the rustling shadows. "Good-by, Cave!" she called softly. "Good-by, Cave!" And once when some tiny woods-animal scuttled out from under her feet she smiled up a bit appealingly at Barton. Several times they stopped for water at some sudden noisy brook. And once, or twice, or even three times perhaps, when some blinding daze of dizziness overwhelmed him, she climbed up with one foot into the roomy stirrup and steadied his swaying, unfeeling body against her own little harsh, reassuring, flannel-shirted breast.

Mile after mile through the jet-black lattice-work of the tree-tops the August moon spotted brightly down on them. Mile after mile through rolling pastures the moon-plaited stubble crackled and sucked like a sheet of wet ice under their feet, then roads began—mere molten bogs of mud and moonlight; and little frail roadside bushes drunk with rain lay wallowing helplessly in every hollow.

Out of this pristine, uninhabited wilderness the hotel buildings loomed at last with startling conventionality. Even before their discreetly shuttered windows Barton winced back again with a sudden horrid new realization of his half-nakedness.

"For Heaven's sake!" he cried, "let's sneak in the back way somewhere! Oh Lordy!—what a sight I am to meet your father!"

"What a sight you are to—meet my father?" repeated Eve Edgarton with astonishment. "Oh, please don't insist on waking up Father," she begged. "He hates so to be waked up. Oh, of course if I'd been hurt it would have been courteous of you to tell him," she explained seriously. "But, oh, I'm sure he wouldn't like your waking him up just to tell him that you got hurt!"

Softly under her breath she began to whistle toward a shadow in the stable-yard. "Usually," she whispered, "there's a sleepy stable-boy lying round here somewhere. Oh—Bob!" she summoned.

Rollingly the shadow named "Bob" struggled to its very real feet.

"Here, Bob!" she ordered. "Come help Mr. Barton. He's pretty badly off. We got sort of struck by lightning. And two of us—got killed. Go help him up-stairs. Do anything he wants. But don't make any fuss. He'll be all right in the morning."

Gravely she put out her hand to Barton, and nodded to the boy.

"Good night!" she said. "And good night, Bob!"

Shrewdly for a moment she stood watching them out of sight, shivered a little at the clatter of a box kicked over in some remote shed, and then swinging round quickly, ripped the hot saddle from the big gray's back, slipped the bit from his tortured tongue, and, turning him loose with one sharp slap on his gleaming flank, yanked off her own riding-boots and went scudding off in her stocking-feet through innumerable doors and else till, reaching the great empty office, she caromed off suddenly up three flights of stairs to her own apartment.

Once in her room her little traveling-clock told her it was a quarter of three.

"Whew!" she said. Just "Whew!" Very furiously at the big porcelain washbowl she began to splash and splash and splash. "If I've got to make four hundred muffins," she said, "I surely have got to be whiter than snow!"

Roused by the racket, her father came irritably and stood in the doorway.

"Oh, my dear Eve!" he complained, "didn't you get wet enough in the storm? And for mercy's sake where have you been?"

Out of the depths of her dripping hair and her big plushy bath-towel little Eve Edgarton considered her father only casually.

"Don't delay me!" she said, "I've got to make four hundred muffins."

"Don't delay me!" she said, "I've got to make four hundred muffins! And I'm so late I haven't even time to change my clothes! We got struck by lightning," she added purely incidentally. "That is—sort of struck by lightning. That is, Mr. Barton got sort of struck by lightning. And oh, glory, Father!" her voice kindled a little. "And, oh, glory, Father, I thought he was gone! Twice in the hours I was working over him he stopped breathing altogether!"

Palpably the vigor died out of her voice again. "Father," she drawled mumblingly through intermittent flops of bath-towel; "Father—you said I could keep the next thing I—saved. Do you think I could—keep him?"

CHAPTER III

"What?" demanded her father.
Altogether unexpectedly little Eve Edgarton threw back her tousled head and burst out laughing.
"Oh, Father!" she jeered. "Can't you take a joke?"
"I don't know as you ever offered me one before," growled her father a bit ungraciously.
"All the same," asserted little Eve Edgarton with sudden seriousness—"all the same, Father, he did stop breathing twice. And I worked and I worked and I worked over him!" Slowly her great eyes widened.
"And oh, Father, his skin!" she whispered simply.
"Hush!" snapped her father with a great gust of resentment that he took to be a gust of propriety. "Hush, I say! I tell you it isn't delicate for a—for a girl to talk about a man's skin!"
"Oh—but his skin was very delicate," mused little Eve Edgarton persistently. "There in the lantern light—"
"What lantern light?" demanded her father.
"And the moonlight," murmured little Eve Edgarton.
"What moonlight?" demanded her father. A trifle quizzically he stepped forward and peered into his daughter's face. "Personally, Eve," he said, "I don't care for the young man. And I certainly don't wish to hear anything about his skin. Not anything! Do you understand? I'm very glad you saved his life," he hastened to affirm. "It was very commendable of you, I'm sure, and some one, doubtless, will be very much relieved. But for me personally the incident is closed! Closed, I said. Do you understand?"
Bruskly he turned back toward his own room, and then swung around again suddenly in the doorway.
"Eve," he frowned. "That was a joke—wasn't it?—what you said about wanting to keep that young man?"
"Why, of course!" said little Eve Edgarton.
"Well, I must say—it was an exceedingly clumsy one!" growled her father irritably.
"Maybe so," droned little Eve Edgarton with unruffled serenity. "It was the first joke, you see, that I ever made." Slowly again her eyes began to widen. "All the same, Father," she said, "his—"
"Hush!" he ordered, and slammed the door conclusively behind him.
Very thoughtfully for a moment little Eve Edgarton kept right on standing there in the middle of the room. In her eyes was just the faintest possible suggestion of a smile. But there was no smile whatsoever about her lips. Her lips indeed were quite drawn and most flagrantly set with the expression of one who, having something determinate to say, will—yet—say it, somewhere, sometime, somehow, though the skies fall and all the waters of the earth dry up.

Then like the dart of a bird, she flashed to her father's door and opened it.

"Father!" she whispered. "Father!"

"Yes," answered the half-muffled, pillowy voice. "What is it?"

"Oh, I forgot to tell you something that happened once—down in Indo-China," whispered little Eve Edgarton. "Once when you were away," she confided breathlessly, "I pulled a half-drowned coolie out of a canal."

"Well, what of it?" asked her father a bit tartly.

"Oh, nothing special," said little Eve Edgarton, "except that his skin was like yellow parchment! And sandpaper! And old plaster!"

Without further ado then, she turned away, and, except for the single ecstatic episode of making the four hundred muffins for breakfast, resumed her pulseless role of being just—little Eve Edgarton.

As for Barton, the subsequent morning hours brought sleep and sleep only—the sort of sleep that fairly souses the senses in oblivion, weighing the limbs with lead, the brain with stupor, till the sleeper rolls out from under the load at last like one half paralyzed with cramp and helplessness.

Certainly it was long after noon-time before Barton actually rallied his aching bones, his dizzy head, his refractory inclinations, to meet the fluctuant sympathy and chaff that awaited him down-stairs in every nook and corner of the great, idle-minded hotel.

Conscientiously, but without enthusiasm, from the temporary retreat of the men's writing-room, he sent up his card at last to Mr. Edgarton, and was duly informed that that gentleman and his daughter were mountain-climbing. In an absurd flare of disappointment then, he edged his way out through the prattling piazza groups to the shouting tennis players, and on from the shouting tennis players to the teasing golfers, and back from the teasing golfers to the peaceful writing-room, where in a great, lazy chair by the open window he settled down once more with unwonted morbidness to brood over the grimly bizarre happenings of the previous night.

In a soft blur of sound and sense the names of other people came wafting to him from time to time, and once or twice at least the word "Barton" shrilled out at him with astonishing poignancy. Still like a man half drugged he dozed again—and woke in a vague, sweating terror—and dozed again—and dreamed again—and roused himself at last with the one violent determination to hook his slipping consciousness, whether or no, into the nearest conversation that he could reach.

The conversation going on at the moment just outside his window was not a particularly interesting one to hook one's attention into, but at least it was fairly distinct. In blissfully rational human voices two unknown men were discussing the non-domesticity of the modern woman. It was not an erudite discussion, but just a mere personal complaint.

"I had a house," wailed one, "the nicest, coziest house you ever saw. We were two years building it. And there was a garden—a real jim-dandy flower and vegetable garden—and there were twenty-seven fruit-trees. But my wife—" the wail deepened—"my wife—she just would live in a hotel! Couldn't stand the 'strain,' she said, of 'planning food three times a day'! Not—'couldn't stand the strain of earning meals three times a day'—you understand," the wailing voice added significantly, "but couldn't stand the strain of ordering 'em. People all around you, you know, starving to death for just—bread; but she couldn't stand the strain of having to decide between squab and tenderloin! Eh?"

"Oh, Lordy! You can't tell me anything!" snapped the other voice more incisively. "Houses? I've had four! First it was the cellar my wife wanted to eliminate! Then it was the attic! Then it was—We're living in an apartment now!" he finished abruptly. "An apartment, mind you! One of those blankety—blank—blank apartments!"

"Humph!" wailed the first voice again. "There's hardly a woman you meet these days who hasn't got rouge on her cheeks, but a man's got to go back—two generations, I guess, if he wants to find one that's got any flour on her nose!"

"Flour on her nose?" interrupted the sharper voice. "Flour on her nose? Oh, ye gods! I don't believe there's a woman in this whole hotel who'd know flour if she saw it! Women don't care any more, I tell you! They don't care!"

Just as a mere bit of physical stimulus the crescendoish stridency of the speech roused Barton to a lazy smile. Then, altogether unexpectedly, across indifference, across drowsiness, across absolute physical and mental non-concern, the idea behind the speech came hurtling to him and started him bolt upright in his chair.

"Ha!" he thought. "I know a girl that cares!" From head to foot a sudden warm sense of satisfaction glowed through him, a throb of pride, a puffiness of the chest. "Ha!" he gloated. "H—"

Then interruptingly from outside the window he heard the click of chairs hitching a bit nearer together.

"Sst!" whispered one voice. "Who's the freak in the 1830 clothes?"

"Why, that? Why, that's the little Edgarton girl," piped the other voice cautiously. "It isn't so much the '1830 clothes' as the 1830 expression that gets me! Where in creation—"

"Oh, upon my soul," groaned the man whose wife "would live in a hotel." "Oh, upon my soul—if there's one thing that I can't stand it's a woman who hasn't any style! If I had my way," he threatened with hissing emphasis, "if I had my way, I tell you, I'd have every homely looking woman in the world put out of her misery! Put out of my misery—is what I mean!"

"Ha! Ha! Ha!" chuckled the other voice.

"Ha! Ha! Ha!" gibed both voices ecstatically together.

With quite unnecessary haste Barton sprang to the window and looked out.

It was Eve Edgarton! And she did look funny! Not especially funny, but just plain, every-day little-Eve-Edgarton funny, in a shabby old English tramping suit, with a knapsack slung askew across one shoulder, a faded Alpine hat yanked down across her eyes, and one steel-wristed little hand dragging a mountain laurel bush almost as big as herself. Close behind her followed her father, equally shabby, his shapeless pockets fairly bulging with rocks, a battered tin botany kit in one hand, a dingy black camera-box in the other.

Impulsively Barton started out to meet them, but just a step from the threshold of the piazza door he sensed for the first time the long line of smokers watching the two figures grinningly above their puffy brown pipes and cigars.

"What is it?" called one smoker to another. "Moving Day in Jungle Town?"

"Ha! Ha! Ha!" tittered the whole line of smokers. "Ha!—Ha! Ha! Ha!—Ha!"

So, because he belonged, not so much to the type of person that can't stand having its friends laughed at, as to the type that can't stand having friends who are liable to be laughed at, Barton changed his mind quite precipitately about identifying himself at that particular moment with the Edgarton family, and whirled back instead to the writing-room. There, by the aid of the hotel clerk, and two bell-boys, and three new blotters, and a different pen, and an entirely fresh bottle of ink, and just exactly the right-sized, the right-tinted sort of letter paper, he concocted a perfectly charming note to little Eve Edgarton—a note full of compliment, of gratitude, of sincere appreciation, a note reiterating even once more his persistent intention of rendering her somewhere, sometime, a really significant service!

Whereupon, thus duly relieved of his truly honest effort at self-expression, he went back again to his own kind—to the prattling, the well-groomed, the ultra-fashionables of both mind and body. And there on the shining tennis-courts and the soft golf greens, through the late yellow afternoon and the first gray threat of twilight, the old sickening ennui came creeping back to his senses, warring chaotically there with the natural nervous reaction of his recent adventure, till just out of sheer morbid unrest, as soon as the flower-scented, candle-lighted dinner hour was over, he went stalking round and round the interminable piazzas, hunting in every dark corner for Mr. Edgarton and his daughter.

Meeting them abruptly at last in the full glare of the office, he clutched fatuously at Mr. Edgarton's reluctant attention with some quick question about the extraordinary moonlight, and stood by, grinning like any bashful schoolboy, while Mr. Edgarton explained to him severely, as if it were his fault, just why and to what extent the radii of mountain moonlight differed from the radii of any other kind of moonlight, and Eve herself, in absolute spiritual remoteness, stood patiently shifting her weight from one foot to the other, staring abstractedly all the time at the floor under her feet.

Right into the midst of this instructive discourse broke one of Barton's men friends with a sharp jog of his elbow, and a brief, apologetic nod to the Edgartons.

"Oh, I say, Barton!" cried the newcomer, breathlessly. "That wedding, you know, over across at the Kentons' to-night, with the Viennese orchestra—and Heaven knows what from New York? Well, we've shanghaied the whole business for a dance here to-morrow night! Music! Flowers! Palms! Catering! Everything! It's going to be the biggest little dancing party that this slice of North American scenery ever saw! And—"

Slowly little Eve Edgarton lifted her great solemn eyes to the newcomer's face.

"A party?" she drawled. "A—a—dancing party—you mean? A real—Christian—dancing party?"

Dully the big eyes drooped again, and as if in mere casual mannerism her little brown hands went creeping up to the white breast of her gown. Then just as startling, just-as unprovable as the flash of a shooting star, her glance flashed up at Barton.

"O—h!" gasped little Eve Edgarton.

"O—h!" said Barton.

Astoundingly in his ears bells seemed suddenly to be ringing. His head was awhirl, his pulses fairly pounding with the weird, quixotic purport of his impulse.

"Miss Edgarton," he began. "Miss—"

Then right behind him two older men joggled him awkwardly in passing.

"—and that Miss Von Eaton," chuckled one man to another. "Lordy! There'll be more than forty men after her for to-morrow night! Smith! Arnold! Hudson! Hazeltine! Who are you betting will get her?"

"I'M BETTING THAT I WILL!" crashed every brutally competitive male instinct in Barton's body. Impetuously he broke away from the Edgartons and darted off to find Miss Von Eaton before "Smith—Arnold—Hudson—Hazeltine"—or any other man should find her!

So he sent little Eve Edgarton a great, gorgeous box of candy instead, wonderful candy, pounds and pounds of it, fine, fluted chocolates, and rose-pink bonbons, and fat, sugared violets, and all sorts of tin-foiled mysteries of fruit and spice.

And when the night of the party came he strutted triumphantly to it with Helene Von Eaton, who already at twenty was beginning to be just a little bit bored with parties; and together through all that riot of music and flowers and rainbow colors and dazzling lights they trotted and tangoed with monotonous perfection—the envied and admired of all beholders; two superbly physical young specimens of manhood and womanhood, desperately condoning each other's dullnesses for the sake of each other's good looks.

And while Youth and its Laughter—a chaos of color and shrill crescendos—was surging back and forth across the flower-wreathed piazzas, and violins were wheedling, and Japanese lanterns drunk with candle light were bobbing gaily in the balsam-scented breeze, little Eve Edgarton, up-stairs in her own room, was kneeling crampishly on the floor by the open window, with her chin on the window-sill, staring quizzically down—down—down on all that joy and novelty, till her father called her a trifle impatiently at last from his microscope table on the other side of the room.

"Eve!" summoned her father. "What an idler you are! Can't you see how worried I am over this specimen here? My eyes, I tell you, aren't what they used to be."

Then, patiently, little Eve Edgarton scrambled to her feet and, crossing over to her father's table, pushed his head mechanically aside and, bending down, squinted her own eye close to his magnifying glass.

"Bell-shaped calyx?" she began. "Five petals of the corollary partly united? Why, it must be some relation to the Mexican rain-tree," she mumbled without enthusiasm. "Leaves—alternate, bi-pinnate, very typically—few foliate," she continued. "Why, it's a—a Pithecolobium."

"Sure enough," said Edgarton. "That's what I thought all the time."

As one eminently relieved of all future worry in the matter, he jumped up, pushed away his microscopic work, and, grabbing up the biggest book on the table, bolted unceremoniously for an easy chair.

Indifferently for a moment little Eve Edgarton stood watching him. Then heavily, like a sleepy, insistent puppy dog, she shambled across the room and, climbing up into her father's lap, shoved aside her father's book, and burrowed her head triumphantly back into the lean, bony curve of his shoulder, her whole yawning interest centered apparently in the toes of her father's slippers.

Then so quietly that it scarcely seemed abrupt, "Father," she asked, "was my mother—beautiful?"

"What?" gasped Edgarton. "What?"

Bristling with a grave sort of astonishment he reached up nervously and stroked his daughter's hair. "Your mother," he winced. "Your mother was—to me—the most beautiful woman that ever lived! Such expression!" he glowed. "Such fire! But of such a spiritual modesty! Of such a physical delicacy! Like a rose," he mused, "like a rose—that should refuse to bloom for any but the hand that gathered it."

Languorously from some good practical pocket little Eve Edgarton extracted a much be-frilled chocolate bonbon and sat there munching it with extreme thoughtfulness. Then, "Father," she whispered, "I wish I was like—Mother."

"Why?" asked Edgarton, wincing.

"Because Mother's—dead," she answered simply.

Noisily, like an over conscious throat, the tiny traveling-clock on the mantelpiece began to swallow its moments. One moment—two moments—three—four—five—six moments—seven moments—on, on, on, gutturally, laboriously—thirteen—fourteen—fifteen—even twenty; with the girl still nibbling at her chocolate, and the man still staring off into space with that strange little whimper of pain between his pale, shrewd eyes.

It was the man who broke the silence first. Precipitately he shifted his knees and jostled his daughter to her feet.

"Eve," he said, "you're awfully spleeny to-night! I'm going to bed." And he stalked off into his own room, slamming the door behind him.

Once again from the middle of the floor little Eve Edgarton stood staring blankly after her father. Then she dawdled across the room and opened his door just wide enough to compass the corners of her mouth.

"Father," she whispered, "did Mother know that she was a rose—before you were clever enough to find her?"

"N—o," faltered her father's husky voice. "That was the miracle of it. She never even dreamed—that she was a rose—until I found her."

Very quietly little Eve Edgarton shut the door again and came back into the middle of her room and stood there hesitatingly for an instant.

Then quite abruptly she crossed to her bureau and pushing aside the old ivory toilet articles, began to jerk her tously hair first one way and then another across her worried forehead.

"But if you knew you were a rose?" she mused perplexedly to herself. "That is—if you felt almost sure that you were," she added with sudden humility. "That is—" she corrected herself—"that is—if you felt almost sure that you could be a rose—if anybody wanted you to be one?"

In impulsive experimentation she gave another tweak to her hair, and pinched a poor bruised-looking little blush into the hollow of one thin little cheek. "But suppose it was the—the people—going by," she faltered, "who never even dreamed that you were a rose? Suppose it was the—Suppose it was—Suppose—"

Dejection unspeakable settled suddenly upon her—an agonizing sense of youth's futility. Rackingly above the crash and lilt of music, the quick, wild thud of dancing feet, the sharp, staccato notes of laughter—she heard the dull, heavy, unrhythmical tread of the oncoming years—gray years, limping eternally from to-morrow on, through unloved lands, on unloved errands.

"This is the end of youth. It is—it is—it is," whimpered her heart.

"It ISN'T!" something suddenly poignant and determinate shrilled startlingly in her brain. "I'll have one more peep at youth, anyway!" threatened the brain.

"If we only could!" yearned the discouraged heart.

Speculatively for one brief instant the girl stood cocking her head toward the door of her father's room. Then, expeditiously, if not fashionably, she began at once to rearrange her tousled hair, and after one single pat to her gown—surely the quickest toilet-making of that festive evening—snatched up a slipper in each hand, crept safely past her father's door, crept safely out at last through her own door into the hall, and still carrying a slipper in each hand, had reached the head of the stairs before a new complexity assailed her.

"Why—why, I've never yet—been anywhere—alone—without my mother's memory!" she faltered, aghast.

Then impetuously, with a little frown of material inconvenience, but no flicker whatsoever in the fixed spiritual habit of her life, she dropped her slippers on the floor, sped back to her room, hesitated on the threshold a moment with real perplexity, darted softly to her trunk, rummaged as noiselessly through it as a kitten's paws, discovered at last the special object of her quest—a filmy square of old linen and lace—thrust it into her belt with her own handkerchief, and went creeping back again to her slippers at the head of the stairs.

As if to add fresh nervousness to the situation, one of the slippers lay pointing quite boldly down-stairs. But the other slipper—true as a compass to the north—toed with unmistakable severity toward the bedroom.

Tentatively little Eve Edgarton inserted one foot in the timid slipper. The path back to her room was certainly the simplest path that she knew—and the dullest. Equally tentatively she withdrew from the timid slipper and tried the adventurous one. "O-u-c-h!" she cried out loud. The sole of the second slipper seemed fairly sizzling with excitement.

With a slight gasp of impatience, then, she reached out and pulled the timid slipper back into line, stepped firmly into it, pointed both slipper-toes unswervingly southward, and proceeded on down-stairs to investigate the "Christian Dance."

At the first turn of the lower landing she stopped short, with every ennui-darkened sense in her body "jacked" like a wild deer's senses before the sudden dazzle of sight, sound, scent that awaited her below. Before her blinking eyes she saw even the empty, humdrum hotel office turned into a blazing bower of palms and roses and electric lights. Beyond this bower a corridor opened out—more dense, more sweet, more sparkling. And across this corridor the echo of the unseen ball came diffusing through the palms—the plaintive cry of a violin, the rippling laugh of a piano, the swarming hum of human voices, the swish of skirts, the agitant thud-thud-thud of dancing feet, the throb, almost, of young hearts—a thousand commonplace, every-day sounds merged here and now into one magic harmony that thrilled little Eve Edgarton as nothing on God's big earth had ever thrilled her before.

Hurriedly she darted down the last flight of steps and sped across the bright office to the dark veranda, consumed by one fuming, passionate, utterly uncontrollable curiosity to see with her own eyes just what all that wonderful sound looked like!

Once outside in the darkness her confusion cleared a little. It was late, she reasoned—very, very late, long after midnight probably; for of all the shadowy, flickering line of evening smokers that usually crowded that particular stretch of veranda only a single distant glow or two remained. Yet even now in the almost complete isolation of her surroundings the old inherent bashfulness swept over her again and warred chaotically with her insistent purpose. As stealthily as possible she crept along the dark wall to the one bright spot that flared forth like a lantern lens from the gay ballroom—crept along—crept along—a plain little girl in a plain little dress, yearning like all the other plain little girls of the world, in all the other plain little dresses of the world, to press her wistful little nose just once against some dazzling toy-shop window.

With her fingers groping at last into the actual shutters of that coveted ballroom window, she scrunched her eyes up perfectly tight for an instant and then opened them, staring wide at the entrancing scene before her.

"O—h!" said little Eve Edgarton. "O—h!"

The scene was certainly the scene of a most madcap summer carnival. Palms of the far December desert were there! And roses from the near, familiar August gardens! The swirl of chiffon and lace and silk was like a rainbow-tinted breeze! The music crashed on the senses like blows that wasted no breath in subtler argument! Naked shoulders gleamed at every turn beneath their diamonds! Silk stockings bared their sheen at each new rompish step! And through the dizzy mystery of it all—the haze, the maze, the vague, audacious unreality,—grimly conventional, blatantly tangible white shirt-fronts surrounded by great black blots of men went slapping by—each with its share of fairyland in its arms!

"Why! They're not dancing!" gasped little Eve Edgarton. "They're just prancing!"

Even so, her own feet began to prance. And very faintly across her cheek-bones a little flicker of pink began to glow.

Then very startlingly behind her a man's shadow darkened suddenly, and, sensing instantly that this newcomer also was interested in the view through the window, she drew aside courteously to give him his share of the pleasure. In her briefest glance she saw that he was no one whom she knew, but in the throbbing witchery of the moment he seemed to her suddenly like her only friend in the world.

"It's pretty, isn't it?" she nodded toward the ballroom.

Casually the man bent down to look until his smoke-scented cheek almost grazed hers. "It certainly is!" he conceded amiably.

Without further speech for a moment they both stood there peering into the wonderful picture. Then altogether abruptly, and with no excuse whatsoever, little Eve Edgarton's heart gave a great, big lurch, and, wringing her small brown hands together so that by no grave mischance should she reach out and touch the stranger's sleeve as she peered up at him, "I—can dance," drawled little Eve Edgarton.

Shrewdly the man's glance flashed down at her. Quite plainly he recognized her now. She was that "funny little Edgarton girl." That's exactly who she was! In the simple, old-fashioned arrangement of her hair, in the personal neatness but total indifference to fashion of her prim, high-throated gown, she represented—frankly—everything that he thought he most approved in woman. But nothing under the starry heavens at that moment could have forced him to lead her as a partner into that dazzling maelstrom of Mode and Modernity, because she looked "so horridly eccentric and conspicuous"—compared to the girls that he thought he didn't approve of at all!

"Why, of course you can dance! I only wish I could!" he lied gallantly. And stole away as soon as he reasonably could to find another partner, trusting devoutly that the darkness had not divulged his actual features.

Five minutes later, through the window-frame of her magic picture, little Eve Edgarton saw him pass, swinging his share of fairyland in his arms.

And close behind him followed Barton, swinging his share of fairyland in his arms! Barton the wonderful—at his best! Barton the wonderful—with his best, the blonde, blonde girl of the marvelous gowns and hats. There was absolutely no doubt whatsoever about them. They were the handsomest couple in the room!

Furtively from her hidden corner little Eve Edgarton stood and watched them. To her appraising eyes there were at least two other girls almost as beautiful as Barton's partner. But no other man in the room compared with Barton. Of that she was perfectly sure! His brow, his eyes, his chin, the way he held his head upon his wonderful shoulders, the way he stood upon his feet, his smile, his laugh, the very gesture of his hands!

Over and over again as she watched, these two perfect partners came circling through her vision, solemnly graceful or rhythmically hoydenish—two fortune-favored youngsters born into exactly the same sphere, trained to do exactly the same things in exactly the same way, so that even now, with twelve years' difference in age between them, every conscious vibration of their beings seemed to be tuned instinctively to the same key.

Bluntly little Eve Edgarton looked back upon the odd, haphazard training of her own life. Was there any one in this world whose training had been exactly like hers? Then suddenly her elbow went crooking up across her eyes to remember how Barton had looked in the stormy woods that night—lying half naked—and almost wholly dead—at her feet. Except for her odd, haphazard training, he would have been dead! Barton, the beautiful—dead? And worse than dead—buried? And worse than—

Out of her lips a little gasp of sound rang agonizingly.

And in that instant, by some trick-fashion of the dance, the rollicking music stopped right off short in the middle of a note, the lights went out, the dancers fled precipitously to their seats, and out of the arbored gallery of the orchestra a single swarthy-faced male singer stepped forth into the wan wake of an artificial moon, and lifted up a marvelous tenor voice in one of those weird folk-songs of the far-away that fairly tear the listener's heart out of his body—a song as sinisterly metallic as the hum of hate along a dagger-blade; a song as rapturously surprised at its own divinity as the first trill of a nightingale; a song of purling brooks and grim, gray mountain fortresses; a song of quick, sharp lights and long, low, lazy cadences; a song of love and hate; a song of all joys and all sorrows—and then death; the song of Sex as Nature sings it—the plaintive, wheedling, passionate song of Sex as Nature sings it yet—in the far-away places of the earth.

To no one else in that company probably did a single word penetrate. Merely stricken dumb by the vibrant power of the voice, vaguely uneasy, vaguely saddened, group after group of hoydenish youngsters huddled in speechless fascination around the dark edges of the hall.

But to little Eve Edgarton's cosmopolitan ears each familiar gipsyish word thus strangely transplanted into that alien room was like a call to the wild—from the wild.

So—as to all repressed natures the moment of full self-expression comes once, without warning, without preparation, without even conscious acquiescence sometimes—the moment came to little Eve Edgarton. Impishly first, more as a dare to herself than as anything else, she began to hum the melody and sway her body softly to and fro to the rhythm.

Then suddenly her breath began to quicken, and as one half hypnotized she went clambering through the window into the ballroom, stood for an instant like a gray-white phantom in the outer shadows, then, with a laugh as foreign to her own ears as to another's, snatched up a great, square, shimmering silver scarf that gleamed across a deserted chair, stretched it taut by its corners across her hair and eyes, and with a queer little cry—half defiance, half appeal—a quick dart, a long, undulating glide—merged herself into the dagger-blade, the nightingale, the grim mountain fortress, the gay mocking brook, all the love, all the rapture, all the ghastly fatalism of that heartbreaking song.

Bent as a bow her lithe figure curved now right, now left, to the lilting cadence. Supple as a silken tube her slender body seemed to drink up the fluid sound. No one could have sworn in that vague light that her feet even so much as touched the ground. She was a wraith! A phantasy! A fluctuant miracle of sound and sense!

Tremulously the singer's voice faltered in his throat to watch his song come gray-ghost-true before his staring eyes. With scant restraint the crowd along the walls pressed forward, half pleasure-mad, to solve the mystery of the apparition. Abruptly the song stopped! The dancer faltered! Lights blazed! A veritable shriek of applause went roaring to the roof-tops!

And little Eve Edgarton in one wild panic-stricken surge of terror went tearing off through a blind alley of palms, dodging a cafe table, jumping an improvised trellis—a hundred pursuing voices yelling: "Where is she? Where is she?"—the telltale tinsel scarf flapping frenziedly behind her, flapping—flapping—till at last, between one high, garnished shelf and another it twined its vampirish chiffon around the delicate fronds of a huge potted fern! There was a jerk,—a blur,—a blow, the sickening crash of fallen pottery—And little Eve Edgarton crumpled up on the floor, no longer "colorless" among the pale, dry, rainbow tints and shrill metallic glints of that most wondrous scene.

Under her crimson mask, when the rescuers finally reached her, she lay as perfectly disguised as even her most bashful mood could have wished.

All around her—kneeling, crowding, meddling, interfering—frightened people queried: "Who is she? Who is she?" Now and again from out of the medley some one offered a half-articulate suggestion. It was the hotel proprietor who moved first. Clumsily but kindly, with a fat hand thrust under her shoulders, he tried to raise her head from the floor. Barton himself, as the most recently returned from the "Dark Valley," moved next. Futilely, with a tiny wisp of linen and lace that he found at the girl's belt, he tried to wipe the blood from her lips.

"Who is she? Who is she?" the conglomerate hum of inquiry rose and fell like a moan.

Beneath the crimson stain on the little lace handkerchief a trace of indelible ink showed faintly. Scowlingly Barton bent to decipher it. "Mother's Little Handkerchief," the marking read. "'Mother's?'" Barton repeated blankly. Then suddenly full comprehension broke upon him, and, horridly startled and shocked with a brand-new realization of the tragedy, he fairly blurted out his astonishing information.

"Why—why, it's the—little Edgarton girl!" he hurled like a bombshell into the surrounding company.

Instantly, with the mystery once removed, a dozen hysterical people seemed startled into normal activity. No one knew exactly what to do, but some ran for water and towels, and some ran for the doctor, and one young woman with astonishing acumen slipped out of her white silk petticoat and bound it, blue ribbons and all, as best she could, around Eve Edgarton's poor little gashed head.

Suddenly full comprehension broke upon him and he fairly blurted out his astonishing information

"We must carry her up-stairs!" asserted the hotel proprietor.

"I'll carry her!" said Barton quite definitely.

Fantastically the procession started upward—little Eve Edgarton white as a ghost now in Barton's arms, except for that one persistent trickle of red from under the loosening edge of her huge Oriental-like turban of ribbon and petticoat; the hotel proprietor still worrying eternally how to explain everything; two or three well-intentioned women babbling inconsequently of other broken heads.

In astonishingly slow response to as violent a knock as they thought they gave, Eve Edgarton's father came shuffling at last to the door to greet them. Like one half paralyzed with sleep and perplexity, he stood staring blankly at them as they filed into his rooms with their burden.

"Your daughter seems to have bumped her head!" the hotel proprietor began with professional tact.

In one gasping breath the women started to explain their version of the accident.

Barton, as dumb as the father, carried the girl directly to the bed and put her down softly, half lying, half sitting, among the great pile of night-crumpled pillows. Some one threw a blanket over her. And above the top edge of that blanket nothing of her showed except the grotesquely twisted turban, the whole of one white eyelid, the half of the other, and just that single persistent trickle of red. Raspishly at that moment the clock on the mantelpiece choked out the hour of three. Already Dawn was more than half a hint in the sky, and in the ghastly mixture of real and artificial light the girl's doom looked already sealed.

Then very suddenly she opened her eyes and stared around.

"Eve!" gasped her father, "what have you been doing?"

Vaguely the troubled eyes closed, and then opened again. "I was—trying—to show people—that I was a—rose," mumbled little Eve Edgarton.

Swiftly her father came running to her side. He thought it was her deathbed statement. "But Eve?" he pleaded. "Why, my own little girl. Why, my—"

Laboriously the big eyes lifted to his. "Mother was a rose," persisted the stricken lips desperately.

"Yes, I know," sobbed her father. "But—but—"

"But—nothing," mumbled little Eve Edgarton. With an almost superhuman effort she pushed her sharp little chin across the confining edge of the blanket. Vaguely, unrecognizingly then, for the first time, her heavy eyes sensed the hotel proprietor's presence and worried their way across the tearful ladies to Barton's harrowed face.

"Mother—was a rose," she began all over again. "Mother—was a rose. Mother—was—a rose," she persisted babblingly. "And Father—g-guessed it—from the very first! But as for me—?" Weakly she began to claw at her incongruous bandage. "But—as—for me," she gasped, "the way I'm fixed!—I have to—announce it!"

CHAPTER IV

The Edgartons did not start for Melbourne the following day! Nor the next—nor the next—nor even the next.

In a head-bandage much more scientific than a blue-ribboned petticoat, but infinitely less decorative, little Eve Edgarton lay imprisoned among her hotel pillows.

Twice a day, and oftener if he could justify it, the village doctor came to investigate pulse and temperature. Never before in all his humdrum winter experience, or occasional summer-tourist vagary, had he ever met any people who prated of camels instead of motor-cars, or deprecated the dust of Abyssinia on their Piccadilly shoes, or sighed indiscriminately for the snow-tinted breezes of the Klondike and Ceylon. Never, either, in all his full round of experience had the village doctor had a surgical patient as serenely complacent as little Eve Edgarton, or any anxious relative as madly restive as little Eve Edgarton's father.

For the first twenty-four hours, of course, Mr. Edgarton was much too worried over the accident to his daughter to think for a moment of the accident to his railway and steamship tickets. For the second twenty-four hours he was very naturally so much concerned with the readjustment of his railway and steamship tickets that he never concerned himself at all with the accident to his plans. But by the end of the third twenty-four hours, with his first two worries reasonably eliminated, it was the accident to his plans that smote upon him with the fiercest poignancy. Let a man's clothes and togs vacillate as they will between his trunk and his bureau—once that man's spirit is packed for a journey nothing but journey's end can ever unpack it again!

With his own heart tuned already to the heart-throb of an engine, his pale eyes focused squintingly toward expected novelties, his thin nostrils half a-sniff with the first salty scent of the Far-Away, Mr. Edgarton, whatever his intentions, was not the most ideal of sick-room companions. Too conscientious to leave his daughter, too unhappy to stay with her, he spent the larger part of his days and nights pacing up and down like a caged beast between the two bedrooms.

It was not till the fifth day, however, that his impatience actually burst the bounds he had set for it. Somewhere between his maple bureau and Eve's mahogany bed the actual explosion took place, and in that explosion every single infinitesimal wrinkle of brow, cheek, chin, nose, was called into play, as if here at last was a man who intended once and for all time to wring his face perfectly dry of all human expression.

"Eve!" hissed her father. "I hate this place! I loathe this place! I abominate it! I despise it! The flora is—execrable! The fauna? Nil! And as to the coffee—the breakfast coffee? Oh, ye gods! Eve, if we're delayed here another week—I shall die! Die, mind you, at sixty-two! With my life-work just begun, Eve! I hate this place! I abominate it! I de—"

"Really?" mused little Eve Edgarton from her white pillows. "Why—I think it's lovely."

"Eh?" demanded her father. "What? Eh?"

"It's so social," said little Eve Edgarton.

"Social?" choked her father.

As bereft of expression as if robbed of both inner and outer vision, little Eve Edgarton lifted her eyes to his. "Why—two of the hotel ladies have almost been to see me," she confided listlessly. "And the chambermaid brought me the picture of her beau. And the hotel proprietor lent me a story-book. And Mr.—"

"Social?" snapped her father.

"Oh, of course—if you got killed in a fire or anything, saving people's lives, you'd sort of expect them to—send you candy—or make you some sort of a memorial," conceded little Eve Edgarton unemotionally. "But when you break your head—just amusing yourself? Why, I thought it was nice for the hotel ladies to almost come to see me," she finished, without even so much as a flicker of the eyelids.

Disgustedly her father started for his own room, then whirled abruptly in his tracks and glanced back at that imperturbable little figure in the big white bed. Except for the scarcely perceptible hound-like flicker of his nostrils, his own face held not a whit more expression than the girl's.

"Eve," he asked casually, "Eve, you're not changing your mind, are you, about Nunko-Nono? And John Ellbertson? Good old John Ellbertson," he repeated feelingly. "Eve!" he quickened with sudden sharpness. "Surely nothing has happened to make you change your mind about Nunko-Nono? And good old John Ellbertson?"

"Oh—no—Father," said little Eve Edgarton. Indolently she withdrew her eyes from her father's and stared off Nunko-Nonoward—in a hazy, geographical sort of a dream. "Good old John Ellbertson—good old John Ellbertson," she began to croon very softly to herself. "Good old John Ellbertson. How I do love his kind brown eyes—how I do—"

"Brown eyes?" snapped her father. "Brown? John Ellbertson's got the grayest eyes that I ever saw in my life!"

Without the slightest ruffle of composure little Eve Edgarton accepted the correction. "Oh, has he?" she conceded amiably. "Well, then, good old John Ellbertson—good old John Ellbertson—how I do love his kind—gray eyes," she began all over again.

Palpably Edgarton shifted his standing weight from one foot to the other. "I understood—your mother," he asserted a bit defiantly.

"Did you, dear? I wonder?" mused little Eve Edgarton.

"Eh?" jerked her father.

Still with the vague geographical dream in her eyes, little Eve Edgarton pointed off suddenly toward the open lid of her steamer trunk.

"Oh—my manuscript notes, Father, please!" she ordered almost peremptorily, "John's notes, you know? I might as well be working on them while I'm lying here."

Obediently from the tousled top of the steamer trunk her father returned with the great batch of rough manuscript. "And my pencil, please," persisted little Eve Edgarton. "And my eraser. And my writing-board. And my ruler. And my—"

Absent-mindedly, one by one, Edgarton handed the articles to her, and then sank down on the foot of her bed with his thin-lipped mouth contorted into a rather mirthless grin. "Don't care much for your old father, do you?" he asked trenchantly.

Gravely for a moment the girl sat studying her father's weather-beaten features, the thin hair, the pale, shrewd eyes, the gaunt cheeks, the indomitable old-young mouth. Then a little shy smile flickered across her face and was gone again.

"As a parent, dear," she drawled, "I love you to distraction! But as a daily companion?" Vaguely her eyebrows lifted. "As a real playmate?" Against the starch-white of her pillows the sudden flutter of her small brown throat showed with almost startling distinctness. "But as a real playmate," she persisted evenly, "you are so—intelligent—and you travel so fast—it tires me."

"Whom do you like?" asked her father sharply.

The girl's eyes were suddenly sullen again—bored, distrait, inestimably dreary. "That's the whole trouble," she said. "You've never given me time—to like anybody."

"Oh, but—Eve," pleaded her father. Awkward as any schoolboy, he sat there, fuming and twisting before this absurd little bunch of nerve and nerves that he himself had begotten. "Oh, but Eve," he deprecated helplessly, "it's the deuce of a job for a—for a man to be left all alone in the world with a—with a daughter! Really it is!"

Already the sweat had started on his forehead, and across one cheek the old gray fretwork of wrinkles began to shadow suddenly. "I've done my best!" he pleaded. "I swear I have! Only I've never known how! With a mother, now," he stammered, "with a wife, with a sister, with your best friend's sister, you know just what to do! It's a definite relation! Prescribed by a definite emotion! But a daughter? Oh, ye gods! Your whole sexual angle of vision changed! A creature neither fish, flesh, nor fowl! Non-superior, non-contemporaneous, non-subservient! Just a lady! A strange lady! Yes, that's exactly it, Eve—a strange lady—growing eternally just a little bit more strange—just a little bit more remote—every minute of her life! Yet it's so—damned intimate all the time!" he blurted out passionately. "All the time she's rowing you about your manners and your morals, all the time she's laying down the law to you about the tariff or the turnips, you're remembering—how you used to—scrub her—in her first little blue-lined tin bath-tub!"

Once again the flickering smile flared up in little Eve Edgarton's eyes and was gone again. A trifle self-consciously she burrowed back into her pillows. When she spoke her voice was scarcely audible. "Oh, I know I'm funny," she admitted conscientiously.

"You're not funny!" snapped her father.

"Yes, I am," whispered the girl.

"No, you're not!" reasserted her father with increasing vehemence. "You're not! It's I who am funny! It's I who—" In a chaos of emotion he slid along the edge of the bed and clasped her in his arms. Just for an instant his wet cheek grazed hers, then: "All the same, you know," he insisted awkwardly, "I hate this place!"

Surprisingly little Eve Edgarton reached up and kissed him full on the mouth. They were both very much embarrassed.

"Why—why, Eve!" stammered her father. "Why, my little—little girl! Why, you haven't kissed me—before—since you were a baby!"

"Yes, I have!" nodded little Eve Edgarton.

"No, you haven't!" snapped her father.

"Yes, I have!" insisted Eve.

Tighter and tighter their arms clasped round each other. "You're all I've got," faltered the man brokenly.

"You're all I've ever had," whispered little Eve Edgarton.

Silently for a moment each according to his thoughts sat staring off into far places. Then without any warning whatsoever, the man reached out suddenly and tipped his daughter's face up abruptly into the light.

"Eve!" he demanded. "Surely you're not blaming me any in your heart because I want to see you safely married and settled with—with John Ellbertson?"

Vaguely, like a child repeating a dimly understood lesson, little Eve Edgarton repeated the phrases after him. "Oh, no, Father," she said, "I surely am not blaming you—in my heart—for wanting to see me married and settled with—John Ellbertson. Good old John Ellbertson," she corrected painstakingly.

With his hand still holding her little chin like a vise, the man's eyes narrowed to his further probing. "Eve," he frowned, "I'm not as well as I used to be! I've got pains in my arms! And they're not good pains! I shall live to be a thousand! But I—I might not! It's a—rotten world, Eve," he brooded, "and quite unnecessarily crowded—it seems to me—with essentially rotten people. Toward the starving and the crippled and the hideously distorted, the world, having no envy of them, shows always an amazing mercy; and Beauty, whatever its sorrows, can always retreat to the thick protecting wall of its own conceit. But as for the rest of us?" he grinned with a sudden convulsive twist of the eyebrow, "God help the unduly prosperous—and the merely plain! From the former—always, Envy, like a wolf, shall tear down every fresh talent, every fresh treasure, they lift to their aching backs. And from the latter—Brutal Neglect shall ravage away even the charm that they thought they had!

"It's a—a rotten world, Eve, I tell you," he began all over again, a bit plaintively. "A rotten world! And the pains in my arms, I tell you, are not—nice! Distinctly not nice! Sometimes, Eve, you think I'm making faces at you! But, believe me, it isn't faces that I'm making! It's my—heart that I'm making at you! And believe me, the pain is not—nice!"

Before the sudden wince in his daughter's eyes he reverted instantly to an air of semi-jocosity. "So, under all existing circumstances, little girl," he hastened to affirm, "you can hardly blame a crusty old codger of a father for preferring to leave his daughter in the hands of a man whom he positively knows to be good, than in the hands of some casual stranger who, just in a negative way, he merely can't prove isn't good? Oh, Eve—Eve," he pleaded sharply, "you'll be so much better off—out of the world! You've got infinitely too much money and infinitely too little—self-conceit—to be happy here! They would break your heart in a year! But at Nunko-Nono!" he cried eagerly. "Oh, Eve! Think of the peace of it! Just white beach, and a blue sea, and the long, low, endless horizon. And John will make you a garden! And women—I have often heard—are very happy in a garden! And—"

Slowly little Eve Edgarton lifted her eyes again to his. "Has John got a beard?" she asked.

"Why—why, I'm sure I don't remember," stammered her father. "Why, yes, I think so—why, yes, indeed—I dare say!"

"Is it a grayish beard?" asked little Eve Edgarton.

"Why—why, yes—I shouldn't wonder," admitted her father.

"And reddish?" persisted little Eve Edgarton. "And longish? As long as—?" Illustratively with her hands she stretched to her full arm's length.

"Yes, I think perhaps it is reddish," conceded her father. "But why?"

"Oh—nothing," mused little Eve Edgarton. "Only sometimes at night I dream about you and me landing at Nunko-Nono. And John in a great big, long, reddish-gray beard always comes crunching down at full speed across the hermit-crabs to meet us. And always just before he reaches us, he—he trips on his beard—and falls headlong into the ocean—and is—drowned."

"Why—what an awful dream!" deprecated her father.

"Awful?" queried little Eve Edgarton. "Ha! It makes me—laugh. All the same," she affirmed definitely, "good old John Ellbertson will have to have his beard cut." Quizzically for an instant she stared off into space, then quite abruptly she gave a quick, funny little sniff. "Anyway, I'll have a garden, won't I?" she said. "And always, of course, there will be—Henrietta."

"Henrietta?" frowned her father.

"My daughter!" explained little Eve Edgarton with dignity.

"Your daughter?" snapped Edgarton.

"Oh, of course there may be several," conceded little Eve Edgarton. "But Henrietta, I'm almost positive, will be the best one!"

So jerkily she thrust her slender throat forward with the speech, her whole facial expression seemed suddenly to have undercut and stunned her father's.

"Always, Father," she attested grimly, "with your horrid old books and specimens you have crowded my dolls out of my steamer trunk. But never once—" her tightening lips hastened to assure him, "have you ever succeeded in crowding—Henrietta—and the others out of my mind!"

Quite incongruously, then, with a soft little hand in which there lurked no animosity whatsoever, she reached up suddenly and smoothed the astonishment out of her father's mouth-lines.

"After all, Father," she asked, "now that we're really talking so intimately, after all—there isn't so specially much to life anyway, is there, except just the satisfaction of making the complete round of human experience—once for yourself—and then once again—to show another person? Just that double chance, Father, of getting two original glimpses at happiness? One through your own eyes, and one—just a little bit dimmer—through the eyes of another?"

With mercilessly appraising vision the starving Youth that was in her glared up at the satiate Age in him.

"You've had your complete round of human experience, Father!" she cried. "Your first—full—untrammeled glimpse of all your Heart's Desires. More of a glimpse, perhaps, than most people get. From your tiniest boyhood, Father, everything just as you wanted it! Just the tutors you chose in just the subjects you chose! Everything then that American colleges could give you! Everything later that European universities could offer you! And then Travel! And more Travel! And more! And more! And then—Love! And then Fame! 'Love, Fame, and Far Lands!' Yes, that's it exactly! Everything just as you chose it! So your only tragedy, Father, lies—as far as I can see—in just little—me! Because I don't happen to like the things that you like, the things that you already have had the first full joy of liking,—you've got to miss altogether your dimmer, second-hand glimpse of happiness! Oh, I'm sorry, Father! Truly I am! Already I sense the hurt of these latter years—the shattered expectations, the incessant disappointments! You who have stared unblinkingly into the face of the sun, robbed in your twilight of even a candle-flame. But, Father?"

Grimly, despairingly, but with unfaltering persistence—Youth fighting with its last gasp for the rights of its Youth—she lifted her haggard little face to his. "But, Father!—my tragedy lies in the fact—that at thirty—I've never yet had even my first-hand glimpse of happiness! And now apparently, unless I'm willing to relinquish all hope of ever having it, and consent to 'settle down,' as you call it, with 'good old John Ellbertson'—I'll never even get a gamble—probably—at sighting Happiness second-hand through another person's eyes!"

"Oh, but Eve!" protested her father. Nervously he jumped up and began to pace the room. One side of his face was quite grotesquely distorted, and his lean fingers, thrust precipitously into his pockets, were digging frenziedly into their own palms. "Oh, but Eve!" he reiterated sharply, "you will be happy with John! I know you will! John is a—John is a—Underneath all that slowness, that ponderous slowness—that—that—Underneath that—"

"That longish—reddish—grayish beard?" interpolated little Eve Edgarton.

Glaringly for an instant the old eyes and the young eyes challenged each other, and then the dark eyes retreated suddenly before—not the strength but the weakness of their opponents.

"Oh, very well, Father," assented little Eve Edgarton. "Only—" ruggedly the soft little chin thrust itself forth into stubborn outline again. "Only, Father," she articulated with inordinate distinctness, "you might just as well understand here and now, I won't budge one inch toward Nunko-Nono—not one single solitary little inch toward Nunko-Nono—unless at London, or Lisbon, or Odessa, or somewhere, you let me fill up all the trunks I want to—with just plain pretties—to take to Nunko-Nono! It isn't exactly, you know, like a bride moving fifty miles out from town somewhere," she explained painstakingly. "When a bride goes out to a place like Nunko-Nono, it isn't enough, you understand, that she takes just the things she needs. What she's got to take, you see, is everything under the sun—that she ever may need!"

With a little soft sigh of finality she sank back into her pillows, and then struggled up for one brief instant again to add a postscript, as it were, to her ultimatum. "If my day is over—without ever having been begun," she said, "why, it's over—without ever having been begun! And that's all there is to it! But when it comes to Henrietta," she mused, "Henrietta's going to have five-inch hair-ribbons—and everything else—from the very start!"

"Eh?" frowned Edgarton, and started for the door.

"And oh, Father!" called Eve, just as his hand touched the door-knob. "There's something I want to ask you for Henrietta's sake. It's rather a delicate question, but after I'm married I suppose I shall have to save all my delicate questions to—ask John; and John, somehow, has never seemed to me particularly canny about anything except—geology. Father!" she asked, "just what is it—that you consider so particularly obnoxious in—in—young men? Is it their sins?"

"Sins!" jerked her father. "Bah! It's their traits!"

"So?" questioned little Eve Edgarton from her pillows. "So? Such as—what?"

"Such as the pursuit of woman!" snapped her father. "The love—not of woman, but of the pursuit of woman! On all sides you see it to-day! On all sides you hear it—sense it—suffer it! The young man's eternally jocose sexual appraisement of woman! 'Is she young? Is she pretty?' And always, eternally, 'Is there any one younger? Is there any one prettier?' Sins, you ask?" Suddenly now he seemed perfectly willing, even anxious, to linger and talk. "A sin is nothing, oftener than not, but a mere accidental, non-considered act! A yellow streak quite as exterior as the scorch of a sunbeam. And there is no sin existent that a man may not repent of! And there is no honest repentance, Eve, that a wise woman cannot make over into a basic foundation for happiness! But a trait? A congenital tendency? A yellow streak bred in the bone? Why, Eve! If a man loves, I tell you, not woman, but the pursuit of woman? So that—wherever he wins—he wastes again? So that indeed at last, he wins only to waste? Moving eternally—on—on—on from one ravaged lure to another? Eve! Would I deliver over you—your mother's reincarnated body—to—to such as that?"

"O—h," said little Eve Edgarton. Her eyes were quite wide with horror. "How careful I shall have to be with Henrietta."

"Eh?" snapped her father.

Ting-a-ling—ling—ling—ling! trilled the telephone from the farther side of the room.

Impatiently Edgarton came back and lifted the receiver from its hook. "Hello?" he growled. "Who? What? Eh?"

With quite unnecessary vehemence he rammed the palm of his hand against the mouth-piece and glared back over his shoulder at his daughter. "It's that—that Barton!" he said. "The impudence of him! He wants to know if you are receiving visitors to-day! He wants to know if he can come up! The—"

"Yes—isn't it—awful?" stammered little Eve Edgarton.

Imperiously her father turned back to the telephone. Ting-a-ling—ling—ling—ling, chirped the bell right in his face. As if he were fairly trying to bite the transmitter, he thrust his lips and teeth into the mouth-piece.

"My daughter," he enunciated with extreme distinctness, "is feeling quite exhausted—exhausted—this afternoon. We appreciate, of course Mr. Barton, your—What? Hello there!" he interrupted himself sharply. "Mr. Barton? Barton? Now what in the deuce?" he called back appealingly toward the bed. "Why, he's rung off! The fool!" Quite accidentally then his glance lighted on his daughter. "Why, what are you smoothing your hair for?" he called out accusingly.

"Oh, just to put it on," acknowledged little Eve Edgarton.

"But what in creation are you putting on your coat for?" he demanded tartly.

"Oh, just to smooth it," acknowledged little Eve Edgarton.

With a sniff of disgust Edgarton turned on his heel and strode off into his own room.

For five minutes by the little traveling-clock, she heard him pacing monotonously up and down—up and down. Then very softly at last she summoned him back to her.

"Father," she whispered, "I think there's some one knocking at the outside door."

"What?" called Edgarton. Incredulously he came back through his daughter's room and, crossing over to the hall door, yanked it open abruptly on the intruder.

"Why—good afternoon!" grinned Barton above the extravagantly large and languourous bunch of pale lavender orchids that he clutched in his hand.

"Good afternoon!" said Edgarton without enthusiasm.

"Er—orchids!" persisted Barton still grinningly. Across the unfriendly hunch of the older man's shoulder he caught a disquieting glimpse of a girl's unduly speculative eyes. In sudden impulsive league with her against this, their apparent common enemy, Age, he thrust the orchids into the older man's astonished hands.

"For me?" questioned Edgarton icily.

"Why, yes—certainly!" beamed Barton. "Orchids, you know! Hothouse orchids!" he explained painstakingly.

"So I—judged," admitted Edgarton. With extreme distaste he began to untie the soft flimsy lavender ribbon that encompassed them. "In their native state, you know," he confided, "one very seldom finds them growing with—sashes on them." From her nest of cushions across the room little Eve Edgarton loomed up suddenly into definite prominence.

"What did you bring me, Mr. Barton?" she asked.

"Why, Eve!" cried her father. "Why, Eve, you astonish me! Why, I'm surprised at you! Why—what do you mean?"

The girl sagged back into her cushions. "Oh, Father," she faltered, "don't you know—anything? That was just 'small talk.'"

With perfunctory courtesy Edgarton turned to young Barton. "Pray be seated," he said; "take—take a chair."

It was the chair closest to little Eve Edgarton that Barton took. "How do you do, Miss Edgarton?" he ventured.

"How do you do, Mr. Barton?" said little Eve Edgarton.

From the splashy wash-stand somewhere beyond them, they heard Edgarton fussing with the orchids and mumbling vague Latin imprecations—or endearments—over them. A trifle surreptitiously Barton smiled at Eve. A trifle surreptitiously Eve smiled back at Barton.

In this perfectly amiable exchange of smiles the girl reached up suddenly to the sides of her head. "Is my—is my bandage on straight?" she asked worriedly.

"Why, no," admitted Barton; "it ought not to be, ought it?"

Again for no special reason whatsoever they both smiled.

"Oh, I say," stammered Barton. "How you can dance!"

Across the girl's olive cheeks her heavy eyelashes shadowed down like a fringe of black ferns. "Yes—how I can dance," she murmured almost inaudibly.

"Why didn't you let anybody know?" demanded Barton.

"Yes—why didn't I let anybody know?" repeated the girl in an utter panic of bashfulness.

"Oh, I say," whispered Barton, "won't you even look at me?"

Mechanically the girl opened her eyes and stared at him fixedly until his own eyes fell.

"Eve!" called her father sharply from the next room, "where in creation is my data concerning North American orchids?"

"In my steamer-trunk," began the girl. "On the left hand side. Tucked in between your riding-boots and my best hat."

"O—h," called her father.

Barton edged forward in his chair and touched the girl's brown, boyish little hand.

"Really, Miss Eve," he stammered, "I'm awfully sorry you got hurt! Truly I am! Truly it made me feel awfully squeamish! Really I've been thinking a lot about you these last few days! Honestly I have! Never in all my life did I ever carry any one as little and hurt as you were! It sort of haunts me, I tell you. Isn't there something I could do for you?"

"Something you could do for me?" said little Eve Edgarton, staring. Then again the heavy lashes came shadowing down across her cheeks.

"I haven't had any very great luck," she said, "in finding you ready to do things for me."

"What?" gasped Barton.

The big eyes lifted and fell again. "There was the attic," she whispered a bit huskily. "You wouldn't rent me your attic!"

"Oh, but—I say!" grinned Barton. "Some real thing, I mean! Couldn't I—couldn't I—read aloud to you?" he articulated quite distinctly, as Edgarton came rustling back into the room with his arms full of papers.

"Read aloud?" gibed Edgarton across the top of his spectacles. "It's a daring man, in this unexpurgated day and generation, who offers to read aloud to a lady."

"He might read me my geology notes," suggested little Eve Edgarton blandly.

"Your geology notes?" hooted her father. "What's this? Some more of your new-fangled 'small talk'? Your geology notes?" Still chuckling mirthlessly, he strode over to the big table by the window and, spreading out his orchid data over every conceivable inch of space, settled himself down serenely to compare one "flower of mystery" with another.

Furtively for a moment Barton sat studying the gaunt, graceful figure. Then quite impulsively he turned back to little Eve Edgarton's scowling face.

"Nevertheless, Miss Eve," he grinned, "I should be perfectly delighted to read your geology notes to you. Where are they?"

"Here," droned little Eve Edgarton, slapping listlessly at the loose pile of pages beside her.

Conscientiously Barton reached out and gathered the flimsy papers into one trim handful. "Where shall I begin?" he asked.

"It doesn't matter," murmured little Eve Edgarton.

"What?" said Barton. Nervously he began to fumble through the pages. "Isn't there any beginning?" he demanded.

"No," moped little Eve Edgarton.

"Nor any end?" he insisted. "Nor any middle?"

"N—o," sighed little Eve Edgarton.

Helplessly Barton plunged into the unhappy task before him. On page nine there were perhaps the fewest blots. He decided to begin there.

"Paleontologically," the first sentence smote him—

"Paleontologically the periods are characterized by absence of the large marine saurians, Dinosaurs and Pterosaurs—"

"eh?" gasped Barton.

"Why, of course!" called Edgarton, a bit impatiently, from the window.

Laboriously Barton went back and reread the phrase to himself. "Oh—oh, yes," he conceded lamely.

"Paleontologically,"

he began all over again. "Oh, dear, no!" he interrupted himself. "I was farther along than that!—Absence of marine saurians? Oh, yes!

"Absence of marine saurians,"

he resumed glibly,

"Dinosaurs and Pterosaurs—so abundant in the—in the Cretaceous—of Ammonites and Belemnites,"

he persisted—heroically. Hesitatingly, stumblingly, without a glimmer of understanding, his bewildered mind worried on and on, its entire mental energy concentrated on the single purpose of trying to pronounce the awful words.

"Of Rudistes, Inocerami—Tri—Trigonias,"

the horrible paragraph tortured on ...

"By the marked reduction in the—Brachiopods compared with the now richly developed Gasteropods and—and sinupalliate—Lamellibranchs,"—

it writhed and twisted before his dizzy eyes.

Every sentence was a struggle; more than one of the words he was forced to spell aloud just out of sheer self-defense; and always against Eve Edgarton's little intermittent nod of encouragement was balanced that hateful sniffing sound of surprise and contempt from the orchid table in the window.

Despairingly he skipped a few lines to the next unfamiliar words that met his eye.

"The Neozoic flora,"

he read,

"consists mainly of—of Angio—Angiosper—"

Still smiling, but distinctly wan around the edges of the smile, he slammed the handful of papers down on his knee. "If it really doesn't make any difference where we begin, Miss Eve," he said, "for Heaven's sake—let's begin somewhere else!"

"Oh—all right," crooned little Eve Edgarton.

Expeditiously Barton turned to another page, and another, and another. Wryly he tasted strange sentence after strange sentence. Then suddenly his whole wonderful face wreathed itself in smiles again.

"Three superfamilies of turtles,"

he began joyously. "Turtles! Ha!—I know turtles!" he proceeded with real triumph. "Why, that's the first word I've recognized in all this—this—er—this what I've been reading! Sure I know turtles!" he reiterated with increasing conviction. "Why, sure! Those—those slow-crawling, box-like affairs that—live in the mud and are used for soup and—er—combs," he continued blithely.

"The—very—same," nodded little Eve Edgarton soberly.

"Oh—Lordy!" groaned her father from the window.

"Oh, this is going to be lots better!" beamed Barton. "Now that I know what it's all about—"

"For goodness' sake," growled Edgarton from his table, "how do you people think I'm going to do any work with all this jabbering going on!"

Hesitatingly for a moment Barton glanced back over his shoulder at Edgarton, and then turned round again to probe Eve's preferences in the matter. As sluggishly determinate as two black turtles trailing along a white sand beach, her great dark eyes in her little pale face seemed headed suddenly toward some Far-Away Idea.

"Oh—go right on reading, Mr. Barton," nodded little Eve Edgarton.

"Three superfamilies of turtles,"

began Barton all over again.

"Three superfamilies of turtles—the—the Amphichelydia, the Cryptodira, and the Tri—the—Tri—the T-r-i-o-n-y-c-h-o-i-d-e-a,"

he spelled out laboriously.

With a vicious jerk of his chair Edgarton snatched up his papers and his orchids and started for the door.

"You're nice," he said. "I like you!"

"When you people get all through this nonsense," he announced, "maybe you'll be kind enough to let me know! I shall be in the writing-room!" With satirical courtesy he bowed first to Eve, then to Barton, dallied an instant on the threshold to repeat both bows, and went out, slamming the door behind him.

"A nervous man, isn't he?" suggested Barton.

Gravely little Eve Edgarton considered the thought. "Trionychoidea," she prompted quite irrelevantly.

"Oh, yes—of course," conceded Barton. "But do you mind if I smoke?"

"No, I don't mind if you smoke," singsonged the girl.

With a palpable sigh of relief Barton lighted a cigarette. "You're nice," he said. "I like you!" Conscientiously then he resumed his reading.

"No—Pleurodira—have yet been found,"

he began.

"Yes—isn't that too bad?" sighed little Eve Edgarton.

"It doesn't matter personally to me," admitted Barton. Hastily he moved on to the next sentence.

"The Amphichelydia—are known there by only the genus Baena,"

he read.

"Two described species: B. undata and B. arenosa, to which was added B. hebraica and B. ponderosa—"

Petulantly he slammed the whole handful of papers to the floor.

"Eve!" he stammered. "I can't stand it! I tell you—I just can't stand it! Take my attic if you want to! Or my cellar! Or my garage! Or anything else of mine in the world that you have any fancy for! But for Heaven's sake—"

With extraordinarily dilated eyes Eve Edgarton stared out at him from her white pillows.

"Why—why, if it makes you feel like that—just to read it," she reproached him mournfully, "how do you suppose it makes me feel to have to write it? All you have to do—is to read it," she said. "But I? I have to write it!"

"But—why do you have to write it?" gasped Barton.

Languidly her heavy lashes shadowed down across her cheeks again. "It's for the British consul at Nunko-Nono," she said. "It's some notes he asked me to make for him in London this last spring."

"But for mercy's sake—do you like to write things like that?" insisted Barton.

"Oh, no," drawled little Eve Edgarton. "But of course—if I marry him," she confided without the slightest flicker of emotion, "it's what I'll have to write—all the rest of my life."

"But—" stammered Barton. "For mercy's sake, do you want to marry him?" he asked quite bluntly.

"Oh, no," drawled little Eve Edgarton.

Impatiently Barton threw away his half-smoked cigarette and lighted a fresh one. "Then why?" he demanded.

"Oh, it's something Father invented," said little Eve Edgarton.

Altogether emphatically Barton pushed back his chair. "Well, I call it a shame!" he said. "For a nice live little girl like you to be packed off like so much baggage—to marry some great gray-bearded clout who hasn't got an idea in his head except—except—" squintingly he stared down at the scattered sheets on the floor—"except—'Amphichelydia,'" he asserted with some feeling.

"Yes—isn't it?" sighed little Eve Edgarton.

"For Heaven's sake!" said Barton. "Where is Nunko-Nono?"

"Nunko-Nono?" whispered little Eve Edgarton. "Where is it? Why, it's an island! In an ocean, you know! Rather a hot—green island! In rather a hot—blue-green ocean! Lots of green palms, you know, and rank, rough, green grass—and green bugs—and green butterflies—and green snakes. And a great crawling, crunching collar of white sand and hermit-crabs all around it. And then just a long, unbroken line of turquoise-colored waves. And then more turquoise-colored waves. And then more turquoise-colored waves. And then more turquoise-colored waves. And then—and then—"

"And then what?" worried Barton.

With a vaguely astonished lift of the eyebrows little Eve Edgarton met both question and questioner perfectly squarely. "Why—then—more turquoise-colored waves, of course," chanted little Eve Edgarton.

"It sounds rotten to me," confided Barton.

"It is," said little Eve Edgarton. "And, oh, I forgot to tell you: John Ellbertson is—sort of green, too. Geologists are apt to be, don't you think so?"

"I never saw one," admitted Barton without shame.

"If you'd like me to," said Eve, "I'll show you how the turquoise-colored waves sound—when they strike the hermit-crabs."

"Do!" urged Barton.

Listlessly the girl pushed back into her pillows, slid down a little farther into her blankets, and closed her eyes.

"Mmmmmmmmm," she began, "Mmm-mmmmmmm—Mmmmm—Mmmmmmm, W-h-i-s-h-h-h! Mmmmmmmmm—Mmmmmmmm—Mmmmmmmm—Mmmmmm—W-h-i-s-h-h-h!—Mmmmmmmm—Mmmmmmm—"

"After a while, of course, I think you might stop," suggested Barton a bit creepishly.

Again the big eyes opened at him with distinct surprise. "Why—why?" said Eve Edgarton. "It—never stops!"

"Oh, I say," frowned Barton, "I do feel awfully badly about your going away off to a place like that to live! Really!" he stammered.

"We're going—Thursday," said little Eve Edgarton.

"THURSDAY?" cried Barton. For some inexplicable reason the whole idea struck him suddenly as offensive, distinctly offensive, as if Fate, the impatient waiter, had snatched away a yet untasted plate. "Why—why, Eve!" he protested, "why, we're only just beginning to get acquainted."

"Yes, I know it," mused little Eve Edgarton.

"Why—if we'd have had half a chance—" began Barton, and then didn't know at all how to finish it. "Why, you're so plucky—and so odd—and so interesting!" he began all over again. "Oh, of course, I'm an awful duffer and all that! But if we'd had half a chance, I say, you and I would have been great pals in another fortnight!"

"Even so," murmured little Eve Edgarton, "there are yet—fifty-two hours before I go."

"What are fifty-two hours?" laughed Barton.

Listlessly like a wilting flower little Eve Edgarton slid down a trifle farther into her pillows. "If you'd have an early supper," she whispered, "and then come right up here afterward, why, there would be two or three hours. And then to-morrow if you got up quite early, there would be a long, long morning, and—we—could get acquainted—some," she insisted.

"Why, Eve!" said Barton, "do you really mean that you would like to be friends with me?"

"Yes—I do," nodded the crown of the white-bandaged head.

"But I'm so stupid," confided Barton, with astonishing humility. "All these botany things—and geology—and—"

"Yes, I know it," mumbled little Eve Edgarton. "That's what makes you so restful."

"What?" queried Barton a bit sharply. Then very absent-mindedly for a moment he sat staring off into space through a gray, pungent haze of cigarette smoke.

"Eve," he ventured at last.

"What?" mumbled little Eve Edgarton.

"Nothing," said Barton.

"Mr. Jim Barton," ventured Eve.

"What?" asked Barton.

"Nothing," mumbled little Eve Edgarton.

Out of some emotional or purely social tensities of life it seems rather that Time strikes the clock than that anything so small as a clock should dare strike the Time. One—two—three—four—five! winced the poor little frightened traveling-clock on the mantelpiece.

Then quite abruptly little Eve Edgarton emerged from her cozy cushions, sitting bolt upright like a doughty little warrior.

"Mr. Jim Barton!" said little Eve Edgarton. "If I stayed here two weeks longer—I know you'd like me! I know it! I just know it!" Quizzically for an instant, as if to accumulate further courage, she cocked her little head on one side and stared blankly into Barton's astonished eyes. "But you see I'm not going to be here two weeks!" she resumed hurriedly. Again the little head cocked appealingly to one side. "You—you wouldn't be willing to take my word for it, would you? And like me—now?"

"Why—why, what do you mean?" stammered Barton.

"What do I mean?" quizzed little Eve Edgarton. "Why, I mean—that just once before I go off to Nunko-Nono—I'd like to be—attractive!"

"Attractive?" stammered Barton helplessly.

With all the desperate, indomitable frankness of a child, the girl's chin thrust itself forward.

"I could be attractive!" she said. "I could! I know I could! If I'd ever let go just the teeniest—tiniest bit—I could have—beaux!" she asserted triumphantly. "A thousand beaux!" she added more explicitly. "Only—"

"Only what?" laughed Barton.

"Only one doesn't let go," said little Eve Edgarton.

"Why not?" persisted Barton.

"Why, you just—couldn't—with strangers," said little Eve Edgarton. "That's the bewitchment of it."

"The bewitchment?" puzzled Barton.

Nervously the girl crossed her hands in her lap. She suddenly didn't look like a doughty little soldier any more, but just like a worried little girl.

"Did you ever read any fairy stories?" she asked with apparent irrelevance.

"Why, of course," said Barton. "Millions of them when I was a kid."

"I read one—once," said little Eve Edgarton. "It was about a person, a sleeping person, a lady, I mean, who couldn't wake up until a prince kissed her. Well, that was all right, of course," conceded little Eve Edgarton, "because, of course, any prince would have been willing to kiss the lady just as a mere matter of accommodation. But suppose," fretted little Eve Edgarton, "suppose the bewitchment also ran that no prince would kiss the lady until she had waked up? Now there!" said little Eve Edgarton, "is a situation that I should call completely stalled."

"But what's all this got to do with you?" grinned Barton.

"Nothing at all to do with me!" said little Eve Edgarton. "It is me! That's just exactly the way I'm fixed. I can't be attractive—out loud—until some one likes me! But no one, of course, will ever like me until I am already attractive—out loud! So that's why I wondered," she said, "if just as a mere matter of accommodation, you wouldn't be willing to be friends with me now? So that for at least the fifty-two hours that remain, I could be released—from my most unhappy enchantment."

Astonishingly across that frank, perfectly outspoken little face, the frightened eyelashes came flickering suddenly down. "Because," whispered little Eve Edgarton, "because—you see—I happen to like you already."

"Oh, fine!" smiled Barton. "Fine! Fine! Fi—" Abruptly the word broke in his throat. "What?" he cried. His hand—the steadiest hand among all his chums—began to shake like an aspen. "WHAT?" he cried. His heart, the steadiest heart among all his chums, began to pitch and lurch in his breast. "Why, Eve! Eve!" he stammered. "You don't mean you like me—like that?"

"Yes—I do," nodded the little white-capped head. There was much shyness of flesh in the statement, but not a flicker of spiritual self-consciousness or fear.

"But—Eve!" protested Barton. Already he felt the goose-flesh rising on his arms. Once before a girl had told him that she—liked him. In the middle of a silly summer flirtation it had been, and the scene had been mawkish, awful, a mess of tears and kisses and endless recriminations. But this girl? Before the utter simplicity of this girl's statement, the unruffled dignity, the mere acknowledgment, as it were, of an interesting historical fact, all his trifling, preconceived ideas went tumbling down before his eyes like a flimsy house of cards. Pang after pang of regret for the girl, of regret for himself, went surging hotly through him. "Oh, but—Eve!" he began all over again. His voice was raw with misery.

"Why, there's nothing to make a fuss about," drawled little Eve Edgarton. "You've probably liked a thousand people, but I—you see?—I've never had the fun of liking—any one—before!"

"Fun?" tortured Barton. "Yes, that's just it! If you'd ever had the fun of liking anything it wouldn't seem half so brutal—now!"

"Brutal?" mused little Eve Edgarton. "Oh, really, Mr. Jim Barton, I assure you," she said, "there's nothing brutal at all in my liking—for you."

With a gasp of despair Barton stumbled across the rug to the bed, and with a shaky hand thrust under Eve Edgarton's chin, turned her little face bluntly up to him to tell her—how proud he felt, but—to tell her how sorry he was, but—

"Any time that you people want me," suggested Edgarton's icy voice, "I am standing here—in about the middle of the floor!"

And as he turned that little face up to his,—inconceivably—incomprehensively—to his utter consternation and rout—he saw that it was a stranger's little face that he held. Gone was the sullen frown, the indifferent glance, the bitter smile, and in that sudden, amazing, wild, sweet transfiguration of brow, eyes, mouth, that met his astonished eyes, he felt his whole mean, supercilious world slip out from under his feet! And just as precipitously, just as inexplainably, as ten days before he had seen a Great Light that had knocked all consciousness out of him, he experienced now a second Great Light that knocked him back into the first full consciousness that he had ever known!

"Why, Eve!" he stammered. "Why, you—mischief! Why, you little—cheeky darling! Why, my own—darned little Story Book Girl!" And gathered her into his arms.

From the farther side of the room the sound of a creaking board smote almost instantly upon their ears.

"Any time that you people want me," suggested Edgarton's icy voice, "I am standing here—in about the middle of the floor!"

With a jerk of dismay Barton wheeled around to face him. But it was little Eve Edgarton herself who found her tongue first.

"Oh, Father dear—I have been perfectly wise!" she hastened to assure him. "Almost at once, Father, I told him that I liked him, so that if he really were the dreadful kind of young man you were warning me about, he would eliminate himself from my horizon—immediately—in his wicked pursuit of—some other lady! Oh, he did run, Father!" she confessed in the first red blush of her life. "Oh, he did—run, Father, but it was—almost directly—toward me!"

"Eh?" snapped Edgarton.

Then in a divine effrontery, half impudence and half humility, Barton stepped out into the middle of the room, and proffered his strong, firm young hand to the older man.

"You told me," he grinned, "to rummage around until I discovered a Real Treasure? Well, I didn't have to do it! It was the Treasure, it seems, who discovered me!"

Then suddenly into his fine young eyes flared up the first glint of his new-born soul.

"Your daughter, sir," said Barton, "is the most beautiful woman in the world! As you suggested to me, I have found out what she is interested in—She is interested in—ME!"

The Sick-a-Bed Lady

HE Sick-A-Bed Lady lived in a huge old-fashioned mahogany bedstead, with solid silk sheets, and three great squashy silk pillows edged with fluffy ruffles. On a table beside the Sick-A-Bed Lady was a tiny little, shiny little bell that tinkled exactly like silver raindrops on a golden roof, and all around this Lady and this Bedstead and this Bell was a big, square, shadowy room with a smutty fireplace, four small paned windows, and a chintzy wall-paper showered profusely with high-handled baskets of lavender flowers over which strange green birds hovered languidly.

The Sick-A-Bed Lady, herself, was as old as twenty, but she did not look more than fifteen with her little wistful white face against the creamy pillows and her soft brown hair braided in two thick pigtails and tied with great pink bows behind each ear.

When the Sick-A-Bed Lady felt like sitting up high against her pillows, she could look out across the footboard through her opposite window. Now through that opposite window was a marvelous vista—an old-fashioned garden, millions of miles of ocean, and then—France! And when the wind was in just the right direction there was a perfectly wonderful smell to be smelled—part of it was Cinnamon Pink and part of it was Salt-Sea-Weed, but most of it, of course, was—France. There were days and days, too, when any one with sense could feel that the waves beat perkily against the shore with a very strong French accent, and that all one's French verbs, particularly "*J'aime, Tu aimes, Il aime*," were coming home to rest. What else was there to think about in bed but funny things like that?

It was the Old Doctor who had brought the Sick-A-Bed Lady to the big white house at the edge of the Ocean, and placed her in the cool, quaint room with its front windows quizzing dreamily out to sea, and its side windows cuddled close to the curving village street. It was a long, tiresome, dangerous journey, and the Sick-A-Bed Lady in feverish fancy had moaned: "I shall die, I shall die, I shall *die*," every step of the way, but, after all, it was the Old Doctor who did the dying! Just like a snap of the finger he went at the end of two weeks, and the Sick-A-Bed Lady rallied to the shock with a plaintive: "Seems to me he was in an *awful* hurry," and fell back on her soft bed into days of unconsciousness that were broken only by riotous visions day and night of an old man rushing frantically up to a great white throne yelling: "One, two, three, for Myself!"

Out of this trouble the Sick-A-Bed Lady woke one day to find herself quite alone and quite alive. She had often felt alone before, but it was a long time since she had felt alive. The world seemed very pleasant. The flowers on the wall-paper were still unwilted, and the green paper birds hung airily without fatigue. The room was full of the most enticing odor of cinnamon pinks, and by raising herself up in bed the merest trifle she could get a smell of good salt, a smell which somehow you couldn't get unless you actually *saw* the Ocean, but just as she was laboriously tugging herself up an atom higher, trying to find the teeniest, weeniest sniff of France, everything went suddenly black and silver before her eyes, and she fell down, down, down, as much as forty miles into Nothing At All.

When she woke up again all limp and wappsy there was a Young Man's Face on the Footboard of the bed; just an isolated, unconnected sort of face that might have blossomed from the footboard, or might have been merely a mirage on the horizon. Whatever it was, though, it kept staring at her fixedly, balancing itself all the while most perfectly on its chin. It was a funny sight, and while the Sick-A-Bed Lady was puckering her forehead trying to think out what it all meant the Young Man's Face smiled at her and said "*Boo!*" and the Sick-A-Bed Lady tiptilted her chin weakly and said—"Boo *yourself!*" Then the Sick-A-Bed Lady fell into her fearful stupor again, and the Young Man's Face ran home as fast as it could to tell its Best Friend that the Sick-A-Bed Lady had spoken her first sane word for five weeks. He thought it was a splendid victory, but when he tried to explain it to his friend, he found that "Boo *yourself!*" seemed a fatuous proof of so startling a truth, and was obliged to compromise with considerable dignity on the statement: "Well, of course, it wasn't so much what she said as the *way* she said it."

For days and days that followed, the Sick-A-Bed Lady was conscious of nothing except the Young Man's Face on the footboard of the bed. It never seemed to wabble, it never seemed to waver, but just stayed there perfectly balanced on the point of its chin, watching her gravely with its blue, blue eyes. There was a cleft in its chin, too, that you could have stroked with your finger if—you could have. Of course, there were some times when she went to sleep, and some times when she just seemed to go *out* like a candle, but whenever she came back from *anything* there was always the Young Man's Face for comfort.

The Sick-A-Bed Lady was so sick that she thought all over her body instead of in her head, so that it was very hard to concentrate any particular thought in her mouth, but at last one afternoon with a mighty struggle she opened her half-closed eyes, looked right in the Young Man's Face and said: "Got any arms?"

The Young Man's Face nodded perfectly politely, and smiled as he raised two strong, lean hands to the edge of the footboard, and hunched his shoulders obligingly across the sky line.

"How do you feel?" he asked very gently.

Then the Sick-A-Bed Lady knew at once that it was the Young Doctor, and wondered why she hadn't thought of it before.

"Am I pretty sick?" she whispered deferentially.

"Yes—I think you are *very pretty*—sick," said the Young Doctor, and he towered up to a terrible, leggy height and laughed joyously, though there was almost no sound to his laugh. Then he went over to the window and began to jingle small bottles, and the Sick-A-Bed Lady lay and watched him furtively and thought about his compliment, and wondered why when she wanted to smile and say "Thank you" her mouth should shut tight and her left foot wiggle, instead.

When the Young Doctor had finished jingling bottles, he came and sat down beside her and fed her something wet out of a cool spoon, which she swallowed and swallowed and swallowed, feeling all the while like a very sick brown-eyed dog that couldn't wag anything but the far-away tip of its tail. When she got through swallowing she wanted very much to stand up and make a low bow, but instead she touched the warm little end of her tongue to the Young Doctor's hand. After that, though, for quite a few minutes her brain felt clean and tidy, and she talked quite pleasantly to the Young Doctor: "Have you got any bones in your arms?" she asked wistfully.

"Why, yes, indeed," said the Young Doctor, "rather more than the usual number of bones. Why?"

"I'd give my life," said the Sick-A-Bed Lady, "if there were bones in my silky pillows." She faltered a moment and then continued bravely: "Would you mind—holding me up stiff and strong for a second? There's no bottom to my bed, there's no top to my brain, and if I can't find a hard edge to something I shall topple right off the earth. So would you mind holding me like an *edge* for a moment—that is—if there's no lady to care? I'm not a little girl," she added conscientiously—"I'm twenty years old."

So the Young Doctor slipped over gently behind her and lifted her limp form up into the lean, solid curve of his arm and shoulder. It wasn't exactly a sumptuous corner like silken pillows, but it felt as glad as the first rock you strike on a life-swim for shore, and the Sick-A-Bed Lady dropped right off to sleep sitting bolt upright, wondering vaguely how she happened to have two hearts, one that fluttered in the usual place, and one that pounded rather noisily in her back somewhere between her shoulder-blades.

On his way home that day the Young Doctor stopped for a long while at his Best Friend's house to discuss some curious features of the Case.

"Anything new turned up?" asked the Best Friend.

"Nothing," said the Young Doctor, pulling moodily at his cigar.

"Well, it certainly beats *me*," exclaimed the Best Friend, "how any long-headed, shrewd old fellow like the Old Doctor could have brought a raving fever patient here and installed her in his own house under that clumsy Old Housekeeper without once mentioning to any one who the girl was, or where to communicate with her people. Great Heavens, the Old Doctor knew what a poor 'risk' he was. He knew absolutely that that heart of his would burst some day like a firecracker."

"The Old Doctor never was very communicative," mused the Young Doctor, with a slight grimace that might have suggested professional memories not strictly pleasant. "But I'll surely never forget him as long as ether exists," he added whimsically. "Why, you'd have thought the old chap invented ether—you'd have thought he ate it, drank it, bathed in it. I hope the *smell* of my profession will never be the only part of it I'm willing to share."

"That's all right," said the Best Friend, "that's all right. If he wanted to go off every Winter to the States and work in the Hospitals, and come back every Spring smelling like a Surgical Ward, with a lot of wonderful information which he kept to himself, why, that was his own business. He was a plucky old fellow anyway to go at all. But what I'm kicking at is his wicked carelessness in bringing this young girl here in a critical illness without taking a single soul into his confidence. Here he's dead and buried for weeks, and the Girl's people are probably worrying themselves crazy about not hearing from her. But why don't they write? Why in thunder don't they write?"

"Don't ask me!" cried the Young Doctor nervously. "I don't know! I don't know anything about it. Why, I don't even know whether the Girl is going to live. I don't even know whether she'll ever be sane again. How can I stop to quiz about her name and her home, when, perhaps, her whole life and reason rests in my foolish hands that have never done anything yet much more vital than usher a perfectly willing baby into life, or tinker with croup in some chunky throat? There's only one thing in the case that I'm sure of, and that is that she doesn't know herself who she is, and the effort to remember might snap her utterly. She's just a thread.

"I have an idea—" the Young Doctor shook his shoulders as though to shake off his more somber thoughts—"I have an idea that the Old Doctor rather counted on building up a sort of informal sanitarium here. He was daft, you know, about the climate on this particular stretch of coast. You remember that he brought home some athlete last Summer—pretty bad case of breakdown, too, but the Old Doctor cured him like a magician; and the Spring before that there was a little lad with epilepsy, wasn't there? The Old Doctor let me look at him once just to tease me. And before that—I can count up half-a-dozen people of that sort, people whom you would have said were 'gone-ers,' too. Oh, the Old Doctor would have brought home a dead man to cure if any one had 'stumped' him. And I guess this present case was a 'stump' fast enough. Why, she was raging like a prairie fire when they brought her here. No other man would have dared to travel. And they put her down in a great silk bed like a fairy-story, and the Old Doctor sat and watched her night and day studying her like a fiend, and she got better after a while: not keen, you know, but funny like a child, cooing and crooning over her pretty room, and tickled to pieces with the ocean, and vain as a kitten over her pink ribbons—the Old Doctor wouldn't let them cut her hair—and everything went on like that, till in a horrid flash the Old Doctor dropped dead that morning at the breakfast table, the little girl went loony again, and every possible clew to her identity was wiped off the earth!"

"No baggage?" suggested the Best Friend.

"Why, of course, there was baggage!" the Young Doctor exclaimed, "a great trunk. Haven't the Housekeeper and I rummaged and rummaged it till I can feel the tickle of lace across my wrists even in my sleep? Why, man alive! she's a *rich* girl. There never were such clothes in our town before. She's no free hospital pauper whom the Old Doctor obligingly took off their hands. That is, I don't see how she can be!

"Oh, well," he continued bitterly, "everybody in town calls her just the Sick-A-Bed Lady, and pretty soon it will be the Death-Bed Lady, and then it will be the Dead-and-Buried Lady—and that's all we'll ever know about it." He shivered clammily as he finished and reached for a scorching glass of whisky on the table.

But the Young Doctor did not feel so lugubrious the next day and the next and the next, when he found the Sick-A-Bed Lady rallying slowly but surely to the skill of his head and hands. To be frank, she still lay for hours at a time in a sort of gentle daze watching the world go by without her, but little by little her body strengthened as a wilted flower freshens in water, and little by little she struggled harder for words that even then did not always match her thoughts.

The village continued to speculate about her lost identity, but the Young Doctor seemed to worry less and less about it as time went on. If the sweetest little girl you ever saw knew perfectly whom you meant when you said "Dear," what was the use of hunting up such prosy names as May or Alice? And as to her funny speeches, was there anything in the world more piquant than to be called a "beautiful horse," when she meant a "kind doctor"? Was there anything dearer than her absurd wrath over her blunders, or the way she shook her head like an angry little heifer, when she occasionally forgot altogether how to talk? It was at one of these latter times that the Young Doctor, watching her desperate struggle to focus her speech, forgot all about her twenty years and stooped down suddenly and kissed her square on her mouth.

"There," he laughed, "*that* will help you remember where your mouth is!" But it was astonishing after that how many times he had to remind her.

He couldn't help loving her. No man could have helped loving her. She was so little and dear and gentle and—lost.

The Sick-A-Bed Lady herself didn't know who she was, but she would have perished with fright if she had realized that no one in the village, and not even the Young Doctor himself, could guess her identity.

The Young Doctor knew everything else in the world; why shouldn't he know who she was? He knew all about France being directly opposite the house; he had known it ever since he was a boy, and had been glad about it. He stopped her trying to count the green birds on the wall-paper because he "knew positively" that there were four hundred and seventeen whole birds, and nineteen half birds cut off by the wainscoting. He never laughed at her when she slid down the side of her bed by the village street window, and went to sleep with her curly head pillowed on the hard, white sill. He never laughed, because he understood perfectly that if you hung one white arm down over the sidewalk when you went to sleep, sometimes little children would come and put flowers in your hand, or, more wonderful still, perhaps, a yellow collie dog would come and lick your fingers.

Nothing could surprise the Young Doctor. Sometimes the Sick-A-Bed Lady took thoughts she did have and mixed them up with thoughts she didn't have, and *sprung* them on the poor Young Doctor, but he always said, "Why, of *course*," as simply as possible.

But more than all the other wise things he knew was the wise one about smelly things. He knew that when you were very, very, *very* sick, nothing pleased you so much as nice, smelly things. He brought wild strawberries, for instance, not so much to eat as to smell, but when he wasn't looking she gobbled them down as fast as she could. And he brought her all kinds of flowers, one or two at a time, and seemed so disappointed when she just sniffed them and smiled; but one day he brought her a spray of yellow jasmine, and she snatched it up and kissed it and cried "*Home,*" and the Young Doctor was so pleased that he wrote it right down in a little book and ran away to study up something. He let her smell the fresh green bank-notes in his pocketbook. Oh, they were good to smell, and after a while she said "Shops." He brought her a tiny phial of gasoline from his neighbor's automobile, and she crinkled up her nose in disgust and called it "gloves" and slapped it playfully out of his hand. But when he brought her his riding-coat she rubbed her cheek against it and whispered some funny chirruppy things. His pipe, though, was the most confusing symbol of all. It was his best pipe, too, and she snuggled it up to her nose and cried "*You, y-o-u!*" and hid it under her pillow and wouldn't give it back to him, and though he tried her a dozen times about it, she never acknowledged any association except that joyous, "*Y-o-u!*"

So day by day she gained in consecutive thought till at last she grew so reasonable as to ask: "Why do you call me *Dear?*"

And the Young Doctor forgot all about his earliest reason and answered perfectly simply: "Because I love you."

Then some of the evenings grew to be almost sweetheart evenings, though the Sick-A-Bed Lady's fragile childishness keyed the Young Doctor into an almost uncanny tenderness and restraint.

Those were wonderful evenings, though, after the Sick-A-Bed Lady began to get better and better. A good deal of the Young Doctor's practice was scattered up and down the coast, and after the dust and sweat and glare and rumble of his long day he would come back to the sleepy village in the early evening, plunge for a freshening swim into the salt water, don his white clothes and saunter round to the quaint old house at the edge of the ocean. Here in the breezy kitchen he often sat for as long as an hour, talking with the Old Housekeeper, till the Sick-A-Bed Lady's tiny silver bell rang out with absurd peremptoriness. Then for as much time as seemed wise he went and sat with the Sick-A-Bed Lady.

One night, one full-moon night, he came back from his day's work extraordinarily tired and fretted after a series of strident experiences, and hurried to the old house as to a veritable Haven of Refuge. The Housekeeper was busy with village company, so he postponed her report and went at once to the Sick-A-Bed Lady's room.

Only fools lit lights on such a night as that, and he threw himself down in the big chair by the bedside, and fairly basked in peacefulness and moonlight and content, while the Sick-A-Bed Lady leaned over and stroked his hair with her little white fingers, crooning some pleasant, childish thing about "nice, smoky Boy." There was no fret or fuss or even sound in the room, except the drowsy murmur of voices in the Garden, and the churky splash of little waves against the shore.

"Hear the French Verbs," said the Sick-A-Bed Lady, at last, with deliberate mischief. Then she shut her lips tight and waved her hands distractedly after a manner she had when she wished to imply that she was suddenly stricken dumb. The Young Doctor laughed and reached over and kissed her.

"*J'aime,*" he said.

"*J'aime,*" the Sick-A-Bed Lady repeated.

"*Tu aimes,*" he persisted.

"*Tu aimes,*" she echoed on his lips.

—Then—"There'll be no '*he* loves' to our story," he cried suddenly, and caught her so fiercely to his breast that she gave a little quick gasp of pain and struggled back on her pillows, and the Young Doctor jumped up in bitter, stinging contrition and strode out of the room. Just across the threshold he met the Old Housekeeper with a clattering tray of dishes.

"I'm going down to the Library to smoke," he said huskily to her. "Come there when you've finished. I want to talk with you."

His thoughts of himself were not kind as he wandered into the library and settled down in the first big chair that struck his fancy.

Then he fell to wondering whether there was anything gross about his love, because it took no heed of mental qualifications. He thought of at least three houses in the village where that very night he would have found lights and laughter and clever talk, and the prodding sympathy of earnest women who made the sternest happening of the day seem nothing more than a dress rehearsal for the evening's narration of it. Then he thought again of the big, quiet room upstairs, with its unquestioning peace and love and restfulness and content. What was the best thing after all that a woman could bring to a man? Yet a year ago he had bragged of the blatant braininess of his best woman friend! He began to laugh at himself.

Slowly the incongruities of the whole situation bore in upon him, and he sat and smoked and smiled in moody silence, staring with skeptical interest at the dimly lighted room around him. It was certainly the Old Doctor's private study, and realization of just what that meant came over him ironically.

The Old Doctor had been very stingy with his house and his books and his knowledge and his patients. It was natural perhaps under the professional circumstances of waning Age and waxing Youth. Yet the fact remained. Never before in five years of village association had the Young Doctor crossed the threshold of the Old Doctor's home, yet now he came and went like the Man of the House. Here he sat at this instant in the Old Doctor's private study, in the Old Doctor's chair, his feet upon the Old Doctor's table, and the whole great room with its tier after tier of bookcases, and its drawer after drawer of probable memoranda *free* before him. He could imagine the Old Doctor's impotent wrath over such a contingency, yet he felt no sentimental mawkishness over his own position. As far as he knew the Dead were dead.

Sitting there in the Old Doctor's study, he conjured up scene after scene of the Old Doctor's irascibility and exclusiveness. Even as late as the Sick-A-Bed Lady's arrival, the Old Doctor had snubbed him unmercifully before a crowd of people. It was at the station when the little sick stranger was being taken off the car and put into a carriage, and the Old Doctor had hailed the Younger with unwonted friendliness.

"I've got a case in there that would make you famous if you could master it," he said.

The Young Doctor remembered perfectly how he had walked into the trap.

"What is it?" he had cried eagerly.

"That's none of your business," chuckled the Old Doctor, and drove away with all the platform loafers shouting with delight.

Well, it seemed to be the Young Doctor's business *now*, and he got up, turned the lamp higher and began to hunt through the Old Doctor's rarest books for some light on certain curious developments in the Sick-A-Bed Lady's case.

He was just in the midst of this hunt when the Old Housekeeper glided in like a ghost and startled him.

"Sit down," he said absent-mindedly, and went on with his reading. He had almost forgotten her presence when she coughed and said: "Excuse me, sir, but I've something very special to say to you."

The Young Doctor looked up in surprise and saw that the Woman's face was ashy white.

"I—don't—think—you quite—understand the case," she stammered. "I think the little lady upstairs is going to be a Mother!"

The Young Doctor put his hand up to his face, and his face felt like parchment. He put his hand down to the book again, and the book cover quivered like flesh.

"What do you m-e-a-n?" he asked.

"I'll tell you what I mean," said the Old Housekeeper, and led him back to the sick room.

Two hours later the Young Doctor staggered into his Best Friend's house clutching a sheet of letter paper in his hand. His shoulders dragged as though under a pack, and every trace of boyishness was wrung like a rag out of his face.

"For Heaven's sake, what's the matter?" cried his friend, starting up.

"Nothing," muttered the Young Doctor, "except the Sick-A-Bed Lady."

"When did she die? What happened?"

The Young Doctor made a gesture of dissent and crawled into a chair and began to fumble with the paper in his hand. Then he shivered and stared his Best Friend straight in the face.

"You might say," he stammered, "that I have just heard from the Sick-A-Bed Lady's Husband—" he choked at the word, and his Friend sat up with astonishment: "You heard me *say* I had heard from the Sick-A-Bed Lady's Husband?" he persisted. "*You* heard me say it, mind you. You heard me say that her Husband is sick in Japan—detained indefinitely—so we are afraid he won't get here in time for her confinement—"

The sweat broke out in great drops on his forehead, and his hand that held the sheet of paper shook like a hand that has strained its muscles with heavy weights.

The Best Friend took a scathing glance at the scribbled words on the paper and laughed mirthlessly.

"You're a good fool," he said, "a good fool, and I'll publish your blessed lie to the whole stupid village, if that's what you want."

But the Young Doctor sat oblivious with his head in his hands, muttering: "Blind fool, blind fool, how could I have been such a blind fool?"

"What is it to *you*?" asked his Best Friend abruptly.

The Young Doctor jumped to his feet and squared his shoulders.

"It's *this* to me," he cried, "that I wanted her for my own! I could have cured her. I tell you I could have cured her. I wanted her for my own!"

"She's only a waif," said the Best Friend tersely.

"Waif?" cried the Young Doctor, "*waif?* No woman whom I love is a *waif!*" His face blazed furiously. "The woman I *love*—that little gentle girl—a waif?—without a home?—I would make a cool home for her out of Hell itself, if it was necessary! Damn, damn,*damn* the brute that deserted her, but *home is all around her* NOW! Do I think the Old Doctor guessed about it? *N-o!* Nobody could have guessed about it. Nobody could have known about it much before this. You say *again* she isn't *anybody's?* I'll prove to you as soon as it's decent that she's *mine*."

His Best Friend took him by the shoulder and shook him roughly.

"It is no time," he said, "for you to be courting a woman."

"I'll court my Sweetheart when and where I choose!" the Young Doctor answered defiantly, and left the house.

The night seemed a thousand miles long to him, but when he slept at last and woke again, the air was fresh and hopeful with a new day. He dressed quickly and hurried off to the scene of last night's tragedy, where he found the Old Housekeeper arguing in the doorway with a small boy. She turned to the Doctor complacently. "He's begging for the postage stamp off the Japanese letter," she exclaimed, "and I'm just telling him I sent it to my Sister's boy in Montreal."

There was no slightest trace of self-consciousness in her manner, and the Young Doctor could not help but smile as he beckoned her into the house and shut the door.

Then, "Have you told her?" he asked eagerly.

The Old Housekeeper humped her shoulders against the door and folded her arms sumptuously. "No, I haven't told her," she said, "and I'm not going to. I don't dar'st! I help you out about your business same as I helped the Old Doctor out about his business. That's all right. That's as it should be. And I'll go skipping up those stairs to tell the little lady any highfaluting, pleasant yarn that you can invent, but I don't budge one single step to tell that poor, innocent, loony Lamb—the *truth*. It isn't ugliness, Doctor. I haven't got the strength, that's all!"

Just then the little silver bell tinkled, and the Doctor went heavily up the few steps that swung the Sick-A-Bed Lady's room just out of line of real upstairs or downstairs.

The Sick-A-Bed Lady was lying in glorious state, arrayed in a wonderful pale green kimono with shimmering silver birds on it.

"You stayed too long downstairs," she asserted and went on trying to cut out pictures from a magazine.

The Young Doctor stood at the window looking out to sea as long as his legs would hold him, and then he came back and sat down on the edge of the bed.

"What's your name, Honey?" he asked with a forced smile.

"Why, 'Dear,' of course," she answered and dropped her scissors in surprise.

"What's my name?" he continued, fencing for time.

"Just '*Boy*,'" she said with sweet, contented positiveness.

The Young Doctor shivered and got up and started to leave the room, but at the threshold he stopped resolutely and came back and sat down again.

This time he took his Mother's wedding ring from his little finger and twirled it with apparent aimlessness in his hands.

Its glint caught the Sick-A-Bed Lady's eye, and she took it daintily in her fingers and examined it carefully. Then, as though it recalled some vague memory, she crinkled up her forehead and started to get out of bed. The Young Doctor watched her with agonized interest. She went direct to her bureau and began to search diligently through all the drawers, but when she reached the lower drawer and found some bright-colored ribbons she forgot her original quest, whatever it was, and brought all the ribbons back to bed with her.

The Young Doctor started to leave her again, this time with a little gesture which she took to be anger, but he had not gone further than the head of the stairs before she called him back in a voice that was startlingly mature and reasonable.

"Oh, Boy, come back," she cried. "I'll be good. What do you want?"

The Young Doctor came doubtfully.

"Do you understand me to-day?" he asked in a voice that sent an ominous chill to her heart. "Can you think pretty clearly to-day?"

She nodded her head. "Yes," she answered; "it's a good day."

"Do you know what marriage is?" he asked abruptly.

"Oh, yes," she said, but her face clouded perceptibly.

Then he took her in his arms and told her plainly, brutally, clumsily, without preface, without comment: "Honey, you are going to have a child."

For a second her mind wavered before him. He could actually see the totter in her eyes, and braced himself for the final hopeless crash, but suddenly all her being focused to the realization of his words, and she pushed at him with her hands and cried: "No—No—Oh, my God—*n-o!*" and fainted in his arms.

When she woke up again the little-girl look was all gone from her face, and though the Young Doctor smiled and smiled and smiled, he could not smile it back again. She just lay and watched him questioningly.

"Sweetheart," he whispered at last, "do you remember what I told you?"

"Yes," she answered gravely, "I remember that, but I don't remember what it means. Is it all right? Is it all right to *you*?"

"Yes," said the Young Doctor, "it's—all—right to—me."

Then the Sick-A-Bed Lady turned her little face wearily away on her pillow and went back to those dreams of hers which no one could fathom.

For all the dragging weeks and months that followed she lay in her bed or groped her way round her room in a sort of timid stupor. Whenever the Young Doctor was there she clung to him desperately and seemed to find her only comfort in his presence, but when she talked to him it was babbling talk of things and places he could not understand. All the village feared for the imminent tragedy in the great white house, and mourned the pathetic absence of the young husband, and the Young Doctor went his sorrowful way cursing that other "boy" who had wrought this final disaster on a girl's life.

But when the Sick-A-Bed Lady's hour of trial came and some one held the merciful cone of ether to her face, the Sick-A-Bed Lady took one deep, heedless breath, then gave suddenly a great gasp, snatched the cone from her face, struggled up and stretched out her arms and cried, "Boy—Boy!"

The Young Doctor came running to her and saw that her eyes were big and startled and sharp with terror:

"Oh, Boy—*Boy*," she cried, "the Ether!—I remember *everything* now—I—was his wife—the Old Doctor's Wife!"

The Young Doctor tried to replace the cone, but she beat at him furiously with her hands, crying:

"No, No, No!—If you give me Ether I shall die thinking of him!—Oh, no!—*n-o!*"

The Young Doctor's face was like chalk. His knees shook under him.

"My God!" he said, "what *can* I give you!"

The Sick-A-Bed Lady looked up at him and smiled a tortured, gallant smile. "Give me something to keep me here," she gasped! "Give me a token of you! Give me your little briarwood pipe to smell—and give it to me—quickly!"

HICKORY DOCK
Used by permission of *Lippincott's Magazine*.

THIS is the story of Hickory Dock, and of a Man and a Girl who trifled with Time.

Hickory Dock was a clock, and, of course, the Man, being a man, called it a clock, but the Girl, being a girl, called it a Hickory Dock for no more legitimate reason than that once upon a time

"Hickory, Dickory, Dock,
A Mouse ran up the Clock."
—Girls are funny things.

The Man and the Girl were very busy collecting a Home—in one room. They were just as poor as Art and Music could make them, but poverty does not matter much to lovers. The Man had collected the Girl, a wee diamond ring, a big Morris chair, two or three green and rose rugs, a shiny chafing-dish, and various incidentals. The Girl was no less discriminating. She had accumulated the Man, a Bagdad couch-cover, half-a-dozen pictures, a huge gilt mirror, three or four bits of fine china and silver, and a fair-sized boxful of lace and ruffles that idled under the couch until the Wedding-Day. The room was strikingly homelike, masculinely homelike, in all its features, but it was by no means home—yet. No place is home until *two* people have latch-keys. The Girl wore *her* key ostentatiously on a long, fine chain round her neck, but its mate hung high and dusty on a brass hook over the fireplace, and the sight of it teased the Man more than anything else that had ever happened to him in his life. The Girl was easily mistress of the situation, but the Man, you see, was not yet Master.

It was tacitly understood that if the Wedding-Day *ever* arrived, the Girl should slip the extra key into her husband's hand the very first second that the Minister closed his eyes for the blessing. She would have chosen to do this openly in exchange for her ring, but the Man contended that it might not be legal to be married with a latch-key—some ministers are so particular. It was a joke, anyway—everything except the Wedding-Day itself. Meanwhile Hickory Dock kept track of the passing hours.

When the Man first brought Hickory Dock to the Girl, in a mysteriously pulsating tissue-paper package, the Girl pretended at once that she thought it was a dynamite bomb, and dropped it precipitously on the table and sought immediate refuge in the Man's arms, from which propitious haven she ventured forth at last and picked up the package gingerly, and rubbed her cheek against it—after the manner of girls with bombs. Then she began to tug at the string and tear at the paper.

"Why, it's a Hickory Dock!" she exclaimed with delight,—"a real, live Hickory Dock!" and brandished the gift on high to the imminent peril of time and chance, and then fled back to the Man's arms with no excuse whatsoever. She was a bold little lover.

"But it's a *c-l-o-c-k*," remonstrated the Man with whimsical impatience. He had spent half his month's earnings on the gift. "Why can't you call it a clock? Why can't you *ever* call things by their right names?"

Then the Girl dimpled and blushed and burrowed her head in his shoulder, and whispered humbly, "Right name? Right names? Call things by their right names? Would you rather I called *you* by your right name—Mr. James Herbert Humphrey Jason?"

That settled the matter—settled it so hard that the Girl had to whisper the Man's wrong name seven times in his ear before he was satisfied. No man is practical about everything.

There are a good many things to do when you are in love, but the Girl did not mean that the *Art of Conversation* should be altogether lost, so she plunged for a topic.

"I think it was beautiful of you to give me a Hickory Dock," she ventured at last.

The Man shifted a trifle uneasily and laughed. "I thought perhaps it would please you," he stammered. "You see, now I have given you *all my time*."

The Girl chuckled with amused delight. "Yes—all your time. And it's nice to have a Hickory Dock that says 'Till he comes! Till he comes! Till he comes!'"

"Till he comes to—*stay*," persisted the Man. There was no sparkle in his sentiment. He said things very plainly, but his words drove the Girl across the room to the window with her face flaming. He jumped and followed her, and caught her almost roughly by the shoulder and turned her round.

"Rosalie, Rosalie," he demanded, "will you love me till the *end of time?*" There was no gallantry in his face but a great, dogged persistency that frightened the Girl into a flippant answer. She brushed her fluff of hair across his face and struggled away from him.

"I will love you," she teased, "until—the clock stops."

Then the Man burst out laughing, suddenly and unexpectedly, like a boy, and romped her back again across the room, and snatched up the clock and stole away the key.

"Hickory Dock shall *never* stop!" he cried triumphantly. "I will wind it till I die. And no one else must ever meddle with it."

"But suppose you forget?" the Girl suggested half wistfully.

"I shall *never* forget," said the Man. "I will wind Hickory Dock every week as long as I live. I *p-r-o-m-i-s-e!*" His lips shut almost defiantly.

"But it isn't fair," the Girl insisted. "It isn't fair for me to let you make such a long promise. You—might—stop—loving me." Her eyes filled quickly with tears. "Promise me just for one year,"—she stamped her foot,—"I won't take any other promise."

So, half provoked and half amused, the Man bound himself then and there for the paltry term of a year. But to fulfil his own sincerity and seriousness he took the clock and stopped it for a moment that he might start it up again with the Girl close in his arms. A half-frightened, half-willing captive, she stood in her prison and looked with furtive eyes into the little, potential face of Hickory Dock.

"You—and I—for—*all time*," whispered the Man solemnly as he started the little mechanism throbbing once more on its way, and he stooped down to seal the pledge with a kiss, but once more the significance of his word and act startled the Girl, and she clutched at the clock and ran across the room with it, and set it down very hard on her desk beside the Man's picture. Then, half ashamed of her flight, she stooped down suddenly and patted the little, ticking surface of ebony and glass and silver.

"It's a wonderful little Hickory Dock," she mused softly. "I never saw one just like it before."

The Man hesitated for a second and drew his mouth into a funny twist. "I don't believe there *is* another one like it in all the world," he acknowledged, half laughingly,—"that is, not *just* like it. I've had it fixed so that it won't strike *eleven*. I'm utterly tired of having you say 'There! it's eleven o'clock and you've *got* to go home.' *Now*, after ten o'clock nothing can strike till twelve, and that gives me two whole hours to use my own judgment in."

The Girl took one eager step towards him, when suddenly over the city roofs and across the square came the hateful, strident chime of midnight. Midnight? *Midnight?* The Girl rushed frantically to her closet and pulled the

Man's coat out from among her fluffy dresses and thrust it into his hands, and he fled distractedly for his train without "Good-by."

That was the trouble with having a lover who lived so far away and was so busy that he could come only one evening a week. Long as you could make that one evening, something always got crowded out. If you made love, there was no time to talk. If you talked, there was no time to make love. If you spent a great time in greetings, it curtailed your good-by. If you began your good-by any earlier, why, it cut your evening right in two. So the Girl sat and sulked a sad little while over the general misery of the situation, until at last, to comfort herself with the only means at hand, she went over to the closet and opened the door just wide enough to stick her nose in and sniff ecstatically.

"Oh! O—h!" she crooned. "O—h! What a nice, smoky smell."

Then she took Hickory Dock and went to bed. This method of bunking was nice for her, but it played sad havoc with Hickory Dock, who lay on his back and whizzed and whirred and spun around at such a rate that when morning came he was minutes and hours, not to say days, ahead of time.

This gain in time seemed rather an advantage to the Girl. She felt that it was a good omen and must in some manner hasten the Wedding-Day, but when she confided the same to the Man at his next visit he viewed the fact with righteous scorn, though the fancy itself pleased him mightily. The Girl learned that night, however, to eschew Hickory Dock as a rag doll. She did not learn this, though, through any particular solicitude for Hickory Dock, but rather because she had to stand by respectfully a whole precious hour and watch the Man's lean, clever fingers tinker with the little, jeweled mechanism. It was a fearful waste of time. "You are so kind to *little* things," she whispered at last, with a catch in her voice that made the Man drop his work suddenly and give all his attention to *big* things. And another evening went, while Hickory Dock stood up like a hero and refused to strike eleven.

So every Sunday night throughout the Winter and the Spring and the Summer, the Man came joyously climbing up the long stairs to the Girl's room, and every Sunday night Hickory Dock was started off on a fresh round of Time and Love.

Hickory Dock, indeed, became a very precious object, for both Man and Girl had reached that particular stage of love where they craved the wonderful sensation of owning some vital thing together. But they were so busy loving that they did not recognize the instinct. The man looked upon Hickory Dock as an exceedingly blessed toy. The Girl grew gradually to cherish the little clock with a certain tender superstition and tingling reverence that sent her heart pounding every time the Man's fingers turned to any casual tinkering.

And the Girl grew so exquisitely dear that the Man thought all women were like her. And the Man grew so sturdily precious that the Girl knew positively there was no person on earth to be compared with him. Over this happiness Hickory Dock presided throbbingly, and though he balked sometimes and bolted or lagged, he never stopped, and he never struck eleven.

Thus things went on in the customary way that things do go on with men and girls—until the Chronic Quarrel happened. The Chronic Quarrel was a trouble quite distinct from any ordinary lovers' disturbance, and it was a very silly little thing like this: The Girl had a nature that was emotionally apprehensive. She was always looking, as it were, for "dead men in the woods." She was always saying, "Suppose you get tired of me?" "Suppose I died?" "Suppose I found out that you had a wife living?" "Suppose you lost all your legs and arms in a railroad accident when you were coming here some Sunday night?"

And one day the Man had snapped her short with "Suppose? Suppose? What arrant nonsense! Suppose?—Suppose I fall in love with the Girl in the Office?"

It seemed to him the most extravagant supposition that he could possibly imagine, and he was perfectly delighted with its effect on his Sweetheart. She grew silent at once and very wistful.

After that he met all her apprehensions with "Suppose?—Suppose I fall in love with the Girl in the Office!"

And one day the Girl looked up at him with hot tears in her eyes and said tersely, "Well, why don't you fall in love with her if you *want* to?"

That, of course, made a little trouble, but it was delicious fun making up, and the "Girl in the Office" became gradually one of those irresistibly dangerous jokes that always begin with laughter and end just as invariably with tears. When the Girl was sad or blue the Man was clumsy enough to try and cheer her with facetious allusions to the "Girl in the Office," and when the Girl was supremely, radiantly happy she used to boast, "Why, I'm so happy I don't care a *rap* about your old 'Girl in the Office.'" But whatever way the joke began, it always ended disastrously, with bitterness and tears, yet neither Man nor Girl could bear to formally taboo the subject lest it should look like the first shirking of their perfect intimacy and freedom of speech. The Man felt that in love like theirs he ought to be able to say anything he wanted to, so he kept on saying it, while the Girl claimed an equal if more caustic liberty of expression, and the Chronic Quarrel began to fester a little round its edges.

One night in November, when Hickory Dock was nearly a year old in love, the Chronic Quarrel came to a climax. The Man was very listless that evening, and absent-minded, and altogether inadequate. The Girl accused him of indifference. He accused her in return of a shrewish temper. She suggested that perhaps he regretted his visit. He failed to contradict her. Then the Girl drew herself up to an absurd height for so small a creature and said stiffly,—

"You don't have to come next Sunday night if you don't want to."

At her scathing words the Man straightened up very suddenly in his chair and gazed over at the little clock in a startled sort of way.

"Why, of course I shall come," he retorted impulsively, "Hickory Dock needs me, if you don't."

"Oh, come and wind the clock by all means," flared the Girl. "I'm glad *something* needs you!"

Then the Man followed his own judgment and went home, though it was only ten o'clock.

"I'm not going to write to him this week," sobbed poor Rosalie. "I think he's very disagreeable."

But when the next Sunday came and the Man was *late*, it seemed as though an Eternity had been tacked onto a hundred years. It was fully quarter-past eight before he came climbing up the stairs.

The Girl looked scornfully at the clock. Her throat ached like a bruise. "You didn't hurry yourself much, did you?" she asked spitefully.

The Man looked up quickly and bit his lip. "The train was late," he replied briefly. He did not stop to take off his coat, but walked over to the table and wound Hickory Dock. Then he hesitated the smallest possible fraction of a moment, but the Girl made no move, so he picked up his hat and started for the door.

The Girl's heart sank, but her pride rose proportionally. "Is that all you came for?" she flushed. "Good! I am very tired to-night."

Then the Man went away. She counted every footfall on the stairs. In the little hush at the street doorway she felt that he must surely turn and come running back again, breathless and eager, with outstretched arms and all the kisses she was starving for. But when she heard the front door slam with a vicious finality she went and threw herself, sobbing on the couch. "Fifty miles just to wind a clock!" she raged in grief and chagrin. "I'll punish him for it if that's all he comes for."

So the next Sunday night she took Hickory Dock with a cruel jerk, and put him on the floor just outside her door, and left a candle burning so that the Man could not possibly fail to see what was intended. "If all he comes for is to wind the clock, just because he *promised*, there's no earthly use of his coming in," she reasoned, and went into her room and shut and locked her door, waiting nervously with clutched hands for the footfall on the stairs. "He loves some one else! He loves some one else!" she kept prodding herself.

Just at eight o'clock the Man came. She heard him very distinctly on the creaky board at the head of the stairs, and her heart beat to suffocation. Then she heard him come close to the door, as though he stooped down, and then he—laughed.

"Oh, very well," thought the Girl. "So he thinks it's funny, does he? He has no business to laugh while I am crying, even if he does love some one else.—I *hate him!*"

The Man knocked on the door very softly, and the Girl gripped tight hold of her chair for fear she should jump up and let him in. He knocked again, and she heard him give a strange little gasp of surprise. Then he tried the door-handle. It turned fatuously, but the door would not open. He pushed his weight against it,—she could almost feel the soft whirr of his coat on the wood,—but the door would not yield.—Then he turned very suddenly and went away.

The Girl got up with a sort of gloating look, as though she liked her pain. "Next Sunday night is the last Sunday night of his year's promise," she brooded; "then everything will be over. He will see how wise I was not to let him promise forever and ever. I will send Hickory Dock to him by express to save his coming for the final ceremony." Then she went out and got Hickory Dock and brought him in and shook him, but Hickory Dock continued to tick, "Till he comes! Till he comes! Till he comes!"

It was a very tedious week. It is perfectly absurd to measure a week by the fact that seven days make it—some days are longer than others. By Wednesday the Girl's proud little heart had capitulated utterly, and she decided not to send Hickory Dock away by express, but to let things take their natural course. And every time she thought of the "natural course" her heart began to pound with expectation. Of course, she would not acknowledge that she really expected the Man to come after her cruel treatment of him the previous week. "Everything is over. Everything is over," she kept preaching to herself with many gestures and illustrations; but next to God she put her faith in promises, and hadn't the Man promised a great, sacred lover's promise that he would come every Sunday for a year? So when the final Sunday actually came she went to her wedding-box and took out her "second best" of everything, silk and ruffles and laces, and dressed herself up for sheer pride and joy, with tingling thoughts of the night when she should wear her "first best" things. She put on a soft, little, white Summer dress that the Man liked better than anything else, and stuck a pink bow in her hair, and big rosettes on her slippers, and drew the big Morris chair towards the fire, and brought the Man's pipe and tobacco-box from behind the gilt mirror. Then she took Hickory Dock very tenderly and put him outside the door, with two pink candles flaming beside him, and a huge pink rose over his left ear. She thought the Man could smell the rose the second he opened the street door. Then she went back to her room, and left her door a wee crack open, and crouched down on the floor close to it, like a happy, wounded thing, and *waited*—

But the Man did not come. Eight o'clock, nine o'clock, ten o'clock, eleven o'clock, twelve o'clock, she waited, cramped and cold, hoping against hope, fearing against fear. Every creak on the stairs thrilled her. Every fresh disappointment chilled her right through to her heart. She sat and rocked herself in a huddled heap of pain, she taunted herself with lack of spirit, she goaded herself with intricate remorse—but she never left her bitter vigil until half-past two. Then some clatter of milkmen in the street roused her to the realization of a new day, and she got up dazed and icy, like one in a dream, and limped over to her couch and threw herself down to sleep like a drunken person.

Late the next morning she woke heavily with a vague, dull sense of loss which she could not immediately explain. She lay and looked with astonishment at the wrinkled folds of the white mull dress that bound her limbs like a shroud. She clutched at the tightness of her collar, and fingered with surprise the pink bow in her hair. Then slowly, one by one, the events of the previous night came back to her in all their significance, and with a muffled scream of heartbreak she buried her face in the pillow. She cried till her heart felt like a clenched fist within her, and then, with her passion exhausted, she got up like a little, cold, rumpled ghost and pattered out to the hall in her silk-stockinged feet, and picked up Hickory Dock with his wilted pink rose and brought him in and put him back on her desk. Then she brought in the mussy, pink-smooched candlesticks and stowed them far away in her closet behind everything else. The faintest possible scent of tobacco-smoke came to her from the closet depths, and as she reached instinctively to take a sad little whiff she became suddenly conscious that there was a strange, uncanny *hush* in the room, as though a soul had left its body. She turned back quickly and cried out with a smothered cry. Hickory Dock had stopped!

"Until—the—end—of—Time," she gasped, and staggered hard against the closet-door. Then in a flash she burst out laughing stridently, and rushed for Hickory Dock and grabbed him by his little silver handle, opened the window with a bang, and threw him with all her might and main down into the brick alley four stories below, where he fell with a sickening crash among a wee handful of scattered rose petals.

—The days that followed were like horrid dreams, the nights, like hideous realities. The fire would not burn. The sun and moon would not shine, and life itself settled down like a pall. Every detail of that Sunday night stamped and re stamped itself upon her mind. Back of her outraged love was the crueller pain of her outraged faith. The Man of his own free will had made a sacred promise and broken it! She realized now for the first time in her life why men went to the devil because women had failed them—not disappointed them, but *failed* them! She could even imagine how poor mothers felt when fathers shirked their fatherhood. She tasted in one week's imagination all possible woman sorrows of the world.

At the end of the second week she began to realize the depth of isolation into which her engagement had thrown her. For a year and a half she had thought nothing, dreamed nothing, cared for nothing except the Man. Now, with the Man swept away, there was no place to turn either for comfort or amusement.

At the end of the third week, when no word came, she began to gather together all the Man's little personal effects, and consigned them to a box out of sight—the pipe and tobacco, a favorite book, his soft Turkish slippers, his best gloves, and even a little poem which he had written for her to set to music. It was a pretty little love-song that they had made together, but as she hummed it over now for the last time she wondered if, after all, *woman's music* did not do more than man's words to make love Singable.

When a month was up she began to strip the room of everything that the Man had brought towards the making of their Home. It was like stripping tendons. She had never realized before how thoroughly the Man's personality had dominated her room as well as her life. When she had crowded his books, his pictures, his college trophies, his Morris chair, his rugs, into one corner of her room and covered them with two big sheets, her little, paltry, feminine possessions looked like chiffon in a desert.

While she was pondering what to do next her rent fell due. The month's idling had completely emptied her pewter savings-bank that she had been keeping as a sort of precious joke for the Honeymoon. The rent-bill startled her into spasmodic efforts at composition. She had been quite busy for a year writing songs for some Educational people, but how could one make harmony with a heart full of discord and all life off the key. A single week convinced her of the utter futility of these efforts. In one high-strung, wakeful night she decided all at once to give up the whole struggle and go back to her little country village, where at least she would find free food and shelter until she could get her grip again.

For three days she struggled heroically with burlap and packing-boxes. She felt as though every nail she pounded was hurting the Man as well as herself, and she pounded just as hard as she possibly could.

When the room was stripped of every atom of personality except her couch, and the duplicate latch-key, which still hung high and dusty, a deliciously cruel thought came to the Girl, and the irony of it set her eyes flashing. On the night before her intended departure she took the key and put it into a pretty little box and sent it to the Man.

"He'll know by that token," she said, "that there's no more 'Home' for him and me. He will get his furniture a few days later, and then he will see that everything is scattered and shattered. Even if he's married by this time, the key will hurt him, for his wife will want to know what it means, and he never can tell her."

Then she cried so hard that her overwrought, half-starved little body collapsed, and she crept into her bed and was sick all night and all the next day, so that there was no possible thought or chance of packing or traveling. But towards the second evening she struggled up to get herself a taste of food and wine from her cupboard, and, wrapping herself in her pink kimono, huddled over the fire to try and find a little blaze and cheer.

Just as the flames commenced to flush her cheeks the lock clicked. She started up in alarm. The door opened abruptly, and the Man strode in with a very determined, husbandly look on his haggard face. For the fraction of a second he stood and looked at her pitifully frightened and disheveled little figure.

"Forgive me," he cried, "but I *had* to come like this." Then he took one mighty stride and caught her up in his arms and carried her back to her open bed and tucked her in like a child while she clung to his neck laughing and sobbing and crying as though her brain was turned. He smoothed her hair, he kissed her eyes, he rubbed his rough cheek confidently against her soft one, and finally, when her convulsive tremors quieted a little, he reached down into his great overcoat pocket and took out poor, battered, mutilated Hickory Dock.

"I found him down in the Janitor's office just now," he explained, and his mouth twitched just the merest trifle at the corners.

"Don't smile," said the Girl, sitting up suddenly very straight and stiff. "Don't smile till you know the whole truth. *I* broke Hickory Dock. I threw him *purposely* four stories down into the brick alley!"

The Man began to examine Hickory Dock very carefully.

"I should judge that it was a *brick* alley," he remarked with an odd twist of his lips, as he tossed the shattered little clock over to the burlap-covered armchair.

Then he took the Girl very quietly and tenderly in his arms again, and gazed down into her eyes with a look that was new to him.

"Rosalie," he whispered, "I will mend Hickory Dock for you if it takes a thousand years,"—his voice choked,—"but I wish to God I could mend my broken promise as easily!"

And Rosalie smiled through her tears and said,—

"Sweetheart-Man, you do love me?"

"With all my heart and soul and body and breath, and past and present and future I *love you!*" said the Man.

Then Rosalie kissed a little path to his ear, and whispered, oh, so softly,—

"Sweetheart-Man, I love *you* just that same way."

And Hickory Dock, the Angel, never ticked the passing of a single second, but lay on his back looking straight up to Heaven with his two little battered hands clasped eternally at Love's *high noon*.

THE VERY TIRED GIRL

On one of those wet, warm, slushy February nights when the vapid air sags like sodden wool in your lungs, and your cheek-bones bore through your flesh, and your leaden feet seem strung directly from the roots of your eyes, three girls stamped their way through the jostling, peevish street crowds with no other object in Heaven or Earth except just to get—HOME.

It was supper time, too, somewhere between six and seven, the caved-in hour of the day when the ruddy ghost of Other People's dinners flaunts itself rather grossly in the pallid nostrils of Her Who Lives by the Chafing-Dish.

One of the girls was a Medical Masseuse, trained brain and brawn in the German Hospitals. One was a Public School Teacher with a tickle of chalk dust in her lungs. One was a Cartoon Artist with a heart like chiffon and a wit as accidentally malicious as the jab of a pin in a flirt's belt.

All three of them were silly with fatigue. The writhing city cavorted before them like a sick clown. A lame cab horse went strutting like a mechanical toy. Crape on a door would have plunged them into hysterics. Were you ever as tired as that?

With no other object, except to get home

It was, in short, the kind of night that rips out every one according to his stitch. Rhoda Hanlan the Masseuse was ostentatiously sewed with double thread and backstitched at that. Even the little Teacher, Ruth MacLaurin, had a physique that was embroidered if not darned across its raveled places. But Noreen Gaudette, the Cartoon Drawer, with her spangled brain and her tissue-paper body, was merely basted together with a single silken thread. It was the knowledge of being only basted that gave Noreen the droll, puckered terror in her eyes whenever Life tugged at her with any specially inordinate strain.

Yet it was Noreen who was popularly supposed to be built with an electric battery instead of a heart.

The boarding-house that welcomed the three was rather tall for beauty, narrow-shouldered, flat-chested, hunched together in the block like a prudish, dour old spinster overcrowded in a street car. To call such a house "Home" was like calling such a spinster "Mother." But the three girls called it "Home" and rather liked the saucy taste of the word in their mouths.

Across the threshold in a final spurt of energy the jaded girls pushed with the joyous realization that there were now only five flights of stairs between themselves and their own attic studio.

On the first floor the usual dreary vision greeted them of a hall table strewn with stale letters—most evidently bills, which no one seemed in a hurry to appropriate.

It was twenty-two stumbling, bundle-dropping steps to the next floor, where the strictly Bachelor Quarters with half-swung doors emitted a pleasant gritty sound of masculine voices, and a sumptuous cloud of cigarette smoke which led the way frowardly up twenty-two more toiling steps to the Old Maid's Floor, buffeted itself naughtily against the sternly shut doors, and then mounted triumphantly like sweet incense to the Romance Floor, where with door alluringly open the Much-Loved Girl and her Mother were frankly and ingenuously preparing for the Monday-Night-Lover's visit.

The vision of the Much-Loved Girl smote like a brutal flashlight upon the three girls in the hall.

Out of curl, out of breath, jaded of face, bedraggled of clothes, they stopped abruptly and stared into the vista.

Before their fretted eyes the room stretched fresh and clean as a newly returned laundry package. The green rugs lay like velvet grass across the floor. The chintz-covered furniture crisped like the crust of a cake. Facing the gilt-bound mirror, the Much-Loved Girl sat joyously in all her lingerie-waisted, lace-paper freshness, while her Mother hovered over her to give one last maternal touch to a particularly rampageous blond curl.

The Much-Loved Girl was a cordial person. Her liquid, mirrored reflection nodded gaily out into the hall. There was no fatigue in the sparkling face. There was no rain or fog. There was no street-corner insult. There was no harried stress of wherewithal. There was just Youth, and Girl, and Cherishing.

She made the Masseuse and the little School Teacher think of a pale-pink rose in a cut-glass vase. But she made Noreen Gaudette *feel* like a vegetable in a boiled dinner.

With one despairing gasp—half-chuckle and half-sob—the three girls pulled themselves together and dashed up the last flight of stairs to the Trunk-Room Floor, and their own attic studio, where bumping through the darkness they turned a sulky stream of light upon a room more tired-looking than themselves, and then, with almost fierce abandon, collapsed into the nearest resting-places that they could reach.

It was a long time before any one spoke.

Between the treacherous breeze of the open window and a withering blast of furnace heat the wilted muslin curtain swayed back and forth with languid rhythm. Across the damp night air came faintly the yearning, lovery smell of violets, and the far-off, mournful whine of a sick hand-organ.

On the black fur hearth-rug Rhoda, the red-haired, lay prostrated like a broken tiger lily with her long, lithe hands clutched desperately at her temples.

"I am so tired," she said. "I am so tired that I can actually feel my hair fade."

Ruth, the little Public School Teacher, laughed derisively from her pillowed couch where she struggled intermittently with her suffocating collar and the pinchy buckles on her overshoes.

"That's nothing," she asserted wanly. "I am so tired that I would like to build me a pink-wadded silk house, just the shape of a slipper, where I could snuggle down in the toe and go to sleep for a—million years. It isn't to-morrow's early morning that racks me, it's the thought of all the early mornings between now and the Judgment Day. Oh, any sentimental person can cry at night, but when you begin to cry in the morning—to lie awake and cry in the morning—" Her face sickened suddenly. "Did you see that Mother downstairs?" she gasped, "fixing that curl? Think of having a Mother!"

Then Noreen Gaudette opened her great gray eyes and grinned diabolically. She had a funny little manner of cartooning her emotions.

"Think of having a Mother?" she scoffed. "What nonsense!—*Think of having a c-u-r-l!*

"You talk like Sunday-Paper débutantes," she drawled. "You don't know anything about being tired. Why, I am so tired—I am so tired—that I wish—I wish that the first man who ever proposed to me would come back and ask me—*again!*"

It was then that the Landlady, knocking at the door, presented a card, "Mr. Ernest T. Dextwood," for Miss Gaudette, and the innocent-looking conversation exploded suddenly like a short-fused firecracker.

Rhoda in an instant was sitting bolt upright with her arms around her knees rocking to and fro in convulsive delight. Ruth much more thoughtfully jumped for Noreen's bureau drawer. But Noreen herself, after one long, hyphenated "Oh, my *H-e-a-v-e-n-s!*" threw off her damp, wrinkled coat, stalked over to the open window, and knelt down quiveringly where she could smother her blazing face in the inconsequent darkness.

For miles and miles the teasing lights of Other Women's homes stretched out before her. From the window-sill below her rose the persistent purple smell of violets, and the cooing, gauzy laughter of the Much-Loved Girl. Fatigue was in the damp air, surely, but Spring was also there, and Lonesomeness, and worst of all, that desolating sense of patient, dying snow wasting away before one's eyes like Life itself.

When Noreen turned again to her friends her eyelids drooped defiantly across her eyes. Her lips were like a scarlet petal under the bite of her teeth. There in the jetty black and scathing white of her dress she loomed up suddenly like one of her own best drawings—pulseless ink and stale white paper vitalized all in an instant by some miraculous emotional power. A living Cartoon of "*Fatigue*" she stood there—"*Fatigue*," as she herself would have drawn it—no flaccid failure of wilted bone and sagging flesh, but *Verve*—the taut Brain's pitiless rally of the Body that can not afford to rest—the verve of Factory Lights blazing overtime, the verve of the Runner who drops at his goal.

"All the time I am gone," she grinned, "pray over and over, 'Lead Noreen not into temptation.'" Her voice broke suddenly into wistful laughter: "Why to meet again a man who used to love you—it's like offering store-credit to a pauper."

Then she slammed the door behind her and started downstairs for the bleak, plush parlor, with a chaotic sense of absurdity and bravado.

But when she reached the middle of the bachelor stairway and looked down casually and spied her clumsy arctics butting out from her wet-edged skirt all her nervousness focused instantly in her shaking knees, and she collapsed abruptly on the friendly dark stair and clutching hold of the banister, began to whimper.

In the midst of her stifled tears a door banged hard above her, the floor creaked under a sturdy step, and the tall, narrow form of the Political Economist silhouetted itself against the feeble light of the upper landing.

One step down he came into the darkness—two steps, three steps, four, until at last in choking miserable embarrassment, Noreen cried out hysterically:

"Don't step on me—I'm *crying!*"

With a gasp of astonishment the young man struck a sputtering match and bent down waving it before him.

"Why, it's *you*, Miss Gaudette," he exclaimed with relief. "What's the matter? Are you ill? What are you crying about?" and he dropped down beside her and commenced to fan her frantically with his hat.

"What *are* you crying about?" he persisted helplessly, drugged man-like, by the same embarrassment that mounted like wine to the woman's brain.

Noreen began to laugh snuffingly.

"I'm not crying about anything special," she acknowledged. "I'm just crying. I'm crying partly because I'm tired—and partly because I've got my overshoes on—but *mostly*"—her voice began to catch again—"but mostly—because there's a *man* waiting to see me in the parlor."

The Political Economist shifted uneasily in his rain coat and stared into Noreen's eyes.

"Great Heavens!" he stammered. "Do you always cry when men come to see you? Is that why you never invited *me* to call?"

Noreen shook her head. "I never have men come to see me," she answered quite simply. "I go to see *them*. I study in their studios. I work on their newspapers. I caricature their enemies. Oh, it isn't *men* that I'm afraid of," she added blithely, "but *this* is something particular. *This* is something really very funny. Did you ever make a wish that something perfectly preposterous would happen?"

"Oh, yes," said the Political Economist reassuringly. "This very day I said that I wished my Stenographer would swallow the telephone."

"But she didn't swallow it, did she?" persisted Noreen triumphantly. "Now I said that I wished some one would swallow the telephone and she *did* swallow it!"

Then her face in the dusky light flared piteously with harlequined emotions. Her eyes blazed bright with toy excitement. Her lips curved impishly with exaggerated drollery. But when for a second her head drooped back against the banister her jaded small face looked for all the world like a death-mask of a Jester.

The Political Economist's heart crinkled uncomfortably within him.

"Why, you poor little girl," he said. "I didn't know that women got as tired as that. Let me take off your overshoes."

Noreen stood up like a well-trained pony and shed her clumsy footgear.

The Man's voice grew peremptory. "Your skirt is sopping wet. Are you crazy? Didn't have time to get into dry things? Nonsense! Have you had any supper? What? *N-o?* Wait a minute."

In an instant he was flying up the stairs, and when he came back there was a big glass of cool milk in his hand.

Noreen drank it ravenously, and then started downstairs with abrupt, quick courage.

When she reached the ground floor the Political Economist leaned over the banisters and shouted in a piercing whisper:

"I'll leave your overshoes outside my door where you can get them on your way up later."

Then he laughed teasingly and added: "I—hope—you'll—have—a—good—time."

And Noreen, cleaving for one last second to the outer edge of the banisters, smiled up at him, so strainingly *up*, that her face, to the man above her, looked like a little flat white plate with a crimson-lipped rose wilting on it.

Then she disappeared into the parlor.

With equal abruptness the Political Economist changed his mind about going out, and went back instead to his own room and plunged himself down in his chair, and smoked and thought, until his friend, the Poet at the big writing-desk, slapped down his manuscript and stared at him inquisitively.

"Lord Almighty! I wish I could draw!" said the Political Economist. It was not so much an exclamation as a reverent entreaty. His eyes narrowed sketchily across the vision that haunted him. "If I could draw," he persisted, "I'd make a picture that would hit the world like a knuckled fist straight between its selfish old eyes. And I'd call that picture 'Talent.' I'd make an ocean chopping white and squally, with *black* clouds scudding like fury across the sky, and no land in sight except rocks. And I'd fill that ocean full of sharks and things—not showing too much, you know, but just an occasional shimmer of fins through the foam. And I'd make a sailboat scooting along, tipped 'way over on her side toward you, with just a slip of an eager-faced girl in it. And I'd wedge her in there, wind-blown, spray-dashed, foot and back braced to the death, with the tiller in one hand and the sheet in the other, and weather-almighty roaring all around her. And I'd make the riskiest little leak in the bottom of that boat rammed desperately with a box of chocolates, and a bunch of violets, and a large paper compliment in a man's handwriting reading: 'Oh, how *clever* you are.' And I'd have that girl's face haggard with hunger, starved for sleep, tense with fear, ravished with excitement. But I'd have her chin*up*, and her eyes *open*, and the tiniest tilt of a quizzical smile hounding you like mad across the snug, gilt frame. Maybe, too, I'd have a woman's magazine blowing around telling in chaste language how to keep the hair 'smooth' and the hands 'velvety,' and admonishing girls above all things not to be eaten by sharks! Good Heavens, Man!" he finished disjointedly, "a girl doesn't know how to sail a boat anyway!"

"*W-h-a-t* are you talking about?" moaned the Poet.

The Political Economist began to knock the ashes furiously out of his pipe.

"What am I talking about?" he cried; "I'm talking about *girls*. I've always said that I'd gladly fall in love if I only could decide what kind of a girl I wanted to fall in love with. Well, I've decided!"

The Poet's face furrowed. "Is it the Much-Loved Girl?" he stammered.

The Political Economist's smoldering temper began to blaze.

"No, it isn't," ejaculated the Political Economist. "The Much-Loved Girl is a sweet enough, airy, fairy sort of girl, but I'm not going to fall in love with just a pretty valentine."

"Going to try a 'Comic'?" the Poet suggested pleasantly.

The Political Economist ignored the impertinence. "I am reasonably well off," he continued meditatively, "and I'm reasonably good-looking, and I've contributed eleven articles on 'Men and Women' to modern economic literature, but it's dawned on me all of a sudden that in spite of all my beauteous theories regarding life in general, I am just one big shirk when it comes to life in particular."

The Poet put down his pen and pushed aside his bottle of rhyming fluid, and began to take notice.

"Whom are you going to fall in love with?" he demanded.

The Political Economist sank back into his chair.

"I don't quite know," he added simply, "but she's going to be some tired girl. Whatever else she may or may not be, she's got to be a tired girl."

"A tired girl?" scoffed the Poet. "That's no kind of a girl to marry. Choose somebody who's all pink and white freshness. That's the kind of a girl to make a man happy."

The Political Economist smiled a bit viciously behind his cigar.

"Half an hour ago," he affirmed, "I was a beast just like you. Good Heavens! Man," he cried out suddenly, "did you ever see a girl cry? Really cry, I mean. Not because her manicure scissors jabbed her thumb, but because her great, strong, tyrant, sexless brain had goaded her poor little woman-body to the very cruelest, last vestige of its strength and spirit. Did you ever see a girl like that Miss Gaudette upstairs—she's the Artist, you know, who did those cartoons last year that played the devil itself with 'Congress Assembled'—did you ever see a girl like *that* just plain thrown down, tripped in her tracks, sobbing like a hurt, tired child? Your pink and white prettiness can cry like a rampant tragedy-queen all she wants to over a misfitted collar, but my hand is going here and now to the big-brained girl who cries like a child!"

"In short," interrupted the Poet, "you are going to help—Miss Gaudette sail her boat?"

"Y-e-s," said the Political Economist.

"And so," mocked the Poet, "you are going to jump aboard and steer the young lady adroitly to some port of your own choosing?"

The older man's jaws tightened ominously. "No, by the Lord Almighty, that's just what I am not going to do!" he promised. "I'm going to help her sail to the port of her own choosing!"

The Poet began to rummage in his mind for adequate arguments. "Oh, allegorically," he conceded, "your scheme is utterly charming, but from any material, matrimonial point of view I should want to remind myself pretty hard that overwrought brains do not focus very easily on domestic interests, nor do arms which have tugged as you say at 'sheets' and 'tillers' curve very dimplingly around youngsters' shoulders."

The Political Economist blew seven mighty smoke-puffs from his pipe.

"That would be the economic price I deserve to pay for not having arrived earlier on the scene," he said quietly.

The Poet began to chuckle. "You certainly are hard hit," he scoffed.

"Political Economy
Gone to rhyme with Hominy!
It's an exquisite scheme!"

"It's a rotten rhyme," attested the Political Economist, and strode over to the mantelpiece, where he began to hunt for a long piece of twine.

"Miss Gaudette," he continued, "is downstairs in the parlor now entertaining a caller—some resurrected beau, I believe. Anyway, she left her overshoes outside my door to get when she comes up again, and I'm going to tie one end of this string to them and the other end to my wrist, so that when she picks up her shoes a few hours later it will wake me from my nap, and I can make one grand rush for the hall and—"

"Propose then and there?" quizzed the Poet.

"No, not exactly. But I'm going to ask her if she'll let me fall in love with her."

The Poet sniffed palpably and left the room.

But the Political Economist lay back in his chair and went to sleep with a great, pleasant expectancy in his heart.

When he woke at last with a sharp, tugging pain at his wrist the room was utterly dark, and the little French clock had stopped aghast and clasped its hands at eleven.

For a second he rubbed his eyes in perplexity. Then he jumped to his feet, fumbled across the room and opened the door to find Noreen staring with astonishment at the tied overshoes.

"Oh, I wanted to speak to you," he began. Then his eyes focused in amazement on a perfectly huge bunch of violets which Noreen was clasping desperately in her arms.

"Good Heavens!" he cried. "Is anybody dead?"

But Noreen held the violets up like a bulwark and commenced to laugh across them.

"He did propose," she said, "and I accepted him! Does it look as though I had chosen to be engaged with violets instead of a ring?" she suggested blithely. "It's only that I asked him if he would be apt to send me violets, and when he said: 'Yes, every week,' I just asked if I please couldn't have them all at once. There must be a Billion dollars' worth here. I'm going to have a tea-party to-morrow and invite the Much-Loved Girl." The conscious, childish malice of her words twisted her lips into an elfish smile. "It's Mr. Ernest Dextwood," she rattled on: "Ernest Dextwood, the Coffee Merchant. He's a widower now—with three children. Do—you—think—that—I—will—make—a—good—stepmother?"

The violets began to quiver against her breast, but her chin went higher in rank defiance of the perplexing *something* which she saw in the Political Economist's narrowing eyes. She began to quote with playful recklessness Byron's pert parody:

"There is a tide in the affairs of women
Which taken at its flood leads—God Knows Where."

But when the Political Economist did not answer her, but only stared with brooding, troubled eyes, she caught her breath with a sudden terrifying illumination. "Ouch!" she said. "O-u-c-h!" and wilted instantly like a frost-bitten rose under heat. All the bravado, all the stamina, all the glint of her, vanished utterly.

"Mr. Political Economist," she stammered, "Life—is—too—hard—for—me. I am not Rhoda Hanlan with her sturdy German peasant stock. I am not Ruth MacLaurin with her Scotch-plaited New Englandism. Nationality doesn't count with me. My Father was a Violinist. My Mother was an Actress. In order to marry, my Father swapped his music for discordant factory noises, and my Mother shirked a dozen successful rôles to give one life-long, very poor imitation of Happiness. My Father died of too much to drink. My Mother died of too little to eat. And I was bred, I guess, of very bitter love, of conscious sacrifice—of thwarted genius—of defeated vanity. Life—is—too—hard—for—me—*alone*. I can not finance it. I can not safeguard it. I can not weather it. *I am not seaworthy!* You might be willing to risk your *own* self-consciousness, but when the dead begin to come back and clamor in you—when you laugh unexpectedly with your Father's restive voice—when you quicken unexplainably to the Lure of gilt and tinsel—" A whimper of pain went scudding across her face, and she put back her head and grinned—"You can keep my overshoes for a souvenir," she finished abruptly. "I'm not allowed any more to go out when it storms!" Then she turned like a flash and ran swiftly up the stairs.

When he heard the door slam hard behind her, the Political Economist fumbled his way back through the darkened room to his Morris chair, and threw himself down again. Ernest Dextwood? He knew him well, a prosperous, kindly, yet domestically tyrannical man, bright in the office, stupid at home. Ernest Dextwood! So much less of a girl would have done for him.

A widower with three children? The eager, unspent emotionalism of Noreen's face flaunted itself across his smoky vision. All that hunger for Life, for Love, for Beauty, for Sympathy, to be blunted once for all in a stale, misfitting, ready-made home? A widower with three children! God in Heaven, was she as tired as that!

It was a whole long week before he saw Noreen again. When he met her at last she had just come in from automobiling, all rosy-faced and out of breath, with her thin little face peering almost plumply from its heavy swathings of light-blue veiling, and her slender figure deeply wrapped in a wondrous covert coat.

Rhoda Hanlan and Ruth MacLaurin were close behind her, much more prosaically garnished in golf capes and brown-colored mufflers. The Political Economist stood by on the stairs to let them pass, and Noreen looked back at him and called out gaily:

"It's lots of fun to be engaged. We're all enjoying it very much. It's bully!"

The next time he saw her she was on her way downstairs to the parlor, in a long-tailed, soft, black evening gown that bothered her a bit about managing. Her dark hair was piled up high on her head, and she had the same mischievous, amateur-theatrical charm that the blue chiffon veil and covert coat had given her.

Quite frankly she demanded the Political Economist's appreciation of her appearance.

"Just see how nice I can look when I really try?" she challenged him, "but it took me all day to do it, and my work went to smash—and my dress cost seventy dollars," she finished wryly.

But the Political Economist was surly about his compliment.

"No, I like you better in your little business suit," he attested gruffly. And he lied, and he knew that he lied, for never before had he seen the shrewd piquancy of her eyes so utterly swamped by just the wild, sweet lure of girlhood.

Some time in May, however, when the shop windows were gay with women's luxuries, he caught a hurried glimpse of her face gazing rather tragically at a splurge of lilac-trimmed hats.

Later in the month he passed her in the Park, cuddled up on a bench, with her shabby business suit scrunched tight around her, her elbows on her knees, her chin burrowed in her hands, and her fiercely narrowed eyes quaffing like some outlawed thing at the lusty new green grass, the splashing fountain, the pinky flush of flowering quince. But when he stopped to speak to her she jumped up quickly and pleaded the haste of an errand.

It was two weeks later in scorching June that the biggest warehouses on the river caught fire in the early part of the evening. The day had been as harsh as a shining, splintery plank. The night was like a gray silk pillow. In blissful, soothing consciousness of perfect comfort every one in the boarding-house climbed up on the roof to watch the gorgeous, fearful conflagration across the city. The Landlady's voice piped high and shrill discussing the value of insurance. The Old Maids scuttled together under their knitted shawls. The Much-Loved Girl sat amiably enthroned among the bachelors with one man's coat across her shoulders, another man's cap on her yellow head, and two deliciously timid hands clutched at the coat-sleeves of the two men nearest her. Whenever she bent her head she trailed the fluff of her hair across the enraptured eyelids of the Poet.

Only Noreen Gaudette was missing.

"Where is Miss Gaudette?" probed the Political Economist.

The Masseuse answered vehemently: "Why, Noreen's getting ready to go to the fire. Her paper sent for her just as we came up. There's an awful row on, you know, about the inefficiency of the Fire Department, and there's no other person in all the city who can make people look as silly as Noreen can. If this thing appeals to her to-night, and she gets good and mad enough, and keeps her nerve, there'll be the biggest overhauling of the Fire Department that *you* ever saw! But I'm sorry it happened. It will be an all-night job, and Noreen is almost dead enough as it is."

"An 'all-night job'?" The Much-Loved Girl gasped out her startled sense of propriety, and snuggled back against the shoulder of the man who sat nearest to her. She was very genuinely sorry for any one who had to be improper.

The Political Economist, noting the incident in its entirety, turned abruptly on his heel, climbed down the tremulous ladder to the trunk-room floor and knocked peremptorily at Noreen's door.

In reply to the answer which he thought he heard, he turned the handle of the door and entered. The gas jet sizzled blatantly across the room, and a tiny blue flame toiled laboriously in a cooking lamp beneath a pot of water. The room was reeking strong with the smell of coffee, the rank brew that wafted him back in nervous terror to his college days and the ghastly eve of his final examinations. A coat, a hat, a mouse-gray sweater, a sketch-book, and a bunch of pencils were thrown together on the edge of the divan. Crouched on the floor with head and shoulders prostrate across her easel chair and thin hands straining at the woodwork was Noreen Gaudette. The startled face that lifted to his was haggard with the energy of a year rallied to the needs of an hour.

"I thought you told me to come in," said the Political Economist. "I came down to go to the fire with you."

Noreen was on her feet in an instant, hurrying into her hat and coat, and quaffing greedily at the reeking coffee.

"You ought to have some one to look after you," persisted the man. "Where's Mr. Dextwood?"

Noreen stood still in the middle of the floor and stared at him.

"Why, I've broken my engagement," she exclaimed, trying hard to speak tamely and reserve every possible fraction of her artificial energy.

"Oh, yes," she smiled wanly, "I couldn't afford to be engaged! I couldn't afford the time. I couldn't afford the money. I couldn't afford the mental distraction. I'm working again now, but it's horribly hard to get back into the mood. My drawing has all gone to smash. But I'll get the hang of it again pretty soon."

"You look in mighty poor shape to work to-night," said the Political Economist. "What makes you go?"

"What makes me go?" cried Noreen, with an extravagant burst of vehemence. "What makes me go?—Why, if I make good to-night on those Fire-Department Pictures I get a Hundred Dollars, as well as the assurance of all the Republican cartooning for the next city election. It's worth a lot of money to me!"

"Enough to kill yourself for?" probed the Man.

Noreen's mouth began to twist. "Yes—if you still owe for your automobile coat, and your black evening gown, and your room rent and a few other trifles of that sort. But come on, if you'll promise not to talk to me till it's all over." Like a pair of youngsters they scurried down the stairs, jumped into the waiting cab, and galloped off toward the river edge of the city.

True to his promise, the Political Economist did not speak to her, but he certainly had not promised to keep his eyes shut as well as his mouth. From the very first she sat far forward on the seat where the passing street-lights blazed upon her unconscious face. The Man, the cab, love-making, debt-paying, all were forgotten in her desperate effort to keep keyed up to the working-point. Her brain was hurriedly sketching in her backgrounds. Her suddenly narrowed eyes foretold the tingling pride in some particular imagining. The flashing twist of her smile predicted the touch of malice that was to make her pictures the sensation of—a day.

The finish of the three-mile drive found her jubilant, prescient, pulsing with power. The glow from the flames lit up the cab like a room. The engine bells clanged around them. Sparks glittered. Steam hissed. When the cabman's horse refused to scorch his nose any nearer the conflagration, Noreen turned to the Political Economist with some embarrassment. "If you really want to help me," she pleaded, "you'll stay here in the cab and wait for me."

Then, before the Political Economist could offer his angry protest, she had opened the door, jumped from the step, and disappeared into the surging, rowdy throng of spectators. A tedious hour later the cab door opened abruptly, and Noreen reappeared.

Her hat was slouched down over her heat-scorched eyes. Her shoulders were limp. Her face was dull, dumb, gray, like a Japanese lantern robbed of its candle. Bluntly she thrust her sketch-book into his hands and threw herself down on the seat beside him.

"Oh, take me home," she begged. "Oh, take me home *quick*. It's no use," she added with a shrug, "I've seen the whole performance. I've been everywhere—inside the ropes—up on the roofs—out on the waterfront. The Fire Department Men are not 'inefficient.' They're simply *bully! And I make no caricatures of heroes!*"

The lurch of the cab wheel against a curbstone jerked a faint smile into her face. "Isn't it horrid," she complained, "to have a Talent and a Living that depend altogether upon your *getting mad?*" Then her eyes flooded with worry. "What *shall* I do?"

"You'll marry me," said the Political Economist.

"Oh, no!" gasped Noreen. "I shall never, never marry any one! I told you that I couldn't afford to be engaged. It takes too much time, and besides," her color flamed piteously, "I didn't like being engaged."

"I didn't ask you to be engaged," persisted the Political Economist. "I didn't ask you to serve any underpaid, ill-fed, half-hearted apprenticeship to Happiness. I asked you to be married."

"Oh, no!" sighed Noreen. "I shall never marry any one."

The Political Economist began to laugh. "Going to be an old maid?" he teased.

The high lights flamed into Noreen's eyes. She braced herself into the corner of the carriage and fairly hurled her defiance at him. Indomitable purpose raged in her heart, unutterable pathos drooped around her lips. Every atom of blood in her body was working instantly in her brain. No single drop of it loafed in her cheeks under the flimsy guise of embarrassment.

"I am not an 'Old Maid!' I am not! No one who creates anything is an 'Old Maid'!"

The passion of her mood broke suddenly into wilful laughter. She shook her head at him threateningly.

"Don't you ever dare to call me an 'Old Maid' again.—But I'll tell you just what you can call me—Women are supposed to be the Poetry of Life, aren't they—the Sonnet, the Lyric, the Limerick? Well—I am blank verse. *That* is the trouble with me. I simply *do not rhyme.*—That is all!"

"Will you marry me?" persisted the Political Economist.

Noreen shook her head. "No!" she repeated. "You don't seem to understand. Marriage is not for me. I tell you that I am Blank Verse. I am *Talent*, and I do not *rhyme* with Love. I am *Talent* and I do not rhyme with *Man*. There is no place in my life for you. You can not come into my verse and rhyme with me!"

"Aren't you a little bit exclusive?" goaded the Political Economist.

Noreen nodded gravely. "Yes," she said, "I am brutally exclusive. But everybody isn't. Life is so easy for some women. Now, the Much-Loved Girl is nothing in the world except 'Miss.' She rhymes inevitably with almost anybody's kiss.—*I* am not just '*Miss*.' The Much-Loved Girl is nothing in the world except 'Girl.'—She rhymes inevitably with 'Curl.' *I* am not just '*Girl*.' She is 'Coy' and rhymes with 'Boy.' She is 'Simple' and rhymes with 'Dimple.' *I am none of those things!* I haven't the Lure of the Sonnet. I haven't the Charm of the Lyric. I haven't the Bait of the Limerick. At the very best I am 'Brain' and rhyme with 'Pain.' And I wish I was*dead!*"

The Political Economist's heart was pounding like a gong smothered in velvet. But he stooped over very quietly and pushed the floor cushion under her feet and snuggled the mouse-gray sweater into a pillowed roll behind her aching neck. Then from his own remotest corner he reached out casually and rallied her limp, cold hand into the firm, warm clasp of his vibrant fingers.

"Of course, you never have rhymed," he said. "How could you possibly have rhymed when—*I am the missing lines of your verse?*" His clasp tightened. "Never mind about Poetry to-night, Dear, but *to-morrow* we'll take your little incomplete lonesome verse and quicken it into a Love-Song that will make the Oldest Angel in Heaven sit up and carol!"

THE HAPPY-DAY

IT was not you, yourself, who invented your Happy-day. It was your Father, long ago in little-lad time, when a Happy-Day or a Wooden Soldier or High Heaven itself lay equally tame and giftable in the cuddling, curving hollow of a Father's hand.

Your Father must have been a very great Genius. How else could he have invented any happy thing in the black-oak library?

The black-oak library was a cross-looking room, dingy, lowering, and altogether boggy. You could not stamp your boot across the threshold without joggling the heart-beats out of the gaunt old clock that loomed in the darkermost corner of the alcove. You could not tiptoe to the candy box without plunging headlong into a stratum of creakiness that puckered your spine as though an electric devil were pulling the very last basting thread out of your little soul. Oh, it must have been a very, very aged room. The darkness was abhorrent to you. The dampness reeked with the stale, sad breath of ancient storms. Worst of all, blood-red curtains clotted at the windows; rusty swords and daggers hung most imminently from the walls, and along the smutted hearth a huge, moth-eaten tiger skin humped up its head in really terrible ferocity.

Through all the room there was no lively spot except the fireplace itself.

Usually, white birch logs flamed on the hearth with pleasant, crackling cheerfulness, but on this special day you noted with alarm that between the gleaming andirons a soft, red-leather book writhed and bubbled with little gray wisps of pain, while out of a charry, smoochy mass of nothingness a blue-flowered muslin sleeve stretched pleadingly toward you for an instant, shuddered, blazed, and was—gone.

It was there that your Father caught you, with that funny, strange sniff of havoc in your nostrils.

It was there that your Father told you his news.

When you are only a little, little boy and your Father snatches you suddenly up in his arms and tells you that he is going to be married again, it is very astonishing. You had always supposed that your Father was perfectly married! In the dazzling sunshine of the village church was there not a thrilly blue window that said quite distinctly, "Clarice Val Dere" (that was your Mother) "Lived" (*Lived*, it said!) "June, 1860—December, 1880"? All the other windows said "Died" on them. Why should your Father marry again?

In your Dear Father's arms you gasped, "Going to be *married?*" and your two eyes must have popped right out of your head, for your Father stooped down very suddenly and kissed them hard—whack, whack, back into place.

"N—o, not going to be married," he corrected, "but going to be married—again."

He spoke as though there were a great difference; but it was man-talk and you did not understand it.

Then he gathered you into the big, dark chair and pushed you way out on his knees and scrunched your cheeks in his hands and ate your face all up with his big eyes. When he spoke at last, his voice was way down deep like a bass drum.

"Little Boy Jack," he said, "you must never, never, never forget your Dear Mother!"

His words and the bir-r-r of them shook you like a leaf.

"But what was my Dear Mother like?" you whimpered. You had never seen your Mother.

Then your Father jumped up and walked hard on the creaky floor. When he turned round again, his eyes were all wet and shiny like a brown stained-glass window.

"What was your Dear Mother like?" he repeated. "Your Dear Mother was like—was like—the flash of a white wing across a stormy sea. And your Dear Mother's name was 'Clarice.' I give it to you for a Memorial. What better Memorial could a little boy have than his Dear Mother's name? And there is a date—" His voice grew suddenly harsh and hard like iron, and his lips puckered on his words as with a taste of rust—"there is a date—the 26th of April—No, that is too hard a date for a little boy's memory! It was a Thursday. I give you Thursday for your—Happy-Day. 'Clarice' for a Memorial, and Thursday for your Happy-Day." His words began to beat on you like blows. "As—long—as—you—live," he cried, "be very kind to any one who is named 'Clarice.' And no matter what

Time brings you—weeks, months, years, centuries—*keep Thursday for your Happy-Day*. No cruelty must ever defame it, no malice, no gross bitterness."

Then he crushed you close to him for the millionth, billionth fraction of a second, and went away, while you stayed behind in the scary black-oak library, feeling as big and achy and responsible as you used to feel when you and your Dear Father were carrying a heavy suit-case together and your Dear Father let go his share just a moment to light his brown cigar. It gave you a beautiful feeling in your head, but way off in your stomach it tugged some.

So you crept away to bed at last, and dreamed that on a shining path leading straight from your front door to Heaven you had to carry all alone two perfectly huge suit-cases packed tight with love, and one of the suit-cases was marked "Clarice" and one was marked "Thursday." Tug, tug, tug, you went, and stumble, stumble, stumble, but your Dear Father could not help you at all because he was perfectly busy carrying a fat leather bag, some golf sticks, and a bull-terrier for a strange lady.

It was not a pleasant dream, and you screamed out so loud in the night that the Housekeeper-Woman had to come and comfort you. It was the Housekeeper-Woman who told you that on the morrow your Father was going far off across the salt seas. It was the Housekeeper-Woman who told you that you, yourself, were to be given away to a Grandmother-Lady in Massachusetts. It was also the Housekeeper-Woman who told you that your puppy dog Bruno—Bruno the big, the black, the curly, the waggy, was not to be included in the family gift to the Grandmother-Lady. Everybody reasoned, it seemed, that you would not need Bruno because there would be so many other dogs in Massachusetts. That was just the trouble. They *would* all be "other dogs." It was Bruno that you wanted, for he was the only *dog*, just as *you* were the only *boy* in the world. All the rest were only "other boys." You could have explained the matter perfectly to your Father if the Housekeeper-Woman had not made you cry so that you broke your explainer. But later in the night the most beautiful thought came to you. At first perhaps it tasted a little bit sly in your mouth, but after a second it spread like ginger, warm and sweet over your whole body except your toes, and you crept out of bed like a flannel ghost and fumbled your way down the black hall to your Dear Father's room and woke him shamelessly from his sleep. His eyes in the moonlight gleamed like two frightened dreams.

"Dear Father," you cried—you could hardly get the words fast enough out of your mouth—"Dear—Father—I—do—not—think—Bruno—is—a—very—good—name—for—a—big—black—dog—I—am—going—to—name—him—Clarice—instead!"

That was how you and Bruno-Clarice happened to celebrate together your first Happy-Day with a long, magic, joggling train journey to Massachusetts—the only original *boy* and the only original *dog* in all the world.

The Grandmother-Lady proved to be a very pleasant purple sort of person. Exactly whose Grandmother she was, you never found out. She was not your Father's mother. She was not your Mother's mother. With these links missing, whose Grandmother could she be? You could hardly press the matter further without subjecting her to the possible mortification of confessing that she was only adopted. Maybe, crudest of all, she was just a Paid-Grandmother.

The Grandmother-Lady lived in a perfectly brown house in a perfectly green garden on the edge of a perfectly blue ocean. That was the Sight of it. Salted mignonette was the Smell of it. And a fresh wind flapping through tall poplar trees was always and forever the Sound of it.

The brown house itself was the living image of a prim, old-fashioned bureau backed up bleakly to the street, with its piazza side yanked out boldly into the garden like a riotous bureau drawer, through which the Rising Sun rummaged every morning for some particular new shade of scarlet or yellow nasturtiums. As though quite shocked by such bizarre untidiness, the green garden ran tattling like mad down to the ocean and was most frantically shooed back again, so that its little trees and shrubs and flowers fluttered in a perpetual nervous panic of not knowing which way to blow.

The blue ocean was the most wonderful thing of all

But the blue ocean was the most wonderful thing of all. Never was there such an ocean! Right from the far-away edge of the sky it came, roaring, ranting, rumpling, till it broke against the beach all white and frilly like the Grandmother-Lady's best ruching. It was morning when you saw the ocean first, and its pleasant waters gleamed like a gorgeous, bright-blue looking-glass covered with paper ships all filled with Other Boys' fathers. It was not till the first night came down—black and mournful and moany—it was not till the first night came down that you saw that the ocean was Much Too Large. There in your chill linen bed, with the fear of Sea and Night and Strangers upon you, you discovered a very strange droll thing—that your Father was a Person and might therefore leave you, but that your Mother was a *feeling* and would never, never, never forsake you. Bruno-Clarice, slapping his fat, black tail against your bedroom floor, was something of a *feeling* too.

Most fortunately for your well-being, the Grandmother-Lady's house was not too isolated from its neighbors. To be sure, a tall, stiff hedge separated the green garden from the lavender-and-pink garden next door, but a great scraggly hole in the hedge gave a beautiful prickly zest to friendly communication.

More than this, two children lived on the other side of the hedge. You had never had any playmates before in all your life!

One of the children was just Another Boy—a duplicate of you. But the other one was—*the only original girl*. Next to the big ocean, she was the surprise of your life. She wore skirts instead of clothes. She wore curls instead of hair. She wore stockings instead of legs. She cried when you laughed. She laughed when you cried. She was funny from the very first second, even when the Boy asked you if your big dog would bite. The Boy stood off and kept right on asking: "Will he bite? Will he bite? *W-i-l-l* he *bite?*" But the Girl took a great rough stick and pried open Bruno-Clarice's tusky mouth *to see if he would*, and when he *g-r-o-w-l-e-d*, she just kissed him smack on his black nose and called him "A Precious," and said, "Why, of course he'll bite."

The Boy was ten years old—a year older, and much fatter than you. His name was Sam. The Girl was only eight years old, and you could not tell at first whether she was thin or fat, she was so ruffledy. She had a horrid dressy name, "Sophia." But everybody called her Ladykin.

Oh, it is fun to make a boat that will flop sideways through the waves. It is fun to make a windmill that will whirl and whirl in the grass. It is fun to make an education. It is fun to make a fortune. But most of anything in the world it is fun to make a *friend!*

You had never made a *friend* before. First of all you asked, "How old are you?" "Can you do fractions?" "Can you name the capes on the west coast of Africa?" "What is your favorite color? Green? Blue? Pink? Red? Or yellow?" Sam voted for green. Ladykin chose green *and* blue *and* pink *and* red *and* yellow, *also* purple. Then you asked, "Which are you most afraid of, the Judgment Day or a Submarine Boat?" Sam chose the Submarine Boat right off, so you had to take the Judgment Day, which was not a very pleasant fear to have for a pet. Ladykin declared that she wasn't afraid of anything in the world except of Being Homely. Wasn't that a silly fear? Then you got a little more intimate and asked, "What is your Father's business?" Sam and Ladykin's Father kept a huge candy store. It was mortifying to have to confess that your Father was only an Artist, but you laid great stress on his large eyes and his long fingers.

Then you three went off to the sandy beach and climbed up on a great huddly gray rock to watch the huge yellow sun go down all shiny and important, like a twenty-dollar gold piece in a wad of pink cotton batting. The tide was going out, too, the mean old "injun-giver," taking back all the pretty, chuckling pebbles, the shining ropes of seaweed, the dear salt secrets it had brought so teasingly to your feet a few hours earlier. You were very lonesome. But not till the gold and pink was almost gone from the sky did you screw your courage up to its supreme point. First you threw four stones very far out into the surf, then—

"What—is—your—Mother—like?" you whispered.

Ladykin went to her answer with impetuous certainty:

"Our Mother," she announced, "is fat and short and wears skin-tight dresses, and is President of the Woman's Club, and is sometimes cross."

A great glory came upon you and you clutched for wonder at the choking neck of your little blouse.

"M-y Mother," you said, "m-y Mother is like the Flash of a White Wing across a Stormy Sea!"

You started to say more, but with a wild war-whoop of amusement, Sam lost his balance and fell sprawling into the sand. "Oh, what a funny Mother!" he shouted, but Ladykin jumped down on him furiously and began to kick him with her scarlet sandals. "Hush! hush!" she cried, "Jack's Mother is dead!" and then in an instant she had clambered back to your side again and snuggled0 her little soft girl-cheek close against yours, while with one tremulous hand she pointed way out beyond the surf line where a solitary, snow-white gull swooped down into the Blue. "Look!" she gasped, "L-o-o-k!" and when you turned to her with a sudden gulping sob, she kissed you warm and sweet upon your lips.

It was not a Father kiss with two tight arms and a scrunching pain. It was not a Grandmother-Lady kiss complimenting your clean face. It was not a Bruno-Clarice kiss, mute and wistful and lappy. There was no pain in it. There was no compliment. There was no doggish fealty. There was just *sweetness*.

Then you looked straight at Ladykin, and Ladykin looked straight at you, looked and *looked* and LOOKED, and you both gasped right out loud before the first miracle of your life, the Miracle of the Mating of Thoughts. Without a word of suggestion, without a word of explanation, you and Ladykin clasped hands and tiptoed stealthily off to the very edge of the water, and knelt down slushily in the sand, and stooped way over, oh, way, way over, with the cold waves squirting up your cuffs; and kissed two perfectly round floaty kisses out to the White Sea-Gull, and after a minute the White Gull rose in the sky, swirled round and round and round, stopped for a second, and then with a wild cry swooped down again into the blue—Once! Twice! and then with a great fountainy splash of wings rose high in the air like a white silk kite and went scudding off like mad into the Grayness, then into the Blackness, then into the Nothingness of the night. And you stayed behind on that pleasant, safe, sandy edge of things with all the sweetness gone from your lips, and nothing left you in all the world but the thudding of your heart, and a queer, sad, salty pucker on your tongue that gave you a thirst not so much for water as for *life*.

Oh, you learned a great deal about living in those first few days and weeks and months at the Grandmother-Lady's house.

You learned, for instance, that if you wanted to *do* things, Boys were best; but if you wanted to *think* things, then Girls were infinitely superior. You, yourself, were part Thinker and part Doer.

Sam was a *doer* from start to finish, strong of limb, long of wind, sturdy of purpose. But Sam was certainly prosy in his head. Ladykin, on the contrary, had "gray matter" that jumped like a squirrel in its cage, and fled hither and yon, and turned somersaults, and leaped through hoops, and was altogether alert beyond description. But she could not *do* things. She could not stay in the nice ocean five minutes without turning blue. She could not climb a tree without falling and bumping her nose. She could not fight without getting mad. Out of these proven facts you evolved a beautiful theory that if Thinky-Girls could only be taught to *do* things, they would make the most perfect playmates in all the wide, wide world. Yet somehow you never made a theory to improve Sam, though Sam's inability to think invariably filled you with a very cross, unholy contempt for him, while Ladykin's inability to *do* only served to thrill you with the most delicious, sweet, puffy pride in *yourself*.

Sam was very evidently a Person. Ladykin was a Feeling. You began almost at once to distinguish between Persons and Feelings. Anything that straightened out your head was a Person. Anything that puckered up your heart was a Feeling. Your Father, you had found out, was a Person. The Grandmother-Lady was a Person. Sam was a Person. Sunshine was a Person. A Horse was a Person. A Chrysanthemum was a Person. But your Mother was a Feeling. And Ladykin was a Feeling. And Bruno-Clarice was a Feeling. And the Ocean Blue was a Feeling. And a Church Organ was a Feeling. And the Smell of a June Rose was a Feeling. Perhaps your Happy-Day was the biggest Feeling of All.

Thursday, to be sure, came only once a week, but—*such a Thursday!* Even now, if you shut your eyes tight and gasp a quick breath, you can sense once more the sweet, crisp joy of fresh, starched clothes, and the pleasant, shiny jingle of new pennies in your small white cotton pockets. White? Yes; your Father had said that always on that day you should go like a little white Flag of Truce on an embassy to Fate. And Happiness? Could anything in the world make more for happiness than to be perfectly clean in the morning and perfectly dirty at night, with something rather frisky to eat for dinner, and Sam and Ladykin invariably invited to supper? Your Happy-Day was your Sacristy, too. Nobody ever punished you on Thursday. Nobody was ever cross to you on Thursday. Even if you were very black-bad the last thing Wednesday night, you were perfectly, blissfully, lusciously safe until Friday morning.

Oh, a Happy-Day was a very simple thing to manage compared with the terrible difficulties of being kind to everybody named "Clarice." There was *nobody* named Clarice! In all the town, in all the directory, in all the telephone books, you and Ladykin could not find a single person named Clarice. Once in a New York newspaper you read about a young Clarice-Lady of such and such a street who fell and broke her hip; and you took twenty shiny pennies of your money and bought a beautiful, hand-painted celluloid brush-holder and sent it to her; but you never, never heard that it did her any good. You did not want your Father to be mad at you, but Ladykin reasoned you out of your possible worry by showing you how if you ever saw your Father again you could at least plant your feet firmly, fold your arms, puff out your chest, and affirm distinctly: "Dear Father, I have *never* been cruel to *any one* named 'Clarice.'" Ladykin knew perfectly well how to manage it. Ladykin knew perfectly well how to manage everything.

Sam was the stupid one. Sam took a certain pleasure in Bruno-Clarice, but he never realized that Bruno-Clarice was a sacred dog. Sam thought that it was very fine for you to have a Happy-Day, with Clean Clothes, and Ice-Cream, and Pennies, but he never almost *burst* with the wonder of the day.

Sam thought that it was pleasant enough for you to have a dead Mother who was like "the flash of a white wing across a stormy sea," but he did not see any possible connection between that fact and stoning all the white sea-gulls in sight. Ladykin, on the contrary, told Sam distinctly that she'd knock his head off if he ever hit a gull, but fortunately—or unfortunately—Ladykin's aim was not so sure as Sam's. It was you who had to stay behind on the beach and pommel more than half the life out of Sam while Ladykin, pink as a posy in her best muslin, scared to death of wet and cold, plunged out to her little neck in the chopping waves to rescue a quivering fluff of feathers that struggled broken-winged against the cruel, drowning water. "Gulls are gulls!" persisted Sam with every blubbering breath. "Gulls are *Mothers!*" gasped Ladykin, staggering from the surf all drenched and dripping like a bursted water-pail. "Well, boy-gulls are gulls!" Sam screamed in a perfect explosion of outraged *truth*. But Ladykin defied him to the last. Through chattering teeth her vehement reassertion sounded like some horrid, wicked blasphemy: "Nnnnnnnnnnnn-oo! Bbb-o-y ggggg-ggulls are MMMMMM-Mothers too!" Then with that pulsing drench of feathers cuddled close to her breast, she struggled off alone to the house to have the Croup, while you and Sam went cheerily up the beach to find some shiners and some seaweed for your new gull hospital. Not till you were quite an old boy did you ever find out what became of that gull. Sacred Bruno-Clarice ate him. Ladykin, it seems, knew always what had happened to him, but she never dreamed of telling you till you were old enough to bear it. To Ladykin, Truth out of season was sourer than strawberries at Christmas time.

Sam would have told you *anything* the very first second that he found it out. Sam was perfectly great for Truth. He could tell more Great Black Truths in one day than there were thunder-clouds in the whole hot summer sky. This quality made Sam just a little bit dangerous in a crowd. He was always and forever shooting people with Truths that he didn't know were loaded. He was always telling the Grandmother-Lady, for instance, that her hair looked *exactly* like a wig. He was always telling Ladykin that she smelled of raspberry jam. He was always telling you that he didn't believe your Father really loved you. Oh, everything that Sam said was as straight and lank and honest as a lady's hair when it's out of crimp. Nothing in the world could be straighter than that.

But sometimes, when you had played sturdily with Sam for a good many hours, you used to coax Ladykin off all alone to the puffy, scorchy-looking smoke tree, where you could cuddle up on the rustic seat and rest your Honesty. And when you were thoroughly rested, you used to stretch your little arms behind your yawning face and beg:

"Oh, Ladykin, wouldn't you, couldn't you *please* say something curly?"

Ladykin's mind seemed to curl perfectly naturally. The crimp of it never came out. Almost any time you could take her words that looked so little and tight, and unwind them and unwind them into yards and yards and yards of pleasant, magic meanings.

There were no magic meanings in Sam's words. Sam, for instance, could throw as many as a hundred stones into the water, yet when he got through he just lay down in the sand and groaned, "Oh, how tired I am! Oh, how tired I am!" But Ladykin, after she'd thrown only two stones—one that hit the beach, and one that hit you—would stand right up and declare that her arm was "*be*-witched." Tired? No, not a bit of it, but "*be*-witched!" Hadn't she seen, hadn't you seen, hadn't everybody seen that *perfectly awful* sea-witch's head that popped out of the wave just after she had thrown her first stone? Oh, indeed, and it wasn't the first time either that she had been so frightened! Once when she was sitting on the sand counting sea-shells, hadn't the Witch swooped right out of the water and grabbed her legs? So, now if you wanted to break the cruel spell, save Ladykin's life, marry Ladykin, and live in a solid turquoise palace—where all the walls were papered with foreign postage-stamps, and no duplicates—you, not Sam, but *you,you*, chosen of all the world, must go down to the little harbor between the two highest, reariest rocks and stick a spiked stick through every wave that came in. There was no other way! Now you, yourself, might possibly have invented the witch, but you never, never would have thought of harpooning the waves and falling in and drowning your best suit, while Ladykin rested her arms.

Yet in the enforced punishment of an early bedtime you were not bereaved, but lay in rapturous delight untangling the minutest detail of Ladykin's words, till turquoise cities blazed like a turquoise flashlight across your startled senses, wonderful little princes and princesses kowtowed perpetually to royal Mother Ladykin and royal Father Yourself, and life-sized postage-stamps loomed so lusciously large that envelopes had to be pasted to the corners of stamps instead of stamps to the corners of envelopes. And before you had half straightened out the whole thought, you were fast asleep, and then fast awake, and it was suddenly morning! Oh, it is very comforting to have a playmate who can say curly things.

Sometimes, too, when Sam's and Ladykin's Mother had been rude to them about brushing their teeth or tracking perfectly good mud into the parlor, and Sam had gone off to ease his sorrow, scating hens or stoning cats, you and Ladykin would steal down to the gray rock on the beach to watch the white, soft, pleasant sea-gulls. There were times, you think, when Ladykin wished that *her* Mother was a sea-gull. Then you used to wonder and wonder about your own Mother, and tell Ladykin all over again about the creaky, black-oak library, and the smoky, smelly hearth-fire with the hurt red book, and the blue-flowered muslin sleeve beckoning and beckoning to you; and Ladykin used to explain to you how, very evidently, you were the only souvenir that your Father did not burn. With that thought in mind, you used to try and guess what could possibly have happened long ago on a Thursday to make a Happy-Day forever and ever. Ladykin said that of course it was something about "Love," but when you ran off to ask the Grandmother-Lady just exactly what Love was, the Grandmother-Lady only laughed and said that Love was a fever that came along a few years after chicken-pox and measles and scarlet fever. Ladykin was saucy about it. "That may be *true*," Ladykin acknowledged, "but *t'aint so!*" Then you went and found Sam and asked him if he knew what Love was. Sam knew at once. Sam said that Love was the feeling that one had for mathematics. Now that was all *bosh*, for the feeling that you and Ladykin had for Mathematics would not have made a Happy-Day for a cow.

But even if there were a great many things that you could not find out, it was a good deal of fun0 to grow up. Apart from a few stomach-aches and two or three gnawing pains in the calves of your legs, aging was a most alluring process.

Springs, summers, autumns, winters, went hurtling over one another, till all of a sudden, without the slightest effort on your part, you were fifteen years old, Bruno-Clarice had grown to be a sober, industrious, middle-aged dog, Sam was idolatrously addicted to geometry, and Ladykin subscribed to a fashion magazine for the benefit of her paper dolls.

Most astonishing of all, however, your Father had invited you to go to Germany and visit him. It was a glorious invitation. You were all athrill with the geography and love of it. Already your nostrils crinkled to the lure of tar and oakum. Already your vision feasted on the parrot-colored crowds of Come-igrants and Go-igrants that huddled along the wharves with their eager, jabbering faces and their soggy, wadded feet.

Oh, the prospect of the journey was a most beautiful experience, but when the actual Eve of Departure came, the scissors of separation gleamed rather hard and sharp in the air, and you hunched your neck a little bit wincingly before the final crunching snip. That last evening was a dreadful evening. The Cook sat sobbing in the kitchen. The Grandmother-Lady's eyes were red with sewing. The air was all heavy with *goingawayness*. To escape the strangle of it, you fled to the beach with Bruno-Clarice tagging in mournful excitement at your heels, his smutty nose all a-sniff with the foreboding leathery smell of trunks and bags. There on the beach in a scoopy hollow of sand backed up against the old gray rock were Sam and Ladykin. Sam's round, fat face was fretted like a pug-dog's, and Ladykin's eyes were blinky-wet with tears.

It was not a pleasant time to say good-by. It had been a beautiful, smooth-skied day, crisp and fresh and bright-colored as a "Sunday supplement"; but now the clouds piled gray and crumpled in the west like a poor stale, thrown-away newspaper, with just a sputtering blaze in one corner like the kindling of a half-hearted match.

"*Please* be kind to Bruno-Clarice," you began; "I shall miss you very much—very, very much. But I will come back—"

"N—o, I do not think you will come back," said Ladykin. "You will go to Germany to live with your Father and your Play-Mother, and you will gargle all your words like a throat tonic till you don't know how to be friends in English any more; and even if you did come back Bruno-Clarice would bark at you, and I shall be married, and Sam will have a long, black beard."

Now you could have borne Ladykin's marriage; you could even have borne Bruno-Clarice's barking at you; but you could not, simply could not bear the thought of Sam's growing a long black beard without you. Even Ladykin with all her wonderfulness sat utterly helpless before the terrible, unexpected climax of her words. It was Sam who leaped into the breach. The clutch of his hand was like the grit of sand-paper. "Jack," he stammered, "Jack, I promise you—anyhow I won't *cut* my beard until you come!"

It was certainly only the thought of Sam's faithful beard that sustained you on your rough, blue voyage to Germany. It was certainly only the thought of Sam's faithful beard that rallied your smitten forces when you met your Father face to face and saw him reel back white as chalk against the silky shoulder of your Play-Mother, and hide his eyes behind the crook of his elbow.

It is not pleasant to make people turn white as chalk, even in Germany. Worse yet, every day your Father grew whiter and whiter and whiter, and every day your pretty Play-Mother wrinkled her forehead more and more in a strange, hurty sort of trouble. Never once did you dare think of Ladykin. Never once did you dare think of Bruno-Clarice. You just named all your upper teeth "Sam," and all your lower teeth "Sam," and ground them into each other all day long—"Sam! Sam! Sam!" over and over and over. There were also no Happy-Days in Germany, and nobody ever spoke of Clarice.

You were pretty glad at last after a month when your Father came to you with his most beautiful face and his most loving hands, and said:

"Little Boy Jack, there is no use in it. You have got to go away again. You are a wound that will not heal. It is your Dear Mother's eyes. It is your Dear Mother's mouth. It is your Dear Mother's smile. God forgive me, but I cannot bear it! I am going to send you away to school in England."

You put your finger cautiously up to your eyes and traced their round, firm contour. Your Mother's eyes? They felt like two heaping teaspoonfuls of tears. Your Mother's mouth? Desperately you poked it into a smile. "Going to send me away to school in England?" you stammered. "Never mind. Sam will not cut his beard until I come."

"*What?*" cried your Father in a great voice. "*W-h-a-t?*"

But you pretended that you had not said anything, because it was boy-talk and your Father would not have understood it.

Never, never, never had you seen your Father so suffering; yet when he took you in his arms and raised your face to his and quizzed you: "Little Boy Jack, do you love me? Do you love me?" you scanned him out of your Mother's made-over eyes and answered him out of your Mother's made-over mouth:

"N—o! N—o! I *don't* love you!"

And he jumped back as though you had knifed him, and then laughed out loud as though he were glad of the pain.

"But I ask you this," he persisted, and the shine in his eyes was like a sunset glow in the deep woods, and the touch of his hands would have lured you into the very heart of the flame. "It is not probable," he said, "that your Dear Mother's child and mine will go through Life without knowing Love. When your Love-Time comes, if you understand all Love's tragedies *then*, and forgive me, will you send me a message?"

"Oh, yes," you cried out suddenly. "Oh, yes! Oh, yes! Oh, yes!" and clung to him frantically with your own boyish hands, and kissed him with your Mother's mouth. But you did not love him. It was your Mother's mouth that loved him.

So you went away to school in England and grew up and up and up some more; but somehow this latter growing up was a dull process without savor, and the years went by as briefly and inconsequently as a few dismissing sentences in a paragraph. There were plenty of people to work with and play with, but almost no one to think with, and your hard-wrought book knowledge faded to nothingness compared to the three paramount convictions of your youthful experience, namely, that neither coffee nor ocean nor Life tasted as good as it smelled.

And then when you were almost twenty-one you met "Clarice"!

It was a Christmas supper party in a café. Some one looked up suddenly and called the name "Clarice! Clarice!" and when your startled eyes shot to the mark and saw her there in her easy, dashing, gorgeous beauty, something in your brain curdled, and all the lonesomeness, all the mystery, all the elusiveness of Life pounded suddenly in your heart like a captured Will-o'-the-Wisp. "Clarice?" Here, then, was the end of your journey? The eternal kindness? The flash of a white wing across *your* stormy sea? "Clarice!" And you looked across unbidden into her eyes and smiled at her a gaspy, astonished smile that brought the strangest light into her face.

Oh, but Clarice was very beautiful! Never had you seen such a type. Her hair was black and solemn as crape. Her eyes were bright and noisy as jet. Her heart was barren as a blot of ink. And she took your dreamy, paper-white boy life and scourged it like a tongue of flame across a field of Easter lilies!

And when the wonder of the flame was gone, you sat aghast in your room among the charred, scorched fragments of your Youth. The thirst for death was very strong upon you, and the little, long, narrow cup of your revolver gleamed very brimming full of death's elixir. Even the June-time could not save you. Your Mother's name was an agony on your lips. The frenzied reiteration of your thoughts scraped on your brain like a sledge on gravel. You would drink very deep, you thought, of your little slim cup of death. Yet the thing that was tortured within you was scarcely Love, and you had no message of understanding for your Father. Just with wrecked life, wrecked faith, wrecked courage, you huddled at your desk, catching your breath for a second before you should reach out your fretted fingers for the little cool cunning, toy hand of Death.

"Once again," you said to yourself, "once again I will listen to the children's voices in the garden. Once again I will lure the smell of June roses into my heart." The children prattled and passed. Your hand reached out and fumbled. Once more you shut your scalding eyes, hunched up your shoulders, and breathed in like an ultimate tide the ravishing sweetness of the June—one breath, another, another—longer—longer. Oh, God in Heaven, if one could only die of such an anesthetic—smothered with sweetbrier, spiced with saffron, buried in bride roses. *Die?* Your wild hand leaped to the task and faltered stricken before the strange, grim fact that blazed across your consciousness. It was Thursday. It was your "Happy-Day!" Your Father's words came pounding back like blows into your sore brain! Your "Happy-Day!" "No cruelty must ever defame it, no malice, no gross bitterness!" Somewhere in air or sky or sea there was a Mother-Woman who must not be *hurt*. Your "Happy-Day?" HAPPY-DAY? Rage and sorrow broke like a fearful storm across your senses, and you put down your head and cried like a child.

Tears? Again you felt on your lips that queer, sad, salty pucker, that taste of the sea that gave you a thirst not so much for water as for Life. *Life? Life?* The thought thrilled through you like new nerves. Your ashy pulses burst into flame. Your dull heart jumped. Your vision woke. Your memory quickened. You saw the ocean, blue, blue, blue before you. You saw a small, rude boy lie sprawling in the sand. You saw a little girl's face, wild with wonder, tremulous with sweetness. You felt again the flutter of a kiss against your cheek. The little girl who—understood. Your salt lips puckered into a smile, and the smile ran back like a fuse into the inherent happiness of your heart. Sam? Ladykin? Home? You began to laugh! Haggard, harried, wrecked, ruined, you began to laugh! Then, faltering like a hysterical girl, you staggered down the stairs, out of the house, along the streets to the cable office, and sent a message to Sam.

"How long is your beard?" the message said. "How long is your beard?" Just that silly, magic message across miles and miles and miles of waves and seaweeds. How the great cable must have simpered with the foolishness of it. How the pink coral must have chuckled. How the big, tin-foiled fishes must have wondered.

You did not wait for an answer. What answer was there? You could picture Sam standing in stupefied awkwardness before the amazing nothingness of such a message. But Ladykin would remember. Oh, yes, Ladykin would remember. You could see her peering past Sam's shoulder and snatching out suddenly for the fluttering paper. Ladykin would remember. What were six years?

Joy sang in your heart like a purr of a sea-shell. The blue blur of ocean, the dear green smell of mignonette, the rush of wind through the poplar trees were tonic memories to you. You did not wait to pack your things. You did not wait to notify your Father. You sped like a wild boy to the first wharf, to the first steamer that you could find.

The week's ocean voyage went by like a year. The silly waves dragged on the steamer like a tired child on the skirts of its mother. Haste raged in your veins like a fever. You wanted to throw all the fat, heavy passengers overboard. You wanted to swim ahead with a towing rope in your teeth. You wanted to kill the Captain when he stuttered. You wanted to flay the cook for serving an extra course for dinner. Yet all the while the huge machinery throbbed in rhythm, "Time *will* pass. It *always does*. It *always does*. It *always does*."

And then at last you stood again on your Native Land, *alive, well, vital, at home!*

With the sensation of an unbroken miracle, you found your way again to the little Massachusetts sea town, along the peaceful village walk to the big brown house that turned so bleakly to the street. There on the steps, wonder of wonders, you found two elderly people, Bruno-Clarice and the Grandmother-Lady, and your knees gave out very suddenly and you sank down beside Bruno-Clarice and smothered the bark right out of him.

"Good lack!" cried the Grandmother-Lady,0 "Good *lack!*" and made so much noise that Sam himself came running like mad from the next house; and though he had no beard, you liked him very much and shook and shook his hand until he squealed.

With the Grandmother-Lady plying you with questions, and Sam feeling your muscle, and Bruno-Clarice trying to crawl into your lap like a pug-dog baby, it was almost half an hour before you had a chance to ask,

"Where is Ladykin?"

"She's down on the beach," said Sam. "I'll go and help you find her."

You looked at Sam speculatively. "I'll give you ten dollars if you won't," you said.

Sam considered the matter gravely before he began to grin. "I wouldn't think of charging you more than five," he acquiesced.

So you went off with Bruno-Clarice hobbling close at your heels to find Ladykin for yourself. When you saw her she was perched up on the very top of the huddly gray rock playing tinkle tunes on her mandolin, and you stole up so quietly behind her that she did not see you till you were close beside her.

Then she turned very suddenly and looked down upon you and pretended that she did not know you, with her color coming and going all luminous and intermittent like a pink and white flashlight. In six years you had not seen such a wonderful playmatey face.

"Who are you?" she asked. "Who are you?"

"I am 'Little Boy Jack' come back to marry you," you began, but something in the wistful, shy girl-tenderness of her face and eyes choked your bantering words right off in your throat.

"Yes, Ladykin," you said, "I have come home, and I am very tired, and I am very sad, and I am very lonesome, and I have not been a very good boy. But please be good to me! I am so lonesome I cannot wait to make love to you. Oh, *please, please* love me*n-o-w*. I *need* you to love me N-O-W!"

Ladykin frowned. It was not a cross frown. It was just a sort of a cosy corner for her thoughts. Surprise cuddled there, and a sorry feeling, and a great tenderness.

"You have not been a very good boy?" she repeated after you.

The memory of a year crowded blackly upon you. "No," you said, "I have not been a very good boy, and I am very suffering-sad. But *please* love me, and forgive me. No one has ever loved me!"

The surprise and the sorry feeling in Ladykin's forehead crowded together to make room for something that was just*womanliness*. She began to smile. It was the smile of a hurt person when the opiate first begins to overtake the pain.

"Oh, I'm sure it was an accidental badness," she volunteered softly. "If I were accidentally bad, you would forgive *me*, wouldn't you?"

"Oh, yes, yes, yes," you stammered, and reached up your lonesome hands to her.

"Then you don't have to make love," she whispered. "It's all made," and slipped down into your arms.

But something troubled her, and after a minute she pushed you away and tried to renounce you.

"But it is not Thursday," she sobbed; "it is Wednesday; and my name is not 'Clarice'; it is Ladykin."

Then all the boyishness died out of you—the sweet, idle reveries, the mystic responsibilities. You shook your Father's dream from your eyes, and squared your shoulders for your own realities.

"A Man must make his own Happy-Day," you cried, "and a Man must choose his own Mate!"

Before your vehemence Ladykin winced back against the rock and eyed you fearsomely.

"Oh, I will love you and cherish you," you pleaded.

But Ladykin shook her head. "That is not enough," she whispered. There was a kind of holy scorn in her eyes.

Then a White Gull flashed like an apparition before your sight. Ladykin's whole figure drooped, her cheek paled, her little mouth quivered, her vision narrowed. There with her eyes on the White Gull and your eyes fixed on hers, you saw her shy thoughts journey into the Future. You saw her eyes smile, sadden, brim with tears, smile again, and come homing back to you with a timid, glad surprise as she realized that your thoughts too had gone all the long journey with her.

She reached out one little hand to you. It was very cold.

"If I should pass like the flash of a white wing," she questioned, "would you be true to me—and *mine?*"

The Past, the Present, the Future rushed over you in tumult. Your lips could hardly crowd so big a vow into so small a word. "Oh, YES, YES, YES!" you cried.

In reverent mastery you raised her face to yours. "A Man must make his own Happy-Day," you repeated. "A Man must make his own Happy-Day!"

Timorously, yet assentingly, she came back to your arms. The whisper of her lips against your ear was like the flutter of a rose petal.

"It will be Wednesday, then," she said, "for us and—ours."

Clanging a strident bell across the magic stillness of the garden, Sam bore down upon you like a steam-engine out of tune.

"Oh, I say," he shouted, "for heaven's sake cut it out and come to supper."

The startled impulse of your refusal faded before the mute appeal in Ladykin's eyes.

"All right," you answered; "but first I must go and cable 'love' to my Father."

"Oh, hurry!" cried Ladykin. Her word was crumpled and shy as a kiss.

"Oh, hurry!" cried Sam. His thought was straight and frank as a knife and fork.

Joy sang in your heart like a prayer that rhymed. Your eager heart was pounding like a race horse. The clouds in the sky were scudding to sunset. The surf on the beach seemed all out of breath. The green meadow path to the village stretched like the paltriest trifle before a man's fleet running pace.

"But I can't hurry," you said, for Bruno-Clarice came poking his grizzled old nose into your hand. "Oh, wait for me," he seemed to plead. "Oh, please, *please* wait for me."

THE RUNAWAY ROAD

THE Road ran spitefully up a steep, hot, rocky, utterly shadeless hill, and then at the top turned suddenly in a flirty little green loop, and looked back, and called "Follow me!"

Wouldn't you have considered that a dare?

The Girl and the White Pony certainly took it as such, and proceeded at once to "follow," though the White Pony stumbled clatteringly on the rolling stones, and the Girl had to cling for dear life to the rocking pommels of her saddle.

It was a cruel climb, puff—pant—scramble—dust—glare—every step of the way, but when the two adventurers really reached the summit at last, a great dark chestnut-tree loomed up for shade, every sweet-smelling breeze in the world was there to welcome them, and the whole green valley below stretched out before them in the shining, woodsy wonder of high noon and high June.

You know, yourself, just how the world looks and feels and smells at high noon of a high June!

Even a pony stands majestically on the summit of a high hill—neck arched, eyes rolling, mane blowing, nostrils quivering. Even a girl feels a tug of power at her heart.

And still the Road cried "Follow me!" though it never turned its head again in doubt or coquetry. It was a kind-looking Road now, all gracious and sweet and tender, with rustly green overhead, and soft green underfoot, and the pleasant, buzzing drone of bees along its clovered edges.

"We might just as well follow it and see," argued the Girl, and the White Pony took the suggestion with a wild leap and cantered eagerly along the desired way.

It was such an extraordinarily lonesome Road that you could scarcely blame it for picking up companionship as best it might. There was stretch after stretch of pasture, and stretch after stretch of woodland, and stretch after stretch of black-stumped clearing—with never a house to cheer it, or a human echo to break its ghostly stillness. Yet with all its isolation and remoteness the landscape had that certain vibrant, vivid air of self-consciousness that thrills you with an uncanny sense of an invisible presence—somewhere. It's just a trick of June!

Tramps, pirates, even cannibals, seemed deliciously imminent. The Girl remembered reading once of a lonely woman bicyclist who met a runaway circus elephant at the turn of a country road. Twelve miles from home is a long way off to have anything happen.

Her heart began to quicken with the joyous sort of fear that is one of the prime sweets of youth. It's only when fear reaches your head that it hurts. The loneliness, the mystery, the uncertainty, were tonic to her. The color spotted in her cheeks. Her eyes narrowed defensively to every startling detail of woods or turf. Her ears rang with the sudden, new acuteness of her hearing. She felt as though she and the White Pony were stalking right across the heartstrings of the earth. Once the White Pony caught his foot and sent a scared sob into her throat.

Oh, everything was magic! A little brown rabbit reared up in the Road as big as a kangaroo, and beckoned her with his ears. A red-winged blackbird bulky as an eagle trumpeted a swamp-secret to her as he passed. A tiny chipmunk in the wall loomed like a lion in his lair, and sent a huge rock crashing like an avalanche into the field. The whole green and blue world seemed tingling with toy noises, made suddenly big.

The White Pony's mouth was frothing with the0 curb. The White Pony's coat was reeking wet with noon and nervousness, but the Girl sat tense and smiling and important in her saddle, as though just once for all time she was the only italicized word in the Book of Life.

"It's just the kind of a road that I like to travel alone," she gasped, a little breathlessly, "but if I were engaged and my man let me do it, I should consider him—careless."

That was exactly the sort of Road it was!

Yet after three or four miles the White Pony shook all the skittishness out of his feet, and settled down to a zigzag, browsing-clover gait, and the Girl relaxed at last, and sat loosely to ease her own muscles, and slid the bridle trustingly across the White Pony's neck.

Then she began to sing. Never in all her life had she sung outside the restricting cage of house or church. A green and blue loneliness on a June day is really the only place in the world that is big enough for singing! In dainty ballad, in impassioned hymn, in opera, in anthem, the Girl's voice, high and sweet and wild as a boy's, rang out in fluttering tremolo. Over and over again, as though half unconscious of the words, but enraptured with the melody, she dwelt at last on that dream-song of every ecstatic young soul who tarries for a moment on the edge of an unfocused exultation:

>The King of Love my Shepherd is
>Whose Goodness faileth never,
>I nothing lack if I am *his*
>And he is *mine f-o-r-e-v-e-r!*
>Forever!—--Is *mine f-o-r-e-v-e-r!*

Her pulsing, passionate crescendo came echoing back to her from a gray granite hillside, and sent a reverent thrill of power across her senses.

Then—suddenly—into her rhapsody broke the astonishing, harsh clash and clatter of a hay-rake. The White Pony lurched, stood stock-still, gave a hideous snort of terror, grabbed the bit in his teeth, and bolted like mad on and on and on and on till a quick curve in the Road dashed him into the very lap of a tiny old gray farmhouse that completely blocked the way.

In another second he would have stumbled across the threshold and hurled his rider precipitously into the front hall if she had not at that very second recovered her "yank-hold" on his churning mouth and wrenched him back so hard that any animal but a horse would have sat down.

Then the girl straightened up very tremblingly in her saddle and said "O—h!"

Some one had to say something, for there in the dooryard close beside her were an Artist, a Bossy, and a White Bulldog, who all instantaneously, without the slightest cordiality or greeting, stopped whatever they were doing and began to stare at her.

Now it's all very well to go dashing like mad into a person's front yard on a runaway horse. Anybody could see that you didn't do it on purpose; but when at last you have stopped dashing, what are you going to do next, particularly when the Road doesn't go any farther? Shall you say, "Isn't this a pleasant summer?" or "What did you really like best at the theater last winter?" If you gallop out it looks as though you were frightened. If you amble out, you might hear some one laugh behind your back, which is infinitely worse than being grabbed on the stairs.

The situation was excessively awkward. And the Artist evidently was not clever in conversational emergencies.

The Girl straightened her gray slouch hat. Then she ran the cool metal butt of her riding-whip back and forth under the White Pony's sweltering mane. Then she swallowed very hard once or twice and remarked inanely:

"Did the Road go right into the house?"

"Yes," said the Artist, with a nervous blue dab at his canvas.

The Girl's ire rose at his churlishness. "If that is so," she announced, "if the Road really went right into the house, I'll just wait here a minute till it comes out again."

But the Artist never smiled an atom to make things easier, though the Bossy began to tug most joyously at his chain, and the White Bulldog rolled over and over with delight.

The Girl would have given anything now to escape at full speed down the Road along which she had come, but escape of that sort had suddenly assumed the qualities of a panicky, ignominious retreat, so she parried for time by riding right up behind the Artist and watching him change a perfectly blue canvas sky into a regular tornado.

"Oh, do you think it's going to rain as hard as that?" she teased. "Perhaps I'd better settle down here until the storm is over."

But the Artist never smiled or spoke. He just painted and sniffed as though he worked by steam, and when his ears had finally grown so crimson that apoplexy seemed impending, she took pity on his miserable embarrassment and backed even the shadow of her pony out of his sight. Then with a desperate effort at perfect ease she remarked:

"Well—I guess I'll ride round to your back door. Perhaps the Road came out that way and went on without me."

But though she and the White Pony hunted in every direction through white birch and swaying alders, they found no possible path by which the Road could have escaped, and were obliged at last to return with some hauteur, and make as dignified an exit as possible from the scene.

The Artist bowed with stiff relief at their departure, but the White Bulldog preceded them with friendly romps and yells, and the Bossy pulled up his iron hitching stake and chain and came clanking after them with furious bounds and jingles.

No one but the White Pony would have stood the racket for a moment, and even the White Pony began to feel a bit staccato in his feet. The Girl kept her saddle like a circus rider, but the amusement on her face was just a trifle studied. It was a fine procession, clamor and all, with the Bulldog scouting ahead, the White Pony following skittishly, and the Bossy see-sawing behind, clanking a dungeon chain that left a cloud of dust as far as you could see.

It must have startled the Youngish Man who loomed up suddenly at a bend of the Road and caught the wriggling Bulldog in his arms.

"Who comes here?" he cried with a regular war-whoop of a challenge. "Who comes here?"

"Just a lady and a bossy," said the Girl, as she reined in the Pony abruptly, and sent the Bossy caroming off into the bushes.

"But it's my brother's Bossy," protested the Youngish Man.

"Oh, no, it isn't," the Girl explained a little wearily. "It's mine now. It chose between us."

The Youngish Man eyed her with some amusement.

"Did you really see my brother at the house?" he probed.

The Girl nodded, flushing. It was very hot, and she was beginning to feel just a wee bit faint and hungry and irritable.

"Yes, I saw your brother," she reiterated, "but I didn't seem to care for him. I rode by mistake right into the picture he was painting. There's probably paint all over me. It was very awkward, and he didn't do a thing to make it easier. I abominate that kind of person. If a man can't do anything else he can always ask you if you wouldn't like a drink of water!" She scowled indignantly. "It was the Road's fault anyway! I was just exploring, and the Road cried 'Follow me,' and I followed—a little faster than I meant to—and the Road ran right into your house and shut the door. Oh, *slammed* the door right in my face!"

"Would you like a drink of water, *now?*" suggested the Youngish Man.

"No, I thank you," said the Girl, with stubborn dignity, and then weakened to the alluring offer with "But my White Pony is very cruelly thirsty."

Both adventurers looked pretty jaded with heat and dust.

The Youngish Man led the way into a tiny, pungent wood-path that ended in a gurgling spring-hole, where the White Pony nuzzled his nose with deep-breathed, dripping satisfaction, while the Girl kept to her saddle and looked down on the Youngish Man with frank interest.

He looked very picturesque and brown and clever in his khaki suit with a game bag slung across his shoulder.

"You're not a hunter," she exclaimed impulsively. "You're not a hunter—because you haven't any gun."

"No," said the Man, "I'm a collector."

The Girl cried out with pleasure and clapped her hands. "A collector?—oh, goody! So am I! What do you collect? Minerals? Oh—dear! *Mine* is lots more interesting. I collect adventures."

"Adventures?" The Man made no slightest effort to conceal his amused curiosity. "Adventures? Now I call that a jolly thing to collect. Is it a good country to work in? And what have you found?"

The Girl smiled at him appreciatively—a little flitting, whimsical sort of smile, and commenced to rummage in the blouse of her white shirt-waist, from which she finally produced a small, red-covered notebook. She fluttered its diminutive pages for a second, and then began to laugh:

"You'd better sit down if you really want to hear what I've found."

The Man dropped comfortably into place beside the spring and watched her. She was very watchable. Some people have to be beautiful to rivet your attention. Some people *don't* have to be. It's all a matter of temperament. Her hair was very, very brown, though, and her eyes were deep and wide and hazel, and the red in her cheeks came and went with every throb of her heart.

"Of course," she explained apologetically, "of course I haven't found a lot of things yet—I've only been working at it a little while. But I've collected a 'Runaway Accident with the Rural Free-Delivery Man.' It was awfully scary and interesting. And I've collected a 'Den of Little Foxes Down in the Woods Back of My House,' and 'Two Sunrises with a Crazy Woman who Thinks that the Sun Can't Get Up Until She Does,' and I've collected a 'Country Camp-Meeting all Hallelujahs and By Goshes,' and a 'Circus Where I Spent All Day with the Snake-Charmer,' and a 'Midnight Ride Alone through the Rosedale Woods in a Thunder-Storm.' Of course, as I say, I haven't found a lot of things yet, but then it's only the middle of June and I have two more weeks' vacation yet."

The Man put back his head and laughed, but it was a pleasant sort of laugh that flooded all the stern lines in his face.

"I'm sure I never thought of making a regular business of collecting adventures," he admitted, "but it certainly is a splendid idea. But aren't you ever afraid?" he asked. "Aren't you ever afraid, for instance, riding round on a lonesome trip like this?"

The Girl laughed. "Yes," she acknowledged, "I'm often afraid of—squirrels—and falling twigs—and black-looking stumps. I'm often afraid of toy noises and toy fears—but I never saw a real fear in all my life. Even when you jumped up in the Road I wasn't afraid of you—because you are a gentleman—and—gentlemen are my friends."

"Have you many friends?" asked the Man. The question seemed amusingly justifiable. "You look to me about eighteen. Girls of your age are usually too busy collecting Love to collect anything else—even ideas. Have you collected any Love?"

The Girl threw out her hands in joking protest. "Collected any Love? Why, I don't even know what Love looks like! Maybe what I'd collect would be—poison ivy." Her eyes narrowed a little. Her voice quivered the merest trifle. "There's a Boy at Home—who talks—a little—about it. But how can I tell that it's Love?"

Her sudden vehemency startled him. "Where *is* 'Home'?" he asked.

For immediate answer the Girl slipped down from the White Pony's back, and loosened the saddle creakingly before she helped herself to a long, dripping draught from the birch cup that hung just over the spring.

"You're nice to talk to," she acknowledged, "and almost no one is nice to talk to. It's a whole year since I've talked right out to any one! Where do I live? Well, my headquarters are in New York, but my heartquarters are over at Rosedale. There's quite a difference, you know!"

"Yes," said the Man, "I remember—there used to—be—quite a difference. But how did you ever happen to think of collecting adventures?"

The girl pulled at the White Pony's mane for a long, hesitating moment, then she turned and looked searchingly into the Man's face. She very evidently liked what she saw.

"I collect adventures because I am lonesome!" Her voice shook a little, but her eyes were frankly untroubled. "I collect adventures because the life0 that interests me doesn't happen to come to me, and I have to go out and search for it!—I'm companion all the year to a woman who doesn't know right from wrong in any dear, big sense, but who could define propriety and impropriety to you till your ears split. And all her friends are just like her. They haven't any mental muscle to them. It's just dress and etiquette, dress and etiquette, dress and etiquette! So I have to live all alone in my head, and think and think and think, till my poor brain churns and overlaps like a surf without any shore. Do you know what I mean? Then when my June vacation comes, I run right off to Rosedale and collect all the adventures I possibly can to take back with me for the long dreary year. Things to think about, you know, when I have to sit up at night giving medicine, or when I have to mend heavy black silk clothes, or when the dinners are so long that I could scream over the extra delay of a salad course. So I make June a sort of pranky, fancy-dress party for my soul. Do you know what I mean?"

"Yes, I know what you mean," said the Man. "I know just what you mean. You mean you're eighteen. That's the whole of it. You mean that there's no fence to your pasture, no bottom to your cup, no crust to your bread. You mean that you can't sleep at night for the pounding of your heart. You mean most of all that there's no limit to your vision. You're inordinately keen after life. That's all. You'll get over it!"

"*I won't get over it!*" There was fire in the Girl's eyes and she drew her breath sharply. "I say I *won't* get over it! There's nothing on earth that could stale me! If I live to be a hundred I sha'n't wither!—why, how could I?"

Buoyant, blooming, aquiver with startled emotions, she threw out her hands with a passionate gesture of protest.

The Man shook his shoulders and jumped up. "Perhaps you're right," he muttered. "Perhaps you *are* the kind that won't ever grow old. If you are—Heaven help you! Youth's nothing but a wound, anyway. Do you want to be a wound that never heals?" He laughed stridently.

Then the Girl began to fumble through sudden tears at the buckles of her saddle. Her growing hunger and faintness and the heat of the day were telling on her.

"You must think me a crazy fool," she confessed, "the way I have plunged into personalities. Why, I could go a whole year with an alien running-mate and never breathe a word or a sigh about myself, but with some people—the second you see them you know they are part of your chord. Chord is the only term in music that I understand, and I understand that as though I had made the word myself." She tried to laugh. "Now I'm going home! I've had a good time. You seem almost like a friend. I've never had a talky friend."

And she was in her saddle and half-way down the wood-path before his mind quickened to cry out "Stop! Wait a minute!"

A little out of breath he caught up with her, and stood for a moment like an embarrassed schoolboy, though his face in the sunlight was as old as young forty.

"I'm afraid you haven't had much of an adventure this morning," he volunteered whimsically. "If you really want an adventure why don't you come back to the house and have dinner with my brother and me? There's no one else there. Think how it would tease my brother! You're twelve or fifteen miles from home, and it's already two o'clock and very hot. My brother has done some pictures that are going to be talked about next winter, and I—I've got rather a conspicuous position ahead of me in Washington. Wouldn't it amuse you a little bit afterward, if any one spoke of us, to remember our little farmhouse dinner to-day?—Would you be afraid to come?" His last question was very direct.

A look came into the Girl's eyes that was very good for a man to see.

"Why, of course I wouldn't be afraid to come," she said. "Gentlemen are my friends."

But she was shy about going, just the same, with a certain frank, boyish shyness that only served to emphasize the general artlessness of her verve.

With a quick dive into the bushes the Man collared the Bossy and transferred his clanking chain to the bit of the astonished White Pony.

"Now you've got to come," he laughed up at her, and the whole party started back for the tiny old gray farmhouse where the Artist greeted them with sad concern.

"I've brought Miss Girl back to have dinner with us," announced the Pony-leader cheerfully, relying on his brother's serious nature to overlook any strangeness of nomenclature. "You evidently didn't remember meeting her at Mrs. Moyne's house-party last spring?"

The Girl fell readily into the game. She turned the White Pony loose in the dooryard, and then went into the queer old kitchen, rolled up her sleeves, wound herself round with a blue-checked apron, and commenced to work. She had a deft touch at household matters, and the Man followed her about as humbly as though he himself had not been adequately providing meals for the past two months.

The color rose high in the Girl's cheeks, and her voice took on the thrill and breathiness of amused excitement. Wherever she found a huddle of best china or linen or silver she raided it for her use, and the table flared forth at last with a dainty, inconsequent prettiness that quite defied the Artist's prescribed rules for beauty.

It was a funny dinner, with an endless amount of significant bantering going on right under the Artist's sunburned nose. Yet for all the mirth of the situation, the Girl had quite a chance to study the face of her special host, in all its full detail of worldliness, of spirituality, of hardness, of sweetness. Her final impression, as her first one, was of a wonderful affinity and congeniality. "His face is like a harbor for all my stormy thoughts," was the way she described it to herself.

After dinner the three washed up the dishes as sedately as though they had been working together day-in, day-out through the whole season, and after that the Artist escaped as quickly as possible to catch a cloud effect which he seemed to consider preposterously vital.

Then with a dreary little feeling of a prize-pleasure all spent and gone, the Girl went over to the mirror in the sitting-room and pinned on her gray slouch hat and patted her hair and straightened her belt.

But it was not her own reflection that interested her most. The mirror made a fine frame for the whole quaint room, with its dingy landscape wall-paper from which the scarlet petticoat of a shepherdess or the vivid green of a garland stood out with cheerful crudity. The battered, blackened fireplace was lurid here and there with gleams of copper kettles, and a huge gray cat purred comfortably in the curving seat of a sun-baked rocking-chair.

It was a good picture to take home in your mind for remembrance, when walls should be brick and rooms ornate and life hackneyed, and the Girl shut her eyes for a second, experimentally, to fix the vision in her consciousness.

When she opened her eyes again the Man was struggling through the doorway dragging a small, heavy trunk.

"Oh, don't go yet!" he exclaimed. "Here are a lot of your things in this trunk. I brought them in to show you."

And he dragged the trunk to the middle of the room and knelt down on the floor and commenced to unlock it.

"*My* things?" cried the Girl in amazement, and ran across the room and sat down on the floor beside him. "*My* things?"

There was a funny little twist to the Man's mouth that never relaxed all the time he was tinkering with the lock. "Yes—*your* things," was all he said till the catch yielded finally, and he raised the cover to display the full contents to his companion's curious eyes.

Instinctively she clasped it to her

"Oh—*books!*" she cried out, with a sudden, sweeping flush of comprehension, and darted her hand into the dusty pile and pulled out a well-worn copy of the Rubaiyat. Instinctively she clasped it to her.

"I thought so!" said the Youngish Man quizzically. "I thought that was one of your books.

"When Time lets slip a little, perfect hour,
Oh, take it—for it will not come again."

His eyes narrowed, and his hands reached nervously to regain possession of the volume. Then he laughed.

"*I*, also, used to think that Life was made for me," he scoffed teasingly. "It's a glorious idea—as long as it lasts! You take every harsh old happening and every flimsy friendship and line it with your own silk, and then sit by and say, 'Oh, *isn't* the World a rustly, shimmery, luxurious place!' And all the time the happening *is* harsh, and the friendship *is* flimsy, and it's just your own perishable silk lining that does the rustle and the shimmer and the luxury act. Oh, I suppose that's 'woman talk' about silk linings, but I know a thing or two, even if I am a man."

But the radiancy of the Girl's face defied his cynicism utterly. Her eyes were absolutely fathomless with Youth.

Then his mood changed suddenly. He reached out with a little brooding gesture of protection. "These are my college books," he confided, "my Dream Library. I've scarcely thought of them for a dozen years. I don't meet many dreamers nowadays. You've probably got a lot of newer books than these, but I'll wager you anything in the world that every book here is a precious friend to you. I shouldn't wonder if your own copies opened exactly to the same places. Here's young Keats with his shadowing tragedy. How you have mooned over it. And here's Tennyson. What about the starlit vision:

"And on her lover's arm she leant,
And round her waist she felt it fold,—"

The Girl took up the words softly in unison:

"And far across the hills they went
To that new world which is the old."

In rushing, eager tenderness she browsed through one book after another, sometimes silently, sometimes with a little crooning quotation, where corners were turned down. And when she had quite finished, her eyes were like stars, and she looked up tremulously, and whispered:

"Why, we—like—just—the—same—things."

But the Youngish Man did not smile back at her. His face in that second turned suddenly old-looking and haggard and gray. He threw the books back into their places, and slammed the trunk-cover with a bang.

For just the infinitesimal fraction of a second the Man and the Girl looked into each other's eyes. For just that infinitesimal fraction of a second the Man's eyes were as unfathomable as the Girl's.

Then with a great sniff and scratching and whine, the White Bulldog pushed his way into the room, and the Girl jumped up in alarm to note that the sun was dropping very low in the west, and that the shadows of late afternoon crept palpably over her companion's face.

For a moment the two stood awkwardly without a word, and then the Girl with a conscious effort at lightness queried:

"But *where* did the Runaway Road go to? I *must* find out."

The Youngish Man turned as though something had startled him.

"Wouldn't you rather leave things just as they are?" he asked.

"NO!" The Girl stamped her foot vehemently. "NO! I want everything. I want the whole adventure."

"The whole adventure?" The Youngish Man winced at the phrase, and then laughed to cover his seriousness.

"All right," he acquiesced. "I'll show you just where the Runaway Road goes to."

Without further explanation he stepped to the dooryard and scooped up two heaping handfuls of gravel from the Road. As he came back into the room he trailed a little line of earth across the floor to the foot of the stairs, and threw the remaining handful up the steps just as a heedless child might have done.

"Go follow your Runaway Road," he smiled, "and see where it leads to, if you are so eager! I'm going down to the woods to see if my brother is quite lost in his clouds."

Wasn't that *another* dare? It seemed a craven thing to tease for a climax and then shirk it. She had never shirked anything yet that was right, no matter how unusual it was.

She started for the stairs. One step, two steps, three steps, four steps—her riding-boots grated on0 the gravel. "Oh, you funny Runaway Road," she trembled, "where *do* you go to?"

At the top stairs a tiny waft of earth turned her definitely into the first doorway.

She took one step across the threshold, and then stood stock-still and stared. It was a *woman's room*. And from floor to ceiling and from wall to wall flaunted an incongruous, moneyed effort to blot out all temperament and pang and trenchant life-history from one spot at least of the little old gray farmhouse. Bauble was there, and fashion and novelty, but the whole gay decoration looked and felt like the sumptuous dressing of a child whom one *hated*.

With a gasp of surprise the Girl went over and looked at herself in the mirror.

"Wouldn't I look queer in a room like this?" she whispered to herself. But she didn't look queer at all. She only felt queer, like a flatted note.

Then she hurried right down the stairs again, and went out in the yard, and caught the White Pony, and climbed up into her saddle.

The Youngish Man came running to say good-by.

"Well?" he said.

The Girl's eyes were steady as her hand. If her heart fluttered there was no sign of it.

"Why, it was a *woman's* room," she answered to his inflection.

"Yes," said the Youngish Man quite simply. "It is my wife's room. My wife is in Europe getting her winter clothes. All people do not happen—to—like—the—same—things."

The Girl put out her hand to him with bright-faced friendliness.

"In Europe?" she repeated. "Indeed, I shall not be so local when I think of her. Wherever she is—all the time—I shall always think of your wife as being—most of anything else—*in luck*."

She drew back her hand and chirruped to the White Pony, but the Youngish Man detained her.

"Wait a second," he begged. "Here's a copy of Matthew Arnold for you to take home as a token, though there's only one thing in it for us, and you won't care for that until you are forty. You can play it's about the mountains that you pass going home. Here it is:

"Unaffrighted by the silence round them,
Undistracted by the sights they see,
THESE demand not that the things about them
Yield them love, amusement, sympathy."

"Rather cracked-ice comfort, isn't it?" the Girl laughed as she tucked the little book into her blouse.

"Rather," said the Youngish Man, "but cracked ice is good for fevers, and Youth is the most raging fever that I know about."

Then he stood back from the White Pony, and smiled quizzically, and the Girl turned the White Pony's head, and started down the Road.

Just before the first curve in the alders, she whirled in her saddle and looked back. The Youngish Man was still standing there watching her, and she held up her hand as a final signal. Then the Road curved her out of sight.

It was chilly now in the gloaming shade of the woods, and home seemed a long way off. After a mile or two the White Pony dragged as though his feet were sore, and when she tried to force him into a jarring canter the sharp corners of the Matthew Arnold book goaded cruelly against her breast.

"It isn't going to be a very pleasant ride," she said. "But it was quite an adventure. I don't know whether to call it the 'Adventure of the Runaway Road' or the 'Adventure of the Little Perfect Hour.'"

Then she shivered a little and tried to keep the White Pony in the rapidly fading sun spots of the Road, but the shadows grew thicker and cracklier and more lonesome every minute, and the only familiar sound of life to be heard was 'way off in the distance, where some little lost bossy was calling plaintively for its mother.

There were plenty of unfamiliar sounds, though. Things—nothing special, but just Things—sighed mournfully from behind a looming boulder. Something dark, with gleaming eyes, scudded madly through the woods. A ghastly, mawkish chill like tomb-air blew dankly from the swamp. Myriads of tiny insects droned venomously. The White Pony shied at a flash of heat lightning, and stumbled bunglingly on a rolling stone. Worst of all, far behind her, sounded the unmistakable tagging step of some stealthy creature.

For the first time in her life the girl was frightened—hideously, sickeningly frightened of Night!

Back in the open clearing round the tiny farmhouse, the light, of course, still lingered in a lulling yellow-gray. It would be an hour yet, she reasoned, before the great, black loneliness settled there. She could picture the little, simple, homely, companionable activities of early evening—the sputter of a candle, the good smell of a pipe, the steamy murmur of a boiling kettle. O—h! But could one go back wildly and say: "It is darker and cracklier than I supposed in the woods, and I am a wilful Girl, and there are fifteen wilful miles between me and home—and there is a cemetery on the way, and a new grave—and a squalid camp of gypsies—and a broken bridge—*and I am afraid! What shall I do?*"

She laughed aloud at the absurdity, and cut at the White Pony sharply with her whip. It would be lighter, she thought, on the open village road below the hill.

Love? Amusement? Sympathy? She shook her young fist defiantly at the hulking contour of a stolid, bored old mountain that loomed up through a gap in the trees. "*Drat* Self-sufficiency," she cursed, with a vehement little-girl curse. "I won't be a bored old Mountain. I *won't! I won't! I won't!*"

All her short, eager life, it seemed, she had been floundering like a stranger in a strange land—no father or mother, no chum, no friend, no lover, no anything—and now just for a flash, just for one "little, perfect hour" she had found a voice at last that *spoke her own language*, and the voice belonged to a Man who belonged to another woman!

She remembered her morning's singing with a bitter pang. "*Nothing* is mine forever. Nothing, *nothing*, NOTHING!" she sobbed.

A great, black, smothering isolation like a pall settled down over her, and seemed to pin itself with a stab through her heart. Everybody, once in his time, has tried to imagine his Dearest-one absolutely nonexistent, unborn, and tortured himself with the possibility of such a ghostly vacuum in his life. To the Girl suddenly it seemed as though puzzled, lonely, unmated, all her short years, she had stumbled now precipitously on the Great Cause Of It—a *vacuum*. It was not that she had lost any one, or missed any one. *It was simply that some one had never been born!*

The thought filled her with a whimsical new terror. She pounded the White Pony into a gallop and covered the last half-mile of the Runaway Road. At the crest of the hill the valley vista brightened palely and the White Pony gave a whimper of awakened home instinct. Cautiously, warily, with legs folding like a jack-knife he began the hazardous descent.

Was he sleepy? Was he clumsy? Was he footsore? Just before the Runaway Road smoothed out into the village highway his knees wilted suddenly under him, and he pitched headlong with a hideous lurch that sent the Girl hurtling over his neck into a pitiful, cluttered heap among the dust and stones, where he came back after his first panicky run, and blew over her with dilated nostrils, and whimpered a little before he strayed off to a clover patch on the highway below.

Twilight deepened to darkness. Darkness quickened at last to stars. It was Night, real Night, black alike in meadow, wood, and dooryard, before the Girl opened her eyes again. Part of an orange moon, waning, wasted, decadent, glowed dully in the sky.

For a long time, stark-still and numb, she lay staring up into space, conscious of nothing except consciousness. It was a floaty sort of feeling. Was she dead? That was the first thought that twittered in her brain. Gradually, though, the reassuring edges of her cheeks loomed into sight, and a beautiful, real pain racked along her spine and through her side. It was the pain that whetted her curiosity. "If it's my neck that's broken," she reasoned, "it's all over. If it's my heart it's only just begun."

Then she wriggled one hand very cautiously, and a White Doggish Something came over and licked her fingers. It felt very kind and refreshing.

Now and then on the road below, a carriage rattled by, or one voice called to another. She didn't exactly care that no one noticed her, or rescued her—indeed, she was perfectly, sluggishly comfortable—but she remembered with alarming distinctness that once, on a scorching city pavement, she had gone right by a bruised purple pansy that lay wilting underfoot. She could remember just how it looked. It had a funny little face, purple and yellow, and all twisted with pain. And she had gone right by. And she felt very sorry about it now.

She was still thinking about that purple pansy an hour later, when she heard the screeching toot of an automobile, the snort of a horse, and the terrified clatter of hoofs up the hill. Then the White Doggish Something leaped up and barked a sharp, fluttery bark like a signal.

The next thing she knew, pleasant voices and a lantern were coming toward her. "They will be frightened," she thought, "to find a body in the Road." So, "Coo-o! Coo-o!" she cried in a faint little voice.

Then quickly a bright light poured into her face, and she swallowed very hard with her eyes for a whole minute before she could see that two men were bending over her. One of the men was just a man, but the other one was the Boy From Home. As soon as she saw him she began to cry very softly to herself, and the Boy From Home took her right up in his great, strong arms and carried her down to the cushioned comfort of the automobile.

"Where—did—you—come—from?" she whispered smotheringly into his shoulder.

The harried, boyish face broke brightly into a smile.

"I came from Rosedale to-night, to find *you!*" he said. "But they sent me up here on business to survey a new Road."

"To survey a new Road?" she gasped. "That's—good. All the Roads that I know—go—to—Other People's Homes."

Her head began to droop limply to one side. She felt her senses reeling away from her again. "If—I—loved—you," she hurried to ask, "would—you—make—me—a—safe Road—*all my own?*"

The Boy From Home gave a scathing glance at the hill that reared like a crag out of the darkness.

"If I couldn't make a safer Road than *that*—" he began, then stopped abruptly, with a sudden flash of illumination, and brushed his trembling lips across her hair.

"I'll make you the safest, smoothest Road that ever happened," he said, "if I have to dig it with my fingers and gnaw it with my teeth."

A little, snuggling sigh of contentment slipped from the Girl's lips.

"Do—you—suppose," she whispered, "do—you—suppose—that—after—all—*this*—was—the real—end—of—the Runaway Road?"

SOMETHING THAT HAPPENED IN OCTOBER

MONDAY, Tuesday, Wednesday, Thursday, Friday, it had rained. Day in, day out, day in, day out, day in, it had rained and rained and rained and rained and rained, till by Friday night the great blue mountains loomed like a chunk of ruined velvet, and the fog along the valley lay thick and gross as mildewed porridge.

It was a horrid storm. Slop and shiver and rotting leaves were rampant. Even in Alrik's snug little house the chairs were wetter than moss. Clothes in the closets hung lank and clammy as undried bathing-suits. Worst of all, across every mirror lay a breathy, sad gray mist, as though ghosts had been back to whimper there over their lost faces.

It had never been so before in the first week of October.

There were seven of us who used to tryst there together every year in the gorgeous Scotch-plaid Autumn, when the reds and greens and blues and browns and yellows lapped and overlapped like a festive little kilt for the Young Winter, and every crisp, sweet day that dawned was like the taste of cider and the smell of grapes.

That is the kind of October well worth living, and seven people make a wonderfully proper number to play together in the country, particularly if six of you are men and women, and one of you is a dog.

Yet, after all, it was October, and October alone, that lured us. We certainly differed astonishingly in most of our other tastes.

Three of us belonged to the peaceful Maine woods—Alrik and Alrik's Wife and his Growly-Dog-Gruff. Four of us came from the rackety cities—the Partridge Hunter, the Blue Serge Man, the Pretty Lady, and Myself—a newspaper woman.

Incidentally, I may add that the Blue Serge Man and the Pretty Lady were husband and wife, but did not care much about it, having been married, very evidently, in some gorgeously ornate silver-plated emotion that they had mistaken at the time for the "sterling" article. The shine and beauty of the marriage had long since worn away, leaving things quite a little bit edgy here and there. Alrik's young spouse was, wonder of wonders, a transplanted New York chorus girl. No other biographical data are necessary except that Growly-Dog-Gruff was a brawling, black, fat-faced mongrel whose complete sense of humor had been slammed in the door at a very early age. For some inexplainable reason, he seemed to hold all the rest of the crowd responsible for the catastrophe, but was wildly devoted to me. He showed this devotion by never biting me as hard as he bit the others.

Yet even with Growly-Dog-Gruff included among our assets, we had always considered ourselves an extremely superior crowd.

There were seven of us, I said, who *used* to tryst there together every autumn. But now, since the year before, three of us had *gone*, Alrik's Wife, Alrik's Dog, and the Blue Serge Man. So the four of us who remained huddled very close around the fire on that stormy, dreary, ghastly first night of our reunion, and talked-talked-talked and laughed-laughed-laughed just as fast as we possibly could for fear that a moment's silence would plunge us all down, whether or no, into the sorrow-chasm that lurked so consciously on every side. Yet we certainly looked and acted like a very jovial quartet.

The Pretty Lady, to be sure, was a black wisp of crape in her prim, four-footed chair; but Alrik's huge bulk tipped jauntily back against the wainscoting in a gaudy-colored Mackinaw suit, with merely a broad band of black across his left sleeve—as one who, neither affirming nor denying the formalities of grief, would laconically warn the public at large to "Keep Off My Sorrow." I liked Alrik, and I had liked Alrik's Wife. But I had loved Alrik's Dog. I do not care especially for temper in women, but a surly dog, or a surly man, is as irresistibly funny to me as Chinese music, there is so little plot to any of them.

The four of us who remained huddled very close around the fire

But now on the hearth-rug at my feet the Partridge Hunter lay in amiable corduroy comfort, with the little puff of his pipe and his lips throbbing out in pleasant, dozy regularity. He had traveled in Japan since last we met, and one's blood flowed pink and gold and purple, one's flesh turned silk, one's eyes onyx, before the wonder of his narrative.

No one was to be outdone in adventurous recital. Alrik had spent the summer guiding a party of amateur sports along the Allagash, and his garbled account of it would have stocked a comic paper for a month. The Pretty Lady had christened a warship, and her eager, brooky voice went rippling and churtling through such major details as blue chiffon velvet and the goldiest kind of champagne. Even Alrik's raw-boned Old Mother, clinking dirty supper dishes out in the kitchen, had a crackle-voiced tale of excitement to contribute about a floundering spring bear that she had soused with soap-suds from her woodshed window.

But all the time the storm grew worse and worse. The poor, tiny old house tore and writhed under the strain. Now and again a shutter blew shrilly loose, or a chimney brick thudded down, or a great sheet of rain sucked itself up like a whirlpool and then came drenching and hurtling itself in a perfect frenzy against the frail, clattering window-panes.

It was a good night for four friends to be housed together in a red, red room, where the low ceiling brooded over you like a face and the warped floor curled around you like the cuddle of a hand. A living-room should always be red, I think, like the walls of a heart, and cluttered, as Alrik's was, with every possible object, mean or fine, funny or pathetic, that typifies the owner's personal experience.

Yet there are people, I suppose, people stuffed with arts, not hearts, who would have monotoned Alrik's bright walls a dull brain-gray, ripped down the furs, the fishing-tackle, the stuffed owls, the gaudy theatrical posters, the shelf of glasses, the spooky hair wreaths, the really terrible crayon portrait of some much-beloved ancient grandame; and, supplementing it all with a single, homesick Japanese print, yearning across the vacuum at a chalky white bust of a perfect stranger like Psyche or Ruskin, would have called the whole effect more "successful." Just as though the crudest possible room that represents the affections is not infinitely more worth while than the most esoteric apartment that represents the intellect.

There were certainly no vacuums in Alrik's room. Everything in it was crowded and scrunched together like a hard, friendly hand-shake. It was the most fiercely, primitively sincere room that I have ever seen, and king or peasant therefore would have felt equally at home in it. Surely no mere man could have crossed the humpy threshold without a blissful, instinctive desire to keep on his hat and take off his boots. Alrik knew how to make a room "homeful." Alrik knew everything in the world except grammar.

Red warmth, yellow cheer, and all-colored jollity were there with us.

Faster and faster we talked, and louder and louder we laughed, until at last, when the conversation lost its breath utterly, Alrik jumped up with a grin and started our old friend the phonograph. His first choice of music was a grotesque *duo* by two back-yard cats. It was one of those irresistibly silly minstrel things that would have exploded any decent bishop in the midst of his sermon. Certainly no one of us had ever yet been able to withstand it. *But now no bristling, injuriated dog jumped from his sleep and charged like a whole regiment on the perfectly innocent garden.* And the duo somehow seemed strangely flat.

"Here is something we used to like," suggested Alrik desperately, and started a splendid barytone rendering of "Drink to Me Only with Thine Eyes." *But no high-pitched, mocking tenor voice took up the solemn velvet song and flirted it like a cheap chiffon scarf.* And the Pretty Lady rose very suddenly and went out to the kitchen indefinitely "for a glass of water." It was funny about the Blue Serge Man. I had not liked him overmuch, but I missed *not-liking-him* with a crick in my heart that was almost sorrow.

"Oh, for heaven's sake try some other music!" cried the Partridge Hunter venomously, and Alrik clutched out wildly for the first thing he could reach. It was "Give My Regards to Broadway." We had practically worn out the record the year before, but its mutilated remains whirred along, dropping an occasional note or word, with the same cheerful spunk and unconcern that characterized the song itself:

"Give my regards to Broadway,
Remember me to Herald Square,
Tell all the—whirry—whirry, whirrrrry—whirrrrrrr
That I will soon be there."

The Partridge Hunter began instantly to beat muffled time with his soft felt slippers. Alrik plunged as usual into a fearfully clever and clattery imitation of an ox shying at a street-car. But what of it? No wakened, sparkling-eyed girl came stealing forth from her corner to cuddle her blazing cheek against the cool, brass-colored jowl of the phonograph horn. An All-Goneness is an amazing thing. It was strange about Alrik's Wife. Her presence had been as negative as a dead gray dove. But her absence was like scarlet strung with bells! The evening began to drag out like a tortured rubber band getting ready to snap.

It was surely eleven o'clock before the Pretty Lady returned from the kitchen with our hot lemonades. The tall glasses jingled together pleasantly on the tray. The height was there, the breadth, the precious, steaming fragrance. *But the Blue Serge Man had always mixed our nightcaps for us.*

With grandiloquent pleasantry, the Partridge Hunter jumped to his feet, raised his glass, toasted "Happy Days," choked on the first swallow, bungled his grasp, and dropped the whole glass in shattering, messy fragments to the floor.

"Lord," he muttered under his breath, "one could stand missing a fellow in a church or a graveyard or a mournful sunset glow—but to miss him in a foolish, folksy—hot lemonade!—Lord!" And he shook his shoulders almost angrily and threw himself down again on the hearth-rug.

The darkening room was warm as an oven now, and the great, soft, glowing pile of apple-wood embers lured one's drowsy eyes like a flame-colored pillow. No one spoke at all until midnight.

But the clock had only just finished complaining about the hour when the Partridge Hunter straightened up abruptly and cried out to no one in particular:

"Well, I simply can't bluff this out any longer. I've just *got* to know how it all happened!"

No one stopped to question his meaning. No one stopped to parry with word or phrase. Like two tense music-boxes wound to their utmost resonance, but with mechanism only just that instant released, Alrik and the Pretty Lady burst into sound.

The Pretty Lady spoke first. Her breath was short and raspy and cross, like the breath of a person who runs for a train—and misses it.

"It was—in—Florida," she gasped, "the—last—of March. The sailboat was a dreadful, flimsy, shattered thing. But he *would* go out in it—*alone*—storm or no storm!" She spoke with a sudden sense of emotional importance, with a certain strange, fierce, new pride in the shortcomings0 of her Man. "He must have swamped within an hour. They found his boat. But they never found his body. Just as one could always find his pocket, but never his watch—his purse, but never his money—his song, but never his soul." Her broken self-control plunged deeper and deeper into bitterness. "It was a stupid—wicked—wilful—accident," she persisted, "and I can see him in his last, smothery—astonished—moment—just—as—as—plainly—as—though—I—had—been—there. Do you think for an instant that he would swallow even—Death—without making a fuss about it? Can't you hear him rage and sputter: '*This* is too salt! *This* is too cold! Take it away and bring me another!' While all the time his frenzied mind was racing up and down some precious, memoried playground like the Harvard Stadium or the New York Hippodrome, whimpering, 'Everybody'll be there except—*me*—except M-E!'"

The Pretty Lady's voice took on a sudden hurt, left-out resentment. "Of course," she hurried on, "he wasn't exactly sad to go—nothing could make him sad. But I know that it must have made him very *mad*. He had just bought a new automobile. And he had rented a summer place at Marblehead. And he wanted to play tennis in June—"

She paused for an instant's breath, and Alrik crashed like a moose into the silence.

"It was lung trouble!" he attested vehemently. "Cough, cough, cough, all the time. It came on specially worse in April, and she died in May. She wasn't never very strong, you know, but she'd been brought up in your wicked old steam-heated New York, and she would persist in wearing tissue-paper clothes right through our rotten icy winters up here. And when I tried to dose her like the doctor said, with cod-liver oil or any of them thick things, I couldn't fool her—she just up an' said it was nothin' but liquid flannel, and spit it out and sassed me. And Gruff—Growly-Dog-Gruff," he finished hastily, "I don't know what ailed him. He jus' kind of followed along about June."

The Partridge Hunter drew a long, heavy breath. When he spoke at last, his voice sounded like the voice of a man who holds his hat in his hand, and the puffs of smoke from his pipe made a sort of little halo round his words.

"Isn't it nice," he mused, "to think that while we four are cozying here to-night in the same jolly old haunts, perhaps they three—Man, Girl, and Dog—are cuddling off together somewhere in the big, spooky Unknown, in the shade of a cloud, or the shine of a star—talking—perhaps—about—*us?*"

The whimsical comfort of the thought pleased me. I did not want any one to be alone on such a night.

But Alrick's tilted chair came crashing down on the floor with a resounding whack. His eyes were blazing.

"She *ain't* with him!" he cried. "She *ain't*, she AIN'T, she A-I-N-'T! I won't have it. Why, it's the middle of the night!"

And in that electric instant I saw the Pretty Lady's face set rigidly, all except her mouth, which twisted in my direction.

"I'll wager she *is* with him," she whispered under her breath. "She always did tag him wherever he went!"

Then I felt the toe of my slipper meet the recumbent elbow of the Partridge Hunter. Had I reached out to him? Or had he reached back to me? There was no time to find out, for the smooth, round conversation shattered prickingly in the hand like a blown-glass bauble, and with much nervous laughter and far-fetched joke-making, we rose, rummaged round for our candles, and climbed upstairs to bed.

Alrik's Old Mother burrowed into a corner under the eaves.

The Pretty Lady had her usual room, and mine was next to hers. For a lingering moment I dallied with her, craving some tiny, absurd bit of loving service. First, I helped her with a balky hook on her collar. Then I started to put her traveling coat and hat away in the closet. On the upper shelf something a little bit scary brushed my hands. *It was the Blue Serge Man's cap, with a ragged gash across it where Growly-Dog-Gruff had worried it on a day I remembered well.* With a hurried glance over my shoulder to make sure that the Pretty Lady had not also spied it, I reached up and shoved it—oh, 'way, 'way back out of sight, where no one but a detective or a lover could possibly find it.

Then I hurried off to my room with a most garish human wonder: How could a *man* be all gone, but his silly cap *last?*

My little room was just as I remembered it, bare, bleak, and gruesomely clean, with a rag rug, a worsted motto, and a pink china vase for really sensuous ornamentation. I opened the cheap pine bureau to stow away my things. *A trinket jingled—a tawdry rhinestone side-comb. Caught in the setting was a tiny wisp of brown hair.* I slammed the drawer with a bang, and opened another. *Metal and leather slid heavily along the bottom.* It might have been my beast's collar, if distinctly across the name-plate had not run the terse phrase "Alrik's Cross Dog." I did not like to have my bureau haunted! When I slammed that drawer, it cracked the looking-glass.

Then, with candle burning just as cheerfully as possible, I lay down on the bed in all my clothes and began to *wake up*—wider and wider and wider.

My reason lay quite dormant like some drugged thing but my memory, photographic as a lens, began to reproduce the ruddy, blond face of the Blue Serge Man beaming across a chafing-dish; the mournful, sobbing sound of a dog's dream; the crisp, starched, Monday smell of the blue gingham aprons that Alrik's Wife used to wear. The vision was altogether too vivid to be pleasant.

Then the wet wind blew in through the window like a splash of alcohol, chilling, revivifying, stinging as a whip-lash. The tormented candle flame struggled furiously for a moment, and went out, hurtling the black night down upon me like some choking avalanche of horror. In utter idiotic panic I jumped from my bed and clawed my way toward the feeble gray glow of the window-frame. The dark dooryard before me was drenched with rain. The tall linden trees waved and mourned in the wind.

"Of course, of course, there are no ghosts," I reasoned, just as one reasons that there is no mistake in the dictionary, no flaw in the multiplication table. But sometimes one's fantastically jaded nerves think they have found the blunder in language, the fault in science. Ghosts or no ghosts—if you *thought* you saw one, wouldn't it be just as bad? My eyes strained out into the darkness. Suppose—I—should—*think*—that I heard the bark of a dog? Suppose—suppose—that from that black shed door where the automobile used to live, I should *think*—even T-H-I-N-K that I saw the Blue Serge Man come stumbling with a lantern? The black shed door burst open with a bang-bang-bang, and I screamed, jumped, snatched a blanket, and fled for the lamp-lighted hall.

A little dazzled by the sudden glow, I shrank back in alarm from a figure on the top stair. It was the Pretty Lady. Wrapped clumsily like myself in a big blanket, she sat huddled there with the kerosene lamp close beside her, mending the Blue Serge Man's cap. On the step below her, smothered in a soggy lavender comforter, crouched Alrik's Old Mother, her dim eyes brightened uncannily with superstitious excitement. I was evidently a welcome addition to the party, and the old woman cuddled me in like a meal-sack beside her.

"Naw one could sleep a night like this," she croaked.

"*Sleep?*" gasped the Pretty Lady. Scorn infinite was in her tone.

But comfortably and serenely from the end of the hall came the heavy, regular breathing of the Partridge Hunter, and from beyond that, Alrik's blissful, oblivious snore. Yet Alrik was the only one among us who claimed an agonizing, personal sorrow.

I began to laugh a bit hysterically. "Men are funny people," I volunteered.

Alrik's Old Mother caught my hand with a chuckle, then sobered suddenly, and shook her wadded head.

"Men *ain't* exactly—people," she confided. "Men *ain't* exactly people—at all!"

The conviction evidently burned dull, steady, comforting as a night-light, in the old crone's eighty years' experience, but the Pretty Lady's face grabbed the new idea desperately, as though she were trying to rekindle happiness with a wet match. Yet every time her fretted lips straightened out in some semblance of Peace, her whole head would suddenly explode in one gigantic sneeze. There was no other sound, I remember, for hours and hours, except the steady, monotonous, slobbery swash of a bursting roof-gutter somewhere close in the eaves.

Certainly Dawn itself was not more chilled and gray than we when we crept back at last to our beds, thick-eyed with drowsy exhaustion, limp-bodied, muffle-minded.

But when we woke again, the late, hot noonday sun was like a scorching fire in our faces, and the drenched dooryard steamed like a dye-house in the sudden burst of unseasonable heat.

After breakfast, the Pretty Lady, in her hundred-dollar ruffles, went out to the barn with shabby Alrik to help him mend a musty old plow harness. The Pretty Lady's brains were almost entirely in her fingers. So were Alrik's. The exclusiveness of their task seemed therefore to thrust the Partridge Hunter and me off by ourselves into a sort of amateur sorrow class, and we started forth as cheerfully as we could to investigate the autumn woods.

Passing the barn door, we heard the strident sound of Alrik's complaining. Braced with his heavy shoulders against a corner of the stall, he stood hurling down his new-born theology upon the glossy blond head of the Pretty Lady who sat perched adroitly on a nail keg with two shiny-tipped fingers prying up the corners of her mouth into a smile. One side of the smile was distinctly wry. But Alrik's face was deadly earnest. Sweat bubbled out on his forehead like tears that could not possibly wait to reach his eyes.

"There ought to be a separate heaven for ladies and gentlemen," he was arguing frantically. "'Tain't fair. 'Tain't right. I won't have it! I'll see a priest. I'll find a parson. If it ain't proper to live with people, it ain't proper to die with 'em. I tell you I won't have Amy careerin' round with strange men. She always was foolish about men. And I'm breakin' my heart for her, and Mother's gettin' old, and the house is goin' to rack and ruin, but how—*how* can a man go and get married comfortable again when his mind's all torturin' round and round and round about his first wife?"

The Partridge Hunter gave a sharp laugh under his breath, yet he did not seem exactly amused. "Laugh for *two!*" I suggested, as we dodged out of sight round the corner and plunged off into the actual Outdoors.

The heat was really intense, the October sun dazzlingly bright. Warmth steamed from the earth, and burnished from the sky. A plushy brown rabbit lolling across the roadway dragged on one's sweating senses like overshoes in June. Under our ruthless, heavy-booted feet the wet green meadow winced like some tender young salad. At the edge of the forest the big pines darkened sumptuously. Then, suddenly, between a scarlet sumach and a slim white birch, the cavernous wood-path opened forthmysteriously, narrow and tall and domed like the arch of a cathedral. Not a bird twitted, not a leaf rustled, and, far as the eye could reach, the wet brown pine-needles lay thick and soft and padded like tan-bark, as though all Nature waited hushed and expectant for some exquisitely infinitesimal tragedy, like the travail of a squirrel.

With brain and body all a-whisper and a-tiptoe, the Partridge Hunter and I stole deeper and deeper into the Color and the Silence and the Witchery, dazed at every step by the material proof of autumn warring against the spiritual insistence of spring. It was the sort of day to make one very tender toward the living just because they were living, and very tender toward the dead just because they were dead.

At the gurgling bowl of a half-hidden spring, we made our first stopping-place. Out of his generous corduroy pockets the Partridge Hunter tinkled two drinking-cups, dipped them deep in the icy water, and handed me one with a little shuddering exclamation of cold. For an instant his eyes searched mine, then he lifted his cup very high and stared off into *Nothingness*.

"To the—*All-Gone People*," he toasted.

I began to cry. He seemed very glad to have me cry. "Cry for two," he suggested blithely, "cry0 for two," and threw himself down on the twiggy ground and began to snap metallically against the cup in his hand.

"Nice little tin cup," he affirmed judicially. "The Blue Serge Man gave it to me. It must have cost as much as fifteen cents. And it will last, I suppose, till the moon is mud and the stars are dough. But the Blue Serge Man himself is—quite *gone*. Funny idea!" The Partridge Hunter's forehead began to knit into a fearful frown. "Of course it *isn't* so," he argued, "but it would certainly seem sometimes as though a man's *things* were the only really immortal, indestructible part of him, and that Soul was nothing in the world but just a composite name for the S-ouvenirs, O-rnaments, U-tensils, L-itter that each man's personality accumulates in the few years' time allotted to him. The man himself, you see, is wiped right off the earth like a chalk-mark, but you can't escape or elude in a million years the wizened bronze elephant that he brought home from India, or the showy red necktie that's down behind his bureau, or the floating, wind-blown, ash-barrel bill for violets that turns up a generation hence in a German prayer-book at a French book-stall.

"And isn't Death a teasing teacher? Holds up a personality suddenly like a map—makes you learn by heart every possible, conceivable pleasant detail concerning that personality, and then, when you are fairly bursting with your happy knowledge, tears up the map in your face and says, 'There's no such country any more, so what you've learned won't do you the slightest good.' And there you'd only just that moment found out that your friend's hair was a beautiful auburn instead of 'a horrid red'; that his blessed old voice was hearty, not 'noisy'; that his table manners were quaint, not 'queer'; that his morals were broad, not 'bad.'"

The Partridge Hunter's mouth began to twist. "It's a horrid thing to say," he stammered, "but there ought to be a sample shroud in every home, so that when your husband is late to dinner, or your daughter smokes a cigarette, or your son decides to marry the cook, you could get out the shroud and try it on the offender, and make a few experiments concerning—well, *values*. Why, I saw a man last week dragged by a train—jerked in and out and over and under, with his head or his heels or the hem of his coat just missing Death every second by the hundred-millionth fraction of an inch. But when he was rescued at last and went home to dinner—shaken as an aspen, sicker than pulp, tongue-tied like a padlock—I suppose, very likely, his wife scolded him for having forgotten the oysters."

The Partridge Hunter's face flushed suddenly.

"I didn't care much for Alrik's Wife," he attested abruptly. "I always thought she was a trivial, foolish little crittur. But if I had known that I was never going to see her again—while the sun blazed or the stars blinked—I should like to have gone back from the buckboard that last morning and stroked her brown hair just once away from her eyes. Does that seem silly to you?"

"Why, no," I said. "It doesn't seem silly at all. If I had guessed that the Blue Serge Man was going off on such a long, long, never-stop journey, I might even have kissed him good-by. But I certainly can't imagine anything that would have provoked or astonished him more! People can't go round petting one another just on the possible chance of never meeting again. And goodness gracious! nobody wants to. It's only that when a person actually *dies*, a sort of subtle, holy sense in you wakes up and wishes that just once for all eternity it might have gotten a signal through to that subtle, holy sense in the other person. And of course when a youngster dies, you feel somehow that he or she must have been different all along from other people, and you simply wish that you might have guessed that fact sooner—before it was too late."

The Partridge Hunter began to smile. "If you knew," he teased, "that I was going to be massacred by an automobile or crumpled by an elevator before next October—would you wish that you had petted me just a little to-day?"

"Yes," I acknowledged.

The Partridge Hunter pretended he was deaf. "Say that once again," he begged.

"Y-e-s," I repeated.

The Partridge Hunter put back his head and roared. "That's just about like kissing through the telephone," he said. "It isn't particularly satisfying, and yet it makes a desperately cunning sound."

Then I put back my head and laughed, too, because it is so thoroughly comfortable and pleasant to be friends for only one single week in all the year. Independence is at best such a scant fabric, and every new friendship you incur takes just one more tuck in that fabric, till before you know it your freedom is quite too short to go out in. The Partridge Hunter felt exactly the same way about it, and after each little October playtime we ripped out the thread with never a scar to show.

Even now while we laughed, we thought we might as well laugh at everything we could think of, and get just that much finished and out of the way.

"Perhaps," said the Partridge Hunter, "perhaps the Blue Serge Man was *glad* to see Amy, and perhaps he was rattled, no one can tell. But I'll wager anything he was awfully mad to see Gruff. There were lots of meteors last June, I remember. I understand now. It was the Blue Serge Man raking down the stars to pelt at Gruff."

"Gruff was a very—nice dog," I insisted.

"He was a very growly dog," acceded the Partridge Hunter.

"If you growl all the time, it's almost the same as a purr," I argued.

The Partridge Hunter smiled a little, but not very generously. Something was on his mind. "Poor little Amy," he said. "Any man-and-woman game is playing with fire, but it's foolish to think that there are only two kinds, just Hearth-Fire and Hell-Fire. Why, there's 'Student-lamp' and 'Cook-stove' and 'Footlights.' Amy and the Blue Serge Man were playing with 'Footlights,' I guess. She needed an audience. And he was New York to her, great, blessed, shiny, rackety New York. I believe she loved Alrik. He must have been a pretty picturesque figure on that first and only time when he blazed his trail down Broadway. But *happy* with him—H-E-R-E? Away from New York? Five years? In just green and brown woods where the posies grow on the ground instead of on hats, and even the Christmas trees are trimmed with nothing except real snow and live squirrels? G-L-O-R-Y! Of course her chest caved in. There wasn't kinky air enough in the whole state of Maine to keep her kind of lungs active. Of course she starved to death. She needed her meat flavored with harp and violin; her drink aerated with electric lights. We might have done something for her if we'd liked her just a little bit better. But I didn't even know her till I heard that she was dead."

He jumped up suddenly and helped me to my feet. Something in my face must have stricken him. "Would you like my warm hand to walk home with?" he finished quite abruptly.

Even as he offered it, one of those chill, quick autumn changes came over the October woods. The sun grayed down behind huge, windy clouds. The leaves began to shiver and shudder and chatter, and all the gorgeous reds and greens dulled out of the world, leaving nothing as far as the eye could reach but dingy squirrel-colors, tawny grays and dusty yellows, with the far-off, panting sound of a frightened brook dodging zigzag through some meadow in a last, desperate effort to escape winter. As a draft from a tomb the cold, clammy, valley twilight was upon us.

Like two bashful children scuttling through a pantomime, we hurried out of the glowery, darkening woods, and then at the edge of the meadow broke into a wild, mirthful race for Alrik's bright hearth-fire, which glowed and beckoned from his windows like a little tame, domesticated sunset. The Partridge Hunter cleared the porch steps at a single bound, but I fell flat on the bruising doormat.

Nothing really mattered, however, except the hearth-fire itself.

Alrik and the Pretty Lady were already there before us, kneeling down with giggly, scorching faces before a huge corn-popper foaming white with little muffled, ecstatic notes of heat and harvest.

The Pretty Lady turned a crimson cheek to us, and Alrik's tanned skin glowed like a freshly shellacked Indian. Even the Old Mother's asthmatic breath purred from the jogging rocker like a specially contented pussy-cat.

Nothing in all the room, I remember, looked pallid or fretted except the great, ghastly white face of the clock. I despise a clock that looks worried. It wasn't late, anyway. It was scarcely quarter-past four.

Indeed, it was only half-past four when the company came. We were making such a racket among ourselves that our very first warning was the sudden, blunt, rubbery *m-o-o* of an automobile directly outside. Mud was the first thing I thought of.

Then the door flew open peremptorily, and there on the threshold stood the Blue Serge Man—not dank and wet with slime and seaweed, but fat and ruddy and warm in a huge gray 'possum coat. Only the fearful, stilted immovability of him gave the lie to his reality.

It was a miracle! I had always wondered a great deal about miracles. I had always longed, craved, prayed to experience a miracle. I had always supposed that a miracle was the supreme sensation of existence, the ultimate rapture of the soul. But it seems I was mistaken. A miracle doesn't do anything to your soul for days and days and days. Your heart, of course, may jump, and your blood foam, but first of all it simply makes you very, very sick in the pit of your stomach. It made a man like Alrik clutch at his belt and jump up and down and "holler" like a lunatic. It smote the Partridge Hunter somewhere between a cramp and a sob. It ripped the Old Mother close at her waist-line, and raveled her out on the floor like a fluff of gray yarn.

But the Pretty Lady just stood up with her hands full of pop-corn, and stared and stared and stared and STARED. From her shining blond head to her jet-black slippers she was like an exploded pulse.

The Blue Serge Man stepped forward into the room and faltered. In that instant's faltering, Alrik jumped for him like a great, glad, loving dog, and ripped the coat right off his shoulders.

The Blue Serge Man's lips were all a-grin, but a scar across his forehead gave a certain tense, stricken dignity to his eyes. Very casually, very indolently, he began to tug at his gloves, staring all the while with malevolent joy on the fearful crayon portrait of the ancient grandame.

"That's the very last face I thought of when I was drowning," he drawled, "and there wasn't room enough in all heaven for the two of us. Bully old face, I'm glad I'm here. I've been in Cuba," he continued quite abruptly, "and I meant to play dead forever and ever. But there was an autumn leaf—a red autumn leaf in a lady's hat—and it made me homesick." His voice broke suddenly, and he turned to his wife with quick, desperate, pleading intensity. "I'm not—much—good," he gasped. "But I've—*come back!*"

I saw the flaky white pop-corn go trickling through the Pretty Lady's fingers, but she just stood there and shook and writhed like a tightly wrung newspaper smoldering with fire. Then her face flamed suddenly with a light I had never, never seen since my world was made.

"I don't care whether you're any good or not," she cried. "You're alive! You're alive! You're alive! You're *alive!* You're—ALIVE!"

I thought she would never stop saying it, on and on and on and on. "You're alive, you're alive, you're alive." Like a defective phonograph disk her shattered sense caught on that one supreme phrase, "You're alive! You're alive! You're alive! You're alive!"

Then the blood that had blazed in her face spread suddenly to her nerveless hands, and she began to pluck at the crape ruffles on her gown. Stitch by stitch I heard the rip-rip-rip like the buzz of a fishing-reel. But louder than all came that maddening, monotonous cry, "You're alive! You're alive! You're alive!" I thought her brain was broken.

Then the Blue Serge Man sprang toward her, and I shut my eyes. But I caught the blessed, clumsy sound of a lover's boot tripping on a ruffle—the crushing out of a breath—the smother of a half-lipped word.

I don't know what became of Alrik. I don't know what became of Alrik's Old Mother. But the Partridge Hunter, with his arm across his eyes, came groping for me through the red, red room.

"Let's get out of this," he whispered. "Let's get out of this."

So once again, amateurs both in sorrow and in gladness, the Partridge Hunter and I fled fast before the Incomprehensible. Out we ran through0 Amy's frost-blighted rose-garden, *where no gay, shrill young voice challenged our desecration*, out through the senile old apple orchard, *where no suspicious dog came bristling forth to question our innocent intrusion*, up through the green-ribbon roadway, up through the stumbling wood-path, to the safe, sound, tangible, moss-covered pasture-bars, where the warm, brown-fur bossies, sweet-breathed and steaming, came lolling gently down through the gauzy dusk to barter their pleasant milk for a snug night's lodging and a troughful of yellow mush.

A dozen mysterious wood-folk crackled close within reach, as though all the little day-animals were laying aside their starched clothes for the night; and the whole earth teemed with the exquisite, sleepy, nestling-down sound of fur and feathers and tired leaves. Out in the forest depths somewhere a belated partridge drummed out his excuses. Across on the nearest stone wall a tawny marauder went hunching his way along. It might have been a fox, it might have been Amy's thrown-away coon-cat. Short and sharp from the house behind us came the fast, furious crash of

Alrik's frenzied young energies, chopping wood enough to warm a dozen houses for a dozen winters for a dozen new brides. But high above even the racket of his ax rang the sweet, wild, triumphant resonance of some French Canadian *chanson*. His heart and his lungs seemed fairly to have exploded in relief.

And over the little house, and the dark woods, and the mellow pasture, and the brown-fur bossies, broke a little, wee, tiny prick-point of a star, as though some Celestial Being were peeping down whimsically to see just what the Partridge Hunter and I thought of it all.

THE AMATEUR LOVER

WITH every night piercing her like a new wound, and every morning stinging her like salt in that wound, Ruth Dudley's broken engagement had dragged itself out for four long, hideous months. There's so much fever in a woman's sorrow.

At first, to be sure, there had been no special outward and visible sign of heartbreak except the thunderstorm shadows under the girl's blue eyes. Then, gradually, very gradually, those same plucky eyes had dulled and sickened as though every individual thought in her brain was festering. Later, an occasional loosened finger ring had clattered off into her untouched plate or her reeking strong cup of coffee. At the end of the fourth month the family doctor was quite busy attesting that she had no tubercular trouble of any sort. There never yet was any stethoscope invented that could successfully locate consumption of the affections.

It was about this time that Ruth's Big Brother, strolling smokily into her room one evening, jumped back in tragic dismay at the astonishing sight that met his eyes. There, like some fierce young sacrificial priestess, with a very modern smutty nose and scorched cheeks, Ruth knelt on the hearth-rug, slamming every conceivable object that she could reach into the blazing fire. The soft green walls of the room were utterly stripped and ravished. The floor in every direction lay cluttered deep with books and pictures and clothes and innumerable small bits of bric-a-brac. Already the brimming fireplace leaked forth across the carpet in little gray, gusty flakes of ash and cinder.

The Big Brother hooted right out loud. "Why, Ruthy Dudley," he gasped. "What *are* you doing? You look like the devil!"

Blissfully unconscious of smoke or smut, the girl pushed back the straggling blond hair from her eyes and grinned, with her white teeth shot like a bolt through her under lip to keep the grin in place.

"I'm not a 'devil,'" she explained. "I'm a god! And what am I doing? I'm creating a new heaven and a new earth."

"You won't have much left to create it with," scoffed the Big Brother, kicking the tortured wreck of a straw hat farther back into the flames.

The girl reached up impatiently and smutted her other hand across her eyes. "Nothing left to create it with?" she mocked. "Why, if I had anything left to create it with, I'd be only a—mechanic!"

Then, blackened like a coal-heaver and tousled like a Skye terrier, she picked up the scarlet bellows and commenced to pump a savage yellow flame into a writhing, half-charred bundle of letters.

Through all the sweet, calm hours of that warm June night the sacrifice progressed with amazing rapacity. By midnight she had just finished stirring the fire-tongs through the ghostly, lacelike ashes of her wedding gown. At two o'clock her violin went groaning into the flames. At three her Big Brother, yawning sleepily back in his nightclothes, picked her up bodily and dumped her into her bed. He was very angry. "Little Sister," he scolded, "there's no man living worth the fuss you're making over Aleck Reese!" And the little sister sat up and rubbed her smutty, scorched cheek against his cool, blue-shaven face as she tilted the drifting ashes from the bedspread. "I'm not making any 'fuss,'" she protested. "I'm only just—burning my bridges." It was the first direct allusion that she had ever made to her trouble.

Twice after that—between three o'clock and breakfast time—the Big Brother woke from his sleep with a horrid sense that the house was on fire. Twice between three o'clock and breakfast time he met the Housekeeper scuttling along the halls on the same sniffy errand. Once with a flickering candle-light Ruth herself crept out to the doorway and laughed at them. "The house isn't on fire, you sillies," she cried. "Don't you know a burnt bridge when you smell it?" But the doctor had said quite distinctly: "You must watch that little girl. Sorrow in the tongue will talk itself cured, if you give it a chance; but sorrow in the eyes has a wicked, wicked way now and then of leaking into the brain."

It was the Housekeeper, though, whose eyes looked worried and tortured at breakfast time. It was the Big Brother's face that showed a bit sharp on the cheek-bones. Ruth herself, for the first time in a listless, uncollared, unbelted, unstarched month, came frisking down to the table as white and fresh and crisp as linen and starch and curls could make her.

"I'm going to town this morning," she announced nonchalantly to her relieved and delighted hearers. The eyes that turned to her brother's were almost mischievous. "Couldn't you meet me at twelve o'clock," she suggested, "and take me off to the shore somewhere for lunch? I'll be shopping on Main Street about that time, so suppose I meet you at Andrew Bernard's office."

Half an hour later she was stealing out of the creaky back door into the garden, along the gray, pebbly gravel walk between the tall tufts of crimson and purple phlox, to the little gay-faced plot of heart's-ease where the family doctor, symbolist and literalist, had bade her dig and delve every day in the good, hot, wholesome, freckly sunshine. Close by in the greensward an absurd pet lamb was tugging and bouncing at the end of its stingy tether. In a moment's time the girl had transferred the clumsy iron tether-stake to the midst of her posy bed. Then she started for the gate.

Pausing for just one repentant second with her hand on the gate latch, she turned and looked back to the ruthlessly trodden spot where the bland-eyed lamb stood eyeing her quizzically with his soft, woolly mouth fairly dripping with the tender, precious blossoms. "Heart's-ease. B-a-a!" mocked the girl, with a flicker of real amusement. "Heart's-ease. B-a-a-a!" scoffed the lamb, just because his stomach and his tongue happened to be made like that. Then with a quick dodge across the lane she ran to meet the electric car and started off triumphantly for the city, shutting her faint eyes resolutely away from all the roadside pools and ponds and gleams of river whose molten, ultimate peace possibilities had lured her sick mind so incessantly for the past dozen weeks.

Two hours later, with a hectic spurt of energy,0 she was racing up three winding, dizzy flights of stairs in a ponderous, old-fashioned office building.

Before a door marked "Andrew Bernard, Attorney at Law," she stopped and waited a frightened moment for breath and courage. As though the pounding of her heart had really sounded as loud as it felt, the door handle turned abruptly, and a very tall, broad-shouldered, grave-faced young man greeted her with attractive astonishment.

"Good morning, Drew," she began politely. "Why, I haven't seen you for a year." Then, with alarming vehemence, she finished: "Are you all alone? I want to talk with you."

Her breathlessness, her embarrassment, her fragile intensity sobered the young man instantly as he led her into his private office and stood for a moment staring inquiringly into her white face. Her mouth was just as he had last seen it a year ago, fresh and whimsical and virginal as a child's; but her eyes were scorched and dazed like the eyes of a shipwreck survivor or any other person who has been forced unexpectedly to stare upon life's big emotions with the naked eye.

"I hear you've been ill this spring," he began gently. "If you wanted to talk with me, Ruthy, why didn't you let me come out to the house and see you? Wouldn't it have been easier?"

She shook her head. "No," she protested, "I wanted to come here. What I've got to talk about is very awkward, and if things get too awkward—why, an embarrassed guest has so much better chance to escape than an embarrassed host." She struggled desperately to smile, but her lips twittered instead into a frightened quiver. With narrowing eyes the young man drew out his big leather chair for her. Then he perched himself on the corner of his desk and waited for her to speak.

"Ruthy dear," he smiled, "what's the trouble? Come, tell your old chum all about it."

The girl scrunched her eyes up tight, like a person who starts to jump and doesn't care where he lands. Twice her lips opened and shut without a sound. Then suddenly she braced herself with an intense effort.

"Drew," she blurted out, "do you remember—three years ago—you asked me to—marry—you?"

"Do I remember it?" gasped Drew. The edgy sharpness of his tone made the girl open her eyes and stare at him. "Yes," he acknowledged, "I remember it."

The girl began to smooth her white skirts with excessive precision across her knees. "What made you—ask me?" she whispered.

"What made me ask you?" cried the man.

"What made me ask you? Why, I asked you because I love you."

The girl bent forward anxiously as though she were deaf. "You asked me because—*what?*" she quizzed him.

"Because I love you," he repeated.

She jumped up suddenly and ran across the room to him. "Because you—love me?" she reiterated. "'Love?' Not 'loved'? Not past tense? Not all over and done with?"

There was no mistaking her meaning. But the man's face did not kindle, except with pain. Almost roughly he put his hands on her shoulders and searched down deep into her eyes. "Ruth," he probed, "what are you trying to do to me? Open an old wound? You know I—love you."

The girl's mouth smiled, but her eyes blurred wet with fright and tears.

"Would you care anything—about—marrying me—now?" she faltered.

Drew's face blanched utterly, and the change gave him such a horridly foreign, alien look that the girl drew away from his hands and scuttled back to the big chair, and began all over again to smooth and smooth the garish white skirt across her knees. "Oh, Drew, Drew," she pleaded, "please look like—*you*. Please—please—don't look like anybody else."

But Drew did not smile at her. He just stood there and stared in a puzzled, tortured sort of way.

"What about Aleck Reese?" he began with fierce abruptness.

The girl met the question with unwonted flippancy. "I've broken my engagement to Aleck Reese," she said coolly. "Broken it all to smash."

But the latent tremor in her voice did not satisfy the man. "Why did you break it?" he insisted. "Isn't Aleck Reese the man you want?"

Her eyes wavered and fell, and then rallied suddenly to Drew's utmost question.

"Yes, Drew," she answered ingenuously, "Aleck Reese *is* the man I want, *but he's not the kind of man I want!*" As the telltale sentence left her lips, every atom of strength wilted out of her, and she sank back into her chair all sick and faint and shuddery.

The impulsive, bitter laugh died dumb on Drew's lips. Instantly he was at her side, gentle, patient, compassionate, the man whom she knew so well. "Do you mean," he stammered in a startled sort of way, "do you mean that—love or no love—I, I am the kind of man that you do want?"

Her hand stole shyly into his and she nodded her head. But her eyes were turned away from him.

For the fraction of a second he wondered just what the future would hold for him and her if he should snatch the situation into his arms and crush her sorrow out against his breast. Then in that second's hesitancy she shook her hair out of her eyes and looked up at him like a sick, wistful child.

"Oh, Drew," she pleaded, "you've never, never failed me yet—all my hard lessons, all my Fourth-of-July accidents, all my broken sleds and lost skates. Couldn't you help me now we're grown up? I'm so unhappy."

The grimness came back to Drew's face.

"Has Aleck Reese been mean to you?" he asked.

Her eyebrows lifted in denial. "Oh, no—not specially," she finished a trifle wearily. "I simply made up my mind at last that I didn't want to marry him."

Drew's frown relaxed. "Then what's the trouble?" he suggested.

Her eyebrows arched again. "What's the trouble?" she queried. "Why, I happen to love him. That's all."

She took her hand away from Drew and began to smooth her skirt once more.

"Yes," she repeated slowly, "as long ago as last winter I made up my mind that I didn't want to marry him—but I didn't make up my courage until Spring. My courage, I think, is just about six months slower than my mind. And then, too, my 'love-margin' wasn't quite used up, I suppose. A woman usually has a 'love-margin,' you know, and, besides, there's always so much more impetus in a woman's love. Even though she's hurt, even though she's heartbroken, even though, worst of all, she's a tiny bit bored, all her little, natural love courtesies go on just the same of their own momentum, for a day or a week, or a month, or half a lifetime, till the love-flame kindles again—or else goes out altogether. Love has to be like that. But if I were a man, Drew, I'd be awfully careful that that love-margin didn't ever get utterly exhausted. Aleck, though, doesn't understand about such things. I smoothed his headaches just as well, and listened to his music just as well, so he shiftlessly took it for granted that I loved him just as well. What nonsense! 'Love?'" Her voice rose almost shrilly. "'Love?' Bah! What's love, anyway, but a wicked sort of hypnotism in the way that a mouth slants, or a cheek curves, or a lock of hair colors? Listen to me. If Aleck Reese were a woman and I were a man, I certainly wouldn't choose his type for a sweetheart—irritable, undomestic, wild for excitement. How's that for a test? And if Aleck Reese and I were both women, I certainly shouldn't want him for my friend. Oughtn't that to decide it? Not a vital taste in common, not a vital interest, not a vital ideal!"

She began to laugh hysterically. "And I can't sleep at night for remembering the droll little way that his hair curls over his forehead, or the hurt, surprised look in his eyes when he ever really did get sorry about anything. My God!

Drew, look at me!" she cried, and rolled up her sleeves to her elbow. The flesh was gone from her as though a fever had wasted her.

The muscles in Drew's throat began to twitch unpleasantly. "Was Aleck Reese mean to you?" he persisted doggedly.

A little faint, defiant smile flickered across her lips. "Never mind, Drew," she said, "whether Aleck Reese was mean to me or not. It really doesn't matter. It doesn't really matter at all just exactly what a man does or doesn't do to a woman as long as, by one route or another, before her wedding day, he brings her to the place where she can honestly say in her heart, 'This man that I want is not the kind of man that I want.' Honor, loyalty, strength, gentleness—why, Drew, the man I marry has *got* to be the kind of man I want.

"I've tried to be fair to Aleck," she mused almost tenderly. "I've tried to remember always that men are different from women, and that Aleck perhaps is different from most men. I've tried to remember always that he is a musician—a real, real musician with all the ghastly, agonizing extremes of temperament. I've tried to remember always that he didn't grow up here with us in our little town with all our fierce, little-town standards, but that he was educated abroad, that his whole moral, mental, and social ideals are different, that the admiration and adulation of—new—women is like the breath of life to him—that he simply couldn't live without it any more than I could live without the love of animals, or the friendship of children, or the wonderfulness of outdoors, all of which bore *him* to distraction.

"Oh, I've reasoned it all out, night after night after night, fought it out, *torn* it out, that he probably really and truly did love me quite a good deal—in his own way—when there wasn't anything else to do. But how can it possibly content a woman to have a man love her as well as *he* knows how—if it isn't as well as *she* knows how? We won't talk about—Aleck Reese's morals," she finished abruptly. "Fickleness, selfishness, neglect, even infidelity itself, are such purely minor, incidental data of the one big, incurably rotten and distasteful fact that—such and such a man is *stupid in the affections*."

With growing weakness she sank back in her chair and closed her eyes.

For an anxious moment Drew sat and watched her. "Is that all?" he asked at last.

She opened her eyes in surprise. "Why, yes," she said, "that's all—that is, it's all if you understand. I'm not complaining because Aleck Reese didn't love me, but because, loving me, he wasn't *intelligent* enough to be true to me. You do understand, don't you? You understand that it wasn't because he didn't pay his love bills, but because he didn't know enough to pay them. He took my loyalty without paying for it with his; he took my devotion, my tenderness, my patience, without ever, ever making any adequate return. Any girl ought to be able to tell in six months whether her lover is using her affection rightly, whether he is taking her affection and investing it with his toward their mutual happiness and home. Aleck invested nothing. He just took all my love that he could grab and squandered it on himself—always and forever on himself. A girl, I say, ought to be able to tell in six months. But I am very stupid. It has taken me three years."

"Well, what do you want *me* to do?" Drew asked a bit quizzically.

"I want you to advise me," she said.

"Advise you—*what?*" persisted Drew.

The first real flicker of comedy flamed in the girl's face. Her white cheeks pinked and dimpled. "Why, advise me to—marry*you!*" she announced. "WELL, WHY NOT?" She fairly hurled the three-word bridge across the sudden, awful chasm of silence that yawned before her.

Drew's addled mind caught the phrase dully and turned it over and over without attempting to cross on it. "Well, why not? Well, why not?" he kept repeating. His discomfiture filled the girl with hysterical delight, and she came and perched herself opposite him on the farther end of his desk and smiled at him.

"It seems to me perfectly simple," she argued. "Without any doubt or question you certainly are the kind of man whom I should like to marry. You are true and loyal and generous and rugged about things. And you like the things that I like. And I like the people that you like. And, most of anything in the world, you are *clever in the affections*. You are heart-wise as well as head-wise. Why, even in the very littlest, silliest thing that could possibly matter, you wouldn't—for instance—remember George Washington's birthday and forget mine. And you wouldn't go away on a lark and leave me if I was sick, any more than you'd blow out the gas. And you wouldn't—hurt me about—other women—any more than you'd eat with your knife." Impulsively she reached over and patted his hand with the tips of0 her fingers. "As far as I can see," she teased, "there's absolutely no fault in you that matters to me except that I don't happen to love you."

Quick as her laugh the tears came scalding back to her eyes.

"Why, Drew," she hurried on desperately, "people seem to think it's a dreadful thing to marry a man whom you don't love; but nobody questions your marrying *any* kind of a man if you do love him. As far as I can make out, then, it's the love that matters, not the man. Then why not love the right man?" She began to smile again. "So here and now, sir, I deliberately choose to love *you*."

But Drew's fingers did not even tighten over hers.

"I want to be a happy woman," she pleaded. "Why, I'm only twenty-two. I can't let my life be ruined now. There's *got* to be some way out. And I'm going to find that way out if I have to crawl on my hands and knees for a hundred years. I'm luckier than some girls. I've got such a shining light to aim for."

Almost roughly Drew pulled his hand away, the color surging angrily into his cheeks. "I'm no shining light," he protested hotly, "and you shall never, never come crawling on your hands and knees to me."

"Yes, I shall," whispered the girl. "I shall come creeping very humbly, if you want me. And you do want me, don't you? Oh, please advise me. Oh, please play you are my Father or my Big Brother and advise me to—marry *you*."

Drew laughed in spite of himself. "Play I was your Father or your Big Brother?" Mimicry was his one talent. "Play I was your Father or your Big Brother and advise you to marry me?"

Instantly his fine, straight brows came beetling down across his eyes in a fierce paternal scrutiny. Then, quick as a wink, he had rumpled his hair and stuck out his chest in a really startling imitation of Big Brother's precious, pompous importance. But before Ruth could clap her hands his face flashed back again into its usual keen, sad gravity, and he shook his head. "Yes," he deliberated, "perhaps if I truly were your Father or your Brother, I really should advise you to marry—me—not because I amount to anything and am worth it, but because I honestly believe that I should be good to you—and I know that Aleck Reese wouldn't be. But if I'm to advise you in my own personal capacity—no, Ruthy, I don't want to marry you!"

"What? What?" Staggering from the desk, she turned and faced him, white as her dress, blanched to her quivering lips.

But Drew's big shoulders blocked her frenzied effort to escape.

"Don't go away like that, Little Girl," he said. "You don't understand. It isn't a question of caring. You know I care. But don't you, don't you understand that a man doesn't like to marry a woman who doesn't love him?"

Her face brightened piteously. "But I *will* love you?" she protested. "I *will* love you. I promise. I promise you faithfully—I will love you—if you'll only give me just a little time." The old flicker of mischief came back to her eyes, and she began to count on her fingers. "Let me see," she said. "It's June now—June, July, August, September, October, November—six months. I promise you that I will love you by November."

"I don't believe it." Drew fairly slashed the words into the air.

Instantly the hurt, frightened look came back to her eyes. "Why, Drew," she whispered, "if it were money that I wanted, if I were starving, or sick, or any all-alone anything, you wouldn't refuse to help me just because you couldn't possibly see ahead just how I was ever going to pay you. Drew, I'm very unhappy and frightened and lost-feeling. I just want to borrow your love. I promise you I will pay it back to you. You won't be sorry. You won't. You won't!"

Drew's hand reached up and smothered the words on her lips. "You can't borrow my love," he said sternly. "It's yours, always, every bit of it. But I won't marry you unless you love me. I tell you it isn't fair to you."

Impulsively she took his hand and led him back to the big chair and pushed him gently into it, and perched herself like a little child on a pile of bulky law books at his feet. The eyes that looked up to his were very hopeful.

"Don't you think, Drew," she argued, "that just being willing to marry you is love enough?"

He scanned her face anxiously for some inner, hidden meaning to her words, some precious, latent confession; but her eyes were only blue, and just a little bit shy.

She stooped forward suddenly, and took Drew's hand and brushed it across her cheek to the edge of her lips. "I feel so safe with you, Drew," she whispered, "so safe, and comforted always. Oh, I'm sure I can teach you how to make me love you—and you're the only man in the world that I'm willing to teach." Her chin stiffened suddenly with renewed stubbornness. "*You* are the Harbor that was meant for me, and Aleck Reese is nothing but a—Storm. If you know it, and I know it, what's the use of dallying?"

Drew's solemn eyes brightened. "Do you truly think," he said, "that Aleck Reese is only an accident that happened to you on your way to me?"

She nodded her head. Weakness and tears were only too evidently overtaking her brave little theories.

"And there's something else, too," she confided tremulously. "My head isn't right. I have such hideous dreams when I do get to sleep. I dream of drowning myself, and it feels good; and I dream of jumping off high buildings, and it feels good; and I dream of throwing myself under railroad trains, and it feels good. And I see the garish announcement in the morning papers, and I picture how Uncle Terry would look when he got the news, and I cry and cry and cry, and it feels good. Oh, Drew, I'm so bored with life! It isn't right to be so bored with life. But I can't seem to help it. Nothing in all the world has any meaning any more. Flowers, sunshine, moonlight—everything I loved has gone stale. There's no taste left to anything; there's no fragrance, there's no rhyme. Drew, I could stand the sorrow part of it, but I simply can't stand the emptiness. I tell you I *can't* stand it. I wish I were dead; and, Drew, there are so many, many easy ways all the time to make oneself dead. I'm not safe. Oh, please take me and make me safe. Oh, please take me and make me want to live!"

Driven almost distracted by this final appeal to all the chivalrous love in his nature, Drew jumped up and paced the floor. Perplexity, combativeness, and ultimate defeat flared already in his haggard face.

The girl sensed instantly the advantage that she had gained. "Of course," she persisted, "of course I see now, all of a sudden, that I'm not offering you very much in offering you a wife who doesn't love you. You are quite right; of course I shouldn't make you a very good wife at first—maybe not for quite a long, long time. Probably it would all be too hard and miserable for you—"

Drew interrupted her fiercely. "Great heavens!" he cried out, "my part would be easy, comfortable, serene, interesting, compared to yours. Don't you know it's nothing except *sad* to be shut up in the same house, in the same life, with a person you love who doesn't love you? Nothing but sad, I tell you; and there's no special nervous strain about being sad. But to be shut up day and night—as long as life lasts—with a person who takes the impudent liberty of loving you against your wish to be loved—oh, the spiritual distastefulness of it, and the physical enmity, and the ghastly, ghastly ennui! That's your part of it. Flower or book or jewel or caress, no agonizing, heart-breaking, utterly wholesome effort to please, but just one hideously chronic, mawkishly conscientious effort to *be* pleased, to act pleased—though it blast your eyes and sear your lips—to *look* pleased. I tell you I won't have it!"

"I understand all that," said Ruth gravely. "I understand it quite perfectly. But underneath it all—I would rather—you had taken me in your arms—as though I were a little, little hurt girl—and comforted me—"

But before Drew's choking throat-cry had reached his lips she had sprung from her seat and was facing him defiantly. Across her face flared suddenly for the first time the full, dark flush of one of Life's big tides, and the fear in her hands reached up and clutched at Drew's shoulders. The gesture tipped her head back like a fagged swimmer's struggling in the water.

"I am pleading for my life, Drew," she gasped, "for my body, for my soul, for my health, for my happiness, for home, for safety!"

He snatched her suddenly into his arms. "My God! Ruth," he cried, "what do you want me to do?"

Triumph came like a holiday laugh to her haggard face.

"What do I want you to do?" she dimpled. "Why, I want you to come with me now and get a license. I want to be married right away this afternoon."

"What!" Drew hurled the word at her like a bomb, but it did not seem to explode.

Laughingly, flushingly, almost delightedly, she stood and watched the anger rekindle in his face.

"Do you think I am going to take advantage of you like this?" he asked hotly. "You would probably change your mind to-morrow and be very, very sorry—"

She tossed her head. It was a familiar little gesture. "I fully and confidently expect to be sorry to-morrow," she affirmed cheerfully. "That's why I want to be married to-day, this afternoon, this minute, if possible, before I have had any chance to change my mind."

Then, with unexpected abruptness, she shook her recklessness aside and walked back to him childishly, pulling a long, loose wisp of hair across her face. "See," she said. "Smell the smoke in my hair. It's the smoke from my burned bridges. I sat up nearly all night and burned everything I owned, everything that could remind me of Aleck Reese, all my dresses, all my books, all my keepsakes, all my doll houses that ever grew up into dreams. So if you decide to marry me I shall be very expensive. You'll have to take me just as I am—quite a little bit crumpled, not an extra collar, not an extra hairpin, not anything. Aleck Reese either loved or hated everything I owned. I haven't left a single bridge on which one of my thoughts could even crawl back to him again—"

Half quizzically, half caressingly, Drew stooped down and brushed his lips across the lock of hair. Fragrant as violets, soft as the ghost of a kiss, the little curl wafted its dearness into his senses. But ranker than violets, harsher than kisses, lurked the blunt, unmistakable odor of ashes.

He laughed. And the laugh was bitter as gall. "Burning your bridges," he mused. "It's a good theory. But if I take your life into my bungling hands and sweat my heart out trying to make you love me, and come home every night to find you crying with fear and heartbreak, will you still protest that the sting in your eyes is nothing in the world except the *smudge* from those burnt bridges? Will you promise?"

With desperate literalness she clutched at the phrase. Everything else in the room began to whirl round and round like prickly stars. "I promise, I promise," she gasped. Then sight—not air, but just sight—seemed to be smothered right out of her, and her brain reeled, and she wilted down unconscious on the floor.

Cursing himself for a brute, Drew snatched her up in a little, white, crumpled heap and started for the window. Halfway there, the office door opened abruptly and Ruth's Big Brother stood on the threshold. Surprise, anxiety, ultimate relief chased flashingly across the newcomer's face, and in an instant both men were working together over the limp little body.

"Well, old man," said the Big Brother, "I'm glad she was here safe with you when she fainted." His spare arm clapped down affectionately across Drew's shoulders and jarred Drew's fingers brownly against the death-like pallor of the girl's throat. The Big Brother gave an ugly gasp. "Damn Aleck Reese," he said.

Drew's eyes shut perfectly tight as though he was smitten by some unbearable agony. Then suddenly, without an instant's warning, he pulled himself together and burst out laughing uproariously like a schoolboy.

"Oh, what's the use of damning Aleck Reese?" he cried. "Aleck Reese is as stale an issue as yesterday morning's paper. If you've no particular objection to me as a brother-in-law as well as a tennis chum, Ruth and I were planning to marry each other this afternoon. Maybe I was just a little bit too vehement about it."

Three hours later, in a dusty, musty, mid-week church vestry, an extraordinarily white and extraordinarily0 vivacious girl was quite busy assuring a credulous minister and a credulous sexton and a credulous Big Brother that she would love till death hushed her the perfectly incredulous bridegroom who stood staring down upon her like a very tall man in a very short dream.

And then, because neither groom nor bride could think of anything specially married to say to each other, they kidnapped Big Brother and bore him away in an automobile to a nervous, rollicking, wonderfully entertaining "shore dinner," where they sat at an open window round a green-tiled table in a marvelously glowering, ice-cool, artificial grotto, and ate bright scarlet lobsters while the great, hot, blowzy yellow moon came wallowing up out of the night-shadowed sea, and the thrilly, thumpy brass band played "I Love You So"; and the only, only light in the whole vague, noisy room seemed to be Big Brother's beaming, ecstatic face gleaming like some glad phosphorescent thing through the clouds of murky tobacco smoke.

Not till the wines and dines and roses and posies and chatter and clatter were all over, and the automobile had carried Big Brother off to his railroad station and whisked the bride and groom back to the wobbly city pavements, did Drew begin to realize that the frolicking, jesting, crisp-tongued figure beside him had wilted down into a piteous little hunch of fear. Stooping to push her slippery new suit case closer under her feet, he caught the sharp, shuddering tremor of her knees, and as the automobile swayed finally into the street that led to his apartment, her lungs seemed to crumple up in a paroxysm of coughing. Under the garish lights that marked his apartment-house doorway her slight figure drooped like a tired flower, and the footsteps that tinkled behind him along the stone corridor rang in his ears with a dear, shy, girlish reluctance. The elevator had stopped running. One flight, two flights, three, four, five they toiled up the harsh, cool, metallic stairway. Four times Ruth stopped to get her breath, and twice to tie her shoe. Drew laughed to himself at the delicious subterfuge of it.

Then at the very top of the strange, gloomy, midnight building, when Drew's nervous fingers fumbled a second with his door-lock, without the slightest possible warning she reached out suddenly with one mad, frenzied impulse and struck the key from his hand. To his startled eyes she turned a face more wild, more agonized than any terror he had ever dreamed in his most hideous, sweating nightmare. Instantly her hands went clutching out to him.

"Oh, Drew, for God's sake take me home!" she gasped. "What have I done? What have I done? What have I done? Oh, ALECK!"

Wrenching himself free from her hands, Drew dropped down on the floor and began to hunt around for the key. The blood surged into his head like a hot tide, and he felt all gritty-lunged and smothered, as though he were crawling under water. After a minute he stumbled to his feet and slipped the recreant key smoothly into the lock, and swung his door wide open, and turned back to Ruth. She stood facing him defiantly, her eyes blazing, her poor hands twisting.

Drew nodded toward the door, and shoved the suit case with his foot across the threshold. His face was very stern and set.

"You want me to take you 'home'?" he said. "*This* is home. What do you mean? Take you back to your Brother's house? You can't go back to your Brother's house on your wedding day. It wouldn't be fair to me. And I won't help you do an unfair thing *even* to me. You've *got* to give me a chance!"

He nodded again toward the open door, but the girl did not budge. His face brightened suddenly, and he stepped back to where she was standing, and lifted her up in his arms and swung her to his shoulder and stumbled through the pitch-black doorway. "Do you remember," he cried, "the day at your grammar-school picnic when I carried you over the railroad trestle because the locomotive that was swooping down upon us round the curve had scared all the starch out of your legs? Look out for your head now, honey, and I'll give you a very good imitation of a cave man bringing home his bride."

In another moment he had switched a blaze of electric light into his diminutive library, and deposited his sobbing burden none too formally in the big easy chair that blocked almost all the open space between his desk and his bookcases. "What! Aren't you laughing, too?" he cried in mock alarm. But the crumpled little figure in the big chair did not answer to his raillery.

Until it seemed as though he would totter from his wavering foothold, Drew stood and watched her dumbly. Then a voice that sounded strange even to himself spoke out of his lips.

"Ruth—come here," he said.

She raised her rumpled head in astonishment, gaged for a throbbing instant the new authoritative glint in his eyes, and then slipped cautiously out of her chair and came to him, reeking with despair. For a second they just stood and stared at each other, white face to white face, a map of anger confronting a map of fear.

"You understand," said Drew, "that to-day, by every moral, legal, religious right and rite, you have delivered your life over utterly into my hands?" His voice was like ice.

"Yes, I understand," she answered feebly, with the fresh tears gushing suddenly into her eyes.

Drew's mouth relaxed. "You understand?" he repeated. "Well—forget it! And never, never, never, as long as you and I are together, never, I say, understand anything but this: you can cry about Aleck Reese all you want to, but you sha'n't cry about me. You can count on that anyway." He started to smile, but his mouth twitched instead with a wince of pain. "And I thought I could really bring you heart's-ease," he scoffed. "Heart's-ease? Bah!"

"Heart's-ease. Bah!" The familiar phrase exploded Ruth's inflammable nerves into hysterical laughter. "Why, that's what the lamb said," she cried, "when I fed him on my pansy posies. 'Heart's-ease. B-a-h!'" And her sudden burst of even unnatural delight cleared her face for the moment of all its haggard tragedy, and left her once more just a very fragile, very plaintive, very helpless, tear-stained child. "You *b-a-a* exactly like the lamb," she suggested with timid, snuffling pleasantry; and at the very first suspicion of a reluctant twinkle at the corner of Drew's eyes she reached up her trembling little hands to his shoulders and held him like a vise with a touch so light, so faint, so timorous that it could hardly have detained the shadow of a humming-bird.

For a moment she stared exploringly round the unfamiliar, bright little room crowded so horribly, cruelly close with herself, her mistake, and the life-long friend loomed so suddenly and undesirably into a man. Then with a quick, shuddery blink her eyes came flashing back wetly and wistfully to the unsolved, inscrutable face before her. Her fingers dug themselves frantically into his cheviot shoulders.

"Oh, Drew, Drew," she blurted out, "I am so very—very—very—frightened! Won't you please take me and play you are my—Mother?"

"Play I am your Mother? *Play I am your Mother!*" The phrase ripped out of Drew's lips like an oath, and twitched itself just in time into explosive, husky mirth. "Play I am your Mother?" The teeniest grimace over his left shoulder outlined the soft silken swish and tug of a lady's train. A most casual tap at his belt seemed to achieve instantly the fashionable hour-glass outline of feminine curves. "Play I am your Mother!" He smiled and, stooping down, took Ruth's scared white face between his hands, and his smile was as bright—and just about as pleasant— as a zigzag of lightning from a storm-black sky.

"Ruthy dear," he said, "I don't feel very much like your Mother. Now if it was a cannibal that you wanted, or a pirate, or a kidnapper, or a body-snatcher, or a general all-round robber of widows and orphans, why, here I am, all dressed and trained and labeled for the part. But a *Mother*—" The smile went zigzagging again across his face just as a big, wet, scalding tear came trickling down the girl's cheek into his fingers. The feeling of that tear made his heart cramp unpleasantly. "Oh, hang it all," he finished abruptly, "what does a Mother do, anyway?"

The little white face in his hands flooded instantly with a great desolation. "I don't know," she moaned wearily. "I *never* knew."

For some inexplicable reason Aleck Reese's devilish, insolent beauty flaunted itself suddenly before Drew's vision, and he gave a bitter gasp, and turned away fiercely, and brushed his arm potently across his forehead as though Sex, after all, were nothing but a trivial mask that fastened loosely to the ears.

When he turned round again, his conquered face had that strange, soft, shining, translucent wonder-look in it which no woman all her life long may reap twice from a man's face. Tenderly, serenely, uncaressingly, without passion and without playfulness, he picked up his sad little bride and carried her back to the big, roomy, restful chair, and snuggled her down in his long arms, with her smoke-scented hair across his cheek, and told her funny, giggly little stories, and crooned her funny, sleepy little songs, till her shuddering sobs soothed themselves—oh, so slowly—into lazy, languid, bashful little smiles, and the lazy, languid, bashful little smiles droned off at last into nestling, contented little sighs, and the nestling, contented little sighs blossomed all of a sudden into merciful, peaceful slumber.

Then, when the warm, gray June dawn was just beginning to flush across the roofs of the city, he put her softly down and slipped away, and took his smallest military brushes, and his smallest dressing-gown, and his smallest slippers, and carried them out to his diminutive guest-room. "It isn't a very big little guest-room," he mused disconsolately, "but then, she isn't a very big little guest. It will hold her, I guess, as long as she's willing to stay."

"As long as she's willing to stay." The phrase puckered his lips. Again Aleck Reese's face flashed before him in all its amazing beauty and magical pathos, a face this time staring across a tiny, ornate café table into the jaded, world-wise eyes of some gorgeous woman of the theatrical demi-monde. At the vision Drew's shoulders squared suddenly as though for a fair fight to the finish, and then wilted down with equal abruptness as his eyes met accidentally in the mirror his own plain, matter-of-fact reflection. The sight fairly mocked him. There was no beauty there. No magic. No brilliance. No talent. No compelling moodiness. No possible promise of "Love and Fame and Far Lands." Nothing. Just eyes and nose and mouth and hair and an ugly baseball scar on his left cheek. Merciful heavens! What had he to fight Aleck Reese with, except the only two virtues that a man may not brag of—a decently clean life and an unstaled love!

Grinning to rekindle his courage, he started tiptoeing back along the hall to his bedroom and his kitchen, and rolled up his sleeves and began to clean house most furiously; for even if you are quite desperately in love, and a fairly good man besides, it is just a little bit crowded-feeling and disconcerting to have the lady walk unannounced right into your life and your neckties and your pictures, to say nothing of your last week's unwashed cream-jars.

Frantically struggling with his coffee-pot at seven o'clock, he had almost forgotten his minor troubles when a little short, gaspy breath sound made him look up. Huddling her tired-out dress into the ample folds of his dressing-gown, Ruth stood watching him bashfully.

"Hello!" he said. "Who are you?"

"I'm—Mrs.—Andrew Bernard, attorney at law," she announced with stuttering nonchalance, and started off exploringly for the cupboard to find Drew's best green Canton china to deck the kitchen breakfast table. All through the tortuous little meal she sat in absolute tongue-tied gravity, carving her omelet into a hundred infinitesimal pieces and sipping like a professional coffee-taster at Drew's over-rank concoction. Only once did her solemn face lighten with an inspirational flash that made Drew's heart jump. Then, "Oh, Drew," she exclaimed, "do you think you could go out to the house to-day and see if they fed the lamb?"

"No, I don't," said Drew bluntly, and poured himself out his fifth cup of coffee.

After breakfast, all the time that he was shaving, she came and sat on the edge of a table and watched him with the same maddening gravity, and when he finally started off for his office she followed him down the whole length of his little hallway. "I like my cave!" she volunteered with sudden sociability, and then with a great, pink-flushing wave of consciousness she lifted up her face to him and stammered, "Do I kiss you good-by?"

Drew shook his head and laughed. "No," he said, "you don't even have to do that; I'm not much of a kisser," and turned abruptly and grabbed at the handle of the door.

But before he had crossed the threshold she reached out and pulled him back for a moment, and he had to stoop down very far to hear what she wanted to tell him. "It's nothing much, Drew,"0 she whispered. "It's nothing much at all. I just wanted to say that—considering how strong they are, and how—wild—and strange—I think men are—very—*gentle* creatures. Thank you." And in another instant she had gone back alone to face by crass daylight the tragedy that she had brought into three people's lives.

Certainly in all the days and weeks that followed, Drew never failed to qualify as a "gentle creature." Not a day passed at his office that he did not telephone home with the most casual-sounding pleasantry, "Is everything all right? Any burnt-bridge smoke in the air?" Usually, clear as his own voice, and sometimes even with a little giggle tucked on at the end, the answer came, "Yes, everything's all right." But now and then over that telephone wire a minor note flashed with unmistakably tremulous vibration: "N-o, Drew. Oh, could you come right home—and take me somewhere?"

Drew's brown cheeks hollowed a bit, perhaps, as time went on, but always smilingly, always frankly and jocosely, he met the occasionally recurrent emergencies of his love-life. Underneath his smile and underneath his frankness his original purpose never flinched and never wavered. With growing mental intimacy and absolute emotional aloofness he forced day by day the image and the consciousness of his personality upon the girl's plastic mind: his picture, for instance, as a matter of course for her locket; his favorite, rather odd, colors for her clothes; his sturdy, adventuresome, fleet-footed opinions to run ahead and break in all her strange new thought-grounds for her. More than this, in every possible way that showed to the world he stamped her definitely as the most carefully cherished wife among all her young married mates.

At first the very novelty of the situation had fed his eyes with rapture and fired the girl's face with a feverish excitement almost as pink as happiness. The surprise and congratulations of their friends, the speech of the janitor, the floral offering of the elevator boy, the long procession of silver spoons and cut-glass dishes, had filled their days with interest and laughter. Trig in her light muslin house gowns or her big gingham aprons, Ruth fluttered blissfully around her house like a new, brainy sort of butterfly. By some fine, instinctive delicacy, shrewder than many women's love, she divined and forestalled Drew's domestic tastes and preferences, and lined his simplest, homespun needs with all the quiver and sheen of silk. Resting his weariness, spurring his laziness; equally quick to divine the need of a sofa pillow or a joke; equally interested in his food and his politics; always ready to talk, always ready to keep still; cramping her free suburban ways into his hampered accommodations; missing her garden and her pets and her piazzas without ever acknowledging it—she tried in every plausible way except loving to compensate Drew for the wrong she had done him.

Only once did Drew's smoldering self-control slip the short leash he had set for himself. Just once, round the glowing coziness of a rainy-night open fire, he had dropped his book slammingly on the floor and reached out his hand to her soft hair that brightened like bronze in the lamplight. "Are you happy?" he had probed before he could fairly bite the words back; and she had jumped up, and tossed her hair out of her eyes, and laughed as she started for the kitchen. "No, I'm not exactly happy," she had said. "But I'm awfully—interested."

So June budded into July, and July bloomed into August, and August wilted into September, and September brittled and crisped and flamed at last into October. Tennis and boating and picnics and horseback riding filled up the edges of the days. Little by little the bright, wholesome red came back to live in Ruth's rounding cheeks. Little by little the good steady gleam of normal interests supplanted the wild will-o'-the-wisp lights in her eyes. Little by little her accumulating possessions began to steel shyly out from her tiny room and make themselves boldly at home in the places where hitherto they had ventured only as guests. Her workbasket crowded Drew's tobacco-jar deliberately from the table to the top of the bookcase. Her daring hands nonchalantly replaced a brutally clever cartoon with a soft-toned sketch of a little child. Once, indeed, an ostentatiously freshly laundered dress, all lace and posies and ruffles, went and hung itself brazenly in Drew's roomy closet right next to his fishing clothes.

And then, just as Drew thought that at last he saw Happiness stop and turn and look at him a bit whimsically, Aleck Reese came back to town—Aleck Reese, not as Fate should have had him, drunken with flattery, riotous with revelry, chasing madly some new infatuation, but Aleck Reese sobered, dazed, temporarily purified by the shock of his loss, if not by the loss itself.

For a week, blissfully unconscious of any cause, Drew had watched with growing perplexity and anxiety the sudden, abrupt flag in the girl's health and spirits and general friendliness. Flowers, fruit, candy, books, excursion plans had all successively, one by one, failed to rouse either her interest or her ordinary civility. And then one night, dragging home extra late from a worried, wearisome day at the office, faint for his dinner, sick for his sleep, he found the apartment perfectly dark and cheerless, the fire unlighted, the table unset, and Ruth herself lying in a paroxysm of grief on the floor under his stumbling feet. With his dizzy head reeling blindly, and his hands shaking like an aspen, he picked her up and tried to carry her to the couch; but she wrenched herself away from him, and walked over to the window and halfway back again before she spoke.

"Aleck Reese has come home," she announced dully, and reached up unthinkingly and turned a blast of electric light full on her ghastly face.

Drew clutched at the back of the nearest chair. "Have you seen him?" he almost whispered.

The girl nodded. "Yes. He's been here a week. I've seen him twice. Once—all day at the tennis club—and this afternoon I met him on the street, and he came home with me to get—a book."

"Why didn't you tell me before that he was here?"

She shrugged her shoulders wearily. "I thought his coming wasn't going to matter," she faltered, "but—"

"But what?" said Drew.

Her arms fell limply down to her sides and her chin began to quiver.

"He kissed me this afternoon," she stammered, "and I—kissed him. And, worse than that, we were both—glad."

Trying to brush the fog away from his eyes, Drew almost sprang across the room at her, and she gave a queer little cry and fled, not away from him, but right into his arms, as though *there* was her only haven. "Would you be apt to hurt me?" she gasped with a funny-sad sort of inquisitiveness. Then she backed away and held out her hand like a man's to Drew's shaking fingers. "I'm very much ashamed," she said, "about this afternoon. Oh, very, very, very much ashamed. I haven't ever been a really good wife to you, you know, but I never have cheated before until to-day. I promise you faithfully that it sha'n't happen again. But, Drew"—her face flushed utterly crimson—"but, Drew—I honestly think that it *had* to happen to-day."

Drew's tortured eyes watched her keenly for a second and then his look softened. "Will you please tell Aleck," he suggested, "that you told me all about it and that I—laughed?"

It was not till some time in December, however, after a nervous, evasive, speechless sort of week, that Ruth appeared abruptly one day at Drew's office, looking for all the world like the frightened child who had sought him out there the June before.

"Drew, you're five years older than I am, aren't you?" she began disconnectedly. "And you've always been older than I am, and stronger than I am, and wiser than I am. And you've always gone ahead in school and play and everything, and learned what you wanted to and then come back—and gotten me. And it always made everything—oh, so much easier for me—and I thought it was a magic scheme that simply couldn't fail to work. But I'm afraid I'm not quite as smart as I used to be—I can't seem to catch up with you this time."

"What do you mean?" said Drew.

She began to fidget with her gloves. "Do you know what month it is?" she asked abruptly.

"Why, yes," said Drew, just a bit drearily. "It's December. What of it?"

Her eyes blurred, but she kept them fixed steadily on her husband. "Why, don't you remember," she gasped, "that when we were married I promised you faithfully that I would love you within six months? The six months were up in November—but I find I'm not quite ready—yet. You'll have to give me a little more time," she pleaded. "You'll have to renew my love-loan. Will you?"

Drew slammed down his law books and forced his mouth into a grin. "I'd forgotten all about that arrangement," he said. "Of course I'll renew what you call your 'love-loan.' Really and truly I didn't expect you to love me before a full year was up. Heart-wounds don't ever even begin to heal until their first anniversaries are passed—all the Christmases and birthdays and Easters. And, really, I'd quite as soon anyway that you didn't love me till Spring," he added casually. "I'm so hideously busy and worried just now with business things."

She gave him an odd little look that barely grazed his face and settled flutteringly on the book in his hand. It was a ponderous-looking treatise on "The Annulment of Marriage." Her heart began to pound furiously. "Drew!" she blurted out, "I simply can't stand things any longer. I shall go mad. I've tried and tried and tried to be good, and it's no use. I must be stupid. I must be a fool. BUT I WANT TO GO HOME!"

"All right," said Drew very quietly, "you—can—go—home."

In another instant, without good-by or regret, she had flashed out of the office and was racing down the stairs. Halfway to the street she missed her handkerchief, and started reluctantly back to get it. The office door was locked, but she tiptoed round to a private side entrance and opened the door very cautiously and peeped in.

Prostrate across his great, cluttered desk, Drew, the serene, the laughing, the self-sufficient, lay sobbing like a woman.

Startled as though she had seen a ghost, the girl backed undetected out of the door, and closed it very softly behind her, nor did she stop tiptoeing until she had reached the street floor. Then, dropping down weak-kneed upon the last step, she sat staring out into the dingy patch of snow that flared now and then through the swinging doorway. Somewhere out in that vista Aleck Reese was waiting and watching for her. Two or three of her husband's business acquaintances paused and accosted her. "Anything the matter?" they probed.

"Oh, no," she answered brightly. "I'm just thinking."

After a while she jumped up abruptly and stole back through a box-cluttered hall to the rear door of the building, and slid out unnoticed into a side street, gathering her great fur coat—Drew's latest gift—closer and closer around her shivering body. The day was gray and bleak and scarily incomplete, like the work of some amateur creator who had slipped up on the one essential secret of how to make the sun shine. The jingliest sound of sleigh-bells, the reddest flare of holiday shop windows, could not cheer her thoughts away from the stinging, shuddering memory of Drew's crumpled shoulders, the gasping catch of his breath, the strange new flicker of gray at his temples. Over and over to herself she kept repeating dully: "I've hurt Drew just the way that Aleck hurt me. It mustn't be. It mustn't be—it mustn't! There's got to be some way out!"

Then most unexpectedly, at the first street corner she was gathered up joyously by a crowd of her young married chums who were starting off in an automobile for their sewing-club in Ruth's own old-home suburb fifteen miles away. It was a long time since she had played very freely with women, and the old associations caught her interest with a novel charm. Showered with candy, gay with questions, happy with laughter, the party whizzed up at last to the end of its journey, and tumbled out rosy with frost and mischief to join the women who had already arrived. From every individual corner of the warm, lazy sewing-room some one seemed to jump up and greet Ruth's return. "Oh, you pampered young bride!" they teased, and "Will you look at the wonderful fur coat and hat that have happened to Ruth!" Even the sad-faced, widowed little dressmaker who always officiated professionally at the club wriggled out of her seat and brought her small boy 'way across the room to stroke the girl's sumptuous mink-brown softness.

"Why, am I so very wonderful?" stammered Ruth, staring down with her hands in her pockets at the great fur length and breadth of her.

"Well, if I had a coat like that," scoffed a shrill voice from the sofa, "I should think that it was the most wonderful thing in life that could happen to me."0

Standing there scorching herself in the fire-glow, Ruth looked up suddenly with a fierce sort of intentness. "You wise old married people," she cried, "tell me truly what really is the most wonderful thing in life that can happen to a woman?"

"Goodness, is it a new riddle?" shouted her hostess, and instantly a dozen noisy answers came rollicking into the contest. "Money!" cried the extravagant one. "A husband who goes to the club every night!" screamed the flirt.

"Health!" "Curls!" "Dresden china!" "Single blessedness!" the suggestions came piling in. Only the dressmaker's haggard face whitened comprehendingly to the hunger underneath Ruth's laughing eyes. Staring scornfully at the heaping luxuries all around her, the shabby, widow-marked woman snatched up her child and cuddled it to her breast. "The most wonderful thing in life that can happen to a woman?" she quoted passionately. "I'll tell you what it is. It's being able to hope that your son will be *exactly* like his father."

"Exactly like his father?" The shrewd sting and lash of the words ripped through Ruth's senses like the scorch of a red-hot fuse. Strength, tenderness, patience, love, loyalty flamed up before her with such dazzling brilliance that she could scarcely fathom the features behind them, and the room whirled dizzily with sudden excessive heat. "Exactly like his father." A dozen feminine voices caught up the phrase and dropped it blisteringly. The wife of the town's *bon vivant* winced a trifle. The most radiant bride of the year jabbed her fingers accidentally with her scissors. Some one started to sigh and laughed instead. A satirical voice suggested, "Well, but of course there's got to be some improvement in every generation."

Smothering for air, Ruth reached up bunglingly and fastened her big fur collar and started for the door. "Oh, no," she protested to every one's detaining hands, "honestly I didn't intend to stay. I've got to hurry over to the house and get some things before dark," and, pleading several equally legitimate excuses, she bolted out into the snowy fields to take the quickest possible short cut to her Big Brother's house.

Every plowing step drove her heart pounding like an engine, and every lagging footfall started her scared thoughts throbbing louder than her heart. Hurry as fast as she could, stumbling over drift-hidden rocks or floundering headlong into some hollow, she could not seem to outdistance the startling, tumultuous memory of the little dressmaker's passion-glorified eyes staring scornfully down on the slowly sobering faces of the women around her. The vision stung itself home to the girl like sleet in her eyes.

"O-h!" she groaned. "What a wicked thing Life is—wasting a man like Drew on a girl—like me. 'To be able to hope that your son will be exactly like his father!'" Her heart jumped. Merciful heavens! If Happiness were really—only as simple a thing as that—just to look in your husband's eyes and find them good. Years and years hence, perhaps, she herself might have a son—with all his father's blessed, winsome virtues. Her eyes flooded suddenly with angry tears. "Oh, could Fate possibly, possibly be so tricky as to make a woman love her son because he *was* like his father, and yet all, all the long years make that woman just miss loving the father himself?"

With a little frightened gasp she began to run. "If I only can get to the house," she reasoned, "then everything will be all right. And I'll never leave it again."

Half an hour later, panting and flushing, she twisted her latch-key through the familiar home door. No one was there to greet her. From attic to cellar the whole house was deserted. At first the emptiness and roominess seemed to ease and rest her, but after a little while she began to get lonesome, and started out to explore familiar corners, and found them unfamiliar. "What an ugly new wall-paper!" she fretted; "and what a silly way to set the table!" Her old room smote upon her with strange surprise—not cunningly, like one's funny little baby clothes, but distastefully, like a last year's outgrown coat. In the large, light pantry a fresh disappointment greeted her. "What an insipid salad!" she mourned. "It isn't half as nice as the salad Drew makes." Cookies, cakes, doughnuts failed her successively. "And I used to think they were the best I ever tasted," she puzzled. In the newly upholstered parlor a queer unrest sickened her. "Why, the house doesn't seem quite to—fit me any more," she acknowledged, and bundled herself into her coat again, and stuffed her pockets with apples, and started off more gladly for the barn.

As she pushed back the heavy sliding doors a horse whinnied, possibly for welcome, but probably for oats. Teased by the uncertainty, the girl threw back her head and laughed. "Hello, all you animals," she cried; "I have come home. Isn't it fine?"

Up from the floor of his pen the lamb rose clatteringly like a mechanical toy, and met the glad news with a peculiarly disdainful "B-a-a-a!" Back to the sheltering wood-pile her old friends the kittens—little cats now—fled from her with precipitous fear. The white-nosed cow reared back with staring eyes. The pet horse snapped at her fingers instead of the apple. The collie dog, to be sure, came jumping boisterously, but the jumpiness was unmistakably because he was "Carlo," and not because she was "Ruth." And yet only six months before every animal on the place had looked like her with that strange, absurd mimicry of human expression that characterizes the faces of all much-cherished birds or beasties. And now even the collie dog had reverted to the plain, blank-featured canine street type—and the pet horse looked like the hired man.

"Hello, all you animals," she cried

The girl's forehead puckered up into a bewildered sort of frown. "I don't quite seem to belong anywhere," she concluded. The thought was unpleasant. Worst of all, the increasing, utterly unexplainable sob in her throat made her feel very reluctant to go back into the house and wait for her Brother and the Housekeeper and the inevitable questions. Dallying there on the edge of the wheelbarrow, munching her red-cheeked apples, it was almost eight o'clock before her mind quickened to a solution of her immediate difficulties. She would hide in the hay all night, there in the sweetness and softness of last summer's beautiful grass, and think out her problems and decide what to do.

Deep in the hay she burrowed out a nest, and lined it with the biggest buffalo robe and the thickest carriage rug. Then one by one she carried up the astonished kittens, and the heavy, fat lamb, and the scrambling collie dog to keep her company, and snuggled herself down, warm and content, to drowse and dream amidst the musty cobwebs, and the short, sharp snap of straws, and the soothing sighs of the sleepy cow, and the stamp, stamp of the horse, and all the extra, indefinite, scary, lonesome night noises that keep your nerves exploding intermittently like torpedoes and start your common sense scouring like a silver polish at all the tarnished values of your everyday life.

Midnight found her lying wide awake and starry-eyed, with her red lips twisted into an oddly inscrutable smile. Close in her left hand the collie dog nestled his grizzly nose. Under her right arm the woolly lamb slumbered. Over her quiet feet the little cats purred with fire-gleaming faces.

Attracted by the barking of his new bulldog, Big Brother came out in the early morning and discovered her in the hay.

"Well, for heaven's sake!" he began. "Where did you come from? Where does Drew think you are? He's been telephoning here all night trying to find you. I guess he's scared to death. Great Scott! what's the matter? What are you hiding out here for? Have you had any trouble with Drew?"

She slid down out of her nest with the jolliest sort of a laugh. "Of course I haven't had any trouble with Drew. I just wanted to come home. That's all. Drew buys me everything else," she dimpled, "but he simply won't buy me any hay—and I'm such a donkey."

Big Brother shrugged his shoulders. "You're just as foolish as ever," he began, and then finished abruptly with "What a perfectly absurd way to do your hair! It looks like fury."

An angry flush rose to her cheeks, and she reached up her hands defensively. "It suits Drew all right," she retorted.

Big Brother laughed. "Well, come along in the house and get your breakfast and telephone Drew."

The funniest sort of an impulse smote suddenly upon Ruth's mind. "I don't want any breakfast," she protested, "and I don't want any telephone. I'm going home this minute to surprise Drew. We were going to have broiled chicken, and a new dining-room table, and a pot of primroses as big as your head. Shall I have time to wash my face before the car comes?"

Ten minutes after that she was running like mad to the main street. An hour later the big, whizzing electric car that was speeding her back to the city crashed headlong at a curve into another brittling, splintering mass of screams and blood and broken glass and shivering woodwork.

When she came to her senses she was lying in her blood-stained furs on some one's piazza floor, and the horrid news of the accident must have traveled very quickly, for a great crowd of people was trampling round over the snowy lawn, and Big Brother and Aleck Reese and the old family doctor seemed to have dropped down right out of the snow-whirling sky. Just as she opened her eyes, Aleck Reese, haggard with fear and dissipation, was kneeling down trying to slip his arms under her.

With the mightiest possible effort she lifted her forefinger warningly.

"Don't you dare touch me," she threatened. "I promised Drew—"

The doctor looked up astonished into her wide-open eyes. "Now, Ruth," he begged, "don't you make any fuss. We've got to get you into a carriage. We'll try not to hurt you any more than is absolutely necessary."

Her shattered nerves failed her utterly. "What nonsense!" she sobbed. "You don't have to hurt me at all. My own man never hurts me at all. I tell you I want my own man."

"But we can't find Drew," protested the doctor.

Then the blood came gushing back into her eyes and some wicked brute took her bruised knees, and her wrenched back, and her broken collar bone, and her smashed head, and jarred them all up together like a bag of junk, and she gave one awful, blood-curdling yell—and a horse whinnied—and everything in the world stopped happening like a run-down clock.

When Time began to tick normally again, she found herself lying with an almost solid cotton face in a pleasant, puffy bed that seemed to rock, and roll, and tug against her straining arm that clutched its fingers like an anchor into somebody's perfectly firm, kind hand. As far away as a voice on a shore, tired, hoarse, desperately incessant, some one was signaling reassurance to her: "You're all right, honey, You're all right, honey."

After a long time her fingers twittered in the warm grasp. "Who are you?" she stammered perplexedly.

"Just your 'own man,'" whispered Drew.

The lips struggling out from the edge of the bandage quivered a little. "My 'own man'?" she repeated with surprise. "Who was the tattletale that told you?" She began to shiver suddenly in mental or physical agony. "Oh, I remember it all now," she gasped. "Was the little boy killed who sat in the corner seat?"

"Why, I don't know," said Drew, and his voice rasped unexpectedly with the sickening strain of the past few hours.

At the sound she gave a panic-stricken sob. "I believe I'm dead myself, Drew," she cried, "and you're trying to keep it from me. Where am I? Tell me instantly where I am."

Drew's laugh rang out before he could control it. "You're here in your own little room," he assured her.

"Prove it," she whimpered hysterically. "Tell me what's on my bureau."

He jumped up and walked across the room to make sure. "Why, there's a silver-backed mirror, and a box of violet powder, and a package of safety pins."

"Pshaw!" she said. "Those might be on any angel's bureau. What else do you see?"

He fumbled a minute among the glass and silver and gave a quick sigh of surprise. "Here's your wedding ring."

"Bring it to me," she pleaded, and took the tiny golden circlet blindly from his hand and slipped it experimentally once or twice up and down her finger. "Yes, that's it," she assented, and handed it back to him. "Hurry—quick—before anybody comes."

"What do you want?" faltered Drew.

She reached up wilfully and yanked the bandage away from the corner of one eye.

"Why, put the ring back on my finger where0 it belongs!" she said. "We're going to begin all over again. Play that I am your wife!" she demanded tremulously.

Drew winced like raw flesh. "You are my wife," he cried. "You are! You are! You are!"

With all the strength that was left to her she groped out and drew his face down to her lips.

"Oh, I've invented a lots better game than that," she whispered. "If we're going to play any game at all—let's—play—that—I—love—you!"

HEART OF THE CITY

THE dining-room was green, as green could be. Under the orange-colored candle-light, the walls, rugs, ceiling, draperies, ferns, glowed verdant, mysterious, intense, like night woods arching round a camp fire. Into this fervid, pastoral verdure the round white table, sparkling with silver, limpid with wine-lights, seemed to roll forth resplendent and incongruous as a huge, tinseled snowball.

Outside, like fire engines running on velvet wheels, the automobiles went humming along the pavement. Inside, the soft, narrow, ribbony voice of a violin came whimpering through the rose-scented air.

It was the midst of dinner-party time. In the oak-paneled hallway a shadowy, tall clock swallowed gutturally on the verge of striking nine.

The moment was distinctly nervous. The *entrée* course was late, and the Hostess, gesticulating tragically to her husband, had slipped one chalky white shoulder just a fraction of an inch too far out of its jeweled strap. The Host, conversing every second with exaggerated blandness about the squirrels in Central Park, was striving frantically all the while with a desperately surreptitious, itchy gesture to signal to his mate. Worse than this, a prominent Sociologist was audibly discussing the American penal system with a worried-looking lady whose brother was even then under indictment for some banking fraud. Some one, trying to kick the Sociologist's ankle bone, had snagged his own foot gashingly through the Woodland Girl's skirt ruffle, and the Woodland Girl, blush-blown yet with country breezes, clear-eyed as a trout pool, sweet-breathed as balsam, was staring panic-stricken around the table, trying to locate the particular man's face that could possibly connect boot-wise with such a horridly profane accident. The sudden, grotesque alertness of her expression attracted the laggard interest of the young Journalist at her left.

"What brought you to New York?" the Journalist asked abruptly. "You're the last victim in from the country, so you must give an account of yourself. Come 'fess up! What brought you to New York?"

The Journalist's smile was at least as conscientious as the smile of daylight down a city airshaft, and the Woodland Girl quickened to the brightening with almost melodramatic delight, for all previous conversational overtures from this neighbor had been about actors that she had never heard of, or operas that she could not even pronounce, and before the man's scrutinizing, puzzled amazement she had felt convicted not alone of mere rural ignorance, but of freckles on her nose.

"What brought me to New York?" she repeated with vehement new courage. "Do you really want to know? It's quite a speech. What brought me to New York? Why, I wanted to see the 'heart of the city.' I'm twenty years old, and I've never in all my life been away from home before. Always and always I've lived in a log bungalow, in a wild garden, in a pine forest, on a green island, in a blue lake. My father is an invalid, you know, one of those people who are a little bit short of lungs but inordinately long of brains. And I know Anglo-Saxon and Chemistry and Hindoo History and Sunrises and Sunsets and Mountains and Moose, and such things. But I wanted to know People. I wanted to know Romance. I wanted to see for myself all this 'heart of the city' that you hear so much about—the great, blood-red, eager, gasping heart of the city. So I came down here last week to visit my uncle and aunt."

"The lone, accentuated figure of a boy violinist"

Her mouth tightened suddenly, and she lowered her voice with ominous intensity. "But there *isn't* any heart to, your city—no!—there is no heart at all at the center of things—just a silly, pretty, very much decorated heart-shaped box filled with candy. If you shake it hard enough, it may rattle, but it won't throb. And I hate—hate—hate your old city. It's utterly, hopelessly, irremediably jejune, and I'm going home to-morrow!" As she leaned toward the Journalist, the gold locket on her prim, high-necked gown swung precipitously forth like a wall picture in a furious little earthquake.

The Journalist started to laugh, then changed his mind and narrowed his eyes speculatively toward something across the room. "No heart?" he queried. "No Romance?"

The Woodland Girl followed his exploring gaze. Between the plushy green*portières* a dull, cool, rose-colored vista opened forth refreshingly, with a fragment of bookcase, the edge of a stained glass window, the polished gleam of a grand piano, and then—lithe, sinuous, willowy, in the shaded lamplight—the lone, accentuated figure of a boy violinist. In the amazing mellow glow that smote upon his face, the Woodland Girl noted with a crumple at her heart the tragic droop of the boy's dark head, the sluggish, velvet passion of his eyes, the tortured mouth, the small chin fairly worn and burrowed away against his vibrant instrument. And the music that burst suddenly forth was like scalding water poured on ice—seething with anguish, shuddering with ecstasy, flame at your heart, frost at your spine.

The Girl began to shiver. "Oh, yes, I know," she whispered. "He plays, of course, as though he knew all sorrows by their first names, but that's Genius, isn't it, not Romance? He's such a little lad. He can hardly have experienced much really truly emotion as yet beyond a—stomach ache—or the loss of a Henty book."

"A stomach ache! A Henty book!" cried the Journalist, with a bitter, convulsive sort of mirth. "Well, I'm ready to admit that the boy is scarcely eighteen. But he happens to have lost a wife and a son within the past two months! While some of us country-born fellows of twenty-eight or thirty were asking our patient girls at home to wait even another year, while we came over to New York and tried our fortunes, this little youngster of scarcely eighteen is already a husband, a father, and a widower.

"He's a Russian Jew—you can see that—and one of our big music people picked him up over there a few months ago and brought him jabberingly to America. But the invitation didn't seem to include the wife and baby—genius and family life aren't exactly guaranteed to develop very successfully together—and right there on the dock at the very last sailing moment the little chap had to choose between a small, wailing family and a great big, clapping New York—just temporarily, you understand, a mere matter of immediate expediency; and families are supposed to keep indefinitely, you know, and keep sweet, too, while everybody knows that New York can go sour in a single night, even in the coldest weather. And just as the youngster was trying to decide, wavering first one way and then the other, and calling on high every moment to the God of all the Russias, the old steamer whistle began to blow, and they rustled him on board, and his wife and the kid pegged back alone to the province where the girl's father lived, and they got snarled up on the way with a band of Cossack soldiers, and the little chap hasn't got any one now even as far off as Russia to hamper his musical career.... So he's playing jig-tunes to people like us that are trying to forget our own troubles, such as how much we owe our tailors or our milliners. But sometimes they say he screams in the night, and twice he has fainted in the midst of a concert.

"No heart in the city? No Romance? Why, my dear child, this whole city fairly teems with Romance. The automobiles throb with it. The great, roaring elevated trains go hustling full of it. There's Romance—Romance—Romance from dawn to dark, and from dark to dawn again. The sweetness of the day-blooming sunshine, the madness of the night-blooming electric lights, the crowds, the colors, the music, the perfume—why, the city is *Romance-mad!* If you stop anywhere for even half an instant to get your breath, Romance will run right over you. It's whizzing past you in the air. It's whizzing past you in the street. It's whizzing past you in the sensuous, ornate theaters, in the jaded department stores, in the calm, gray churches. Romance?—Love?

"The only trouble about New York Romance lies just in the fact that it is so whizzingly premature. You've simply got to grab Love the minute before you've made up your mind—because the minute after you've made up your mind, it won't be there. Grab it—or lose it. Grab it—or lose it. That's the whole Heart-Motto of New York. Sinner or Saint—RUSH—RUSH—RUSH—like Hell!"

"Grab it—or lose it. Grab it, or—l-o-s-e it." Like the impish raillery of a tortured devil, the violin's passionate, wheedling tremolo seemed to catch up the phrase, and mouth it and mock it, and tear it and tease it, and kiss it and curse it—and0 SMASH it at last into a great, screeching crescendo that rent your eardrums like the crash of steel rails.

With strangely parched lips, the Woodland Girl stretched out her small brown hand to the fragile, flower-stemmed glass, and tasted for the first time in her life the sweety-sad, molten-gold magic of champagne. "Why, what is it?" she asked, with the wonder still wet on her lips. "Why, what is it?"

The Journalist raised his own glass with staler fingers, and stared for a second through narrowing eyes into the shimmering vintage. "What is it?" he repeated softly. "This particular brand? The Italians call it '*Lacrymæ Christi*.' So even in our furies and our follies, in our cafés and carousals, in our love and all our laughter—we drink—you see—the—'Tears of Christ.'" He reached out suddenly and covered the Girl's half-drained glass with a quivering hand. "Excuse me," he stammered. "Maybe—our thirst is partly of the soul; but '*Lacrymæ Christi*' was never meant for little girls like you. *Go back to your woods!*"

Scuttle as it might, the precipitate, naked passion in his voice did not quite have time to cover itself with word-clothes. A little gasping breath escaped. And though the Girl's young life was as shiningly empty as an unfinished house, her brain-cells were packed like an attic with all the inherent experiences of her mother's mother's mother, and she flinched instinctively with a great lurch of her heart.

"Oh, let's talk about something—dressy," she begged. "Let's talk about Central Park. Let's talk about the shops. Let's talk about the subway." Her startled face broke desperately into a smile. "Oh, don't you think the subway is perfectly dreadful," she insisted. "There's so much underbrush in it!" Even as she spoke, her shoulders hunched up the merest trifle, and her head pushed forward, after the manner of people who walk much in the deep woods. The perplexity in her eyes spread instantly to her hands. Among the confusing array of knives and forks and spoons at her plate, her fingers began to snarl nervously like a city man's feet through a tangle of blackberry vines.

With a good-natured shrug of his shoulders, the Journalist turned to his more sophisticated neighbor, and left her quite piteously alone once more. An enamored-looking man and woman at her right were talking transmigration of souls, but whenever she tried to annex herself to their conversation they trailed their voices away from her in a sacred, aloof sort of whisper. Across the table the people were discussing city politics in a most clandestine sort of an undertone. Altogether it was almost half an hour before the Journalist remembered to smile at her again. The very first flicker of his lips started her red mouth mumbling inarticulately.

"Were you going to say something?" he asked.

She shook her head drearily. "No," she stammered. "I've tried and tried, but I can't think of anything at all to say. I guess I don't know any secrets."

The Journalist's keen eyes traveled shrewdly for a second round the cautious, worldly-wise table, and then came narrowing back rather quizzically to the Woodland Girl's flushing, pink and white face.

"Oh, I don't know," he smiled. "You look to me like a little girl who might have a good many secrets."

She shook her head. "No," she insisted, "in all the whole wide world I don't know one single thing that has to be whispered."

"No scandals?" teased the Journalist.

"No!"

"No love affairs?"

"No!"

The Journalist laughed. "Why, what do you think about all day long up in your woods?" he quizzed.

"Anglo-Saxon and Chemistry and Hindoo History and Sunsets and Mountains and Moose," she repeated glibly.

"Now you're teasing me," said the Journalist.

She nodded her head delightedly. "I'm trying to!" she smiled.

The Journalist turned part way round in his chair, and proffered her a perfectly huge olive as though it had been a crown jewel. When he spoke again, his voice was almost as low as the voice of the man who was talking transmigration of souls. But his smile was a great deal kinder. "Don't you find any Romance at all in your woods?" he asked a bit drawlingly.

"No," said the Girl; "that's the trouble. Of course, when I was small it didn't make any difference; indeed, I think that I rather preferred it lonesome then. But this last year, somehow, and this last autumn especially—oh, I know you'll think I'm silly—but two or three times in the woods—I've hoped and hoped and hoped—at the turn of a trail, or the edge of a brook, or the scent of a camp fire—that I might run right into a real, live Hunter or Fisherman. And—one night I really prayed about it—and the next morning I got up early and put on my very best little hunting suit—all coats and leggings and things just like yours, you know—and I stayed out all day long—tramping—tramping—tramping, and I never saw *any one*. But I did get a fox. Yes!—and then—"

"And then what?" whispered the Journalist very helpfully.

The Girl began to smile, but her lips were quite as red as a blush. "Well—and—then," she continued softly, "it occurred to me all of a sudden that the probable reason why the Man-Who-Was-Meant-for-Me didn't come was because he—*didn't know I was there!*" She began to laugh, toying all the while a little bit nervously with her ice-cream fork. "So I thought that perhaps—if I came down to New York this winter—and then went home again, that maybe—not probably you know, but just possibly—some time in the spring or summer—I might look up suddenly through the trees and he *would* be there! But I've been ten days in New York and I haven't seen one single man whom I'd exactly like to meet in the woods—in my little hunting suit."

"Wouldn't you be willing to meet me?" pried the Journalist injudiciously.

The Girl looked up and faltered. "Why, of course," she hurried, "I should be very glad to see you—but I had always sort of hoped that the man whom I met in the woods wouldn't be bald."

The Journalist choked noisily over his salted almonds. His heightened color made him look very angry.

"Oh, I trust I wasn't rude," begged the Woodland Girl. Then as the Journalist's galloping laughter slowed down into the gentlest sort of a single-foot smile, her eyes grew abruptly big and dark with horror. "Why, I never thought of it," she stammered, "but I suppose that what I have just said about the man in the woods and my coming to New York is—'husband hunting.'"

The Journalist considered the matter very carefully. "N—o," he answered at last, "I don't think I should call it 'husband hunting' nor yet, exactly, 'the search for the Holy Grail'; but, really now, I think on the whole I should call it more of a sacrament than a sport."

"O—h," whispered the Girl with a little sigh of relief.

It must have been fully fifteen minutes before the Journalist spoke to her again. Then, in the midst of his salad course, he put down his fork and asked quite inquisitively: "Aren't there any men at all up in your own special Maine woods?"

"Oh, yes," the Girl acknowledged with a little crinkle of her nose, "there's Peter."

"Who's Peter?" he insisted.

"Why, Peter," she explained, "is the Philadelphia boy who tutors with my father in the summers."

Her youthfulness was almost as frank as fever, and, though taking advantage of this frankness seemed quite as reprehensible as taking advantage of any other kind of babbling delirium, the Journalist felt somehow obliged to pursue his investigations.

"Nice boy?" he suggested tactfully.

The Girl's nose crinkled just a little bit tighter.

The Journalist frowned. "I'll wager you two dozen squirrels out of Central Park," he said, "that Peter is head over heels in love with you!"

The Girl's mouth twisted a trifle, but her eyes were absolutely solemn. "I suppose that he is," she answered gravely, "but he's never taken the trouble to tell me so, and he's been with us three summers. I suppose lots of men are made like that. You read about it in books. They want to sew just as long—long—long a seam as they possibly can without tying any knot in the thread. Peter, I know, wants to make perfectly Philadelphia-sure that he won't meet any girl in the winters whom he likes better."

"I think that sort of thing is mighty mean," interposed the Journalist sympathetically.

"Mean?" cried the Girl. "Mean?" Her tousley yellow hair seemed fairly electrified with astonishment, and her big blue eyes brimmed suddenly with uproarious delight. "Oh, of course," she added contritely, "it may be mean for the person who sews the seam, but it's heaps of fun for the cloth, because after awhile, you know, Pompous Peter will discover that there isn't any winter girl whom he likes better, and in the general excitement of the discovery he'll remember only the long, long seam—three happy summers—and forget altogether that he never tied any knot. And then! And then!" her cheeks began to dimple. "And then—just as he begins triumphantly to gather me in—all my yards and yards and yards of beautiful freedom fretted into one short, puckery, worried ruffle—then—

Hooray—swish—slip—slide—*out comes the thread*—and Mr. Peter falls right over bump-backward with surprise. Won't it be fun?"

"Fun?" snapped the Journalist. "What a horrid, heartless little cynic you are!"

The Girl's eyebrows fairly tiptoed to reach his meaning. "Cynic?" she questioned. "You surely don't mean that I am a cynic? Why, I think men are perfectly splendid in every possible way that—doesn't matter to a woman. They can build bridges and wage wars, and spell the hardest, homeliest words. But Peter makes life so puzzling," she added wryly. "Everybody wants me to marry Peter; everybody says 'slow but sure,' 'slow but sure.' But it's a lie!" she cried out hotly. "Slow is *not* sure. It is not! It is not! The man who isn't excited enough to *run* to his goal is hardly interested enough to walk. And yet"—her forehead crinkled all up with worry—"and yet—you tell me that 'quick' isn't sure, either. *What is sure?*"

"Nothing!" said the Journalist.

She tossed her head. "All the same," she retorted, "I'd rather have a man propose to me three years before, rather than three years after, I'd made up my mind whether to accept him or not."

"Don't—marry—Peter," laughed the Journalist.

"Why not?" she asked—so very bluntly that the Journalist twisted a bit uneasily.

"Oh—I—don't—know," he answered cautiously. Then suddenly his face brightened. "Any trout fishing up in your brooks about the first of May?" he asked covertly.

Again the knowledge of her mother's mother's mother blazed red-hot in the Girl's cheeks. "Y—e—s," she faltered reluctantly, "the trout-fishing is very generous in May."

"Will Peter be there?" persisted the Journalist.

Her eyes began to shine again with amusement. "Oh, no," she said. "Peter never comes until July." With mock dignity she straightened herself up till her shoulder almost reached the Journalist's. "I was very foolish," she attested, "even to mention Peter, or mankind—at all. Of course, I'm commencing to realize that my ideas about men are exceedingly countrified—'disgustingly countrified,' my aunt tells me. Why, just this last week at my aunt's sewing club I learned that the only two real qualifications for marriage are that a man should earn not less than a hundred dollars a week, and be a perfectly kind hooker."

"A perfectly kind hooker?" queried the Journalist.

"Why, yes," she said. "Don't you know—now—that all our dresses fasten in the back?" Her little tinkling, giggling laugh rang out with startling incongruity through the formal room, and her uncle glanced at her and frowned with the slightest perceptible flicker of irritation. She leaned her face a wee bit closer to the Journalist. "Now, uncle, for instance," she confided, "is not a particularly kind hooker. He's accurate, you understand, but not exactly kind."

The Journalist started to smile, but instantly her tip-most finger ends brushed across his sleeve. "Oh, please, don't smile any more," she pleaded, "because every time you smile you look so pleasant that some lady sticks out a remark like a hand0 and grabs you into her own conversation." But the warning came too late. In another moment the Journalist was most horridly involved with the people on his left in a prosy discussion regarding Japanese servants.

For another interminable length of time the Woodland Girl sat in absolute isolation. Some of the funerals at home were vastly more social, she thought—people at least inquired after the health of the survivors. But now, even after she had shredded all her lettuce into a hundred pieces and bitten each piece twice, she was still quite alone. Even after she had surreptitiously nibbled up all the cracker crumbs around her own plate and the Journalist's plate, she was still quite alone. Finally, in complete despair, she folded her little, brown, ringless hands and sat and stared frankly about her.

Across the sparkly, rose-reeking table a man as polished as poison ivy was talking devotedly to a white-faced Beauty in a most exciting gown that looked for all the world like the Garden of Eden struck by lightning—black and billowing as a thunder cloud, zigzagged with silver, ravished with rose-petals, rain-dropped with pearls. Out of the gorgeous, mysterious confusion of it the Beauty's bare shoulders leaped away like Eve herself fleeing before the storm. But beyond the extravagant sweep of gown and shoulder the primitive likeness ended abruptly in one of those utterly well-bred, worldly-wise, perfected young faces, with that subtle, indescribable sex-consciousness of expression which makes the type that men go mad over, and the type that older women tersely designate as looking just a little bit "too kissed."

But the Woodland Girl did not know the crumpled-rose-leaf stamp of face which characterizes the coquette. Utterly fascinated, tremulous with excitement, heartsick with envy, she reached out very softly and knocked with her finger on the Journalist's plate to beg readmission to his mind.

"Oh, who is that beautiful creature?" she whispered.

"Adele Reitzen," said the Journalist, "your uncle's ward."

"My own uncle's ward?" The Woodland Girl gave a little gasp. "But why does she worry so in her eyes every now and then?" she asked abruptly.

Even as she asked, Adele Reitzen began to cough. The trouble started with a trivial clearing of her throat, caught up a disjointed swallow or two, and ended with a rack that seemed to rip like a brutal knife right across her silver-spangled lungs. Somebody patted her on the back. Somebody offered her a glass of water. But in the midst of the choking paroxysm she asked to be excused for a moment and slipped away to the dressing-room. The very devoted man seemed rather piteously worried by the incident, and the Hostess looked straight into his eyes and shook her head ominously.

"I hope you are planning a southern wedding trip next week," she said. "I don't like that cough of Adele's. I've sat at three dinner parties with her this week, and each individual night she has had an attack like this and been obliged to leave the table."

In the moment's lull, the butler presented a yellow telegram on a shiny, Sheffield tray, and the Hostess slipped her pink fingers rustlingly through the envelope and brightened instantly. "Oh, here's a surprise for you, Chloe," she called to the Woodland Girl. "Peter is coming over to-night to see you." Like a puckering electric tingle the simple announcement seemed to run through the room, and a little wise, mischievous smile spread from face to face among the guests. In another instant everybody turned and peeped at the Woodland Girl, and the Woodland Girl felt her good cool, red blood turn suddenly to bubbling, boiling water, and steam in horrid, clammy wetness across her forehead and along the prickling palms of her hands, and the Journalist laughed right out loud, and the whole green, definite room swam dizzily like the flaunting scarlet messiness of a tropical jungle.

Every nook and corner of the house, indeed, was luxuriously heated, but when Adele Reitzen came sauntering back to her seat, pungent around her, telltale as an alien perfume, lurked the chill, fresh aroma of the wintry, blustering street. Only the country girl's smothering lungs noted the astonishing fact. Like a little caged animal scenting the blessed outdoors, her nostrils began to crinkle, and she straightened up with such abrupt alertness that she loomed to Adele Reitzen's startled senses like the only visible person at the table, and for just the fraction of a heart-beat the two girls fathomed down deep and understandingly into each other's eyes, before Adele Reitzen fluttered her white lids with a little piteous gesture of appeal.

Breathlessly the Woodland Girl turned to the Journalist, and touched his arm. "New York *is* interesting, isn't it!" she stammered. "I've decided just this minute to stay another week."

"Oh, ho," said the Journalist. "So you love it better than you did an hour ago?"

"No!" cried the Woodland Girl. "I love it worse. I love it worse every moment like a—ghost story, but I'm going to stick it out a week longer and see how it ends. And I've learned one clue to New York's plot this very night. I've learned that most every face is a 'haunted house.' The mouths slam back and forth all the time like pleasant doors, and the jolliest kind of speeches come prancing out, and all that—but in the eyes ghosts are peering out the windows every minute."

"Cheerful thought," said the Journalist, taking off his glasses. "Who's the ghost in my eyes?"

The Woodland Girl stared at him wonderingly. "The ghost in your eyes?" she blundered. "Why—I guess—it's 'the patient girl at home' whom you asked to wait 'even another year.'"

Like two fever spots the red flared angrily on the Journalist's cheek bones.

Not even the Journalist spoke to her again.

Finally, lonesome as a naughty child, she followed the dozen dinner guests back into the huge drawing-room, and wandered aimlessly around through the incomprehensible mysteries of Chinese idols and teakwood tabourets and soft, mushy Asiatic rugs. Then at last, behind a dark, jutting bookcase, in a corner most blissfully safe and secret like a cave, she stumbled suddenly upon a great, mottled leopard skin with its big, humpy head, and its sad glass eyes yearning out to her reproachfully. As though it had been a tiny, lost kitten, she gave a wee gasp of joy, and dropped down on the floor and tried to cuddle the huge, felt-lined, fur bulk into her lap. Just as the clumsy face flopped across her knees, she heard the quick swish of silk, and looked up to see Adele Reitzen bending over her.

The older girl's eyes were tortured with worry, and her white fingers teased perpetually at the jeweled watch on her breast. "Chloe Curtis," she whispered abruptly, "will you do something for me? Would you be afraid? You are visiting here in the house, so no one would question your disappearance. Will you go up to the dressing-room—quick—and get my black evening coat—the one with the gold embroidery and the big hood—and go out to the street corner where the cars stop—and tell the man who is waiting there—that I couldn't—simply couldn't—get out again? Would you be afraid?"

The Woodland Girl jumped to her feet. At that particular instant the lump in her throat seemed the only really insurmountable obstacle in the whole wide world. "Would I be afraid?" she scoffed. "Afraid of what? Of New York? Of the electric lights? Of the automobiles? Of the cross policemen? Afraid of nothing!" Her voice lowered suddenly. "Is it—Love?" she whispered.

The older girl's face was piteous to see. "Y—e—s," she stammered. "It is Love."

The Woodland Girl's eyes grew big with wonder. "But the other man?" she gasped. "You are going to be married next week!"

Adele Reitzen's eyes blurred. "Yes," she repeated, "I am going to be married next week." A little shiver went flickering across her shoulders.

The Woodland Girl's heart began to plunge and race. "What's the matter with the man out on the street corner?" she asked nervously.

Adele Reitzen caught her breath. "He's a civil engineer," she said. "His name is Brian Baird. He's just back from Central America. I met him on the steamer once. He was traveling second cabin. My—family—won't—let—me—have—him."

The Woodland Girl threw back her head and laughed, and smothered her laugh contritely with her hand. "Your family won't let you have him?" she mumbled. "What a funny idea! What has your family got to do about it?" Her breath began to quicken, and she reached out suddenly and clutched Adele Reitzen's shoulder. "Do you know where my uncle's musty old law library is?" she hurried. "It's downstairs, you know, close to the store room—nobody ever uses it. You go down there just as fast as you possibly can, and wait there, and I'll be back in five minutes with the—Love Man."

Before Adele Reitzen's feebler courage could protest, the Woodland Girl was scurrying up the short flight to the dressing-room and pawing like a prankish terrier through the neatly folded evening coats that snuggled across the bed. Tingling with excitement, she arrayed herself finally in the luxuriantly muffling black and gold splendor, and started cautiously down the long, creaky front stairs.

Like the inimitable, familiar thrill of little wild, phosphorescent eyes looming suddenly out of the black night-woods at home, the adventure challenged her impetuous curiosity. Bored puzzlingly by the big city's utter inability to reproduce the identical, simple lake-and-forest emotionalism that was the breath of life to her, she quickened now precipitately to the possible luring mystery in human eyes. Through the dark mahogany stripes of the balustrade, the drawing-room candles flared and sputtered like little finger-pinches of fluid flame, and the violin's shuddering voice chased after her, taunting, "Hurry! Hurry! Or it won't be there!" Beyond the lights and music, and the friendly creaking stairs, the strange black night opened forth like the scariest sort of a bottomless pit; but as yet, in all the girl's twenty coltish years nothing except headache and heart-beat had ever made her feel perfectly throbbing-positive that she was alive. She could spare the headache, but she could not spare the heart-beat. Paddling with muscle-strained shoulder and heaving breast across a November-tortured lake, or huddling under forbidden pine trees in a rackety August thunder storm, or floundering on broken snowshoes into the antlered presence of an astounded moose—Fun and Fear were synonymous to her.

Once on the street, like water to thirst, the cold night air freshened and vivified her. Over her head the electric lights twinkled giddily like real stars. On either side of her the huge, hulking houses reared up like pleasant imitation mountains. Her trailing cloak slipped now and then from her clutching fingers, but she trudged along toward the corner with just one simple, supreme sense of pleasurable excitement—somewhere out of the unfathomed shadows a real, live Adventure was going to rise up and scare her.

But the man, when he came, did not scare her one hundredth part as much as she scared him, though he jumped at her from the snuggling fur robe of a stranded automobile, and snatched at her arm with an almost bruising intensity.

"Oh, Adele," he cried huskily, "I thought you had failed me again."

The Woodland Girl threw back her somber hood and stood there all blonde and tousle-haired and astonishing under the electric light. "I'm not your Adele," she explained breathlessly. "I'm just Chloe Curtis. Adele sent me out to tell you that she absolutely couldn't—couldn't come. You yourself would have seen that it was horridly impossible. But you are to go back to the house now with me—to my uncle's old unused library and see Adele yourself for as much as fifteen minutes. No one—oh, I'm sure that no one—could persuade a woman to be brave—on a street corner; but I think that perhaps if you had a chance to see Adele all alone, she would be very—extraordinarily brave."

Anger, resentment, confusion, dismay flared like successive explosions in the man's face, and faded again, leaving his flesh utter ash gray.

"It was plucky of you to come," he muttered grimly, "but I haven't quite reached the point yet—thank you—where I go sneaking round people's unused rooms to meet any one!"

"Is it so very different from sneaking round street corners?" said the Woodland Girl.

The man's head lifted proudly. "I don't go 'sneaking' round street corners," he answered simply. "All Outdoors *belongs* to me! But I won't go secretly to any house that doesn't welcome me."

The Woodland Girl began to stamp her foot. "But the house does welcome you," she insisted. "It's my visity-house, and you are to come there as my friend."

In her ardor she turned and faced him squarely under the light, and winced to see how well worth0 facing he was—for the husband of a coward. There was no sleek New York about him, certainly, but rather the merge of all cities and many countries, a little breath of unusualness, a touch of mystery, a trifling suggestion, perhaps, of more dusty roads than smug pavements, twenty-eight or thirty years, surely, of adventurous youth. Impulsively she put out her hand to him. "Oh, please come," she faltered. "I—think you are so nice."

With a little laugh that had no amusement in it, nor pleasure, nor expectation, nor any emotion that the Woodland Girl had ever experienced, he stood and stared at her with some sudden impulse. "Does Adele really want me to come?" he asked trenchantly.

"Why yes," insisted the Woodland Girl. "It's life or death for you and Adele."

Ten minutes later, standing on guard at the edge of the library door, the Woodland Girl heard, for the first time in her life, the strange, low, vibrant, mysterious mate-tone of a human voice. If she had burrowed her head in a dozen pillows, she could not have failed to sense the amazing wonder of the sound, though the clearer-worded detail of hurried plans and eager argument and radiant acquiescence passed by her unobserved. "But I must be perfectly sure that you love me," persisted the man's voice.

"You and—you only," echoed the woman's passion.

Then suddenly, like a practical joke sprung by a half-witted Fate, the store room door opened with casual, exploring pleasantness, and the Journalist and Adele Reitzen's promised husband and big Peter himself stepped out into the hallway.

Before the surprised greeting in two men's faces the Woodland Girl retreated step by step, until at last with a quick turn she whirled back into the dingy, gas-lit library—her chalky face, her staring eyes proclaiming only too plainly the calamity which she had no time to stuff into words.

Close behind her followed the three smiling, unsuspicious intruders. Even then the incident might have passed without gross awkwardness if the Woodland Girl's uncle and aunt had not suddenly joined the company. From the angry, outraged flush on the two older faces it was perfectly evident that these two, at least, had been waylaid by kitchen gossip.

Brian Baird laughed. Like a manly lover goaded and hectored and cajoled too long into unworthy secrecy, his pulses fairly jumped to meet the frank, forced issue. But with a quick, desperate appeal Adele Reitzen silenced the triumphant speech on his lips. "Let me manage it!" she whispered, so vehemently that the man yielded to her, and stepped back against the fireplace, and spread his arms with studied, indolent ease along the mantel, like a rustic cross tortured out of a supple willow withe. One of his hands played teasingly with a stale spray of Christmas greens. Nothing but the straining, white-knuckled grip of his other hand modified the absolute, wilful insolence of his pose.

As for Adele, her face was ghastly.

With crude, uncontrolled venom the Woodland Girl's aunt plunged into the emergency. "Adele," she cried shrilly, "I think you owe your *fiancé* an explanation! You promised us faithfully last year that you would never, never see Mr. Baird again—and now to-night our chauffeur saw you steal out to the street corner to meet him—like a common shop-girl. And you dare to bring him back—to my house! What have you to say for yourself?"

For the fraction of a moment Adele Reitzen's superb beauty straightened up to its full majestic height, and all the love-pride that was in her white, white flesh flamed gloriously in her face. Then her sleek, prosperous, arrogant city lover stepped suddenly forward where the yellow light struck bleakly across his shrewd, small eyes and his thin, relentless mouth.

"I should be very glad, indeed, to hear what you have to say," he announced, and his voice was like a nicked knife blade.

Flush by flush by flush the red glory fled from Adele Reitzen's face. Her throat began to flutter. Her knees crumpled under her. Fear went over her like a gray fog.

With one despairing hand she reached back to the Woodland Girl. "Oh, tell them it was you," she whispered hotly. "Oh, tell them it was you." Her scared face brightened viciously. "It *was* you—you know! Tell them—oh, tell them anything—only save me!"

The Woodland Girl's eyes were big with horror. She started to speak, she started to protest, but before the jumbled words could leave her lips Adele Reitzen turned to the others and blurted out hysterically:

"Surely I can't be expected to keep even a love-secret under these—distressing circumstances. *It was Chloe who went out to the street corner to-night—like a common shop-girl—to meet Brian Baird. She wore my cloak on purpose to disguise her.*"

Like the blaring scream of a discordant trumpet, the treacherous, flatted truth crashed into the Woodland Girl's startled senses, and the man in the shape of a sagging willow cross started up and cried out, "My God!"

For a second the Woodland Girl stood staring into his dreadful, chaotic face, then she squared her shoulders and turned to meet the wrathful, contemptuous surprise in her uncle's and aunt's features.

"So it was you," sneered the uncle, "embroiling our decent household in a common, vulgar intrigue?"

"So it was you," flamed her aunt, "you who have been posing all these days as an Innocent?"

Frantic with perplexity, muddled with fear, torn by conflicting chivalries, the Woodland Girl stared back and forth from Adele Reitzen's agonized plea to the grim, inscrutable gleam in Brian Baird's eyes. As though every living, moving verb had been ripped out of that night's story, and all the inflexible nouns were printing themselves slam-bang one on top of another—Roses, Wine, Music, Silver, Diamonds, Fir-Balsam telescoped each other in her senses.

"Your father sent you down here," persisted her aunt brutally, "on the private plea to me that he was planning to be married again—but I can readily see that perhaps no one would exactly want you."

The Woodland Girl's heart began to pound.

"We—are—waiting," prodded her uncle's icy voice.

Suddenly the Girl's memory quickened. Once, long ago, her father had said to her: "Little Daughter, if you are ever in fear and danger by sea or land—or city, which is neither sea nor land—turn always to that man, and to that man only, whom you would trust in the deep woods. Put your imagination to work, not your reason. You have no reason!"

Desperately she turned to Peter. His face, robbed utterly of its affection, was all a-shock with outraged social proprieties, merging the merest bit unpleasantly into the racy appreciation of a unique adventure. Panic-stricken, she turned to the Journalist. Already across the Journalist's wine-flushed face the pleasant, friendly smile was souring into worldly skepticism and mocking disillusionment.

She shut her eyes. "O Big Woods, help me!" she prayed. "O Cross Storm, warn me! O Rough Trail, guide me!"

Behind her tightly scrunched lids her worried brain darkened like a jumbled midnight forest. Jaded, bedraggled, aching with storm and terror, she saw herself stumbling into the sudden dazzling splurge of a stranger's camp fire. Was it a man like Peter? Was it the Journalist? She began to shiver. Then her heart gave a queer, queer jump, and she opened her eyes stark wide and searched deep into Brian Baird's livid face. One of his hands still strained at the wooden mantel. The other still bruised the pungent balsam tip between its restive fingers. His young hair was too gray about his temples. His shoulders were too tired with life's pack burdens. His eyes had probably grown more bitter that night than any woman's lips could ever sweeten again. And yet—

Down from the far-away music room floated the quavering, passionate violin wail of the boy who had dared to temporize with Fate. Up from the close-nudging street crashed the confusing slap of hoofs and the mad whir of wheels racing not so much for the Joy of the Destination as for the Thrill of the Journey. She gave a little gasping sob, and Brian Baird stooped forward incredulously, as though from the yellow glare of his camp fire he had only just that instant sensed the faltering footfall of a wayfarer in acute distress, and could scarcely distinguish even yet through the darkness the detailed features of the apparition.

For a second, startled eyes defied startled eyes, and then suddenly, out of his own meager ration of faith or fortune or immediate goodness, the man straightened up, and *smiled*—the simple, honest, unquestioning camp-fire smile—the smile of food and blanket, the smile of welcome, the smile of shelter, the signal of the gladly-shared crust—and the Woodland Girl gave a low, wild cry of joy, and ran across the room to him, and wheeled back against him, close, tight, with her tousled hair grazing his haggard cheek and her brown hands clutching hard at the sweep of his arms along the mantel.

"Adele Reitzen is right," she cried out triumphantly. "This is my—man!"

THE PINK SASH

NO man could have asked the question more simply. The whole gaunt, gigantic Rocky Mountain landscape seemed indeed most peculiarly conducive to simple emotions.

Yet Donas Guthrie's original remark had been purely whimsical and distinctly apropos of nothing at all. The careless knocking of his pipe against the piazza's primitive railing had certainly not prepared the way for any particularly vital statement.

"Up—to—the—time—he's—thirty," drawled the pleasant, deep, distinctly masculine voice, "up—to—the—time—he's—thirty, no man has done the things that he's really wanted to do—but only the things that happened to come his way. He's forced into business to please his father, and cajoled into the Episcopal Church to gratify his mother, and bullied into red neckties to pacify his sister Isabel. But once having reached the grown-up, level-headed, utterly independent age of thirty, a man's a fool, I tell you, who doesn't sit down deliberately, and roll up his sleeves, and square his jaw, and list out, one by one, the things that *he* wants in the presumable measure of lifetime that's left him—and go ahead and get them!"

"Why, surely," said the young woman, without the slightest trace of surprise. Something in her matter-of-fact acquiescence made Donas Guthrie smile a trifle shrewdly.

"Oh! So you've got your own list all made out?" he quizzed. Around the rather tired-looking corners of Esther Davidson's mouth the tiniest possible flicker of amusement began to show.

"No, not all made out," she answered frankly. "You see, I wasn't thirty—until yesterday."

Stooping with cheerful unconcern to blow a little fluff of tobacco ash from his own khaki-colored knees to hers, Guthrie eyed her delightedly from under his heavy brows.

"Oh, this is working out very neatly and pleasantly," he mused, all agrin. "Ever since you joined our camping party at Laramie, jumping off the train as white-faced and out of breath as though you'd been running to catch up with us all the way from Boston—indeed, ever since you first wrote me at Morristown, asking full particulars about the whole expedition and begging us to go to the Sierra Nevadas instead and blotted 'Sierra' twice and crossed it out once—and then in final petulance spelled it with three 'r's,' I've been utterly consumed with curiosity to know just how old you are."

"Thirty years—and one morning," said the young woman—absent-mindedly.

"W-h-e-w!" gasped Guthrie. "But that's a ripe old age! Surely, you've no time to lose!"

Rummaging through his pockets with mock intensity he thrust into her hands, at last, a small pad of paper and a pencil.

"Now quick!" he insisted. "Make out your list before it's too late to profit by it!"

The woman was evidently perfectly willing to comply with every playful aspect of his mood, but it was equally evident that she did not intend to be hurried about it. Quite perversely she began to dally with the pencil.

"But, you see, I don't know exactly just what kind of a list you mean," she protested.

"Oh, shucks!" laughed the man. "Here, give me the paper! Now—head it like this: 'I, Esther Davidson, spinster, *æt.* thirty years and a few minutes over, do hereby promise and attest that no matter how unwilling to die I may be when my time comes, I shall, at least, not feel that life has defrauded me if I have succeeded in achieving and possessing the following brief list of experiences and substances.' There!" he finished triumphantly. "Now do you see how easy and business-like it all is? Just the plainest possible rating of the things you'd like to have before you're willing to die."

Cautiously Esther Davidson took the paper from his hand and scanned it with slow-smiling eyes.

"The—things—I'd—like to have—before I'm—willing—to—die," she mused indolently. Then suddenly into her placid face blazed an astonishing flame of passion that vanished again as quickly as it came. "My God!" she said. "The things I've *got* to have before I'm willing to die!"

Stretching the little paper taut across her knees, she began to scribble hasty, impulsive words and phrases, crossing and recrossing, making and erasing, now frowning fiercely down on the unoffending page, now staring off narrow-eyed and smilingly speculative into the blue-green spruce tops.

It was almost ten minutes before she spoke again. Then: "How do you spell amethyst?" she asked meditatively.

The man gave a groan of palpable disgust. "Oh, I say," he reproached her. "You're not playing fair! This was to be a really *bona fide* statement you know."

Without looking up the young woman lifted her hand and gesticulated across the left side of her mannish, khaki-colored flannel shirt.

"Cross my heart!" she affirmed solemnly. "This is a perfectly 'honest-injun' list!"

Then she tore up everything she had written and began all over again, astonishingly slowly, astonishingly neatly, on a fresh sheet of paper.

"Of course, at first," she explained painstakingly, "you think there are just about ten thousand things that you've simply got to have, but when you really stop to sort them out, and pick and choose a bit, and narrow them all down to actual essentials; narrow them all down to just the 'Passions of the Soul,' as it were, why, then, there really aren't so many after all! Only one, two, three, four, five, six, seven, eight," she counted on her fingers. "At first, for instance," she persisted frankly, "it seemed to me that I could never, never die happy until I had possessed a very large—oh, I mean an inordinately large amethyst brooch that simply wallowed in pearls, but honestly now as a real treasure-trove, I can see that I'd infinitely rather be able to remember that once upon a time I'd—stroked a lion's face; just one, long, slow, soft-furred, yellow stroke from the browny-pink tip of his nose to the extremest shaggy end of his mane—and he hadn't bitten me!"

"My Heavens!" gasped the man. "Are you crazy? What kind of a list have you been making out anyway?"

A little acridly she thrust both her list and her hands into the side pockets of her riding skirt.

"What kind of a list did you think I would make out?" she asked sharply. "Something all about machinery? And getting a contract for city paving stones? Or publicly protesting the new football rules? Goodness! Does it have to be a 'wise' list? Does it have to be a worthy list? Something that would really look commendable in a church magazine? This was all your idea, you know! You asked me, didn't you, to write out, just for fun, the things I'd got to have before I'd be willing to die?"

"Oh, come now," laughed the man. "Please don't get stuffy about it. You surprised me so about stroking the lion's face that I simply had to chaff you a little. Truly, I care a great deal about seeing that list. When you got off the train that day it rattled me a confounded lot to see that your camping togs were cut out of exactly the same piece of cloth that mine were. Professor Ellis and his wife and Doctor Andrews jollied me a good bit about it in fact, but—hang it all—it's beginning to dawn on me rather cozily, though I admit still embarrassingly, that maybe your mind and mine are cut out of the same piece of cloth, too. Please let me see what you've written!"

With a grimace that was half reluctance, half defiance, the young woman pulled the paper from her pocket, smoothed it out on her knees for an instant and handed it to him.

"Oh, very well, then," she said. "Help yourself to the only authentic list of my 'Heart's Desires.'" Then suddenly her whole face brightened with amusement and she shook a sun-browned finger threateningly at him. "Now remember," she warned him, "I don't have to justify this list, no matter how trivial it sounds, no matter how foolish even; it is excuse enough for it—it is dignity enough for it, that it happens to be so."

"Yes, surely," acknowledged the man.

Either consciously or unconsciously—then—he took off his battered slouch hat and placed it softly on the seat beside him. The act gave the very faintest possible suggestion of reverence to the joke. Then, rather slowly and hesitatingly, after the manner of a man who is not specially accustomed to reading aloud, he began:

"Is—a—pink—sash—exactly a—a—passion?"

"Things That I, Esther Davidson, Am Really Obliged to Have Before I'm Willing to Die: No. 1. A solid summer of horseback riding on a rusty brown pony among really scary mountains. No. 2. A year's work at Oxford in Social Economics. No. 3. One single, solitary sunset view of the Bay of Naples. No. 4. A very, very large oil-painting portrait of a cloud—a great white, warm, cotton-battinglooking, summer Sunday afternoon sort of a cloud—I mean; the kind that you used to see as a child when all 'chock full' of chicken and ice cream and serene thoughts about Heaven, you lay stretched out flat on the cool green grass and stared right up into the face of God, and never even guessed what made you blink so. No. 5. The ability to buy one life-saving surgical operation for some one who probably wouldn't otherwise have afforded it. No. 6. A perfectly good dinner. No. 7. A completely happy Christmas. No. 8. A pink sash. That's all."

With really terrifying gravity, the man put down the finished page and lifted his searching eyes to the woman's flushing, self-conscious face.

"Is—a—pink—sash—exactly a—a—passion?" he probed in much perplexity.

"Oh, yes!" nodded the young woman briskly. "Oh, yes, indeed! It's an obsession in my life. It's a groove in my brain. In the middle of the night I wake and find myself sitting bolt upright in bed saying it. The only time I ever took ether I prattled persistently concerning it. When a Spring sunshine is so marvelous that it makes me feel faint, when the Vox Humana stop in a church-organ snarls my heart-strings like an actual hand, when the great galloping, tearing fire-engine horses come clanging like mad around the street corner, it's the one definite idea that explodes in my consciousness. It began way back when I was a tiny six-year-old child at a Maine woods 'camp meeting.' Did you ever see a really primitive 'camp meeting'? All fir-balsam trees and little rustic benches and pink calicoes and Grand Army suits and high cheek-bones and low insteps and—lots of noise? Rather inspiring too, sometimes, or at least soul excitative. It might do a good deal to any high-strung six-year-old kiddie. Anyway, I saw the old village drunkard jump up and wave his arms and wail ingenuously: 'I want to be a Christian!' And a palsied crone beside me moaned and sobbed 'I want to be baptized!' And even my timid, gentle mother leaped impetuously to her feet and announced quite publicly to every one 'I want to be washed in the Blood of the Lamb!' And all about me I saw frenzied neighbors and strangers dashing about making these uncontrollable, confidential proclamations. And suddenly, to my meager, indefinite baby-brain, there rushed such an exultancy of positive personal conviction that my poor little face must have been literally transfigured with it, for my father lifted me high to his tight-coated shoulders and cried out ecstatically: 'A little child shall lead them! Hear! Hear!' And with an emphasis on the personal pronoun0 which I hate to remember even at this remote date, I screamed forth at the top of my lungs: 'I want—a pink sash!'"

"And didn't you get it?" said Donas Guthrie.

The young woman crooked one eyebrow rather comically. "N-o," she said, "I never got it!"

"But you could get it any time now," argued the man.

Helplessly she threw out the palms of her hands and the unexpected gesture displayed an amazing slimness and whiteness of wrist.

"Stupid!" she laughed. "What would I do with a pink sash now?" Ruthlessly her quick eyes traveled down the full length of her scant, rough skirt to the stubbed toes of her battered brown riding boots. "Dust on the highway and chalk in the classroom and 'grown-up-ness' everywhere!" she persisted dully. "That's the real tragedy of growing up—not that we outgrow our original desires, but that retaining those desires, we outgrow the ability to find satisfaction in them. People ought to think of that, you know, when they thwart a child's ten-cent passion for a tin trumpet. Fifty years later, when that child is a bank president, it may drive him almost crazy to have a toy-shop with a whole window-full of tin trumpets come and cuddle right next door to his bank—and nothing that the man can do with them!"

Like a little gray veil the tired look fell again over her face. The man saw it and shuddered.

"Psychology is my subject at Varndon College, you know," she continued listlessly, "and so I suppose I'm rather specially interested in freakish mental things. Anyway—pink sashes or Noah's arks or enough sugar in your cocoa—I have a theory that no child ever does outgrow its ungratified legitimate desires; though subsequent maturity may bring him to the point where his original desire has reached such astounding proportions that the original object can no longer possibly appease it."

Reminiscently, her narrowing eyes turned back their inner vision to the far-away grotesque incident of the camp meeting. "It isn't as though a child asked for a thing the very first time that he thought of it," she protested a trifle pathetically. "An idea has been sown and has grown and germinated in his mind a pretty long time before he gets up his courage to speak to anybody about it. Oh, I tell you, sir, the time to grant anybody a favor is the day the favor is asked, for that day is the one psychological moment of the world when supply and demand are keyed exactly to each other's limits, and can be mated beatifically to grow old, or die young, together. But after that day—!

"Why, even with grown people," she added hastily. "Did you ever know a marriage to turn out to be specially successful where the man had courted a reluctant woman for years and years before she finally yielded to him? It's perfectly astonishing how soon a wife like that is forced to mourn: 'Why did he court me so long and so furiously if he really cared as little as this? I'm just exactly the same person that I was in the beginning!'—Yes, that's precisely the trouble. In the long time that she has kept her man waiting, she has remained just exactly the same small object that she was in the beginning, but the man's hunger for her has materialized and spiritualized and idealized a thousandfold beyond her paltry capacity to satisfy it."

"That's a funny way to look at it," mused Donas Guthrie.

"Is it?" said the young woman, a trifle petulantly. "It doesn't seem funny to me!"

Then to Guthrie's infinite astonishment and embarrassment the tears welled up suddenly into her eyes and she turned her head abruptly away and began to beat a nervous tattoo with one hand on the flimsy piazza railing.

In the moment's awkward silence that ensued, the little inn's clattery kitchen wafted up its pleasant, odorous, noon-day suggestion of coffee and bacon.

"W-h-e-w!" gloated Guthrie desperately, "but that smells good!"

"It doesn't smell good to me," said the young woman tartly.

With a definite thud the tilting leg of Guthrie's chair came whacking down on the piazza floor.

"Why, you inconsistent little gourmand!" he exclaimed. "Then why did you give 'one perfectly good dinner' a place on your list of necessities?"

"I don't know," whispered the young woman, a trifle tremulously. Then abruptly she burst out laughing, and the face that she turned to Guthrie again was all deliciously mussed up like a child's, with tears and smiles and breeze-blown wisps of hair.

"That dinner item was just another silly thing," she explained half bashfully, half defiantly. "It's only that although I practically never eat much of anything on ordinary occasions, whenever I get into any kind of danger, whenever the train runs off the track, or the steamer threatens to sink, or my car gets stuck in the subway, I'm seized with the most terrific gnawing hunger—as though—as though—" Furiously the red flushed into her face again. "Well—eternity sounds so l-long," she stammered, "and I have a perfect horror, somehow—of going to Heaven—on an empty stomach."

In mutual appreciation of a suddenly relaxed tension, the man's laughter and the woman's rang out together throughout the dooryard and startled a grazing pony into a whimpering whinny of sympathy.

"I knew you'd think my list was funny," protested the young woman. "I knew perfectly well that every single individual item on it would astonish you."

Meditatively Donas Guthrie refilled his pipe and evidently illuminated both the tobacco and the situation with the same match.

"It isn't the things that are on your list that astonish me," he remarked puffingly. "It's the things that aren't on it that have given me the bit of a jolt."

"Such as what?" frowned the young woman, sliding jerkily out to the edge of her chair.

"Why, I'd always supposed that women were inherently domestic," growled Guthrie. "I'd always somehow supposed that Love and Home would figure pretty largely on any woman's 'List of Necessities.' But you! For Heaven's sake, haven't you ever even thought of man in any specific relation to your own life?"

"No, except in so far as he might retard my accomplishment of the things on my list," she answered frankly. Out of the gray film of pipe-smoke, her small face loomed utterly serene, utterly honest, utterly devoid of coquetry or self-consciousness.

"Any man would be apt to 'retard' your desire to stroke a lion's face," said Guthrie grimly. "But then," with a flicker of humor, "but then I see you've omitted that item from your revised list. Your only thought about man then," he continued slowly, "is his probable tendency to interfere with your getting the things out of life that you most want."

"Yes."

"Oh, this is quite a novel idea to me," said Guthrie, all a-smile again. "You mean then—if I judge your premises correctly—you mean then that if on the contrary you found a man who would really facilitate the accomplishment of your 'heart's desires,' you'd be willing to think a good deal about him?"

"Oh, yes!" said the young woman.

"You mean then," persisted Guthrie, "you mean then, just for the sake of the argument, that if I, for instance, could guarantee for you every single little item on this list, you'd be willing to marry even me?"

"Yes."

Altogether unexpectedly Guthrie burst out laughing.

Instantly a little alarmed look quickened in the young woman's sleepy eyes. "Does it seem cold-blooded to you?" she asked anxiously.

"No, not exactly 'cold' blooded, but certainly a little cooler blooded than any man would have dared to hope for," smiled Guthrie.

The frowning perplexity deepened in the young woman's face. "You surely don't misunderstand me?" she pleaded. "You don't think I'm mercenary or anything horrid like that? Suppose I do make a man's aptitude for gratifying my eight particular whims the supreme test of his marital attractiveness for me—it's not, you must understand, by the sign of his material ability in the matter that I should recognize the Man Who Was Made for Me—but by the sign of his spiritual willingness."

"O—h!" said Guthrie very leisurely. Then, with a trifle more vigor, he picked up the small list again and scanned it carefully.

"It—wouldn't—be—such—a hard—list to—fulfil!" he resumed presently. "'A summer in the mountains?' You're having that now. 'Oxford?' 'Glimpse of Naples?' 'Cloud Picture?' 'Surgical Operation?' 'Pink Sash?' 'Good Dinner?' 'Christmas?' Why there's really nothing here that I couldn't provide for you, myself, if you'd only give me time."

With mischievous unconcern he smiled at the young woman. With equally mischievous unconcern the young woman smiled back at him.

"What an extraordinary conversation we've had this morning," she said. As though quite exhausted by the uniqueness of it, she slid a little further down into her seat and turned her cheek against the firm support of the chair-back.

"What an extraordinary understanding it has brought us to!" exclaimed the man, scanning her closely.

"I don't see anything particularly—understandy about it," denied the young woman wearily.

It was then that Donas Guthrie asked his simple question, boring his khaki-colored elbows into his khaki-colored knees.

"Little Psychology Teacher," he said very gently, "Little Psychology Teacher, Dr. Andrews says that you've got typhoid fever. He's feared it now for some time, and you know it's against his orders—your being up to-day. So as long as I've proved myself here and now, by your own test, the Man-Whom-You-Were-Looking-For, I suggest that you and I be—married this afternoon—before that itinerant shiny-shouldered preacher out in the corral escapes us altogether—and then we'll send the rest of the party on about their business, and you and Dr. Andrews and Hanlon's Mary and I will camp right down here where we are—and scrap the old typhoid fever to its finish. Will you, Little Psychology Teacher?"

Lifting her white hands to her throbbing temples the young woman turned her astonished face jerkily toward him.

"What—did—you—say?" she gasped.

"I said: 'Will you marry me this afternoon?'" repeated Guthrie.

Bruskly she pushed that part of the phrase aside. "What did you really say?" she insisted. "What did Dr. Andrews say?"

"Dr. Andrews says that you've got typhoid fever," repeated Guthrie.

Inertly she blinked her big brown eyes for an instant. Then suddenly her hands went groping out to the arms of her chair. Her face was horror-stricken. "Why didn't he tell me, himself?"

"Because I asked him to let me tell you," said Guthrie quietly.

"When did he tell you?" she persisted.

"Just before I came up on the piazza," said Guthrie.

"How did he tell you?" she demanded.

"How did he tell me?" mused Guthrie wretchedly. After all, underneath his occasional whimsicality he was distinctly literal-minded. "How did he tell me? Why I saw them all powwowing together in the corral, and Andrews looked up sort of queer and said: 'Say, Guthrie, that little Psychology friend of yours has got typhoid fever. What in thunder are we going to do?'"

The strained lines around Esther Davidson's mouth relaxed for a second.

"Well, what in thunder am I going to do?" she joked heroically. But the effort at flippancy was evidently quite too much for her. In another instant her head pitched forward against the piazza railing and her voice, when she spoke again, was almost indistinguishable.

"And you knew all this an hour ago!" she accused him incoherently. "Knew my predicament—knew my inevitable weakness and fear and mortification—knew me a stranger among strangers. And yet you came up here to jolly me inconsequently—about a million foolish things!"

"It was because at the end of the hour I hoped to be something to you that would quite prevent your feeling a 'stranger among strangers,'" said Guthrie very quietly. "I have asked you to marry me this afternoon, you must remember."

The young woman's lip curled tremulously. "You astonish me!" she scoffed. "I had always understood that men did not marry very easily. Quick to love, slow to marry, is supposed to be your most striking characteristic—and here are0 you asking marriage of me, and you haven't even loved me yet!"

235

"You women do not seem to marry any too easily," smiled Guthrie gazing nervously from his open watch to the furthest corner of the corral, where the preacher's raw-boned pony, nose in air, was stubbornly refusing to take his bit.

"Indeed we do marry—perfectly easily—when we once love," retorted the woman contentiously! "It's the love part of it that we are reluctant about!"

"But I haven't asked you to love me," protested the man with much patience. "I merely asked you to marry me."

The woman's jaw dropped. "Out of sympathy for my emergency, out of mistaken chivalry, you're asking me to marry you, and not even pretending that you love me?" she asked in astonishment.

"I haven't had time to love you yet. I've only known you such a little while," said the man quite simply. Almost sternly he rose and began to pace up and down the narrow confines of the little piazza. "All I know is," he asserted, "that the very first moment you stepped off the train at Laramie, I knew you were the woman whom I was—going to love—sometime."

Very softly he slid back into the rustic seat he had just vacated, and taking the woman's small clenched hands in his began to smooth out her fingers like poor crumpled ribbons.

"Now, Little Psychology Teacher," he said, "I want you to listen very, very carefully to everything I say. Do you like me all right?"

"Y—e—s."

"Better than you like Andrews or Ellis or even the old Judge?"

"Oh, yes!"

"Ever since we all started out together on the Trail you've just sort of naturally fallen to my lot, haven't you? Whenever you needed your pony's girth tightened, or whenever you wanted a drink of water, or whenever the big canyons scared you, or whenever the camp fire smoked you, you've just sort of naturally turned to me, haven't you? And it would be fair enough, wouldn't it, to say that at least I've never made any situation worse for you? So that if anything ugly or awkward were going to happen—perhaps you really would rather have me around than any one else?"

"Yes—surely."

"Maybe even, when we've been watching Ellis and his Missis riding ahead, all hand in hand and smile in smile, you've wondered a bit, woman-like, how it would seem, for instance, to be riding along hand in hand and smile in smile with me?"

"P-o-s-s-i-b-l-y."

"Never had any special curiosity about how it would seem to go hand and hand with—Andrews?"

"Foolish!"

"Hooray!" cried Guthrie. "That's all that I really needed to know! Oh, don't feel bashful about it. It surely is an absolutely impersonal compliment on your part. It isn't even you that I'm under obligations to for the kindness, but Nature with a great big capital 'N.' Somehow I always have had an idea that you women instinctively do divide all mankind into three classes: first, Those Whom You Couldn't Possibly Love; second, Those Whom You Could Possibly Love, and third, the One Man of the World Whom You Actually Do Love. And unless this mysterious Nature with a capital 'N' has already qualified a man for the second class, God himself can't promote that man into the third class. So it seems to me that every fellow could save himself an awful lot of misunderstanding and wasted time if he'd do just what I've done—make a distinctly preliminary proposal to his lady; not 'Do you love me?' which might take her fifteen years to decide, but: 'Could you love me?' which any woman can tell the first time she sees you. And if she can't possibly love you, that settles everything neatly then and there, but if she can possibly, why, with Nature once on his side, a man's a craven who can't put up a mighty good scrap for his coveted prize. Doesn't this all make sense to you?"

Cannily the young woman lifted her eyes to his and fathomed him mutely for an instant. Then:

"Perfectly good 'sense' but no feeling," she answered dully.

"It's only 'sense' that I'm trying to make," acknowledged Guthrie. "Now look here, you Little Teacher Person, I'm going to talk to you just as bluntly as I would to another fellow. You are in a hole—the deuce of a hole! You have got typhoid fever, and it may run ten days and it may run ten weeks! And you are two thousand miles from home—among strangers! And no matter how glad I personally may be that you did push on and join us, sick or well, from every practical standpoint, of course, it surely was heedless and ill-considered of you to start off in poor health on a trip like this and run the risk of forcing perfectly unconcerned strangers to pay for it all. Personally, you seem so much to belong to me already that it gives me goose-flesh to think of your having to put yourself under obligations to any purely conscientious person. Mrs. Ellis, of course, will insist, out of common humanity, upon giving up her trip and staying behind with you, but Mrs. Ellis, Little Teacher, is on her honeymoon, and Ellis couldn't stay behind—it's his party—he'd have to go on with his people—and you'd never be able to compensate anybody for a broken honeymoon, and the Judge's youngster couldn't nurse a sick kitten, and the two women teachers from New

York have been planning seven years for this trip, they told me, and we couldn't decently take it away from them. But you and I, Little Psychology Lady, are not strangers to each other. Hanlon's Mary here at the ranch house, rough as she is, has at least the serving hands of a woman, and Andrews belongs naturally to the tribe which is consecrated to inconveniences, and both can be compensated accordingly. And I would have married you, anyway, before another year was out! Yes, I would!"

Apparently ignoring everything that he had said, she turned her face scowlingly toward the sound of hammering that issued suddenly through the piazza door.

"Oh, Glory!" she complained. "Are they making my coffin already?"

With a little laugh, Guthrie relinquished her limp fingers, and jumping up, took another swift turn along the piazza, stopping only to bang the door shut again. When he faced her once more the twinkle was all gone from his eyes.

"You're quite right, what you said about men," he resumed with desperate seriousness. "We are a heap sight quicker in our susceptibilities than in our mentalities! Therefore, no sane man ever does marry till his brain has caught up with his emotions! But sometimes, you know, something happens that hustles a man's brain along a bit, and this time my brain seems fairly to have jumped to its destination and clean-beaten even the emotions in the race. In cool, positive judgment I tell you I want to marry you this afternoon."

"You've confessed yourself, haven't you, that you've no severer ideal for marriage than that a man should be generous enough to give your personality, no matter how capricious, a chance to breathe? Haven't I qualified sufficiently as that amiable man? More than that, I'm free to love you; I'm certainly keen to serve you; I'm reasonably well able to provide for you, and you naturally have a right to know that I've led a decent life. It's ten good years now since I was thirty and first found nerve enough to break away from the stifling business life I hated and get out into the open, where there's surely less money but infinitely more air. And in ten years I've certainly found considerable chance to fulfil a few of the items in my own little 'List of Necessities.' I've seen Asia and I've seen Africa, and I've written the book I've always wanted to write on North American mountain structures.

"But there's a lot more that I crave to do. Maybe I've got a bit of a 'capricious personality' myself! Maybe I also have been hunting for the mate who would give my personality a chance to breathe. Certainly I've never wanted any home yet, except when the right time came, the arms of the right woman. And I guess you must be she, because you're the first woman I've ever seen whom I'd trust to help me just as hard to play my chosen games as I'd help her to play hers! I tell you—I want—very much—to marry you this afternoon."

"Why do you dally with me so? Isn't it your own argument that there's only just one day in the love-life of a man and woman when the question and the answer mate exactly, and the books are balanced perfectly even for the new start together? Demand and supply, debit and credit, hunger and food? You, wild for help, and I wild to help you! What difference does it make what you call it? Isn't this our day?"

"For a man who's usually as silent as you are, don't you think you're talking a good deal, considering how sick you said I was?" asked the young woman, not unmirthfully.

Guthrie's square jaws snapped together like a trap. "I was merely trying to detain you," he mumbled, "until Hanlon had finished knocking the windows out of your room. We're going to give you all the air you can breathe, anyway."

A little sullenly he started for the stairs. Then just at the door he turned unexpectedly and his face was all smiles again.

"Little Psychology Teacher," he said, "I have made you a formal, definite offer of marriage. And in just about ten minutes from now I am coming back for my answer."

When he did return a trifle sooner than he had intended, he met her in the narrow upper hallway, with hands outstretched, groping her way unsteadily toward her room. As though her equilibrium was altogether disturbed by his sudden advent, she reeled back against the wall.

"Mr. Donas Guthrie," she said, "I'm feeling pretty wobbly! Mr. Donas Guthrie," she said, "I guess I'm pretty sick."

"It's a cruel long way down the hall," suggested Guthrie. "Wouldn't you like me to carry you?"

"Yes—I—would," sighed the Little Psychology Teacher.

Even to Guthrie's apprehensive mind, her weight proved most astonishingly light. The small head drooping limply back from the slender neck seemed actually the only heavy thing about her, yet there were apparently only two ideas in that head.

"I'm afraid of Hanlon's Mary, and I don't like Dr. Andrews—very—specially—much," she kept repeating aimlessly. Then halfway to her room her body stiffened suddenly.

"Mr. Donas Guthrie," she asked. "Do you think I'm probably going to die?"

"N-a-w!" said Guthrie, his nose fairly crinkling with positiveness.

"But they don't give you much of anything to eat in typhoid, do they?" she persisted hectically.

"I suppose not," acknowledged Guthrie.

With disconcerting unexpectedness she began to cry—a soft, low, whimpery cry like a sleepy child's.

"If any day should come when—they think—that I am going to die," she moaned, "who will there be to see that I do get—something awfully good to eat?"

"I'll see to it," said Guthrie, "if you'll only put me in authority."

As though altogether indifferent to anything that he might say, her tension relaxed again and without further parleying she let Guthrie carry her across the threshold of her room and set her down cautiously in the creaky rocking chair. The eyes that lifted to his were as vague and turbid as brown velvet.

"There's one good thing about typhoid," she moaned. "It doesn't seem to hurt any, does it? In fact, I think I rather like it. It feels as warm and snug and don't-care as a hot lemonade at bed time. But what?" brightening suddenly, "but what was it you asked me to think about? I feel sort of confused—but it was something, I remember, that I was going to argue with you about."

"It was what I said about marrying me," prompted Guthrie.

"Oh, y-e-s," smiled the Little Psychology Teacher. Hazily for a moment she continued staring at him with her fingers prodded deep into her temples. Then suddenly, like a flower blasted with heat, she wilted down into her chair, groping blindly out with one hand toward the sleeve of his coat.

"Whatever you think best to do about it," she faltered, "I guess you'd better arrange pretty quickly—'cause I think—I'm—going—out."

This is how it happened that Mr. and Mrs. Donas Guthrie and Dr. Andrews stayed behind at the ranch house with Hanlon and Hanlon's Mary, and a piebald pony or two, and a herd of Angora goats, and a pink geranium plant, and the strange intermittent smell of a New England farmhouse which lurked in Hanlon's goods and chattels even after thirty years, and three or four stale, tattered magazines—and typhoid fever.

It was typhoid fever that proved essentially the0 most incalculable companion of them all. Hanlon's austerity certainly never varied from day to day, nor the inherent sullenness of Hanlon's Mary.

The meager sick-room, stripped to its bare pine skin of every tawdry colored print and fluttering cheese-cloth curtain, faced bluntly toward the west—a vital little laboratory in which the unknown quantity of a woman's endurance and the fallible skill of one man, the stubborn bravery of another, and the quite inestimable will of God were to be fused together in a desperate experiment to precipitate Life rather than Death.

So October waxed into November, and so waxed misgiving into apprehension, and apprehension into actual fear. In any more cheerful situation it would have been at least interesting to have watched the infuriated expletives issue from Andrew's perennially smiling lips.

"Oh, hang not having anything to work with!" he kept reiterating and reiterating. "Hang being shut off like this on a ranch where there aren't anything but sheep and goats and one old stingy cow that Hanlon's Mary guards with her life 'cause the lady's only a school teacher, but a baby is a baby.' Hang Hanlon's Mary! And hang not being altogether able to blame her! And hang not knowing, anyway, just what nanny-goat's milk would do for a typhoid patient! And hang—"

But before the expletives, and through the expletives, and after the expletives, Andrews was all hero, working, watching, experimenting, retrenching, humanly comprehensive, more than humanly vigilant.

So, with the brain of a doctor and the heart of a lover, the two men worked and watched and waited through the tortuous autumn days and nights, blind to the young dawn stealing out like a luminous mist from the night-smothered mountains; deaf to the flutter of sun-dried leaves in the radiant noon-time; dull to the fruit-scented fragrance of the early twilight, seeing nothing, hearing nothing, sensing nothing, except the flicker of a pulse or the rise of a temperature.

And then at last there came a harsh, wintry feeling day, when Andrews, stepping out into the hall, called Guthrie softly to him and said, still smiling:

"Guthrie, old man, I don't think we're going to win this game!"

"W-h-a-t?" gasped Guthrie.

With his mouth still curling amiably around his words, Andrews repeated the phrase. "I said, I don't think we're going to win this game. No, nothing new's happened. She's simply burning out. Can't you understand? I mean she's probably—going to die!"

Out of the jumble of words that hurtled through Guthrie's mind only four slipped his lips.

"But—she's—my—wife!" he protested.

"Other men's wives have died before this," said Andrews still smiling.

"Man," cried Guthrie, "if you smile again, I'll break your head!"

With his tears running down like rain into the broadening trough of his smile, Andrews kept right on smiling. "You needn't be so cross about it," he said. "You're not the only one who likes her! I wanted her myself! You're nothing but a tramp on the face of the earth—and I could have given her the snuggest home in Yonkers!"

With their arms across each other's shoulders they went back into the sick room.

Rousing from her lethargy, the young woman opened her eyes upon them with the first understanding that she had shown for some days. Inquisitively she stared from Guthrie's somber eyes to Andrews' distorted cheerfulness.

Taking instant advantage of her unwonted rationality, Andrews blurted out the question that was uppermost in his professional responsibility.

"Don't you think, maybe, your people ought to know about your being sick?" he said. "Now, if you could give us any addresses."

For a second it really seemed as though the question would merely safely ignite her common sense.

"Why yes, of course," she acquiesced. "My brother."

Then suddenly, without any warning, her most dangerous imagination caught fire.

"You mean," she faltered, "that—I—am—not—going to get well?"

Before either man was quick enough to contradict her, the shock had done its work. Piteously she turned her face to the pillow.

"Never—never—to—go—to—Oxford?" she whispered in mournful astonishment. "Never—even—to—see my—Bay of Naples?—Never to—have a—a—perfectly happy Christmas?" A little petulantly then her brain began to clog. "I think I—might at least have had—the pink sash!" she complained. Then, equally suddenly her strength rallied for an instant and the eyes that she lifted to Guthrie's were filled with a desperate effort at raillery. "Bring on your—anchovies and caviar," she reminded him, "and the stuffed green peppers—and remember I don't like my fillet too well done—and—"

Five minutes later in the hallway Andrews caught Guthrie just as he was chasing downstairs after Hanlon.

"What are you going to do?" he asked curiously.

"I am going to send Hanlon out to the telegraph station," said Guthrie. "I'm going to wire to Denver for a pink sash!"

"What she was raving about?" quizzed Andrews. "Are you raving too?"

"It's the only blamed thing in the whole world that she's asked for that I can get her," said Guthrie.

"It'll take five days," growled Andrews.

"I know it!"

"It won't do her any good."

"I can't help that!"

"She'll—be gone before it gets here."

"You can't help that!"

But she wasn't "gone," at all before it came. All her vitalities charred, to be sure, like a fire-swept woodland, but still tenacious of life, still fighting for reorganization, a little less feverish, a little stronger-pulsed, she opened her eyes in a puzzled, sad sort of little smile when Guthrie shook the great, broad, shimmering gauze-like ribbon ticklingly down across her wasted hands, and then apparently drowsed off to sleep again. But when both men came back to the room a few moments later, almost half the pink sash was cuddled under her cheek. And Hanlon's Mary came and peered through the doorway, with the whining baby still in her arms, and reaching out and fretting a piece of pink fringe between her hardy fingers, sniffed mightily.

"And you sent my man all the way to the wire," she asked, "and grubbed him three whole days waitin' round, just for that?"

"Yes, sure," said Guthrie.

"G-a-w-d!" said Hanlon's Mary.

And, the next week the patient was even better, and the next week, better still. Then, one morning after days and days of seemingly interminable silence and stupor, she opened her eyes perfectly wide and asked Guthrie abruptly:

"Whom did I marry? You or Dr. Andrews?"

And Guthrie in a sudden perversity of shock and embarrassment lied grimly:

"Dr. Andrews!"

"I didn't either!—it was you!" came the immediate, not too strong, but distinctly temperish response.

Something in the new vitality of the tone made Guthrie stop whatever he was doing and eye her suspiciously.

"How long have you been conscious like this?" he queried in surprise.

The faintest perceptible flicker of mischief crossed her haggard face.

"Three—days," she acknowledged.

"Then why—?" began Guthrie.

"Because I—didn't know—just what to call you," she faltered.

After that no power on earth apparently could induce any further speech from her for another three days. Solemn and big-eyed and totally unfathomable, she lay watching Guthrie's every gesture, every movement. From the door to the chair, from the chair to the window, from the window back to the chair, she lay estimating him altogether disconcertingly. Across the hand that steadied her drinking glass, she studied the poise of his lean, firm wrist. Out from the shadow-mystery of her heavy lashes, she questioned the ultimate value of each frown or smile.

And then, suddenly—just as abruptly as the first time she had spoken:

"What day is it?" she asked.

"It's Christmas," said Guthrie softly.

"O-h!—O-h!—O-h!" she exclaimed, very slowly. Then with increasing interest and wonder, "Is there snow on the ground?" she whispered.

"No," said Guthrie.

"Is it full moon to-night?" she questioned.

"No," said Guthrie.

"Is there any small, freckle-faced, alto-voiced choir boy in the house, trotting around humming funny little tail-ends of anthems and carols, while he's buckling up his skates?" she stammered.

"No," said Guthrie.

"Are there any old, white-haired loving people cuddled in the chimney corner?" she persisted.

"No," said Guthrie.

"Isn't there—any Christmas tree?"

"No."

"Aren't there even any presents?"

"No."

"Oh!" she smiled. "Isn't it funny!"

"What's funny?" asked Guthrie perplexedly.

The eyes that lifted to his were brimming full of a strange, wistful sort of astonishment. "Why, it's funny," she faltered, "it's funny—that without—any of these things—that I thought were so necessary to it—I've found my 'perfectly happy Christmas.'"

Then, almost bashfully, her wisp-like fingers went straying out toward the soft silken folds of the precious pink sash which she kept always close to her pillow.

"If—you—don't—mind," she said, "I think I'll cut my sash in two and give half of it to Hanlon's Mary to make a dress for her baby."

The medicine spoon dropped rather clatteringly out of Guthrie's hand.

"But I sent all the way to Denver for it," he protested.

"Oh, yes, I know all about that," she acknowledged. "But—what—can—a great big girl—like me—do with a—pink sash?"

"But you said you wanted it!" cried Guthrie. "Why, it took a man and a pony and a telegraph station five entire days to get it, and they had to flag the express train specially for it—and—and—"

A little wearily she closed her eyes and then opened them again blinkingly.

"I'm pretty tired, now," she said, "so I don't want to talk about it—but don't you—understand? I've revised my whole list of necessities. Out of the wide—wide—world—I find that I don't really want anything—except—just—you!"

WOMAN'S ONLY BUSINESS

THE men at the club were horridly busy that night discussing the silly English law about marrying your dead wife's sister. The talk was quite rabid enough even before an English High-churchman infused his pious venom into the subject-matter. When the argument was at its highest and the drinks were at their lowest, Bertus Sagner, the biology man at the university, jumped up from his seat with blazing eyes and said

"Rats!"—not anything long and Latin, not anything obscure and evasive, not even "rodents," but just plain "Rats!" The look on his face was inordinately disgusted, or indeed more than disgusted, unless disgust is perhaps an emotion that may at times be served red-hot. As he broke away from the gabbling crowd and began to hunt noisily round the room for his papers, I gathered up my own chemistry notebook and started after him. I was a new man in town and a comparative stranger. But Sagner and I had been chums once long ago in Berlin.

At the outside door he turned now and eyed me a bit shamefacedly. "Barney, old man," he said, "are you going my way? Well, come along." The broad-shouldered breadth of the two of us blocked out the light from the shining chandelier and sent our clumsy feet fairly stumbling down the harsh granite steps. The jarring lurch exploded Sagner's irritation into a short, sharp, damny growl, and I saw at once that his nerves were raw like a woman's.

As we turned into the deep-shadowed, spooky-black college roadway, the dormitories' yellow lights and laughter flared forth grotesquely like the Fruit of the Tree of Knowledge cut up for a Jack-o'-Lantern. At the edge of the Lombardy poplars I heard Sagner swallowing a little bit overhard.

"I suspect that I made rather a fool of myself back there," he confided abruptly, "but if there's anything under the day or night sky that makes me mad, it's the idiotic babble, babble, babble, these past few weeks about the 'dead wife's sister' law."

"What's your grouch?" I asked. "You're not even a married man, let alone a widower."

He stopped suddenly with a spurting match and a big cigar and lighted up unconsciously all the extraordinary frowning furrows of his face. The match went out and he struck another, and that match went out and he struck another—and another, and all the time it seemed to me as though just the flame in his face was hot enough to kindle any ordinary cigar. After each fruitless, breeze-snuffed effort he snapped his words out like so many tiny, tempery torpedoes. "Of—all—the—rot!" he ejaculated. "Of—all—the nonsense!" he puffed and mumbled. "A—whole—great, grown-up empire fussing and brawling about a 'dead wife's sister.' A dead wife! What does a dead wife care who marries her sister? Great heavens! If they really want to make a good moral law that will help somebody, why—don't—they—make—a—law—that will forbid a man's flirting with his living wife's sister?"

When I laughed I thought he would strike me, but after a husky second he laughed, too, through a great blue puff of smoke and a blaze like the headlight of an engine. In another instant he had vaulted the low fence and was starting off across lots for his own rooms, but before I could catch up with him he whirled abruptly in his tracks and came back to me.

"Will you come over to the Lennarts' with me for a moment?" he asked. "I was there at dinner with them to-night and I left my spectacles."

Very willingly I acquiesced, and we plunged off single file into the particular darkness that led to Professor Lennart's rose-garden. Somewhere remotely in my mind hummed and halted a vague, evasive bit of man-gossip about Lennart's amazingly pretty sister-in-law. Yet Sagner did not look exactly to me like a man who was going courting. Even in that murky darkness I could visualize perfectly from Sagner's pose and gait the same strange, bleak, facial furnishings that had attracted me so astoundingly in Berlin—the lean, flat cheeks cleaned close as the floor of a laboratory; the ugly, short-cropped hair; the mouth, just for work; the nose, just for work; the ears, just for work—not a single, decorative, pleasant thing from crown to chin except those great, dark, gorgeous, miraculously virgin eyes, with the huge, shaggy eyebrows lowering down prudishly over them like two common doormats on which every incoming vision must first stop and wipe its feet. Once in a café in Berlin I saw a woman try to get into Sagner's eyes—without stopping. Right in the middle of our dinner I jumped as though I had been shot. "Why, what was *that*?" I cried. "What was *that*?"

"What was what?" drawled Sagner. Try as I might the tiniest flicker of a grin tickled my lips. "Oh, nothing," I mumbled apologetically. "I just thought I heard a door slam-bang in a woman's face."

"What door?" said Sagner stupidly. "What woman?"

Old Sagner was deliciously stupid over many things, but he dissected the darkness toward Professor Lennart's house as though it had been his favorite kind of cadaver. Here, was the hardening turf, compact as flesh. There, was the tough, tight tendon of the ripping ground pine. Farther along under an exploring match a great vapid peony loomed like a dead heart. Somewhere out in an orchard the May-blooms smelled altogether too white. Almost at the edge of the Lennarts' piazza he turned and stepped back to my pace and began talking messily about some stale biological specimen that had just arrived from the Azores.

College people, it seemed, did not ring bells for one another, and the most casual flop of Sagner's knuckles against the door brought Mrs. Lennart almost immediately to welcome us. "Almost immediately," I say, because the slight, faltering delay in her footfall made me wonder even then whether it was limb or life that had gone just a little bit lame. But the instant the hall light struck her face my hand clutched down involuntarily on Sagner's shoulder. It was the same, same face whose brighter, keener, shinier pastelled likeness had been the only joyous object in Sagner's homesick German room. With almost embarrassing slowness now we followed her lagging steps back to the library.

It was the first American home that I had seen for some years, and the warmth of it, and the color, and the glow, and the luxurious, deep-seated comfort, mothered me like the notes of an old, old song. Between the hill-green walls the long room stretched like a peaceful valley to the very edge of the huge, gray field-stone fireplace that blocked the final vista like a furious breastwork raised against all the invading tribes of history. Red books and gold frames and a chocolate-colored bronze or two caught up the flickering glint from the apple-wood fire, and out of some shadowy corner flanked by a grand piano a young girl's contralto voice, sensuous as liquid plush, was lipping its magic way up and down the whole wonderful, molten scale.

The corner was rather small, but out of it loomed instantly the tall, supple figure of Professor Lennart with his thousand-year-old brown eyes and his young gray hair. We were all big fellows, but Lennart towered easily three inches over anybody else's head. Professionally, too, he had outstripped the rest of us. People came gadding from all over the country to consult his historical criticisms and interpretations. And I hardly know how to express the man's vivid, luminous, incandescent personality. Surely no mother in a thousand would have chosen to have her son look like me, and I hope that no mother in a million would really have yearned to have a boy look like Sagner, but any mother, I think, would gladly have compromised on Lennart. I suppose he was handsome. Rising now, as he did, from the murkiest sort of a shadow, the mental and physical radiance of him made me want to laugh right out loud just for sheer pleasure.

Following closely behind his towering bulk, the girl with the contralto voice stepped out into the lamplight, and I made my most solemn and profound German bow over her proffered hand before the flaming mischief in her finger tips sent my eyes staring up into her astonishing face.

I have never thought that American women are extraordinarily beautiful, but rather that they wear their beauty like a thinnish sort of veil across the adorable, insistent expressiveness of their features. But this girl's face was so thick with beauty that you could not tell in one glance, or even two glances, or perhaps three, whether she had any expression at all. Kindness or meanness, brightness or dullness, pluck or timidity, were absolutely undecipherable in that physically perfect countenance. She was very small, and very dark, and very active, with hair like the color of eight o'clock—daylight and darkness and lamplight all snarled up together—and lips all crude scarlet, and eyes as absurdly big and round as a child's good-by kiss. Yet never for one instant could you have called her anything so impassive as "attractive." "Attracting" is the only hasty, ready-made word that could possibly fit her. Personally I do not like the type. The prettiest picture postal that ever was printed could not lure me across the borders of any unknown country. When I travel even into Friendship Land I want a good, clear face-map to guide my explorations.

There was a boy, too, in the room—the Lennarts' son—a brown-faced lad of thirteen whose algebraic séance with his beloved mother we had most brutally interrupted.

Professor Lennart's fad, as I have said, was history. Mrs. Lennart's fad was presumably housekeeping. The sister-in-law's fad was unmistakably men. Like an electric signboard her fascinating, spectacular sex-vanity flamed and flared from her coyly drooped eyes to her showy little feet. Every individual gesture signaled distinctly, "I am an extraordinarily beautiful little woman." Now it was her caressing hand on Lennart's shoulder; now it was her maddening, dazzling smile hurled like a bombshell into Sagner's perfectly prosy remark about the weather, now it was her teasing lips against the boy's tousled hair; now it was her tip-toeing, swaying, sweet-breathed exploration of a cobweb that the linden trees had left across my shoulder.

Lennart was evidently utterly subjugated. Like a bright moth and a very dull flame the girl chased him unceasingly from one chair, or one word, or one laugh to another. A dozen times their hands touched, or their smiles met, or their thoughts mated in distinctly personal if not secret understanding. Once when Mrs. Lennart stopped suddenly in the midst of my best story and asked me to repeat what I had been saying, I glanced up covertly and saw the girl kissing the tip of her finger a little bit over-mockingly to her brother-in-law. Never in any country but America could such a whole scene have been enacted in absolute moral innocence. It made me half ashamed and half very proud of my country. In continental Europe even the most trivial, innocent audacity assumes at once such utterly preposterous proportions of evil. But here before my very eyes was the most dangerous man-and-woman game in the world being played as frankly and ingenuously and transiently as though it had been croquet.

Through it all, Sagner, frowning like ten devils, sat at the desk with his chin in his hands, staring—staring0 at the girl. I suppose that she thought he was fascinated. He was. He was fairly yearning to vivisect her. I had seen that expression before in his face—reverence, repulsion, attraction, distaste, indomitable purpose, blood-curdling curiosity—SCIENCE.

When I dragged him out of the room and down the steps half an hour later my sides were cramped with laughter. "If we'd stayed ten minutes longer," I chuckled, "she would have called you 'Bertie' and me 'Boy.'"

But Sagner would not laugh.

"She's a pretty girl all right," I ventured again.

"Pretty as h—," whispered Sagner.

As we rounded the corner of the house the long French window blazed forth on us. Clear and bright in the lamplight stood Lennart with his right arm cuddling the girl to his side. "Little sister," he was saying, "let's go back to the piano and have some more music." Smiling her kindly good night we saw Mrs. Lennart gather up her books and start off limpingly across the hall, with the devoted boy following close behind her.

"Then she's really lame?" I asked Sagner as we swung into the noisy gravel path.

"Oh, yes," he said; "she got hurt in a runaway accident four years ago. Lennart doesn't know how to drive a *goat!*"

"Seems sort of too bad," I mused dully.

Then Sagner laughed most astonishingly. "Yes, sort of too bad," he mocked me.

It was almost ten o'clock when we circled back to the college library. Only a few grinds were there buzzing like June-bugs round the low-swinging green lamps. Even the librarian was missing. But Madge Hubert, the librarian's daughter, was keeping office hours in his stead behind a sumptuous old mahogany desk. At the very first college party that I had attended, Madge Hubert had been pointed out to me with a certain distinction as being the girl that Bertus Sagner was *almost* in love with. Then, as now, I was startled by the surprising youthfulness of her. Surely she was not more than three years ahead of the young girl whom we had left at Professor Lennart's house. With unmistakable friendly gladness she welcomed Sagner to the seat nearest her, and accorded me quite as much chair and quite as much smile as any new man in a university town really deserved. In another moment she had closed her book, pushed a full box of matches across the table to us, and switched off the electric light that fairly threatened to scorch her straight blond hair.

One by one the grinds looked up and nodded and smiled, and puckered their vision toward the clock, and "folded their tents like the Arabs and silently stole away," leaving us two men there all alone with the great silent room, and the long, rangy, echoing metal book-stacks, and the duddy-looking portraits, and the dopy-acting busts, and the sleek gray library cat—and the girl. Maybe Sagner came every Wednesday night to help close the library.

Certainly I liked the frank, almost boyish manner in which the two friends included me in their friendship by seeming to ignore me altogether.

"What's the matter, Bertus?" the girl began quite abruptly. "You look worried. What's the matter?"

"Nothing is ever the matter," said Sagner.

The girl laughed, and began to build a high, tottering paper tower out of a learned-looking pack of catalogue cards. Just at the moment of completion she gave a sharp little inadvertent sigh and the tower fluttered down.

"What's the matter with *you?*" quizzed Sagner.

"Nothing is ever the matter with me, either," she mocked smilingly.

Trying to butt into the silence that was awkward for me, if not for them, I rummaged my brain for speech, and blurted out triumphantly, "We've just come from Professor Lennart's."

"Just come from Professor Lennart's?" she repeated slowly, lifting her eyebrows as though the thought was a little bit heavy.

"Yes," said Sagner bluntly. "I've been there twice this evening."

With a rather playful twist of her lips the girl turned to me. "What did you think of 'Little Sister'?" she asked.

But before I could answer, Sagner had pushed me utterly aside once more and was shaking his smoke-stained finger threateningly in Madge Hubert's face. "Why—didn't—you—come—to the—Lennarts'—to—dinner—to-night—as—you—were—invited?" he scolded.

The girl put her chin in her hand and cuddled her fingers over her mouth and her nose and part of her blue eyes.

"I don't go to the Lennarts' any more—if I can help it," she mumbled.

"Why not?" shouted Sagner.

She considered the question very carefully, then "Go ask the other girls," she answered a trifle hotly. "Go ask any one of them. We all stay away for exactly the same reason."

"WHAT IS THE REASON?" thundered Sagner in his most terrible laboratory manner.

When Sagner speaks like that to me, I always grab hold of my head with both hands and answer just as fast as I possibly can, for I remember only too distinctly all the shining assortment of different sized knives and scalpels in his workshop and I have always found that a small, narrow, quick question makes the smallest, narrowest, quickest, soon-overest incision into my secret.

But Madge Hubert only laughed at the laboratory manner.

"Say 'Please,'" she whispered.

"Please!" growled Sagner, with his very own blood flushing all over his face and hands.

"Now—what is it you want to know?" she asked, frittering her fingers all the time over that inky-looking pack of catalogue cards.

Somehow, strange as it may seem, I did not feel an atom in the way, but rather that the presence of a third person, and that person myself, gave them both a certain daring bravado of speech that they would scarcely have risked alone with each other.

"What do I want to know?" queried Sagner. "I want to know—in fact—I'm utterly mad to know—just what your kind of woman thinks of 'Little Sister's' kind of woman."

With a startled gesture Madge Hubert looked back over her shoulder toward a creak in the literature book-stack, and Sagner jumped up with a great air of mock conspiracy, and went tip-toeing all around among the metal corridors in search of possible eavesdroppers, and then came flouncing back and stuffed tickly tissue paper into the gray cat's ears.

Then "Why don't you girls go to the Lennarts' any more?" he resumed with quickly recurrent gravity.

For a moment Madge Hubert dallied to shuffle one half of her pack of cards into the other half. Then she looked up and smiled the blond way a white-birch tree smiles in the sunshine.

"Why—we don't go any more because we don't have a good time," she confided. "After you've come home from a party once or twice and cried yourself to sleep, it begins to dawn on you very gradually that you didn't have a very good time. We don't like 'Little Sister.' She makes us feel ashamed."

"Oh!" said Sagner, rather brutally. "You are all jealous!"

But if he had expected for a second to disconcert Madge Hubert he was most ingloriously mistaken.

"Yes," she answered perfectly simply. "We are all jealous."

"Of her beauty?" scowled Sagner.

"Oh, no," said Madge Hubert. "Of her innocence."

Acid couldn't have eaten the fiber out of Madge Hubert's emotional honesty. "Why, yes," she hurried on vehemently, "among all the professors' daughters here in town there isn't one of us who is innocent enough to do happily even once the things that 'Little Sister' does every day of her life. You are quite right. We are all furiously jealous."

With sudden professional earnestness she ran her fingers through the catalogue cards and picked out one and slapped it down in front of Sagner. "There!" she said. "That's the book that explains all about it. It says that jealousy is an emotion that is aroused only by business competition, which accounts, of course, for the fact that, socially speaking, you very rarely find any personal enmity between men. There are so many, many different kinds of businesses for men, that interests very seldom conflict—so that the broker resents *only* the broker, and the minister resents *only* the minister, and the merchant resents *only* the merchant. Why, Bertus Sagner," she broke off abruptly, "you fairly idolize your chemistry friend here, and Lennart for history, and Dudley for mathematics, and all the others, and you glory in their achievements, and pray for their successes. But if there were another biology man here in town, you'd tear him and his methods tooth and nail, day and night. Yes, you would!—though you'd cover your hate a foot deep with superficial courtesies and 'professional etiquette.'"

She began to laugh. "Oh, the book is very wise," she continued more lightly. "It goes on to say that woman's only business in the whole wide world is LOVE—that Love is really the one and only, the Universal Profession for Women—so that every mortal feminine creature, from the brownest gypsy to the whitest queen, is in brutal, acute competition with her neighbor. It's funny, isn't it!" she finished brightly.

"Very funny," growled Sagner.

"So you see," she persisted, "that we girls are jealous of 'Little Sister' in just about the same way in which an old-fashioned, rather conservative department store would be jealous of the first ten-cent store that came to town." A sudden rather fine white pride paled suddenly in her cheeks. "It isn't, you understand," she said, "it isn't because the ten-cent store's rhinestone comb, or tinsel ribbon, or slightly handled collar really competes with the other store's plainer but possibly honester values, but—because in the long run the public's frittered taste and frittered small change is absolutely bound to affect the general receipts of the more conservative store."

"And it isn't," she added hastily, "it isn't, you know, because we're not used to men. There isn't one of us—from the time we were sixteen years old—who hasn't been quite accustomed to entertain anywhere from three to a dozen men every evening of her life. But we can't entertain them the way 'Little Sister' does." A hot, red wave of mortification flooded her face. "We tried it once," she confessed, "and it didn't work. Just before the last winter party seven of us girls got together and deliberately made up our minds to beat 'Little Sister' at her own game. Wasn't it disgusting of us to start out actually and deliberately with the intention of being just a little wee bit free and easy with men?"

"How did it work?" persisted Sagner, half agrin.

The color flushed redder and redder into Madge Hubert's cheeks.

"I went to the party with the new psychology substitute," she continued bravely, "and as I stepped into the carriage I called him 'Fred'—and he looked as though he thought I was demented. But fifteen minutes afterward I heard 'Little Sister' call him 'Psyche'—and he laughed." She began to laugh herself.

"But how did the party come out?" probed Sagner, going deeper and deeper.

The girl sobered instantly. "There were seven of us," she said, "and we all were to meet at the house of one of the girls at twelve o'clock and compare experiences. Three of us came home at ten o'clock—crying. And four of us didn't turn up till half-past one—laughing. But the ones who came home crying were the only ones who really had any fun out of it. The game was altogether too easy—that was the trouble with it. But the four who came home laughing had been bored to death with their *un*-successes."

"Which lot were you in?" cried Sagner.

She shook her head. "I won't tell you," she whispered.

With almost startling pluck she jumped up suddenly and switched the electric light full blast into her tense young face and across her resolute shoulders.

"Look at me!" she cried. "Look at me! As long as men are men—what have I that can possibly, possibly compete with a girl like 'Little Sister'? Can I climb up into a man's face every time I want to speak to him? Can I pat a man's shoulder every time he passes me in a room? Can I hold out my quivering white hand and act perfectly helpless in a man's presence every time that I want to step into a carriage, or out of a chair? Can I cry and grieve and mope into a man's arms at a dance just because I happen to cut my finger on the sharp edge of my dance-order? Bah! If a new man came to town and made not one single man-friend but called all of us girls by our first names the second time he saw us, and rolled his eyes at us, and fluttered his hands, you people would0 call him the biggest fool in Christendom—but you flock by the dozens and the hundreds and the millions every evening to see 'Little Sister.' And great, grown-up, middle-aged boys like *you*, Bertus Sagner, flock *twice* in the same evening!"

With astounding irrelevance Sagner burst out laughing. "Why, Madge," he cried, "you're perfectly superb when you're mad. Keep it up. Keep it up. I didn't know you had it in you! Why, you dear, gorgeous girl—WHY AREN'T YOU MARRIED?"

Like a scarlet lightning-bolt spiked with two-edged knives the red wrath of the girl descended then and there on Sagner's ugly head. With her heaving young shoulders braced like a frenzied creature at bay, against a great, silly, towering tier of "Latest Novels," she hurled her flaming, irrevocable answer crash-bang into Sagner's astonished, impertinent face.

"You want to know why I'm not married?" she cried. "You want to know why I'm not married? Well, I'll tell you—why—I'm—not married, Bertus Sagner, and I'll use yourself for an illustration—for when I do come to marry, it is written in the stars that I must of necessity marry your kind, a mature, cool, calculating, emotionally-tamed man, a man of brain as well as brawn, a man of fame if not of fortune, a man bred intellectually, morally, socially, into the same wonderfully keen, thinky corner of the world where I was born—nothing but a woman.

"For four years, Bertus Sagner, ever since I was nineteen years old, people have come stumbling over each other at college receptions to stare at me because I am 'the girl that Bertus Sagner, the big biologist, is *almost* in love with.' And you *are* 'almost' in love with me, Bertus Sagner. You can't deny it! And what is more, you will stay 'almost' in love with me till our pulses run down like clocks, and our eyes burn out like lamps, and the Real Night comes. If I remain here in this town, even when I am middle-aged—people will come and stare at me—because of you. And when I am old, and you are gone—altogether, people will still be talking about it. 'Almost in love' with me. Yes, Bertus Sagner, but if next time you came to see me, I should even so much as dally for a second on the arm of your chair, and slip my hand just a little bit tremulously into yours, and brush my lips like the ghost of a butterfly's wing across your love-starved face, you would probably find out then and there in one great, blinding, tingling, crunching flash that you LOVE ME NOW! But I don't want *you*, Bertus Sagner, nor any other man, at that price. The man who was made for me will love me first and get his petting afterward. There! Do you understand now?"

As though Sagner's gasp for breath was no more than the flutter of a book-leaf, she plunged on, "And as for Mrs. Lennart—"

Sagner jumped to his feet. "We weren't talking about Mrs. Lennart," he exclaimed hotly.

It has always seemed to me that very few things in the world are as quick as a woman's anger. But nothing in the world, I am perfectly positive, is as quick as a woman's amusement. As though an anarchist's bomb had exploded into confetti, Madge Hubert's sudden laughter sparkled through the room.

"Now, Bertus Sagner," she teased, "you just sit down again and listen to what I have to say."

Sagner sat down.

And as casually as though she were going to pour afternoon tea the girl slipped back into her own chair, and gave me a genuinely mirthful side-glance before she resumed her attack on Sagner.

"You were, too, talking about Mrs. Lennart," she insisted. "When you asked me to tell you exactly what a girl of my kind thinks of a girl like 'Little Sister,' do you suppose for a second I didn't understand that the thing you really wanted to find out was whether Mrs. Lennart was getting hurt or not in this 'Little Sister' business? Oh, no, Mrs. Lennart hasn't been hurt for a long, long time—several months perhaps. I think she looks a little bit bored now and then, but not hurt."

"Lennart's a splendid fellow," protested Sagner.

"He's a splendid fool," said Madge Hubert. "And after a woman once discovers that her husband is a fool I don't suppose that any extra illustrations on his part make any particular difference to her."

"Why, you don't—really think," stammered Sagner, "that there's any actual harm in Lennart's perfectly frank infatuation with 'Little Sister'?"

"Oh, no," said Madge Hubert, "of course there's no real harm in it at all. It's only that Mrs. Lennart has got to realize once for all that the special public that she has catered to so long and faithfully with honest values and small profit, has really got a ten-cent taste! Most men have. And it isn't, you know, because Professor Lennart really wants or needs all these ten-cent toys and favors, but because he probably never before in all his studious, straight, idealistic life saw glittering nonsense so inordinately cheap and easy to get. Talk about women being 'bargain-hunters'!

"But, of course, it's all pretty apt to ruin Mrs. Lennart's business. Anybody with half a heart could see that her stock is beginning to run down. She hasn't put in a new idea for months. She's wearing last year's clothes. She's thinking last year's thoughts. Even that blessed smile of hers is beginning to get just a little bit stale. You can't get what you want from her any more. Dust and indifference have already begun to set in. How will it end? Oh, I'll tell you how it will end. Pretty soon now college will be over and the men will scatter in five hundred different directions, and 'Little Sister' will be smitten suddenly with conscientious scruples about the 'old folks at home,' and will pack up her ruffles and her fraternity pins and go back to the provincial little town that has made her what she is. And Professor Lennart will mope around the house like a lost soul—for as much as five days—moaning, 'Oh, I wish "Little Sister" was here to-night to sing to me,' and 'I wish "Little Sister" was going to be here to-morrow to go canoeing with me,' and 'I wish "Little Sister" could see this moonlight,' and 'I wish "Little Sister" could taste this wild-strawberry pie.' And then somewhere about the sixth day, when he and Mrs. Lennart are at breakfast or dinner or supper, he'll look up suddenly like a man just freed from a delirium, and drop his cup, or his knife, or his fork 'ker-smash' into his plate, and cry out, 'My Heavens, Mary! But it's pretty good just for *you* and *me* to be alone together again!'"

"And what will Mrs. Lennart say?" interposed Sagner hastily, with a great puff of smoke.

For some unaccountable reason Madge Hubert's eyes slopped right over with tears.

"What will Mary Lennart say?" she repeated. "Mary Lennart will say: 'Excuse me, dear, but I wasn't listening. I didn't hear what you said. I was trying to remember whether or not I'd put moth-balls in your winter suit.' Though he live to be nine hundred and sixty-two, Harold Lennart's love-life will never rhyme again. But prose, of course, is a great deal easier to live than verse."

As though we had all been discussing the latest foreign theory concerning microbes, Sagner jumped up abruptly and began to rummage furiously through a pile of German bulletins. When he had found and read aloud enough things that he didn't want, he looked up and said nonchalantly, "Let's go home."

"All right," said Madge Hubert.

"Maybe you hadn't noticed that I was here," I suggested, "but I think that perhaps I should like to go home, too."

As we banged the big, oaken, iron-clamped door behind us, Madge Hubert lingered a second and turned her white face up to the waning, yellow moonlight. "I think I'd like to go home through the dark woods," she decided.

Silently we all turned down into the soft, padded path that ran along the piny shore of our little college lake. Sagner of course led the way. Madge Hubert followed close. And I tagged along behind as merrily as I could. Twice I saw the girl's shoulders shudder.

"Don't you like the woods, Miss Hubert?" I called out experimentally.

She stopped at once and waited for me to catch up with her. There was the very faintest possible suggestion of timidity in the action.

"Don't you like the woods?" I repeated.

She shook her head. "No, not especially," she answered. "That is, not all woods. There's such a difference. Some woods feel as though they had violets in them, and some woods feel as though they had—Indians."

I couldn't help laughing. "How about these woods?" I quizzed.

She gave a little gasp. "I don't believe there are violets in any woods to-night," she faltered.

Even as she spoke we heard a swish and a crackle ahead of us and Sagner came running back. "Let's go round the other way," he insisted.

"I won't go round the other way," said Madge Hubert. "How perfectly absurd! What's the matter?"

Even as she argued we stepped out into the open clearing and met Harold Lennart and "Little Sister" singing their way home hand in hand through the witching night. For an instant our jovial greetings parried together, and then we passed. Not till we had reached Madge Hubert's doorstep did I lose utterly the wonderful lilting echo of that young contralto voice with the man's older tenor ringing in and out of it like a shimmery silver lining.

Ten minutes later in Sagner's cluttered workroom we two men sat and stared through our pipe-smoke into each other's evasive eyes.

"Madge didn't—hesitate at all—to tell me a thing or two to-night, did she?" Sagner began at last, gruffly.

I smiled. The relaxation made me feel as though my mouth had really got a chance at last to sit down.

"Am I so very old?" persisted Sagner. "I'm not forty-five."

I shrugged my shoulders.

Pettishly he reached out and clutched at a scalpel, cleansed it for an instant in the flame, and jabbed the point of it into his wrist. The red blood spurted instantly.

"There!" he cried out triumphantly. "I have blood in me! It isn't embalming fluid at all."

"Oh, quit your fooling, you old death-digger," I said. And then with overtense impulse I asked, "Sagner, man, do you really understand Life?"

Sagner's jaw-bones stiffened instantly. "Oh, yes," he exclaimed. "Oh, yes, of course I understand Life. That is," he added, with a most unusual burst of humility, "I understand everything, I think, except just why the gills of a fish—but, oh, bother, you wouldn't know what I meant; and there's a new French theory about odylic forces that puzzles me a little, and I never, never have been able to understand the particular mental processes of a woman who violates the law of species by naming her firstborn son for any man but his father. I'm not exactly criticising the fish," he added vehemently, "nor the new odylic theory, nor even the woman; I'm simply stating baldly and plainly the only three things under God's heaven that I can't quite seem to fathom."

"What's all this got to do with Mary Lennart?" I asked impatiently.

"Nothing at all to do with Mary Lennart," he answered proudly. "Mary Lennart's son is named Harold." He began to smoke very hard. "Considering the real object of our being put here in the world," he resumed didactically, "it has always seemed to me that the supreme test of character lay in the father's and mother's mental attitude toward their young."

"Couldn't you say 'toward their children'?" I protested.

He brushed my interruption aside. "I don't care," he persisted, "how much a man loves a woman or how much a woman loves a man—the man who deserts his wife during her crucial hour and goes off on a lark to get out of the fuss, and the woman who names her firstborn son for any man except his father, may qualify in all the available moral tenets, but they certainly have slipped up somehow, mentally, in the Real Meaning of things. Thank God," he finished quickly, "that neither Harold Lennart nor Mary has failed the other like that—no matter what else happens." His face whitened. "I stayed with Harold Lennart the night little Harold was born," he whispered rather softly.

Before I could think of just the right thing to say, he jumped up awkwardly and strode over to the looking-glass, and puffed out his great chest and stood and stared at himself.

"I wish I had a son named Bertus Sagner," he said.

"It's all right, of course, to have him named after you," I laughed, "but you surely wouldn't choose to have him look like you, would you?"

He turned on me with absurd fierceness. "I wouldn't marry any woman who didn't love me0 enough to want her son to look like me!" he exclaimed.

I was still laughing as I picked up my hat. I was still laughing as I stumbled and fumbled down the long, black, steep stairs. Half an hour later in my pillows I was still laughing. But I did not get to sleep. My mind was too messy. After all, when you really come to think of it, a man's brain ought to be made up fresh and clean every night like a hotel bed. Sleep seems to be altogether too dainty a thing to nest in any brain that strange thoughts have rumpled. Always there must be the white sheet of peace edging the blanket of forgetfulness. And perhaps on one or two of life's wintrier nights some sort of spiritual comforter thrown over all.

It was almost a week before I saw any of the Lennarts again. Then, on a Saturday afternoon, as Sagner and I were lolling along the road toward town we met Lennart and "Little Sister" togged out in a lot of gorgeous golf duds. Lennart was delighted to see us, and "Little Sister" made Sagner get down on his knees and tie her shoe lacings twice. I escaped with the milder favor of a pat on the wrist.

"We're going out to the Golf Club," beamed Lennart, "to enter for the tournament."

"Oh," said Sagner, turning to join them. "Shall we find Mrs. Lennart out at the club? Is she going to play?"

A flicker of annoyance went over Lennart's face. "Why, Sagner," he said, "how stupid you are! Don't you know that Mary is lame and couldn't walk over the golf course now to save her life?"

As Sagner turned back to me, and we passed on out of hearing, I noted two red spots flaming hectically in his cheeks.

"It seems to me," he muttered, "that if I had crippled or incapacitated my wife in any way so that she couldn't play golf any more, I wouldn't exactly take another woman into the tournament. I think that singles would just about fit me under the circumstances."

"But Lennart is such a 'splendid fellow,'" I quoted wryly.

"He's a splendid fool," snapped Sagner.

"Why, you darned old copy-cat," I taunted. "It was Miss Hubert who rated him as a 'splendid fool.'"

"Oh," said Sagner.

"Oh, yourself," said I.

Involuntarily we turned and watched the two bright figures skirting the field. Almost at that instant they stopped, and the girl reached up with all her clinging, cloying coquetry and fastened a great, pink wild rose into the lapel of the man's coat. Sagner groaned. "Why can't she keep her hands off that man?" he muttered; then he shrugged his shoulders with a grim little gesture of helplessness. "If a girl doesn't know," he said, "that it's wrong to chase another woman's man she's too ignorant to be congenial. If she does know it's wrong, she's too—vicious. But never mind," he finished abruptly, "Lennart's foolishness will soon pass. And meanwhile Mary has her boy. Surely no lad was ever so passionately devoted to his mother. They are absolutely inseparable. I never saw anything like it." He began to smile again.

Then, because at a turn of the road he saw a bird that reminded him of a beast that reminded him of a reptile, he left me unceremoniously and went back to the laboratory.

Feeling a bit raw over his desertion, I gave up my walk and decided to spend the rest of the afternoon at the library.

At the edge of the reading-room I found Madge Hubert brandishing a ferocious-looking paper-knife over the perfectly helpless new magazines. With a little cry of delight she summoned me to her by the wave of a *Science Monthly*. Looking over her shoulder I beheld with equal delight that the canny old Science paper had stuck in Sagner's great, ugly face for a frontispiece. At arm's length, with opening and narrowing eyes, I studied the perfect, clever likeness: the convict-cropped hair; the surly, aggressive, relentlessly busy features; the absurd, overwrought, deep-sea sort of eyes. "Great Heavens, Miss Hubert," I said, "did you ever see such a funny-looking man?"

The girl winced. "Funny?" she gasped. "Funny? Why, I think Bertus Sagner is the most absolutely fascinating-looking man that I ever saw in my life." She stared at me in astonishment.

To hide my emotions I fled to the history room. Somewhat to my surprise Mrs. Lennart and her little lad were there, delving deep into some thrilling grammar-school problem concerning Henry the Eighth. I nodded to them, thought they saw me, and slipped into a chair not far behind them. There was no one else in the room. Maybe my thirst for historical information was not very keen. Certainly every book that I touched rustled like a dead, stale autumn leaf. Maybe the yellow bird in the acacia tree just outside the window teased me a little bit. Anyway, my eyes began only too soon to stray from the text-books before me to the little fluttering wisp of Mrs. Lennart's hair that tickled now and then across the lad's hovering face. I thought I had never seen a sweeter picture than those two cuddling, browsing faces. Surely I had never seen one more entrancingly serene.

"Oh, I wish I had a sister," fretted the boy

Then suddenly I saw the lad push back his books with a whimper of discontent.

"What is it?" asked his mother. I could hear her words plainly.

"Oh, I wish I had a sister," fretted the boy.

"Why?" said the mother in perfectly happy surprise.

The lad began to drum on the table. "Why do I want a sister?" he repeated a trifle temperishly. "Why, so I could have some one to play with and walk with and talk with and study with. Some one jolly and merry and frisky."

"Why—what about *me?*" she quizzed. Even at that moment I felt reasonably certain that she was still smiling.

The little lad looked bluntly up into her face. "Why you are—*so old!*" he said quite distinctly.

I saw the woman's shoulders hunch as though her hands were bracing against the table. Then she reached out like a flash and clutched the little lad's chin in her fingers. If a voice-tone has any color, hers was corpse-white. "I never—let—*you*—know—that—you—were—too—*young!*" she almost hissed.

And I shut my eyes.

When I looked up again the woman was gone, and the little lad was running after her with a queer, puzzled look on his face.

Life has such a strange way of foreshortening its longest plots with a startling, snapped-off ending. Any true story is a tiny bit out of rhetorical proportion.

The very next day, under the railroad trestle that hurries us back and forth to the big, neighboring city, we found Mrs. Lennart's body in a three-foot pool of creek water. It was the little lad's birthday, it seems, and he was to have had a supper party, and she had gone to town in the early afternoon to make a few festive purchases. A package of tinsel-paper bonbons floated safely, I remember, in the pool beside her. For some inexplicable reason she had stepped off the train at the wrong station and, realizing presumably how her blundering tardiness would blight the little lad's pleasure, she had started to walk home across the trestle, hoping thereby to beat the later train by as much as half an hour. The rest of the tragedy was brutally plain. Somehow between one safe, friendly embankment and another she had slipped and fallen. The trestle was ticklish walking for even a person who wasn't lame.

Like a slim, white, waxen altar candle snuffed out by a child's accidental, gusty pleasure-laugh, we brought her home to the sweet, green, peaceful library, with its resolute, indomitable hearthstone.

Out of all the crowding people who jostled me in the hallway I remember only—Lennart's ghastly, agonized face.

"Go and tell Sagner," he said.

Even as I crossed the campus the little, fluttery, flickery, hissing word "suicide" was in the air. From the graduates' dormitory I heard a man's voice argue, "But why did she get off deliberately at the wrong station?" Out of the president's kitchen a shrill tone cackled, "Well, she ain't been herself, they say, for a good many weeks. And who wonders?"

In one corner of the laboratory, close by an open window, I found Sagner working, as I had expected, in blissful ignorance.

"What's the matter?" he asked bluntly.

I was very awkward. I was very clumsy. I was very frightened. My face was all condensed like a telegram.

"Madge Hubert was right," I stammered. "Mrs. Lennart's—business—has gone into the hands of a—receiver."

The glass test tube went brittling out of Sagner's fingers. "Do you mean that she is—dead?" he asked.

I nodded.

For the fraction of a moment he rolled back his great, shaggy brows, and lifted his face up wide-eyed and staring to the soft, sweet, dove-colored, early evening sky. Then his eyelids came scrunching down again perfectly tight, and I saw one side of his ugly mouth begin to smile a little as a man might smile—as he closes the door—when the woman whom he loves comes home again. Then very slowly, very methodically, he turned off all the gas-burners and picked up all the notebooks, and cleansed all the knives, and just as I thought he was almost ready to go with me he started back again and released a fair, froth-green lunar moth from a stifling glass jar. Then, with his arm across my cringing shoulders, we fumbled our way down the long, creaky stairs. And all the time his heart was pounding like an oil-soused engine. But I had to bend my head to hear the questions that crumbled from his lips.

As we crunched our way across the Lennarts' garden with all the horrible, rackety noise that the living inevitably make in the presence of the dead, we ran into Lennart's old gardener crouching there in the dusk, stuffing cold, white roses into a huge market basket. Almost brutally Sagner clutched the old fellow by the arm. "Dunstan," he demanded, "how—did—this—thing—happen?"

The old gardener shook with fear and palsy. "There's some," he whispered, "as says the lady-dear was out of her mind. A-h, no," he protested, "a-h, no. She may ha' been out of her heart, but she weren't never out of her mind. There's some," he choked, "as calls it suicide, there's some," he gulped, "as calls it accident. I'm a rough-spoke man and I don' know the tongue o' ladies, but it weren't suicide, and it weren't accident. If it had be'n a man that had done it, you'd 'a' called it just a 'didn't-give-a-damn.'"

As we neared the house Sagner spoke only once. "Barney," he asked quite cheerfully, "were you ever rude to a woman?"

My hands went instinctively up to my head. "Oh, yes," I hurried, "once in the Arizona desert I struck an Indian squaw."

"Does it hurt?" persisted Sagner.

"You mean 'Did it hurt?'" I answered a bit impatiently. "Yes, I think it hurt her a little, but not nearly as much as she deserved."

Sagner reached forward and yanked me back by the shoulder. "I mean," he growled, "do you remember it now in the middle of the night, and are you sorry you did it?"

My heart cramped. "Yes," I acknowledged, "I remember it now in the middle of the night. But I am distinctly not sorry that I did it."

"Oh," muttered Sagner.

With the first creaking sound of our steps in the front hall "Little Sister" came gliding down the stairway with the stark-faced laddie clutching close at her sash. All the sparkle and spangle were gone from the girl. Her eyes were like two bruises on the flesh of a calla lily. Slipping one ice-cold tremulous hand into mine she closed down her other frightened hand over the two. "I'm so very glad you've come," she whispered huskily. "Mr. Lennart isn't any comfort to me at all to-night—and Mary was the only sister I had." Her voice caught suddenly with a rasping sob. "You and Mr. Sagner have always been so kind to me," she plunged on blindly, with soft-drooping eyelids, "and I shall probably never see either of you again. We are all going home to-morrow. And I expect to be married in July to a boy at home." Her icy fingers quickened in mine like the bloom-burst of a sun-scorched Jacqueminot.

"You—expect—to—be—married—in—July to—a—boy—at—home?" cried Sagner.

The awful slicing quality in his voice brought Lennart's dreadful face peering out through a slit in the library curtains.

"Hush!" I signaled warningly to Sagner. But again his venomous question ripped through the quiet of the house.

"You—expected—all—the—time—to—be—married—in—July?"

"Why, yes," said the girl, with the faintest dimpling flicker of a smile. "Won't you congratulate0 me?" Very softly she drew her right hand away from me and held it out whitely to Sagner.

"Excuse me," said Sagner, "but I have just—washed—my—hands."

"What?" stammered the girl. "W-h-a-t?"

"Excuse—me," said Sagner, "but I have just—washed my hands."

Then, bowing very, very low, like a small boy at his first dancing-school, Sagner passed from the house.

When I finally succeeded in steering my shaking knees and flopping feet down the long front steps and the pleasant, rose-bordered path, I found Sagner waiting for me at the gateway. Under the basking warmth of that mild May night his teeth were chattering as with an ague, and his ravenous face was like the face of a man whose soul is utterly glutted, but whose body has never even so much as tasted food and drink.

I put both my hands on his shoulders. "Sagner," I begged, "if there is anything under God's heaven that you want to-night—go and get it!"

He gave a short, gaspy laugh and wrenched himself free from me. "There is nothing *under* God's heaven—to-night—that I want—except Madge Hubert," he said.

In another instant he was gone. With a wh-i-r and a wh-i-s-h and a snow-white fragrance, his trail cut abruptly through the apple-bush hedge. Then like a huge, black, sweet-scented sponge the darkening night seemed to swoop down and wipe him right off the face of the earth.

Very softly I knelt and pressed my ear to the ground. Across the young, tremulous, vibrant greensward I heard the throb-throb-throb of a man's feet—*running*.

The White Linen Nurse

CHAPTER I

The White Linen Nurse was so tired that her noble expression ached.

Incidentally her head ached and her shoulders ached and her lungs ached and the ankle-bones of both feet ached quite excruciatingly. But nothing of her felt permanently incapacitated except her noble expression. Like a strip of lip-colored lead suspended from her poor little nose by two tugging wire-gray wrinkles her persistently conscientious sickroom smile seemed to be whanging aimlessly against her front teeth. The sensation certainly was very unpleasant.

Looking back thus on the three spine-curving, chest-cramping, foot-twinging, ether-scented years of her hospital training, it dawned on the White Linen Nurse very suddenly that nothing of her ever had felt permanently incapacitated except her noble expression!

Impulsively she sprang for the prim white mirror that capped her prim white bureau and stood staring up into her own entrancing, bright-colored Novia Scotian reflection with tense and unwonted interest.

Except for the unmistakable smirk which fatigue had clawed into her plastic young mouth-lines there was certainly nothing special the matter with what she saw.

"Perfectly good face!" she attested judicially with no more than common courtesy to her progenitors. "Perfectly good and tidy looking face! If only—if only—" her breath caught a trifle. "If only—it didn't look so disgustingly noble and—hygienic—and dollish!"

All along the back of her neck little sharp prickly pains began suddenly to sting and burn.

"Silly—simpering—pink and white puppet!" she scolded squintingly,

"I'll teach you how to look like a real girl!"

Very threateningly she raised herself to her tiptoes and thrust her glowing, corporeal face right up into the moulten, elusive, quick-silver face in the mirror. Pink for pink, blue for blue, gold for gold, dollish smirk for dollish smirk, the mirror mocked her seething inner fretfulness.

"Why—darn you!" she gasped. "Why—darn you! Why, you looked more human than that when you left the Annapolis Valley three years ago! There were at least—tears in your face then, and—cinders, and—your mother's best advice, and the worry about the mortgage, and—and—the blush of Joe Hazeltine's kiss!"

Furtively with the tip of her index-finger she started to search her imperturbable pink cheek for the spot where Joe Hazeltine's kiss had formerly flamed.

"My hands are all right, anyway!" she acknowledged with infinite relief. Triumphantly she raised both strong, stub-fingered, exaggeratedly executive hands to the level of her childish blue eyes and stood surveying the mirrored effect with ineffable satisfaction. "Why my hands are—dandy!" she gloated. "Why they're perfectly—dandy! Why they're wonderful! Why they're—." Then suddenly and fearfully she gave a shrill little scream. "But they don't go with my silly doll-face!" she cried. "Why, they don't! They don't! They go with the Senior Surgeon's scowling Heidelberg eyes! They go with the Senior Surgeon's grim gray jaw! They go with the—! Oh! what shall I do? What shall I do?"

Dizzily, with her stubby finger-tips prodded deep into every jaded facial muscle that she could compass, she staggered towards the air, and dropping down into the first friendly chair that bumped against her knees, sat staring blankly out across the monotonous city roofs that flanked her open window,—trying very, very hard for the first time in her life, to consider the General-Phenomenon-of-Being-a-Trained-Nurse.

All around and about her, inexorable as anesthesia, horrid as the hush of tomb or public library, lurked the painfully unmistakable sense of institutional restraint. Mournfully to her ear from some remote kitcheny region of pots and pans a browsing spoon tinkled forth from time to time with soft-muffled resonance. Up and down every clammy white corridor innumerable young feet, born to prance and stamp, were creeping stealthily to and fro in rubber-heeled whispers. Along the somber fire-escape just below her windowsill, like a covey of snubbed doves, six or eight of her classmates were cooing and crooning together with excessive caution concerning the imminent graduation exercises that were to take place at eight o'clock that very evening. Beyond her dreariest ken of muffled voices, beyond her dingiest vista of slate and brick, on a far faint hillside, a far faint streak of April green went roaming jocundly skyward. Altogether sluggishly, as though her nostrils were plugged with warm velvet, the smell of spring and ether and scorched mutton-chops filtered in and out, in and out, in and out, of her abnormally jaded senses.

Taken all in all it was not a propitious afternoon for any girl as tired and as pretty as the White Linen Nurse to be considering the general phenomenon of anything—except April!

In the real country, they tell me, where the Young Spring runs wild and bare as a nymph through every dull brown wood and hay-gray meadow, the blasé farmer-lad will not even lift his eyes from the plow to watch the pinkness of her passing. But here in the prudish brick-minded city where the Young Spring at her friskiest is nothing more audacious than a sweltering, winter-swathed madcap, who has impishly essayed some fine morning to tiptoe down street in her soft, sloozily, green, silk-stockinged feet, the whole hob-nailed population reels back aghast and agrin before the most innocent flash of the rogue's green-veiled toes. And then, suddenly snatching off its own cumbersome winter foot-habits, goes chasing madly after her, in its own prankish, vari-colored socks.

Now the White Linen Nurse's socks were black, and cotton at that, a combination incontestably sedate. And the White Linen Nurse had waded barefoot through too many posied country pastures to experience any ordinary city thrill over the sight of a single blade of grass pushing scarily through a crack in the pavement, or puny, concrete-strangled maple tree flushing wanly to the smoky sky. Indeed for three hustling, square-toed, rubber-heeled city years the White Linen Nurse had never even stopped to notice whether the season was flavored with frost or thunder. But now, unexplainably, just at the end of it all, sitting innocently there at her own prim little bed-room window, staring innocently out across indomitable roof-tops,—with the crackle of glory and diplomas already ringing in her ears,—she heard, instead, for the first time in her life, the gaily dare-devil voice of the spring, a hoydenish challenge flung back at her, leaf-green, from the crest of a winter-scarred hill.

"Hello, White Linen Nurse!" screamed the saucy city spring. "Hello, White Linen Nurse! Take off your homely starched collar! Or your silly candy-box cap! Or any other thing that feels maddeningly artificial! And come out! And be very wild!"

Like a puppy dog cocking its head towards some strange, unfamiliar sound, the White Linen Nurse cocked her head towards the lure of the green-crested hill. Still wrestling conscientiously with the General-Phenomenon-of-Being-a-Trained-Nurse she found her collar suddenly very tight, the tiny cap inexpressibly heavy and vexatious. Timidly she removed the collar—and found that the removal did not rest her in the slightest. Equally timidly she removed the cap—and found that even that removal did not rest her in the slightest. Then very, very slowly, but very, very permeatingly and completely, it dawned on the White Linen Nurse that never while eyes were blue, and hair gold, and lips red, would she ever find rest again until she had removed her noble expression!

With a jerk that started the pulses in her temples throbbing like two toothaches she straightened up in her chair. All along the back of her neck the little blonde curls began to crisp very ticklingly at their roots.

Still staring worriedly out over the old city's slate-gray head to that inciting prance of green across the farthest horizon she felt her whole being kindle to an indescribable passion of revolt against all Hushed Places. Seething with fatigue, smoldering with ennui, she experienced suddenly a wild, almost uncontrollable impulse to sing, to shout, to scream from the housetops, to mock somebody, to defy everybody, to break laws, dishes, heads,—anything in fact that would break with a crash! And then at last, over the hills and far away, with all the outraged world at her heels, to run! And run! And run! And run! And run! And laugh! Till her feet raveled out! And her lungs burst! And there was nothing more left of her at all,—ever—ever—any more!

Discordantly into this rapturously pagan vision of pranks and posies broke one of her room-mates all awhiff with ether, awhirr with starch.

Instantly with the first creak of the door-handle the White Linen Nurse was on her feet, breathless, resentful, grotesquely defiant.

"Get out of here, Zillah Forsyth!" she cried furiously. "Get out of here—quick!—and leave me alone! I want to think!"

Perfectly serenely the newcomer advanced into the room. With her pale, ivory-tinted cheeks, her great limpid brown eyes, her soft dark hair parted madonna-like across her beautiful brow, her whole face was like some exquisite, composite picture of all the saints of history. Her voice also was amazingly tranquil.

"Oh, Fudge!" she drawled. "What's eating you, Rae Malgregor? I won't either get out! It's my room just as much as it is yours! And Helene's just as much as it is ours! And besides," she added more briskly, "it's four o'clock now, and with graduation at eight and the dance afterwards, if we don't get our stuff packed up now, when in thunder shall we get it done?" Quite irrelevantly she began to laugh. Her laugh was perceptibly shriller than her speaking voice. "Say, Rae!" she confided. "That minister I nursed through pneumonia last winter wants me to pose as 'Sanctity' for a stained-glass window in his new church! Isn't he the softie?"

"Shall—you—do—it?" quizzed Rae Malgregor a trifle tensely.

"Shall I do it?" mocked the newcomer. "Well, you just watch me! Four mornings a week in June—at full week's wages? Fresh Easter lilies every day? White silk angel-robes? All the high-souls and high-paints kowtowing around me? Why it would be more fun than a box of monkeys! Sure I'll do it!"

Expeditiously as she spoke the newcomer reached up for the framed motto over her own ample mirror and yanking it down with one single tug began to busy herself adroitly with a snarl in the picture-cord. Like a withe of willow yearning over a brook her slender figure curved to the task. Very scintillatingly the afternoon light seemed to brighten suddenly across her lap. *You'll Be a Long Time Dead!* glinted the motto through its sun-dazzled glass.

Still panting with excitement, still bristling with resentment, Rae Malgregor stood surveying the intrusion and the intruder. A dozen impertinent speeches were rioting in her mind. Twice her mouth opened and shut before she finally achieved the particular opprobrium that completely satisfied her.

"Bah! You look like a—Trained Nurse!" she blurted forth at last with hysterical triumph.

"So do you!" said the newcomer amiably.

With a little gasp of dismay Rae Malgregor sprang suddenly forward. Her eyes were flooded with tears.

"Why, that's just exactly what's the matter with me!" she cried. "My face is all worn out trying to look like a Trained Nurse! Oh, Zillah, how do you know you were meant to be a Trained Nurse? How does anybody know? Oh, Zillah! Save me! Save me!"

Languorously Zillah Forsyth looked up from her work, and laughed. Her laugh was like the accidental tinkle of sleighbells in mid-summer, vaguely disquieting, a shiver of frost across the face of a lily.

"Save you from what, you great big overgrown, tow-headed doll-baby?" she questioned blandly. "For Heaven's sake, the only thing you need is to go back to whatever toy-shop you came from and get a new head. What in Creation's the matter with you lately, anyway? Oh, of course, you've had rotten luck this past month, but what of it? That's the trouble with you country girls. You haven't got any stamina."

With slow, shuffling-footed astonishment Rae Malgregor stepped out into the center of the room. "Country girls," she repeated blankly. "Why, you're a country girl yourself!"

"I *am* not!" snapped Zillah Forsyth. "I'll have you understand that there are nine thousand people in the town I come from—and not a rube among them. Why I tended soda fountain in the swellest drug-store there a whole year before I even thought of taking up nursing. And I wasn't as green—when I was six months old—as you are now!"

Slowly with a soft-snuggling sigh of contentment she raised her slim white fingers to coax her dusky hair a little looser, a little farther down, a little more madonna-like across her sweet, mild forehead, then snatching out abruptly at a convenient shirt-waist began with extraordinary skill to apply its dangly lace sleeves as a protective bandage for the delicate glass-faced motto still in her lap, placed the completed parcel with inordinate scientific precision in the exact corner of her packing-box, and then went on very diligently, very zealously, to strip the men's photographs from the mirror on her bureau. There were twenty-seven photographs in all, and for each one she had already cut and prepared a small square of perfectly fresh, perfectly immaculate white tissue wrapping-paper. No one so transcendently fastidious, so exquisitely neat, in all her personal habits had ever trained in that particular hospital before.

Very soberly the doll-faced girl stood watching the men's pleasant paper countenances smooth away one by one into their chaste white veilings, until at last quite without warning she poked an accusing, inquisitive finger directly across Zillah Forsyth's shoulder.

"Zillah!" she demanded peremptorily. "All the year I've wanted to know! All the year every other girl in our class has wanted to know! Where did you ever get that picture of the Senior Surgeon? He never gave it to you in the world! He didn't! He didn't! He's not that kind!"

Deeply into Zillah Forsyth's pale, ascetic cheek dawned a most amazing dimple. "Sort of jarred you girls some, didn't it," she queried, "to see me strutting round with a photo of the Senior Surgeon?" The little cleft in her chin showed suddenly with almost startling distinctness. "Well, seeing it's you," she grinned, "and the year's all over, and there's nobody left that I can worry about it any more, I don't mind telling you in the least that I—bought it out of a photographer's show-case! There! Are you satisfied now?"

With easy nonchalance she picked up the picture in question and scrutinized it shrewdly.

"Lord! What a face!" she attested. "Nothing but granite! Hack him with a knife and he wouldn't bleed but just chip off into pebbles!" With exaggerated contempt she shrugged her supple shoulders. "Bah! How I hate a man like that! There's no fun in him!" A little abruptly she turned and thrust the photograph into Rae Malgregor's hand. "You can have it if you want to," she said. "I'll trade it to you for that lace corset-cover of yours!"

Like water dripping through a sieve the photograph slid through Rae Malgregor's frightened fingers. With nervous apology she stooped and picked it up again and held it gingerly by one remotest corner. Her eyes were quite wide with horror.

"Oh, of course I'd like the—picture, well enough," she stammered. "But it wouldn't seem—exactly respectful to—to trade it for a corset-cover."

"Oh, very well," drawled Zillah Forsyth. "Tear it up then!"

Expeditiously with frank, non-sentimental fingers Rae Malgregor tore the tough cardboard across, and again across, and once again across, and threw the conglomerate fragments into the waste-basket. And her expression all the time was no more, no less, than the expression of a person who would infinitely rather execute his own pet dog or cat than risk the possible bungling of an outsider. Then like a small child trotting with infinite relief to its own doll-house she trotted over to her bureau, extracted the lace corset-cover, and came back with it in her hand to lean across Zillah Forsyth's shoulder again and watch the men's faces go slipping off into oblivion. Once again, abruptly without warning, she halted the process with a breathless exclamation.

"Oh, of course this waist is the only one I've got with ribbons in it," she asserted irrelevantly. "But I'm perfectly willing to trade it for that picture!" she pointed out with unmistakably explicit finger-tip.

Chucklingly Zillah Forsyth withdrew the special photograph from its half-completed wrappings.

"Oh! Him?" she said. "Oh, that's a chap I met on the train last summer. He's a brakeman or something. He's a—"

Perfectly unreluctantly Rae Malgregor dropped the fluff of lace and ribbons into Zillah's lap and reached out with cheerful voraciousness to annex the young man's picture to her somewhat bleak possessions. "Oh, I don't care a rap who he is," she interrupted briskly. "But he's sort of cute-looking, and I've got an empty frame at home just that odd size, and Mother's crazy for a new picture to stick up over the kitchen mantelpiece. She gets so tired of seeing nothing but the faces of people she knows all about."

Sharply Zillah Forsyth turned and stared up into the younger girl's face, and found no guile to whet her stare against.

"Well of all the ridiculous—unmitigated greenhorns!" she began. "Well—is that all you wanted him for? Why, I supposed you wanted to write to him! Why, I supposed—"

For the first time an expression not altogether dollish darkened across Rae Malgregor's garishly juvenile blondeness.

"Maybe I'm not quite as green as you think I am!" she flared up stormily. With this sharp flaring-up every single individual pulse in her body seemed to jerk itself suddenly into conscious activity again like the soft, plushy pound-pound-pound of a whole stocking-footed regiment of pain descending single file upon her for her hysterical undoing. "Maybe I've had a good deal more experience than you give me credit for!" she hastened excitedly to explain. "I tell you—I tell you I've been engaged!" she blurted forth with a bitter sort of triumph.

With a palpable flicker of interest Zillah Forsyth looked back across her shoulder. "Engaged? How many times?" she asked quite bluntly.

As though the whole monogamous groundwork of civilization was threatened by the question, Rae Malgregor's hands went clutching at her breast. "Why, once!" she gasped. "Why, once!"

Convulsively Zillah Forsyth began to rock herself to and fro. "Oh Lordy!" she chuckled. "Oh Lordy, Lordy! Why I've been engaged four times just this past year!" In a sudden passion of fastidiousness she bent down over the particular photograph in her hand and snatching at a handkerchief began to rub diligently at a small smouch of dust in one corner of the cardboard. Something in the effort of rubbing seemed to jerk her small round chin into almost angular prominence. "And before I'm through," she added, at least two notes below her usual alto tones, "And before I'm through—I'm going to get engaged to—every profession that there is on the surface of the globe!" Quite helplessly the thin paper skin of the photograph peeled off in company with the smouch of dust. "And when I marry," she ejaculated fiercely, "and when I marry—I'm going to marry a man who will take me to every place that there is—on the surface of the globe! And after that—!"

"After what?" interrogated a brand new voice from the doorway.

CHAPTER II

It was the other room-mate this time. The only real aristocrat in the whole graduating class, high-browed, high-cheekboned,—eyes like some far-sighted young prophet,—mouth even yet faintly arrogant with the ineradicable consciousness of caste,—a plain, eager, stripped-for-a-long-journey type of face,—this was Helene Churchill. There was certainly no innocuous bloom of country hills and pastures in this girl's face, nor any seething small-town passion pounding indiscriminately at all the doors of experience. The men and women who had bred Helene Churchill had been the breeders also of brick and granite cities since the world was new.

Like one infinitely more accustomed to treading on Persian carpets than on painted floors she came forward into the room.

"Hello, children!" she said casually, and began at once without further parleying to take down the motto that graced her own bureau-top.

It was the era when almost everybody in the world had a motto over his bureau. Helene Churchill's motto was: *Inasmuch As Ye Have Done It Unto One Of The Least Of These Ye Have Done It Unto Me*. On a scroll of almost priceless parchment the text was illuminated with inimitable Florentine skill and color. A little carelessly, after the manner of people quite accustomed to priceless things, she proceeded now to roll the parchment into its smallest possible circumference, humming exclusively to herself all the while an intricate little air from an Italian opera.

So the three faces foiled each other, sober city girl, pert town girl, bucolic country girl,—a hundred fundamental differences rampant between them, yet each fervid, adolescent young mouth tamed to the same monotonous, drolly exaggerated expression of complacency that characterizes the faces of all people who, in a distinctive uniform, for a reasonably satisfactory living wage, make an actual profession of righteous deeds.

Indeed among all the thirty or more varieties of noble expression which an indomitable Superintendent had finally succeeded in inculcating into her graduating class, no other physiognomies had responded more plastically perhaps than these three to the merciless imprint of the great *hospital machine* which, in pursuance of its one repetitive design, *discipline*, had coaxed Zillah Forsyth into the semblance of a lady, snubbed Helene Churchill into the substance of plain womanhood, and, still uncertain just what to do with Rae Malgregor's rollicking rural immaturity, had frozen her face temporarily into the smugly dimpled likeness of a fancy French doll rigged out as a nurse for some gilt-edged hospital fair.

With characteristic desire to keep up in every way with her more mature, better educated classmates, to do everything, in fact, so fast, so well, that no one should possibly guess that she hadn't yet figured out just why she was doing it at all, Rae Malgregor now with quickly readjusted cap and collar began to hurl herself into the task of her own packing. From her open bureau drawer, with a sudden impish impulse towards worldly wisdom, she extracted first of all the photograph of the young brakeman.

"See, Helene! My new beau!" she giggled experimentally.

In mild-eyed surprise Helene Churchill glanced up from her work. "*Your* beau?" she corrected. "Why, that's Zillah's picture."

"Well, it's mine now!" snapped Rae Malgregor with unexpected edginess. "It's mine now all right. Zillah said I could have him! Zillah said I could—write to him—if I wanted to!" she finished a bit breathlessly.

Wider and wider Helene Churchill's eyes dilated. "Write to a man—whom you don't know?" she gasped. "Why, Rae! Why, it isn't even—very nice—to have a picture of a man you don't know!"

Mockingly to the edge of her strong white teeth Rae Malgregor's tongue crept out in pink derision. "Bah!" she taunted. "What's 'nice'? That's the whole matter with you, Helene Churchill! You never stop to consider whether anything's fun or not; all you care is whether it's 'nice'!" Excitedly she turned to meet the cheap little wink from Zillah's sainted eyes. "Bah! What's 'nice'?" she persisted a little lamely. Then suddenly all the pertness within her crumbled into nothingness. "That's—the—whole trouble with you, Zillah Forsyth!" she stammered. "You never give a hang whether anything's nice or not; all you care is whether it's fun!" Quite helplessly she began to wring her hands. "Oh, how do I know which one of you girls to follow?" she demanded wildly. "How do I know anything? How does anybody know anything?"

Like a smoldering fuse the rambling query crept back into the inner recesses of her brain and fired once more the one great question that lay dormant there. Impetuously she ran forward and stared into Helene Churchill's face. "How do you know you were meant to be a Trained Nurse, Helene Churchill?" she began all over again. "How does anybody know she was really meant to be one? How can anybody, I mean, be perfectly sure?" Like a drowning man clutching out at the proverbial straw, she clutched at the parchment in Helene Churchill's hand. "I mean—where did you get your motto, Helene Churchill?" she persisted with increasing irritability. "If—you don't tell me—I'll tear the whole thing to pieces!"

With a startled frown Helene Churchill jerked back out of reach. "What's the matter with you, Rae?" she quizzed sharply, and then turning round quite casually to her book-case began to draw from the shelves one by one her beloved Marcus Aurelius, Wordsworth, Robert Browning. "Oh, I did so want to go to China," she confided irrelevantly. "But my family have just written me that they won't stand for it. So I suppose I'll have to go into tenement work here in the city instead." With a visible effort she jerked her mind back again to the feverish question in Rae Malgregor's eyes. "Oh, you want to know where I got my motto?" she asked. A flash of intuition brightened suddenly across her absent-mindedness. "Oh!" she smiled, "you mean you want to know—just what the incident was that first made me decide to—devote my life to—to humanity?"

"Yes!" snapped Rae Malgregor.

A little shyly Helene Churchill picked up her copy of Marcus Aurelius and cuddled her cheek against its tender Morocco cover. "Really?" she questioned with palpable hesitation. "Really you want to know? Why, why—it's rather a—sacred little story to me. I wouldn't exactly want to have anybody—laugh about it."

"I'll laugh if I want to!" attested Zillah Forsyth forcibly from the other side of the room.

Like a pugnacious boy, Rae Malgregor's fluent fingers doubled up into two firm fists.

"I'll punch her if she even looks as though she wanted to!" she signaled surreptitiously to Helene.

Shrewdly for an instant the city girl's narrowing eyes challenged and appraised the country girl's desperate sincerity. Then quite abruptly she began her little story.

"Why, it was on an Easter Sunday—Oh, ages and ages ago," she faltered. "Why, I couldn't have been more than nine years old at the time." A trifle self-consciously she turned her face away from Zillah Forsyth's supercilious smile. "And I was coming home from a Sunday school festival in my best white muslin dress with a big pot of purple pansies in my hand," she hastened somewhat nervously to explain. "And just at the edge of the gutter there was a dreadful drunken man lying in the mud with a great crowd of cruel people teasing and tormenting him. And, because—because I couldn't think of anything else to do about it, I—I walked right up to the poor old creature,—scared as I could be—and—and I presented him with my pot of purple pansies. And everybody of course began to laugh, to scream, I mean, and shout with amusement. And I, of course, began to cry. And the old drunken man straightened up very oddly for an instant, with his battered hat in one hand and the pot of pansies in the other,—and he raised the pot of pansies very high, as though it had been a glass of rarest wine—and bowed to me as—reverently as though he had been toasting me at my father's table at some very grand dinner. And 'Inasmuch!' he said. Just that,—'Inasmuch!' So that's how I happened to go into nursing!" she finished as abruptly as she had begun. Like some wonderful phosphorescent manifestation her whole shining soul seemed to flare forth suddenly through her plain face.

With honest perplexity Zillah Forsyth looked up from her work.

"So that's—how you happened to go into nursing?" she quizzed impatiently. Her long, straight nose was all puckered tight with interrogation. Her dove-like eyes were fairly dilated with slow-dawning astonishment. "You—don't—mean?" she gasped. "You don't mean that—just for that—?" Incredulously she jumped to her feet and stood staring blankly into the city girl's strangely illuminated features.

"Well, if I were a swell—like you!" she scoffed, "it would take a heap sight more than a drunken man munching pansies and rum and Bible-texts to—to jolt me out of my limousines and steam yachts and Adirondack bungalows!"

Quite against all intention Helene Churchill laughed. She did not often laugh. Just for an instant her eyes and Zillah Forsyth's clashed together in the irremediable antagonism of caste,—the Plebeian's scornful impatience with the Aristocrat, equaled only by the Aristocrat's condescending patience with the Plebeian.

It was no more than right that the Aristocrat should recover her self-possession first. "Never mind about your understanding. Zillah dear," she said softly. "Your hair is the most beautiful thing I ever saw in my life!"

Along Zillah Forsyth's ivory cheek an incongruous little flush of red began to show. With much more nonchalance than was really necessary she pointed towards her half-packed trunk.

"It wasn't—Sunday school—I was coming home from—when I got my motto!" she remarked dryly, with a wink at no one in particular. "And, so far as I know," she proceeded with increasing sarcasm, "the man who inspired my noble life was not in any way—particularly addicted to the use of alcoholic beverages!" As though her collar was suddenly too tight she rammed her finger down between her stiff white neck-band and her soft white throat. "He was a—New York doctor!" she hastened somewhat airily to explain. "Gee! But he was a swell! And he was spending his summer holiday up in the same Maine town where I was tending soda fountain. And he used to drop into the drug-store, nights, after cigars and things. And he used to tell me stories about the drugs and things, sitting up there on the counter swinging his legs and pointing out this and that,—quinine, ipecac, opium, hasheesh,—all the silly patent medicines, every sloppy soothing syrup! Lordy! He knew 'em as though they were people! Where they come from! Where they're going to! Yarns about the tropics that would kink the hair along the nape of your neck! Jokes about your own town's soup-kettle pharmacology that would make you yell for joy! Gee! But the things that man had seen and known! Gee! But the things that man could make you see and know! And he had an automobile," she confided proudly. "It was one of those billion dollar French cars. And I lived just round the corner from the drug-store. But we used to ride home by way of—New Hampshire!"

Almost imperceptibly her breath began to quicken. "Gee! Those nights!" she muttered. "Rain or shine, moon or thunder,—tearing down those country roads at forty miles an hour, singing, hollering, whispering! It was him that taught me to do my hair like this—instead of all the cheap rats and pompadours every other kid in town was wearing," she asserted, quite irrelevantly; then stopped with a quick, furtive glance of suspicion towards both her listeners and mouthed her way delicately back to the beginning of her sentence again. "It was *he* that taught me to do my hair like this," she repeated with the faintest possible suggestion of hauteur.

For one reason or another along the exquisitely chaste curve of her cheek a narrow streak of red began to show again.

"And he went away very sudden at the last," she finished hurriedly. "It seems he was married all the time." Blandly she turned her wonderful face to the caressing light. "And—I hope he goes to Hell!" she added perfectly simply.

With a little gasp of astonishment, shock, suspicion, distaste, Helene Churchill reached out an immediate conscientious hand to her.

"Oh, Zillah!" she began. "Oh, poor Zillah dear! I'm so—sorry! I'm so—"

Absolutely serenely, through a mask of insolence and ice, Zillah Forsyth ignored the proffered hand.

"I don't know what particular call you've got to be sorry for me, Helene Churchill," she drawled languidly. "I've got my character, same as you've got yours. And just about nine times as many good looks. And when it comes to nursing—" Like an alto song pierced suddenly by one shrill treble note, the girl's immobile face sharpened transiently with a single jagged flash of emotion. "And when it comes to nursing? Ha! Helene Churchill! You can lead your class all you want to with your silk-lined manners and your fuddy-duddy book-talk! But when genteel people like you are moping round all ready to fold your patients' hands on their breasts and murmur 'Thy will be done,'—why, that's the time that little 'yours truly' is just beginning to roll up her sleeves and get to work!"

With real passion her slender fingers went clutching again at her harsh linen collar. "It isn't you, Helene Churchill," she taunted, "that's ever been to the Superintendent on your bended knees and begged for the rabies cases—and the small-pox! Gee! You like nursing because you think it's pious to like it! But I like it—*because I like it!*" From brow to chin as though fairly stricken with sincerity her whole bland face furrowed startlingly with crude expressiveness. "The smell of ether!" she stammered. "It's like wine to me! The clang of the ambulance gong? I'd rather hear it than fire-engines! I'd crawl on my hands and knees a hundred miles to watch a major operation! I wish there was a war! I'd give my life to see a cholera epidemic!"

Abruptly as it came the passion faded from her face, leaving every feature tranquil again, demure, exaggeratedly innocent. With saccharine sweetness she turned to Rae Malgregor.

"Now, Little One," she mocked, "tell us the story of your lovely life. Having heard me coyly confess that I went into nursing because I had such a crush on this world,—and Helene here brazenly affirm that she went into nursing because she had such a crush on the world to come,—it's up to you now to confide to us just how you happened to take up so noble an endeavor! Had you seen some of the young house doctors' beautiful, smiling faces depicted in the hospital catalogue? Or was it for the sake of the Senior Surgeon's grim, gray mug that you jilted your poor plow-boy lover way up in the Annapolis Valley?"

"Why, Zillah!" gasped the country girl. "Why, I think you're perfectly awful! Why, Zillah Forsyth! Don't you ever say a thing like that again! You can joke all you want to about the flirty young Internes. They're nothing but fellows. But it isn't—it isn't respectful—for you to talk like that about the Senior Surgeon. He's too—too terrifying!" she finished in an utter panic of consternation.

"Oh, now I know it was the Senior Surgeon that made you jilt your country beau!" taunted Zillah Forsyth with soft alto sarcasm.

"I didn't, either, jilt Joe Hazeltine!" stormed Rae Malgregor explosively. Backed up against her bureau, eyes flaming, breast heaving, little candy-box cap all tossed askew over her left ear, she stood defying her tormentor. "I didn't, either, jilt Joe Hazeltine!" she reasserted passionately. "It was Joe Hazeltine that jilted me! And we'd been going together since we were kids! And now he's married the dominie's daughter and they've got a kid of their own most as old as he and I were when we first began courting each other. And it's all because I insisted on being a trained nurse," she finished shrilly.

With an expression of real shock Helene Churchill peered up from her lowly seat on the floor.

"You mean?" she asked a bit breathlessly. "You mean that he didn't want you to be a trained nurse? You mean that he wasn't big enough,—wasn't fine enough to appreciate the nobility of the profession?"

"Nobility nothing!" snapped Rae Malgregor. "It was me scrubbing strange men with alcohol that he couldn't stand for! And I don't know as I exactly blame him," she added huskily. "It certainly is a good deal of a liberty when you stop to think about it."

Quite incongruously her big, childish, blue eyes narrowed suddenly into two dark, calculating slits. "It's comic," she mused, "how there isn't a man in the world who would stand letting his wife or daughter or sister have a male nurse. But look at the jobs we girls get sent out on! It's very confusing!"

With sincere appeal she turned to Zillah Forsyth. "And yet—and yet," she stammered. "And yet—when everything scary that's in you has once been scared out of you,—why, there's nothing left in you to be scared *with* any more, is there?"

"What? What?" pleaded Helene Churchill. "Say it again! What?"

"That's what Joe and I quarreled about my first vacation home!" persisted Rae Malgregor. "It was a traveling salesman's thigh. It was broken bad. Somebody had to take care of it. So I did! Joe thought it wasn't modest to be so willing." With a perplexed sort of defiance she raised her square little chin. "But you see I was willing!" she said. "I was perfectly willing. Just one single solitary year of hospital training had made me perfectly willing. And you can't *un*-willing a willing—even to please your beau, no matter how hard you try!" With a droll admixture of shyness and disdain she tossed her curly blonde head a trifle higher. "Shucks!" she attested. "What's a traveling salesman's thigh?"

"Shucks yourself!" scoffed Zillah Forsyth. "What's a silly beau or two up in Nova Scotia to a girl with looks like you? You could have married that typhoid case a dozen times last winter if you'd crooked your little finger! Why, the fellow was crazy about you. And he was richer than Croesus. What queered it?" she demanded bluntly. "Did his mother hate you?"

Like one fairly cramped with astonishment Rae Malgregor doubled up very suddenly at the waist-line, and thrusting her neck oddly forward after the manner of a startled crane, stood peering sharply round the corner of the rocking-chair at Zillah Forsyth.

"Did his mother hate me?" she gasped. "Did—his—mother—hate—me? Well, what do you think? With me who never even saw plumbing till I came down here, setting out to explain to her with twenty tiled bathrooms how to be hygienic though rich? Did his mother hate me? Well, what do you think? With her who bore him, her who *bore* him, mind you, kept waiting down stairs in the hospital ante-room—half an hour every day—on the raw edge of a rattan chair—waiting—worrying—all old and gray and scared—while little young, perky, pink and white *me* is upstairs—brushing her own son's hair and washing her own son's face—and altogether getting her own son ready to see his own mother! And then me obliged to turn her out again in ten minutes, flip as you please, for fear she'd stayed too long,—while I stay on the rest of the night? *Did his mother hate me!*"

Stealthily as an assassin she crept around the corner of the rocking-chair and grabbed Zillah Forsyth by her astonished linen shoulder.

"Did his mother hate me?" she persisted mockingly. "Did his mother hate me? Well rather! Is there any woman from here to Kamchatka who doesn't hate us? Is there any woman from here to Kamchatka who doesn't look upon a trained nurse as her natural born enemy? I don't blame 'em!" she added chokingly. "Look at the impudent jobs we get sent out on! Quarantined upstairs for weeks at a time with their inflammable, diphtheritic bridegrooms—while they sit down stairs—brooding over their wedding teaspoons! Hiked off indefinitely to Atlantic City with their gouty bachelor uncles! Hearing their own innocent little sisters' blood-curdling deathbed deliriums! Snatching their own new-born babies away from their breasts and showing them, virgin-handed, how to nurse them better! The impudence of it, I say! The disgusting, confounded impudence! Doing things perfectly—flippantly—*right*—for twenty-five dollars a week—and washing—that all the achin' love in the world don't know how to do right—just for love!"

Furiously she began to jerk her victim's shoulder. "I tell you it's awful, Zillah Forsyth!" she insisted. "I tell you I just won't stand it!"

With muscles like steel wire Zillah Forsyth scrambled to her feet, and pushed Rae Malgregor back against the bureau.

"For Heaven's sake, Rae, shut up!" she said. "What in Creation's the matter with you to-day? I never saw you act so before!" With real concern she stared into the girl's turbid eyes. "If you feel like that about it, what in thunder did you go into nursing for?" she demanded not unkindly.

Very slowly Helene Churchill rose from her lowly seat by her precious book-case and came round and looked at Rae Malgregor rather oddly. "Yes," faltered Helene Churchill. "What did you go into nursing for?" The faintest possible taint of asperity was in her voice.

Quite dumbly for an instant Rae Malgregor's natural timidity stood battling the almost fanatic professional fervor in Helene Churchill's frankly open face, the raw, scientific passion, of very different caliber, but no less intensity, hidden so craftily behind Zillah Forsyth's plastic features. Then suddenly her own hands went clutching back at the bureau for support, and all the flaming, raging red went ebbing out of her cheeks, leaving her lips with hardly blood enough left to work them.

"I went into nursing," she mumbled, "and it's God's own truth,—I went into nursing because—because I thought the uniforms were so cute."

Furiously, the instant the words were gone from her mouth, she turned and snarled at Zillah's hooting laughter.

"Well, I had to do something!" she attested. The defense was like a flat blade slapping the air.

Desperately she turned to Helene Churchill's goading, faintly supercilious smile, and her voice edged suddenly like a twisted sword. "Well, the uniforms *are* cute!" she parried. "They are! They are! I bet you there's more than one girl standing high in the graduating class to-day who never would have stuck out her first year's bossin' and slops and worry and death—if she'd had to stick it out in the unimportant looking clothes she came from home in! Even you, Helene Churchill, with all your pious talk,—the day they put your coachman's son in as new Interne and you got called down from the office for failing to stand when Mr. Young Coachman came into the room, you bawled all night,—you did,—and swore you'd chuck your whole job and go home the next day—if it wasn't that you'd just had a life-size photo taken in full nursing costume to send to your brother's chum at Yale! So there!"

With a gasp of ineffable satisfaction she turned from Helene Churchill.

"Sure the uniforms are cute!" she slashed back at Zillah Forsyth. "That's the whole trouble with 'em. They're so awfully—masqueradishly—cute! Sure, I could have got engaged to the Typhoid Boy. It would have been as easy as robbing a babe! But lots of girls, I notice, get engaged in their uniforms, feeding a patient perfectly scientifically out of his own silver spoon, who don't seem to stay engaged so especially long in their own street clothes, bungling just plain naturally with their own knives and forks! Even you, Zillah Forsyth," she hacked, "even you who trot round like the Lord's Anointed in your pure white togs, you're just as Dutchy looking as anybody else, come to put you in a red hat and a tan coat and a blue skirt!"

Mechanically she raised her hands to her head as though with some silly thought of keeping the horrid pain in her temples from slipping to her throat, her breast, her feet.

"Sure the uniforms are cute," she persisted a bit thickly. "Sure the Typhoid Boy was crazy about me! He called me his 'Holy Chorus Girl,' I heard him—raving in his sleep. Lord save us! What are we to any man but just that?" she questioned hotly with renewed venom. "Parson, actor, young sinner, old saint—I ask you frankly, girls, on your word of honor, was there ever more than one man in ten went through your hands who didn't turn out soft somewhere before you were through with him? Mawking about your 'sweet eyes' while you're wrecking your optic nerves trying to decipher the dose on a poison bottle! Mooning over your wonderful likeness to the lovely young sister they—never had! Trying to kiss your finger tips when you're struggling to brush their teeth! Teasin' you to smoke cigarettes with 'em—when they know it would cost you your job!"

Impishly, without any warning, she crooked her knee and pointed at one homely square-toed shoe in a mincy dancing step. Hoydenishly she threw out her arms and tried to gather Helene and Zillah both into their compass.

"Oh, you Holy Chorus Girls!" she chuckled with maniacal delight.

"Everybody, all together, now! Kick your little kicks! Smile your little
smiles! Tinkle your little thermometers! Steady,—there!
One—two—three—One—two—three!"

Laughingly Zillah Forsyth slipped from the grasp. "Don't you dare 'holy' me!" she threatened.

In real irritation Helene released herself. "I'm no chorus girl," she said coldly.

With a little shrill scream of pain Rae Malgregor's hands went flying back to her temples. Like a person giving orders in a great panic she turned authoritatively to her two room-mates, her fingers all the while boring frenziedly into her temples.

"Now, girls," she warned, "stand well back! If my head bursts, you know, it's going to burst all to slivers and splinters—like a boiler!"

"Rae, you're crazy!" hooted Zillah.

"Just plain vulgar—looney," faltered Helene.

Both girls reached out simultaneously to push her aside.

Somewhere in the dusty, indifferent street a bird's note rang out in one wild, delirious ecstasy of untrammeled springtime. To all intents and purposes the sound might have been the one final signal that Rae Malgregor's jangled nerves were waiting for.

"Oh, I *am* crazy, am I?" she cried with a new, fierce joy. "Oh, I *am* crazy, am I? Well, I'll go ask the Superintendent and see if I am! Oh, surely they wouldn't try and make me graduate if I really was crazy!"

Madly she bolted for her bureau, and snatching her own motto down, crumpled its face securely against her skirt and started for the door. Just what the motto was no one but herself knew. Sprawling in paint-brush hieroglyphics on a great flapping sheet of brown wrapping-paper, the sentiment, whatever it was, had been nailed face down to the wall for three tantalizing years.

"No you don't!" cried Zillah now, as she saw the mystery threatening so meanly to escape her.

"No you don't!" cried Helene. "You've seen our mottoes—and now we're going to see yours!"

Almost crazed with new terror Rae Malgregor went dodging to the right,—to the left,—to the right again,—cleared the rocking-chair,—a scuffle with padded hands,—climbed the trunk,—a race with padded feet,—reached the door-handle at last, yanked the door open, and with lungs and temper fairly bursting with momentum, shot down the hall,—down some stairs,—down some more hall,—down some more stairs, to the Superintendent's office where, with her precious motto still clutched securely in one hand, she broke upon that dignitary's startled, near-sighted vision like a young whirl-wind of linen and starch and flapping brown paper. Breathlessly, without prelude or preamble, she hurled her grievance into the older woman's grievance-dulled ears.

"Give me back my own face!" she demanded peremptorily. "Give me back my own face, I say! And my own hands! I tell you I want my own hands! Helene and Zillah say I'm insane! And I want to go home!"

CHAPTER III

Like a short-necked animal elongated suddenly to the cervical proportions of a giraffe, the Superintendent of Nurses reared up from her stoop-shouldered desk-work and stared forth in speechless astonishment across the top of her spectacles.

Exuberantly impertinent, ecstatically self-conscious, Rae Malgregor repeated her demand. To her parched mouth the very taste of her own babbling impudence refreshed her like the shock and prickle of cracked ice.

"I tell you I want my own face again! And my own hands!" she reiterated glibly. "I mean the face with the mortgage in it, and the cinders—and the other human expressions!" she explained. "And the nice grubby country hands that go with that sort of a face!"

Very accusingly she raised her finger and shook it at the Superintendent's perfectly livid countenance.

"Oh, of course I know I wasn't very much to look at. But at least I matched! What my hands knew, I mean, my face knew! Pies or plowing or May-baskets, what my hands knew my face knew! That's the way hands and faces ought to work together! But you? you with all your rules and your bossing and your everlasting 'S—sh! S—sh!' you've snubbed all the know-anything out of my face—and made my hands nothing but two disconnected machines—for somebody else to run! And I hate you! You're a Monster! You're a ——, everybody hates you!"

Mutely then she shut her eyes, bowed her head, and waited for the Superintendent to smite her dead. The smite she felt quite sure would be a noisy one. First of all, she reasoned it would fracture her skull. Naturally then of course it would splinter her spine. Later in all probability it would telescope her knee-joints. And never indeed now that she came to think of it had the arches of her feet felt less capable of resisting so terrible an impact. Quite unconsciously she groped out a little with one hand to steady herself against the edge of the desk.

But the blow when it came was nothing but a cool finger tapping her pulse.

"There! There!" crooned the Superintendent's voice with a most amazing tolerance.

"But I won't 'there—there'!" snapped Rae Malgregor. Her eyes were wide open again now, and extravagantly dilated.

The cool fingers on her pulse seemed to tighten a little. "S—sh! S—sh!" admonished the Superintendent's mumbling lips.

"But I won't 'S—sh—S—sh'!" stormed Rae Malgregor. Never before in her three years' hospital training had she seen her arch-enemy, the Superintendent, so utterly disarmed of irascible temper and arrogant dignity, and the sight perplexed and maddened her at one and the same moment. "But I won't 'S—sh—S—sh'!" Desperately she jerked her curly blonde head in the direction of the clock on the wall. "Here it's four o'clock now!" she cried. "And in less than four hours you're going to try and make me graduate—and go out into the world—God knows where—and charge innocent people twenty-five dollars a week and washing, likelier than not, mind you, for these hands," she gestured, "that don't co-ordinate at all with this face," she grimaced, "but with the face of one of the House Doctors—or the Senior Surgeon—or even you—who may be way off in Kamchatka—when I need him most!" she finished with a confused jumble of accusation and despair.

Still with unexplainable amiability the Superintendent whirled back into place in her pivot-chair and with her left hand which had all this time been rummaging busily in a lower desk drawer proffered Rae Malgregor a small fold of paper.

"Here, my dear," she said. "Here's a sedative for you. Take it at once. It will quiet you perfectly. We all know you've had very hard luck this past month, but you mustn't worry so about the future." The slightest possible tinge of purely professional manner crept back into the older woman's voice. "Certainly, Miss Malgregor, with your judgment—"

"With my judgment?" cried Rae Malgregor. The phrase was like a red rag to her. "With my judgment? Great Heavens! That's the whole trouble! I haven't got any judgment! I've never been allowed to have any judgment! All I've ever been allowed to have is the judgment of some flirty young medical student—or the House Doctor!—or the Senior Surgeon!—or you!"

Her eyes were fairly piteous with terror.

"Don't you see that my face doesn't know anything?" she faltered, "except just to smile and smile and smile and say 'Yes, sir—No, sir—Yes, sir'?" From curly blonde head to square-toed, commonsense shoes her little body began to quiver suddenly like the advent of a chill. "Oh, what am I going to do," she begged, "when I'm way off alone—somewhere—in the mountains—or a tenement—or a palace—and something happens—and there isn't any judgment round to tell me what I ought to do?"

Abruptly in the doorway as though summoned by some purely casual flicker of the Superintendent's thin fingers another nurse appeared.

"Yes, I rang," said the Superintendent. "Go and ask the Senior Surgeon if he can come to me here a moment, immediately."

"The Senior Surgeon?" gasped Rae Malgregor. "The Senior Surgeon?" With her hands clutching at her throat she reeled back against the wall for support. Like a shore bereft in one second of its tide, like a tree stripped in one second of its leafage, she stood there, utterly stricken of temper or passion or any animating human emotion whatsoever.

"Oh, now I'm going to be expelled! Oh, now I know I'm going to be—expelled!" she moaned listlessly.

Very vaguely into the farthest radiation of her vision she sensed the approach of a man. Gray-haired, gray-bearded, gray-suited, grayly dogmatic as a block of granite, the Senior Surgeon loomed up at last in the doorway.

"I'm in a hurry," he growled. "What's the matter?"

Precipitously Rae Malgregor collapsed into the breach.

"Oh, there's—nothing at all the matter, sir," she stammered. "It's only—it's only that I've just decided that I don't want to be a trained nurse."

With a gesture of ill-concealed impatience the Superintendent shrugged the absurd speech aside.

"Dr. Faber," she said, "won't you just please assure Miss Malgregor once more that the little Italian boy's death last week was in no conceivable way her fault,—that nobody blames her in the slightest, or holds her in any possible way responsible."

"Why, what nonsense!" snapped the Senior Surgeon. "What—!"

"And the Portuguese woman the week before that," interrupted Rae Malgregor dully.

"Stuff and nonsense!" said the Senior Surgeon. "It's nothing but coincidence! Pure coincidence! It might have happened to anybody!"

"And she hasn't slept for almost a fortnight." the Superintendent confided, "nor touched a drop of food or drink, as far as I can make out, except just black coffee. I've been expecting this break-down for some days."

"And-the-young-drug-store-clerk-the-week-before-that," Rae Malgregor resumed with sing-song monotony.

Brusquely the Senior Surgeon stepped forward and taking the girl by her shoulders, jerked her sharply round to the light, and, with firm, authoritative fingers, rolled one of her eyelids deftly back from its inordinately dilated pupil. Equally brusquely he turned away again.

"Nothing but moonshine!" he muttered. "Nothing in the world but too much coffee dope taken on an empty stomach,—'empty brain,' I'd better have said! When will you girls ever learn any sense?" With searchlight shrewdness his eyes flashed back for an instant over the haggard gray lines that slashed along the corners of her quivering, childish mouth. A bit temperishly he began to put on his gloves. "Next time you set out to have a 'brain-storm,' Miss Malgregor," he suggested satirically, "try to have it about something more sensible than imagining that anybody is trying to hold you personally responsible for the existence of death in the world. Bah!" he ejaculated fiercely. "If you are going to fuss like this over cases hopelessly moribund from the start, what in thunder are you going to do some fine day when out of a perfectly clear and clean sky Security itself turns septic and you lose the President of the United States—or a mother of nine children—with a hang-nail?"

"But I wasn't fussing, sir!" protested Rae Malgregor with a timid sort of dignity. "Why, it never had occurred to me for a moment that anybody blamed me for—anything!" Just from sheer astonishment her hands took a new clutch into the torn flapping corner of the motto that she still clung desperately to even at this moment.

"For Heaven's sake stop crackling that brown paper!" stormed the Senior Surgeon.

"But I wasn't crackling the brown paper, sir! It's crackling itself," persisted Rae Malgregor very softly. The great blue eyes that lifted to his were brimming full of misery. "Oh, can't I make you understand, sir?" she stammered. Appealingly she turned to the Superintendent. "Oh, can't I make anybody understand? All I was trying to say,—all I was trying to explain, was—that I *don't want to be a trained nurse—after all!*"

"Why not?" demanded the Senior Surgeon with a rather noisy click of his glove fasteners.

"Because—my—face—is—tired," said the girl quite simply.

The explosive wrath on the Senior Surgeon's countenance seemed to be directed suddenly at the Superintendent.

"Is this an afternoon tea?" he asked tartly. "With six major operations this morning and a probable meningitis diagnosis ahead of me this afternoon I think I might be spared the babblings of an hysterical nurse!" Casually over his shoulder he nodded at the girl. "You're a fool!" he said, and started for the door.

Just on the threshold he turned abruptly and looked back. His forehead was furrowed like a corduroy road and the one rampant question in his mind at the moment seemed to be mired hopelessly between his bushy eyebrows.

"Lord!" he exclaimed a bit flounderingly. "Are *you* the nurse that helped me last week on that fractured skull?"

"Yes, sir," said Rae Malgregor.

Jerkily the Senior Surgeon retraced his footsteps into the office and stood facing her as though with some really terrible accusation.

"And the freak abdominal?" he quizzed sharply. "Was it *you* who threaded that needle for me so blamed slowly—and calmly—and surely, while all the rest of us were jumping up and down and cursing you—for no brighter reason than that we couldn't have threaded it ourselves if we'd had all eternity before us and—all creation bleeding to death?"

"Y-e-s, sir," said Rae Malgregor.

Quite bluntly the Senior Surgeon reached out and lifted one of her hands to his scowling professional scrutiny.

"Gad!" he attested. "What a hand! You're a wonder! Under proper direction you're a wonder! It was like myself working with twenty fingers and no thumbs! I never saw anything like it!"

Almost boyishly the embarrassed flush mounted to his cheeks as he jerked away again. "Excuse me for not recognizing you," he apologized gruffly. "But you girls all look so much alike!"

As though the eloquence of Heaven itself had suddenly descended upon a person hitherto hopelessly tongue-tied, Rae Malgregor lifted an utterly transfigured face to the Senior Surgeon's grimly astonished gaze.

"Yes! Yes, sir!" she cried joyously. "That's just exactly what the trouble is! That's just exactly what I was trying to express, sir! My face is all worn out trying to 'look alike'! My cheeks are almost sprung with artificial smiles! My eyes are fairly bulging with unshed tears! My nose aches like a toothache trying never to turn up at anything! I'm smothered with the discipline of it! I'm choked with the affectation! I tell you—I just can't breathe through a trained nurse's face any more! I tell you, sir, I'm sick to death of being nothing but a type. I want to look like *myself*! I want to see what Life could do to a silly face like mine—if it ever got a chance! When other women are crying, I want the fun of crying! When other women look scared to death, I want the fun of looking scared to death!" Hysterically again with shrewish emphasis she began to repeat: "I won't be a nurse! I tell you, I won't! I *won't*!"

"Pray what brought you so suddenly to this remarkable decision?" scoffed the Senior Surgeon.

"A letter from my father, sir," she confided more quietly. "A letter about some dogs."

"Dogs?" hooted the Senior Surgeon.

"Yes, sir," said the White Linen Nurse. A trifle speculatively for an instant she glanced at the Superintendent's face and then back again to the Senior Surgeon's. "Yes, sir," she repeated with increasing confidence. "Up in Nova Scotia my father raises hunting-dogs. Oh, no special fancy kind, sir," she hastened in all honesty to explain. "Just dogs, you know,—just mixed dogs,—pointers with curly tails,—and shaggy-coated hounds,—and brindled spaniels, and all that sort of thing,—just mongrels, you know, but very clever; and people, sir, come all the way from Boston to buy dogs of him, and once a man came way from London to learn the secret of his training."

"Well, what is the secret of his training?" quizzed the Senior Surgeon with the sudden eager interest of a sportsman. "I should think it would be pretty hard," he acknowledged, "in a mixed gang like that to decide just which particular dog was suited to what particular game!"

"Yes, that's just it, sir," beamed the White Linen Nurse. "A dog, of course, will chase anything that runs,—that's just dog,—but when a dog really begins to *care* for what he's chasing he—wags! That's hunting! Father doesn't calculate, he says, on training a dog on anything he doesn't wag on!"

"Yes, but what's that got to do with you?" asked the Senior Surgeon a bit impatiently.

With ill-concealed dismay the White Linen Nurse stood staring blankly at the Senior Surgeon's gross stupidity.

"Why, don't you see?" she faltered. "I've been chasing this nursing job three whole years now—and there's no wag to it!"

"Oh Hell!" said the Senior Surgeon. If he hadn't said "Oh Hell!" he would have grinned. And it hadn't been a grinning day, and he certainly didn't intend to begin grinning at any such late hour as that in the afternoon. With his dignity once reassured he relaxed then a trifle. "For Heaven's sake, what *do* you want to be?" he asked not unkindly.

With an abrupt effort at self-control Rae Malgregor jerked her head into at least the outer semblance of a person lost in almost fathomless thought.

"Why I'm sure I don't know, sir," she acknowledged worriedly. "But it would be a great pity, I suppose, to waste all the grand training that's gone into my hands." With sudden conviction her limp shoulders stiffened a trifle. "My oldest sister," she stammered, "bosses the laundry in one of the big hotels in Halifax, and my youngest sister teaches school in Moncton. But I'm so strong, you know, and I like to move things round so,—and everything,—maybe—I could get a position somewhere as general housework girl."

With a roar of amusement as astonishing to himself as to his listeners, the Senior Surgeon's chin jerked suddenly upward.

"You're crazy as a loon!" he confided cordially. "Great Scott! If you can work up a condition like this on coffee,—what would you do on," he hesitated grimly, "malted milk?" As unheralded as his amusement, gross irritability overtook him again. "Will—you—stop—rattling that brown paper?" he thundered at her.

Innocently as a child she rebuffed the accusation and ignored the temper.

"But I'm not rattling it, sir!" she protested. "I'm simply trying to hide what's on the other side of it."

"What is on the other side of it?" demanded the Senior Surgeon bluntly.

With unquestioning docility the girl turned the paper around.

From behind her desk the austere Superintendent twisted her neck most informally to decipher the scrawling hieroglyphics. "*Don't—Ever—Be—bumptious*!" she read forth jerkily with a questioning, incredulous sort of emphasis.

"Don't ever be bumptious?" squinted the Senior Surgeon perplexedly through his glasses.

"Yes," said Rae Malgregor very timidly. "It's my—motto."

"Your motto?" sniffed the Superintendent.

"Your motto?" chuckled the Senior Surgeon.

"Yes, my motto," repeated Rae Malgregor with the slightest perceptible tinge of resentment. "And it's a perfectly good motto, too! Only, of course, it hasn't got any style to it. That's why I didn't want the girls to see it," she confided a bit drearily. Then palpably before their eyes they saw her spirit leap into ineffable pride. "My Father gave it to me," she announced briskly. "And my Father said that, when I came home in June, if I could honestly say that I'd never once been bumptious—all my three years here,—he'd give me a—heifer! And—"

"Well I guess you've lost your heifer!" said the Senior Surgeon bluntly.

"Lost my heifer?" gasped the girl. Big-eyed and incredulous she stood for an instant staring back and forth from the Superintendent's face to the Senior Surgeon's. "You mean?" she stammered, "you mean—that I've—been—bumptious—just now? You mean—that after all these years of—meachin' meekness—I've lost—?"

Plainly even to the Senior Surgeon and the Superintendent the bones in her knees weakened suddenly like knots of tissue paper. No power on earth could have made her break discipline by taking a chair while the Senior Surgeon stood, so she sank limply down to the floor instead, with two great solemn tears welling slowly through the fingers with which she tried vainly to cover her face.

"And the heifer was brown, with one white ear; it was awful cunning," she confided mumblingly. "And it ate from my hand—all warm and sticky, like—loving sandpaper." There was no protest in her voice, nor any whine of complaint, but merely the abject submission to Fate of one who from earliest infancy had seen other crops blighted by other frosts. Then tremulously with the air of one who, just as a matter of spiritual tidiness, would purge her soul of all sad secrets, she lifted her entrancing, tear-flushed face from her strong, sturdy, utterly unemotional fingers and stared with amazing blueness, amazing blandness into the Senior Surgeon's scowling scrutiny.

"And I'd named her—for you!" she said. "I'd named her—Patience—for you!"

Instantly then she scrambled to her knees to try and assuage by some miraculous apology the horrible shock which she read in the Senior Surgeon's face.

"Oh, of course, sir, I know it isn't scientific!" she pleaded desperately. "Oh, of course, sir, I know it isn't scientific at all! But up where I live, you know, instead of praying for anybody, we—we name a young animal—for the virtue that that person—seems to need the most. And if you tend the young animal carefully—and train it right—! Why—it's just a superstition, of course, but—Oh, sir!" she floundered hopelessly, "the virtue you needed most in your business was what I meant! Oh, really, sir, I never thought of criticizing your character!"

Gruffly the Senior Surgeon laughed. Embarrassment was in the laugh, and anger, and a fierce, fiery sort of resentment against both the embarrassment and the anger,—but no possible trace of amusement. Impatiently he glanced up at the fast speeding clock.

"Good Lord!" he exclaimed, "I'm an hour late now!" Scowling like a pirate he clicked the cover of his watch open and shut for an uncertain instant. Then suddenly he laughed again, and there was nothing whatsoever in his laugh this time except just amusement.

"See here, Miss—Bossy Tamer," he said. "If the Superintendent is willing, go get your hat and coat, and I'll take you out on that meningitis case with me. It's a thirty mile run if it's a block, and I guess if you sit on the front seat it will blow the cobwebs out of your brain—if anything will," he finished not unkindly.

Like a white hen sensing the approach of some utterly unseen danger the Superintendent seemed to bristle suddenly in every direction.

"It's a bit—irregular," she protested in her most even tone.

"Bah! So are some of the most useful of the French verbs!" snapped the Senior Surgeon. In the midst of authority his voice could be inestimably soft and reassuring, but sometimes on the brink of asserting said authority he had a tone that was distinctly unpleasant.

"Oh, very well," conceded the Superintendent with some waspishness.

Hazily for an instant Rae Malgregor stood staring into the Superintendent's uncordial face. "I'd—I'd apologize," she faltered, "but I—don't even know what I said. It just blew up!"

Perfectly coldly and perfectly civilly the Superintendent received the overture. "It was quite evident, Miss Malgregor, that you were not altogether responsible at the moment," she conceded in common justice.

Heavily then, like a person walking in her sleep the girl trailed out of the room to get her coat and hat.

Slamming one desk-drawer after another the Superintendent drowned the sluggish sound of her retreating footsteps.

"There goes my best nurse!" she said grimly. "My very best nurse! Oh no, not the most brilliant one, I didn't mean that, but the most reliable! The most nearly perfect human machine that it has ever been my privilege to see turned out,—the one girl that week in, week out, month after month, and year after year, has always done what she's told,—when she was told,—and the exact way she was told,—without questioning anything, without protesting anything, without supplementing anything with some disastrous original conviction of her own—*and look at her now*!" Tragically the Superintendent rubbed her hand across her worried brow. "Coffee, you said it was?" she asked skeptically. "Are there any special antidotes for coffee?"

With a queer little quirk to his mouth the gruff Senior Surgeon jerked his glance back from the open window where with the gleam of a slim torn-boyish ankle the frisky young Spring went scurrying through the tree-tops.

"What's that you asked?" he quizzed sharply. "Any antidotes for coffee? Yes. Dozens of them. But none for Spring."

"Spring?" sniffed the Superintendent. A little shiveringly she reached out and gathered a white knitted shawl around her shoulders. "Spring? I don't see what Spring's got to do with Rae Malgregor or any other young outlaw in my graduating class. If graduation came in November it would be just the same! They're a set of ingrates, every one of them!" Vehemently she turned aside to her card-index of names and slapped the cards through one by one without finding one single soothing exception. "Yes, sir, a set of ingrates!" she repeated accusingly. "Spend your life trying to teach them what to do and how to do it! Cram ideas into those that haven't got any, and yank ideas out of those who have got too many! Refine them, toughen them, scold them, coax them, everlastingly drill and discipline them! And then, just as you get them to a place where they move like clock-work, and you actually believe you can trust them, then graduation day comes round, and they think they're all safe,—and every single individual member of the class breaks out and runs a-muck with the one dare-devil deed she's been itching to do every day the past three years! Why this very morning I caught the President of the Senior Class with a breakfast tray in her hands—stealing the cherry out of her patient's grape fruit. And three of the girls reported for duty as bold as brass with their hair frizzed tight as a nigger doll's. And the girl who's going into a convent next week was trying on the laundryman's derby hat as I came up from lunch. And now, now—" the Superintendent's voice went suddenly a little hoarse, "and now—here's Miss Malgregor—intriguing—to get an automobile ride with—*you!*"

"Eh?" cried the Senior Surgeon with a jump. "What? Is this an Insane Asylum? Is it a Nervine?" Madly he started for the door. "Order a ton of bromides!" he called back over his shoulder. "Order a car-load of them! Saturate the whole place with them! Drown the whole damned place!"

Half way down the lower hall, all his nerves on edge, all his unwonted boyish impulsiveness quenched noxiously like a candle flame, he met and passed Rae Malgregor without a sign of recognition.

"God! How I hate women!" he kept mumbling to himself as he struggled clumsily all alone into the torn sleeve lining of his thousand dollar mink coat.

CHAPTER IV

Like a train-traveler coming out of a long, smoky, smothery tunnel Into the clean-tasting light, the White Linen Nurse came out of the prudish-smelling hospital into the riotous mud-and-posie promise of the young April afternoon.

The God of Hysteria had certainly not deserted her! In all the full effervescent reaction of her brain-storm,—fairly bubbling with dimples, fairly foaming with curls,—light-footed, light-hearted, most ecstatically light-headed, she tripped down into the sunshine as though the great, harsh, granite steps that marked her descent were nothing more nor less than a gigantic, old, horny-fingered hand passing her blithely out to some deliciously unknown Lilliputian adventure.

As she pranced across the soggy April sidewalk to what she supposed was the Senior Surgeon's perfectly empty automobile she became conscious suddenly that the rear seat of the car was already occupied.

Out from an unseasonable snuggle of sable furs and flaming red hair a small, peevish face peered forth at her with frank curiosity.

"Why, hello!" beamed the White Linen Nurse. "Who are you?"

With unmistakable hostility the haughty little face retreated into its furs and its red hair. "Hush!" commanded a shrill childish voice. "Hush, I say! I'm a cripple—and very bad-tempered. Don't speak to me!"

"Oh, my Glory!" gasped the White Linen Nurse. "Oh my Glory, Glory, Glory!" Without any warning whatsoever she felt suddenly like Nothing-At-All, rigged out in an exceedingly shabby old ulster and an excessively homely black slouch hat. In a desperate attempt at tangible tom-boyish nonchalance she tossed her head and thrust her hands down deep into her big ulster pockets. That the bleak hat reflected no decent featherish consciousness of being tossed, that the big threadbare pockets had no bottoms to them, merely completed her startled sense of having been in some way blotted right out of existence.

Behind her back the Senior Surgeon's huge fur-coated approach dawned blissfully like the thud of a rescue party.

But if the Senior Surgeon's blunt, wholesome invitation to ride had been perfectly sweet when he prescribed it for her in the Superintendent's office, the invitation had certainly soured most amazingly in the succeeding ten minutes. Abruptly now, without any greeting, he reached out and opened the rear door of the car, and nodded curtly for her to enter there.

Instantly across the face of the little crippled girl already ensconced in the tonneau a single flash of light went zig-zagging crookedly from brow to chin,—and was gone again. "Hello, Fat Father!" piped the shrill little voice. "Hello,—Fat Father!" Yet so subtly was the phrase mouthed, to save your soul you could not have proved just where the greeting ended and the taunt began.

There was nothing subtle however about the way in which the Senior Surgeon's hand shot out and slammed the tonneau door bang-bang again on its original passenger. His face was crimson with anger. Brusquely he pointed to the front seat.

"You may sit in there, with me, Miss Malgregor!" he thundered.

"Yes, sir," crooned the White Linen Nurse.

Meek as an oiled machine she scuttled to her appointed place. Once More in smothered giggle and unprotesting acquiescence she sensed the resumption of eternal discipline. Already in just this trice of time she felt her rampant young mouth resettle tamely into lines of smug, determinate serenity. Already across her idle lap she felt her clasped fingers begin to frost and tingle again like a cheerfully non-concerned bunch of live wires waiting the one authoritative signal to connect somebody,—anybody,—with this world or the next. Already the facile tip of her tongue seemed fairly loaded and cocked like a revolver with all the approximate "Yes, sirs," "No, sirs," that she thought she should probably need.

But the only immediate remarks that the Senior Surgeon addressed to any one were addressed distinctly to the crank of his automobile.

"Damn having a chauffeur who gets drunk the one day of the year when you need him most!" he muttered under his breath, as with the same exquisitely sensitive fingers that could have dissected like a caress the nervous system of a humming bird, or re-set unbruisingly the broken wing of a butterfly, he hurled his hundred and eighty pounds of infuriate brute-strength against the calm, chronic, mechanical stubbornness of that auto crank. "Damn!" he swore on the upward pull. "Damn!" he gasped on the downward push. "Damn!" he cursed and sputtered and spluttered. Purple with effort, bulging-eyed with strain, reeking with sweat, his frenzied outburst would have terrorized the entire hospital staff.

With an odd little twinge of homesickness, the White Linen Nurse slid cautiously out to the edge of her seat so that she might watch the struggle better. For thus, with dripping foreheads and knotted neck-muscles and breaking backs and rankly tempestuous language, did the untutored men-folk of her own beloved home-land hurl their great strength against bulls and boulders and refractory forest trees. Very startlingly as she watched, a brand new thought went zig-zagging through her consciousness. Was it possible,—was it even so much as remotely possible—that the great Senior Surgeon,—the great, wonderful, altogether formidable, altogether unapproachable Senior Surgeon,—was just a—was just a—? Stripped ruthlessly of all his social superiority,—of all his professional halo,—of all his scientific achievement, the Senior Surgeon stood suddenly forth before her—a mere man—just like other men! *Just exactly* like other men? Like the sick drug-clerk? Like the new-born millionaire baby? Like the doddering old Dutch gaffer? The very delicacy of such a thought drove the blood panic-stricken from her face. It was the indelicacy of the thought that brought the blood surging back again to brow, to cheeks, to lips, even to the tips of her ears.

Glancing up casually from the roar and rumble of his abruptly repentant engine the Senior Surgeon swore once more under his breath to think that any female sitting perfectly idle and non-concerned in a seven thousand dollar car should have the nerve to flaunt such a furiously strenuous color.

Bristling with resentment and mink furs he strode around the fender and stumbled with increasing irritation across the White Linen Nurse's knees to his seat. Just for an instant his famous fingers seemed to flash with apparent inconsequence towards one bit of mechanism and another. Then like a huge, portentous pill floated on smoothest syrup the car slid down the yawning street into the congested city.

Altogether monotonously in terms of pain and dirt and drug and disease the city wafted itself in and out of the White Linen Nurse's well-grooved consciousness. From every filthy street corner sodden age or starved babyhood reached out its fluttering pulse to her. Then, suddenly sweet as a draught through a fever-tainted room, the squalid city freshened into jocund, luxuriant suburbs with rollicking tennis courts, and flaming yellow forsythia blossoms, and green velvet lawns prematurely posied with pale exotic hyacinths and great scarlet splotches of lusty tulips.

Beyond this hectic horticultural outburst the leisurely Spring faded out again into April's naturally sallow colors.

Glossy and black as an endless typewriter ribbon, the narrow, tense State Road seemed to wind itself everlastingly in—and in—and in—on some hidden spool of the car's mysterious mechanism. Clickety-Click-Click-Clack,—faster than any human mind could think,—faster than any human hand could finger,—hurtling up hazardous hills of thought,—sliding down facile valleys of fancy,—roaring with emphasis,—shrieking with punctuation,—the great car yielded itself perforce to Fate's dictation.

Robbed successively of the city's humanitarian pang, of the suburb's esthetic pleasure, the White Linen Nurse found herself precipitated suddenly into a mere blur of sight, a mere chaos of sound. In whizzing speed and crashing breeze,—houses—fences—meadows—people—slapped across her eyeballs like pictures on a fan. On and on and on through kaleidoscopic yellows and rushing grays the great car sped, a purely mechanical factor in a purely mechanical landscape.

Rigid with concentration the Senior Surgeon stared like a dead man into the intrepid, on-coming road.

Intermittently from her green, plushy laprobes the little crippled girl struggled to her feet, and sprawling clumsily across whose-ever shoulder suited her best, raised a brazenly innocent voice, deliberately flatted, in a shrill and maddeningly repetitive chant of her own making, to the effect that

> All the birds were there
> With yellow feathers instead of hair,
> And bumble bees crocheted in the trees—
> And bumble bees crocheted in the trees—
> And all the birds were there—
> And—And—

Intermittently from the front seat the Senior Surgeon's wooden face relaxed to the extent of a grim mouth twisting distractedly sideways in one furious bellow.

"Will—you—stop—your—*noise*—and—go—back—to—your—seat!"

Nothing else happened at all until at last, out of unbroken stretches of winter-staled stubble, a high, formal hemlock hedge and a neat, pebbled driveway proclaimed the Senior Surgeon's ultimate destination.

Cautiously now, with an almost tender skill, the big car circled a tiny, venturesome clump of highway violets and crept through a prancing, leaping fluff of yellow collie dogs to the door of the big stone house.

Instantly from inestimable resources a liveried serving man appeared to help the Surgeon from his car; another, to take the Surgeon's coat; another, to carry his bag.

Lingering for an instant to stretch his muscles and shake his great shoulders, the Senior Surgeon breathed into his cramped lungs a friendly impulse as well as a scent of budding cherry trees.

"You may come in with me, if you want to, Miss Malgregor." he conceded. "It's an extraordinary case. You will hardly see another one like it." Palpably he lowered his already almost indistinguishable voice. "The boy is young," he confided, "about your age, I should guess, a college foot-ball hero, the most superbly perfect specimen of young manhood it has ever been my privilege to behold. It will be a long case. They have two nurses already, but would like another. The work ought not to be hard. Now if they should happen to—fancy you!" In speechless expressiveness his eyes swept estimatingly over sun-parlors, stables, garages, Italian gardens, rapturous blue-shadowed mountain views—every last intimate detail of the mansion's wonderful equipment.

Like a drowning man feeling his last floating spar wrenched away from him, the White Linen Nurse dug her finger-nails frantically into every reachable wrinkle and crevice of the heavily upholstered seat.

"Oh, but sir, I don't want to go in!" she protested passionately. "I tell you, sir, I'm quite done with all that sort of thing! It would break my heart! It would! Oh, sir, this worrying about people for whom you've got no affection,—it's like sledding without any snow! It grits right down on your naked nerves. It—"

Before the Senior Surgeon's glowering, incredulous stare her heart began to plunge and pound again, but it plunged and pounded no harder, she realized suddenly, than when in the calm, white hospital precincts she was obliged to pass his terrifying presence in the corridor and murmur an inaudible "Good Morning" or "Good Evening." "After all, he's nothing but a man—nothing but a man—nothing but a mere—ordinary—two-legged man," she reasoned over and over to herself. With a really desperate effort she smoothed her frightened face into an expression of utter guilelessness and peace and smiled unflinchingly right into the Senior Surgeon's rousing anger as she had once seen an animal-trainer smile into the snarl of a crouching tiger.

"Th—ank you very much!" she said. "But I think I won't go in, sir,—thank you! My—my face is still pretty tired!"

"Idiot!" snapped the Senior Surgeon as he turned on his heel and started up the steps.

From the green plushy robes on the back seat the White Linen Nurse could have sworn that she heard a sharply ejaculated, maliciously joyful "Ha!" piped out. But when both she and the Senior Surgeon turned sharply round to make sure, the Little Crippled Girl, in apparently complete absorption, sat amiably extracting tuft after tuft of fur from the thumb of one big sable glove, to the rumbling, sing-song monotone of "He loves me—Loves me not—Loves me—Loves me not."

Bristling with unutterable contempt for all femininity, the Senior Surgeon proceeded up the steps between two solemn-faced lackeys.

"Father!" wailed a feeble little voice. "Father!" There was no shrillness in the tone now, nor malice, nor any mischievous thing,—just desolation, the impulsive, panic-stricken desolation of a little child left suddenly alone with a stranger. "Father!" the frightened voice ventured forth a tiny bit louder. But the unheeding Senior Surgeon had already reached the piazza. "Fat Father!" screamed the little voice. Barbed now like a shark-hook the phrase ripped through the Senior Surgeon's dormant sensibilities. As one fairly yanked out of his thoughts he whirled around in his tracks.

"What do you want?" he thundered.

Helplessly the little girl sat staring from a lackey's ill-concealed grin to her Father's smoldering fury. Quite palpably she began to swallow with considerable difficulty. Then quick as a flash a diminutively crafty smile crooked across one corner of her mouth.

"Father?" she improvised dulcetly. "Father? May—may I—sit—in the White Linen Nurse's lap?"

Just for an instant the Senior Surgeon's narrowing eyes probed mercilessly into the reekingly false little smile. Then altogether brutally he shrugged his shoulders.

"I don't care where in blazes you sit!" he muttered, and went on into the house.

With an air of unalterable finality the massive oak door closed after him. In the resonant click of its latch the great wrought-iron lock seemed to smack its lips with ineffable satisfaction.

Wringing suddenly round with a whish of starched skirts the White Linen Nurse knelt up in her seat and grinned at the Little Crippled Girl.

"'Ha'—yourself!" she said.

Against all possible expectancy the Little Crippled Girl burst out laughing. The laugh was wild, ecstatic, extravagantly boisterous, yet awkward withal, and indescribably bumpy, like the first flight of a cage-cramped bird.

Quite abruptly the White Linen Nurse sat down again, and commenced nervously with the wrist of her chamois glove to polish the slightly tarnished brass lamp at her elbow. Equally abruptly after a minute she stopped polishing and looked back at the Little Crippled Girl.

"Would—you—like—to sit in my lap?" she queried conscientiously.

Insolent with astonishment the Little Girl parried the question. "Why in blazes—should I want to sit in your lap?" she quizzed harshly. Every accent of her voice, every remotest intonation, was like the Senior Surgeon's at his worst. The suddenly forked eyebrow, the snarling twitch of the upper lip, turned the whole delicate little face into a grotesque but desperately unconscious caricature of the grim-jawed father.

As though the father himself had snubbed her for some unimaginable familiarity the White Linen Nurse winced back in hopeless confusion. Just for sheer shock, short-circuited with fatigue, a big tear rolled slowly down one pink cheek.

Instantly to the edge of her seat the Little Girl jerked herself forward. "Don't cry, Pretty!" she whispered. "Don't cry! It's my legs. I've got fat iron braces on my legs. And people don't like to hold me!"

Half the professional smile came flashing back to the White Linen Nurse's mouth.

"Oh, I just adore holding people with iron braces on their legs," she affirmed, and, leaning over the back of the seat, proceeded with absolutely perfect mechanical tenderness to gather the poor, puny, surprised little body into her own strong, shapely arms. Then dutifully snuggling her shoulder to meet the stubborn little shoulder that refused to snuggle, to it, and dutifully easing her knees to suit the stubborn little knees that refused to be eased, she settled down resignedly in her seat again to await the return of the Senior Surgeon. "There! There! There!" she began quite instinctively to croon and pat.

"Don't say 'There! There!'" wailed the Little Girl peevishly. Her body was suddenly stiff as a ram-rod. "Don't say 'There! There!' If you've got to make any noise at all, say 'Here! Here!'"

"Here! Here!" droned the White Linen Nurse. "Here! Here! Here! Here!" On and on and interminably on, "Here! Here! Here! Here!"

At the end of about the three-hundred-and-forty-seventh "Here!" the Little Girl's body relaxed, and she reached up two fragile fingers to close the White Linen Nurse's mouth. "There! That will do," she sighed contentedly. "I feel better now. Father does tire me so."

"Father tires—*you*?" gasped the White Linen Nurse. The giggle that followed the gasp was not in the remotest degree professional. "Father tires *you*?" she repeated accusingly. "Why, you silly Little Girl! Can't you see it's you that makes Father so everlastingly tired?" Impulsively with her one free hand she turned the Little Girl's listless face to the light. "What makes you call your nice father 'Fat Father'?" she asked with real curiosity. "What makes you? He isn't fat at all. He's just big. Why, what ever possesses you to call him 'Fat Father,' I say? Can't you see how mad it makes him?"

"Why, of course it made him mad!" said the Little Girl with plainly reviving interest. Thrilled with astonishment at the White Linen Nurse's apparent stupidity she straightened up perkily with inordinately sparkling eyes. "Why, of course it makes him mad!" she explained briskly. "That's why I do it! Why, my Parpa—never even looks at me—unless I make him mad!"

"S—sh!" said the White Linen Nurse. "Why, you mustn't ever say a thing like that! Why, your Marma wouldn't like you to say a thing like that!"

Jerking bumpily back against the White Linen Nurse's unprepared shoulder the Little Girl prodded a pallid finger-tip into the White Linen Nurse's vivid cheek. "Silly—Pink and White—Nursie!" she chuckled, "Don't you know there *isn't* any Marma?" Cackling with delight over her own superior knowledge she folded her little arms and began to rock herself convulsively to and fro.

"Why, stop!" cried the White Linen Nurse. "Now you stop! Why, you wicked little creature laughing like that about your poor dead mother! Why, just think how bad it would make your poor Parpa feel!"

With instant sobriety the Little Girl stopped rocking, and stared perplexedly into the White Linen Nurse's shocked eyes. Her own little face was all wrinkled up with earnestness.

"But the Parpa—didn't like the Marma!" she explained painstakingly. "The Parpa—*never* liked the Marma! That's why he doesn't like me! I heard Cook telling the Ice Man once when I wasn't more than ten minutes old!"

Desperately with one straining hand the White Linen Nurse stretched her fingers across the Little Girl's babbling mouth. Equally desperately, with the other hand, she sought to divert the Little Girl's mind by pushing the fur cap back from her frizzly red hair, and loosening her sumptuous coat, and jerking down vainly across two painfully obtrusive white ruffles, the awkwardly short, hideously bright little purple dress.

"I think your cap is too hot," she began casually, and then proceeded with increasing vivacity and conviction to the objects that worried her most. "And those—those ruffles," she protested, "they don't look a bit nice being so long!" Resentfully she rubbed an edge of the purple dress between her fingers. "And a little girl like you,—with such bright red hair,—oughtn't to wear—purple!" she admonished with real concern.

"Now whites and blues—and little soft pussy-cat grays—"

Mumblingly through her finger-muzzled mouth the Little Girl burst into explanations again.

"Oh, but when I wear gray," she persisted, "the Parpa—never sees me! But when I wear purple he cares,—he cares—most awfully!" she boasted with a bitter sort of triumph. "Why when I wear purple and frizz my hair hard enough,—no matter who's there, or anything,—he'll stop right off short in the middle of whatever he's doing—and rear right up so perfectly beautiful and mad and glorious—and holler right out 'For Heaven's sake, take that colored Sunday supplement away!'"

"Your Father's nervous," suggested the White Linen Nurse.

Almost tenderly the Little Girl reached up and drew the White Linen Nurse's ear close down to her own snuggling lips.

"Damned nervous!" she confided laconically.

Quite against all intention the White Linen Nurse giggled. Floundering to recover her dignity she plunged into a new error. "Poor little dev—," she began.

"Yes," sighed the Little Girl complacently. "That's just what the Parpa calls me." Fervidly she clasped her little hands together. "Yes, if I can only make him mad enough daytimes," she asserted, "then at night when he thinks I'm all asleep he comes and stands by my cribby-house like a great black shadow-bear and shakes and shakes his most beautiful head and says, 'Poor little devil—poor little devil.' Oh, if I can only make him mad enough daytimes!" she cried out ecstatically.

"Why, you naughty little thing!" scolded the White Linen Nurse with an unmistakable catch in her voice. "Why, you—naughty—naughty—little thing!"

Like the brush of a butterfly's wing the child's hand grazed the White Linen Nurse's cheek. "I'm a lonely little thing," she confided wistfully. "Oh, I'm an awfully lonely little thing!" With really shocking abruptness the old malicious smile came twittering back to her mouth. "But I'll get even with the Parpa yet!" she threatened joyously, reaching out with pliant fingers to count the buttons on the White Linen Nurse's dress. "Oh, I'll get even with the Parpa yet!" In the midst of the passionate assertion her rigid little mouth relaxed in a most mild and innocent yawn.

"Oh, of course," she yawned, "on wash days and ironing days and every other work day in the week he has to be away cutting up people 'cause that's his lawful business. But Sundays, when he doesn't really need to at all, he goes off to some kind of a green, grassy club—all day long—and plays golf."

Very palpably her eyelids began to droop. "Where was I?" she asked sharply. "Oh, yes, 'the green, grassy club.' Well, when I die," she faltered, "I'm going to die specially on some Sunday when there's a big golf game,—so he'll just naturally have to give it up and stay home and—amuse me—and help arrange the flowers. The Parpa's crazy about flowers. So am I," she added broodingly. "I raised almost a geranium once. But the Parpa threw it out. It was a good geranium, too. All it did was just to drip the tiniest-teeniest bit over a book and a writing and somebody's brains in a dish. He threw it at a cat. It was a good cat, too. All it did was to—"

A little jerkily her drooping head bobbed forward and then back again. Her heavy eyes were almost tight shut by this time, and after a moment's silence her lips began moving dumbly like one at silent devotions. "I'm making a little poem, now," she confided at last. "It's about—you and me. It's a sort of a little prayer." Very, very softly she began to repeat.

> Now I sit me down to nap
> All curled up in a Nursie's lap,
> If *she* should die before I wake—

Abruptly she stopped and stared up suspiciously into the White Linen Nurse's eyes. "Ha!" she mocked, "you thought I was going to say 'If I should die before I wake,'—didn't you? *Well, I'm not!*"

"It would have been more generous," acknowledged the White Linen Nurse.

Very stiffly the Little Girl pursed her lips. "It's plenty generous enough—when it's all done!" she said severely. "And I'll thank you,—Miss Malgregor,—not to interrupt me again!" With excessive deliberateness she went back to the first line of her poem and began all over again,

> Now I sit me down to nap,
> All curled up in a Nursie's lap,
> If *she* should die before I wake,
> Give her—give her ten cents—for Jesus' sake!

"Why that's a—a cunning little prayer," yawned the White Linen Nurse. Most certainly of course she would have smiled if the yawn hadn't caught her first. But now in the middle of the yawn it was a great deal easier to repeat the "very cunning" than to force her lips into any new expression. "Very cunning—very cunning," she kept crooning conscientiously.

Modestly like some other successful authors the Little Girl flapped her eyelids languidly open and shut for three or four times before she acknowledged the compliment. "Oh, cunning as any of 'em," she admitted off-handishly. Only once again did she open either mouth or eyes, and this time it was merely one eye and half a mouth. "Do my fat iron braces—hurt you?" she mumbled drowsily.

"Yes, a little," conceded the White Linen Nurse.

"Ha! They hurt me—all the time!" gibed the Little Girl.

Five minutes later, the child who didn't particularly care about being held, and the girl who didn't particularly care about holding her, were fast asleep in each other's arms,—a naughty, nagging, restive little hornet all hushed up and a-dream in the heart of a pink wild-rose!

Stalking out of the house in his own due time the Senior Surgeon reared back aghast at the sight.

"Well—I'll be hanged!" he muttered. "Most everlastingly hanged! Wonder what they think this is? A somnolent kindergarten show? Talk about fiddling while Rome burns!"

Awkwardly, on the top step, he struggled alone into his cumbersome coat. Every tingling nerve in his body, every shuddering sensibility, was racked to its utmost capacity over the distressing scenes he had left behind him in the big house. Back in that luxuriant sickroom, Youth Incarnate lay stripped, root, branch, leaf, bud, blossom, fruit, of All its manhood's promise. Back in that erudite library, Culture Personified, robbed of all its fine philosophy, sat babbling illiterate street-curses into its quivering hands. Back in that exquisite pink and gold boudoir, Blonded Fashion, ravished for once of all its artistry, ran stumbling round and round in interminable circles like a disheveled hag. In shrill crescendos and discordant basses, with heartpiercing jaggedness, with blood-curdling raspishness, each one, boy, father, mother, meddlesome relative, competent or incompetent assistant, indiscriminate servant, filing his separate sorrow into the Senior Surgeon's tortured ears!

With one of those sudden revulsions to materialism which is liable to overwhelm any man who delves too long at a time in the brutally unconventional issues of life and death, the Senior Surgeon stepped down into the subtle, hyacinth-scented sunshine with every latent human greed in his body clamoring for expression—before it, too, should be hurtled into oblivion. "Eat, you fool, and drink, you fool, and be merry,—you fool,—for to-morrow—*even you,—Lendicott R. Faber—may have to die*!" brawled and re-brawled through his mind like a ribald phonograph tune.

At the edge of the bottom step a precipitous lilac branch that must have budded and bloomed in a single hour smote him stingingly across his cheek. "Laggard!" taunted the lilac branch.

With the first crunching grit of gravel under his feet, something transcendently naked and unashamed that was neither Brazen Sorrow nor Brazen Pain thrilled across his startled consciousness. Over the rolling, marshy meadow, beyond the succulent willow-hedge that hid the winding river, up from some fluent, slim canoe, out from a chorus of virile young tenor voices, a little passionate Love Song—divinely tender—most incomparably innocent—came stealing palpitantly forth into that inflammable Spring world without a single vestige of accompaniment on it!

Kiss me, Sweet, the Spring is here,
And Love is Lord of you and me,
There's no bird in brake or brere,
But to his little mate sings he,
"Kiss me, Sweet, the Spring is here
And Love is Lord of you—and me!"

Wrenched like a sob out of his own lost youth the Senior Surgeon's faltering college memories took up the old refrain.

As I go singing, to my dear,
"Kiss me, Sweet, the Spring is here,
And Love is Lord of you and me!"

Just for an instant a dozen long-forgotten pictures lanced themselves poignantly into his brain,—dingy, uncontrovertible old recitation rooms where young ideas flashed bright and futile as parade swords,—elm-shaded slopes where lithe young bodies lolled on green velvet grasses to expound their harshest cynicisms! Book-history, book-science, book-economics, book-love,—all the paper passion of all the paper poets swaggering imperiously on boyish lips that would have died a thousand bashful deaths before the threatening imminence of a real girl's kiss! Magic days, with Youth the one glittering, positive treasure on the Tree of Life—and Woman still a mystery!

"Woman a mystery?" Harshly the phrase ripped through the Senior Surgeon's brain. Croakingly in that instant all the grim gray scientific years re-overtook him, swamped him, strangled him. "Woman a *mystery*? Oh ye Gods! And Youth? Bah! Youth,—a mere tinsel tinkle on a rotting Christmas tree!"

Furiously with renewed venom he turned and threw his weight again upon the stubbornly resistant crank of his automobile.

Vaguely disturbed by the noise and vibration the White Linen Nurse opened her big, drowsy, blue eyes upon him.

"Don't—jerk—it—so!" she admonished hazily, "You'll wake the Little Girl!"

"Well, what about my convenience, I'd like to know?" snapped the Senior Surgeon in some astonishment.

Heavily the White Linen Nurse's lashes shadowed down again across her sleep-flushed cheeks.

"Oh, never mind—about—that," she mumbled non-concernedly.

"Oh, for Heaven's sake—wake up there!" bellowed the Senior Surgeon above the sudden roar of his engine.

Adroitly for a man of his bulk he ran around the radiator and jumped into his seat. Joggled unmercifully into wakefulness, the Little Girl greeted his return with a generous if distinctly non-tactful demonstration of affection. Grabbing the unwitting fingers of his momentarily free hand she tapped them proudly against the White Linen Nurse's plump pink cheek.

"See! I call her 'Peach'!" she boasted joyously with all the triumphant air of one who felt assured that mental discrimination such as this could not possibly fail to impress even a person so naturally obtuse as—a father.

"Don't be foolish!" snarled the Senior Surgeon.

"Who? Me?" gasped the White Linen Nurse in a perfect agony of confusion.

"Yes! You!" snapped the Senior Surgeon explosively half an hour later after interminable miles of absolute silence—and dingy yellow field-stubble—and bare brown alder bushes.

Truly out of the ascetic habit of his daily life, "where no rain was," as the Bible would put it, it did seem to him distinctly foolish, not to say careless, not to say out and out incendiary, for any girl to go blushing her way like a fire-brand through a world so palpably populated by young men whose heads were tow, and hearts indisputably tinder, rather than tender.

"Yes! You!" he reasserted vehemently at the end of another silent mile.

Then plainly begrudging this second inexcusable interruption of his most vital musings concerning Spinal Meningitis he scowled his way savagely back again into his own grimly established trend of thought.

Excited by so much perfectly good silence that nobody seemed to be using the Little Crippled Girl ventured gallantly forth once more into the hazardous conversational land of grown-ups.

"Father?" she experimented cautiously with most commendable discretion.

Fathoms deep in abstraction the Senior Surgeon stared unheeding into the whizzing black road. Pulses and temperatures and blood-pressures were seething in his mind; and sharp sticks and jagged stones and the general possibilities of a puncture; and murmurs of the heart and râles of the lungs; and a most unaccountable knock-knock-knocking in the engine; and the probable relation of middle-ear disease; and the perfectly positive symptoms of optic neuritis; and a damned funny squeak in the steering gear!

"Father?" the Little Girl persisted valiantly.

To add to his original concentration the Senior Surgeon's linen collar began to chafe him maddeningly under his chin. The annoyance added two scowls to his already blackly furrowed face, and at least ten miles an hour to his running time; but nothing whatsoever to his conversational ability.

"Father!" the Little Girl whimpered with faltering courage. Then panic-stricken, as wiser people have been before her, over the dreadful spookish remoteness of a perfectly normal human being who refuses either to answer or even to notice your wildest efforts at communication, she raised her waspish voice in its shrillest, harshest war-cry. "Fat Father! *Fat Father! F-a-t F-a-t-h-e-r!*" she screeched out frenziedly at the top of her lungs.

The gun-shot agony of a wounded rabbit was in the cry, the last gurgling gasp of strangulation under a murderer's reeking fingers,—catastrophe unspeakable,—disaster now irrevocable!

Clamping down his brakes with a wrench that almost tore the insides out of his engine the Senior Surgeon brought the great car to a staggering standstill.

"What is it?" he cried in real terror. "What is it?"

Limply the Little Girl stretched down from the White Linen Nurse's lap till she could nick her toe against the shiniest woodwork in sight. Altogether aimlessly her small chin began to burrow deeper and deeper into her big fur collar.

"For Heaven's sake, what do you want?" demanded the Senior Surgeon. Even yet along his spine the little nerves crinkled with shock and apprehension. "For Heaven's sake what do you want?"

Helplessly the child lifted her turbid eyes to his. With unmistakable appeal her tiny hand went clutching out at one of the big buttons on his coat. Desperately for an instant she rummaged through her brain for some remotely adequate answer to this most thunderous question,—and then retreated precipitously as usual to the sacristy of her own imagination.

"All the birds *were* there, Father!" she confided guilelessly. "All the birds *were* there,—with yellow feathers instead of hair! And bumblebees—crocheted in the trees. And—"

Short of complete annihilation there was no satisfying vengeance whatsoever that the Senior Surgeon's exploding passion could wreak upon his offspring. Complete annihilation being unfeasible at the moment he merely climbed laboriously out of the car, re-cranked the engine, climbed laboriously back into his place and started on his way once more. All the red blustering rage was stripped completely from him. Startlingly rigid, startlingly white, his face was like the death-mask of a pirate.

Pleasantly excited by she-didn't-know-exactly-what, the Little Girl resumed her beloved falsetto chant, rhythmically all the while with her puny iron-braced legs beating the tune into the White Linen Nurse's tender flesh.

All the birds were there
With yellow feathers instead of hair,
And bumblebees crocheted in the trees
And—and—all the birds were there,
With yellow feathers instead of hair,
And—

Frenziedly as a runaway horse trying to escape from its own pursuing harness and carriage the Senior Surgeon poured increasing speed into both his own pace and the pace of his tormentor. Up hill,—down dale,—screeching through rocky echoes,—swishing through blue-green spruce-lands,—dodging indomitable boulders,—grazing lax, treacherous embankments,—the great car scuttled homeward. Huddled behind his steering wheel like a warrior behind his shield, every body-muscle taut with strain, every facial muscle diabolically calm, the Senior Surgeon met and parried successively each fresh onslaught of yard, rod, mile.

Then suddenly in the first precipitous descent of a mighty hill the whole earth seemed to drop out from under the car. Down-down-down with incredible swiftness and smoothness the great machine went diving towards abysmal space! Up-up-up with incredible bumps and bouncings, trees, bushes, stonewalls went rushing to the sky!

Gasping surprisedly towards the Senior Surgeon the White Linen Nurse saw his grim mouth yank round abruptly in her direction as it yanked sometimes in the operating-room with some sharp, incisive order of life or death. Instinctively she leaned forward for the message.

Not over-loud but strangely distinct the words slapped back into her straining ears.

"If—it will rest your face any—to look scared—by all means—do so! I've lost control of the machine!" called the Senior Surgeon sardonically across the roar of the wind.

The phrase excited the White Linen Nurse but it did not remotely frighten her. She was not in the habit of seeing the Senior Surgeon lose control of any situation. Merely intoxicated with speed, delirious with ozone, she snatched up the Little Girl close, to her breast.

"We're flying!" she cried. "We're dropping from a parachute! We're—!"

Swoopingly like a sled striking glare, level ice the great car swerved from the bottom of the hill into a soft rolling meadow. Instantly from every conceivable direction, like foes in ambush, trees, stumps, rocks reared up in threatening defiance.

Tighter and tighter the White Linen Nurse crushed the Little Girl to her breast. Louder and louder she called in the Little Girl's ear.

"*Scream!*" she shouted. *"There might be a bump! Scream louder than a bump! Scream! Scream! Scream!"*

In that first over-whelming, nerve-numbing, heart-crunching terror of his whole life as the great car tilted up against a stone,—plowed down into the mushy edge of a marsh,—and skidded completely round, *crash-bang*—into a tree, it was the last sound that the Senior Surgeon heard,—the sound of a woman and child screeching their lungs out in diabolical exultancy!

CHAPTER V

When the White Linen Nurse found anything again she found herself lying perfectly flat on her back in a reasonably comfortable nest of grass and leaves. Staring inquisitively up into the sky she thought she noticed a slight black and blue discoloration towards the west, but more than that, much to her relief, the firmament did not seem to be seriously injured. The earth, she feared had not escaped so easily. Even way off somewhere near the tip of her fingers the ground was as sore—as sore—as could be—under her touch. Impulsively to her dizzy eyes the hot tears started, to think that now, tired as she was, she should have to jump right up in another minute or two and attend to the poor earth. Fortunately for any really strenuous emergency that might arise there seemed to be nothing about her own body that hurt at all except a queer, persistent little pain in her cheek. Not until the Little Crippled Girl's dirt-smouched face intervened between her own staring eyes and the sky did she realize that the pain in her cheek was a pinch.

"Wake up! Wake up!" scolded the Little Crippled Girl shrilly. "Naughty—Pink and White Nursie! I wanted to hear the bump! You screamed so loud I couldn't hear the bump!"

With excessive caution the White Linen Nurse struggled up at last to a sitting posture, and gazed perplexedly around her.

It seemed to be a perfectly pleasant field,—acres and acres of mild old grass tottering palsiedly down to watch some skittish young violets and bluets frolic in and out of a giggling brook. Up the field? Up the field? Hazily the White Linen Nurse ground her knuckles into her incredulous eyes. Up the field, just beyond them, the great empty automobile stood amiably at rest. From the general appearance of the stone-wall at the top of the little grassy slope it was palpably evident that the car had attempted certain vain acrobatic feats before its failing momentum had forced it into the humiliating ranks of the back-sliders.

Still grinding her knuckles into her eyes the White Linen Nurse turned back to the Little Girl. Under the torn, twisted sable cap one little eye was hidden completely, but the other eye loomed up rakish and bruised as a prizefighter's. One sable sleeve was wrenched disastrously from its arm-hole, and along the edge of the vivid little purple skirt the ill-favored white ruffles seemed to have raveled out into hopeless yards and yards and yards of Hamburg embroidery.

A trifle self-consciously the Little Girl began to gather herself together.

"We—we seem to have fallen out of something!" she confided with the air of one who halves a most precious secret.

"Yes, I know," said the White Linen Nurse. "But what has become of—your Father?"

Worriedly for an instant the Little Girl sat scanning the remotest corners of the field. Then abruptly with a gasp of real relief she began to explore with cautious fingers the geographical outline of her black eye.

"Oh, never mind about Father," she asserted cheerfully. "I guess—I guess he got mad and went home."

"Yes—I know," mused the White Linen Nurse. "But it doesn't seem—probable."

"Probable?" mocked the Little Girl most disagreeably. Then suddenly her little hand went shooting out towards the stranded automobile.

"Why, there he is!" she screamed. "Under the car! Oh, Look—Look—Lookey!"

Laboriously the White Linen Nurse scrambled to her knees. Desperately she tried to ram her fingers like a clog into the whirling dizziness round her temples.

"Oh, my God! Oh, my God! What's the dose for anybody under a car?" she babbled idiotically.

Then with a really herculean effort,—both mental and physical, she staggered to her feet, and started for the automobile.

But her knees gave out, and wilting down to the grass she tried to crawl along on all-fours, till straining wrists sent her back to her feet again.

Whenever she tried to walk the Little Girl walked,—whenever she tried to crawl the Little Girl crawled.

"Isn't it fun!" the shrill childish voice piped persistently. "Isn't it just like playing ship-wreck!"

When they reached the car both woman and child were too utterly exhausted with breathlessness to do anything except just sit down on the ground and—stare.

Sure enough under that monstrous, immovable looking machine the Senior Surgeon's body lay rammed face-down deep, deep into the grass.

It was the Little Girl who recovered her breath first.

"I think he's dead!" she volunteered sagely. "His legs look—awfully dead—to me!" Only excitement was in the statement. It took a second or two for her little mind to make any particularly personal application of such excitement. "I hadn't—exactly—planned—on having him dead!" she began with imperious resentment. A threat of complete emotional collapse zig-zagged suddenly across her face. "I won't have him dead! I won't! I *won't*!" she screamed out stormily.

In the amazing silence that ensued the White Linen Nurse gathered her trembling knees up into the circle of her arms and sat there staring at the Senior Surgeon's prostrate body, and rocking herself feebly to and fro in a futile effort to collect her scattered senses.

"Oh, if some one would only tell me what to do,—I know I could do it! Oh, I know I could do it! If some one would only tell me what to do!" she kept repeating helplessly.

Cautiously the Little Girl crept forward on her hands and knees to the edge of the car and peered speculatively through the great yellow wheel-spokes. "Father!" she faltered in almost inaudible gentleness. "Father!" she pleaded in perfectly impotent whisper.

Impetuously the White Linen Nurse scrambled to her own hands and knees and jostled the Little Girl aside.

"Fat Father!" screamed the White Linen Nurse. "Fat Father! Fat Father! *Fat Father!*" she gibed and taunted with the one call she knew that had never yet failed to rouse him.

Perceptibly across the Senior Surgeon's horridly quiet shoulders a little twitch wrinkled and was gone again.

"Oh, his heart!" gasped the White Linen Nurse. "I must find his heart!"

Throwing herself prone upon the cool meadowy ground and frantically reaching out under the running board of the car to her full arm's length she began to rummage awkwardly hither and yon beneath the heavy weight of the man in the desperate hope of feeling a heart-beat.

"Ouch! You tickle me!" spluttered the Senior Surgeon weakly.

Rolling back quickly with fright and relief the White Linen Nurse burst forth into one maddening cackle of hysterical laughter. "Ha! Ha! Ha!" she giggled. "Hi! Hi! Titter! Titter! Titter!"

Perplexedly at first but with increasing abandon the Little Girl's voice took up the same idiotic refrain. "Ha-Ha-Ha," she choked. And "Hi-Hi-Hi!" And "Titter! Titter! Titter!"

With an agonizing jerk of his neck the Senior Surgeon rooted his mud-gagged mouth a half inch further towards free and spontaneous speech. Very laboriously, very painstakingly, he spat out one by one two stones and a wisp of ground pine and a brackish, prickly tickle of stale golden-rod.

"Blankety-blank-blank—BLANK!" he announced in due time, "Blankety-blank-blank-blank—BLANK! Maybe when you two—blankety-blank—imbeciles have got through your blankety-blank cackling you'll have the—blankety-blank decency to save my—my blankety-blank-blank—blank—*blank-blank* life!"

"Ha! Ha! Ha!" persisted the poor helpless White Linen Nurse with the tears streaming down her cheeks.

"Hi! Hi! Hi!" snickered the poor Little Girl through her hiccoughs.

Feeling hopelessly crushed under two tons and a half of car, the Senior Surgeon closed his eyes for death. No man of his weight, he felt quite sure, could reasonably expect to survive many minutes longer the apoplectic, blood-red rage that pounded in his ear-drums. Through his tight-closed eyelids very, very slowly a red glow seemed to permeate. He thought it was the fires of Hell. Opening his eyes to meet his fate like a man he found himself staring impudently close instead into the White Linen Nurse's furiously flushed face that lay cuddled on one plump cheek staring impudently close at him.

"Why—why—get out!" gasped the Senior Surgeon.

Very modestly the White Linen Nurse's face retreated a little further into its blushes.

"Yes, I know," she protested. "But I'm all through giggling now. I'm sorry—I'm—"

In sheer apprehensiveness the Senior Surgeon's features crinkled wincingly from brow to chin as though struggling vainly to retreat from the appalling proximity of the girl's face.

"Your—eyelashes—are too long," he complained querulously.

"Eh?" jerked the White Linen Nurse's face. "Is it your brain that's hurt? Oh, sir, do you think it's your brain that's hurt?"

"It's my stomach!" snapped the Senior Surgeon. "I tell you I 'm not hurt,—I'm just—squashed! I'm paralyzed! If I can't get this car off me—"

"Yes, that's just it," beamed the White Linen Nurse's face. "That's just what I crawled in here to find out,—how to get the car off you. That's just what I want to find out. I could run for help, of course,—only I couldn't run, 'cause my knees are so wobbly. It would take hours—and the car might start or burn up or something while I was gone. But you don't seem to be caught anywhere on the machinery," she added more brightly, "it only seems to be sitting on you. So if I could only get the car off you! But it's so heavy. I had no idea it would be so heavy. Could I take it apart, do you think? Is there any one place where I could begin at the beginning and take it all apart?"

"Take it apart—Hell!" groaned the Senior Surgeon.

A little twitch of defiance flickered across the White Linen Nurse's face. "All the same," she asserted stubbornly, "if some one would only tell me what to do—I know I could do it!"

Horridly from some unlocatable quarter of the engine an alarming little tremor quickened suddenly and was hushed again.

"Get out of here—quick!" stormed the Senior Surgeon's ghastly face.

"I won't!" said the White Linen Nurse's face. "Until you tell me—what to do!"

Brutally for an instant the ingenuous blue eyes and the cynical gray eyes battled each other.

"*Can* you do what you're told?" faltered the Senior Surgeon.

"Oh, yes," said the White Linen Nurse.

"I mean can you do exactly—what you're told?" gasped the Senior Surgeon. "Can you follow directions, I mean? Can you follow them—explicitly? Or are you one of those people who listens only to her own judgment?"

"Oh, but I haven't got any—judgment," protested the White Linen Nurse.

Palpably in the Senior Surgeon's blood-shot eyes the leisurely seeming diagnosis leaped to precipitous conclusions.

"Then get out of here—quick—for God's sake—and get to work!" he ordered.

Cautiously the White Linen Nurse jerked herself back into freedom and crawled around and stared at the Senior Surgeon through the wheel-spokes again. Like one worrying out some intricate mathematical problem his mental strain was pulsing visibly through his closed eyelids.

"Yes, sir?" prodded the White Linen Nurse.

"Keep still!" snapped the Senior Surgeon. "I've got to think," he said. "I've got to work it out! All in a moment you've got to learn to run the car. All in a moment! It's awful!"

"Oh, I don't mind, sir," affirmed the White Linen Nurse serenely.

Frenziedly the Senior Surgeon rooted one cheek into the mud again. "You don't—*mind*?" he groaned. "You don't—*mind*? Why, you've got to learn—everything! Everything—from—the very beginning!"

"Oh, that's all right, sir," crooned the White Linen Nurse.

Ominously from somewhere a horrid sound creaked again. The Senior Surgeon did not stop to argue any further.

"Now come here," ordered the Senior Surgeon. "I'm going to—I'm going to—" Startlingly his voice weakened,—trailed off into nothingness,—and rallied suddenly with exaggerated bruskness. "Look here now! For Heaven's sake use your brains! I'm going to dictate to you—very slowly—one thing at a time—just what to do!"

Quite astonishingly the White Linen Nurse sank down on her knees and began to grin at him. "Oh, no, sir," she said. "I couldn't do it that way,—not 'one thing at a time.' Oh, no indeed, sir! No!" Absolute finality was in her voice,—the inviolable stubbornness of the perfectly good-natured person.

"You'll do it the way I tell you to!" roared the Senior Surgeon struggling vainly to ease one shoulder or stretch one knee-joint.

"Oh, no, sir," beamed the White Linen Nurse. "Not one thing at a time! Oh, no, I couldn't do it that way! Oh, no, sir, I won't do it that way—one thing at a time," she persisted hurriedly. "Why, you might faint away or something might happen—right in the middle of it—right between one direction and another—and I wouldn't know at all—what to turn on or off next—and it might take off one of your legs, you know, or an arm. Oh, no,—not one thing at a time!"

"Good-by—then," croaked the Senior Surgeon. "I'm as good as dead now." A single shudder went through him,—a last futile effort to stretch himself.

"Good-by," said the White Linen Nurse. "Good-by, sir.—I'd heaps rather have you die—perfectly whole—like that—of your own accord—than have me run the risk of starting the car full-tilt and chopping you up so—or dragging you off so—that you didn't find it convenient to tell me—how to stop the car."

"You're a—a—a—" spluttered the Senior Surgeon indistinguishably.

"Crinkle-crackle," went that mysterious, horrid sound from somewhere in the machinery.

"Oh my God!" surrendered the Senior Surgeon. "Do it your own—damned way! Only—only—" His voice cracked raspingly.

"Steady! Steady there!" said the White Linen Nurse. Except for a sudden odd pucker at the end of her nose her expression was still perfectly serene. "Now begin at the beginning," she begged. "Quick! Tell me everything—just the way I must do it! Quick—quick—quick!"

Twice the Senior Surgeon's lips opened and shut with a vain effort to comply with her request.

"But you can't do it," he began all over again. "It isn't possible. You haven't got the mind!"

"Maybe I haven't," said the White Linen Nurse. "But I've got the memory. Hurry!"

"Creak," said the funny little something in the machinery.

"Creak—drip—bubble!"

"Oh, get in there quick!" surrendered the Senior Surgeon. "Sit down behind the wheel!" he shouted after her flying footsteps. "Are you there? For God's sake—are you there? Do you see those two little levers where your right hand comes? For God's sake—don't you know what a lever is? Quick now! Do just what I tell you!"

A little jerkily then, but very clearly, very concisely, the Senior Surgeon called out to the White Linen Nurse just how every lever, every pedal should be manipulated to start the car!

Absolutely accurately, absolutely indelibly the White Linen Nurse visualized each separate detail in her abnormally retentive mind!

"But you can't—possibly remember it!" groaned the Senior Surgeon. "You can't—possibly! And probably the damn car's *bust* and won't start—anyway—and—!" Abruptly the speech ended in a guttural snarl of despair.

"Don't be a—blight!" screamed the White Linen Nurse. "I've never forgotten anything yet, sir!"

Very tensely she straightened up suddenly in her seat. Her expression was no longer even remotely pleasant. Along her sensitive, fluctuant nostrils the casual crinkle of distaste and suspicion had deepened suddenly into sheer dilating terror.

"Left foot—press down—hard—left pedal!" she began to sing-song to herself.

"No! *Right* foot!—*right* foot!" corrected the Little Girl blunderingly from somewhere close in the grass.

"Inside lever—pull—way—back!" persisted the White Linen Nurse resolutely as she switched on the current.

"No! *Outside* lever! *Outside! Outside!*" contradicted the Little Girl.

"Shut your darned mouth!" screeched the White Linen Nurse, her hand on the throttle as she tried the self starter.

Bruised as he was, wretched, desperately endangered there under the car the Senior Surgeon could almost have grinned at the girl's terse, unconscious mimicry of his own most venomous tones.

Then with all the forty-eight lusty, ebullient years of his life snatched from his lips like an untasted cup, and one single noxious, death-flavored second urged,—forced,—crammed down his choking throat, he felt the great car quicken and start.

"God!" said the Senior Surgeon. Just "God!" The God of mud, he meant! The God of brackish grass! The God of a man lying still hopeful under more than two tons' weight of unaccountable mechanism, with a novice in full command.

Up in her crimson leather cushions, free-lunged, free-limbed, the White Linen Nurse heard the smothered cry. Clear above the whirr of wheels, the whizz of clogs, the one word sizzled like a red-hot poker across her chattering consciousness. Tingling through the grasp of her fingers on the vibrating wheel, stinging through the sole of her foot that hovered over the throbbing clutch, she sensed the agonized appeal. "Short lever—spark—long lever—gas!" she persisted resolutely. "It must be right! It must!"

Jerkily then, and blatantly unskilfully, with riotous puffs and spinning of wheels, the great car started,—faltered,—balked a bit,—then dragged crushingly across the Senior Surgeon's flattened body, and with a great wanton burst of speed tore down the sloping meadow into the brook—rods away. Clamping down the brakes with a wrench and a racket like the smash of a machine-shop the White Linen Nurse jumped out into the brook, and with one wild terrified glance behind her staggered back up the long grassy slope to the Senior Surgeon.

Mechanically through her wooden-feeling lips she forced the greeting that sounded most cheerful to her. "It's not much fun, sir,—running an auto," she gasped. "I don't believe I'd like it!"

Half propped up on one elbow,—still dizzy with mental chaos, still paralyzed with physical inertia,—the Senior Surgeon lay staring blankly all around him. Indifferently for an instant his stare included the White Linen Nurse. Then glowering suddenly at something way beyond her, his face went perfectly livid.

"Good God! The—the car's on fire!" he mumbled.

"Yes, sir," said the White Linen Nurse. "Why! Didn't you know it, sir?"

CHAPTER VI

Headlong the Senior Surgeon pitched over on the grass,—his last vestige of self-control stripped from him,—horror unspeakable racking him sobbingly from head to toe.

Whimperingly the Little Girl came crawling to him, and settling down close at his feet began with her tiny lace handkerchief to make futile dabs at the mud-stains on his gray silk stockings. "Never mind, Father," she coaxed, "we'll get you clean sometime."

Nervously the White Linen Nurse bethought her of the brook. "Oh, wait a minute, sir—and I'll get you a drink of water!" she pleaded.

Bruskly the Senior Surgeon's hand jerked out and grabbed at her skirt.

"Don't leave me!" he begged. "For God's sake—don't leave me!"

Weakly he struggled up again and sat staring piteously at the blazing car. His unrelinquished clutch on the White Linen Nurse's skirt brought her sinking softly down beside him like a collapsed balloon. Together they sat and watched the gaseous yellow flames shoot up into the sky.

"It's pretty, isn't it?" piped the Little Girl.

"Eh?" groaned the Senior Surgeon.

"Father," persisted the shrill little voice. "Father,—do people ever burn up?"

"*Eh?*" gasped the Senior Surgeon. Brutally the harsh, shuddering sobs began to rack and tear again through his great chest.

"There! There!" crooned the White Linen Nurse, struggling desperately to her knees. "Let me get—everybody—a drink of water."

Again the Senior Surgeon's unrelinquished clutch on her skirt jerked her back to the place beside him.

"I said *not to leave me!*" he snapped out as roughly as he jerked.

Before the affrighted look in the White Linen Nurse's face a sheepish, mirthless grin flickered across one corner of his mouth.

"Lord! But I'm shaken!" he apologized. "Me—of all people!" Painfully the red blood mounted to his cheeks. "Me—of all people!" Bluntly he forced the White Linen Nurse's reluctant gaze to meet his own. "Only yesterday," he persisted, "I did a laparotomy on a man who had only one chance in a hundred of pulling through—and I—I scolded him for fighting off his ether cone,—scolded him—I tell you!"

"Yes, I know," soothed the White Linen Nurse. "But—"

"But *nothing!*" growled the Senior Surgeon. "The fear of death? Bah! All my life I've scoffed at it! *Die*? Yes, of course,—when you have to,—but with no kick coming! Why, I've been wrecked in a typhoon in the Gulf of Mexico. And I didn't care! And I've lain for nine days more dead than alive in an Asiatic cholera camp. And I didn't care! And I've been locked into my office three hours with a raving maniac and a dynamite bomb. And I didn't care! And twice in a Pennsylvania mine disaster I've been the first man down the shaft. And I didn't care! And I've been shot, I tell you,—and I've been horse-trampled,—and I've been wolf-bitten. And I've never cared! But to-day—to-day—" Piteously all the pride and vigor wilted from his great shoulders, leaving him all huddled up like a woman, with his head on his knees. "But to-day, I've *got mine!*" he acknowledged brokenly.

Once again the White Linen Nurse tried to rise. "Oh, please, sir, let me get you a—drink of water," she suggested helplessly.

"I said *not to leave me!*" jerked the Senior Surgeon.

Perplexedly with big staring eyes the Little Crippled Girl glanced up at this strange fatherish person who sounded so suddenly small and scared like herself. Jealous instantly of her own prerogatives she dropped her futile labors on the mud-stained silk stockings and scrambled precipitously for the White Linen Nurse's lap where she nestled down finally after many gyrations, and sat glowering forth at all possible interlopers.

"Don't leave any of us!" she ordered with a peremptoriness not unmixed with supplication.

"Surely some one will see the fire and come and get us," conceded the Senior Surgeon.

"Yes—surely," mused the White Linen Nurse. Just at that moment she was mostly concerned with adjusting the curve of her shoulder to the curve of the Little Girl's head. "I could sit more comfortably," she suggested to the Senior Surgeon, "if you'd let go my skirt."

"Let go of your skirt? Who's touching your skirt?" gasped the Senior

Surgeon incredulously. Once again the blood mounted darkly to his face.

"I think I'll get up—and walk around a bit," he confided coldly.

"Do, sir," said the White Linen Nurse.

Ouchily with a tweak of pain through his sprained back the Senior Surgeon sat suddenly down again. "I sha'n't get up till I'm good and ready!" he attested.

"I wouldn't, sir," said the White Linen Nurse.

Very slowly, very complacently, all the while she kept right on renovating the Little Girl's personal appearance, smoothing a wrinkled stocking, tucking up obstreperous white ruffles, tugging down parsimonious purple hems, loosening a pinchy hook, tightening a wobbly button. Very slowly, very complacently the Little Girl drowsed off to sleep with her weazened little iron-cased legs stretched stiffly out before her. "Poor little legs! Poor little legs! Poor little legs!" crooned the White Linen Nurse.

"I don't know—as you need to—make a song about it!" winced the Senior Surgeon. "It's just about the crudest case of complete muscular atrophy that I've ever seen!"

Blandly the White Linen Nurse lifted her big blue eyes to his. "It wasn't her 'complete muscular atrophy' that I was thinking about!" she said. "It's her panties that are so unbecoming!"

"Eh?" jumped the Senior Surgeon.

"Poor little legs—poor little legs—poor little legs," resumed the White Linen Nurse droningly.

Very slowly, very complacently, all around them April kept right on—being April.

Very slowly, very complacently, all around them the grass kept On growing, and the trees kept right on budding. Very slowly, very complacently, all around them the blue sky kept right on fading into its early evening dove-colors.

Nothing brisk, nothing breathless, nothing even remotely hurried was there in all the landscape except just the brook,—and the flash of a bird,—and the blaze of the crackling automobile.

The White Linen Nurse's nostrils were smooth and calm with the lovely sappy scent of rabbit-nibbled maple bark and mud-wet arbutus buds. The White Linen Nurse's mind was full of sumptuous, succulent marsh marigolds, and fluffy white shad-bush blossoms.

The Senior Surgeon's nostrils were all puckered up with the stench of burning varnish. The Senior Surgeon's mind was full of the horrid thought that he'd forgotten to renew his automobile fire-insurance,—and that he had a sprained back,—and that his rival colleague had told him he didn't know how to run an auto anyway—and that the cook had given notice that morning,—and that he had a sprained back,—and that the moths had gnawed the knees out of his new dress suit,—and that the Superintendent of Nurses had had the audacity to send him a bunch of pink roses for his birthday,—and that the boiler in the kitchen leaked,—and that he had to go to Philadelphia the next day to read a paper on "Surgical Methods at the Battle of Waterloo,"—and he hadn't even begun the paper yet,—and that he had a sprained back,—and that the wall-paper on his library hung in shreds and tatters waiting for him to decide between a French fresco effect and an early English paneling,—and that his little daughter was growing up in wanton ugliness under the care of coarse, indifferent hirelings,—and that the laundry robbed him weekly of at least five socks,—and that it would cost him fully seven thousand dollars to replace this car,—and that he had a sprained back!

"It's restful, isn't it?" cooed the White Linen Nurse.

"Isn't *what* restful?" glowered the Senior Surgeon.

"Sitting down!" said the White Linen Nurse.

Contemptuously the Senior Surgeon's mind ignored the interruption and reverted precipitously to its own immediate problem concerning the gloomy, black-walnut shadowed entrance hall of his great house, and how many yards of imported linoleum at $3.45 a yard it would take to recarpet the "damned hole,"—and how it would have seemed anyway if—if he hadn't gone home—as usual to the horrid black-walnut shadows that night—but been carried home instead—feet first and—quite dead—dead, mind you, with a red necktie on,—and even the cook was out! And they wouldn't even know where to lay him—but might put him by mistake in that—in that—in his dead wife's dead—bed!

Altogether unconsciously a little fluttering sigh of ineffable contentment escaped the White Linen Nurse.

"I don't care how long we have to sit here and wait for help," she announced cheerfully, "because to-morrow, of course, I'll have to get up and begin all over again—and go to Nova Scotia."

"Go *where*?" lurched the Senior Surgeon.

"I'd thank you kindly, sir, not to jerk my skirt quite so hard!" said the White Linen Nurse just a trifle stiffly.

Incredulously once more the Senior Surgeon withdrew his detaining hand. "I'm not even touching your skirt!" he denied desperately. Nothing but denial and reiterated denial seemed to ease his self-esteem for an instant. "Why, for Heaven's sake, should I want to hold on to your skirt?" he demanded peremptorily. "What the deuce—?" he began blusteringly. "Why in—?"

Then abruptly he stopped and shot an odd, puzzled glance at the White Linen Nurse, and right there before her startled eyes she saw every vestige of human expression fade out of his face as it faded out sometimes in the operating-room when in the midst of some ghastly, unforeseen emergency that left all his assistants blinking helplessly around them, his whole wonderful scientific mind seemed to break up like some chemical compound into all its meek component parts,—only to reorganize itself suddenly with some amazing explosive action that fairly knocked the breath out of all on-lookers—but was pretty apt to knock the breath into the body of the person most concerned.

When the Senior Surgeon's scientific mind had reorganized itself to meet *this* emergency he found himself infinitely more surprised at the particular type of explosion that had taken place than any other person could possibly have been.

"Miss Malgregor!" he gasped. "Speaking of preferring 'domestic service,' as you call it,—speaking of preferring domestic service to—nursing,—how would you like to consider—to consider a position of—of—well,—call it a—a position of general—heartwork—for a family of two? Myself and the Little Girl here being the 'two,'—as you understand," he added briskly.

"Why, I think it would be grand!" beamed the White Linen Nurse.

A trifle mockingly the Senior Surgeon bowed his appreciation. "Your frank and immediate—enthusiasm," he murmured, "is more, perhaps, than I had dared to expect."

"But it would be grand!" said the White Linen Nurse. Before the odd little smile in the Senior Surgeon's eyes her white forehead puckered all up with perplexity. Then with her mind still thoroughly unawakened, her heart began suddenly to pitch and lurch like a frightened horse whose rider has not even remotely sensed as yet the approach of an unwonted footfall. "What—did—you—say?" she repeated worriedly. "Just exactly what was it that you said? I guess—maybe—I didn't understand just exactly what it was that you said."

The smile in the Senior Surgeon's eyes deepened a little. "I asked you," he said, "how you would like to consider a position of 'general heartwork' in a family of two,—myself and the Little Girl here being the 'two.' 'Heartwork' was what I said. Yes,—'Heartwork,'—not housework!"

"*Heartwork?*" faltered the White Linen Nurse. " *Heartwork?* I don't know what you mean, sir." Like two falling rose-petals her eyelids fluttered down across her affrighted eyes. "Oh, when I shut my eyes, sir, and just hear your voice, I know of course, sir, that it's some sort of a joke. But when I look right at you—I—don't know—what it is!"

"Open your eyes and keep them open then till you do find out!" suggested the Senior Surgeon bluntly.

Defiantly once again the blue eyes and the gray eyes challenged each other.

"'Heartwork' was what I said," persisted the Senior Surgeon. Palpably his narrowing eyes shut out all meaning but one definite one.

The White Linen Nurse's face went almost as blanched as her dress.

"You're—you're not asking me to—marry you, sir?" she stammered.

"I suppose I am!" acknowledged the Senior Surgeon.

"Not marry you!" cried the White Linen Nurse. Distress was in her voice,—distaste,—unmitigated shock, as though the high gods themselves had fallen at her feet and splintered off into mere candy fragments.

"Oh—not *marry* you, sir?" she kept right on protesting. "Not be—*engaged*, you mean? Oh, not be *engaged*—and everything?"

"Well, why not?" snapped the Senior Surgeon.

Like a smitten flower the girl's whole body seemed to wilt down into incalculable weariness.

"Oh—no—no! I couldn't!" she protested. "Oh, no,—really!" Appealingly she lifted her great blue eyes to his, and the blueness was all blurred with tears. "I've—I've been engaged—once—you know," she explained falteringly. "Why—I was engaged, sir, almost as soon as I was born, and I stayed engaged till two years ago. That's almost twenty years. That's a long time, sir. You don't get over it—easy." Very, very gravely she began to shake her head. "Oh—no—sir! No! Thank you—very much—but I—I just simply couldn't begin at the beginning and go all through it again! I haven't got the heart for it! I haven't got the spirit! Carvin' your initials on trees and—and gadding round to all the Sunday school picnics—"

Brutally like a boy the Senior Surgeon threw back his head in one wild hoot of joy. Infinitely more cautiously as the agonizing pang in his shoulder lulled down again he proceeded to argue the matter, but the grin in his face was even yet faintly traceable.

"Frankly, Miss Malgregor," he affirmed, "I'm infinitely more addicted to carving people than to carving trees. And as to Sunday school picnics? Well, really now—I hardly believe that you'd find my demands in that direction—excessive!"

Perplexedly the White Linen Nurse tried to stare her way through his bantering smile to his real meaning. Furiously, as she stared, the red blood came flushing back into her face.

"You don't mean for a second that you—that you love me?" she asked incredulously.

"No, I don't suppose I do!" acknowledged the Senior Surgeon with equal bluntness. "But my little kiddie here loves you!" he hastened somewhat nervously to affirm. "Oh, I'm almost sure that my little kiddie here—loves you! She needs you anyway! Let it go at that! Call it that we both—need you!"

"What you mean is—" corrected the White Linen Nurse, "that needing somebody—very badly, you've just suddenly decided that that somebody might as well be me?"

"Well—if you choose to put it—like that!" said the Senior Surgeon a bit sulkily.

"And if there hadn't been an auto accident?" argued the White Linen Nurse just out of sheer inquisitiveness, "if there hadn't been just this particular kind of an auto accident—at this particular hour—of this particular day—of this particular month—with marigolds and—everything, you probably never would have realized that you did need anybody?"

"Maybe not," admitted the Senior Surgeon.

"U—m—m," said the White Linen Nurse. "And if you'd happened to take one of the other girls to-day—instead of me,—why then I suppose you'd have felt that she was the one you really needed? And if you'd taken the Superintendent of Nurses—instead of any of us girls—you might even have felt that *she* was the one you most needed?"

With surprising agility for a man with a sprained back the Senior
Surgeon wrenched himself around until he faced her quite squarely.

"Now see here, Miss Malgregor!" he growled. "For Heaven's sake listen to sense, even if you can't talk it! Here am I, a plain professional man—making you a plain professional offer. Why in thunder should you try to fuss me all up because my offer isn't couched in all the foolish, romantic, lace-paper sort of flub-dubbery that you think such an offer ought to be couched in? Eh?"

"Fuss you all up, sir?" protested the White Linen Nurse with real anxiety.

"Yes—fuss me all up!" snarled the Senior Surgeon with increasing venom. "I'm no story-writer! I'm not trying to make up what might have happened a year from next February in a Chinese junk off the coast of—Nova Zembla—to a Methodist preacher—and a—and a militant suffragette! What I'm trying to size up is—just what's happened to you and me—to-day! For the fact remains that it is to-day! And it is you and I! And there has been an accident! And out of that accident—and everything that's gone with it—I have come out—thinking of something that I never thought of before! And there were marigolds!" he added with unexpected whimsicality. "You see I don't deny—even the marigolds!"

"Yes, sir," said the White Linen Nurse.

"Yes what?" jerked the Senior Surgeon.

Softly the White Linen Nurse's chin burrowed down a little closer against the sleeping child's tangled hair. "Why—yes—thank you very much—but I never shall love again," she said quite definitely.

"Love?" gasped the Senior Surgeon. "Why, I'm not asking you to love me!"

His face was suddenly crimson. "Why, I'd hate it, if you—loved me! Why,
I'd—"

"O—h—h," mumbled the White Linen Nurse in new embarrassment. Then suddenly and surprisingly her chin came tilting bravely up again. "What do you want?" she asked.

Helplessly the Senior Surgeon threw out his hands. "My goodness!" he said. "What do you suppose I want? *I want some one to take care of us!*"

Gently the White Linen Nurse shifted her shoulder to accommodate the shifting little sleepyhead on her breast.

"You can hire some one for that," she suggested with real relief.

"I was trying to hire—you!" said the Senior Surgeon quite tersely.

"Hire me?" gasped the White Linen Nurse. "Why! Why!"

Adroitly she slipped both hands under the sleeping child and delivered the little frail-fleshed, heavily ironed body into the Senior Surgeon's astonished arms.

"I—I don't want to hold her," he protested.

"She—isn't mine!" argued the White Linen Nurse.

"But I can't talk while I'm holding her!" insisted the Senior Surgeon.

"I can't listen—while I'm holding her!" persisted the White Linen Nurse.

Freely now, though cross-legged like a Turk, she jerked herself forward on the grass and sat probing up into the Senior Surgeon's face like an excited puppy trying to solve whether the gift in your up-raised hand is a lump of sugar—or a live coal.

"You're trying to hire—*me*?" she prompted him nudgingly with her voice. "Hire me—for money?"

"Oh my Lord, no!" said the Senior Surgeon. "There are plenty of people I can hire for money! But they won't stay!" he explained ruefully. "Hang it all,—they won't stay!" Above his little girl's white, pinched face his own ruddy countenance furrowed suddenly with unspeakable anxiety.

"Why, just this last year," he complained, "we've had nine different housekeepers—and thirteen nursery governesses!" Skilfully as a surgeon, but awkwardly as a father, he bent to re-adjust the weight of the little iron leg-braces. "But I tell you—no one will stay with us!" he finished hotly. "There's—something the matter—with us! I don't seem to have money enough in the world to make anybody—stay with us!"

Very wryly, very reluctantly, at one corner of his mouth his sense of humor ignited in a feeble grin.

"So you see what I'm trying to do to you, Miss Malgregor, is to—hire you with something that will just—naturally compel you to stay!"

If the grin round his mouth strengthened a trifle, so did the anxiety in his eyes.

"For Heaven's sake, Miss Malgregor," he pleaded. "Here's a man and a house and a child all going to—rack and ruin! If you're really and truly tired of nursing—and are looking for a new job,—what's the matter with tackling us?"

"It would be a job!" admitted the White Linen Nurse demurely.

"Why, it would be a deuce-of-a-job!" confided the Senior Surgeon with no demureness whatsoever.

CHAPTER VII

Very soberly, very thoughtfully then, across the tangled, snuggling head of his own and another woman's child, he urged the torments—and the comforts of his home upon this second woman.

"What is there about my offer—that you don't like?" he demanded earnestly. "Is it the whole idea that offends you? Or just the way I put it? 'General Heartwork for a Family of Two?' What is the matter with that? Seems a bit cold to you, does it, for a real marriage proposal? Or is it that it's just a bit too ardent, perhaps, for a mere plain business proposition?"

"Yes, sir," said the White Linen Nurse.

"Yes what?" insisted the Senior Surgeon.

"Yes—*sir*," flushed the White Linen Nurse.

Very meditatively the Senior Surgeon reconsidered his phrasing. "'General Heartwork for a Family of Two'? U—m—m." Quite abruptly even the tenseness of his manner faded from him, leaving his face astonishingly quiet, astonishingly gentle. "But how else, Miss Malgregor," he queried, "How else should a widower with a child proffer marriage to a—to a young girl like yourself? Even under conditions directly antipodal to ours, such a proposition can never be a purely romantic one. Yet even under conditions as cold and business-like as ours, there's got to be some vestige of affection in it,—some vestige at least of the *intelligence* of affection,—else what gain is there for my little girl and me over the purely mercenary domestic service that has racked us up to this time with its garish faithlessness?"

"Yes, sir," said the White Linen Nurse.

"But even if I had loved you, Miss Malgregor," explained the Senior Surgeon gravely, "my offer of marriage to you would not, I fear, have been a very great oratorical success. Materialist as I am,—cynic—scientist,—any harsh thing you choose to call me,—marriage in some freak, boyish corner of my mind, still defines itself as being the mutual sharing of a—mutually original experience. Certainly whether a first marriage be instigated in love or worldliness,—whether it eventually proves itself bliss, tragedy, or mere sickening ennui, to two people coming mutually virgin to the consummation of that marriage, the thrill of establishing publicly a man-and-woman home together is an emotion that cannot be reduplicated while life lasts."

"Yes, sir," said the White Linen Nurse.

Bleakly across the Senior Surgeon's face something gray that was not years shadowed suddenly and was gone again.

"Even so, Miss Malgregor," he argued, "even so—without any glittering romance whatsoever, no woman I believe is very grossly unhappy in any—affectional place—that she knows distinctly to be her *own* place. It's pretty much up to a man then I think,—though it tear him brain from heart, to explain to a second wife quite definitely just exactly what place it is that he is offering her in his love,—or his friendship,—or his mere desperate need. No woman can ever hope to step successfully into a second-hand home who does not know from her man's own lips the measure of her predecessor. The respect we owe the dead is a selfish thing compared to the mercy we owe the living. In my own case—"

Unconsciously the White Linen Nurse's lax shoulders quickened, and the sudden upward tilt of her chin was as frankly interrogative as a French inflection. "Yes, sir," she said.

"In my own case," said the Senior Surgeon bluntly, "in my own case, Miss Malgregor, it is no more than fair to tell you that I—did not love my wife. And my wife did not love me." Only the muscular twitch in his throat betrayed the torture that the confession cost him. "The details of that marriage are unnecessary," he continued with equal bluntness. "It is enough perhaps to say that she was the daughter of an eminent surgeon with whom I was exceedingly anxious at that time to be allied, and that our mating, urged along on both sides as it was by strong personal ambitions was one of those so-called 'marriages of convenience' which almost invariably turn out to be marriages of such dire inconvenience to the two people most concerned. For one year we lived together in a chaos of experimental acquaintanceship. For two years we lived together in increasing uncongeniality and distaste. For three years we lived together in open and acknowledged enmity. At the last, I am thankful to remember, that we had one year together again that was at least an—armed truce."

Darkly the gray shadow and the red flush chased each other once more across the man's haggard face.

"I had a theory," he said, "that possibly a child might bridge the chasm between us. My wife refuted the theory, but submitted herself reluctantly to the fact. And when she—in giving birth to—my theory,—the shock, the remorse, the regret, the merciless self-analysis that I underwent at that time almost convinced me that the whole miserable failure of our marriage lay entirely on my own shoulders." Like the stress of mid-summer the tears of sweat started suddenly on his forehead. "But I am a fair man, I hope,—even to myself, and the cooler, less-tortured judgment of the subsequent years has practically assured me that, for types as diametrically opposed as ours, such a thing as mutual happiness never could have existed."

Mechanically he bent down and smoothed a tickly lock of hair away from the little girl's eyelids.

"And the child is the living physical image of her," he stammered. "The violent hair,—the ghost-white skin,—the facile mouth,—the arrogant eyes,—staring—staring—maddeningly reproachful, persistently accusing. My own stubborn will,—my own hideous temper,—all my own ill-favored mannerisms—mocked back at me eternally in her mother's—unloved features." Mirthless as the grin of a skull, the Senior Surgeon's mouth twisted up a little at one corner. "Maybe I could have borne it better if she'd been a boy," he acknowledged grimly. "But to see all your virile—masculine vices come back at you—so sissified—in *skirts*!"

"Yes, sir," said the White Linen Nurse.

With an unmistakable gasp of relief the Senior Surgeon expanded his great chest.

"There! That's done!" he said tersely. "So much for the Past! Now for the Present! Look at us pretty keenly and judge for yourself! A man and a very little girl,—not guaranteed,—not even recommended,—offered merely 'As Is' in the honest trade-phrase of the day,—offered frankly in an open package,—accepted frankly,—if at all—'at your own risk.' Not for an instant would I try to deceive you about us! Look at us closely, I ask, and—decide for yourself! I am forty-eight years old. I am inexcusably bad-tempered,—very quick to anger, and not, I fear, of great mercy. I am moody. I am selfish. I am most distinctly unsocial. But I am not, I believe, stingy,—nor ever intentionally unfair. My child is a cripple,—and equally bad-tempered as myself. No one but a mercenary has ever coped with her. And she shows it. We have lived alone for six years. All of our clothes, and most of our ways, need mending. I am not one to mince matters, Miss Malgregor, nor has your training, I trust, made you one from whom truths must be veiled. I am a man with all a man's needs,—mental, moral, physical. My child is a child with all a child's needs,—mental, moral, physical. Our house of life is full of cobwebs. The rooms of affection have long been closed. There will be a great deal of work to do! And it is not my intention, you see, that you should misunderstand in any conceivable way either the exact nature or the exact amount of work and worry involved. I should not want you to come to me afterwards with a whine, as other workers do, and say 'Oh, but I didn't know you would expect me to do *this*! Oh, but I hadn't any idea you would want me to do *that*! And I certainly don't see why you should expect me to give up my Thursday afternoon just because you, yourself, happened to fall down stairs in the morning and break your back!'"

Across the Senior Surgeon's face a real smile lightened suddenly.

"Really, Miss Malgregor," he affirmed, "I'm afraid there isn't much of anything that you won't be expected to do! And as to your 'Thursdays out'? Ha! If you have ever yet found a way to temper the wind of your obligations to the shorn lamb of your pleasures, you have discovered something that I myself have never yet succeeded in discovering! And as to 'wages'? Yes! I want to talk everything quite frankly! In addition to my average yearly earnings,—which are by no means small,—I have a reasonably large private fortune. Within normal limits there is no luxury I think that you cannot hope to have. Also, exclusive of the independent income which I would like to settle upon you, I should be very glad to finance for you any reasonable dreams that you may cherish concerning your family in Nova Scotia. Also,—though the offer looks small and unimportant to you now, it is liable to loom pretty large to you later,—also, I will personally guarantee to you—at some time every year, an unfettered, perfectly independent two months' holiday. So the offer stands,—my 'name and fame,'—if those mean anything to you,—financial independence,—an assured 'breathing spell' for at least two months out of twelve,—and at last but not least,—my eternal gratitude! 'General Heartwork for a Family of Two'! *There!* Have I made the task perfectly clear to you? Not everything to be done all at once, you know. But immediately where necessity urges it,—gradually as confidence inspires it,—ultimately if affection justifies it,—every womanish thing that needs to be done in a man's and a child's neglected lives? Do you understand?"

"Yes, sir," said the White Linen Nurse.

"Oh, and there's one thing more," confided the Senior Surgeon. "It's something, of course, that I ought to have told you the very first thing of all!" Nervously he glanced down at the sleeping child, and lowered his voice to a mumbling monotone. "As regards my actual morals you have naturally a right to know that I've led a pretty decent sort of life,—though I probably don't deserve any special credit for that. A man who knows enough to be a doctor isn't particularly apt to lead any other kind. Frankly,—as women rate vices I believe I have only one. What—what—I'm trying to tell you—now—is about that one." A little defiantly as to chin, a little appealingly as to eye, he emptied his heart of its last tragic secret. "Through all the male line of my family, Miss Malgregor, dipsomania runs rampant. Two of my brothers, my father, my grandfather, my great grandfather before him, have all gone down as the temperance people would say into 'drunkards' graves.' In my own case, I have chosen to compromise with the evil. Such a choice, believe me, has not been made carelessly or impulsively, but out of the agony and humiliation of—several less successful methods." Hard as a rock, his face grooved into its granite-like furrows again. "Naturally, under these existing conditions," he warned her almost threateningly, "I am not peculiarly susceptible to the mawkishly ignorant and sentimental protests of—people whose strongest passions are an appetite for—chocolate candy! For eleven months of the year," he hurried on a bit huskily, "for eleven months of the year,—eleven months,—each day reeking from dawn to dark with the driving, nerve-wracking, heart-wringing work that falls to my profession, I lead an absolutely abstemious life, touching neither wine nor liquor, nor even indeed tea or coffee. In the twelfth month,—June always,—I go way, way up into Canada,—way, way off in the woods to a little log camp I own there,—with an Indian who has guided me thus for eighteen years. And live like a—wild man for four gorgeous, care-free, trail-tramping, salmon-fighting,—whisky-guzzling weeks. It is what your temperance friends would call a—'spree.' To be quite frank, I suppose it is what—anybody would call a 'spree.' Then the first of July,—three or four days past the first of July perhaps,—I come out of the woods—quite tame again. A little emotionally nervous, perhaps,—a little temperishly irritable,—a little unduly sensitive about being greeted as a returned jail-bird,—but most miraculously purged of all morbid craving for liquor, and with every digital muscle as coolly steady as yours, and every conscious mental process clamoring cleanly for its own work again."

Furtively under his glowering brows he stopped and searched the White Linen Nurse's imperturbable face. "It's an—established custom, you understand," he rewarned her. "I'm not advocating it, you understand,—I'm not defending it. I'm simply calling your attention to the fact that it is an established custom. If you decide to come to us, I—I couldn't, you know, at forty-eight—begin all over again to—to have some one waiting for me on the top step the first of July to tell me—what a low beast I am—till I go down the steps again—the following June."

"No, of course not," conceded the White Linen Nurse. Blandly she lifted her lovely eyes to his. "Father's like that!" she confided amiably. "Once a year,—just Easter Sunday only,—he always buys him a brand new suit of clothes and goes to church. And it does something to him,—I don't know exactly what, but Easter afternoon he always gets drunk,—oh mad, fighting drunk is what I mean, and goes out and tries to tear up the whole county." Worriedly two black thoughts puckered between her eyebrows. "And always," she said, "he makes Mother and me go up to Halifax beforehand to pick out the suit for him. It's pretty hard sometimes," she said, "to find anything dressy enough for the morning, that's serviceable enough for the afternoon."

"Eh?" jerked the Senior Surgeon. Then suddenly he began to smile again like a stormy sky from which the last cloud has just been cleared. "Well, it's all right then, is it? You'll take us?" he asked brightly.

"Oh, no!" said the White Linen Nurse. "Oh, no, sir! Oh, no indeed, sir!" Quite perceptibly she jerked her way backward a little on the grass. "Thank you very much!" she persisted courteously. "It's been very interesting! I thank you very much for telling me, but—"

"But what?" snapped the Senior Surgeon.

"But it's too quick," said the White Linen Nurse. "No man could tell like that—just between one eye-wink and another what he wanted about anything,—let alone marrying a perfect stranger."

Instantly the Senior Surgeon bridled. "I assure you, my dear young lady," he retorted, "that I am entirely and completely accustomed to deciding between 'one wink and another' just exactly what it is that I want. Indeed, I assure you that there are a good many people living to-day who wouldn't be living, if it had taken me even as long as a wink and three-quarters to make up my mind!"

"Yes, I know, sir," acknowledged the White Linen Nurse. "Yes, of course, sir," she acquiesced with most commendable humility. "But all the same, sir, I couldn't do it!" she persisted with inflexible positiveness. "Why, I haven't enough education," she confessed quite shamelessly.

"You had enough, I notice, to get into the hospital," drawled the Senior Surgeon a bit grumpily. "And that's quite as much as most people have, I assure you! 'A High School education or its equivalent,'—that is the hospital requirement, I believe?" he questioned tartly.

"'A High School education or its—equivocation' is what we girls call it," confessed the White Linen Nurse demurely. "But even so, sir," she pleaded, "it isn't just my lack of education! It's my brains! I tell you, sir, I haven't got enough brains to do what you suggest!"

"I don't mean at all to belittle your brains," grinned the Senior Surgeon in spite of himself. "Oh, not at all, Miss Malgregor! But you see it isn't especially brains that I'm looking for! Really what I need most," he acknowledged frankly, "is an extra pair of hands to go with the—brains I already possess!"

"Yes, I know, sir," persisted the White Linen Nurse. "Yes, of course, sir," she conceded. "Yes, of course, sir, my hands work—awfully—well—with your face. But all the same," she kindled suddenly, "all the same, sir, I can't! I won't! I tell you sir, I won't! Why, I'm not in your world, sir! Why, I'm not in your class! Why—my folks aren't like your folks! Oh, we're just as good as you—of course—but we aren't as nice! Oh, we're not nice at all! Really and truly we're not!" Desperately through her mind she rummaged up and down for some one conclusive fact that would close this torturing argument for all time. "Why—my father—eats with his knife," she asserted triumphantly.

"Would he be apt to eat with mine?" asked the Senior Surgeon with extravagant gravity.

Precipitously the White Linen Nurse jumped to the defense of her father's intrinsic honor. "Oh, no!" she denied with some vehemence. "Father's never cheeky like that! Father's simple sometimes,—plain, I mean. Or he might be a bit sharp. But, oh, I'm sure he'd never be—cheeky! Oh, no, sir! No!"

"Oh, very well then," grinned the Senior Surgeon. "We can consider everything all comfortably settled then I suppose?"

"No, we can't!" screamed the White Linen Nurse. A little awkwardly with cramped limbs she struggled partly upward from the grass and knelt there defying the Senior Surgeon from her temporarily superior height. "No, we can't!" she reiterated wildly. "I tell you I can't, sir! I won't! I won't! I've been engaged once and it's enough! I tell you, sir, I'm all engaged out!"

"What's become of the man you were engaged to?" quizzed the Senior Surgeon sharply.

"Why—he's married!" said the White Linen Nurse. "And they've got a kid!" she added tempestuously.

"Good! I'm glad of it!" smiled the Senior Surgeon quite amazingly. "Now he surely won't bother us any more."

"But I was engaged so long!" protested the White Linen Nurse. "Almost ever since I was born, I said. It's too long. You don't get over it!"

"He got over it," remarked the Senior Surgeon laconically.

"Y-e-s," admitted the White Linen Nurse. "But I tell you it doesn't seem decent. Not after being engaged—twenty years!" With a little helpless gesture of appeal she threw out her hands. "Oh, can't I make you understand, sir?"

"Why, of course, I understand," said the Senior Surgeon briskly. "You mean that you and John—"

"His name was 'Joe,'" corrected the White Linen Nurse.

With astonishing amiability the Senior Surgeon acknowledged the correction. "You mean," he said, "you mean that you and—Joe—have been cradled together so familiarly all your babyhood that on your wedding night you could most naturally have said 'Let me see—Joe,—it's two pillows that you always have, isn't it? And a double-fold of blanket at the foot?' You mean that you and Joe have been washed and scrubbed together so familiarly all your young childhood that you could identify Joe's headless body twenty years hence by the kerosene-lamp scar across his back? You mean that you and Joe have played house together so familiarly all your young tin-dish days that even your rag dolls called Joe 'Father'? You mean that since your earliest memory,—until a year or so ago,—Life has never once been just You and Life, but always You and Life and Joe? You and Spring and Joe,—You and Summer and Joe,—You and Autumn and Joe,—You and Winter and Joe,—till every conscious nerve in your body has been so everlastingly Joed with Joe's Joeness that you don't believe there's any experience left in life powerful enough to eradicate that original impression? Eh?"

"Yes, sir," flushed the White Linen Nurse.

"Good! I'm glad of it!" snapped the Senior Surgeon. "It doesn't make you seem quite so alarmingly innocent and remote for a widower to offer marriage to. Good, I say! I'm glad of it!"

"Even so—I don't want to," said the White Linen Nurse. "Thank you very much, sir! But even so, I don't want to."

"Would you marry—Joe—now if he were suddenly free and wanted you?" asked the Senior Surgeon bluntly.

"Oh, my Lord, no!" said the White Linen Nurse.

"Other men are pretty sure to want you," admonished the Senior Surgeon. "Have you made up your mind—definitely that you'll never marry anybody?"

"N—o, not exactly," confessed the White Linen Nurse.

An odd flicker twitched across the Senior Surgeon's face like a sob in the brain.

"What's your first name, Miss Malgregor?" he asked a bit huskily.

"Rae," she told him with some surprise.

The Senior Surgeon's eyes narrowed suddenly again.

"Damn it all, Rae," he said, "*I—want you!*"

Precipitously the White Linen Nurse scrambled to her feet. "If you don't mind, sir," she cried, "I'll run down to the brook and get myself a drink of water!"

Impishly like a child, muscularly like a man, the Senior Surgeon clutched out at the flapping corner of her coat.

"No you don't!" he laughed, "till you've given me my definite answer—yes or no!"

Breathlessly the White Linen Nurse spun round in her tracks. Her breast was heaving with ill-suppressed sobs. Her eyes were blurred with tears. "You've no business—to hurry me so!" she protested passionately. "It isn't fair!—It isn't kind!"

Sluggishly in the Senior Surgeon's jolted arms the Little Girl woke from her feverish nap and peered up perplexedly through the gray dusk into her father's face.

"Where's—my kitty?" she asked hazily.

"Eh?" jerked the Senior Surgeon.

Harshly the little iron leg-braces clanked together.

In an instant the White Linen Nurse was on her knees in the grass. "You don't hold her right, sir!" she expostulated. Deftly with little soft, darting touches, interrupted only by rubbing her knuckles into her own tears, she reached out and eased successively the bruise of a buckle or the dragging weight on a little cramped hip.

Still drowsily, still hazily, with little smacking gasps and gulping swallows, the child worried her way back again into consciousness.

"All the birds *were* there, Father," she droned forth feebly from her sweltering mink-fur nest.

All the birds *were* there

With yellow feathers instead of—hair,

And bumble bees—and bumble bees—

And bumble bees?—And bumble bees—?

Frenziedly she began to burrow the back of her head into her Father's shoulder. "And bumble bees?—And bumble bees—?"

"Oh, for Heaven's sake—'buzzed' in the trees!" interpolated the Senior Surgeon.

Rigidly from head to foot the little body in his arms stiffened suddenly. As one who saw the supreme achievement of a life-time swept away by some one careless joggle of an infinitesimal part, the Little Girl stared up agonizingly into her father's face. "Oh, I don't think—'buzzed' was the word!" she began convulsively. "Oh, I don't think—!"

Startlingly through the twilight the Senior Surgeon felt the White Linen Nurse's rose-red lips come smack against his ear.

"Darn you! Can't you say 'crocheted' in the trees?" sobbed the White Linen Nurse.

Grotesquely for an instant the Senior Surgeon's eyes and the White Linen Nurse's eyes glared at each other in frank antagonism.

Then suddenly the Senior Surgeon burst out laughing. "Oh, very well!" he surrendered. "'Crocheted in the trees'!"

Precipitously the White Linen Nurse sank back on her heels and began to clap her hands.

"Oh, now I will! Now I will!" she cried exultantly.

"Will what?" frowned the Senior Surgeon.

Abruptly the White Linen Nurse stopped clapping her hands and began to wring them nervously in her lap instead. "Why—will—will!" she confessed demurely.

"Oh!" jumped the Senior Surgeon. "*Oh!*" Then equally jerkily he began to pucker his eyebrows. "But for Heaven's sake—what's the 'crocheted in the trees' got to do with it?" he asked perplexedly.

"Nothing much," mused the White Linen Nurse very softly. With sudden alertness she turned her curly blonde head towards the road. "There's somebody coming!" she said. "I hear a team!"

Overcome by a bashfulness that tried to escape in jocosity, the Senior Surgeon gave an odd little choking chuckle.

"Well, I never thought I should marry a—trained nurse!" he acknowledged with somewhat hectic blitheness.

Impulsively the White Linen Nurse reached for her watch and lifted it close to her twilight-blinded eyes. A sense of ineffable peace crept suddenly over her.

"You won't, sir!" she said amiably.

"It's twenty minutes of nine, now. And the graduation was at eight!"

CHAPTER VIII

For any real adventure except dying, June is certainly a most auspicious month.

Indeed it was on the very first rain-green, rose-red morning of June that the White Linen Nurse sallied forth upon her extremely hazardous adventure of marrying the Senior Surgeon and his naughty little crippled daughter.

The wedding was at noon in some kind of a gray granite church. And the Senior Surgeon was there, of course,—and the necessary witnesses. But the Little Crippled Girl never turned up at all, owing—it proved later,—to a more than usually violent wrangle with whomever dressed her, concerning the general advisability of sporting turquoise-colored stockings with her brightest little purple dress.

The Senior Surgeon's stockings, if you really care to know, were gray. And the Senior Surgeon's suit was gray. And he looked altogether very huge and distinguished,—and no more strikingly unhappy than any bridegroom looks in a gray granite church.

And the White Linen Nurse,—no longer now truly a White Linen Nurse but just an ordinary, every-day, silk-and-cloth lady of any color she chose, wore something rather coat-y and grand and bluish, and was distractingly pretty of course but most essentially unfamiliar,—and just a tiny bit awkward and bony-wristed looking,—as even an Admiral is apt to be on his first day out of uniform.

Then as soon as the wedding ceremony was over, the bride and groom went to a wonderful green and gold café all built of marble and lined with music, and had a little lunch. What I really mean, of course, is that they had a very large lunch, but didn't eat any of it!

Then in a taxi-cab, just exactly like any other taxi-cab, the White Linen Nurse drove home alone to the Senior Surgeon's great, gloomy house to find her brand new step-daughter still screaming over the turquoise colored stockings.

And the Senior Surgeon in a Canadian-bound train, just exactly like any other Canadian-bound train, started off alone,—as usual, on his annual June "spree."

Please don't think for a moment that it was the Senior Surgeon who was responsible for the general eccentricities of this amazing wedding day. No indeed! The Senior Surgeon didn't *want* to be married the first day of June! He *said* he didn't! He *growled* he didn't! He *snarled* he didn't! He *swore* he didn't! And when he finished saying and growling and snarling and swearing,—and looked up at the White Linen Nurse for a confirmation of his opinion, the White Linen Nurse smiled perfectly amiably and said, "Yes, sir!"

Then the Senior Surgeon gave a great gasp of relief and announced resonantly, "Well, it's all settled then? We'll be married some time in July,—after I get home from Canada?" And when the White Linen Nurse kept on smiling perfectly amiably and said, "Oh, no, sir! Oh, no, thank you, sir! It wouldn't seem exactly legal to me to be married any other month but June!" Then the Senior Surgeon went absolutely dumb with rage that this mere chit of a girl,—and a trained nurse, too,—should dare to thwart his personal and professional convenience. But the White Linen Nurse just drooped her pretty blonde head and blushed and blushed and blushed and said, "I was only marrying you, sir, to—accommodate you—sir,—and if June doesn't accommodate you—I'd rather go to Japan with that monoideic somnambulism case. It's very interesting. And it sails June second." Then "Oh, Hell with the 'monoideic somnambulism case'!" the Senior Surgeon would protest.

Really it took the Senior Surgeon quite a long while to work out the three special arguments that should best protect him, he thought, from the horridly embarrassing idea of being married in June.

"But you can't get ready so soon!" he suggested at last with real triumph. "You've no idea how long it takes a girl to get ready to be married! There are so many people she has to tell,—and everything!"

"There's never but two that she's got to tell—or bust!" conceded the

White Linen Nurse with perfect candor. "Just the woman she loves the most—and the woman she hates the worst. I'll write my mother to-morrow.

But I told the Superintendent of Nurses yesterday."

"The deuce you did!" snapped the Senior Surgeon.

Almost caressingly the White Linen Nurse lifted her big blue eyes to his. "Yes, sir," she said, "and she looked as sick as a young undertaker. I can't imagine what ailed her."

"Eh?" choked the Senior Surgeon. "But the house now," he hastened to contend. "The house now needs a lot of fixing over! It's all run down! It's all—everything! We never in the world could get it into shape by the first of June! For Heaven's sake, now that we've got money enough to make it right, let's go slow and make it perfectly right!"

A little nervously the White Linen Nurse began to fumble through the pages of her memorandum book. "I've always had money enough to 'go slow and make things perfectly right,'" she confided a bit wistfully. "Never in all my life have I had a pair of boots that weren't guaranteed, or a dress that wouldn't wash, or a hat that wasn't worth at least three re-pressings. What I was hoping for now, sir, was that I was going to have enough money so that I could go fast and make things wrong if I wanted to,—so that I could afford to take chances, I mean. Here's this wall-paper now,"—tragically she pointed to some figuring in her note-book—"it's got peacocks on it—life size—in a queen's garden—and I wanted it for the dining-room. Maybe it would fade! Maybe we'd get tired of it! Maybe it would poison us! Slam it on one week—and slash it off the next! I wanted it just because I wanted it, sir! I thought maybe—while you were way off in Canada—"

Eagerly the Senior Surgeon jerked his chair a little nearer to his—fiancée's.

"Now, my dear girl," he said. "That's just what I want to explain!

That's just what I want to explain! Just what I want to explain!

To—er—explain!" he continued a bit falteringly.

"Yes, sir," said the White Linen Nurse.

Very deliberately the Senior Surgeon removed a fleck of dust from one of his cuffs.

"All this talk of yours—about wanting to be married the same day I start off on my—Canadian trip!" he contended. "Why, it's all damned nonsense!"

"Yes, sir," said the White Linen Nurse.

Very conscientiously the Senior Surgeon began to search for a fleck of dust on his other cuff.

"Why my—my dear girl," he persisted. "It's absurd! It's outrageous! Why people would—would hoot at us! Why they'd think—!"

"Yes, sir," said the White Linen Nurse.

"Why, my dear girl," sweated the Senior Surgeon. "Even though you and I understand perfectly well the purely formal, business-like conditions of our marriage, we must at least for sheer decency's sake keep up a certain semblance of marital conventionality—before the world! Why, if we were married at noon the first day of June—as you suggest,—and I should go right off alone as usual—on my Canadian trip—and you should come back alone to the house—why, people would think—would think that I didn't care anything about you!"

"But you don't," said the White Linen Nurse serenely.

"Why, they'd think," choked the Senior Surgeon. "They'd think you were trying your—darndest—to get rid of me!"

"I am," said the White Linen Nurse complacently.

With a muttered ejaculation the Senior Surgeon jumped to his feet and stood glaring down at her.

Quite ingenuously the White Linen Nurse met and parried the glare.

"A gentleman—and a red-haired kiddie—and a great walloping house—all at once! It's too much!" she confided genially. "Thank you just the same, but I'd rather take them gradually. First of all, sir, you see, I've got to teach the little kiddie to like me! And then there's a green-tiled paper with floppity sea gulls on it—that I want to try for the bath-room! And—and—" Ecstatically she clapped her hands together. "Oh, sir! There are such loads and loads of experiments I want to try while you are off on your spree!"

"S—h—h!" cried the Senior Surgeon. His face was suddenly blanched,—his mouth, twitching like the mouth of one stricken with almost insupportable pain. "For God's sake, Miss Malgregor!" he pleaded, "can't you call it my—Canadian trip?"

Wider and wider the White Linen Nurse opened her big blue eyes at him.

"But it is a 'spree,' sir!" she attested resolutely. "And my father says—" Still resolutely her young mouth curved to its original assertion, but from under her heavy-shadowing eyelashes a little blue smile crept softly out. "When my father's got a lame trotting horse, sir, that he's trying to shuck off his hands," she faltered, "he doesn't ever go round mournful-like with his head hanging—telling folks about his wonderful trotter that's just 'the littlest, teeniest, tiniest bit—lame.' Oh no! What father does is to call up every one he knows within twenty miles and tell 'em, 'Say Tom,—Bill,—Harry,'—or whatever his name is—'what in the deuce do you suppose I've got over here in my barn? A lame horse—that wants to trot! Lamer than the deuce, you know! But can do a mile in 2.40.'" Faintly the little blue smile quickened again in the White Linen Nurse's eyes. "And the barn will be full of men in half an hour!" she said. "Somehow nobody wants a trotter that's lame! But almost anybody seems willing to risk a lame horse—that's plucky enough to trot!"

"What's the 'lame trotting horse' got to do with—me?" snarled the Senior Surgeon incisively.

Darkly the White Linen Nurse's lashes fringed down across her cheeks.

"Nothing much," she said, "Only—"

"Only what?" demanded the Senior Surgeon. A little more roughly than he realized he stooped down and took the White Linen Nurse by her shoulders, and jerked her sharply round to the light. "Only *what?*" he insisted peremptorily.

Almost plaintively she lifted her eyes to his. "Only—my father says," she confided obediently, "my father says if you've got a worse foot—for Heaven's sake put it forward—and get it over with!

"So—I've *got* to call it a 'spree'!" smiled the White Linen Nurse. "'Cause when I think of marrying a—*surgeon*—that goes off and gets drunk every June—it—it scares me almost to my death! But—" Abruptly the red smile faded from her lips, the blue smile from her eyes. "But—when I think of marrying a—June drunk—that's got the grit to pull up absolutely straight as a die and be a *surgeon*—all the other 'leven months in the year—" Dartingly she bent down and kissed the Senior Surgeon's astonished wrist. "Oh, then I think you're perfectly *grand*!" she sobbed.

Awkwardly the Senior Surgeon pulled away and began to pace the floor.

"You're a—good little girl, Rae Malgregor," he mumbled huskily. "A good little girl. I truly believe you're the kind that will—see me through." Poignantly in his eyes humiliation overwhelmed the mist. Perversely in its turn resentment overtook the humiliation. "But I won't be married in June!" he reasserted bombastically. "I won't! I won't! I won't! I tell you I positively refuse to have a lot of damn fools speculating about my private affairs! Wondering why I didn't take you! Wondering why I didn't stay home with you! I tell you I won't! I simply won't!"

"Yes, sir," stammered the White Linen Nurse.

With a real gasp of relief the Senior Surgeon stopped his eternal pacing of the floor.

"Bully for you!" he said. "You mean then we'll be married some time in July after I get back from my—trip?"

"Oh, no, sir," stammered the White Linen Nurse.

"But Great Heavens!" shouted the Senior Surgeon.

"Yes, sir," the White Linen Nurse began all over again. Dreamily planning out her wedding gown, her lips without the slightest conscious effort on her part were already curving into shape for her alternate "No, sir."

"You're an idiot!" snapped the Senior Surgeon.

A little reproachfully the White Linen Nurse came frowning out of her reverie. "Would it do just as well for traveling, do you think?" she asked, with real concern.

"Eh? What?" said the Senior Surgeon.

"I mean—does Japan spot?" queried the White Linen Nurse. "Would it spot a serge, I mean?"

"Oh, Hell with Japan!" jerked the Senior Surgeon.

"Yes, sir," said the White Linen Nurse.

Now perhaps you will understand just exactly how it happened that the Senior Surgeon and the White Linen Nurse *were* married on the first day of June, and just exactly how it happened that the Senior Surgeon went off alone as usual on his Canadian trip, and just exactly how it happened that the White Linen Nurse came home alone to the Senior Surgeon's great, gloomy house, to find her brand new step-daughter still screaming over the turquoise-colored stockings. Everything now is perfectly comfortably explained except the turquoise-colored stockings. Nobody could explain the turquoise-colored stockings!

But even a little child could explain the ensuing June! Oh, June was perfectly wonderful that year! Bud, blossom, bird-song, breeze,—rioting headlong through the Land. Warm days sweet and lush as a green-house vapor! Crisp nights faintly metallic like the scent of stars! Hurdy-gurdies romping tunefully on every street-corner! Even the Ash-Man flushing frankly pink across his dusty cheek-bones!

Like two fairies who had sublet a giant's cave the White Linen Nurse and the Little Crippled Girl turned themselves loose upon the Senior Surgeon's gloomy old house.

It certainly was a gloomy old house, but handsome withal,—square and brown and substantial, and most generously gardened within high brick walls. Except for dusting the lilac bushes with the hose, and weeding a few rusty leaves out of the privet hedge, and tacking up three or four scraggly sprays of English ivy, and re-greening one or two bay-tree boxes, there was really nothing much to do to the garden. But the house? Oh ye gods! All day long from morning till night,—but most particularly from the back door to the barn, sweating workmen scuttled back and forth till nary a guilty piece of black walnut furniture had escaped. All day long from morning till night,—but most particularly from ceilings to floors, sweltering workmen scurried up and down step-ladders stripping dingy papers from dingier plasterings.

When the White Linen Nurse wasn't busy renovating the big house—or the little step-daughter, she was writing to the Senior Surgeon. She wrote twice.

"Dear Dr. Faber," the first letter said.

* * * * *

DEAR DR. FABER,

How do you do? Thank you very much, for saying you didn't care what in thunder I did to the house. It looks *sweet*. I've put white fluttery muslin curtains most everywhere. And you've got a new solid-gold-looking bed in your room. And the Kiddie and I have fixed up the most scrumptious light blue suite for ourselves in the ell. Pink was wrong for the front hall, but it cost me only $29.00 to find out. And now that's settled for all time.

I am very, very, very, very busy. Something strange and new happens every day. Yesterday it was three ladies and a plumber. One of the ladies was just selling soap, but I didn't buy any. It was horrid soap. The other two were calling ladies,—a silk one and a velvet one. The silk one tried to be nasty to me. Right to my face she told me I was more of a lady than she had dared to hope. And I told her I was sorry for that as you'd had one "lady" and it didn't work. Was that all right? But the other lady was nice. And I took her out in the kitchen with me while I was painting the woodwork, and right there in her white kid gloves she laughed and showed me how to mix the paint pearl gray. *She* was nice. It was your sister-in-law.

I like being married, Dr. Faber. I like it lots better than I thought I would. It's fun being the biggest person in the house. Respectfully yours, RAE MALGREGOR,—AS WAS.

P.S. Oh, I hope it wasn't wrong, but in your ulster pocket, when I went to put it away, I found a bottle of something that smelt as though it had been forgotten.—I threw it out.

* * * * *

It was this letter that drew the only definite message from the itinerant bridegroom.

"Kindly refrain from rummaging in my ulster pockets," wrote the Senior Surgeon quite briefly. "The 'thing' you threw out happened to be the cerebellum and medulla of an extremely eminent English Theologian!"

"Even so,—it was sour," telegraphed the White Linen Nurse in a perfect agony of remorse and humiliation.

The telegram took an Indian with a birch canoe two days to deliver, and cost the Senior Surgeon twelve dollars. Just impulsively the Senior Surgeon decided to make no further comments on domestic affairs,—at that particular range.

Very fortunately for this impulse the White Linen Nurse's second letter concerned itself almost entirely with matters quite extraneous to the home.

"Dear Dr. Faber," the second letter ran.

* * * * *

DEAR DR. FABER,

Somehow I don't seem to care so much just now about being the biggest person in the house. Something awful has happened. Zillah Forsyth is dead. Really dead, I mean. And she died in great heroism. You remember Zillah Forsyth, don't you? She was one of my room-mates,—not the gooder one, you know,—not the swell,—that was Helene Churchill. But Zillah? Oh you know! Zillah was the one you sent out on that Fractured Elbow case. It was a Yale student, you remember? And there was some trouble about kissing,—and she got sent home? And now everybody's crying because Zillah *can't* kiss anybody any more! Isn't everything the limit? Well, it wasn't a fractured Yale student she got sent out on this time. If it had been, she might have been living yet. What they sent her out on this time was a Senile Dementia,—an old lady more than eighty years old. And they were in a sanitarium or something like that. And there was a fire in the night. And the old lady just up and positively refused to escape. And Zillah had to push her and shove her and yank her and carry her—out the window—along the gutters—round the chimneys. And the old lady bit Zillah right through the hand,—but Zillah wouldn't let go. And the old lady tried to drown Zillah under a bursted water tank,—but Zillah wouldn't let go. And everybody hollered to Zillah to cut loose and save herself,—but Zillah wouldn't let go. And a wall fell, and everything, and oh, it was awful,—but Zillah never let go. And the old lady that wasn't any good to any one,—not even herself, got saved of course. But Zillah? Oh, Zillah got hurt bad, sir! We saw her at the hospital, Helene and I. She sent for us about something. Oh, it was awful! Not a thing about her that you'd know except just her great solemn eyes mooning out at you through a gob of white cotton, and her red mouth lipping sort of twitchy at the edge of a bandage. Oh it was awful! But Zillah didn't seem to care so much. There was a new Interne there,—a Japanese, and I guess she was sort of taken with him. "But my God, Zillah," I said, "*your* life was worth more than that old dame's!"

"Shut your noise!" says Zillah. "It was my job. And there's no kick coming." Helene burst right out crying, she did. "Shut *your* noise, too!" says Zillah, just as cool as you please. "Bah! There's other lives and other chances!"

"Oh, you do believe that now?" cries Helene. "Oh, you do believe that now,—what the Bible promises you?" That was when Zillah shrugged her shoulders so funny,—the little way she had. Gee, but her eyes were big! "I don't pretend to know—what—your old Bible says," she choked. "It was—the Yale feller—who was tellin' me."

That's all, Dr. Faber. It was her shrugging her shoulders so funny that brought on the hemorrhage.

Oh, we had an awful time, sir, going home in the carriage,—Helene and I. We both cried, of course, because Zillah was dead, but after we got through crying for that, Helene kept right on crying because she couldn't understand why a brave girl like Zillah *had* to be dead. Gee! But Helene takes things hard. Ladies do, I guess.

I hope you're having a pleasant spree.

Oh, I forgot to tell you that one of the wall-paperers is living here at the house with us just now. We use him so much it's truly a good deal more convenient. And he's a real nice young fellow, and he plays the piano finely, and he comes from up my way. And it seemed more neighborly anyway. It's so large in the house at night, just now, and so creaky in the garden.

With kindest regards, good-by for now, from RAE.

P.S.

Don't tell your guide or *any one!* But Helene sent Zillah's mother a check for fifteen hundred dollars. I saw it with my own eyes. And all Zillah asked for that day was just a little blue serge suit. It seems she'd promised her kid sister a little blue serge suit for July. And it sort of worried her.

Helene sent the little blue serge suit too! And a hat! The hat had bluebells on it. Do you think when you come home—if I haven't spent too much money on wall-papers—that I could have a blue hat with bluebells on it? Excuse me for bothering you—but you forgot to leave me enough money.

* * * * *

It was some indefinite, pleasant time on Thursday, the twenty-fifth of June, that the Senior Surgeon received this second letter.

It was Friday the twenty-sixth of June, exactly at dawn, that the Senior Surgeon started homeward.

Nobody looks very well in the dawn. Certainly the Senior Surgeon didn't. Heavily as a man wading through a bog of dreams, he stumbled out of his cabin into the morning. Under his drowsy, brooding eyes appalling shadows circled. Behind his sunburn,—deeper than his tan, something sinister and uncanny lurked wanly like the pallor of a soul.

Yet the Senior Surgeon had been most blamelessly abed and asleep since griddle-cake time the previous evening.

Only the mountains and the forest and the lake had been out all night. For seventy miles of Canadian wilderness only the mountains and the forest and the lake stood actually convicted of having been out all night. Dank and white with its vaporous vigil the listless lake kindled wanly to the new day's breeze. Blue with cold a precipitous mountain peak lurched craggedly home through a rift in the fog. Drenched with mist, bedraggled with dew, a green-feathered pine tree lay guzzling insatiably at a leaf-brown pool. Monotonous as a sob the waiting birch canoe slosh-sloshed against the beach.

There was no romantic smell of red roses in this June landscape. Just tobacco smoke, and the faint reminiscent fragrance of fried trout, and the mournful, sizzling, pungent consciousness of a camp-fire quenched for a whole year with a tinful of wet coffee grounds.

Gliding out cautiously into the lake as though the mere splash of a paddle might shatter the whole glassy surface, the Indian Guide propounded the question that was uppermost in his mind.

"Cutting your trip a bit short this year,—ain't you, Boss?" quizzed the Indian guide.

Out from his muffling mackinaw collar the Senior Surgeon parried the question with an amazingly novel sense of embarrassment.

"Oh, I don't know," he answered with studied lightness. "There are one or two things at home that are bothering me a little."

"A woman, eh?" said the Indian Guide laconically.

"A woman?" thundered the Senior Surgeon. "A—woman? Oh, ye gods! No! It's wall paper!"

Then suddenly and unexpectedly in the midst of his passionate refutation the Senior Surgeon burst out laughing,—boisterously, hilariously like a crazy school-boy. Bluntly from an overhanging ledge of rock the echo of his laugh came mocking back at him. Down from some unvisioned mountain fastness the echo of that echo came wafting faintly to him.

The Senior Surgeon's laugh was made of teeth and tongue and palate and a purely convulsive physical impulse. But the echo's laugh was a phantasy of mist and dawn and inestimable balsam-scented spaces where little green ferns and little brown beasties and soft-breasted birdlings frolicked eternally in pristine sweetness.

Seven miles further down the lake, at the beginning of the rapids, the Indian Guide spoke again. Racking the canoe between two rocks,—paddling, panting, pushing, sweating, the Indian Guide lifted his voice high,—piercing, above the swirling roar of waters.

"Eh, Boss!" shouted the Indian Guide. "I ain't never heard you laugh before!"

Neither man spoke again more than once or twice during the long, strenuous hours that were left to them.

The Indian Guide was very busy in his stolid mind trying to figure out just how many rows of potatoes could be planted fruitfully between his front door and his cow-shed. I don't know what the Senior Surgeon was trying to figure out.

It was just four days later from a rolling, musty-cushioned hack that the Senior Surgeon disembarked at his own front gate.

Even though a man likes home no better than he likes—tea, few men would deny the soothing effect of home at the end of a long fussy railroad journey. Five o'clock, also, of a late June afternoon is a peculiarly wonderful time to be arriving home,—especially if that home has a garden around it so that you are thereby not rushed precipitously upon the house itself, as upon a cup without a saucer, but can toy visually with the whole effect before you quench your thirst with the actual draught.

Very, very deliberately, with his clumsy rod-case in one hand, and his heavy grip in the other, the Senior Surgeon started up the long, broad gravel path to the house. For a man walking as slow as he was, his heart was beating most extraordinarily fast. He was not accustomed to heart-palpitation. The symptom worried him a trifle. Incidentally also his lungs felt strangely stifled with the scent of June. Close at his right an effulgent white and gold syringa bush flaunted its cloying sweetness into his senses. Close at his left a riotous bloom of phlox clamored red-blue-purple-lavender-pink into his dazzled vision. Multi-colored pansies tiptoed velvet-footed across the grass. In soft murky mystery a flame-tinted smoke tree loomed up here and there like a faintly rouged ghost. Over everything, under everything, through everything, lurked a certain strange, novel, vibrating consciousness of *occupancy*. Bees in the rose bushes! Bobolinks in the trees! A woman's work-basket in the curve of the hammock! A doll's tea set sprawling cheerfully in the middle of the broad gravel path!

It was not until the Senior Surgeon had actually stepped into the tiny cream pitcher that he noticed the presence of the doll's tea set.

It was what the Senior Surgeon said as he stepped out of the cream pitcher that summoned the amazing apparition from a ragged green hole in the privet hedge. Startlingly white, startlingly professional,—dress, cap, apron and all,—a miniature white linen nurse sprang suddenly out at him like a tricky dwarf in a moving picture show. Just at that particular moment the Senior Surgeon's nerves were in no condition to wrestle with apparitions. Simultaneously as the clumsy rod-case dropped from his hand, the expression of enthusiasm dropped from the face of the miniature white linen nurse.

"Oh, dear—oh, dear—oh, dear! Have *you* come home?" wailed the familiar, shrill little voice.

Sheepishly the Senior Surgeon picked up his rod-case. The noises in his head were crashing like cracked bells. Desperately with a boisterous irritability he sought to cover also the lurching pound-pound-pound of his heart.

"What in Hell are you rigged out like that for?" he demanded stormily.

With equal storminess the Little Girl protested the question.

"Peach said I could!" she attested passionately. "Peach said I could! She did! She did! I tell you I didn't want her to marry us—that day! I was afraid, I was! I cried, I did! I had a convulsion! They thought it was stockings! So Peach said if it would make me feel any gooderer, I could be the cruel new step-mother. And she'd be the unloved offspring—with her hair braided all yellow fluffikins down her back!"

"Where *is*—Miss Malgregor?" asked the Senior Surgeon sharply.

Irrelevantly the Little Girl sank down on the gravel walk and began to gather up her scattered dishes.

"And it's fun to go to bed—now," she confided amiably. "'Cause every night I put Peach to bed at eight o'clock and she's so naughty always I have to stay with her! And then all of a sudden it's morning—like going through a black room without knowing it!"

"I said—where *is* Miss Malgregor?" repeated the Senior Surgeon with increasing sharpness.

Thriftily the Little Girl bent down to lap a bubble of cream from the broken pitcher.

"Oh, she's out in the summer house with the Wall Paper Man," she mumbled indifferently.

CHAPTER IX

Altogether jerkily the Senior Surgeon started up the walk for his own perfectly formal and respectable brown stone mansion. Deep down in his lurching heart he felt a sudden most inordinate desire to reach that brown stone mansion just as quickly as possible. But abruptly even to himself he swerved off instead at the yellow sassafras tree and plunged quite wildly through a mass of broken sods towards the rickety, no-account cedar summer house.

Startled by the crackle and thud of his approach the two young figures in the summer house jumped precipitously to their feet, and limply untwining their arms from each other's necks stood surveying the Senior Surgeon in unspeakable consternation,—the White Linen Nurse and a blue overalled lad most unconscionably mated in radiant youth and agonized confusion.

"Oh, my Lord, Sir!" gasped the White Linen Nurse. "Oh, my Lord, Sir! I wasn't looking for *you*—for another week!"

"Evidently not!" said the Senior Surgeon incisively. "This is the second time this evening that I've been led to infer that my home-coming was distinctly inopportune!"

Very slowly, very methodically, he put down first his precious rod-case and then his grip. His brain seemed fairly foaming with blood and confusion. Along the swelling veins of his arms a dozen primitive instincts went surging to his fists.

Then quite brazenly before his eyes the White Linen Nurse reached out and took the lad's hand again.

"Oh, forgive me, Dr. Faber!" she faltered. "This is my brother!"

"Your *brother?—what?—eh?*" choked the Senior Surgeon. Bluntly he reached out and crushed the young fellow's fingers in his own. "Glad to see you, Son!" he muttered with a sickish sort of grin, and turning abruptly, picked up his baggage again and started for the big house.

Half a step behind him his White Linen Bride followed softly.

At the edge of the piazza he turned for an instant and eyed her a bit quizzically. With her big credulous blue eyes, and her great mop of yellow hair braided childishly down her back, she looked inestimably more juvenile and innocent than his own little shrewd-faced six-year-old whom he had just left domestically ensconced in the middle of the broad gravel path.

"For Heaven's sake, Miss Malgregor," he asked. "For Heaven's sake—why didn't you tell me that the Wall Paper Man was your—brother?"

Very contritely the White Linen Nurse's chin went burrowing down into the soft collar of her dress and as bashfully as a child one finger came stealing up to the edge of her red, red lips.

"I was afraid you'd think I was—cheeky—having any of my family come and live with us—so soon," she murmured almost inaudibly.

"Well, what did you think I'd think you were—if he wasn't your brother?" asked the Senior Surgeon sardonically.

"Very—economical, I hoped!" beamed the White Linen Nurse.

"All the same!" snapped the Senior Surgeon, with an irrelevance surprising even to himself. "All the same do you think it sounds quite right and proper for a child to call her—step-mother—'Peach'?"

Again the White Linen Nurse's chin went burrowing down into the soft collar of her dress. "I don't suppose it is—usual," she admitted reluctantly. "The children next door, I notice, call theirs—'Cross-Patch.'"

With a gesture of impatience the Senior Surgeon proceeded up the steps,—yanked open the old-fashioned shuttered door, and burst quite breathlessly and unprepared upon his most amazingly reconstructed house. All in one single second chintzes,—muslins,—pale blonde maples,—riotous canary birds,—stormed revolutionary upon his outraged eyes. Reeling back utterly aghast before the sight, he stood there staring dumbly for an instant at what he considered,—and rightly too,—the absolute wreck of his black walnut home.

"It looks like—Hell!" he muttered feebly.

"Yes, *isn't* it sweet?" conceded the White Linen Nurse with unmistakable joyousness. "And your library—" Triumphantly she threw back the door to his grim work-shop.

"Good God!" stammered the Senior Surgeon. "You've made it—pink!"

Rapturously the White Linen Nurse began to clasp and unclasp her hands. "I knew you'd love it!" she said.

Half dazed with bewilderment the Senior Surgeon started to brush an imaginary haze from his eyes but paused mid-way in the gesture and pointed back instead to a dapper little hall-table that seemed to be exhausting its entire blonde strength in holding up a slender green vase with a single pink rose in it. Like a caged animal buffeting for escape against each successive bar that incased it, the man's frenzied irritation hurled itself hopefully against this one more chance for explosive exit.

"What—have—you—done—with the big—black—escritoire that stood—there?" he demanded accusingly.

"Escritoire?—Escritoire?" worried the White Linen Nurse. "Why—why—I'm afraid I must have mislaid it."

"Mislaid it?" thundered the Senior Surgeon. "Mislaid it? It weighed three hundred pounds!"

"Oh, it did?" questioned the White Linen Nurse with great, blue-eyed interest. Still mulling apparently over the fascinating weight of the escritoire she climbed up suddenly into a chair and with the fluffy broom-shaped end of her extraordinarily long braid of hair went angling wildy off into space after an illusive cobweb.

Faster and faster the Senior Surgeon's temper began to search for a new point of exit.

"What do you suppose the—servants think of you?" he stormed. "Running round like that with your hair in a pig-tail like a—kid?"

"Servants?" cooed the White Linen Nurse. "Servants?" Very quietly she jumped down from the chair and came and stood looking up into the Senior Surgeon's hectic face. "Why, there aren't any servants," she explained patiently. "I've dismissed every one of them. We're doing our own work now!"

"Doing 'our own work'?" gasped the Senior Surgeon.

Quite worriedly the White Linen Nurse stepped back a little. "Why, wasn't that right?" she pleaded. "Wasn't it right? Why, I thought people always did their own work when they were first married!" With sudden apprehensiveness she glanced round over her shoulder at the hall clock, and darting out through a side door, returned almost instantly with a fierce-looking knife.

"I'm so late now and everything," she confided. "Could you peel the potatoes for me?"

"No, I couldn't!" said the Senior Surgeon shortly. Equally shortly he turned on his heel, and reaching out once more for his rod-case and grip went on up the stairs to his own room.

One of the pleasantest things about arriving home very late in the afternoon is the excuse it gives you for loafing in your own room while other people are getting supper. No existent domestic sound in the whole twenty-four hours is as soothing at the end of a long journey as the sound of other people getting supper.

Stretched out full length in a big easy chair by his bed-room window, with his favorite pipe bubbling rhythmically between his gleaming white teeth, the Senior Surgeon studied his new "solid gold bed" and his new sage green wall-paper and his new dust-colored rug, to the faint, far-away accompaniment of soft thudding feet, and a girl's laugh, and a child's prattle, and the tink-tink-tinkle of glass,—china,—silver,—all scurrying consciously to the service of one man,—and that man,—*himself*.

Very, very slowly, in that special half hour an inscrutable little smile printed itself experimentally across the right hand corner of the Senior Surgeon's upper lip.

While that smile was still in its infancy he jumped up suddenly and forced his way across the hall to his dead wife's room,—the one ghost-room of his house and his life,—and there with his hand on the turning door knob,—tense with reluctance,—goose-fleshed with strain,—his breath gasped out of him whether or no with the one word—"Alice!"

And behold! There was no room there!

Lurching back from the threshold, as from the brink of an elevator well, the Senior Surgeon found himself staring foolishly into a most sumptuous linen closet, tiered like an Aztec cliff with home after home for pleasant prosy blankets, and gaily fringed towels, and cheerful white sheets reeking most conscientiously of cedar and lavender. Tiptoeing cautiously into the mystery he sensed at one astonished, grateful glance how the change of a partition, the re-adjustment of a proportion, had purged like a draft of fresh air the stale gloom of an ill-favored memory. Yet so inevitable did it suddenly seem for a linen closet to be built right there,—so inevitable did it suddenly seem for the child's meager play-room to be enlarged just there, that to save his soul he could not estimate whether the happy plan had originated in a purely practical brain or a purely compassionate heart.

Half proud of the brain, half touched by the heart, he passed on exploringly through the new play-room out into the hall again.

Quite distinctly now through the aperture of the back stairs the kitchen voices came wafting up to him.

"Oh, dear! Oh, dear!" wailed his Little Girl's peevish voice. "Now that—that Man's come back again—I suppose we'll have to eat in the dining-room—all the time!"

"'That Man' happens to be your darling father!" admonished the White Linen Nurse's laughing voice.

"Even so," wailed the Little Girl, "I love you best."

"Even so," laughed the White Linen Nurse, "I love *you* best!"

"Just the same," cried the Little Girl shrilly, "just the same—let's put the cream pitcher way up high somewhere—so he can't step in it!"

As though from a head tilted suddenly backward the White Linen Nurse's laugh rang out in joyous abandon.

Impulsively the Senior Surgeon started to grin. Then equally impulsively the grin soured on his lips. So they thought he was clumsy? Eh? Resentfully he stared down at his hands,—those wonderfully dexterous,—yes, ambidexterous hands that were the aching envy of all his colleagues. Interruptingly as he stared the voice of the young Wall Paper Man rose buoyantly from the lower hallway.

"Supper's all ready, sir!" called the cordial voice.

For some inexplicable reason, at that particular moment, almost nothing in the world could have irritated the Senior Surgeon more keenly than to be invited to his own supper,—in his own house,—by a stranger. Fuming with a new sense of injury and injustice he started heavily down the stairs to the dining-room.

Standing patiently behind the Senior Surgeon's chair with a laudable desire to assist his carving in any possible emergency that might occur, the White Linen Nurse experienced her first direct marital rebuff.

"What do you think this is? An autopsy?" demanded the Senior Surgeon tartly. "For Heaven's sake—sit down!"

Quite meekly the White Linen Nurse subsided into her place.

The meal that ensued could hardly have been called a success though the room was entrancing,—the cloth, snow-white—the silver, radiant,—the guinea chicken beyond reproach.

Swept and garnished to an alarming degree the young Wall Paper Man presided over the gravy and did his uttermost, innocent country-best to make the Senior Surgeon feel perfectly at home.

Conscientiously, as in the presence of a distinguished stranger, the Little Crippled Girl most palpably from time to time repressed her insatiable desire to build a towering pyramid out of all the salt and pepper shakers she could reach.

Once when the young Wall Paper Man forgot himself to the extent of putting his knife in his mouth, the White Linen Nurse jarred the whole table with the violence of her warning kick.

Once when the Little Crippled Girl piped out impulsively, "Say, Peach,—what was the name of that bantam your father used to fight against the minister's bantam?" the White Linen Nurse choked piteously over her food.

Twice some one spoke about this year's weather.

Twice some one volunteered an illuminating remark about last year's weather.

Except for these four diversions restraint indescribable hung like a horrid pall over the feast.

Next to feeling unwelcome in your friend's house, nothing certainly is more wretchedly disconcerting than to feel unwelcome in your own house!

Grimly the Senior Surgeon longed to grab up all the knives within reach and ram them successively into his own mouth just to prove to the young Wall Paper Man what a—what a devil of a good fellow he was himself! Grimly the Senior Surgeon longed to tell the White Linen Nurse about the pet bantam of his own boyhood days—that he bet a dollar could lick any bantam her father ever dreamed of owning! Grimly the Senior Surgeon longed to talk dolls,—dishes,—kittens,—yes, even cream pitchers, to his Little Daughter, to talk anything in fact—to *any one*,—to talk—sing—shout *anything*—that should make him, at least for the time being, one at heart, one at head, one at table, with this astonishingly offish bunch of youngsters!

But grimly instead,—out of his frazzled nerves,—out of his innate spiritual bashfulness, he merely roared forth, "Where are the potatoes?"

"Potatoes?" gasped the White Linen Nurse. "Potatoes? Oh, potatoes?" she finished more blithely. "Why, yes, of course! Don't you remember—you didn't have time to peel them for me? I was so disappointed!"

"You were so disappointed?" snapped the Senior Surgeon. "You?—you?"

Janglingly the Little Crippled Girl knelt right up in her chair and shook her tiny fist right in her father's face.

"Now, Lendicott Paber!" she screamed. "Don't you start in—sassing—my darling little Peach!"

"*Peach?*" snorted the Senior Surgeon. With almost supernatural calm he put down his knife and fork and eyed his offspring with an expression of absolutely inflexible purpose. "Don't you—ever," he warned her, "ever—ever—let me hear you call—this woman 'Peach' again!"

A trifle faint-heartedly the Little Crippled Girl reached up and straightened her absurdly diminutive little white cap, and pursed her little mouth as nearly as possible into an expression of ineffable peace.

"Why—Lendicott Faber!" she persisted heroically.

"*Lendicott?*" jumped the Senior Surgeon. "What are *you*—'Lendicotting' *me* for?"

Hilariously with her own knife and fork the Little Crippled Girl began to beat upon the table.

"Why, you dear Silly!" she cried. "Why, if I'm the new Marma, I've got to call you 'Lendicott'! And Peach has got to call you 'Fat Father'!"

Frenziedly the Senior Surgeon pushed back his chair, and jumped to his feet. The expression on his face was neither smile nor frown, nor war nor peace, nor any other human expression that had ever puckered there before.

"God!" he said. "This gives me the *willies*!" and strode tempestuously from the room.

Out in his own work-shop fortunately,—whatever the grotesque new pinkness,—whatever the grotesque new perkiness—his great free walking-spaces had not been interfered with. Slamming his door triumphantly behind him, he resumed once more the monotonous pace-pace-pace that had characterized for eighteen years his first night's return to—the obligations of civilization.

Sharply around the corner of his old battered desk the little path started,—wanly along the edge of his dingy book-shelves the little path furrowed,—wistfully at the deep bay-window where his favorite lilac bush budded whitely for his departure, and rusted brownly for his return, the little path faltered,—and went on again,—on and on and on,—into the alcove where his instruments glistened,—up to the fireplace where his college trophy-cups tarnished! Listlessly the Senior Surgeon re-commenced his yearly vigil. Up and down,—up and down,—round and round,—on and on and on,—through interminable dusks to unattainable dawns,—a glutted, bacchanalian Soul sweating its own way back to sanctity and leanness! Nerves always were in that vigil,—raw, rattling nerves clamoring vociferously to be repacked in their sedatives. Thirst also was in that vigil,—no mere whimpering tickle of the palate, but a drought of the tissues,—a consuming fire of the bones! Hurt pride was also there, and festering humiliation!

But more rasping, this particular night, than nerves, more poignant than thirst, more dangerously excitative even than remorse, hunger rioted in him,—hunger, the one worst enemy of the Senior Surgeon's cause,—the simple, silly, no-account,—gnawing,—drink-provocative hunger of an empty stomach. And 'one other hunger was also there,—a sudden fierce new lust for Life and Living,—a passion bare of love yet pure of wantonness,—a passion primitive,—protective,—inexorably proprietary,—engendered strangely in that one mad, suspicious moment at the edge of the summer house when every outraged male instinct in him had leaped to prove that—love or no love—the woman was—*his*. Up and down,—up and down,—round and round,—eight o'clock found the Senior Surgeon still pacing.

At half past eight the young Wall Paper Man came to say good-by to him.

"As long as Sister won't be alone any more, I guess I'll be moving on," beamed the Wall Paper Man. "There's a dance at home Saturday night. And I've got a girl of my own!" he confided genially.

"Come again," urged the Senior Surgeon. "Come again when you can stay longer!"

With one honest prayer in stock, and at least two purely automatic social speeches of this sort, no man needs to flounder altogether hopelessly for words in any ordinary emergency of life. Thus with no more mental interruption than the two-minute break in time, the Senior Surgeon then resumed his bitter-thoughted pacing.

At nine o'clock, however,—patroling his long rangy book-shelves, he sensed with a very different feeling through his heavy oak door, the soft whirring swish of skirts and the breathy twitter of muffled voices. Faintly to his acute ears came the sound of his little daughter's temperish protest, "I won't! I won't!" and the White Linen Nurse's fervid pleading, "Oh, you must,—you must!" and the Little Girl's mumbled ultimatum, "Well, I won't unless *you* do!"

Irascibly he crossed the room and yanked the door open abruptly upon their surprise and confusion. His nerves were very sore.

"What in thunder do you want?" he snarled.

Nervously for an instant the White Linen Nurse tugged at the Little Girl's hand. Nervously for an instant the Little Girl tugged at the White Linen Nurse's hand. Then with a swallow like a sob the White Linen Nurse lifted her glowing face to his.

"K—kiss us good night!" said the White Linen Nurse.

Telescopically all in that startling second, vision after vision beat down like blows upon the Senior Surgeon's senses! The pink, pink flush of the girl! The lure of her! The amazing sweetness! The physical docility! Oh ye gods,—the docility! Every trend of her birth,—of her youth,—of her training,—forcing her now—if he chose it—to unquestioning submission to his will and his judgment! Faster and faster the temptation surged through his pulses! The path from her lips to her ear was such a little path,—the plea so quick to make, so short,—"I want you *now!*"

"K—kiss us good night!" urged the Big Girl's unsuspecting lips. "Kiss us good night!" mocked the Little Girl's tremulous echo.

Then explosively with the noblest rudeness of his life, "No, I *won't!*" said the Senior Surgeon, and slammed the door in their faces.

Falteringly up the stairs he heard the two ascending,—speechless with surprise, perhaps,—stunned by his roughness,—still hand in hand, probably,—still climbing slowly bed-ward,—the soft, smooth, patient footfall of the White Linen Nurse and the jerky, laborious clang-clang-clang of a little dragging iron-braced leg.

Up and down,—round and round,—on and on and on,—the Senior Surgeon resumed his pacing. Under his eyes great shadows darkened. Along the corners of his mouth the lines furrowed like gray scars. Up and down,—round and round,—on and on and on—and on!

At ten o'clock, sitting bolt upright in her bed with her worried eyes straining bluely out across the Little Girl's somnolent form into unfathomable darkness, the White Linen Nurse in the throb of her own heart began to keep pace with that faint, horrid thud-thud-thud in the room below. Was he passing the book-case now? Had he reached the bay-window? Was he dawdling over those glistening scalpels? Would his nerves remember the flask in that upper desk drawer? Up and down,—round and round,—on and on,—the harrowing sound continued.

Resolutely at last she scrambled out of her snug nest, and hurrying into her great warm, pussy-gray wrapper began at once very practically, very unemotionally, with matches and alcohol and a shiny glass jar to prepare a huge steaming cup of malted milk. Beef-steak was infinitely better, she knew, or eggs, of course, but if she should venture forth to the kitchen for real substantiate the Senior Surgeon, she felt quite positive, would almost certainly hear her and stop her. So very stealthily thus like the proverbial assassin she crept down the front stairs with the innocent malted milk cup in her hand, and then with her knuckles just on the verge of rapping against the grimly inhospitable door, went suddenly paralyzed with uncertainty whether to advance or retreat.

Once again through the sombre inert wainscoting, exactly as if a soul had creaked, the Senior Surgeon sensed the threatening, intrusive presence of an unseen personality. Once again he strode across the room and jerked the door open with terrifying anger and resentment.

As though frozen there on his threshold by Her own little bare feet,—as though strangled there in his doorway by her own great mop of golden hair,—stolid and dumb as a pink-cheeked graven image the White Linen Nurse thrust the cup out awkwardly at him.

Absolutely without comment, as though she trotted on purely professional business and the case involved was of mutual concern to them both, the Senior Surgeon took the cup from her hand and closed the door again in her face.

At eleven o'clock she came again,—just as pink,—just as blue,—just as gray,—just as golden. And the cup of malted milk she brought with her was just as huge,—just as hot,—just as steaming,—only this time she had smuggled two raw eggs into it.

Once more the Senior Surgeon took the cup without comment and shut the door in her face.

At twelve o'clock she came again. The Senior Surgeon was unusually loquacious this time.

"Have you any more malted milk?" he asked tersely.

"Oh, yes, sir!" beamed the White Linen Nurse.

"Go and get it!" said the Senior Surgeon.

Obediently the White Linen Nurse pattered up the stairs and returned with the half depleted bottle. Frankly interested she recrossed the threshold of the room and delivered her glass treasure into the hands of the Senior Surgeon as he stood by his desk. Raising herself to her tiptoes she noted with eminent satisfaction that the three big cups on the other side of the desk had all been drained to their dregs.

Then very bluntly before her eyes the Senior Surgeon took the malted milk bottle and poured its remaining contents out quite wantonly into his waste basket. Then equally bluntly he took the White Linen Nurse by the shoulders and marched her out of the room.

"For God's sake!" he said, "get out of this room! And stay out!"

Bang! the big door slammed behind her. Like a snarling fang the lock bit into its catch.

"Yes, sir," said the White Linen Nurse. Even just to herself—all alone there in the big black hall, she was perfectly polite. "Y-e-s, sir," she repeated softly.

With a slightly sardonic grin on his face the Senior Surgeon resumed his pacing. Up and down,—round and round,—on and on and on!

At one o'clock in the dull, clammy chill of earliest morning he stopped long enough to light his hearthfire.

At two o'clock he stopped again to pile on a trifle more wood.

At three o'clock he dallied for an instant to close a window. The new day seemed strangely cold.

At four o'clock, dawn the wonder,—the miracle,—the long despaired of,—quickened wanly across the East. Then suddenly,—more like a phosphorescent breeze than a glow, the pale, pale yellow sunshine came wafting through the green gloom of the garden. The vigil was over!

Stumbling out into the shadowy hall to greet the new day and the new beginning, the Senior Surgeon almost tripped and fell over the White Linen Nurse sitting all huddled up and drowsy-eyed in a little gray heap on his outer threshold. The sensation of stepping upon a human body is not a pleasant one. It smote the Senior Surgeon nauseously through the nerves of his stomach.

"What are you doing here?" he fairly screamed at her.

"Just keeping you company, sir," yawned the White Linen Nurse. Before her hand could reach her mouth again another great childish yawn overwhelmed her. "Just—watching with you, sir," she finished more or less inarticulately.

"Watching with—me?" snarled the Senior Surgeon resentfully. "Why—should—you—watch—with—me?"

Like the frightened flash of a bird the heavy lashes went swooping down across the pink cheeks and lifted as suddenly again. "Because you're my—*man*!" yawned the White Linen Nurse.

Almost roughly the Senior Surgeon reached down and pulled the White Linen Nurse to her feet.

"God!" said the Senior Surgeon. In his strained, husky voice the word sounded like an oath. Grotesquely a little smile went scudding zig-zag across his haggard face. With an impulse absolutely alien to him he reached out abruptly again and raised the White Linen Nurse's hand to his lips. "*'Good* God' was what I meant—Miss Malgregor!" he grinned a bit sheepishly.

Quite bruskly then he turned and looked at his watch.

"I'd like my breakfast just as soon now as you can possibly get it!" he ordered peremptorily,—in his own morbid pathological emergency no more stopping to consider the White Linen Nurse's purely normal fatigue, than he in any pathological emergency of hers would have stopped to consider his own comfort,—safety,—or even perhaps, life!

Joyously then like a prisoner just turned loose, he went swinging up the stairs to recreate himself with a smoke and a shave and a great, splashing, cold shower-bath.

Only one thing seemed to really trouble him now. At the top of the stairs he stopped for an instant and cocked his head a bit worriedly towards the drawing-room where from some slow-brightening alcove bird-carol after bird-carol went fluting shrilly up into the morning.

"Is that—those blasted canaries?" he asked briefly.

Very companionably the White Linen Nurse cocked her own towsled head on one side and listened with him for half a moment.

"Only four of them are blasted canaries," she corrected very gently. "The fifth one is a paroquet that I got at a mark-down because it was a widowed bird and wouldn't mate again."

"Eh?" jerked the Senior Surgeon.

"Yes, sir," said the White Linen Nurse and started for the kitchen.

No one but the Senior Surgeon himself breakfasted in state at five o'clock that morning. Snug and safe in her crib upstairs the Little Crippled Girl slumbered peacefully on through the general disturbance. And as for the White Linen Nurse herself,—what with chilling and rechilling melons,—and broiling and unbroiling steaks,—and making and remaking coffee,—and hunting frantically for a different-sized water glass,—or a prettier colored plate, there was no time for anything except an occasional hurried surreptitious nibble half way between the stove and the table.

Yet in all that raucous early morning hour together neither man nor girl suffered towards the other the slightest personal sense of contrition or resentment, for each mind was trained equally fairly,—whether reacting on its own case or another's—to differentiate pretty readily between mean nerves and a—mean spirit.

Only once in fact across the intervening chasm of crankiness did the Senior Surgeon hurl a smile that was even remotely self-conscious or conciliatory. Glancing up suddenly from a particularly sharp and disagreeable speech, he noted the White Linen Nurse's red lips mumbling softly one to the other.

"Are you specially—religious,—Miss Malgregor?" he grinned quite abruptly.

"No, not specially, sir," said the White Linen Nurse. "Why, sir?"

"Oh, it's only—" grinned the Senior Surgeon dourly, "it's only that every time I'm especially ugly to you, I see your lips moving as though in 'silent prayer' as they call it—and I was just wondering—if there was any special formula you used with me—that kept you so—everlastingly—damned serene. Is there?"

"Yes, sir," said the White Linen Nurse.

"What is it?" demanded the Senior Surgeon quite bluntly.

"Do I have to tell?" gasped the White Linen Nurse. A little tremulously in her hand the empty cup she was carrying rattled against its saucer. "Do I have to tell?" she repeated pleadingly.

A delirious little thrill of power went fluttering through the Senior Surgeon's heart.

"Yes, you have to tell me!" he announced quite seriously.

In absolute submission to his demand, though with very palpable reluctance, the White Linen Nurse came forward to the table, put down the cup and saucer, and began to finger a trifle nervously at the cloth.

"Oh, I'm sure I didn't mean any harm, sir," she stammered. "But all I say is,—honest and truly all I say is,—'Bah! He's nothing but a man—nothing but a man—nothing but a man!' over and over and over,—just that, sir!"

Uproariously the Senior Surgeon pushed back his chair, and jumped to his feet.

"I guess after all I'll have to let the little kid call you—'Peach'—one day a week!" he acknowledged jocosely.

With infinite seriousness then he tossed back his great splendid head,—shook himself free apparently from all unhappy memories,—and started for his work-room,—a great gorgeously vital, extraordinarily talented, gray-haired *boy* lusting joyously for his own work and play again—after a month's distressing illness!

From the edge of the hall he turned round and made a really boyish grimace at her.

"Now if I only had the horns or the cloven hoof—that you think I have," he called, "what an easy time I'd make of it, raking over all the letters and ads. that are stacked up on my desk!"

"Yes, sir," said the White Linen Nurse.

Only once did he come back into the kitchen or dining-room for anything. It was at seven o'clock. And the White Linen Nurse was still washing dishes.

As radiant as a gray-haired god he towered up in the doorway. The boyish rejuvenation in him was even more startling than before.

"I'm feeling so much like a fighting cock this morning," he said, "I think I'll tackle that paper on surgical diseases of the pancreas that I have to read at Baltimore next month!" A little startlingly the gray lines furrowed into his cheeks again. "For Heaven's sake—see that I'm not disturbed by anything!" he admonished her warningly.

It must have been almost eight o'clock when the ear-splitting scream from upstairs sent the White Linen Nurse plunging out panic-stricken into the hall.

"Oh, Peach! Peach!" yelled the Little Girl's frenzied voice. "Come quick and see—what Fat Father's doing *now*—out on the piazza!"

Jerkily the White Linen Nurse swerved off through the French door that opened directly on the piazza. Had the Senior Surgeon hung himself, she tortured, in some wild, temporary aberration of the "morning after"?

But staunchly and reassuringly from the further end of the *piazza* the Senior Surgeon's broad back belied her horrid terror. Quite prosily and in apparently perfect health he was standing close to the railing of the piazza. On a table directly beside him rested four empty bird cages. Just at that particular moment he was inordinately busy releasing the last canary from the fifth cage. Both hands were smouched with ink and behind his left ear a fountain pen dallied daringly.

At the very first sound of the White Linen Nurse's step the Senior Surgeon turned and faced her with a sheepish sort of defiance.

"Well, now, I imagine," he said, "well, now, I imagine I've really made you—mad!"

"No, not mad, sir," faltered the White Linen Nurse. "No, not mad, sir,—but very far from well." Coaxingly with a perfectly futile hand she tried to lure one astonished yellow songster back from a swaying yellow bush. "Why, they'll die, sir!" she protested. "Savage cats will get them!"

"It's a choice of their lives—or mine!" said the Senior Surgeon tersely.

"Yes, sir," droned the White Linen Nurse.

Quite snappishly the Senior Surgeon turned upon her. "For Heaven's sake—do you think—canary birds are more valuable than I am?" he demanded stentoriously.

Most disconcertingly before his glowering eyes a great, sad, round tear rolled suddenly down the White Linen Nurse's flushed cheek.

"N—o,—not more valuable," conceded the White Linen Nurse. "But more—c-cunning."

Up to the roots of the Senior Surgeon's hair a flush of real contrition spread hotly.

"Why—Rae!" he stammered. "Why, what a beast I am! Why—! Why!" In sincere perplexity he began to rack his brains for some adequate excuse,—some adequate explanation. "Why, I'm sure I didn't mean to make you feel badly," he persisted. "Only I've lived alone so long that I suppose I've just naturally drifted into the way of having a thing if I wanted it and—throwing it away if I didn't! And canary birds, now? Well—really—" he began to glower all over again. "Oh, thunder!" he finished abruptly, "I guess I'll go on down to the hospital where I belong!"

A little wistfully the White Linen Nurse stepped forward. "The hospital?" she said. "Oh,—the hospital? Do you think that perhaps you could come home a little bit earlier than usual—to-night—and—and help me catch—just one of the canaries?"

"What?" gasped the Senior Surgeon. Incredulously with a very inky finger he pointed at his own breast. "What? I?" he demanded. "I? Come home—early—from the hospital to help—you—catch a canary?"

Disgustedly without further comment he turned and stalked back again into the house.

The disgust was still in his walk as he left the house an hour later. Watching his exit down the long gravel path the Little Crippled Girl commented audibly on the matter.

"Peach! Peach!" called the Little Crippled Girl. "What makes Fat Father walk so—surprised?"

People at the hospital also commented upon him.

"Gee!" giggled the new nurses. "We bet he's a Tartar! But isn't his hair cute? And say—" gossiped the new nurses, "is it really true that that Malgregor girl was pinned down perfectly helpless under the car and he wouldn't let her out till she'd promised to marry him? Isn't it *awful?* Isn't it *romantic?*"

"Why! Dr. Faber's back!" fluttered the senior nurses. "Isn't he wonderful? Isn't he beautiful? But, oh, say," they worried, "what do you suppose Rae ever finds to talk with him about? Would she ever dare talk *things* to him,— just plain every-day *things*,—hats, and going to the theater, and what to have for breakfast?—breakfast?" they gasped. "Why, yes, of course!" they reasoned more sanely. "Steak? Eggs? Even oatmeal? Why, people had to eat— no matter how wonderful they were! But evenings?" they speculated more darkly. "But evenings?" In the whole range of human experience—was it even so much as remotely imaginable that—evenings—the Senior Surgeon and—Rae Malgregor—sat in the hammock and held hands? "Oh, Gee!" blanched the senior nurses.

"Good-morning, Dr. Faber!" greeted the Superintendent of Nurses from behind her austere office desk.

"Good-morning, Miss Hartzen!" said the Senior Surgeon.

"Have you had a pleasant trip?" quizzed the Superintendent of Nurses.

"Exceptionally so, thank you!" said the Senior Surgeon.

"And—Mrs. Faber,—is she well?" persisted the Superintendent of Nurses conscientiously.

"Mrs. Faber?" gasped the Senior Surgeon. "Mrs. Faber? Oh, yes! Why, of course! Yes, indeed—she's extraordinarily well! I never saw her better!"

"She must have been—very lonely without you—this past month?" rasped the Superintendent of Nurses—perfectly politely.

"Yes—she was," flushed the Senior Surgeon. "She—she suffered—keenly!"

"And you, too?" drawled the Superintendent of Nurses. "It must have been very hard for you."

"Yes, it was!" sweated the Senior Surgeon. "I suffered keenly, too!"

Distractedly he glanced back at the open door. An extraordinarily large number of nurses, internes, orderlies, seemed to be having errands up and down the corridor that allowed them a peculiarly generous length of neck to stretch into the Superintendent's office.

"Great Heavens!" snapped the Senior Surgeon. "What's the matter with everybody this morning?" Tempestuously he started for the door. "Hurry up my cases, please, Miss Hartzen!" he ordered. "Send them to the operating room! And let me get to work!"

At eleven o'clock, absolutely calm, absolutely cool,—pure as a girl in his fresh, white operating clothes—cleaner,—skin, hair, teeth, hands,—than any girl who ever walked the face of the earth, in a white tiled room as surgically clean as himself, with three or four small, glistening instruments still boiling, steaming hot—and half a dozen breathless assistants almost as immaculate as himself, with his gown, cap and mask adjusted, his gloves finally on, and the faintest possible little grin twitching oddly at the corner of his mouth, he "went in" as they say, to a new born baby's tortured, twisted spine—and took out—fifty years perhaps of hunched-back pain and shame and morbid passions flourishing banefully in the dark shades of a disordered life.

At half-past twelve he did an appendix operation on the only son of his best friend. At one o'clock he did another appendix operation. Whom it was on didn't matter. It couldn't have been worse on—any one. At half-past one no one remembered to feed him. At two, in another man's operation, he saw the richest merchant in the city go wafted out into eternity on the fumes of ether taken for the lancing of a stye. At three o'clock, passing the open door of one of the public waiting-rooms, an Italian peasant woman rushed out and spat in his face because her tubercular daughter had just died at the sanitarium where the Senior Surgeon's money had sent her. Only in this one wild, defiling moment did the lust for alcohol surge up in him again, surge clamorously, brutally, absolutely mercilessly, as though in all the known cleansants of the world only interminable raw whisky was hot enough to cauterize a polluted consciousness. At half past three, as soon as he could change his clothes again, he re-broke and re-set an acrobat's priceless leg. At five o'clock, more to rest himself than anything else, he went up to the autopsy amphitheater to look over an exhibit of enlarged hearts, whose troubles were permanently over.

At six o'clock just as he was leaving the great building with all its harrowing sights, sounds, and smells, a peremptory telephone call from one of the younger surgeons of the city summoned him back into the stuffy office again.

"Dr. Faber?"

"Yes."

"This is Merkley!"

"Yes."

"Can you come immediately and help me with that fractured skull case I was telling you about this morning? We'll have to trepan right away!"

"Trepan nothing!" grunted the Senior Surgeon. "I've got to go home early to-night—and help catch a canary."

"Catch a—what?" gasped the younger surgeon.

"A canary!" grinned the Senior Surgeon mirthlessly.

"A—*what?*" roared the younger man.

"Oh, shut up, you damned fool! Of course I'll come!" said the Senior Surgeon.

There was no "boy" left in the Senior Surgeon when he reached home that night.

Gray with road-travel, haggard with strain and fatigue, it was long, long after the rosy sunset time,—long, long after the yellow supper light, that he came dragging up through the sweet-scented dusk of the garden and threw himself down without greeting of any sort on the top step of the piazza where the White Linen Nurse's skirts glowed palely through the gloom.

"Well, I put a canary bird back into its cage for you!" he confided laconically. "It was a little chap's soul. It sure would have gotten away before morning."

"Who was the man that tried to turn it loose—*this* time?" asked the White Linen Nurse.

"I didn't say that anybody did!" growled the Senior Surgeon.

"Oh," said the White Linen Nurse. "Oh." Quite palpably a little shiver of flesh and starch went rustling through her. "I've had a wonderful day, too!" she confided softly. "I've cleaned the attic and darned nine pairs of your stockings and bought a sewing-machine—and started to make you a white silk negligee shirt for a surprise!"

"Eh?" jerked the Senior Surgeon.

The jerk seemed to liberate suddenly the faint vibration of dishes and the sound of ice knocking lusciously against a glass.

"Oh, have you had any supper, sir?" asked the White Linen Nurse.

With a prodigious sigh the Senior Surgeon threw his head back against the piazza railing and stretched his legs a little further out along the piazza floor.

"Supper?" he groaned. "No! Nor dinner! Nor breakfast! Nor any other—blankety-blank meal as far back as I can remember!" Janglingly in his voice, fatigue, hunger, nerves, crashed together like the slammed notes of a piano. "But I wouldn't—move—now," he snarled, "if all the blankety-blank-blank foods in Christendom—were piled blankety-blank-blank high—on all the blankety-blank-blank tables—in this whole blankety-blank-blank house!"

Ecstatically the White Linen Nurse clapped her hands. "Oh, that's just exactly what I hoped you'd say!" she cried. "'Cause the supper's—right here!"

"Here?" snapped the Senior Surgeon. Tempestuously he began all over again. "I—tell—you—I—wouldn't—lift—my—little finger—if all the blankety-blank-blank-blank—"

"Oh, Goody then!" said the White Linen Nurse. "'Cause now I can feed you! I sort of miss fussing with the canary birds," she added wistfully.

"Feed me?" roared the Senior Surgeon. Again something started a lump of ice tinkling faintly in a thin glass. "Feed me?" he began all over again.

Yet with a fragrant strawberry half as big as a peach held out suddenly under his nose, just from sheer, irresistible instinct he bit out at it—and nipped the White Linen Nurse's finger instead.

"Ouch—sir!" said the White Linen Nurse.

Mumblingly down from an upstairs window, as from a face flatted smouchingly against a wire screen, a peremptory summons issued.

"Peach!—Peach!" called an angry little voice. "If you don't come to bed—now—I'll—I'll say my curses instead of my prayers!"

A trifle nervously the White Linen Nurse scrambled to her feet.

"Maybe I'd—better go?" she said.

"Maybe—you had!" said the Senior Surgeon quite definitely.

At the edge of the threshold the White Linen Nurse turned for an instant.

"Good-night, Dr. Faber!" she whispered.

"Good-night, Rae Malgregor—Faber!" said the Senior Surgeon.

"Good-night—*what?*" gasped the White Linen Nurse.

"Good-night, Rae Malgregor—Faber," repeated the Senior Surgeon.

Clutching at her skirts as though a mouse were after her, the White Linen Nurse went scuttling up the stairs.

Very late—on into the night—the Senior Surgeon lay there on his piazza floor staring out into his garden. Very companionably from time to time, like a tame firefly, a little bright spark hovered and glowed for an instant above the bowl of his pipe. Puff-puff-puff, doze-doze-doze, throb-throb-throb,—on and on and on and on—into the sweet-scented night.

CHAPTER X

So the days passed. And the nights. And more days. And more nights. July—August,—on and on and on.

Strenuous, nerve-racking, heart-breaking surgical days—broken maritally only by the pleasant, soft-worded greeting at the gate, or the practical, homely appeal of good food cooked with heart as well as hands, or the tingling, inciting masculine consciousness of there being a woman's—blush in the house!

Strenuous, house-working, child-nursing, home-making, domestic days—broken maritally only by the jaded, harsh word at the gate, the explosive criticism of food, the deadening, depressing, feminine consciousness of there being a man's—vicious temper in the house!

Now and again in one big automobile or another the White Linen Nurse and the Senior Surgeon rode out together, always and forever with the Little Crippled Girl sitting between them,—the other woman's little crippled girl. Now and again in the late summer afternoons the White Linen Nurse and the Senior Surgeon strolled together through the rainbow-colored garden, always and forever with the Little Crippled Girl,—the other woman's little crippled girl, tagging close behind them with her little sad, clanking leg. Now and again in the long sweet summer evenings the White Linen Nurse and the Senior Surgeon sat on the clematis-shadowed porch together, always and forever with the Little Crippled Girl,—the other woman's little crippled girl, mocking them querulously from some vague upper window.

Now and again across the mutually ghost-haunted chasm that separated them flashed the incontrovertible signal of sex and sense, as once when a new Interne, grossly bungling, stepped to the hospital window with a colleague to watch the Senior Surgeon's car roll away as usual with its two feminine passengers.

"What makes the Chief so stingy with that big handsome girl of his?" queried the new Interne a bit resentfully. "He won't ever bring her into the hospital!—won't ever ask any of us young chaps out to his house! And some of us come mighty near to being eligible, too!—Who's he saving her for, anyway?—A saint?—A miracle-worker?—A millionaire medicine man?—They don't exist, you know!"

"I'm saving her for myself!" snapped the Senior Surgeon most disconcertingly from the doorway. "She—she happens to be my wife, not my daughter,—thank you!"

When the Senior Surgeon went home that night he carried a big bunch of magazines and a box of candy as large as his head tucked courtly under his arm.

Now and again across the chasm that separated them flashed the incontrovertible signal of mutual trust and appreciation, as when once, after a particularly violent vocal outburst on the Senior Surgeon's part, he sobered down very suddenly and said:

"Rae Malgregor,—do you realize that in all the weeks we've been together you've never once nagged me about my swearing? Not a word,—not a single word!"

"I'm not very used to—words," smiled the White Linen Nurse hopefully. "All I know how to nag with is—is raw eggs! If we could only get those nerves of yours padded just once, sir! The swearing would get well of itself."

In August the Senior Surgeon suggested sincerely that the house was much too big for the White Linen Nurse to run all alone, but conceded equally sincerely, under the White Linen Nurse's vehement protest, that servants, particularly new servants did creak considerably round a house, and that maybe "just for the present" at least, until he finished his very nervous paper on brain tumors perhaps it would be better to stay "just by ourselves."

In September the White Linen Nurse wanted very much to go home to Nova Scotia to her sister's wedding but the Senior Surgeon was trying a very complicated and worrisome new brace on the Little Girl's leg and it didn't seem quite kind to go. In October she planned her trip all over again. She was going to take the Little Crippled Girl with her this time. But with their trunks already packed and waiting in the hall, the Senior Surgeon came home from the hospital with a septic finger—and it didn't seem quite best to leave him.

"Well, how do you like being married *now*?" asked the Senior Surgeon a bit ironically in his work-room that night, after the White Linen Nurse had stood for an hour with evil-smelling washes, and interminable bandages trying to fix that finger the precise, particular way that he thought it ought to be fixed. "Well—how do you like—being married *now*?" he insisted trenchantly.

"Oh, I like it all right, sir!" said the White Linen Nurse. A little bit wanly this time she smiled her pluck up into the Senior Surgeon's questioning face. "Oh, I like it all right, sir! Oh, of course, sir," she confided thoughtfully—"Oh, of course, sir—it isn't quite as fancy as being engaged—or quite as free and easy as being—single. But still—" she admitted with desperate honesty—"but still there's a sort of—a sort of a combination importance and—and comfort about it, sir, like a—like a velvet suit—the second year, sir."

"Is that—all?" quizzed the Senior Surgeon bluntly.

"That's all—so far, sir," said the White Linen Nurse.

In November the White Linen Nurse caught a bit of cold that pulled her down a little. But the Senior Surgeon didn't notice it specially among all the virulent ills he lived and worked with from day to day. And then when the cold disappeared, Indian Summer came like a reeking sweat after a chill! And the house *was* big! And the Little Crippled Girl *was* pretty difficult to manage now and then! And the Senior Surgeon, no matter how hard he tried not to, did succeed somehow in creating more or less of a disturbance—at least every other day or two!

And then suddenly, one balmy gold and crimson Indian Summer morning, standing out on the piazza trying to hear what the Little Crippled Girl was calling from the window and what the Senior Surgeon was calling from the gate, the White Linen Nurse fell right down in her tracks, brutally, bulkily, like a worn-out horse, and lay as she fell, a huddled white heap across the gray piazza.

"Oh, Father! Come quick! Come quick! Peach has deaded herself!" yelled the Little Girl's frantic voice.

Just with his foot on the step of his car the Senior Surgeon heard the cry and came speeding back up the long walk. Already there before him the Little Girl knelt raining passionate, agonized kisses on her beloved playmate's ghastly white face.

"Leave her alone!" thundered the Senior Surgeon. "Leave her alone, I say!"

Bruskly he pushed the Little Girl aside and knelt to cradle his own ear against the White Linen Nurse's heart.

"Oh, it's all right," he growled, and gathered the White Linen Nurse right up in his arms—she was startlingly lighter than he had supposed—and carried her up the stairs and put her to bed like a child in the great sumptuous guest-room, in a great sumptuous nest of all the best linens and blankets, with the Little Crippled Girl superintending the task with many hysterical suggestions and sharp staccato interruptions. For once in his life the Senior Surgeon did not stop to quarrel with his daughter.

Rallying limply from her swoon the White Linen Nurse stared out with hazy perplexity at last from her dimpling white pillows to see the Senior Surgeon standing amazingly at the guest-room bureau with a glass and a medicine-dropper in his hand, and the Little Crippled Girl hanging apparently by her narrow peaked chin across the foot-board of the bed.

Gazing down worriedly at the lace-ruffled sleeve of her night-dress the White Linen Nurse made her first public speech to the—world at large.

"Who—put—me—to—bed?" whispered the White Linen Nurse.

Ecstatically the Little Crippled Girl began to pound her fists on the foot-board of the bed.

"Father did!" she cried in unmistakable triumph. "All the little hooks! All the little buttons!—*wasn't* it cunning?"

The Senior Surgeon would hardly have been human if he hadn't glanced back suddenly over his shoulder at the White Linen Nurse's precipitously changing color. Quite irrepressibly, as he saw the red, red blood come surging home again into her cheeks, a little short chuckling laugh escaped him.

"I guess you'll live—now," he remarked dryly.

Then because a Senior Surgeon can't stay home on the mere impulse of the moment from a great rushing hospital, just because one member of his household happens to faint perfectly innocently in the morning, he hurried on to his work again. And saved a little boy, and lost a little girl, and mended a fractured thigh, and eased a gunshot wound, and came dashing home at noon in one of his thousand-dollar hours to feel the White Linen Nurse's pulse and broil her a bit of tenderloin steak with his own thousand-dollar hands,—and then went dashing off again to do one major operation or another, telephoned home once or twice during the afternoon to make sure that everything was all right, and finding that the White Linen Nurse was comfortably up and about again, went sprinting off fifty miles somewhere on a meningitis consultation, and came dragging home at last, somewhere near midnight, to a big black house brightened only by a single light in the kitchen where the White Linen Nurse went tiptoeing softly from stove to pantry in deft preparation of an appetizing supper for him.

Quite roughly again without smile or appreciation the Senior Surgeon took her by the shoulders and turned her out of the kitchen, and started her up the stairs.

"Are you an—idiot?" he said. "Are you an—imbecile?" he came back and called up the stairs to her just as she was disappearing from the upper landing.

Then up and down, round and round, on and on and on, the Senior Surgeon began suddenly to pace again.

Only, for some unexplainable reason to the White Linen Nurse upstairs, his work-room didn't seem quite large enough for his pacing this night Along the broad piazza she heard his footsteps creak. Far, far into the morning, lying warm and snug in her own little bed, she heard his footsteps crackling through the wet-leafed garden paths.

Yet the Senior Surgeon didn't look an atom jaded or forlorn when he came down to breakfast the next morning. He had on a brand new gray suit that fitted his big, powerful shoulders to perfection, and the glad glow of his shower-bath was still reddening faintly in his cheeks as he swung around the corner of the table and dropped down into his place with an odd little grin on his lips directed intermittently towards the White Linen Nurse and the Little Crippled Girl who already waited him there at either end of the table.

"Oh, Father, isn't it lovely to have my darling—darling Peach all well again!" beamed the Little Crippled Girl with unusual friendliness.

"Speaking of your—'darling Peach,'" said the Senior Surgeon quite abruptly. "Speaking of your 'darling Peach,'—I'm going to—take her away with me to-day—for a week or so."

"Eh?" jumped the Little Crippled Girl.

"What? What, sir?" stammered the White Linen Nurse.

Quite prosily the Senior Surgeon began to butter a piece of toast. But the little twinkle around his eyes belied in some way the utter prosiness of the act.

"For a little trip," he confided amiably. "A little holiday!"

A trifle excitedly the White Linen Nurse laid down her knife and fork and stared at him, blue-eyed and wondering as a child.

"A holiday?" she gasped. "To a—beach, you mean? Would there be a—a roller-coaster? I've never seen a roller-coaster!"

"Eh?" laughed the Senior Surgeon.

"Oh, I'm going, too! I'm going, too!" piped the Little Crippled Girl.

Most jerkily the Senior Surgeon pushed back his chair from the table and swallowed half a cup of coffee at one single gulp.

"Going *three*, you mean?" he glowered at his little daughter. "Going *three*?" His comment that ensued was distinctly rough as far as diction was concerned, but the facial expression of ineffable peace that accompanied it would have made almost any phrase sound like a benediction. "Not by a—damned sight!" beamed the Senior Surgeon. "This little trip is just for Peach and me!"

"But—sir?" fluttered the White Linen Nurse. Her face was suddenly pinker than any rose that ever bloomed.

With an impulse absolutely novel to him the Senior Surgeon turned and swung his little daughter very gently to his shoulder.

"Your Aunt Agnes is coming to stay with *you*—in just about ten minutes!" he affirmed. "That's—what's going to happen to *you*! And maybe there'll be a pony—a white pony."

"But Peach is so—pleasant!" wailed the Little Crippled Girl. "Peach is so pleasant!" she began to scream and kick.

"So it seems!" growled the Senior Surgeon. "And she's—dying of it!"

Tearfully the Little Girl wriggled down to the ground, and hobbled around and thrust her finger-tip into the White Linen Nurse's blushiest cheek.

"I don't want—Peach—to—die," she admitted worriedly. "But I don't want anybody to take her away!"

"The pony is—very white," urged the Senior Surgeon with a diplomacy quite alien to him.

Abruptly the Little Girl turned and faced him. "What color is Aunt Agnes?" she asked vehemently.

"Aunt Agnes is—pretty white, too," attested the Senior Surgeon.

With the faintest possible tinge of superciliousness the Little Girl lifted her sharp chin a trifle higher.

"If it's just a perfectly plain white pony," she said, "I'd rather have Peach. But if it's a white pony with black blots on it, and if it can pull a little cart, and if I can whip it with a little switch, and if it will eat sugar-lumps out of my hand,—and if its name is—is—'Beautiful Pretty-Thing'—"

"Its name has always been—'Beautiful Pretty-Thing,' I'm quite sure!" insisted the Senior Surgeon. Inadvertently as he spoke he reached out and put a hand very lightly on the White Linen Nurse's shoulder.

Instantly into the Little Girl's suspicious face flushed a furiously uncontrollable flame of jealousy and resentment. Madly she turned upon her father.

"You're a liar!" she screamed. "There *is* no white pony! You're a robber! You're a—a—drunk! You shan't have my darling Peach!" And threw herself frenziedly into the White Linen Nurse's lap.

Impatiently the Senior Surgeon disentangled the little clinging arms, and raising the White Linen Nurse to her feet pushed her emphatically towards the hall.

"Go to my work-room," he said. "Quickly! I want to talk with you!"

A moment later he joined her there, and shut and locked the door behind him. The previous night's loss of sleep showed plainly in his face now, and the hospital strain of the day before, and of the day before that, and of the day before *that*.

Heavily, moodily, he crossed the room and threw himself down in his desk chair with the White Linen Nurse still standing before him as though she were nothing but a—white linen nurse. All the splendor was suddenly gone from him, all the radiance, all the exultant purpose.

"Well, Rae Malgregor," he grinned mirthlessly. "The little kid is right, though I certainly don't know where she got her information. I *am* a Liar. The pony's name is not yet 'Beautiful Pretty-Thing'! I *am* a—Drunk. I was drunk most of June! I *am* a Robber! I have taken you out of your youth—and the love-chances of your youth,—and shut you up here in this great, gloomy old house of mine—to be my slave—and my child's slave—and—"

"Pouf!" said the White Linen Nurse. "It would seem—silly—now, sir,—to marry a boy!"

"And I've been a beast to you!" persisted the Senior Surgeon. "From the very first day you belonged to me I've been a—beast to you,—venting brutally on your youth, on your sweetness, on your patience,—all the work, the worry, the wear and tear, the abnormal strain and stress of my disordered days—and years,—and I've let my little girl vent also on you all the pang and pain of *her* disordered days! And because in this great, gloomy, rackety house it seemed suddenly like a miracle from heaven to have service that was soft-footed, gentle-handed, pleasant-hearted, I've let you shoulder all the hideous drudgery,—the care,—one horrid homely task after another piling up-up-up—till you dropped in your tracks yesterday—still smiling!"

"But I got a good deal out of it, even so, sir!" protested the White Linen Nurse. "See, sir!" she smiled. "I've got real lines in my face—now—like other women! I'm not a doll any more! I'm not a—"

"Yes!" groaned the Senior Surgeon. "And I might just as kindly have carved those lines with my knife! But I was going to make it all up to you to-day!" he hurried. "I swear I was! Even in one short little week I could have done it! You wouldn't have known me! I was going to take you away,—just you and me! I would have been a Saint! I swear I would! I would have given you such a great, wonderful, child-hearted holiday—as you never dreamed of in all your unselfish life! A holiday all *you—you—you!* You could have—dug in the sand if you'd wanted to! Gad! I'd have dug in the sand—if you'd wanted me to! And now it's all gone from me, all the will, all the sheer positive self-assurance that I could have carried the thing through—absolutely selflessly. That little girl's sneering taunt? The ghost of her mother—in that taunt? God! When anybody knocks you just in your decency it doesn't harm you specially! But when they knock you in your Wanting-To-Be-Decent it—it undermines you somewhere. I don't know exactly how! I'm nothing but a man again—now, just a plain, every day, greedy, covetous, physical man—on the edge of a holiday, the first clean holiday in twenty years,—that he no longer dares to take!"

A little swayingly the White Linen Nurse shifted her standing weight from one foot to the other.

"I'm sorry, sir!" said the White Linen Nurse. "I'd like to have seen a roller-coaster, sir!"

Just for an instant a gleam of laughter went brightening across the Senior Surgeon's brooding face, and was gone again.

"Rae Malgregor, come here!" he ordered quite sharply.

Very softly, very glidingly, like the footfall of a person who has never known heels, the White Linen Nurse came forward swiftly and sliding in cautiously between the Senior Surgeon and his desk, stood there with her back braced against the desk, her fingers straying idly up and down the edges of the desk, staring up into his face all readiness, all attention, like a soldier waiting further orders.

So near was she that he could almost hear the velvet heart-throb of her,—the little fluttering swallow,—yet by some strange, persistent aloofness of her, some determinate virginity, not a fold of her gown, not an edge, not a thread, seemed to even so much as graze his knee, seemed to even so much as shadow his hand,—lest it short-circuit thereby the seething currents of their variant emotions.

With extraordinary intentness for a moment the Senior Surgeon sat staring into the girl's eyes, the blue, blue eyes too full of childish questioning yet to flinch with either consciousness or embarrassment.

"After all, Rae Malgregor," he smiled at last, faintly—"After all, Rae Malgregor,—Heaven knows when I shall ever get—another holiday!"

"Yes, sir?" said the White Linen Nurse.

With apparent irrelevance he reached for his ivory paper-cutter and began bending it dangerously between his adept fingers.

"How long have you been with me, Rae Malgregor?" he asked quite abruptly.

"Four months—actually with you, sir," said the White Linen Nurse.

"Do you happen to remember the exact phrasing of my—proposal of marriage to you?" he asked shrewdly.

"Oh, yes, sir!" said the White Linen Nurse. "You called it 'general heartwork for a family of two'!"

A little grimly before her steady gaze the Senior Surgeon's own eyes fell, and rallied again almost instantly with a gaze as even and direct as hers.

"Well," he smiled. "Through the whole four months I seem to have kept my part of the contract all right—and held you merely as a—drudge in my home. Have you then decided, once and for all time,—whether you are going to stay on with us—or whether you will 'give notice' as other drudges have done?"

With a little backward droop of one shoulder the White Linen Nurse began to finger nervously at the desk behind her, and turning half way round as though to estimate what damage she was doing, exposed thus merely the profile of her pink face, of her white throat, to the Senior Surgeon's questioning eyes.

"I shall never—give notice, sir!" fluttered the white throat.

"Are you perfectly sure?" insisted the Senior Surgeon.

The pink in the White Linen Nurse's profiled cheek deepened a little.

"Perfectly sure, sir!" attested the carmine lips.

Like the crack of a pistol the Senior Surgeon snapped the ivory paper cutter in two.

"All right then!" he said. "Rae Malgregor, look at me! Don't take your eyes from mine, I say! Rae Malgregor, if I should decide in my own mind, here and now, that it was best for you—as well as for me—that you should come away with me now—for this week,—not as my guest as I had planned,—but as my wife,—even if you were not quite ready for it in your heart,—even if you were not yet remotely ready for it,—would you come because I told you to come?"

Heavily under her white, white eyelids, heavily under her black, black lashes, the girl's eyes struggled up to meet his own.

"Yes, sir," whispered the White Linen Nurse.

Abruptly the Senior Surgeon pushed back his chair from the desk, and stood up. The important decision once made, no further finessing of words seemed either necessary or dignified to him.

"Go and pack your suit-case quickly then!" he ordered. "I want to get away from here within half an hour!"

But before the girl had half crossed the room he called to her suddenly, his whole bearing and manner miraculously changed, and his face in that moment as haggard as if a whole lifetime's struggle was packed into it.

"Rae Malgregor," he drawled mockingly. "This thing shall be—barter way through to the end,—with the credit always on your side of the account. In exchange for the gift—of yourself—your—wonderful self—and the trust that goes with it, I will give you,—God help me,—the ugliest thing in my life. And God knows I have broken faith with myself once or twice but—never have I broken my word to another! From now on,—in token of your trust in me,—for whatever the bitter gift is worth to you,—as long as you stay with me,—my Junes shall be yours—to do with—as you please!"

"What, sir?" gasped the White Linen Nurse. "*What*, sir?"

Softly, almost stealthily, she was half way back across the room to him, when she stopped suddenly and threw out her arms with a gesture of appeal and defiance.

"All the same, sir!" she cried passionately, "all the same, sir,—the place is too hard for the small pay I get! Oh, I will do what I promised!" she attested with increasing passion. "I will never leave you! And I will mother your little girl! And I will servant your big house! And I will go with you wherever you say! And I will be to you whatever you wish! And I will never flinch from any hardship you impose on me—nor whine over any pain,—on and on and on—all my days—all my years—till I drop in my tracks again and—die—as you say 'still smiling'! All the same!" she reiterated wildly, "the place is too hard! It always was too hard! It always will be too hard—for such small pay!"

"For such small pay?" gasped the Senior Surgeon.

Around his heart a horrid clammy chill began to settle. Sickeningly through his brain a dozen recent financial transactions began to rehearse themselves.

"You mean, Miss Malgregor," he said a bit brokenly. "You mean—that I—haven't been generous enough with you?"

"Yes, sir," faltered the White Linen Nurse.

All the storm and passion died suddenly from her, leaving her just a frightened girl again, flushing pink-white, pink-white, pink-white, before the Senior Surgeon's scathing stare. One step, two steps, three, she advanced towards him.

"Oh, I mean, sir," she whispered, "oh, I mean, sir,—that I'm just an ordinary, ignorant country girl and you—are further above me than the moon from the sea! I couldn't expect you to—love me, sir! I couldn't even dream of your loving me! *But I do think you might like me just a little bit with your heart!*"

"What?" flushed the Senior Surgeon. "*What?*"

Whacketty-bang against the window pane sounded the Little Crippled Girl's knuckled fists! Darkly against the window pane squashed the Little Crippled Girl's staring face.

"Father!" screamed the shrill voice. "Father! There's a white lady here with two black ladies washing the breakfast dishes! Is it Aunt Agnes?"

With a totally unexpected laugh, with a totally unexpected desire to laugh, the Senior Surgeon strode across the room and unlocked his door. Even then his lips against the White Linen Nurse's ear made just a whisper, not a kiss.

"God bless you!—*hurry!*" he said. "And let's get out of here before any telephone message catches me!"

Then almost calmly he walked out on the piazza, and greeted his sister-in-law.

"Hello, Agnes!" he said.

"Hello, yourself!" smiled his sister-in-law.

"How's everything?" he enquired politely.

"How's everything with you?" parried his sister-in-law.

Idly for a few moments the Senior Surgeon threw out stray crumbs of thought to feed the conversation, while smilingly all the while from her luxuriant East Indian chair his sister-in-law sat studying the general situation. The Senior Surgeon's sister-in-law was always studying something. Last year it was archaeology,—the year before, basketry,—this year it happened to be eugenics, or something funny like that,—next year again it might be book-binding.

"So you and your pink and white shepherdess are going off on a little trip together?" she queried banteringly. "The girl's a darling, Lendicott! I haven't had as much sport in a long time as I had that afternoon last June when I came in my best calling-clothes and—helped her paint the kitchen woodwork! And I had come prepared to be a bit nasty, Lendicott! In all honesty, Lendicott, I might just as well 'fess up that I had come prepared to be just a little bit nasty!"

"She seems to have a way," smiled the Senior Surgeon, "she seems to have a way of disarming people's unpleasant intentions."

A trifle quizzically for an instant the woman turned her face to the Senior Surgeon's. It was a worldly face, a cold-featured, absolutely worldly face, with a surprisingly humorous mouth that warmed her nature just about as cheer fully, and just about as effectually, as one open fireplace warms a whole house. Nevertheless one often achieved much comfort by keeping close to "Aunt Agnes's" humorous mouth, for Aunt Agnes knew a thing or two,—Aunt Agnes did,—and the things that she made a point of knowing were conscientiously amiable.

"Why, Lendicott Faber," she rallied him now. "Why, you're as nervous as a school-boy! Why, I believe—I believe that you're going courting!"

More opportunely than any man could have dared to hope, the White Linen Nurse appeared suddenly on the scene in her little blue serge wedding-suit with her traveling-case in her hand. With a gasp of relief the Senior Surgeon took her case and his own and went on down the path to his car and his chauffeur leaving the two women temporarily alone.

When he returned to the piazza the Woman-of-the-World and the Girl-not-at-all-of-the-World were bidding each other a really affectionate good-by, and the woman's face looked suddenly just a little bit old but the girl's cheeks were most inordinately blooming.

In unmistakable friendliness his sister-in-law extended her hand to him.

"Good-by, Lendicott, old man!" she said. "And good luck to you!" A little slyly out of her shrewd gray eyes, she glanced up sideways at him. "You've got the devil's own temper, Lendicott dear," she teased, "and two or three other vices probably, and if rumor speaks the truth you've run a-muck more than once in your life,—but there's one thing I will say for you,—though it prove you a dear Stupid: you never were over-quick to suspect that any woman could possibly be in love with you!"

"To what woman do you particularly refer?" mocked the Senior Surgeon impatiently.

Quite brazenly to her own heart which never yet apparently had stirred the laces that enshrined it, his sister-in-law pointed with persistent banter.

"Maybe I refer to—myself," she laughed, "and maybe to the only—other lady present!"

"Oh!" gasped the White Linen Nurse.

"You do me much honor, Agnes," bowed the Senior Surgeon. Quite resolutely he held his gaze from following the White Linen Nurse's quickly averted face.

A little oddly for an instant the older woman's glance hung on his. "More honor perhaps than you think, Lendicott Faber!" she said, and kept right on smiling.

"Eh?" jerked the Senior Surgeon. Restively he turned to the White Linen Nurse.

Very flushingly on the steps the White Linen Nurse knelt arguing with the Little Crippled Girl.

"Your father and I are—going away," she pleaded. "Won't you—please—kiss us good-by?"

"I've only got one kiss," sulked the Little Crippled Girl.

"Give it to your—father!" pleaded the White Linen Nurse.

Amazingly all in a second the ugliness vanished from the little face. Dartlingly like a bird the Child swooped down and planted one large round kiss on the Senior Surgeon's astonished boot.

"Beautiful Father!" she cried, "I kiss your feet!"

Abruptly the Senior Surgeon plunged from the step and started down the walk. His cheek-bones were quite crimson.

Two or three rods behind him the White Linen Nurse followed falteringly. Once she stopped to pick up a tiny stick or a stone. And once she dallied to straighten out a snarled spray of red and brown woodbine.

Missing the sound or the shadow of her the Senior Surgeon turned suddenly to wait. So startled was she by his intentness, so flustered, so affrighted, that just for an instant the Senior Surgeon thought that she was going to wheel in her tracks and bolt madly back to the house. Then quite unexpectedly she gave an odd, muffled little cry, and ran swiftly to him like a child, and slipped her bare hand trustingly into his. And they went on together to the car.

With his foot already half lifted to the step the Senior Surgeon turned abruptly around and lifted his hat and stood staring back bareheaded for some unexplainable reason at the two silent figures on the piazza.

"Rae," he said perplexedly, "Rae, I don't seem to know just why—but somehow I'd like to have you kiss your hand to Aunt Agnes!"

Obediently the White Linen Nurse withdrew her fingers from his and wafted two kisses, one to "Aunt Agnes" and one to the Little Crippled Girl.

Then the White Linen Nurse and the Senior Surgeon climbed up into the tonneau of the car where they had never, never sat alone before, and the Senior Surgeon gave a curt order to his man and the big car started off again into—interminable spaces.

Mutely without a word, without a glance passing between them the Senior Surgeon held out his hand to her once more, as though the absence of her hand in his was suddenly a lonesomeness not to be endured again while life lasted.

Whizz—whizz—whizz—whirr—whirr—whirr the ribbony road began to roll up again on that hidden spool under the car.

When the chauffeur's mind seemed sufficiently absorbed in speed and sound the Senior Surgeon bent down a little mockingly and mumbled his lips inarticulately at the White Linen Nurse.

"See!" he laughed. "I've got a text, too, to keep my courage up! Of course you look like an angel!" he teased closer and closer to her flaming face. "But all the time to myself—to reassure myself—I just keep saying—' Bah! She 's nothing but a Woman—nothing but a Woman—nothing but a Woman'!"

Within the Senior Surgeon's warm, firm grasp the White Linen Nurse's calm hand quickened suddenly like a bud forced precipitously into full bloom.

"Oh, don't—talk, sir," she whispered. "Oh, don't talk, sir!

Just—listen!"

"Listen? Listen to what?" laughed the Senior Surgeon.

From under the heavy lashes that shadowed the flaming cheeks the Soul of the Girl who was to be his peered up at the Soul of the Man who was to be hers,—*and saluted what she saw!*

"Oh, my heart, sir!" whispered the White Linen Nurse. "Oh, my heart! My heart! my *heart*!"

THE END

Rainy Week

CHAPTER I

IN the changes and chances of our New England climate it is not so much what a Guest can endure outdoors as what he can originate indoors that endears him most to a weather-worried Host.

Take Rollins, for instance, a small man, dour, insignificant— a prude in the moonlight, a duffer at sailing, a fool at tennis—yet once given a rain-patter and a smoky fireplace, of an audacity so impertinent, so altogether absurd, that even yawns must of necessity turn to laughter—or curses. The historic thunderstorm question, for instance, which he sprang at the old Bishop's house-party after five sweltering days of sunshine and ecclesiastical argument: "Who was the last person you kissed before you were married?"

A question innocent as milk if only swallowed! But unswallowed? Gurgled? Spat like venom from Bishop to Bishop? And from Bishop's Wife to Bishop's Wife? Oh la! Yet that Rollins himself was the only unmarried person present on that momentous occasion shows not at all, I still contend, the slightest "natural mendacity" of the man, but merely the perfectly normal curiosity of a confirmed Anchoret to learn what truths he may from those who have been fortunate—or unfortunate enough to live.

Certainly neither my Husband nor myself would ever dream of running a house-party without Rollins!

Yet equally certain it is not at all on Rollins's account but distinctly on our own that we invariably set the date for our annual house-party in the second week of May.

For twenty years, in the particular corner of the New England sea-coast which my husband and I happen to inhabit, it has never, with one single exception only, failed to rain from morning till night and night till morning again through the second week of May!

With all weather-uncertainties thus settled perfectly definitely, even for the worst, it is a comparatively easy matter for any Host and Hostess to *Stage* such events as remain. It is with purely confessional intent that I emphasize that word "stage." Every human being acknowledges, if honest, some one supreme passion of existence. My Husband's and mine is for what Highbrows call "the experimental drama."

We call it "Amateur Theatricals."

Yet even this innocent passion has not proved a serene one!

After inestimable seasons of devotion to that most ruthless of all goddesses, the Goddess of Amateur Theatricals, involving, as it does, wrangles with

Guests who refuse to accept unless they areassured that there will be a Play,

wrangles with

Guests who refuse to accept unless assured that there will not be a Play,

wrangles with

Guests already arrived, unpacked, tubbed, seated at dinner, who discover suddenly that their lines are too long,

wrangles with

Guests already arrived, unpacked, tubbed, seated at dinner, who discover equally suddenly that their lines are too short.

wrangles with

Guests who "can't possibly play in blue."

wrangles with

Guests who "can't possibly play in pink."

wrangles with

Guests who insist upon kissing in every act.

wrangles with

Guests who refuse to kiss in any act, it was my Husband's ingenious idea to organize instead an annual Play that should never dream it was a Play, acted by actors who never even remotely suspected that they were acting, evolving a plot that no one but the Almighty, Himself, could possibly foreordain.

We call this Play "*Rainy Week.*"

Yet, do not, I implore you, imagine for a moment that by any such simple little trick as shifting all blame to the weather, all praise to the Almighty, *Care* has been eliminated from the enterprise.

It is only indeed at the instigation of this trick that the real hazard begins. For a Play after all is only a Play, be it humorous, amorous, murderous, adulterous,—a soap-bubble world combusting spontaneously of its own effervescence. But life is life and starkly real if not essentially earnest. And the merest flicker of the merest eyelid in one of life's real emotions has short-circuited long ere this with the eternities themselves! It's just this chance of "short- circuiting with the eternities" that shifts the pucker from a Host's brow to his spine!

No lazy, purring, reunion of old friends this *Rainy Week* of ours, you understand? No dully congenial convocation of in- bred relatives? No conference on literature,—music,— painting? No symposium of embroidery stitches? Nor of billiard shots? But the deliberate and relentlessly-planned assemblage of such distinctly diverse types of men and women as prodded by unusual conditions of weather, domicile, and propinquity, will best act and re-act upon each other in terms inevitably dramatic, though most naively unrehearsed!

"Vengeance is mine!" said the Lord. "Very considerable psychologic, as well as dramatic satisfaction is now at last ours!" confess your humble servants.

In this very sincere if somewhat whimsical dramatic adventure of *Rainy Week*, the exigencies of our household demand that the number of actors shall be limited to eight.

Barring the single exception of Husband and Wife no two people are invited who have ever seen each other before. Destiny plays very much more interesting tricks we have noticed with perfect strangers than she does with perfect friends!

Barring nothing no one is ever warned that the week will be rainy. It is astonishing how a guest's personality strips itself right down to the bare sincerities when he is forced unexpectedly to doff his extra-selected, super-fitting, ultra-becoming visiting clothes for a frankly nondescript costume chosen only for its becomingness to a—situation! In this connection, however, it is only fair to ourselves to attest that following the usual managerial custom of furnishing from its own pocket such costumes as may not for bizarre or historical reasons be readily converted by a cast to street and church wear, we invariably provide the *Rainy Week* costumes for our cast. This costume consists of one yellow oil-skin suit or "slicker," one yellow oil-skin hat, one pair of rubber boots. One dark blue jersey. And very warm woolen stockings.

Reverting also to dramatic sincerity no professional manager certainly ever chose his cast more conscientiously than does my purely whimsical Husband!

After several years of experiment and readjustment the ultimate cast of *Rainy Week* is fixed as follows:

A Bride and Groom
One Very Celibate Person
Someone With a Past
Someone With a Future
A Singing Voice
A May Girl
And a Bore. (Rollins, of course, figuring as the Bore.)

Always there must be that Bride and Groom (for the Celibate Person to wonder about). And the Very Celibate Person (for the Bride and Groom to wonder about). Male or Female, one Brave Soul who had Rebuilt Ruin. Male or Female, one Intrepid Brain that Dares to Boast of Having Made Tryst with the Future. Soprano, Alto, Bass or Tenor, one Singing Voice that can Rip the Basting Threads out of Serenity. One Young Girl so May-Blossomy fresh and new that Everybody Instinctively Changes the Subject When She Comes into the Room . . . . And Rollins!

To be indeed absolutely explicit experience has proved, with an almost chemical accuracy, that, quite regardless of "age, sex, or previous condition of servitude," this particular combination of

Romantic Passion
Psychic Austerity
Tragedy
Ambition
Poignancy
Innocence
And Irritation

cannot be housed together for even one Rainy Week without producing drama!

But whether that drama be farce or fury—? Whether he who came to *star* remains to *supe*? Who yet shall prove the hero? And who the villain! Who—? Oh, la! It's God's business now!

"All the more reason," affirms my Husband, "why all such details as light and color effects, eatments, drinkments and guest-room reading matter should be attended to with extra conscientiousness."

Already through a somewhat sensational motor collision in the gay October Berkshires we had acquired the tentative Bride and Groom, Paul Brenswick and Victoria Meredith, as ardent and unreasonable a pair of young lovers as ever rose unscathed from a shivered racing car to face, instead of annihilation, a mere casual separation of months until such May-time as Paul himself, returning from Heaven knows what errand in China, should mate with her and meet with us.

And to New York City, of course, one would turn instinctively for the Someone With a Future. At a single round of studio parties in the brief Thanksgiving Holiday we found Claude Kennilworth. Not a moment's dissension occurred between us concerning his absolute fitness for the part. He was beautiful to look at, and not too young, twenty-five perhaps, the approximate age of our tentative Bride and Groom. And he made things with his hands in dough, clay, plaster, anything he could reach very insolently, all the time you were talking to him, modeling the thing he was thinking about, instead!

"Oh, just wait till you see him in bronze?" thrilled all the young Satellites around him.

"Till you see me in bronze!" thrilled young Kennilworth himself.

Never in all my life have I beheld anyone as beautiful as Claude Kennilworth—with a bit of brag in him! That head sharply uplifted, the pony-like forelock swished like smoke across his flaming eyes, the sudden wild pulse of his throat. Heavens! What a boy!

"You artist-fellows are forever reproducing solids with liquids," remarked my Husband quite casually. "All the effects I mean! All the illusion! Crag or cathedral out of a dime-sized mud-puddle in your water-color box! Flesh you could kiss from a splash of turpentine! But can you reproduce liquids with solids? Could you put the ocean into bronze, I mean?"

"The ocean?" screamed the Satellites.

"No mere skinny bas-relief," mused my Husband, "of the front of a wave hitched to the front of a wharf or the front of a beach but waves corporeally complete and all alone— shoreless—skyless—like the model of a village an ocean rolling all alone as it were in the bulk of its three dimensions?"

"In—bronze?" questions young Kennilworth. "*Bronze?*" His voice was very faintly raspish.

"Oh, it wasn't a blue ocean especially that I was thinking about," confided my Husband, genially, through the mist of his cigarette. "Any chance pick-up acquaintance has seen the ocean when it's blue. But my wife and I, you understand, we live with the ocean! Call it by its first name,—'Oh Ocean!' —and all that sort of thing!" he smiled out abruptly above the sudden sharp spurt of a freshly-struck match. "The—the ocean I was thinking of," he resumed with an almost exaggerated monotone, "was a brown ocean—brown as boiled sea-weeds—mad as mud under a leaden sky—seething—souring—perfectly lusterless—every brown billow-top pinched-up as though by some malevolent hand into a vivid verdigris bruise——"

"But however in the world would one know where to begin?" giggled the Satellites. "Or how to break it off so it wouldn't end like the edge of a tin roof! Even if you started all right with a nice molten wave? What about the—last wave? The problem of the horizon sense? Yes! What about the horizon sense?" shouted everybody at once.

From the shadowy sofa-pillowed corner just behind the supper table, young Kennilworth's face glowed suddenly into view. But a minute before I could have sworn that a girl's cheek lay against his. Yet now as he jumped to his feet the feminine glove that dropped from his fidgety fingers was twisted with extraordinary maliciousness, I noted, into a doll-sized caricature of a "Vamp."

"I could put the ocean into bronze, Mr. Delville," he said, "if anybody would give me a chance!"

Perhaps it was just this very ease and excitement of having booked anyone as perfect as young Kennilworth for the part of Someone with a Future that made me act as impulsively as I did regarding Ann Woltor.

We were sitting in our room in a Washington hotel before a very smoky fireplace one rather cross night in late January when I confided the information to my Husband.

"Oh, by the way, Jack," I said quite abruptly, "I've invited Ann Woltor for Rainy Week."

"Invited whom?" questioned my Husband above the rim of his newspaper.

"Ann Woltor," I repeated.

"Ann—what?" persisted my Husband.

"Ann Woltor," I re-emphasized.

"Who's she?" quickened my Husband's interest very faintly.

"Oh, she's a woman," I explained—"or a Girl—that I've been meeting 'most every day this last month at my hair-dresser's. She runs the accounts there or something and tries to keep everybody pacified. And reads the darndest books, all highbrow stuff. You'd hardly expect it! Oh, not modern highbrow, I mean, essays as bawdy as novels, but the old, serene highbrow,—Emerson and Pater and Wordsworth,—books that smell of soap and lavender, as well as brains. Reads 'em as though she liked 'em, I mean! Comes from New Zealand I've been told. Really, she's rather remarkable!"

"Must be!" said my Husband. "To come all the way from New Zealand to land in your hair-dresser's library!"

"It isn't my hair-dresser's library!" I corrected with faint asperity. "It's her own library! She brings the books herself to the office.

"And just what part," drawled my Husband, "is this New Zealand paragon, Miss Stoltor, to play in our Rainy Week?"

"Woltor," I corrected quite definitely. "Ann Woltor."

"Wardrobe mistress?" teased my Husband. "Or——?"

"She is going to play the part of the Someone With a Past," I said.

"What?" cried my Husband. His face was frankly shocked. "*What?*" he repeated blankly. "The most delicate part of the cast? The most difficult? The most hazardous? It seemed best to you, without consultation, without argument, to act so suddenly in the matter, and so—so all alone?"

"I had to act very suddenly," I admitted. "If I hadn't spoken just exactly the minute I did she would have been off to Alaska within another forty-eight hours."

"U-m-m," mused my Husband, and resumed his reading. But the half-inch of eye brow that puckered above the edge of his newspaper loomed definitely as the sample of a face that was still distinctly shocked.

When he spoke again I was quite ready for his question.

"How do you know that this Ann Woltor has got a past?" he demanded.

"How do we know young Kennilworth's got a future?" I counter-checked.

"Because he makes so much noise about it I suppose," admitted my Husband.

"By which very same method," I grinned, "I deduct the fact that Ann Woltor has got a past,—inasmuch as she doesn't make the very slightest sound whatsoever concerning it."

"You concede no personal reticence in the world?" quizzed my Husband.

"Yes, quite a good deal," I admitted. "But most of it I honestly believe is due to sore throat. A normal throat keeps itself pretty much lubricated I've noticed by talking about itself."

"Herself," corrected my Husband.

"Himself," I compromised.

"But this Ann Woltor has told you that she came from New Zealand," scored my Husband.

"Oh, no, she hasn't!" I contradicted. "It was the hair-dresser who suggested New Zealand. All Ann Woltor has ever told me was that she was going to Alaska! Anybody's willing to tell you where he's going! But the person who never tells you where he's been—! The person who never by word, deed or act correlates to-day with yesterday! The Here with the There—! I've been home with her twice to her room! I've watched her unpack the Alaska trunk! Not a thing in it older than this winter! Not a shoe nor a hat nor a glove that confides anything! No scent of fir-balsam left over from a summer vacation! No photograph of sister or brother! Yet it's rather an interesting little room, too,—awfully small and shabby after the somewhat plushy splendor of the hairdressing job—but three or four really erudite English Reviews on the table, a sprig of blue larkspur thrust rather negligently into a water glass, and a man's——"

"Blue larkspur in January?" demanded my Husband. "How—how old is this—this Woltor person?"

"Oh—twenty-five, perhaps," I shrugged.

With a gesture of impatience my Husband threw down his paper and began to poke the fire.

"Oh, Pshaw!" he said, "is our whole dramatic endeavor going to be wrecked by the monotony of everybody being 'twenty-five'?"

"Well—call it 'thirty-five' if you'd rather," I conceded. "Or a hundred and five! Arm Woltor wouldn't care! That's the remarkable thing about her face," I hastened with some fervor to explain. "There's no dating on it! This calamity that has happened to her,—whatever it is, has wrung her face perfectly dry of all contributive biography except the mere structural fact of at least reasonably conservative birth and breeding."

A little bit abruptly my Husband dropped the fire-tongs.

"You like this Ann Woltor, don't you?" he said.

"I like her tremendously," I acknowledged.

"Tremendously *as* a person and tremendously *for* the part!" I insisted.

"Yet there's something about it that worries you?" quizzed my Husband not unamiably.

"There is," I said, "just one thing. She's got a broken tooth."

With a gesture of real irritation my Husband sank down in his chair again and snatched up the paper.

It was ten minutes before he spoke again.

"Is it a front tooth?" he questioned without lifting his eyes from the page.

"It is," I said.

When my Husband jumped up from his chair this time he showed no sign at all of ever intending to return to it. As he reached for his hat and coat and started for the door, he tried very hard to grin. But the effort was poor. This was no mere marital disagreement, but a real professional shock.

"I simply can't stand it," he grinned. "One's prepared, of course, for a tragedy queen to sport a broken heart but when it comes to a broken tooth—!"

"Wait till you see her!" I said. There was nothing else to say. "Wait till you see her!"

Even with the door closed behind him he came back once more to tell me how he felt.

"Oh!" he shivered. "O—H!"

Truly if we hadn't gone out together the very next day and found George Keets I don't know what would have happened. Depression still hung very heavily over my Husband's heart.

"Here it is almost February," he brooded, "and even with what we've got, we're still short the Celibate and the Singing Voice and the May Girl."

It was just then that we turned the street corner and met George Keets.

"Why—why the Celibate—of all persons!" we both gasped in a single breath, and rushed upon him.

Now it may seem a little strange instead of this that we have never thought to feature poor Rollins as the Celibate. To "double" him as it were as Celibate and Bore. Conserving thereby one by no means inexpensive outfit of water-proof clothes, twenty-one meals, a week's wash, and Heaven knows how many rounds of Scotch at a time of imminent drought. But Rollins—though as far as anybody knows, a bachelor and eminently chaste—is by no means my idea of a Celibate. Oh, not Rollins! Not anybody with a mind like Rollins! For Rollins, poor dear, would marry every day in the week if anybody would have him. It's the "other people" who have kept Rollins virgin. But George Keets on the other hand is a good deal of a "fascinator" in spite of his austerity, perhaps indeed because of his austerity, tall, lean, good-looking, extravagantly severe, thirty-eight years old, and a classmate of my Husband at college. Whether Life would ever succeed or not in breaking down his unaccountable intention never-to- mate, that intention,—physical, mental, moral, psychic, call it whatever you choose,—was stamped indelibly and for all time on the curiously incongruous granite-like finish of his originally delicate features. Life had at least done interesting historical things to George Keets's face.

"Oh, George!" cried my Husband, "I thought you were in Egypt digging mummies."

"I was," admitted George without any further palaver of greeting.

"When did you get back?" cried my Husband, "And what are you doing now!"

"And where are you going to be in May?" I interposed with perfectly uncontrollable interest.

"Why, I'm just off the boat, you know," brightened George. "A drink would be good, of course. But first I'd just like to run into the library for a minute to see if they've put in any new thrillers while I've been gone. There's a corking new book on Archselurus that ought to be due about now."

"On w-what?" I stammered.

"Oh, fossil cats, you know, and all that sort of thing," explained George chivalrously. "But, of course—you, Mrs. Delville," he hastened now to appease me, "would heaps rather hear about Paris fashions, I know. So if you-people really should want me in May I'll try my best, I promise you, to remember every latest wrinkle of lace, or feather. Only, of course," he explained with typical conscientiousness, "in the museums and the libraries one doesn't see just—of course— the———"

"On the contrary, Mr. Keats," I interrupted hectically, "there is no subject in the world that interests me more—at the moment—than Mummies. And by the second week in May that interest will have assumed proportions that———"

"S-sh!" admonished my Husband. "But really, George," he himself hastened to cut in, "if you could come to us the second week in May———"

"May?" considered George. "Second week? Why, certainly I will." And bolted for the library, while my Husband and I in a perfectly irresistible impulse drew aside on the curbing to watch him disappear.

Equally unexplainably three totally non-concerned women turned also to watch him.

"It's his shoulders," I ventured. "The amazing virility of his shoulders contrasted with the stinginess of his smile."

"Stinginess nothing!" snapped my Husband. "Devil take him!"

"He may—yet," I mused as we swung into step again.

So now we had nothing to worry about—or rather no uncertainty to worry about except the May Girl and the Singing Voice.

"The Singing Voice," my Husband argued, "might be picked up by good fortune at most any cabaret show or choral practise. Not any singing voice would do, of course. It must be distinctly poignant. But even poignancy may be found sometimes where you least expect it,—some reasonably mature, faintly disappointed sort of voice, usually, lilting with unquestionable loveliness, just this side of real professional success.

"But where in the world should we find a really ingenuous Ingénue?"

"They don't exist any more!" I asserted. "Gone out of style like the Teddy Bear—! Old Ingénues you see, of course, sometimes, sweet and precious and limp—as old Teddy Bears. But a brand new Ingénue—? Don't you remember the awful search we had last year and even then———?"

"Maybe you're right," worried my Husband.

And then the horrid attack of neuralgia descended on poor Mr. Husband so suddenly, so acutely, that we didn't worry at all about anything else for days! And even when that worry was over, instead of starting off gaily together for the Carolinas as we had intended, to search through steam-heated corridors, and green velvet golfways, and jessamine scented lanes, for the May Girl, my poor Husband had to dally at home instead, in a very cold, slushy and disagreeable city, to be X-rayed, tooth-pulled, ear-stabbed, and every thing but Bertilloned, while I, for certain business reason, went on ahead to meet the Spring.

But even at parting it was the dramatic anxiety that worried my Husband most.

"Now, don't you dare do a thing this time," he warned me, "until I come! Look around all you want to! Get acquainted! Size things up! But if ever two people needed to work together in a matter it's in this question of choosing a May Girl!"

Whereupon in an impulse quite as amazing to himself as to me— he went ahead and chose the May Girl all by himself!

Before I had been in the Carolinas three days the telegram came.

"Have found May Girl. Success beyond wildest dreams. Doubles with Singing Voice. Absolute miracle. Explanations."

Himself and the explanations arrived a week later. Himself, poor dear, was rather depleted. But the explanations were full enough to have pleased anybody.

He had been waiting, it seems, on the day of the discovery, an interminably long time in the doctor's office. All around him, in the dinginess and general irritability of such an occasion, loomed the bulky shapes of other patients who like himself had also been waiting interminable eons of time. Everybody was very cross. And it was snowing outside,—one of those dirty gray late-winter snows that don't seem really necessary.

And when *She* came! Just a girl's laugh at first from the street door! An impish prance of feet down the dark, unaccustomed hallway! A little trip on the threshold! And then personified—laughing—blushing, stumbling fairly headlong at last into the room—the most radiantly lovely young girl that you have ever had the grace to imagine, dangling exultantly from each frost-pinked hand a very large, wriggly, and exceedingly astonished rabbit.

"Oh, Uncle Charles!" she began, "s-ee what I've found! And in an ash-barrel, too! In—a—" She blinked the snow from her lashes, took a sudden startled glance round the room, another at the clock, and collapsed with confusion into the first chair that she could reach.

A very tall "little girl" she was, and very young, not a day more than eighteen surely. And even in the encompassing bulk of her big coon-skin coat with its broad arms hugging the brown rabbits to her breast she gave an impression of extraordinary slimness and delicacy, an impression accentuated perhaps by a slender silk-stockinged ankle, the frilly cuff of a white sleeve, and the aura of pale gold hair that radiated in every direction from the brim of her coon- skin hat. For fully fifteen minutes my Husband said she sat huddled-up in all the sweet furry confusion of a young animal, till driven apparently by that very confusion to essay some distinctly normal-appearing, every-day gesture, she reached out impulsively to the reading table and picked up a book which some young man had just relinquished rather suddenly at a summons to the doctor's inner office. Relaxing ever so slightly into the depths of her chair with the bunnies' noses twinkling contentedly to the rhythm of her own breathing, she made a wonderful picture, line, color, spirit, everything of *Youth*. Reading, with that strange, extra, inexplainable touch of the sudden little pucker in the eyebrows, sheer intellectual perplexity was in that pucker!

But when the young man returned from the inner office he did not leave at once as every cross, irritable person in the room hoped that he would, but fidgeted around instead with hat and coat, stamped up and down crowding other people's feet, and elbowing other people's elbows. With a gaspy glance at his watch he turned suddenly on the girl with the rabbits. "Excuse me," he floundered, "but I have to catch a train— *please* may I have my book?"

"Your book?" deprecated the Girl. Confusion anew overwhelmed her! "Your—book? Why, I beg your pardon! Why—why—" Pink as a rose she slammed the covers and glanced for the first time at the title. The title of the book was "What Every Young Husband Should Know." . . . With a sigh like the sigh of a breeze in the ferns the tension of the room relaxed! A very fat, cross-looking woman in black satin ripped audibly at a side seam. . . . A frail old gentleman who really had very few laughs left, wasted one of them in the smothering depths of his big black-bordered handkerchief. . . . The lame newsboy on the stool by the door emitted a single snort of joy. Then the doctor himself loomed suddenly from the inner office, and started right through everybody to the girl with the rabbits. "Why, May," he laughed, "I told you not to get here till four o'clock!"

"Oh, not May?" I protested to my Husband. "It simply couldn't be! Not *really*?"

"Yes, really," affirmed my Husband. "Isn't it the limit? But wait till you hear the rest! She's Dr. Brawne's ward, it seems, and has been visiting him for the winter. . . . Comes from some little place way off somewheres. . . . And she's got one of those sweet, clear, absolutely harrowing 'boy soprano' types of voices that sound like incense and altar lights even in rag-time. But weirder than any thing—" triumphed my Husband.

"Oh, not than 'anything'?" I gasped.

"But weirder than anything," persisted my Husband, "is the curious way she's marked."

"M-marked?" I stammered.

"Yes. After I saw her with her hat off," said my Husband, "I saw the 'mark'. I've seen it in boys before, but never in a girl—an absolutely isolated streak of gray hair! In all that riot of blondness and sparkle and youth, just as riotous, just as lovely, a streak of gray hair! It's bewitching! Bewildering! Like May itself! Now sunshine! Now cloud! You'll write to her immediately, won't you?" he begged. "And to Dr. Brawne, too? I told Dr. Brawne quite frankly that it was going to be rather an experimental party, but that, of course, we'd take the best possible care of her. And he said he'd never seen an occasion yet when she wasn't perfectly capable of taking care of herself. And that he'd be delighted to have her come——" laughed my Husband quite suddenly, "if we were sure that we didn't mind animals."

"Animals?" I questioned.

"Yes, dogs, cats, birds!" explained my Husband. "It isn't apt to be a large animal such as a horse or a cow, Dr. Brawne was kind enough to assure me. But he never knew her yet, he said, to arrive anywhere without a guinea pig, squirrel, broken- winged bat, lame dove, or half-choked mouse that she had acquired on the way! She's very tender-hearted. And younger than——"

Blankly for a moment my Husband and I sat staring into each other's eyes. Then, quite impulsively, I reached over and kissed him.

"Oh, Jack," I admitted, "it's too perfect! Truly it makes me feel nervous!—Suppose she should roll her hoop off the cliff or——"

"Or—blow out the gas!" chuckled my Husband.

So you see now our cast was all assembled.

Radiant, "runctious," impatient Paul Brenswick and Victoria Meredith for the Bride and Groom.

George Keets for the Very Celibate Person.

Ann Woltor for the Someone With a Past.

Claude Kennilworth for the Someone With a Future.

May Davies for the May Girl and the Singing Voice.

And Rollins for the Bore. About Rollins I must now confess that I have not been perfectly frank. We hire Rollins! How else could we control him! Even with a mushroom mind like his,—fruiting only in bad weather, one can't force him on one's guests morning, noon, *and* night! Very fortunately here, for such strategy as is necessary, my Husband concedes one further weakness than what I have previously designated as his passion for amateur theatricals and his tolerance of me. That weakness is sea shells—mollusca, you know, and that sort of thing. . . . From all over the world, smelling saltily of coral and palms, iceberg or arctic,—and only too often alas of their dead selves, these smooth-spikey-pink- blue-yellow-or-mottled shells arrive with maddening frequency. And Rollins is a born cataloguer! What easier thing in the world to say than, "Oh, by the way, Rollins, old man, here's an invoice that might interest you from a Florida Key that I've just located. . . . How about the second week in May? Could you come then, do you think? I'm all tied up to be sure with a houseful of guests that week, but they won't bother you any. And, at least, you'll have your evenings for fun. Clothes? Haven't got 'em? Oh, Pshaw! Let me see. It rained last year, didn't it? . . . Well, I guess we can raise the same umbrella that we raised for you then! S'long!"

Everything settled then! Everything ready but the springtime and the scenery! . . . And God Himself at work on that!— Hist! What is it? The flash of a blue-bird?

A bell tinkles! A pulley-rope creaks! And the Curtain Rises!

May always comes so amazingly soon after February! So infinitely much sooner than anyone dares hope that it would! Peering into snow-smeared shop windows some rather particularly bleak morning you notice with a half-contemptuous sort of amusement a precocious display of ginghams and straw hats. And before you can turn round to tell anybody about it, tulips have happened!—And It's May!

More than seeming extravagantly early this year, May dawned also with extravagant lavishness. Through every prismatic color of the world, sunshine sang to the senses!

"What shall we do," fretted my Husband, "if this perfection lasts?" The question indeed was a leading one!

The scenery for Rainy Week did not arrive until the afternoon of the eighth.

From his frowning survey of bright lawns, gleaming surf, radiant sky, I saw my Husband turn suddenly with a little gasping sigh that might have meant anything.

"What is it?" I cried.

"Look!" he said, "it's come."

Silently, shoulder to shoulder, we stood and watched the gigantic storm-bales roll into the sky—packed in fleece, corded with ropes of mist, gorgeous, portentous,—To-morrow's Rain! It is not many hosts and hostesses under like circumstances who turn to each other as we did with a single whoop of joy!

An hour later, hatless and coatless in the lovely warm May twilight, we stood by the larch tree waiting for our guests. We like to have them sup in town at their own discretion or indiscretion, that first night, and all arrive together reasonably sleek and sleepy, and totally unacquainted, on the eight o'clock train. But the larch tree has always been our established point for meeting the *Rainy Week* people. Conceding cordially the truth of the American aphorism that while charity may perfectly legitimately begin at home, hospitality should begin at the railroad station! We personally have proved beyond all doubt that for our immediate interests at stake dramatic effect begins at the entrance to our driveway.

Yet it is always with mingled feelings of trepidation and anticipation that we first sense the blurry rumble of motor wheels on the highway. If the station bus were only blue or green! But palest oak! And shuttered like a roll-top desk! Spilling out strange personalities at you like other people's ideas brimming from pigeon-holes!

For some unfathomable reason of constraint this night, no one was talking when the bus arrived. Shy, stiff-spined, non- communicative, still questioning, perhaps. Who was who and what was what, these seven guests who by the return ride a week hence might even be mated, such things have happened, or once more not speaking to each other, this also has happened, loomed now like so many dummies in the gloom.

"Why, Hello!" we cried, jumping to the rear step of the bus as it slowed slightly at the curb, and thrusting our faces as genially as possible into the dark, unresponsive doorway.

"Hello!" rallied someone—I think it was Rollins. Whoever it was he seemed to be having a terrible time trying to jerk his suitcase across other people's feet.

"Oh, is this where you live?" questioned George Keets's careful voice from the shadows. The faintest possible tinge of relief seemed to be in the question.

"Here?" brightened somebody else.

A window-fastener clicked, a shutter crashed, an aperture opened, and everybody all at once, scenting the sea, crowded to stare out where the gray dusk merging into gray rocks merged in turn with the gray rocks into a low rambling gray fieldstone house silhouetted with indescribable weirdness at the moment against that delicate, pale gold, French-drawing- room sort of sky cluttered so incongruously with the clump of dark clouds.

"The road—doesn't go any farther?" puzzled someone. "There's no other stopping place you mean—just a little bit farther along? This is the end,—the last house,—the——?"

High from a cliff-top somewhere a sea bird lifted a single eerie cry.

"Oh, how—how dramatic!" gasped somebody.

Reaching out to nudge my Husband's hand I collided instead with a dog's cold nose.

Following apparently the same impulse my Husband's hand met the dog's startling nose at almost the same instant.

Except for a second's loss of balance on the bus-step neither of us resented the incident. But it was my Husband who recovered his conversation as well as his balance first.

"Oh, you Miss Davies!" he called blithely into the bus. "What's your Pom's name? Nose-Gay? Skip-a-bout? Cross-Patch? What?—Lucky for you we knew your propensity for arriving with pets! The kennel's all ready and the cat sent away!"

In the nearest shadow of all it was almost as though one heard an *ego* bristle.

"I beg your pardon, but the Pomeranian is mine," affirmed Claude Kennilworth's un-mistakable voice with what seemed like quite unnecessary hauteur.

"What the deuce is the matter with everybody?" whispered my Husband.

With a jerk and a bump the bus grazed a big boulder and landed us wheezily at our own front door.

As expeditiously as possible my Husband snatched up the lantern that gleamed from the doorstep and brandishing it on high, challenged the shadowy occupants of the bus to disembark and proclaim themselves.

Ann Woltor stepped down first. As vague as the shadows she merged from her black-garbed figure faded un-outlined into the shadow of the porch. For an instant only the uplifted lantern flashed across her strange stark face—and then went crashing down into a shiver of glass on the gravelly path at my Husband's feet. "Ann—Stoltor!" I heard him gasp. My Husband is not usually a fumbler either with hand or tongue. In the brightening flare of the flash-light that some one thrust into his hands his face showed frankly rattled. "Ann *Woltor!*" I prompted him hastily. For the infinitesimal fraction of a second our eyes met. I hope my smile was as quick. "What is the matter with everybody?" I said.

With extravagant exuberance my Husband jumped to help the rest of our guests alight. "Hi, there, Everybody!" he greeted each new face in turn as it emerged somewhat hump-shouldered and vague through the door of the bus into the flare of his lantern light.

Poor Rollins, of course, tumbled out.

Fastidiously, George Keets illustrated how a perfect exit from a bus should be made,—suitcase, hat-box, English ulster, everything a model of its kind. Even the constraint of his face, absolutely perfect.

With the Pomeranian clutched rather drastically under one arm, Claude Kennilworth followed Keets. All the time, of course, you knew that it was the Pomeranian who was growling, but from the frowning irritability of young Kennilworth's eyes one might almost have concluded that the boy was a ventriloquist and the Pom a puppet instead of a puppy. "Her name is 'Pet'," he announced somewhat succinctly to my Husband. "And she sleeps in no—kennel!"

A trifle paler than I had expected, but inexpressively young, lovely, palpitant, and altogether adorable, the May Girl sprang into my vision—and my arms. Her heart was beating like a wild bird's.

With the incredibility of their miracle still stamped almost embarrassingly on their faces, our Bride-and-Groom-of-a-Week completed the list. It wasn't just the material physical fact that Love was consummated, that gave them that look. But the spiritual amazement that Love was consummatable! No other "look" in life ever compasses it, ever duplicates it!

It made my Husband quite perceptibly quicken the tempo of his jocosity.

"One—two—three—four—five—six—seven," he enumerated. "All good guests come straight from Heaven! One—two—three— four—five—six—Seven—" he repeated as though to be perfectly sure, "*seven?* Why—Why, what the——?" he interrupted himself suddenly.

With frank bewilderment I saw him jump back to the rear step of the bus and flash his light into the farthest corner where the huddled form of an *eighth* person loomed weirdly from the shadows.

It was a man—a young man. And at first glimpse he was quite dead. But on second glimpse, merely drunk. Hopelessly,— helplessly,—sodden drunk, with his hat gone, his collar torn away, his haggard face sagging like some broken thing against his breast.

With a tension suddenly relaxed, a faint sigh seemed to slip from the group outside. In the crowding faces that surrounded us instantly, it must have been something in young Kennilworth's expression, or in the Pomeranian's, that made my Husband speak just exactly as he did. With his arms held under the disheveled, uncouth figure, he turned quite abruptly and scanned the faces of his guests, "And whose little pet—may this be?" he asked trenchantly.

From the shadow of the Porte-cochere somebody laughed. It was rather a vacuous little laugh. Sheer nerves! Rollins, I think.

Framed in the half-shuttered window of the bus the May Girl's face pinked suddenly like a flare of apple blossoms.

"He—came with—me," said the May Girl.

No matter how informally one chooses to run his household there is almost always some one rule I've noticed on which the smoothness of that informality depends.

In our household that rule seems to be that no explanations shall ever be asked either in the darkness or by artificial light. . . . It being the supposition I infer that most things explain themselves by daylight. . . . Perfectly cordially I concede that they usually do. . . . But some nights are a great deal longer to wait through than others.

It wasn't, on this particular night, that anyone refused to explain. But that nobody even had time to think of explaining. The young Stranger was in a bad way. Not delirium tremens nor anything like that, but a fearful alcoholic disorganization of some sort. The men were running up and down stairs half the night. Their voices rang through the halls in short, sharp orders to each other. No one else spoke above a whisper. With silly comforts like talcum powder, and hot water bottles, and sweet chocolate, and new novels, I put the women to bed. Their comments if not explanatory were at least reasonably characteristic.

From a swirl of pink chiffon and my best blankets, with her ear cocked quite frankly toward a step on the stairs, her eyes like stars, her mouth all a-kiss, the Bride reported her own emotions in the matter.

"No,—no one, of course had ever believed for a moment," the Bride assured me, "that the Drunken Man was one of the guests. . . . And yet, when he didn't get off at any of the stops, and this house was so definitely announced as the 'end of the road'—why it did, of course, make one feel just a little bit nervous," flushed the Bride, perfectly irrelevantly, as the creak on the stairs drew nearer.

Ann Woltor registered only a very typical indifference.

"A great many different kinds of things," she affirmed, "were bound to happen in any time as long as a day. . . . One simply had to get used to them, that was all." She was unpacking her sombre black traveling bag as she spoke, and the first thing she took out from it was a man's gay, green- plaided golf cap. It looked strange with the rest of her things. All the rest of her things were black.

I thought I would never succeed in putting the May Girl to bed. With a sweet sort of stubbornness she resisted every effort. The first time I went back she was kneeling at her bedside to say her "forgotten prayers." The second time I went back she had just jumped up to "write a letter to her Grandfather." "Something about the sea," she affirmed, "had made her think of her grandfather." "It was a long time," she acknowledged, since she "had thought of her grandfather." "He was very old," she argued, "and she didn't want to delay any longer about writing." Slim and frank as a boy in her half- adjusted blanket-wrapper dishabille she smiled up at me through the amazing mop of gold hair with the gray streak floating like a cloud across the sunshine of her face. She was very nervous. She must have been nervous. It darkened her eyes to two blue sapphires. It quickened her breath like the breath of a young fawn running. "And would I please tell her—how to spell 'oceanic'?" she implored me. As though answering intuitively the unspoken question on my lips, she shrugged blame from her as some exotic songbird might have shrugged its first snow. "No—she didn't know who the young man was! Truly—as far as she knew—she had never—never seen the young man before!—o-c-e-a-n-i-c—was it?——"

The rain was not actually delivered until one o'clock in the morning. Just before dawn I heard the storm-bales rip. In sheets of silver and points of steel, with rage and roar, and a surf like a picture in a Sunday supplement, the weather broke loose!

Thank heaven the morning was so dark that no one appeared in the breakfast-room an instant before the appointed hour of nine.

George Keets, of course, appeared exactly at nine, very trim, very *distingué*, in a marvelously tailored gray flannel suit, and absolutely possessed to make his own coffee.

Claude Kennilworth's morning manner was very frankly peevish. "His room had a tin roof and he hardly thought he should be able to stand it. . . . Rain? Did you call this rain? It was a *Flood!* . . . Were there any Movie Palaces near? . . . And were they open mornings? . . . And he'd like an underdone chop, please, for the Pomeranian. . . . And it wasn't his dog anyway, darn the little fool, but belonged to the girl who had the studio next to his and she was possessed with the idea that a week at the shore would put the pup on its feet again. . . . Women were so blamed temperamental. . . . If there was one thing in the world that he hated it was temperamental people." And all the time he was talking he wasn't making anything with his hands, because he wasn't thinking anything instead, "And how in Creation," he scolded, "did we ever happen to build a house out on the granite edge of Nowhere? . . . How did we stand it? How———? . . . Hi there! . . . Wait a moment! . . . *God*—what *Form!* That wave with the tortured top! . . . Hush! . . . Don't speak! . . . *Please* leave him alone! Breakfast? Not yet! When a fellow could watch a—a thing like that! . . . For heaven's sake, pass him that frothy-edged napkin! . . . Did anybody mind if he *tore* it? . . . While he watched that other froth tear!"

Dear, honest, ardent, red-blooded Paul Brenswick came down so frankly interested in the special device by which our house gutters took care of such amazing torrents of water that everybody felt perfectly confident all at once that no bride of his would ever suffer from leaky roofs or any other mechanical defect. Paul Brenswick liked the rain just as much as he liked the gutters! And he liked the sea! And he liked the house! And he liked the sky! And he liked everything! Even when a clumsy waitress joggled coffee into his grapefruit he seemed to like that just as much as he liked everything else. Paul Brenswick was a real Bridegroom. I am not, I believe, a particularly envious person, and have never as far as I know begrudged another woman her youth or her beauty or her talent or her wealth. But if it ever came to a chance of swapping facial expressions, just once in my life, some very rainy morning, I wish I could look like a Bridegroom!

But the expression on the Bride's face was distinctly worried. Joy worried! Any woman who had ever been a bride could have read the expression like an open book. Victoria Brenswick had not counted on rain. Moonlight, of course, was what she had counted on! Moonlight, day and night in all probability! And long, sweet, soft stretches of beach! And cavernous rocks! And incessantly mirthful escapades of escape from the crowd! But to be shut up all day long in a houseful of strange people! . . . With a Bridegroom who after all was still more or less of a strange Bridegroom? The panic in her face was almost ghastly! The panic of the Perfectly-Happy! The panic of the person hanging over-ecstatically on the absolute perfection of a singer's prolonged high note, driven all at once to wonder if this is the moment when the note must break! . . . To be all alone and bored on a rainy day is no more than anyone would expect. . . . But to be with one's Lover and have the day prove dull? . . . If God in the terrible uncertainty of Him should force even one dull day into the miracle of their life together———?

Ann Woltor, dragging down to breakfast just a few moments late, had not noticed especially, it seemed, that the day was rainy. She met my Husband's eyes as she met the eyes of her fellow-guests, calmly, indifferently, and with perfect sophistication. If his presence or personality was in any way a shock to her she certainly gave no sign of it.

The May Girl didn't appear till very late, so late indeed that everybody started to tease her for being such a Sleepy Head. Her face was very flushed. Her hair in a riot of gold— and gray. Her appetite like the appetite of a young cannibal. Across the rim of her cocoa cup she hurled a lovely defiance at her traducers. "Sleepy Head!" she exulted. "Not much! Hadn't she been up since six? And out on the beach? And all over the rocks? . . . Way, way out to the farthest point? . . . There was such a heavenly suit of yellow oil-skins in her closet! . . . She hoped it wasn't cheeky of her but she just couldn't resist 'em! . . . And the fishes? . . . The poor, poor little bruised fishes dashed up, by that terrible surf on the rocks! . . . . She thought she never, never would get them all put back! . . . They kept coming and coming so! Every new wave! Flopping!—Flopping———"

Rollins's breakfast had been sent to his room. You yourself wouldn't have wanted to spring Rollins on any one quite so early in the day. And with my best breakfast tray, my second best china, and sherry in the grape fruit, there was no reason certainly why Rollins in any way should feel discriminated against. Surely, as far as Rollins knew, every guest was breakfasting in bed.

Even without Rollins there was quite enough uncertainty in the air.

Everybody was talking—talking about the morning, I mean—not about yesterday morning; most certainly not about yesterday night! Babble, chatter, drawl, laughter, the voices rose and fell. Breakfast indeed was just about over when a faint stir on the threshold made everybody look up.

It was the Drunken Stranger of the night before.

Heaven knows he was sober enough now. But very shaky! Yet collarless as he was and still unshaven—our men had evidently not expected quite so early a resuscitation—he loomed up now in the doorway with a certain tragic poise and dignity that was by no means unattractive.

"Why, hello!" said everybody.

"Hello!" said the Stranger. With a palpable flex of muscle he leaned back against the wainscoting of the door and narrowed his haggard eyes to the cheerful scene before him. "I don't know where I am," he said, "or how I got here. . . . Or who you are." "I can't seem to remember anything." The faintly sheepish smile that quickened suddenly in his eyes, if not distinctly humorous, was at least plucky. "I think I must have had a drink," he said.

"I wouldn't wonder!" grinned Paul Brenswick.

"You are perfectly right," conceded George Keets.

"Have another!" suggested my Husband. "A straight and narrow this time! You look wobbly. There's nothing like coffee."

And still the Stranger stood undecided in the doorway. "I'm not very fit," he acknowledged. "Not with ladies. . . . But I *had* to know where I was." Blinking with perplexity he stared and stared at the faces before him. "I'm three thousand miles from home," he worried. "I don't know a soul this side of the Sierras. . . . I—I don't know how it happened——"

"Oh, Shucks!" shrugged young Kennilworth. "Easiest thing in the world to happen to a stranger in a new town! 'Welcome to our City Welcome to our City' from night till morning and morning till night again! Any crowd once it gets started——"

"Crowd!" brightened the Stranger. "I—I was in some sort of a—a crowd?" he rummaged hopefully through his poor bruised brain.

From her concentrated interest in a fried chicken-bone, the May Girl glanced up with her first evidence of divided attention.

"Yes! You were!" she confided genially. "It was at the railroad junction. And when the officer arrived, he said, 'I hate like the dickens to run this gentleman in, but if there's nobody to look after him—?' So I said you belonged to me! I saw the crape on your sleeve!" said the May Girl.

"Crape—on—my—sleeve?" stammered the Stranger. With a dreadful gesture of incredulity he lifted his black-banded arm into vision. It was like watching a live heart torn apart to see his memory waken. "My—God!" he gasped. "My *God!*" Still wavering but with a really heroic effort to square his stricken shoulders, he swung back toward the company. His face was livid, his voice, barely articulate. Over face and voice lay still that dreadful blight of astonishment. But when he spoke his statement was starkly simple. "I—I buried my wife and unborn child—yesterday," he said. "In a strange land—among strangers I—I——"

More quickly than I could possibly have imagined it, George Keets was on his feet beckoning the Stranger to the place which he himself had just vacated. And with his hands on the Stranger's shoulders he bent down suddenly over him with a curiously twisted little smile.

"Welcome to our—Pity!" said George Keets.

Between Paul Brenswick and his Bride there flashed a sharp glance of terror. It was as though the bride's heart had gasped out. "What if I have to die some day?—And *this* day was wasted in rain?"

I saw young Kennilworth flush and turn away from that glance. I saw the May Girl open her eyes with a new baffled sort of perplexity.

It was then that Rollins came puttering in, grinning like a Chessy Cat, with his half-demolished breakfast sliding round rather threateningly on his ill-balanced tray. The strange exultancy of rain was in his eye.

"I thought I heard voices," he beamed. "Merry voices!" With mounting excitement he began to beat tunes with his knife and fork upon the delicate porcelain dome of his toast dish. "Am I a—King," he began to intone, "that I should call my own, this—?" Struck suddenly by the somewhat strained expression of Ann Woltor's face, he dropped his knife and fork and fixed his eye upon her for the first time with an unmistakable intentness.

"How did you break your tooth?" beamed Rollins.

CHAPTER II

FOR a single horrid moment everybody's heart seemed to lurch off into space to land only too audibly in a gaspy thud of dismay.

Then Ann Woltor with unprecedented presence of mind jumped up from the table and ran to the mirror over the fireplace. Only the twittering throat-muscle reflected in that mirror belied for an instant the sincerity of either her haste or her astonishment.

"Broken tooth!" she protested incredulously. "Why! Have I got a—broken tooth?"

People acknowledge their mental panics so divergently. My Husband acknowledged his by ramming his elbow into his coffee cup. Claude Kennilworth lit one cigarette after another. The May Girl started to butter a picture post card that someone had just passed her. Quite starkly before my very eyes I saw the Sober Stranger, erstwhile drunken, reach out and slip a silver salt-shaker into his pocket. Meeting his glance my own nerves exploded in a single hoot of mirth.

Into the unhappy havoc of the Stranger's face a rather sick but very determinate little smile shot suddenly.

"Well, I certainly am rattled?" he acknowledged.

His embarrassment was absolutely perfect. Not a whit too much, not a whit too little, at a moment when the slightest under-emphasis or over-emphasis of his awkwardness would have stamped him ineradicably as either boor—or bounder. More indeed by his chair's volition than by his own he seemed to jerk aside then and there from any further responsibility for the incident. Turbid as the storm at the window his eyes racked back to the eyes of his companions.

"Surely," he besought us, "there must be some place—some hotel—somewhere in this town where I can crawl into for a day or two till I can yank myself together again? . . . Taking me in this way from the streets—or worse the way you- people have—" Along the stricken pallor of his forehead a glisten of sweat showed faintly. From my eyes to my Husband's eyes, and back to mine again he turned with a sharply impulsive gesture of appeal. "How do you-people know but what I *am* a burglar?" he demanded.

"Even so," I suggested blithely, "can't you see that we'd infinitely rather have you visiting here as our friend than boarding at the hotel as our foe!"

The mirthless smile on the Stranger's face twitched ever so faintly at one corner.

"You really believe then—" he quickened, "that there is 'honor among thieves'?"

"All proverbs," intercepted my Husband a bit abruptly, "are best proved by their antithesis. We do at least know that there is at times—a considerable streak of dishonor among saints!"

"Eh?—What's that—I didn't quite catch it," beamed the Bridegroom.

But my Husband's entire attention seemed focused rather suddenly on the Stranger.

"So you'd much better stay right on here where you are!" he adjured him with some accent of authority. "Where all explanations are already given and taken! . . . Ourselves quite opportunely short one guest and long one guest-room, and—No! I won't listen for a moment to its being called an 'imposition'!" protested my Husband. "Not for a moment! Only, of course, I must admit," he confided genially, above the flare of a fresh cigarette, "that it would be a slight convenience to know your name."

"My name?" flushed the Stranger. "Why, of course! It's Allan John."

"You mean 'John Allan'," corrected the May Girl very softly.

"No," insisted the Stranger. "It's Allan John." Quite logically he began to rummage through his pockets for the proof. "It's written on my bill-folder," he frowned. "It's in my check-book. . . . It's written on no-end of envelopes." With his face the color of half-dead sedge grass he sank back suddenly into his chair and turned his empty hands limply outward as though his wrist-bones had been wrung. "Gone!" he gasped. "Stripped!—Everything!"

"There you have it!" I babbled hysterically. "Now, how do you know but what *we* are burglars? . . . This whole house a Den of Thieves? . . . The impeccable Mr. George Keets there at your right,—no more, no less, than exactly what he looks,— an almost perfect replica of a stage 'Raffles'?"

"Eh? What's that?" bridled George Keets.

"Dragging you here to this house the way we did," I floundered desperately. "Quite helpless as you were. So—so——"

"'Spifflicated,'" prompted the May Girl. The word on her lips was like the flutter of a rose petal.

With a little gasp of astonishment young Kennilworth rose from his place, and dragging his chair in one hand, his plate of fruit in the other, moved round to the May Girl's elbow to finish his breakfast. Like a palm trying to patronize a pine tree, his crisp exotic young ego swept down across her young serenity.

"Really, I don't quite make you out," he said. "I think I shall have to study you!"

"Study—me!" reflected the May Girl. "Make a lesson about me, you mean! On a holiday?" The vaguely dawning dimple in her smooth cheek faded suddenly out again.

The Stranger—Allan John—it seemed, was rising from the table.

"If you'll excuse me, I think I'll go to my room," he explained. "I'm still pretty shaky. I'm——"

But half way to the stairs, as though drawn by some irresistible impulse, he turned, and fumbling his way back across the dining-room opened the big glass doors direct into the storm. Tripping ever so slightly on the threshold he lurched forward in a single wavering step. In an instant the May Girl was at his side, her steadying hand held out to his! Recovering his balance almost instantly he did not however release her hand, but still holding tight to it, indescribably puzzled, indescribably helpless, stood shoulder to shoulder with her, staring out into the tempestuous scene. Lashed by the wind the May Girl's mop of hair blew gold, blew gray, across his rain-drenched eyes. Blurred in a gusty flutter of white skirts his whole tragic, sagging figure loomed suddenly like some weird, symbolic shadow against the girl's bright beauty.

Frankly the picture startled me! "S-s-h!" warned my Husband. "It won't hurt her any! He doesn't even know whether she's young or old."

"Or a boy—or a girl," interposed George Keets, a bit drily.

"Or an imp or a saint," grinned young Kennilworth. "Or——"

"Or anything at all," persisted my Husband, "except that she says '*Kindness*' and nothing else, you notice, except just '*Kindness*.' No suggestions, you observe? No advice? And at an acid moment in his life of such unprecedented shock and general nervous disorganization when his only conceivable chance of 'come-back' perhaps, hangs on the alkaline wag of a strange dog's tail or the tune of a street piano proving balm not blister. By to-morrow—I think—you won't see him holding hands with the May Girl nor with any other woman. Personally," confided my Husband a bit abruptly, "I rather like the fellow! Even in the worst of his plight last night there was a certain fundamental sort of poise and dignity about him as of one who would say, 'Bad as this is, you chaps must see that I'd stand ready with my life to do the same for you'!"

"To—do—the same—for you?" gasped the Bride. Very quietly, like an offended young princess, she rose from the table and stood for that single protesting moment with her hand on her Bridegroom's shoulder. Her eager, academic young face was frankly aghast,—her voice distinctly strained. "I'm sorry," she said, "but I quite fail to see how the word 'dignity' could possibly be applied to any man who had so debased himself as to go and get drunk because his wife and child were dead!"

"You talk," said my Husband, "as though you thought 'getting drunk' was some sort of jocular sport. It isn't! That is, not inevitably, you know!"

"No—I didn't—know," murmured the Bride coldly.

"Deplorable as the result proved to be," interposed George Keets's smooth, carefully modulated voice, "it's hardly probable I suppose that the poor devil started out with the one deliberate purpose of—of debasing him self, as Mrs. Brenswick calls it."

"N-o?" questioned the Bride.

"It isn't exactly, you mean, as though he'd leapt from the church shouting, 'Yo—ho—, and a bottle of rum,'" observed young Kennilworth with one faintly-twisted eyebrow.

"S-s-h!" admonished everybody.

"Maybe he simply hadn't eaten for days," suggested my Husband.

"Or slept for nights and nights," frowned George Keets.

"And just absolutely was obliged to have a bracer," said my Husband, "to put the bones back into his knees again so that he could climb up the steps of his train and fumble some sort of way to his seat without seeming too conspicuous. Whatever religion may do, you know, to starch a man's soul or stiffen his upper lip, he's got to have bones in his knees if he's going to climb up into railroad trains. . . . And our poor young friend here, it would seem, merely mis——"

"Mis—calculated," mused Kennilworth, "how many knees he had."

"Paul wouldn't do it!" flared the Bride.

"Do what?" demanded young Kennilworth.

"Hush!" protested everybody.

"Make a beast of himself—if I died—if I died!" persisted the Bride.

"Pray excuse me for contradicting either your noun or your preposition," apologized my Husband. "But even at its worst I'm quite willing to wager that the only thing in the world poor Allan John started out to 'make' was an oblivion—for— himself."

"An oblivion?" scoffed the Bride.

"Yes—even for one night!" persisted my Husband. "Even for one short little night! . . . Before the horror of 365 nights to the year and God knows how many years to the life—rang on again! Some men really like their wives you know,—some men— so no matter how thin-skinned and weak this desire for oblivion seems to you—" quickened my Husband, "it is at least a——"

"Paul wouldn't!" frowned the Bride.

In the sudden accentuation of strain everybody turned as quickly as possible to poor Paul to decide as cheerfully as seemed compatible with good taste just what that gorgeously wholesome looking specimen of young manhood would or would not do probably under suggested circumstances. Nobody certainly wanted to consider the matter seriously, yet nobody with the Bride's scared eyes still scorching through his senses would have felt quite justified I think in mere shrugging the issue aside.

"No, I don't think Paul—would!" rallied my Husband with commendable quickness. "Not with those eyes! Not with that particular shade of crisp, controlled hair! . . . Complexions like his aren't made in one generation of righteous nerves and digestions! . . . Oh no—! Even in the last ditch the worst thing Paul would do would be to stalk round putting brand new gutters on a brand new house!"

"Bridge-building is my job—not gutters," grinned Paul unhappily.

"Stalk round building brand new bridges," corrected my Husband.

"Intoxicated with bridges!" triumphed young Kennilworth. "Doped with specifications!"

"But perhaps Allan John—doesn't know how to build bridges," murmured my Husband. "And perhaps in Allan John's family an occasional Maiden Aunt *or* Uncle has strayed just a———"

"With the faintest possible gesture of impatience, but still smiling, the Bridegroom rose from the table and lifted his Bride's hand very gently from his shoulder.

"Who started this conversation, anyway?" he quizzed.

"I did!" laughed everybody.

"Well, I end it!" said the Bridegroom.

"Oh, thunder!" protested young Kennilworth. In the hollow of his hand something that once had been the spongy shapeless center of a breakfast roll crushed back into sponge again. But in the instant of its crushing, crude as the modeling was, half jest, half child's play, I sensed the unmistakable parody of a woman's finger-prints bruising into the soft crest of a man's shoulder. Even in the absurdity of its substance the sincerity of the thing was appalling. Catching my eye alone, young Kennilworth gave an amused but distinctly worldly-wise little laugh.

"Women do care so much, don't they?" he shrugged.

A trifling commotion in the front hall stayed the retort on my lips.

The commotion was Ann Woltor. Coated and hatted and already half-gloved she loomed blackly from the shadows, trying very hard to attract my attention.

In my twinge of anxiety about the May Girl I had quite forgotten Ann Woltor. And in the somewhat heated discussion of Allan John's responsibilities and irresponsibilities, the May Girl also, it would seem, had passed entirely from my mind.

"I'm very sorry," explained Ann Woltor, "but with this unfortunate accident to my tooth I shall have to hurry, of course, right back to town." Even if you had never heard Ann Woltor speak you could have presaged perfectly from her face just what her voice would be like, gravely contralto, curiously sonorous, absolutely without either accent or emphasis, yet carrying in some strange, inex-plainable way a rather goose-fleshy sense of stubbornness and finality. "One can't exactly in a Christian land," droned Ann Woltor, "go round looking like the sole survivor of a massacre."

Across the somewhat sapient mutual consciousness that ever since we had first laid eyes on each other five months ago— and goodness knows how long before that—she had been going round perfectly serenely 'looking like the sole survivor of a massacre,' Ann Woltor and I stared just a bit deeply into each other's eyes. The expression in Ann's eyes was an expression of peculiar poignancy.

"No, of course not!" I conceded with some abruptness. "But surely if you can find the right dentist and he's clever at all, you ought to be able to get back here on the six-thirty train to-night!"

"The six-thirty train? Perhaps," murmured Ann Woltor. Once again her eyes hung upon mine. And I knew and Ann Woltor knew and Ann Woltor knew that I knew,—that she hadn't the slightest intention in the world of returning to us on any train whatsoever. But for some reason known only to herself and perhaps one other, was only too glad to escape from our party—anatomically impossible as that escape sounds—through the loop-hole of a broken tooth. Already both black gloves were fastened, and her black traveling-bag swayed lightly in one slim, determinate hand. "Your maid has ordered the station bus for me," she confided; "and tells me that by changing cars at the Junction and again at Lees—Truly I'm sorry to make any trouble," she interrupted herself. "If there had been any possible way of just slipping out without anybody noticing———!"

"Without anybody noticing?" I cried. "Why, Ann, you dear silly!"

At this, my first use of her Christian name, she flashed back at me a single veiled glance of astonishment, and started for the door. But before I could reach her side my Husband stepped forward and blocked her exit by the seemingly casual accident of plunging both arms rather wildly into the sleeves of his great city-going raincoat.

"Why the thing is absurd!" he protested. "You can't possibly make train connections! And there isn't even a covered shed at the Junction! If this matter is so important I'll run you up to town myself in the little closed car!"

Across Ann Woltor's imperturbable face an expression that would have meant an in-growing scream on any other person's countenance flared up in a single twitching lip-muscle and was gone again. Behind the smiling banter in my Husband's eyes she also perhaps had noted a determination quite as stubborn as her own.

"Why—if you insist," she acquiesced, "but it has always distressed me more than I can say to inconvenience anybody."

"Inconvenience—nothing!" beamed my Husband. Ordinarily speaking my Husband would not be described I think as having a beaming expression.

With a chug like the chug of a motor-boat the little closed car came splashing laboriously round the driveway. Its glassy face was streaked with tears. Depressant as black life-preservers its two extra tires gleamed and dripped in their jetty enamel-cloth casings. A jangle as of dungeon chains clanked heavily from each fresh revolution of its progress.

Everybody came rushing helpfully to assist in the embarkation.

My Husband's one remark to me flung back in a whisper from the steering wheel, though frankly confidential, concerned Allan John alone.

"Don't let Allan John want for anything to-day," he admonished me. "Keep his body and mind absolutely glutted with bland things like cocoa and reading aloud . . . And don't wait supper for us!"

With her gay jonquil-colored oil-skin coat swathing her sombre figure, Ann Woltor slipped into the seat beside him and slammed the door behind her. Her face was certainly a study.

"Sixty miles to town if it's an inch! How—cosy," mused young Kennilworth.

"Good-bye!" shouted everybody.

"Good-bye!" waved Ann Woltor and my Husband.

As for Rollins, he was almost beside himself with pride and triumph. Shuffling joyously from one foot to the other he crowded to the very edge of the vestibule and with his small fussy face turned up ecstatically to the rain, fairly exploded into speech the instant the car was out of earshot.

"She'll look better!" gloated Rollins.

"Who?—the car?" deprecated young Kennilworth.

Then, because everybody laughed out at nothing, it gave me a very good chance suddenly to laugh out at "nothing" myself. And most certainly I had been needing that chance very badly for at least the last fifteen minutes. Because really when you once stopped to consider the whole thrilling scheme of this "Rainy Week" Play, and how you and your Husband for years and years had constituted yourself a very eager, earnest-minded Audience-of-Two to watch how the Lord Almighty,—the one unhampered Dramatist of the world, would work out the scenes and colors—the exits and entrances—the plots and counter plots of the material at hand—it was just a bit astonishing to have your Husband jump up from his place in the audience and leap to the stage to be one of the players instead!

It wasn't at all that the dereliction worried your head or troubled your heart. But it left your elbow so lonely! Who was there left for your elbow to nudge? When the morning curtain rose on a flight of sea gulls slashing like white knives through a sheet of silver rain, or the Night Scene set itself in a plushy black fog that fairly crinkled your senses; when the Leading Lady's eyes narrowed for the first time to the Leading Man's startled stare, and the song you had introduced so casually at the last moment in the last act proved to be the reforming point in the Villain's nefarious career, and the one character you had picked for "Comic Relief" turned out to be the Tragedienne, who in the world was left for your elbow to nudge?

Swinging back to the breakfast-room I heard the clock strike ten—only ten?

It was going to be a nice little Play all right! Starting off already with several quite unexpected situations! And it wouldn't be the first time by any means that in an emergency I had been obliged to "double" as prompter and stage hand or water carrier and critic. But how to double as elbow-nudger I couldn't quite figure.

"Let's go for a tramp on the beach!" suggested the Bridegroom. Always on the first rainy morning immediately after breakfast some restive business man suggests "a tramp on the beach!" Frankly we have reached a point where we quite depend on it for a cue.

Everybody hailed the proposition with delight except Allan John and Rollins. A zephyr would have blown Allan John from his footing. And Rollins had to stay in his room to catalogue shells. . . . Rollins was paid to stay in his room and catalogue shells!

Of the five adventurers who essayed to sally forth, only one failed to clamor for oil skins. You couldn't really blame the Bride for her lack of clamoring. . . . The Bride's trousseau was wonderful as all trousseaux are bound perforce to be that are made up of equal parts of taste,—money,—fashion,—and passion. No one who had "saved up" such a costume as the Bride had for the first rainy day together, could reasonably be expected to doff it for yellow oil-skins. Of some priceless foreign composition, half cloth, half mist, indescribably shimmering, almost indecently feminine, with the frenchiest sort of a little hat gaily concocted of marshgrass and white rubber pond-lilies, it gave her lovely, somewhat classic type, all the sudden audacious effect somehow of a water-proofed valentine.

Young Kennilworth sensed the inherent contrast at once.

"Beside you," he protested, "we look like Yellow Telegrams! . . . Your Husband there is some Broker's Stock Quotation— sent 'collect!' . . . Mr. Keets is a rather heavily-worded summons to address the Alumnae of Something-or-other College! . . . I am a Lunch Invitation to 'Miss Dancy-Prancy of the Sillies!' . . . And you, of course, Miss Davies," he quickened delightedly, "are a Night Letter, because you are so long—and inconsequent—all about rabbits—and puppies— and kiddie things like checked gingham pinafores!"

Laughing, teasing, arguing, jeering each other's oil-skins, praising the Bride's splendor, they swept, a young hurricane of themselves, out into the bigger hurricane of sea and sky, and still five abreast, still jostling, still teasing, still arguing, passed from sight around the storm-swept curve of the beach, while I stayed behind to read aloud to Allan John.

Not that Allan John listened at all. But merely because every time I stopped reading he struggled up from the lovely soggy depths of his big leather chair and began to worry. We read two garden catalogues and a chapter on insect pests. We read a bit of Walter Pater, and five exceedingly scurrilous poems from a volume of free verse. It seemed to be the Latin names in the garden catalogues that soothed him most. And when we weren't reading, we drank malted milk. Allan John, it seemed, didn't care for cocoa.

But even if I hadn't had Allan John on my mind I shouldn't have gone walking on the beach. We have always indeed made it a point not to walk on the beach with our guests on the first rainy, restive morning of their arrival. In a geographical environment where every slushy step of sand, every crisp rug of pebbles, every wind-tortured cedar root, every salt-gnawed crag is as familiar to us as the palms of our own hands, it is almost beyond human nature not to try and steer one's visitors to the preferable places, while the whole point of this introductory expedition demands that the visitors shall steer themselves. In the inevitable mood of uneasiness and dismay that overwhelms most house party guests when first thrust into each other's unfamiliar faces, the initial gravitations that ensue are rather more than usually significant. To be perfectly explicit, for instance, people who start off five abreast on that first rainy walk never come home five abreast!

In the immediate case at hand, nobody came home at all until long after Allan John and I had finished our luncheon, and in the manner of that coming, George Keets had gravitated to leadership with the Bride and Bridegroom. Very palpably with the Bridegroom's assistance he seemed to be coaxing and urging the Bride's frankly jaded footsteps, while young Kennilworth and the May Girl brought up the rear staggering and lurching excitedly under the weight of a large and somewhat mysteriously colored wooden box.

The Bridegroom and George Keets and young Kennilworth and the May Girl were as neat as yellow paint. But the poor Bride was ruined. Tattered and torn, her diaphanous glory had turned to real mist before the onslaught of wind and rain. Her hat was swamped, her face streaked with inharmonious colors. She was drenched to the skin. Her Bridegroom was distracted with anxiety and astonishment.

Everybody was very much excited! Lured by some will-o-the- wisp that lurks in waves and beaches they had lost their way it seems between one dune and another, staggered up sand- hills, fallen down sand-hills, sheltered themselves at last during the worst gust of all "in a sort of a cave in a sort of a cliff" and sustained life very comfortably "thank you" on some cakes of sweet chocolate which George Keets had discovered most opportunely in his big oil-skin pockets!

But most exciting of all they had found a wreck! "Yes, a real wreck! A perfectly lovely—beautiful—and quite sufficiently gruesome real wreck!" the May Girl reported.

Not exactly a whole wreck it had proved to be . . . Not shattered spars and masts and crumpled cabins with plush cushions floating messily about. But at least it was a real trunk from a real wreck! Mrs. Brenswick had spied it first. Just back of a long brown untidy line of flotsam and jetsam, the sea-weeds, the dead fish, the old bales and boxes, that every storm brings to the beach, Mrs. Brenswick had spied the trunk lurching up half-imbedded in the sand. It must have come in on the biggest wave of all some time during the night. It was "awfully wet" and yet "not so awfully wet." Everybody agreed that is, that it wasn't water-logged, that it hadn't, in short, been rolling around in the sea for weeks or months but bespoke a disaster as poignantly recent as last night, on the edge of this very storm indeed that they themselves were now frivoling in. For fully half an hour, it appeared before even so much as touching the trunk, they had raced up and down the beach hunting half hopefully, half fearfully for some added trace of wreckage, the hunched body even of a survivor. But even with this shuddering apprehension once allayed, the original discovery had not proved an altogether facile adventure.

It had taken indeed at the last all their combined energies and ingenuities to open the trunk. The Bride had broken two finger nails. George Keets had lost his temper. Paul Brenswick in a final flare of desperation had kicked in the whole end with an abandon that seemed to have been somewhat of an astonishment to everybody. Even from the first young Kennilworth had contested "that the thing smelt dead." But this unhappy odor had been proved very fortunately to be nothing more nor less than the rain-sloughed coloring matter of the Bride's pond-lily hat.

"And here is what we found in the trunk!" thrilled the Bride. In the palm of her extended hand lay a garnet necklace,— fifty stones perhaps, flushing crimson-dark in a silver setting of such unique beauty and such unmistakable Florentine workmanship as stamped the whole trinket indisputably "precious," if not the stones themselves.

"And there were women's dresses in it," explained Paul Brenswick. "Rather queer-looking dresses and———"

"Oh, it was the—the—funniest trunk!" cried the May Girl. "All—" Her eyes were big with horror.

"Anybody could have Sherlocked at a glance," sniffed young Kennilworth, "that it had been packed by a crazy person!"

"No, I don't agree to that at all!" protested the Bride, whose own trunk-packing urgencies and emergencies were only too recent in her mind. "Anybody's liable to pack a trunk like that when he's moving! The last trunk of all! Every left-over thing that you thought was already packed or that you had planned to tuck into your suitcase and found suddenly that you couldn't."

"Why, there was an old-fashioned copper chafing dish!" sniffed young Kennilworth. "And the top-drawer of a sewing- table fairly rattling with spools!"

"And books!" frowned George Keets. "The weirdest little old edition of 'Pilgrim's Progress'!"

"And toys!" quivered the May Girl. "A perfectly gorgeous brand new box of 'Toy Village'! As huge as—Oh it was awful!"

"As huge as—that!" kicked young Kennilworth wryfully against the box at his feet. "I wanted to bring the chafing dish," he scolded, "but nothing would satisfy this young idiot here except that we lug the Toy Village.——"

"One couldn't bring—everything all at once," deprecated the May Girl. "Perhaps to-morrow—if it isn't too far—and we ever could find it again——"

"But why such haste about the 'Toy Village'?" I questioned. "Why not the dresses? The——"

Hopelessly, but with her eyes like blue skies, her cheeks like apple-blossoms, the May Girl tried to justify her mental processes. "Probably I can't explain exactly," she admitted, "but books and dishes and dresses being just things wouldn't mind being drowned but toys, I think, would be frightened." With a frank expression of shock she stopped suddenly and stared all around her. "It doesn't quite make sense when you say it out loud, does it?" she reflected. "But when you just feel it—inside——"

"I brought the little 'Pilgrim's Progress' back with me," confessed George Keets with the faintest possible smile. "Not exactly perhaps because I thought it would be 'frightened.' But two nights shipwreck on a New England coast in this sort of weather didn't seem absolutely necessary."

"And I brought the dinkiest little pearl-handled pistol," brightened Paul Brenswick. "It's a peach! Tucked into the pocket of an old blue cape it was! Wonder I ever found it!"

From a furious rummaging through her pockets the May Girl suddenly withdrew her hand.

"Of course, we'll have to watch the shipwreck news," said the May Girl. "Or even advertise, perhaps. So maybe there won't be any real treasure-trove after all. But just to show that I thought of you, Mrs. Delville," she dimpled, "here are four very damp spools of red sewing-silk for your own work-table drawer! Maybe they came all the way from China! And here's a— I don't know what it is, for Allan John—I think it's a whistle! And here's a little not-too-soggy real Morocco-bound blank book for Mr. Rollins when he comes down-stairs again! And——"

"And for Mr. Delville?" I teased. "And for Ann Woltor?"

With her hand slapped across her mouth in a gesture of childish dismay, the May Girl stared round at her companions.

"Oh dear—Oh dear—Oh *dear!*" she stammered. "None of us ever thought once of poor Mr. Delville and Miss Woltor!"

"It's hot eatments and drinkments that you'd better be thinking of now!" I warned them all with real concern. "And blanket-wrappers! And downy quilts! Be off to your rooms and I'll send your lunches up after you! And don't let one of you dare show his drenched face down-stairs again until suppertime!"

Then Allan John and I resumed our reading aloud. We read Longfellow this time, and a page or two of Marcus Aurelius, and half a detective story. And substituted orange juice very mercifully for what had grown to be a somewhat monotonous carousal in malted milk. Allan John seemed very much gratified with the little silver whistle from the shipwreck, and showed quite plainly by various pursings of his strained lips that he was fairly yearning to blow it, but either hadn't the breath, or else wasn't sure that such a procedure would be considered polite. Really by six o'clock I had grown quite fond of Allan John. It was his haunted eyes, I think and the lovely lean line of his cheek. But whether he was animal—vegetable—mineral—Spirituelle—or Intellectuelle, I, myself, was not yet prepared to say.

The supper hour passed fortunately without fresh complications. Everybody came down! Everybody's eyes were like stars! And every body's complexion lashed into sheer gorgeous-ness by the morning's mad buffet of wind and wave! Best of all, no one sneezed.

Our little Bride was a dream again in a very straight, very severe gray velvet frock that sheathed her young suppleness like the suppleness of a younger Crusader. Her regenerated beauty was an object-lesson to all young husbands' pocket- books for all time to come that beauty like love is infinitely more susceptible to bad weather than is either homeliness or hate, and as such must be cherished by a man's brain as well as by his brawn. Paul Brenswick, goodness knows, would never need to choose his Bride's clothes for her. But lusty young beauty-lover that he was by every right of clean heart and clean living, it was up to him to see that his beloved was never financially hampered in her own choosing! A non-extravagant bride, wrecked as his bride had been by the morning's tempest, might not so readily have recovered her magic.

The May Girl, as usual, was like a spray of orchard bloom in some white, frothy, middy blouse sort of effect. With the May Girl's peculiarly fragrant and insouciant type of youthfulness one never noted somehow just what she wore, nor rated one day's mood of loveliness against another. The essential miracle, as of May-time itself, lay merely in the fact that she was here.

Everybody talked, of course, about the shipwreck.

The Bride did not wear her necklace. "It was too ghostly," she felt. But she carried it in her hand and brooded over it with the tender, unshakable conviction that once at least it must have belonged to "another Bride."

Rollins, I thought, was rather unduly enthusiastic about his share of the booty. Yet no one who knew Rollins could ever possibly have questioned the absolute sincerity of him. Note- books, it appeared, were a special hobby of his! Morocco- bound note-books particularly. And when it came to faintly soggy Morocco-bound note-books, words were inadequate it seemed to express his appreciation. Nothing would do but the May Girl must inscribe it for him. "Aberner Rollins," she wrote very carefully in her round, childish hand, with a giggly flourish at the tail-tip of each word. "For Aberner Rollins from his friend May Davies. Awful Shipwreck Time, May 10th, 1919." Rollins used an inestimable number of note-books it appeared in the collection of his statistics. "The collection of statistics was the consuming passion of his life," he confided to everybody. "The consuming passion!" he reiterated emphatically. "Already," he affirmed, "he had revised and reaudited the whole fresh-egg-account of his own family for the last three generations! In a single slender tome," he bragged, "he held listed the favorite flowers of all living novelists both of America and England! Another tome bulged with the evidence that would-be suicides invariably waited for pleasant weather in which to accomplish their self-destruction! In regard to the little black Morocco volume," he kindled ecstatically, "he had already dedicated it to a very interesting new thought which had just occurred to him that evening, apropos of a little remark—a most significant little remark that had been dropped during the breakfast chat. . . . If anyone was really interested—" he suggested hopefully.

Nobody was the slightest bit interested! Nobody paid the remotest attention to him! Everybody was still too much excited about the shipwreck, and planning how best to salvage such loot as remained.

"And maybe by to-morrow there'll be even more things washed up!" sparkled the May Girl. "A real India shawl perhaps! A set of chess-men carved from a whale's tooth! Only, of course—if it should rain as hard—" she drooped as suddenly as she had sparkled.

"It can't!" said young Kennilworth. Even with the fresh crash of wind and rain at the casement he made the assertion arrogantly. "It isn't in the mind of God," he said, "to make two days as rainy as this one." The little black Pomeranian believed him anyway, and came sniffing out of the shadows to see if the arrogantly gesticulative young hand held also the gift of lump sugar as well as of prophecy.

It was immediately after supper that the May Girl decided to investigate the possibilities and probabilities of her "toy village."

Somewhat patronizingly at first but with a surprisingly rapid kindling of enthusiasm, young Kennilworth conceded his assistance.

The storm outside grew wilder and wilder. The scene inside grew snugger and snugger. The room was warm, the lamps well shaded, the tables piled with books, the chairs themselves deep as waves. "Loaf and let loaf" was the motto of the evening.

By pulling the huge wolf-skin rug away from the hearth, the May Girl and young Kennilworth achieved for their village a plane of smoothness and light that gleamed as fair and sweet as a real village common at high noon. Curled up in a fluff of white the May Girl sat cross-legged in the middle of it superintending operations through a maze of sunny hair. Stretched out at full-length on the floor beside her, looking for all the world like some beautiful exotic-faced little lad, young Kennilworth lay on his elbows, adjusting, between incongruous puffs of cigarette smoke, the faintly shattered outline of a miniature church and spire, or soothing a blister of salt sea tears from the paint-crackled visage of a tiny villa. Softly the firelight flickered and flamed across their absorbed young faces. Mysteriously the wisps of cigarette smoke merged realities with unrealities.

It was an entrancing picture. And one by one everybody in the room except Rollins and myself became drawn more or less into it.

"If you're going to do it at all," argued Paul Brenswick, "you might as well do it right! When you start in to lay out a village you know there are certain general scientific principles that must be observed. Now that list to the floor there! What about drainage? Can't you see that you've started the whole thing entirely wrong?"

"But I wanted it to face toward the fire," drooped the May Girl, "like a village looking on the wonders of Vesuvius."

"Vesuvius nothing!" insisted Paul Brenswick. "It's got to have good drainage!"

Enchanted by his seriousness, the Bride rushed off up-stairs with her scissors to rip the foliage off her second-best hat to make a hedge for the church-yard. Even Allan John came sliding just a little bit out of his chair when he noted that there was a large, rather humpy papier-mache mountain in the outfit that seemed likely to be discarded.

"I would like to have that mountain put—there!" he pointed. "Against that table shadow . . . And the mountain's name is Blue Blurr!"

"Oh, very well," acquiesced everybody. "The mountain's name is Blue Blurr!" It was George Keets who suggested taking the little bronze Psyche from the mantelpiece to make a monument for the public square. "Of course there'll be some in your village," he deprecated, "who'll object to its being a nude. But as a classic it——"

"It's a bear! It's a bear! It's a bear!" chanted Kennilworth in exultant falsetto. "Speaking of classics!"

"Hush!" said George Keets. . . . George Keets really wanted very much to play, I think, but he didn't know exactly how to, so he tried to talk highbrow instead. "This village of yours," he frowned, "I—I hope it's going to have good government?"

"Well, it isn't!" snapped young Kennilworth. "It's going to be a terror! But at least it shall be pretty!"

Under young Kennilworth's crafty hand the little village certainly had bloomed from a child's pretty toy into the very real beauty of an artist's ideal. The skill of laying out little streets one way instead of another, the decision to place the tiny red schoolhouse here instead of there, the choice of a linden rather than a pinetree to shade an infinitesimal green-thatched cottage, had all combined in some curious twinge of charm to make your senses yearn—not that all that cunning perfection should swell suddenly to normal real estate dimensions—but that you, reduced by some lovely miracle to toy-size, might slip across that toy-sized greensward into one of those toy-sized houses, and live with toy-sized passions and toy-sized ambitions and toy-sized joys and toy-sized sorrows, one single hour of a toy-sized life.

Everybody, I guess, experienced the same strange little flutter.

"That house shall be mine!" affirmed George Keets quite abruptly. "That gray stone one with the big bay-window and the pink rambler rose. The bay-window room I'm sure would make me a fine study. And——"

From an excessively delicate readjustment of a loose shutter on a rambling brown bungalow young Kennilworth looked up with a certain flicker of exasperation.

"Live anywhere you choose!" he snapped. "Miss Davies and I are going to live—here!"

"W—What?" stammered the May Girl. "What?"

"Here!" grinned young Kennilworth.

"Oh—no," said the May Girl. Without showing the slightest offense she seemed suddenly to be quite positive about it. "Oh, no!—If I live anywhere it's going to be in the gray stone house with Mr. Keets. It's so infinitely more convenient to the schools."

"To the what?" chuckled Kennilworth. Before the very evident astonishment and discomfiture in George Keets's face, his own was convulsed with joy.

"To the schools," dimpled the May Girl.

"You do me a—a very great honor," bowed George Keets. His face was scarlet.

"Thank you," said the May Girl.

In the second's somewhat panicky pause that ensued Rollins flopped forward with his note-book. Rollins evidently had been waiting a long and impatient time for such a pause.

"Now speaking of drinking to drown one's Sorrows——" beamed Rollins.

"But we weren't!" observed George Keets coldly.

"But you were this morning!" triumphed Rollins. From the flapping white pages of the little black note-book he displayed with pride the entries that he had already made, a separate name heading each page—Mrs. Delville—Mr. Delville—Mr. Keets—Miss Davies—the list began. "Now take the hypothesis," glowed Rollins, "that everybody has got just two bottles stowed away for all time, the very last bottles I mean that he will ever own, rum—rye—Benedictine—any thing you choose—and eliminating the first bottle as the less significant of the two—what are you saving the last one for!" demanded Rollins.

From a furtive glance at Allan John's graying face and the May Girl's somewhat startled stare, young Kennilworth looked up with a rather peculiarly glinting smile.

"Oh, that's easy," said he, "I'm saving mine to break the head of some bally fool!"

"And my last bottle," interposed George Keets quickly. "My last bottle—?" In his fine ascetic face the flush deepened suddenly again, but with the flush the faintest possible little smile showed also at the lip-line. "Oh, I suppose if I'm really going to have a wedding—in that little gray toy house, it's up to me to save mine for a 'Loving Cup' . . . claret . . . Something very mild and rosy . . . Yes, mine shall be claret."

With her pretty nose crinkled in what seemed like a particularly abstruse reflection, the May Girl glanced up.

"Bene—benedictine?" she questioned. "Is that the stuff that smells the way stars would taste if you ate them raw?"

"I really can't say," mused Kennilworth. "I don't think I ever ate a perfectly raw star. At the night-lunch carts I think they almost invariably fry them on both sides."

"Night-lunch carts?" scoffed Keets, with what seemed to me like rather unnecessary acerbity. "N-o, somehow I don't seem to picture you in a night-lunch cart when it comes time to share your last bottle of champagne with—with—'Miss Dancy- Prancy of the Sillies,' wasn't it?"

"My last bottle isn't champagne!" flared young Kennilworth. "It's scotch! . . . And there'll be no Miss Anybody in it, thank you!" His face was really angry, and one twitch of his foot had knocked half his village into chaos. "Oh, all right, I'll tell you what I'm going to do with my last bottle!" he frowned. "The next-to-the-last-one, as you say, is none of your business! But the last one is going to my Old Man! . . . I come from Kansas," he acknowledged a bit shamefacedly. "From a shack no bigger than this room . . . And my Old Man lives there yet . . . And he's always been used to having a taste of something when he wanted it and I guess he misses it some. . . . And he'll be eighty years old the 15th of next December. I'm going home for it. . . . I haven't been home for seven years. . . . But my Old Man is going to get his scotch! . . . If they yank me off at every railroad station and shoot me at sunrise each new day,—my Old Man is going to get his scotch!

"Bully for you," said George Keets.

"All the same," argued the May Girl, "I think benedictine smells better."

With a little gaspy breath somebody discovered what had happened to the Village.

"Who did that?" demanded Paul Brenswick.

"You did!" snapped young Kennilworth.

"I didn't, either," protested Brenswick.

"Why of all cheeky things!" cried the Bride.

"Now see here," I admonished them, "you're all very tired and very irritable. And I suggest that you all pack off to bed."

Helping the May Girl up from her cramped position, George Keets bent low for a single exaggerated moment over her proffered hand.

"I certainly think you are making a mistake, Miss Davies," bantered young Kennilworth. "For a long run, of course, Mr. Keets might be better, but for a short run I am almost sure that you would have been jollier in the brown bungalow with me."

"Time will tell," dimpled the May Girl.

"Then I really may consider us—formally engaged?" smiled George Keets, still bending low over her hand. He was really rather amused, I think—and quite as much embarrassed as he was amused.

"No, not exactly formally," dimpled the May Girl. "But until breakfast time to-morrow morning."

"Until breakfast time to-morrow morning," hooted young Kennilworth. "That's the deuce of a funny time-limit to put on an engagement . . . It's like asking a person to go skating when there isn't any ice!..."

"Is it?" puzzled the May Girl.

"What the deuce do you expect Keets to get out of it?" quizzed young Kennilworth.

In an instant the May Girl was all smiles again. "He'll get mentioned in my prayers," she said. "'Please bless Mr. Keets, my fiancé-till-to-morrow-morning.'"

"That's certainly—something," conceded George Keets.

"It isn't enough,"—protested Kennilworth.

The May Girl stared round appealingly at her interlocutors.

"But the time is so awfully short," she said, "and I did want to get engaged to as many boys as possible in the week I was here."

"What—what!" I babbled.

"Yes, for very special reasons," said the May Girl, "I *would* like to get engaged to as many———"

With a strut like the strut of a young ban tam rooster, Rollins pushed his way suddenly into the limelight.

"If it will be the slightest accommodation to you," he affirmed, "you may consider your self engaged to me to-morrow!"

Disconcerted as she was, the May Girl swallowed the bitter, unexpected dose with infinitely less grimace than one would have expected. She even smiled a little.

"Very well, Mr. Rollins," she said, "I will be engaged to you—to-morrow."

Young Kennilworth's dismay exploded in a single exclamation. "Well—you—certainly are an extraordinary young person!"

"Yes, I know," deprecated the May Girl. "It's because I'm so tall, I suppose———"

Before the unallayed breathlessness of my expression she wilted like a worried flower.

"Yes, of course, I know, Mrs. Delville," she acknowledged, "that mock marriages aren't considered very good taste . . . But a mock engagement?" she wheedled. "If it's conducted, oh, very—very—very properly?" Her eyes were wide with pleading.

"Oh, of course," I suggested, "if it's conducted very— *very*—*very* properly!"

Across the May Girl's lovely pink and white cheeks the dark lashes fringed down.

"There—will—be—no—kissing, affirmed the May Girl.

"Oh, Shucks!" protested young Kennilworth. "Now you've spoiled everything."

Out of the corner of one eye I saw Rollins nudge Paul Brenswick. It was not a facetious nudge, but one quite markedly earnest. The whole expression indeed on Rollins's face was an expression of acute determination.

With laughter and song and a flicker of candlelight everybody filed up-stairs to bed.

Rollins carried his candle with the particularly unctuous pride of one who leads a torchlight procession. And as he turned on the upper landing and looked back, I noted that- behind the almost ribald excitement on his face there lurked a look of poignant wistfulness.

"I've never been engaged before," he confided grinningly to Paul Brenswick. "I'd like to make the most of it . . ."

Passing into my own room I flung back the casement windows for a revivifying slash of wind and rain, before I should collapse utterly into the white scrumptiousness of my bed. Frankly, I was very tired.

It must have been almost midnight when I woke to see my Husband's dark figure silhouetted in the bright square of the door. Through the depths of my weariness a consuming curiosity struggled.

"Did Ann Woltor come back?" I asked.

"She did!" said my Husband succinctly.

"And how did you get on with Allan John?"

"Oh, I'm crazy about Allan John," I yawned amiably. And then with one of those perfectly inexplicable nerve-explosions that astonishes no one as much as it astonishes oneself I struggled up on my elbow.

"But he's still got my best silver saltshaker in his pocket!" I cried.

It was then that the scream of a siren whistle tore like some fear-maddened voice through the whole house. Shriller than knives it ripped and screeched into the senses! Doors banged! Feet thudded!

"There's Allan John now!" I gasped. "It's the whistle the May Girl gave him!"

CHAPTER III

EVERYBODY looked pretty tired when they came down to breakfast the next morning. But at least everybody came down. Even Rollins! Never have I seen Rollins so really addicted to coming down to breakfast!

Poor Allan John, of course, was all overwhelmed again with humiliation and despair, and quite heroically insistent on removing his presence as expeditiously as possible from our house party. It *was* his whistle that had screeched so in the night. And as far as he knew he hadn't the slightest reason or excuse for so screeching it beyond the fact that, rousing half-awake and half-asleep from a most horrible nightmare, he had reached instinctively for the little whistle under his pillow, and not realizing what he was doing, cried for help, not just to man alone it would seem, but to High Heaven itself!

"But however in the world did you happen to have the whistle under your pillow?" puzzled the Bride.

"What else have I got?" answered Allan John.

He was perfectly right! Robbed for all time of his wife and child, stripped for the ill-favored moment of all personal moneys and proofs of identity, sojourning even in other men's linen, what did Allan John hold as a nucleus for the New Day except a little silver toy from another person's shipwreck? (Once I knew a smashed man who didn't possess even a toy to begin a new day on so he didn't begin it!)

"Well, of course, it was pretty rackety while it lasted," conceded young Kennilworth. "But at least it gave us a chance to admire each other's lingeries."

"Negligées," corrected George Keets.

"I said 'scare-clothes'!" snapped young Kennilworth. "Everybody who travels by land or sea or puts in much time at house parties ought to have at least one round of scare- clothes, one really chic 'escaping suit.'"

"The silver whistle is mine," intercepted the May Girl with some dignity. "Mine and Allan John's. I found it and gave it to Allan John. And he can blow it any time he wants to, day or night. But as long as you people all made so much fuss about it—and looked so funny," dimpled the May Girl transiently, "we will consider that after this—any time the whistle blows—the call is just for me." The May Girl's gravely ingenuous glance swept down in sudden challenge across the somewhat amused faces of her companions, "Allan John—is mine!" she confided with some incisiveness. "I found him—too!"

"Do you acknowledge that ownership, Allan John!" demanded young Kennilworth.

Even Allan John's sombre eyes twinkled the faintest possible glint of amusement.

"I acknowledge that ownership," acquiesced Allan John.

"Now see here!—I protest," rallied George Keets. "Most emphatically I protest against my fiancée assuming any masculine responsibilities except me during the brief term of our engagement!"

"But your engagement is already over!" jeered young Kennilworth. "Nice kind of Lochinvar you are—drifting down-stairs just exactly on the stroke of the breakfast bell!—'until breakfast time' were the terms, I believe. Now Rollins here has been up since dawn! Banging in and out of the house! Racing up and down the front walk in the rain! Now that's what I call real passion!"

At the very first mention of his name Rollins had come sliding way forward to the edge of his chair. He hadn't apparently expected to be engaged till after breakfast. But if there was any conceivable chance, of course——

"All ready—any time!" beamed Rollins.

"*Through*—breakfast time was what I understood," said George Keets coldly.

"Through breakfast time was—was what I meant," stammered the May Girl. From the only too palpable excitement on Rollins's face to George Keets's chill immobility she turned with the faintest possible gesture of appeal. Her eyes looked suddenly just a little bit frightened. "A—after all," she confided, "I—I didn't know as I feel quite well enough to-day to be engaged so much. Maybe I caught a little cold yesterday. Sometimes I don't sleep very well. Once——"

"Oh, come now," insisted young Kennilworth. "Don t, for Heaven's sake, be a quitter!"

"A—'quitter'?" bridled the May Girl. Her cheeks went suddenly very pink. And then suddenly very white. Like an angry little storm-cloud that absurd fluff of gray hair shadowed down for an instant across her sharply averted face. A glint of tears threatened. Then out of the gray and the gold and the blue and the pink and the tears, the jolliest sort of a little-girl-giggle issued suddenly. "Oh, all right!" said the May Girl and slipped with perfect docility apparently into the chair that George Keets had drawn out for her.

George Keets I really think was infinitely more frightened than she was, but in his case, at least, a seventeen years' lead in experience had taught him long since the advisability of disguising such emotions. Even at the dining-table of a sinking ship George Keets I'm almost certain would never have ceased passing salts and peppers, proffering olives and radishes, or making perfectly sure that your coffee was just exactly the way you liked it. In the present emergency, to cover not only his own confusion but the May Girl's, he proceeded to talk archaeology. By talking archaeology in an undertone with a faintly amorous inflection to the longest and least intelligible words, George Keets really believed I think that he was giving a rather clever imitation of an engaged man. What the May Girl thought no one could possibly have guessed. The May Girl's face was a study, but it was at least turning up to his! Whether she understood a single thing he said, or was only resting, whether she was truly amused or merely deferring as long as possible her unhappy fate with Rollins, she sat as one entranced.

Slipping into the chair directly opposite them, young Kennilworth watched the proceedings with malevolent joy. Between his very frank contempt for the dulness of George Keets's methods, and his perfectly palpable desire to keep poor Rollins tantalized as long as possible, he scarcely knew which side to play on.

Everybody indeed except Ann Woltor seemed to take a more or less mischievous delight in prolonging poor Rollins's suspense. Allan John never lifted his eyes from his coffee cup, but at least he showed no signs of disapproval or haste. Even George Keets, to the eyes of a close observer, seemed to be dallying rather unduly with his knife and fork as well as with his embarrassment.

As the breakfast hour dragged along, poor Rollins's impatience grew apace. Fidgeting round and round in his chair, scowling ferociously at anyone who dared to ask for a second service of anything, dashing out into the hall every now and then on perfectly inexplicable errands, he looked for all the world like some wry-faced clown performing by accident in a business suit.

"Really, Rollins," admonished my Husband. "I think it would have been a bit more delicate of you if you'd kept out of sight somehow till Keets' affair was over—this hovering round so through the harrowing last moments—all ready to pounce—hanged if I don't think it's crude!"

"Crude?—it's plain buzzard-y!" scoffed Kennilworth.

It was the Bride's warm, romantic heart that called the time- limit finally on George Keets's philandering.

"Really, I don't think it's quite fair," whispered the Bride. Taken all in all I think the Bridegroom was inclined to agree with her. But stronger than anybody's sense of justice, it was a composite sense of humor that sped Rollins to his heart's desire. Even Ann Woltor, I think, was curious to see just how Rollins would figure as an engaged man.

The May Girl's parting with George Keets was at least mercifully brief.

"Does he kiss my hand?" questioned the May Girl.

"No—I think not," flushed George Keets. Having no intention in the world of kissing any woman in earnest, it was not in his code, apparently, to kiss a young girl in fun. Very formally, with that frugal, tight-lipped smile of his which contrasted so curiously with the rather accentuated virility of his shoulders, he rose and bowed low over the May Girl's proffered fingers. "Really it's been a great honor. I've enjoyed it immensely!" he conceded.

"Thank you," murmured the May Girl. In a single impulse everybody turned to look at Rollins, only to find that Rollins had disappeared.

"Hi, there, Rollins! *Rollins!*" shouted young Kennilworth. "You're losing time!"

As though waiting dramatically for just this cue, the hall portieres parted slightly, and there stood Rollins grinning like a Cheshire Cat, with a great bunch of purple orchids clasped in one hand! Now we are sixty miles from a florist and the only neighbor of our acquaintance who boasts a greenhouse is a most estimable but exceedingly close-fisted flower-fancier, who might under certain conditions, I must admit, give bread at the back door, but who never under any circumstances whatsoever has been known to give orchids at the front door. Nor did I quite see Rollins even in a rain-storm actually breaking laws or glass to achieve his floral purpose. Yet there stood Rollins in our front hall, at half-past nine in the morning, with a very extravagant bunch of purple orchids in his hand.

"Well—bully for you!" gasped young Kennilworth. "Now that's what I call not being a mutt!"

Beaming with pride Rollins stepped forward and presented his offering, the grin on his face never wavering.

"Just a—just a trifling token of my esteem, Miss Davies!" he affirmed. "To say nothing of—of——"

The May Girl, I think, had never had orchids presented to her before. It is something indeed of an experience all in itself to see a young girl receive her first orchids. The faint astonishment and regret to find that after all they're not nearly as darling and cosy as violets or roses or even carnations—the sudden contradictory flare of sex-pride and importance—flashed like so much large print across the May Girl's fluctuant face.

"Why—why they're—wonderful!" she stammered.

Producing from Heaven knows what antique pin-cushion a hat-pin that would have easily impaled the May Girl like a butterfly against the wall, Rollins completed the presentation. But the end it seemed was not yet. Fumbling through his pockets he produced a small wad of paper, and from that small wad of paper a large old-fashioned seal ring with several strands of silk thread dangling from it.

"Of course at such short notice," beamed Rollins, "one couldn't expect to do much. But if you don't mind things being a bit old-timey,—this ring of my great uncle Aberner's—if we tie it on—perhaps?"

Whereupon, lashing the ring then and there to the May Girl's astonished finger, Rollins proceeded to tuck the May Girl's whole astonished hand into the crook of his arm, and start off with her—still grinning—to promenade the long sheltered glassed-in porch, across whose rain-blurred windows the storm raged by more like a sound than a sight.

The May Girl's face was crimson!

"Well it was all your own idea, you know, this getting engaged!" taunted Kennilworth.

It was not a very good moment to taunt the May Girl. My Husband saw it I think even before I did.

"Really, Rollins," he suggested, "you mustn't overdo this arm-in-arm business. Not all day long! It isn't done! Not this ball-and-chain idea any more! Not this shackling of the betrothed!"

"No, really, Rollins, old man," urged young Kennilworth, "you've got quite the wrong idea. You say yourself you've never been engaged before, so you'd better let some of us wiser guys coach you up a bit in some of the essentials."

"Coach me up a bit?" growled Rollins.

"Why, you didn't suppose for a minute, did you," persisted young Kennilworth tormentingly, "that there was any special fun about being engaged? You didn't think for a moment, I mean, that you were really going to have any sort of good time to-day? Not both of you, I mean?"

"Eh?" jerked Rollins, stopping suddenly short in his tracks, but with the May Girl's reluctant hand still wedged fast into the crook of his arm, he stood defying his tormentor. "Eh? *What?*"

"Why I never in the world," mused Kennilworth, "ever heard of two engaged people having a good time the same day. One or the other of them always has to give up the one thrilling thing that he yearned most to do and devote his whole time to pretending that he's perfectly enraptured doing some stupid fuddy-duddy stunt that the other one wanted to do. It's simply the question always—of who gives up! Now, Miss Davies for instance—" Mockingly he fixed his eyes on the May Girl's unhappy face. "Now, Miss Davies," he insisted, "more than anything else in the world to-day what would you like to do?"

"Sew," said the May Girl.

"And you, Mr. Rollins," persisted Kennilworth. "If it wasn't for Miss Davies here—what would you be doing to-day?"

"I?" quickened Rollins. "I?" across his impatient, irritated face, an expression of frankly scientific ecstasy flared up like an explosion. "Why those shells, you know!" glowed Rollins. "That last consignment! Why I should have been cataloging shells!"

"There you have it!" cried Kennilworth. "Either you've got to sew all day long with Miss Davies—or else she'll have to catalog shells with you!"

"Sew?" hooted Rollins.

"Oh, I'd just love to catalog shells!" cried the May Girl. In that single instant the somewhat indeterminate quiver of her lips had bloomed into a real smile. By a dexterous movement, released from Rollins's arm, she turned and fled for the door. "Up-stairs, you mean, don't you?" she cried. The smile had reached her eyes now. In another minute it seemed as though even her hair would be all laughter. "At the big table in the upper hall? Where you were working yesterday? One, on one side of the table—and one—the other? And one, the *other!*" she giggled triumphantly.

With unflagging agility Rollins started after her.

"What I had really planned," he grinned, "was a walk on the beach."

"Arm—in—arm!" mused young Kennilworth.

"Eh! You think you're smart, don't you!" grinned Rollins.

"Yes, quite so," acknowledged Kennilworth. "But if you really want to see smartness on its native heath just pipe your eye to-morrow when I dawn on the horizon as an engaged man!"

"You?" called the May Girl. Staring back through the mahogany banisters her face looked fairly striped with astonishment.

"You certainly announced your desire," said Kennilworth, "to go right through the whole list. Didn't you?"

"Oh, but I didn't mean—everybody," parried the May Girl. Her mouth and her eyes and her hair were all laughing together now. "Oh, Goodness me—not *everybody!*" she gesticulated, with a fine air of disdain.

"Not the married men," explained the Bride.

"No, I'm sure she discriminated against the married men," chuckled the Bridegroom.

"Well—she sha'n't discriminate against *me!*" snapped young Kennilworth. Absurd as it was he looked angry. Young Kennilworth, one might infer, was not accustomed to having women discriminate against him. "You made the plan and you'll jolly-well keep to it!" affirmed young Kennilworth.

"Oh, all right," laughed the May Girl. "If you really insist! But for a boy who's as truly unselfish as you are about nursery-governessing other people's Pom dogs, and saving your last taste of anything for your old Old Daddy—you've certainly got the worst manners!"

"Manners!" drawled George Keets. "This is no test. Wait—till you see his engagement manners!"

"Oh, she'll 'wait' all right!" sniffed young Kennilworth, and turned on his heel.

Paul Brenswick, searching hard through the shipping news in the morning paper, looked up with a faint shadow of concern.

"What's the grouch?" he questioned.

Standing with her hands on her Bridegroom's shoulders the Bride glanced back from the stormy window to Kennilworth's face with a somewhat provocative smile.

"Well—it *was* in the mind of God, wasn't it?" she said.

"What was!" demanded young Kennilworth.

"The rain," shrugged the Bride.

"Oh—damn the rain!" cried young Kennilworth. "I wish people wouldn't speak to me! It drives me crazy I tell you to have everybody babbling so! Can't you see I want to work? Can't anybody see—anything?" Equally furious all of a sudden at everybody, he swung around and darted up the stairs. "Don't anybody call me to lunch," he ordered. "For Heaven's sake don't let anyone be idiot enough to call me to lunch."

Even Ann Woltor's jaw dropped a bit at the amazing rudeness and peevishness of it.

It was then that the beaming grin on Rollins's face flickered out for a single instant of incredulity and reproach.

"Why—Miss Woltor!" he choked, "you didn't have your tooth fixed—after all!"

With a great crackle of paper every man's face seemed buried suddenly in the shipping news.

"No!" I heard my Husband's voice affirm with extravagant precision, "not the slightest mention anywhere of any maritime disaster."

"Not the slightest!" agreed George Keets.

"Not the slightest!" echoed Paul Brenswick with what seemed to me like quite unnecessary monotony.

It was the Bride who showed the only real tact. Slipping her hand casually into Ann Woltor's hand she started for the Library.

"Let's go see if we can't find something awfully exciting to read to-day," she suggested. Once across the library threshold her voice lowered slightly. "Really, Miss Woltor," she confided, "there are times when I think that Mr. Rollins is sort of crazy."

"So many people are," acquiesced Ann Woltor without emotion.

Caroming off to my miniature conservatory on the pretext of watering my hyacinths I met my Husband bent evidently on the same errand. My Husband's sudden interest in potted plants was bewitching. Even the hyacinths were amused I think. Yet even to prolong the novelty of the situation there was certainly no time to be lost about Rollins.

"Truly Jack," I besought him, "this Rollins man has got to be suppressed."

"Oh, not to-day—surely?" pleaded my Husband. "Not on the one engagement day of his life? Poor Rollins—when he's having such a thrill?"

"Well—not to-day perhaps," I conceded with some reluctance. "But to-morrow surely! We never have been used you know to starting off the day with Rollins! And two breakfasts in succession? Well, really, it's almost more than the human heart can stand. Far be it from me," I argued, "to condone poor Allan John's lapse from sobriety or advocate any plan whatsoever for the ensnaring of the very young or the unwary; but all other means failing," I argued, "I should consider it a very great mercy to the survivors if Rollins should wake to-morrow with a slight headache. No real cerebral symptoms you understand—nothing really acute. Just——!"

"Oh, stop your fooling!" said my Husband. "What I came in here to talk to you about was Miss Woltor."

"'Woltor' or 'Stoltor'?" I questioned.

"Who said 'Stoltor'?" jerked my Husband.

"Oh, sometimes you say 'Woltor' and sometimes you say 'Stoltor'!" I confided. "And it's so confusing. Which is it— really?"

"Hanged if I know!" said my Husband.

"Then let's call her Ann," I suggested.

With an impulse that was quite unwonted in him my Husband stepped suddenly forward to my biggest, rosiest, most perfect pot of pink hyacinths, and snapping a succulent stem in two thrust the great gorgeous bloom incongruously into his button-hole. Never in fifteen years had I seen my Husband with a flower in his button-hole. Neither, in all that time, had I ever seen him flush across the cheek-bones just exactly the shade of a rose-pink Hyacinth. I could have hugged him! He looked so confused.

"Oh, I say—" he ventured quite abruptly, "Miss Woltor and I, you know,—we never went near the dentist yesterday!"

"So I inferred," I said, "from Rollins's observation. What *were* you doing?" Truly I didn't mean to ask, but the long- suppressed wonder most certainly slipped.

"Why we were just arguing!" groaned my Husband. "Round and round and round!"

"Round—what?" I questioned—now that the slipping had started. "Round and round the country?"

"Country, no indeed!" grinned my Husband unhappily. "We never left the place!"

"Never—left the place?" I stammered. "Why, where in Creation were you?"

"Why, first," said my Husband, "we were down at the end of the driveway right there by the acacia trees, you know. She was crying so I didn't exactly like to strike the state highway for fear somebody would notice her. And then afterward—when I saw that she really couldn't stop——"

"Crying?" I puzzled. "Ann Woltor—crying?"

"And then afterward," persisted my Husband, "we went over to the Bungalow on the Rock and commenced the argument all over again! Fortunately there was some tea there and crackers and sardines and enough firewood. But it was the devil and all getting over! We ran the car into the boat-house and took the punt! I thought the surf would smash us, but——"

"But what was the 'argument'?" I questioned.

"Why about her coming back!" said my Husband. "She was so absolutely determined not to come back! I never in my life saw such stubbornness! And if she once got away I knew perfectly well that she never would come back! That she'd drop out of sight just as—And such crying!" he interrupted himself with apparent irrelevance. "Everything smashed up altogether at once!—Hadn't cried before, she said, for eight years!"

"Well, it's time she cried, the poor dear!" I affirmed sincerely. "But——"

"But I couldn't bring her back to the house!" insisted my Husband. "Not crying so, not arguing so!"

"No, of course not," I agreed.

"I kept thinking she'd stop!" shivered my Husband.

"Jack," I asked quite abruptly, "Who is Ann Woltor?"

"Search me!" said my Husband, "I never saw her before."

"You—never saw her—before!" I stammered. "Why—why you called her by name!—you——"

"I knew her face," said my Husband. "I've seen her picture. In London it was. In Hal Ferry's studio. Fifteen years ago if it's a day. A huge charcoal sketch all swoops and smouches.— Just a girl holding up a small hand-mirror to her astonished face.—'*The woman with the broken tooth*' it was called."

"Fifteen years ago?" I gasped. "'*The—the woman with the broken tooth!*' What a—what a name for a picture!

"Yes, wasn't it?" said my Husband. "And you'd have thought somehow that the picture would be funny, wouldn't you? But it wasn't! It was the grimmest thing I ever saw in my life! Sketched just from memory too it must have been. No man would have had the cheek to ask a woman to pose for him like that,— to reduplicate just for fun I mean that particular expression of bewilderment which he had by such grim chance surprised on her unwitting face. Such shock! Such *astonishment!* It wasn't just the astonishment you understand of Marred Beauty worrying about a dentist. But a look the stark, staring, chain-lightning sort of look of a woman who, back of the broken tooth, linked up in some way with the accident of the broken tooth, saw something, suddenly, that God Himself couldn't repair! It was horrid, I tell you! It haunted you! Even if you started to hoot you ended by arguing! Arguing and—wondering! Ferry finally got so that he wouldn't show it to anybody. People quizzed him so."

"Yes, but Ferry?" I questioned.

"No," said my Husband. "It was only by the merest chance that I heard the name Ann Stoltor associated in any way with the picture. Hal Ferry never told anything. Not a word. But he never exhibited the picture, I noticed. It was a point of honor with him, I suppose. If one lives long enough, of course, one's pretty apt to catch every friend off guard at least once in his facial expression. But one doesn't exhibit one's deductions I suppose. One mustn't at least make professional presentation of them."

"Yes, but Ann Woltor—Stoltor," I puzzled. "When she tried to bolt so? Was it because she knew that you knew Hal Ferry? When you called her Stoltor and dropped the lantern so funnily when you first saw her, was it then that she linked you up with this something—whatever it is that has hurt her so?—And determined even then to bolt at the very first chance she could get? But why in the world should she want to bolt?" I puzzled. "Certainly she's had to take us on faith quite as much as we've taken her. And I?—I *love* her!"

In the flare of the open doorway George Keets loomed quite abruptly.

"Oh, is this where you bad people are?" he reproached us. "We've been searching the house for you."

"Oh, of course, if you really need us," conceded my Husband. "But even you, I should think, would know a flirtation when you saw it and have tact enough not to butt in."

"A flirtation?" scoffed Keets. "You? At ten o'clock in the morning? All trimmed up like an Easter bonnet! And acting half scared to death? It looks a bit fishy to me, not to say mysterious!"

"All Husbands move in a mysterious way their flirtations to perform," observed my Husband.

From one pair of half-laughing eyes to the other George Keets glanced up with the faintest possible suggestion of a sigh.

"Really, you know," said George Keets, "there are times when even *I* can imagine that marriage might be just a little bit jolly."

"Oh never jolly," grinned my Husband, "but there are times I frankly admit—when it seems a heap more serious than it does at other times."

"Less serious, you mean," corrected Keets.

"More serious," grinned my Husband.

"Oh, for goodness sake, let's stop talking about us," I protested, "and talk about the weather!"

"It was the weather that I came to talk about," exclaimed George Keets. "Do you think it will clear to-day?" he questioned.

For a single mocking instant my Husband's glance sought mine.

"No, not to-day, George," he said.

"U—m!" mused George Keets. "Then in that case," he brightened suddenly, "if Mrs. Delville is really willing to put up a water-proof lunch we think it would be rather good sport to go back to the cave and explore a bit more of the beach perhaps and bring home Heaven knows what fresh plunder from the shipwrecked trunk."

"Oh, how jolly!" I agreed. "But will Mrs. Brenswick go?"

"Mrs. Brenswick isn't exactly keen about it," admitted Keets. "But she says she'll go. And Brenswick himself and Miss Woltor and Allan John—" It was amusing how everybody called Allan John "Allan John" without title or subterfuge or self-consciousness of any kind.

With their arms across each other's shoulders the Bride and Bridegroom came frolicking by on their way to the foot of the stairs.

"Oh, Miss Davies!—Miss Davies!" they called up teasingly. "Are you willing that Allan John should go to the cave to-day?"

Smiling responsively but not one atom teased, the May Girl jumped up from her tableful of shells and came out to the edge of the balustrade to consider the matter.

"Allan John! Allan John!" she called. "Do you really want to go?"

"Why, yes," admitted Allan John, "if everybody's going."

Behind the May Girl's looming height and loveliness the little squat figure of Rollins shadowed suddenly.

"Miss Davies and I are not going," said Rollins.

"Not—going?" questioned the May Girl.

"Not going," chuckled Rollins, "unless she walks with me!" He didn't say "arm-in-arm." He didn't need to. That inference was entirely expressed by the absurdly triumphant little glint in his eye.

I don't think the May Girl intended to laugh. But she did laugh. And all the laugh in the world seemed suddenly "on" Rollins.

"No—really, People," rallied the May Girl, "I'd heaps rather stay here with Mr. Rollins and work on these perfectly darling shells. One—on one side of the table—and one on the other."

"We are going to have lunch up here—in fact," counterchecked that rascally Rollins with a blandness that was actually malicious. "There is a magnificent specimen here I notice of 'Triton's Trumpet'. The Pacific Islanders I understand use it very successfully for a tea-kettle. And for tea-cups. With the aid of one or two Hare's Ears which I'm almost sure I've seen in the specimen cabinet———"

"'Hare's Ears'?" gasped the May Girl.

"It's the name of a shell, my dear,—just the name of a shell," explained Rollins with some unctuousness. "Very comfortable here we shall be, I am sure!" beamed Rollins. "Very cosy, very scientific, very ro-romantic, if I may take the liberty of saying so. Very———"

"Oh, Shucks!" interrupted George Keets quite surprisingly. "If Miss Davies isn't going there's no good in anybody going!"

"Thank—you," murmured Ann Woltor. At the astonishingly new and relaxed timbre of her voice everybody turned suddenly and stared at her. It wasn't at all that she spoke meltingly, but the fact of her speaking meltedly, that gave every one of us that queer little gasp of surprise. Still icy cold, but fluid at last, her voice flowed forth as it were for the very first time with some faint suggestion of the real emotion in her mind. "Thank you—Mr. Keets," mocked Ann Woltor, "for your enthusiasm concerning the rest of us."

"Oh, I say!" deprecated George Keets. "You know what I meant!" His face was crimson. "It—it was only that Miss Davies was so awfully keen about it all yesterday! Everybody, you know, doesn't find it so exhilarating."

"No-o?" murmured Ann Woltor. In the plushy black somberness of her eyes a highlight glinted suddenly. Suppressed tears make just that particular kind of glint. So also does suppressed laughter. "I was out in a storm—once," drawled Ann Woltor, "I found it very—exhilarating."

With a flash of rather quizzical perplexity I saw my Husband's glance rake hers.

Wincing just a little she turned back to me with a certain gesture of appeal.

"Cry one day and laugh another, is it?" she ventured experimentally.

"Going to the dentist isn't very jolly—you're quite right," interposed the Bride.

"No, it certainly isn't," sympathized every body.

It was perfectly evident that no one in the party except my Husband and myself knew just what had happened to the dentistry expedition. And Ann Woltor wasn't quite sure even yet, I could see, whether I knew or not. The return home the night before had been so late the commotion over Allan John's whistle so immediate—the breakfast hour itself such a chaos of nonsense and foolery. Certainly there was no object in prolonging her uncertainty. I liked her infinitely too much to worry her. Very fortunately also she had a ready eye, the one big compensating gift that Fate bestows on all people who have ever been caught off their guard even once by a real trouble. She never muffed any glance I noticed that you wanted her to catch.

"Oh, I hate to think, Ann dear," I smiled, "about there being any tears yesterday. But if tears yesterday really should mean a laugh to-day———"

"Oh, to-day!" quickened Ann Woltor. "Who can tell about to-day!"

"Then you really would like to go?" said George Keets.

Across Ann Woltor's shoulders a little shrug quivered.

"Why, of course, I'm going!" said Ann Woltor.

"Good! Famous!" rallied George Keets. "Now that makes how many of us?" he reckoned. "Kenmlworth?"

"No, let's not bother about Kennilworth," said my Husband.

"You?" queried George Keets.

"Yes, I'm going," acquiesced my Husband.

"And you, Mrs. Delville, of course?"

"No, I think not," I said.

"Just the Brenswicks then," counted George Keets. "And Allan John and———"

Once again, from the railing of the upper landing, the May Girl's wistfully mirthful face peered down through that amazing cloud of gold-gray hair.

"Allan John—Allan John!" she called very softly. "I'd like to have you dress warmly—you know! And not get just too absolutely tired out! And be sure and take the whistle," she laughed very resolutely, "and if anybody isn't good to you— you just blow it hard—and I'll come."

As befitted the psychic necessities of a very cranky Person-With-a-Future, young Kennilworth was not disturbed for lunch.

And Rollins, it seemed, was grotesquely genuine in his desire to picnic up-stairs with the May Girl and the shells. Even the May Girl herself rallied with a fluttering sort of excitement to the idea. The shell table fortunately was quite large enough to accommodate both work and play. Rollins certainly was beside himself with triumph, and on Rollins's particular type of countenance there is no conceivable synonym for the word "triumph" except "ghoulish glee." Really it was amazing the way the May Girl rallied her gentleness and her patience and her playfulness to the absurd game. She opposed no contrary personality whatsoever even to Rollins's most vapid desires. Unable as he was either to simulate or stimulate "the light that never was on land or sea," it was Rollins's very evident intention apparently to "blue" his Lady's eyes and "pink" his Lady's cheeks by the narration at least of such sights as "never were on land or sea"! Flavored by moonlight, rattling with tropical palms, green as Arctic ice, wild as a loon's hoot, science and lies slipped alike from Rollins's lips with a facility that even I would scarcely have suspected him of! Lands he had never visited— adventures he had never dreamed of cannibals not yet born—babble—babble—*babble—babble!*

As for the May Girl herself, as far as I could observe, not a single sound emanated from her the entire day, except the occasional clank of her hugely over-sized "betrothal ring" against the Pom dog's collar, or the little gasping phrase, "Oh, no, Mr. Rollins! Not*really?*" that thrilled now and then from her astonished lips, as, elbows on table, chin cupped in hand, she sat staring blue-eyed and bland at her— tormentor.

It must have been five o'clock, almost, before the beach party returned. Gleaming like a great bunch of storm-drenched jonquils, the six adventurers loomed up cheerfully in the rain-light. Once again George Keets and the Bridegroom were dragging the Bride by her hand. Ann Woltor and my Husband followed just behind. Allan John walked alone.

Even young Kennilworth came out on the porch to hail them.

"Hi, there!" called my Husband.

"Hi, there, yourself!" retaliated Kennilworth.

"Oh, we've had a perfectly wonderful day! gasped the Bride.

"Found the cave all right!" triumphed Keets.

"Allan John found a—found an old-fashioned hoop-skirt!" giggled the Bride.

"The devil he did!" hooted Rollins.

"But we never found the trunk at all!" scolded the Bridegroom. "Either we were way off in our calculations or else the sand———"

In a sudden gusty flutter of white the May Girl came round the corner into the full buffet of the wind. It hadn't occurred to me before just exactly how tired she looked. "Why, hello, everybody—" she began, faltered an instant— crumpled up at the waist-line—and slipped down in a white heap of unconsciousness to the floor.

It was George Keets who reached her first, and gathering her into his long, strong arms, bore her into the house. It was the first time in his life I think that George Keets had ever held a woman in his arms. His eyes hardly knew what to make of it. And his tightened lips, quite palpably, didn't like it at all. But after all it was those extraordinarily human shoulders of his that were really doing the carrying?

Very fortunately though for all concerned the whole scare was over in a minute. Ensconced like a queen in the deep pillows of the big library sofa the May Girl rallied almost at once to joke about the catastrophe. But she didn't want any supper, I noticed, and dallied behind in her cushions, when the supper-hour came.

"You look like a crumpled rose," said the Bride.

"Like a poor crumpled—white rose," supplemented Ann Woltor.

"Like a very long-stemmed—poor crumpled—white rose," deprecated the May Girl herself.

Kennilworth brought her a knife and fork, but no smiles.

George Keets brought her several different varieties of his peculiarly tight-lipped smile, and all the requisite table- silver besides.

Paul Brenswick sent her the cherry from his cocktail and promised her the frosting from his cake.

The Bride sent her love.

Ann Woltor remembered the table napkin.

Allan John watched the proceedings without comment.

It was Rollins who insisted on serving the May Girl's supper. "It was his right," he said. More than this he also insisted on gathering up all his own supper on one quite inadequate plate, and trotting back to the library to eat it with the May Girl. This also was his right, he said. Truly he looked very funny there all huddled up on a low stool by the May Girl's side. But at least he showed sense enough now not to babble very much. And once, at least, without reproof I saw him reach up to the May Girl's fork and plate and urge some particularly nourishing morsel of food into her languidly astonished mouth.

It was just as everybody drifted back from the dining-room into the library that the May Girl wriggled her long, silken, childish legs out of the steamer-rug that encompassed her, struggled to her feet, wandered somewhat aimlessly to the piano, fingered the keys for a single indefinite moment and burst ecstatically into song!

None of us, except my Husband, had heard her sing before. None of us indeed, except my Husband and myself, knew even that she could sing. The proof that she could smote suddenly across the ridge of one's spine like the prickle of a mild electric shock.

My Husband was perfectly right. It was a typical "Boy Soprano" voice, a chorister's voice—clear as flame—passionless as syrup. As devoid of ritual as the multiplication table it would have made the multiplication table fairly reek with incense and Easter lilies! Absolutely lacking in everything that the tone sharks call "color"—yet it set your mind a-haunt with all the sad crimson and purple splendors of memorial windows! Shadows were back of it! And sorrows! And mysteries! Bridals! And deaths! The prattle alike of the very young and the very old! Carol! And Threnody! And a fearful Transiency as of youth itself passing!

She sang—
"There is a Green Hill far away
Without a city wall,
Where our dear Lord was crucified,
Who died to save us—all."
and she sang
"From the Desert I come to thee,
On a stallion shod with fire!
And the winds are not more fleet
Than the wings of my de-sire!"

Like an Innocent pouring kerosene on the Flame-of-the-World the young voice soared and swelled to that lovely, limpid word "desire." (In the darkness I saw Paul Brenswick's hand clutch suddenly out to his Mate's. In the darkness I saw George Keets switch around suddenly and begin to whisper very fast to Allan John.) And then she sang a little nonsense rhyme about "Rabbits" which she explained rather shyly she had just made up. "She was very fond of rabbits," she explained. "And of dogs, too—if all the truth were to be told. Also cats."

"Also—shells!" sniffed young Kennilworth.

"Yes, also shells," conceded the May Girl without resentment.

"Ha!" sniffed young Kennilworth.

"O—h, a—jealous lover, this," deprecated George Keets. "Really, Miss Davies," he condoned, "I'm afraid to-morrow is going to be somewhat of a strain on you."

"To-morrow?" dimpled the May Girl.

"Ha!—To-morrow!" shrugged young Kennilworth.

"It was the rabbits," dimpled the May Girl, "that I was going to tell you about now. It's a very moral song written specially to deplore the—the thievish habits of the rabbits. But I can't seem to get around to the 'deploring' until the second verse. All the first verse is just scientific description." Adorably the young voice lifted into the nonsense—

"Oh, the habit of a rabbit
Is a fact that would amaze
From the pinkness of his blinkness and the blandness of his gaze,
In a nose that's so a-twinkle like a merri—perri—winkle—
And—"

Goodness me!—That *voice!*—The babyishness of it!—And the poignancy! Should one laugh? Or should one cry? Clap one's hands? Or bolt from the room? I decided to bolt from the room.

Both my Husband and myself thought it would be only right to telephone Dr. Brawne about the fainting spell. There was a telephone fortunately in my own room. And there is one thing at least very compensatory about telephoning to doctors. If you once succeed in finding them, there is never an undue lag in the conversation itself.

"But tell me only just one thing," I besought my Husband, "so I won't be talking merely to a voice! This Dr. Brawne of yours?—Is he old or young? Fat or thin? Jolly? Or——?"

"He's about fifty," said my Husband. "Fifty-five perhaps. Stoutish rather, I think you'd call him. And jolly. Oh, I——"

"Ting-a-ling—ling—*ling!*" urged the telephone-bell.

Across a hundred miles of dripping, rain-bejeweled wires, Dr. Brawne's voice flamed up at last with an almost metallic crispness.

"Yes?"

"This is Dr. Brawne?"

"Yes."

"This is Mrs. Delville—Jack Delville's wife."

"Yes?"

"We just thought we'd call up and report the safe arrival of your ward and tell you how much we are enjoying her!"

"Yes? I trust she didn't turn up with any more lame, halt, or blind pets than you were able to handle."

"Oh no—*no*—not—at all!" I hastened to affirm. (Certainly it seemed no time to explain about poor Allan John.)

"But what I really called up to say," I hastened to confide, "is that she fainted this afternoon, and——"

"Yes?" crisped the clear incisive voice again.

"Fainted," I repeated.

"Yes?"

"*Fainted!*" I fairly shouted.

"Oh, I hardly think that's anything," murmured Dr. Brawne. His voice sounded suddenly very far away and muffled as though he were talking through a rather soggy soda biscuit. "She faints very easily. I don't find anything the matter. It's just a temporary instability, I think. She's grown so very fast."

"Yes, she's tall," I admitted.

"Everything else all right?" queried the voice. The wires were working better now. "I don't need to ask if she's having a good time," essayed the voice very courteously. "She's always so essentially original in her ways of having a good time—even with strangers—even when she's really feeling rather shy."

"Oh, she's having a good time, all right," I hastened to assure him. "Three perfectly eligible young men all competing for her favor!"

"Only three?" laughed the voice. "You surprise me!"

"And speaking of originality," I rallied instantly to that laugh, "she has invented the most diverting game! She is playing at being-engaged-to-a-different-man—every day of her visit. Oh *very* circumspectly, you understand," I hastened to affirm. "Nothing serious at all!"

"No, I certainly hope not," mumbled the voice again through some maddeningly soggy connection. "Because, you see, I'm rather expecting to marry her myself on the fifteenth of September next."

CHAPTER IV

SLEEP is a funny thing! Really comical I mean! A magician's trick! "Now you have it—and now you don't!"

Certainly I had very little of it the night of Dr. Brawne's telephone conversation. I was too surprised.

Yet staring up through those long wakeful hours into the jetty black heights of my bedroom ceiling it didn't seem to be so much the conversation itself as the perfectly irrelevant events succeeding that conversation that kept hurtling back so into my visual consciousness—The blueness of the May Girl's eyes! The brightness of her hair!—Rollins's necktie! The perfectly wanton hideousness of Rollins's necktie!—The bang—*bang*—*bang* of a storm-tortured shutter way off in the ell somewhere.

Step by step, item by item, each detail of events reprinted itself on my mind. Fumbling back from the shadowy telephone- stand into the brightly lighted upper hall with the single desire to find my Husband and confide to him as expeditiously as possible this news which had so amazed me, I had stumbled instead upon the May Girl herself, climbing somewhat listlessly up the stairs toward bed, Rollins was close behind her carrying her book and a filmy sky-blue scarf. George Keets followed with a pitcher of water.

"Oh, it isn't Good Night, dear, is it?" I questioned.

"Yes," said the May Girl. "I'm—pretty tired." She certainly looked it.

Rollins quite evidently was in despair. He was not to accomplish his 'kiss' after all, it would seem. All the long day, I judged, he had been whipping up his cheeky courage to meet some magic opportunity of the evening. And now, it appeared, there wasn't going to be any evening! Even the last precious moment indeed was to be ruined by George Keets's perfidious intrusion!

It was the Bride's voice though that rang down the actual curtain on Rollins's "Perfect Day."

"Oh, Miss Davies!—Miss Davies!" called the Bride. "You mustn't forget to return your ring, you know!"

"Why, no, so I mustn't," rallied the May Girl.

Twice I heard Rollins swallow very hard. Any antique was sacred to him, but a family antique. Oh, ye gods!

"K—K—Keep the ring!" stammered Rollins. It was the nearest point to real heroism surely that funny little Rollins would ever attain.

"Oh, no, indeed," protested the May Girl. Very definitely she snapped the silken threads, removed the clumsy bauble from her finger, and handed it back to Rollins. "But—but it's a beautiful ring!" she hastened chivalrously to assure him. "I'll—I'll keep the orchids!" she assented with real dimples.

On Rollins's sweating face the symptoms of acute collapse showed suddenly. With a glare that would have annihilated a less robust soul than George Keets's he turned and laid bare his horrid secret to an unfeeling Public.

"I'd rather you kept the *ring*," sweated Rollins. "The—The orchids have got to go back!—I only hired the orchids!—That is I—I bribed the gardener. They've got to be back by nine o'clock to-night. For some sort of a—a party."

"To-night?" I gasped. "In all this storm f Why, what if the May Girl had refused to—to———?"

In Rollins's small, blinking eyes, Romance and Thrift battled together in terrible combat.

"I gotta go back," mumbled Rollins. "He's got my watch!"

"Oh, for goodness sake you mustn't risk losing your watch!" laughed the May Girl.

George Keets didn't laugh. He hooted! I had never heard him hoot before, and ribald as the sound seemed emanating from his distinctly austere lips, the mechanical construction of that hoot was in some way strangely becoming to him.

The May Girl quite frankly though was afraid he had hurt Rollins's feelings. Returning swiftly from her bedroom with the lovely exotics bunched cautiously in one hand she turned an extravagantly tender smile on Rollins's unhappy face.

"Just—Just one of them," she apologized, "is crushed a little. I know you told me to be awfully careful of them. I'm very sorry. But truly," she smiled, "it's been perfectly Wonderful—just to have them for a day! Thank you!—Thank you a whole lot, I mean! And for the day itself—it's—it's been very—pleasant," she lied gallantly.

Snatching the orchids almost roughly from her hand Rollins gave another glare at George Keets and started for his own room. With his fingers on the door-handle he turned and glared back with particular ferocity at the May Girl herself. "Pleasant?" he scoffed. "*Pleasant?*" And crossing the threshold he slammed the door hard behind him.

Never have I seen anything more boorish!

"Why—Why, how tired he must be," exclaimed the May Girl.

"Tired?" hooted George Keets. He was still hooting when he joined the Bride and Bridegroom in the library.

It must have been fifteen minutes later that, returning from an investigation of the banging blind, I ran into Rollins stealing surreptitiously to the May Girl's door. Quite unconsciously, doubtless, but with most rapacious effect, his sparse hair was rumpled in innumerable directions, and the stealthy boy-pirate hunch to his shoulders added the last touch of melodrama to the scene. Rollins, as a gay Lothario, was certainly a new idea. I could have screamed with joy. But while I debated the ethics of screaming for joy only, the May Girl herself, as though in reply to his crafty knock, opened her door and stared frankly down at him with a funny, flushed sort of astonishment. She was in her great boyish blanket- wrapper, with her gauzy gold hair wafting like a bright breeze across her neck and shoulders, and the radiance of her I think would have startled any man. But it knocked the breath out of Rollins.

"P-p-pleasant!" gasped Rollins, quite abruptly. "It was a—a *Miracle!*"

"—Miracle?" puzzled the May Girl.

"Wall-papers!" babbled Rollins. "Suppose it had been true?" he besought her. "To-day, I mean? Our betrothal?" With total unexpectedness he began to flutter a handfull of wall-paper samples under the May Girl's astonished nose. "I've got a little flat you know in town," babbled Rollins. "Just one room and bath. It's pretty dingy. But for a long time now I've been planning to have it all repapered. And if you'd choose the wallpaper for it—it would be pleasant to think of during—during the years!" babbled Rollins.

"*What?*" puzzled the May Girl. Then quite suddenly she reached out and took the papers from Rollins's hand and bent her lovely head over them in perfectly solemn contemplation. "Why—why the pretty gray one with the white gulls and the flash of blue!" she decided almost at once, looked up for an instant, smiled straight into Rollins's fatuous eyes, and was gone again behind the impregnable fastness of her closed door, leaving Rollins gasping like a fool, his shoulders drooping, his limp hands clutching the sheet of white gulls with all the absurd manner of an amateur prima donna just on the verge of bursting into song!

And all of a sudden starting to laugh I found myself crying instead. It was the expression in Rollins's eyes, I think. The one "off-guard" expression perhaps of Rollins's life! A scorching flame of self-revelation, as it were, that consumed even as it illuminated, leaving only gray ashes and perplexity. Not just the look it was of a Little-Man-Almost- Old-who-had-Never-Had-a-Chance-to-Play. But the look of a Little-Man-Almost-Old who sensed suddenly for the first time that he never *would* have a chance to play! That Fate denying him the glint of wealth, the flash of romance, the scar even of tragedy, had stamped him merely with the indelible sign of a Person-Who wasn't—Meant-to-be-Liked!

Truly I was very glad to steal back into my dark room for a moment before trotting downstairs again to join all those others who were essentially intended for liking and loving, so eminently fitted, whether they refused or accepted it, for the full moral gamut of human experience.

On my way down it was only human, of course, to stop in the May Girl's room. Rollins or no Rollins it was the May Girl's problem that seemed to me the only really maddening one of the moment. What in creation was life planning to proffer the May Girl?—Dr. Brawne?—Dr. Brawne?—It wasn't just a question of Dr. Brawne! But a question of the May Girl herself?

She was still in her blanket-wrapper when I entered the room, but had hopped into bed, and sat bolt-up-right rocking vaguely, with her knees gathered to her chin in the circle of her slender arms.

"What seems to be the matter?" I questioned.

"That's what I don't know," she dimpled almost instantly. "But I seem to be worrying about something.

"Worrying?" I puzzled.

"Well,—maybe it's about the Pom dog," suggested the May Girl helpfully. "His mouth is so very—very tiny. Do you think he had enough supper?"

"Oh, I'm sure he had enough supper," I hastened to reassure her.

Very reflectively she narrowed her eyes to review the further field of her possible worries.

"That cat—that your Husband said he sent away just before I came for fear I'd bring some—some contradictory animals—are you quite sure that he's got a good home?" she worried.

"Oh, the best in the world," I said. "A Maternity Hospital!"

"Kittens?" brightened the May Girl for a single instant only. "Oh, you really mean kittens? Then surely there's nothing to worry about in that direction!"

"Nothing but—kittens," I conceded.

"Then it must be Allan John," said the May Girl. "His feet! Of course, I can't exactly help feeling pretty responsible for Allan John. Are you sure—are you quite sure, I mean, that he hasn't been sitting round with wet feet all the evening? He isn't exactly the croupy type, of course, but—" With a sudden irrelevant gesture she unclasped her knees, and shot her feet straight out in front of her. "Whatever in the world," she cried out, "am I going to do with Allan John when it comes time to go home! Now gold-fish," she reflected, "in a real emergency,—can always be tucked away in the bath-tub. And once when I brought home a Japanese baby," she giggled in spite of herself, "they made me keep it in my own room. But——"

"But I've got a worry of my own," I interrupted. "It's about your fainting. It scared me dreadfully. I've just been telephoning to Dr. Brawne about it."

Across the May Girl's supple body a curious tightness settled suddenly.

"You—told—Dr. Brawne that—I fainted?" she said. "You—you oughtn't to have done that!" It was only too evident that she was displeased.

"But we were worried," I repeated. "We had to tell him. We didn't like to take the responsibility."

With her childish hands spread flatly as a brace on either side of her she seemed to retreat for a moment into the gold veil of her hair. Then very resolutely her face came peering out again.

"And just what did Dr. Brawne—tell *you*?" asked the May Girl.

"Why something very romantic," I admitted. "The somewhat astonishing news, in fact, that you were engaged—to him."

"Oh, but you know, I'm *not!*" protested the May Girl with unmistakable emphasis. "No—No!"

"And that he was hoping to be married next September. On the 15th to be perfectly exact," I confided.

"Well, very likely I *shall* marry him," admitted the May Girl somewhat bafflingly. "But I'm not engaged to him now! Oh, I'm much too young to be engaged to him now! Why, even my grandmother thinks I'm much too young to be engaged to him now!—Why, he's most fifty years old!" she affirmed with widely dilating eyes. "—And I—I've scarcely been off my grandmother's place, you know, until this last winter! But if I'm grown-up enough by September, they say—you see I'll be eighteen and a half by September," she explained painstakingly, "so that's why I wanted to get engaged as much as I could this week!" she interrupted herself with quite merciless irrelevance. "If I've got to be married in September—without ever having been engaged or courted at all—I just thought I'd better go to work and pick up what experience I could—on my own hook!"

"Dr.—Dr. Brawne will, of course, make you a very distinguished husband," I stammered, "but are you sure you love him?"

"I love everybody!" dimpled the May Girl.

"Yes, dogs, of course," I conceded, "and Rabbits—and horses and——"

"And kittens," supplemented the May Girl.

"Your mother is—not living?" I asked rather abruptly.

"My father is dead," said the May Girl. "But my mother is in Egypt." Her lovely face was suddenly all excitement. "My mother ran away!"

"Oh! An elopement, you mean?" I laughed. "Ran away with your father. Youngsters used to do romantic things like that."

"Ran away *from* my father," said the May Girl. "And from me. It was when I was four years old. None of us have ever seen her since. It was with one of Dr. Brawne's friends that she ran away. That's one reason, I think, why Dr. Brawne has always felt so sort of responsible for me."

"Oh, dear—oh, dear, this is very sad," I winced.

"N-o," said the May Girl perfectly simply. "Maybe it was bad but I'm almost sure it's never been sad. Dr. Brawne hears from her sometimes. Mother's always been very happy, I think. But everybody somehow seems to be in an awful hurry to get me settled."

"Why?" I asked quite starkly, and could have bitten my tongue out for my impertinence.

"Why—because I'm so tall, I suppose," said the May Girl. "And not so very specially bright. Oh, not nearly as bright as I am tall!" she hastened to assure me with her pretty nose all crinkled up for the sheer emphasis of her regret. "Life's rather hard, you know, on tall women," she confided sagely. "Always trying to take a tuck in them somewhere! Mother was tall," she observed; "and Father, they say, was always and forever trying to make her look smaller—especially in public! Pulling her opinions out from under her! Belittling all her great, lovely fancies and ideas! Not that he really meant to be hateful, I suppose. But he just couldn't help it. It was just the natural male-instinct I guess of wanting to be the everythinger—himself!"

"What do you know of the natural male 'instinct'?" I laughed out in spite of myself.

"Oh—lots," smiled the May Girl. "I have an uncle. And my grandmother always keeps two hired men. And for almost six months now I've been at the Art School. And there are twenty-seven boys at the Art School. Why there's Jerry and Paul and Richard and—and——"

"Yes, but your father and mother?" I pondered. "Just how——?"

"Oh, it was when they were walking downtown one day past a great big mirror," explained the May Girl brightly. "And Mother saw that she was getting round-shouldered trying to keep down to Father's level—it was then that she ran away! It was then that she began to run away I mean! To run away in her mind! I heard grandmother and Dr. Brawne talking about it only last summer. But I?" she affirmed with some pride, "oh, I've known about being tall ever since I first had starch enough in my knees to stand up! While I stayed in my crib I don't suppose I noticed it specially. But just as soon as I was big enough to go to school. Why, even at the very first," she glowed, "when every other child in the room had failed without the slightest reproach some perfectly idiotic visitor would always pipe up and say, 'Now ask that tall child there! The one with the yellow hair!' And everyone would be as vexed as possible because I failed, too! It isn't my head, you know that's tall," protested the May Girl with some feeling, "it's just my neck and legs!

"You certainly are entrancingly graceful," I smiled. How anybody as inexpressibly lovely as the May Girl could be so oblivious of the fact was astonishing!

But neither smile nor compliment seemed to allay to the slightest degree the turmoil that was surging in the youngster's mind.

"Why, even at the Art School," she protested, "it's just as bad! Especially with the boys! Being so tall—and with yellow hair besides—you just can't possibly be as important as you are conspicuous! And yet every individual boy seems obliged to find out for himself just exactly how important you are! But no matter what he finds," she shrugged with a gesture of ultimate despair, "it always ends by everybody getting mad!"

"Mad?" I questioned.

"Yes—very mad," said the May Girl. "Either he's mad because he finds you're not nearly as nice as you are conspicuous, or else, liking you most to death, he simply can't stand it that anyone as nice as he thinks you are is able to outplay him at tennis or—that's why I like animals best—and hurt things!" she interrupted herself with characteristic impetuosity. "Animals and hurt things don't care how rangy your arms are as long as they're loving! Why if you were as tall as a tree," she argued, "little deserted birds in nests would simply be glad that you could reach them that much sooner! But men? Why, even your nice Mr. Keets," she cried; "even your nice Mr. Keets, with his fussy old Archaeology, couldn't even play at being engaged without talking down—down—down at me! Tall as he is, too! And funny little old Mr. Rollins," she flushed. "Little—*little*—old Mr. Rollins—Mr. Rollins really liked me, I think, but he—he'd torture me if he thought it would make him feel any burlier!"

"And Claude Kennilworth," I questioned.

The shiver across the May Girl's shoulders looked suddenly more like a thrill than a distaste.

"Oh, Claude Kennilworth," she acknowledged quite ingenuously. "He's begun already to try to 'put me in my place'! Altogether too independent is what he thinks I am. But what he really means is 'altogether too tall'!" Once again the little shiver flashed across her shoulders. "He's so—so awfully temperamental!" she quickened. "Goodness knows what fireworks he'll introduce tomorrow! I can hardly wait!"

"Is—is Dr. Brawne—tall?" I asked a bit abruptly.

"N—o," admitted the May Girl. "He's quite short! But—his years are so tall!" she cried out triumphantly. "He's so tall in his attainments! I've thought it all out—oh very—very carefully," she attested. "And if I've got to be married in order to have someone to look out for me I'm almost perfectly positive that Dr. Brawne will be quite too amused at having so young a wife to bully me very much about anything that goes with the youngness!"

"Oh—h," I said.

"Yes,—exactly," mused the May Girl.

With a heart and an apprehension just about as gray and as heavy as lead I rose and started for the door.

"But, May Girl?" I besought her in a single almost hysterical desire to rouse her from her innocence and her ignorance. "Among all this great array of men and boys that you know— the uncle—yes, even the hired men," I laughed, "and all those blue-smocked boys at the Art School—whom do you really like the best?"

So far her eyes journeyed off into the distance and back again I thought that she had not heard me. Then quite abruptly she answered me. And her voice was all boy-chorister again.

"The best?—why, Allan John!" she said.

Taken all in all there were several things said and done that evening that would have kept any normal hostess awake, I think.

The third morning dawned even rainier than the second! Infinitely rainier than the first! It gave everybody's coming-down-stairs expression a curiously comical twist as though Dame Nature herself had been caught off-guard somehow in a moment of dishabille that though inexpressibly funny, couldn't exactly be referred to—not among mere casual acquaintances—not so early in the morning, anyway!

Yet even though everybody rushed at once to the fireplace instead of to the breakfast-table nobody held us responsible for the weather. Everyone in fact seemed to make rather an extra effort to assure us that he or she—as the case might be, most distinctly did not hold us responsible.

Paul Brenswick indeed grew almost eloquent telling us about an accident to the weather which he himself had witnessed in a climate as supposedly well-regulated as the climate of South Eastern Somewhere was supposed to be! Ann Woltor raked her cheerier memories for the story of a four days' rain-storm which she had experienced once in a very trying visit to her great aunt somebody-or-other on some peculiarly stormbound section of the Welsh coast. George Keet's chivalrous anxiety to set us at our ease was truly heroic. He even improvised a parody about it: "Rain," observed George Keets, "makes strange umbrella-mates!" A leak had developed during the night it seemed in the ceiling directly over his bed—and George, the finicky, the fastidious, the silk-pajamered—had been obliged to crawl out and seek shelter with Rollins and his flannel night-cap in the next room. And Rollins, it appeared, had not proved a particularly genial host.

"By the way, where is Mr. Rollins this morning?" questioned the Bride from her frowning survey of the storm-swept beach.

"Mr. Rollins," confided my Husband, "has a slight headache this morning."

"Why, that's too bad," sympathized Ann Woltor.

"No, it isn't a bad one at all," contradicted my Husband. "Just the very mildest one possible—under the circumstances. It was really very late when he got in again last night. And very wet." From under his casually lowered eyes a single glance of greeting shot out at me.

"Now, there you are again!" cried George Keets. "Flirting! You married people! Something that anyone else would turn out as mere information,—'The Ice Man has just left two chunks of ice!' or 'Mr. Rollins has a headache'!—you go and load up with some mysterious and unfathomable significance! Glances pass! Your wife flushes!" "Mysterious?" shrugged my Husband. "Unfathomable? Why it's clear as crystal. The madam says, 'Let there be a headache'—and there *is* a headache!"

As Allan John joined the group at the fireplace everybody began talking weather again. From the chuckle of the birch-logs to the splash on the window-pane the little groups shifted and changed. Everybody seemed to be waiting for something. On the neglected breakfast table even the gay upstanding hemispheres of grapefruit rolled over on their beds of ice to take another nap.

In a great flutter of white and laughter the May Girl herself came prancing over the threshold. It wasn't just the fact of being in white that made her look so astonishingly festal; she was almost always in white. Not yet the fact of laughter. Taken all in all I think she was the most radiantly laughing youngster that I have ever known. But most astonishingly festal she certainly looked, nevertheless. Maybe it was the specially new and chic little twist which she had given her hair. Maybe it was the absurdly coquettish dab of black court-plaster which she had affixed to one dimply cheek.

"Oh, if I'm going to be engaged to-day to a real artist," she laughed, "I've certainly got to take some extra pains with my personal appearance. Why, I've hardly slept all night," she confided ingenuously, "I was so excited!"

"Yes, won't it be interesting," whispered the Bride to George Keets, "to see what Mr. Kennilworth will really do? He's so awfully temperamental! And so—so inexcusably beautiful. Whatever he does is pretty sure to be interesting. Now up-stairs—all day yesterday—wouldn't it——?"

"Yes, wouldn't it be interesting," glowed Ann Woltor quite unexpectedly, "if he'd made her something really wonderful? Something that would last, I mean, after the game was over? Even just a toy, something that would outlast Time itself. Something that even when she was old she could point to and say, 'Claude Kennilworth made that for me when—we were young'."

"Why, Ann Woltor!" I stammered. "Do you feel that way about him? Does—does he make you feel that way, too!"

"I think—he would make—anyone feel that way—too," intercepted Allan John quite amazingly. In three days surely it was the only voluntary statement he had made, and everybody turned suddenly to stare at him. But it was only too evident from the persistent haggardness of his expression that he had no slightest intention in the world of pursuing his unexpected volubility.

"And it isn't just his good looks either!" resumed the Bride as soon as she had recovered from her own astonishment at the interpolation.

"Oh, something, very different," mused Ann Woltor. "The queer little sense he gives you of—of wires humming! Whether you like him or not that queer little sense of 'wires humming' that all really creative people give you! As though—as though—they were being rather specially re-charged all the time from the Main Battery!"

"The 'Main Battery,'" puzzled the Bridegroom, "being——?"

"Why God,—of course!" said the Bride with a vague sort of surprise.

"When women talk mechanics and religion in the same breath," laughed the Bridegroom, "it certainly——"

"I was talking neither mechanics nor religion," affirmed the Bride, with the faintest possible tinge of asperity.

"Oh, of course, anyone can see," admitted the Bridegroom, "that Kennilworth is a clever chap."

"Clever as the deuce!" acquiesced George Keets.

With an impatient tap of her foot the May Girl turned suddenly back from the window.

"Yes! But where *is* he?" she laughed.

"That's what I say!" cried my Husband. "We've waited quite long enough for him!"

"Dallying up-stairs probably to put a dab of black court-plaster on *his* cheek!" observed George Keets drily.

With one accord everybody but the May Girl rushed impulsively to the breakfast table.

"Seems as though—somebody ought to wait," dimpled the May Girl.

"Oh, nonsense!" asserted everybody.

A little bit reluctantly she came at last to her place. Her face was faintly troubled.

"On—on an engagement morning," she persisted, "it certainly seems as though—somebody ought to wait."

In the hallway just outside a light step sounded suddenly. It was really astonishing with what an air of real excitement and expectancy everybody glanced up.

But the step in the hall proved only the step of a maid.

"The young gentleman upstairs sent a message," said the maid. "Most particular he was that I give it exact. 'It being so rainy again,' he says, 'and there not being anything specially interesting on the—the docket as far as he knows, he'll stay in bed—thank you.'"

For an instant it seemed as though everybody at the table except Allan John jerked back from his plate with a knife, fork or spoon, brandished half-way in mid air. There was no jerk left in Allan John, I imagine. It was Allan John's color that changed. A dull flush of red where once just gray shadows had lain.

"So he'll stay in bed, thank you," repeated the maid sing-songishly.

"What?" gasped my Husband.

"W-w-what?" stammered the May Girl.

"Well—of all the—nerve!" muttered Paul Brenswick.

"Why—why how extraordinary," murmured Ann Woltor.

"*There's* your 'artistic temperament' for you, all right!" laughed the Bride a bit hectically. "Peeved is it because he thought Miss Davies——?"

"Don't you think you're just a bit behind the times in your interpretation of the phrase 'artistic temperament'?" interrupted George Keets abruptly. "Except in special neurasthenic cases it is no longer the fashion I believe to lay bad manners to the artistic temperament itself but rather to the humble environment from which most artistic temperaments are supposed to have sprung."

"Eh? What's that?" laughed the Bride.

Very deliberately George Keets lit a fresh cigarette. "No one person, you know, can have everything," he observed with the thinnest of all his thin-lipped smiles. "Three generations of plowing, isn't it, to raise one artist? Oh, Mr. Kennilworth's social eccentricities, I assure you, are due infinitely more to the soil than to the soul."

"Oh, can your statistics!" implored my Husband a bit sharply, "and pass Miss Davies the sugar!"

"And some coffee!" proffered Paul Brenswick.

"And this heavenly cereal!" urged the Bride.

"Oh, now I remember," winced the May Girl suddenly. "He said 'she'll wait all right'—but, of course, it does seem just a little—wee bit—f-funny! Even if you don't care a—a rap," she struggled heroically through a glint of tears. "Even if you don't care a rap—sometimes it's just a little bit hard to say a word like f-funny!"

"Damned hard," agreed my Husband and Paul Brenswick and George Keets all in a single breath.

The subsequent conversation fortunately was not limited altogether to expletives. Never, I'm sure, have I entertained a more vivacious not to say hilarious company at breakfast. Nobody seemed contented just to keep dimples in the May Girl's face. Everybody insisted upon giggles. The men indeed treated themselves to what is usually described as "wild guffaws."

Personally I think it was a mistake. It brought Rollins down-stairs just as everybody was leaving the table in what had up to that moment been considered perfectly reestablished and invulnerable glee. Everybody, of course, except poor Allan John. No one naturally would expect any kind of glee from Allan John.

In the soft pussy-footed flop of his felt slippers none of us heard Rollins coming. But I—I saw him! And such a Rollins! Stripped of the single significant facial expression of his life which I had surprised so unexpectedly in his eyes the night before, Rollins would certainly never be anything but just Rollins! Heavily swathed in his old plaid ulster with a wet towel bound around his brow he loomed cautiously on the scene bearing an empty coffee cup, and from the faintly shadowing delicacy of the parted portieres affirmed with one breath how astonished he was to find us still at breakfast, while with the next he confided equally fatuously, "I thought I heard merry voices!"

It was on Claude Kennilworth's absence, of course, that his maddening little mind fixed itself instantly with unalterable concentration.

"What ho! The—engagement?" he demanded abruptly.

"There isn't any engagement," said my Husband with a somewhat vicious stab at the fire.

From his snug, speculative scrutiny of the storm outside, George Keets swung round with what quite evidently was intended to be a warning frown.

"Mr. Kennilworth has—defaulted," he murmured.

"Defaulted!" grinned Rollins. Then with perfectly unprecedented perspicacity his roving glance snatched up suddenly the unmistakable tremor of the May Girl's chin. "Oh, what nonsense!" he said. "There are plenty of other eligible men in the party!"

"Oh, but you see—there are not!" laughed Paul Brenswick. "Mr. Delville and I are Married—and our wives won't let us."

"Oh, nonsense!" grinned Rollins. Once again his roving glance swept the company.

Everybody saw what was coming, turned hot, turned cold, shut his eyes, opened them again, but was powerless to avert.

"Why, what's the matter with trying Allan John?" grinned Rollins.

The thing was inexcusable! Brutal! Blundering! Absolutely doltish beyond even Rollins's established methods of doltishness. But at last when everybody turned inadvertently to scan poor Allan John's face—there was no Allan John to be scanned. Somewhere through a door or a window—somehow between one blink of the eye and another—Allan John had slipped from the room.

"Why—why, Mr. Rollins!" gasped everybody all at once. "Whatever in the world were you thinking of?"

"Maybe—maybe—he didn't hear it—after all!" rallied the Bride with the first real ray of hope.

"Maybe he just saw it coming," suggested the Bridegroom.

"And dodged in the nick of time," said George Keets.

"To save not only himself but ourselves," frowned my Husband, "from an almost irretrievable awkwardness.

"Why just the minute before it happened," deprecated Ann Woltor, "I was thinking suddenly how much better he looked, how his color had improved,—why his cheeks looked almost red."

"Yes, the top of his cheeks," said the May Girl, "were really quite red." Her own cheeks at the moment were distinctly pale. "Where do you suppose he's gone to?" she questioned. "Don't you think that—p'raps—somebody ought to go and find him?"

"Oh, for heaven's sake leave him alone!" cried Paul Brenswick.

"Leave him alone," acquiesced all the other men.

In the moment's nervous reaction and letdown that ensued it was really a relief to hear George Keets cry out, with such poignant amazement from his stand at the window:

"Why what in the world is that red-roof out on the rocks?" he cried.

In the same impulse both my Husband and myself ran quickly to his side.

"Oh, that's all right!" laughed my Husband. "I thought maybe it had blown off or something. Why, that's just the 'Bungalow on the Rocks,'" he explained.

"My Husband's study and work-room," I exemplified. "'Forbidden-Ground' is its real name! Nobody is ever allowed to go there without an invitation from—himself!"

"Why—but it wasn't there yesterday!" asserted George Keets.

"Oh, yes, it was!" laughed my Husband.

"It was not!" said George Keets.

The sheer unexpected primitiveness of the contradiction delighted us so that neither of us took the slightest offense.

"Oh, I beg your pardon, of course," George Keets recovered himself almost in an instant—"that right here before our eyes—that same vivid scarlet roof was looming there yesterday against the gray rocks and sea—and none of us saw it?"

"Saw what?" called Paul Brenswick. "Where?" And came striding to the window.

"Gad!" said Paul Brenswick. "Victoria! Come here, quick!" he called.

With frank curiosity the Bride joined the group. "Why of all things!" she laughed. "Why it never in the world was there yesterday!"

A trifle self-consciously Ann Woltor joined the group. "Bungalow?" she questioned. "A Bungalow out on the rocks." Her face did certainly look just a little bit queer. Anyone who wanted to, was perfectly free of course, to interpret the look as one of incredulity.

"No, of course not! Miss Woltor agrees with me perfectly," triumphed George Keets. "It was not there yesterday!"

"Oh, but it must have been!" dimpled the May Girl. "If Mr. and Mrs. Delville say so! It's their bungalow!"

"It—was—not there—yesterday," puzzled George Keets. More than having his honor at stake he spoke suddenly as though he thought it was his reason that was being threatened.

With her cheeks quite rosy again the May Girl began to clap her hands. Her eyes were sparkling with excitement.

"Oh, I don't care whether it was there yesterday or not!" she triumphed. "It's there to-day! Let's go and explore it! And if it's magic, so much the better! Oh, loo—loo—look!" she cried as a great roar and surge of billows broke on the rocks all around the little red roof and churned the whole sky-line into a chaos of foam. "Oh, come—*come!*" she besought everybody.

"Oh, but, my dear!" I explained, "How would you get there? No row-boat could live in that sea! And by way of the rocky ledge there's no possible path except at the lowest tide! And besides," I reminded her, "it's named 'Forbidden Ground', you know! No body is supposed to go there without——"

With all the impulsiveness of an irresponsible baby the May Girl dashed across the room and threw her arms round my neck.

"Why, you old dear," she laughed, "don't you know that that's just the reason why I want to explore it! I want to know why it's 'Forbidden Ground'! Oh, surely—surely," she coaxed, "even if it is a work-room, there couldn't be any real sin in just prying a little?"

"No, of course, no real sin," I laughed back at her earnestness. "Just an indiscretion!"

Quite abruptly the May Girl relaxed her hug, and narrowed her lovely eyes dreamily to some personal introspection.

"I've—never yet—committed a real indiscretion," she confided with apparent regret.

"Well, pray don't begin," laughed George Keets in spite of himself, "by trying to explore something that isn't there."

"And don't you and Keets," flared Paul Brenswick quite unexpectedly, "by denying the existence of something that is there!"

"Well, if it is there to-day," argued George Keets, "it certainly wasn't there yesterday!"

"Well, if it wasn't there yesterday, it is at least there to- day!" argued Paul Brenswick.

"Rollins! Hi there—Rollins!" they both called as though in a single breath.

From his humble seat on the top stair to which he had wisely retreated at his first inkling of having so grossly outraged public opinion, Rollins's reply came wafting some what hopefully back.

"H—h—iii," rallied Rollins.

"That red roof on the rocks—" shouted Paul Brenswick.

"Was it there—yesterday?" demanded George Keets.

"Wait!" cackled Rollins. "Wait till I go look!" A felt footstep thudded. A window opened. The felt footstep thudded again. "No," called Rollins. "Now that I come to think of it— I don't remember having noticed a red roof there yesterday."

"Now!" laughed George Keets.

"But, oh, I say!" gasped Rollins, in what seemed to be very sudden and altogether indisputable confusion. "Why—why it must have been there! Because that's the shack where we've catalogued the shells every year—for the last seven years!"

"Now!" laughed Paul Brenswick.

Without another word everybody made a bolt for the hat-rack and the big oak settle, snatched up his or her oil-skin clothes—anybody's oil-skin clothes—and dashed off through the rain to the edge of the cliff to investigate the phenomenon at closer range.

Truly the thing was almost too easy to be really righteous! Just a huge rock-colored tarpaulin stripped at will from a red-tiled roof and behold, mystery looms on an otherwise drab-colored day! And a mystery at a houseparty? Well— whoever may stand proven as the mother of invention— *Curiosity*, you know just as well as I do, is the father of a great many very sprightly little adventures!

Within ten minutes from the proscenium box of our big bay- window, my Husband and I could easily discern the absurd little plot and counterplots that were already being hatched.

It was the Bride and George Keets who seemed to be thinking, pointing, gesticulating, in the only perfect harmony. Even at this distance, and swathed as they were in hastily adjusted oil-skins, a curiously academic sort of dignity stamped their every movement. Nothing but sheer intellectual determination to prove that their minds were normal would ever tempt either one of them to violate a Host's "No Trespass" sign!

Nothing academic about Paul Brenswick's figure! With one yellow elbow crooked to shield the rain from his eyes he stood estimating so many probable feet of this, so many probable feet of that. He was an engineer! Perspectives were his playthings! And if there was any new trick about perspectives that he didn't know—he was going to solve it now no matter what it cost either him or anybody else!

More like a young colt than anything else, like a young colt running for its pasture-bars, the May Girl dashed vainly up and down the edge of the cliff. Nothing academic, nothing of an engineer—about any young colt! If the May Girl reached "the Bungalow on the Rocks" it would be just because she wanted to!

Ann Woltor's reaction was the only one that really puzzled me. Drawn back a little from the others, sheltered transiently from the wind by a great jagged spur of gray rock but with her sombre face turned almost eagerly to the rain, she stood there watching with a perfectly inexplicable interest the long white blossomy curve of foam and spray which marked the darkly submerged ledge of rock that connected the red-tiled bungalow with the beach just below her. Ann Woltor certainly was no prankish child. Neither was it to be supposed that any particular problem of perspective had flecked her mind into the slightest uneasiness. Ann Woltor knew that the bungalow was there! Had spent at least nine hours in it on the previous day! Lunched in it! Supped in it! Proved its inherent prosiness! Yet even I was puzzled as she crept out from the shelter of her big boulder to the very edge of the cliff, and leaned away out still staring, always at that wave-tormented ledge.

From the hyacinth-scented shadows just behind me I heard a sudden little laugh.

"I'll wager you a new mink muff," said my Husband quite abruptly, "that Ann Woltor gets there first!"

CHAPTER V

IN this annual *Rainy Week* drama of ours, one of the very best parts I "double" in, is with the chambermaid, making beds!

Once having warned my guests of this occasional domestic necessity, I ought, I suppose, to feel absolutely relieved of any embarrassing sense of intrusion incidental to the task. But there is always, somehow, such an unwarrantable sense of spiritual rather than material intimacy connected with the sight of a just deserted guest-room. Particularly so, I think, in a sea-shore guest-room. A beach makes such big babies of us all!

Country-house hostesses have never mentioned it as far as I can remember. Mountains evidently do not recover for us that particular kind of lost rapture. Nor even green pine woods revive the innocent lusts of the little. But in a sea-shore guest-room, every fresh morning of the world, as long as time lasts, you will find on bureau-top desk or table, mixed up with chiffons and rouges, crowding the tennis rackets or base balls, blurring the open sophisticate page of the latest French novel, that dear, absurd, ever-increasing little hoard of childish treasures! The round, shining pebbles, the fluted clam shell, the wopse of dried sea-weed, a feather perhaps from a gull's wing! Things common as time itself, repetitive as sand! Yet irresistibly covetable! How do you explain it?

Who in the world, for instance, would expect to find a cunningly contrived toy-boat on Rollins's bureau with two star-fish listed as the only passengers! Or Paul Brenswick's candle thrust into a copperas-tinted knot of water-logged cedar? In the snug confines of a small cigar box on a lovely dank bed of maroon and gray sea-weed Victoria Brenswick had nested her treasure-trove. Certainly the quaint garnet necklace could hardly have found a more romantic and ship- wrecky sort of a setting. Even Allan John had started a little procession of sand-dollars across his mantelpiece. But there was no silver whistle figuring as the band, I noticed.

What would Victoria Brenswick have said, I wondered, what would Allan John have thought if they had even so much as dreamed that these precious "ship-wreck treasures" of theirs had been purchased brand new in Boston Town within a week and "planted" most carefully by my Husband with all those other pseudo mysteries in the old trunk in the sand? But goodness me, one's got to "start" something on the first day of even the most ordinary house-party!

With so much to watch outside the window, figures still moving eagerly up and down the edge of the cliff, and so much to think about inside, all the little personal whims and fancies betrayed by the various hoards, the bed-making industry I'm afraid was somewhat slighted on this particular morning. Was my Husband still standing at that down-stairs window, I wondered, speculating about that bungalow on the rocks even as I stood at the window just above him speculating on the same subject? Why did he think that Ann Woltor would be the one to get there first? What had Ann Woltor left there the day before that made her specially anxious to get there first? Truly this *Rainy Week* experiment develops some rather unique puzzles. Maybe if I tried, I thought, I could add a little puzzle of my own invention! Just for sheer restiveness I turned and made another round of the guest-rooms. Now that I remembered it there was a bit more sand oozing from the Bride's necklace box to the mahogany bureau-top than was really necessary.

The rest of the morning passed without special interest. But the luncheon hour developed a most extraordinary interest in the principles of physical geography which beginning with all sorts of valuable observations concerning the weight of the atmosphere or the conformation of mountains or the law of tides, ended invariably with the one direct question: "At just what hour this evening, for instance, will the tide be low again?"

My Husband was almost beside himself with concealed delight.

"Oh, but you don't think for a moment, do you—" I implored him in a single whisper of privacy snatched behind the refilling of the coffee urn. "You don't think for a moment that anybody would be rash enough to try and make the trip in the big dory?"

"Well—hardly," laughed my Husband. "If you'd seen where I've hidden the oars!"

The oars apparently were not the only things hidden at the moment from mortal ken. Claude Kennilworth and Ego still persisted quite brutally in withholding their charms from us. Rollins had retreated to the sacristy of his own room to complete his convalescence. And even Allan John seemed to have wandered for the time being beyond the call of either voice or luncheon bell. Allan John's deflection worried the May Girl a little I think, but not unduly. It didn't worry the men at all.

"When a chap wants to be alone he wants to be alone!" explained Paul Brenswick with unassailable conciseness.

"It's a darned good sign," agreed my Husband, "that he's ready to be alone! It's the first time, isn't it?"

"Yes, that's all right, of course," conceded the May Girl amiably, "if you're quite sure that he was dressed right for it."

"Maybe a hike on the beach at just this moment, whether he's dressed right for it or not," asserted George Keets, "is just the one thing the poor devil needs to sweep the last cobweb out of his brain."

"I agree with you perfectly," said Victoria Brenswick.

It was really astonishing in a single morning how many things George Keets and the Bride had discovered that they agreed on perfectly. It teased the Bridegroom a little I think. But anyone could have seen that it actually puzzled the Bride. And women, when they are puzzled, I've noticed, are pretty apt to insist upon tracing the puzzle to its source. So that when George Keets suggested a further exploration of the dunes as the most plausible diversion for the afternoon, it wouldn't have surprised me at all if Victoria Brenswick had not only acquiesced in the suggestion for herself and her Bridegroom but exacted its immediate fulfillment. She did not, however. Quite peremptorily, in fact, she announced instead her own and her Bridegroom's unalterable intent to remain at home in the big warm library by the apple-wood fire.

It was the May Girl who insisted on forging forth alone with George Keets into the storm.

"Why, I shall perish," dimpled the May Girl, "if I don't get some more exercise to-day!—Weather like this—why—why it's so glorious!" she thrilled. "So maddeningly glorious!—I—I wish I was a seagull so I could breast right off into the foam and blast of it! I wish—I wish——!" But what page is long enough to record the wishes of Eighteen?

My Husband evidently had no wish in the world except to pursue the cataloging of shells in Rollins's crafty company.

Ann Woltor confessed quite frankly that her whole human interest in the afternoon centred solely on the matter of sleep.

Hyacinths, of course, are my own unfailing diversion.

Tracking me just a little bit self-consciously to my hyacinth lair, the Bride seemed rather inclined to dally a moment, I noticed, before returning to her Bridegroom and the library fire. Her eyes were very interesting. What bride's are not? Particularly that Bride whose intellect parallels even her emotions.

"Maybe," she essayed quite abruptly, "Maybe it was a trifle funny of me not to tramp this afternoon. But the bridge-building work begins again next week, you know. It's pretty strenuous, everybody says. Men come home very tired from it. Not specially sociable. So I just made up my mind," she said, in a voice that though playfully lowered was yet rather curiously intense. "So I just made up my mind that I would stay at home this afternoon and get acquainted with my Husband." Half-proud, half-shamed, her puzzled eyes lifted to mine. "Because it's dawned on me very suddenly," she laughed, "that I don't know my Husband's opinion on one solitary subject in the world except—just me!" With a rather amusing little flush she stooped down and smothered her face in a pot of blue hyacinths. "Oh—hyacinths!" she murmured. "And May rain! The smell of them! Will I ever forget the fragrance of this week—while Time lasts?" But the eyes that lifted to mine again were still puzzled. "Now—that Mr. Keets," she faltered. "Why in just an hour or two this morning, why in just the little time that luncheon takes, I know his religion and his Mother's first name. I know his philosophies, and just why he adores Buskin and disagrees with Bernard Shaw. I know where he usually stays when he's in Amsterdam and just what hotel we both like best in Paris. Why I know even where he buys his boots, and why. And I buy mine at the same place and for just exactly the same reason. But my Husband." Quite in spite of herself a little laugh slipped from her lips. "Why—I don't even know how my Husband votes!" she gasped. In some magic, excitative flash of memory her breath began to quicken. "It—It was at college, you know, that we met—Paul and I," she explained. "At a dance the night before my graduation." Once again her face flamed like a rose. "Why, we were engaged, you know, within a week! And then Paul went to China!—Oh, of course, we wrote," she said, "and almost every day, too. But——"

"But lovers, of course, don't write a great deal about buying boots," I acquiesced, "nor even so specially much about Buskin nor even their mothers."

In the square of the library doorway a man's figure loomed a bit suddenly.

"Vic! Aren't you ever coming?" fretted her impatient Bridegroom.

Like a homing bird she turned and sped to her mate!

Yet an hour later, when I passed the library door, I saw Paul Brenswick lying fast asleep in the depth of his big leather chair. Fire wasted—books neglected—Chance itself forgotten or ignored! But the Bride was nowhere to be seen.

I was quite right though when I thought that I should find her in her room. Just as I expected, too, she was standing by the window staring somewhat blankly out at the Dunes.

But the eyes that she lifted to me this time were not merely puzzled—they were suffering. If Paul Brenswick could have seen his beloved at this moment and even so much as hoped that there was a God, he would have gone down on his knees then and there and prayed that for Love's sake the very real shock which he had just given her would end in laughter rather than tears. Yet her speech, when it came at last, was perfectly casual.

"He—he wouldn't talk," she said.

"Couldn't, you mean!" I contradicted her quite sharply. "Husbands can't, you know! Marriage seems to do something queer to their vocal chords."

"Your husband talks," smiled the Bride very faintly.

"Oh—beautifully," I admitted. "But not to me! It doesn't seem to be quite compatible with established romance somehow, this talking business, between husbands and wives."

"Romance?" rallied the Bride. "Would you call Mr. Delville ex—exactly romantic!"

"Oh—very!" I boasted. "But not conversationally."

"But I wanted to talk," said the Bride, very slowly.

"Why, of course, you did, you dear darling!" I cried out impulsively. "Most brides do! You wanted to discuss and decide in about thirty minutes every imaginable issue that is yet to develop in all the long glad years you hope to have together! The friends you are going to build. Why you haven't even glimpsed a child's picture in a magazine, this the first week of your marriage, without staying awake half the night to wonder what your children's children's names will be."

"How do you know?" asked the Bride, a bit incisively.

"Because once I was a Bride myself," I said. "But this Paul of yours," I insisted. "This Paul of yours, you see, hasn't finished wondering yet about just you——!"

"For Heaven's sake," called my own husband through the half open doorway, "what's all this pow-wow about?"

"About husbands," I answered, quite frankly. "An argument in fact as to whether taken all in all a husband is ever very specially amusing to talk to."

"Amusing to talk to?" hooted my Husband. "Never! The most that any poor husband can hope for is to prove amusing to talk about!"

"Who said Paul?" called that young person himself from the further shadows of the hallway.

"No one has," I laughed, "for as much as two minutes."

A trifle flushed from his nap, and most becomingly dishevelled as to hair, the Bridegroom stepped into the light. I heard his Bride give a little sharp catch of her breath.

"I—I think I must have been asleep," said the Bridegroom.

Twice the Bride swallowed very hard before she spoke.

"I—I think you must have, you rascal!" she said. It was a real victory!

Really my Husband and I would have been banged in the door if we hadn't jumped out as fast as we did!

George Keets and the May Girl came in from their walk just before supper. Judging from their personal appearances it had at least been a long walk if not a serene one. George Keets indeed seemed quite unnecessarily intent in the vestibule on taking the May Girl to task for what he evidently considered her somewhat careless method of storing away her afternoon's accumulation of pebble and shell. Every accent of his voice, every carefully enunciated syllable reminded me only too absurdly of what the May Girl had confided to me about "boys always trying to make her feel small." He was urging her now, I inferred, to stop and sort out her specimens according to some careful cotton-batting plan which he suggested.

"Whatever is worth doing at all, you know, Miss Davies," he said, "is worth doing well."

The May Girl's voice sounded very tired, not irritable, but very tired.

"Oh, if there's anything in the world that I hate," I heard her cry out, "it's that proverb! What people really mean by it," she protested, "is, 'Whatever's worth doing at all is worth doing *Swell*.' And it isn't either! I tell you I like simple things best! All I ever want to do with my shells tonight is just to chuck 'em behind the door!"

Truly if Claude Kennilworth hadn't turned up for supper all in white flannels and looking like a young god, I don't know just what I should have done. Everybody seemed either so tired or so distrait.

The tide would be low at ten o'clock. It was eight when we sat down to supper.

Ann Woltor I'm sure never took her eyes from the clock.

But to be perfectly frank everybody else at the table except the May Girl seemed to be diverting such attention as he or she retained to the personal appearance of Claude Kennilworth. Truly it wasn't right that anyone who had been so hateful all day long should be able to look so perfectly glorious in the evening.

"Where did you get the suit?" said Rollins. "Is it your own?"

"And the permanent wave?" questioned the Bride. "I think you and the ocean must patronize the same hair dresser."

"Dark men always do look so fine in white flannels," whispered Ann Woltor to my Husband.

"Personally," beamed Paul Brenswick, "you look to me like a person who had imported his own Turkish bath."

"Turkish?" scoffed George Keets. "Nobody works up a shine like that by being washed only in one language! Russian, too, it must be! Flemish——"

"Flemish are rabbits," observed the May Girl gravely. But even with this observation she did not lift her eyes from her plate. Whether she was consciously and determmingly ignoring Claude Kennilworth's only too palpable efforts to impress her with the fact that now at last he was ready to forgive her and subjugate her, or whether she really hadn't noticed him, I couldn't quite make out. And then quite suddenly at the end of her first course she put down her knife and fork and folded her hands in her lap. "Where is Allan John?" she demanded.

"Why, yes, that's so! Where is Allan John!" questioned everybody all at once.

"Some walk he's taking," reflected Paul Brenswick.

"Not too long I hope," worried my Husband very faintly.

"Hang it all, I do like that lad," acknowledged George Keets.

"Who wouldn't?" said Young Kennilworth.

"Yes, but why?" demanded Keets.

"It's his eyes," said the Bride.

"Eyes nothing!" scoffed young Kennilworth. "It's the way he came out of his fuss without fussing! To make a fool of yourself but never a fuss—that's my idea of a fellow being a good sport!"

"It was his tragedy that I was thinking of," said George Keets very quietly.

"Yes, where in the world," questioned my Husband with quite unwonted emotion, "would you have found another chap in the same harrowing circumstances, even among your own friends, I mean, a chum, a pal, who could have dropped in here the way he has, without putting a damper on everything? Not intentionally, of course, but just in the inevitable human nature of things. But I don't get the slightest sense somehow of Allan John being a damper!"

"'Damper?'" said the Bride. "Why he's like a sick man basking in the sun. Hasn't a word to say himself, not a single prance in his own feet. But I'd as soon think of shutting out the sun from a sick man as shutting out a laugh from Allan John. Why, Allan John needs us!" attested the Bride, "and Allan John knows that he needs us!"

With a sideways glance at the vacant chair George Keets's thin lips parted into a really sweet smile.

"Where in creation is the boy!" he insisted. "Frankly I think we rather need him."

"All of which being the case," conceded my Husband, "it behooves me even once more, I should say, to tell Allan John that the next time he speaks about moving on I shall hide his clothes. Certainly I haven't trusted him yet with even a quarter. He's so extraordinarily fussy about thinking that he ought to clear out."

It was just at that moment that the telephone rang. I decided to answer it myself, for some reason, from the instrument upstairs in my own room, rather than from the library. A minute's delay, and I held the transmitter to my lips.

"Yes," I called.

"Is this Mrs. Jack Delville?" queried the voice.

"Yes. Who's speaking?"

"It's Allan John," said the voice.

"Why, Allan John!" I laughed. "Of course it would be you! We were just speaking about you, and that's always the funny way that things happen. But wherever in the world are you? We'd begun to worry a bit!"

"I'm in town," said Allan John.

"In town," I cried. "Town! How did you get there?"

In Allan John's voice suddenly it was as though tone itself was fashion. "That's what I want to tell you," said Allan John. "I've done a horrid thing, a regular kid college-boy sort of thing. I've taken something from your house, that silver salt cellar you know that I forgot to give back, and left it with a man in the village as security for the price of a railroad ticket to town, and a telegram to my brother and this phone message. I didn't have a cent you know. But the instant I hear from my brother——"

"Why, you silly!" I cried. "Why didn't you speak to my Husband?"

"Oh, your Husband," said Allan John, just a bit drily, "would have given me the whole house. But he wouldn't let me leave it! And it was quite time I was leaving," the voice quickened sharply. "I had to leave some time you know. And all of a sudden I—I had to leave at once! Rollins, you know! His break about the little girl. After young Kennilworth's cubbishness I simply couldn't put another slight on that lovely little girl. But—" His voice was all gray and again spent, like ashes. "But I just couldn't play," he said. "Not that!"

"Why of course you couldn't play," I cried. "Nobody expected you to! Rollins is a—a horror!"

"Oh, Rollins is all right enough," said Allan John. "It's life that is the horror."

"Yes, but Allan John—!" I parried.

"You people have been angels to me," he interrupted me sharply. "I shall never forget it. Nor the lovely little girl. I'm going back to Montana to see how my ranch looks. I can't talk now. Not to anybody. For God's sake don't call anybody. But if I get straightened out again, ever, you'll hear from me. And if I don't——"

"But, Allan John," I protested. "Everybody will be desolated, your going off like this! Why, you're not even equipped in the simplest way! Not a single bit of baggage! Not a personal possession!"

Across the buzzing wires it seemed suddenly as though I could actually hear Allan John making one last really desperate effort to smile.

"I've got my little silver whistle," said Allan John. As though in confirmation of the fact he lifted the silver bauble to his lips and blew a single flutey note across the sixty miles.

"Goodbye!" he said.

Before I had fairly dropped the receiver back into its place, the May Girl was at my elbow. Her lovely childish eyes were strangely alert, her radiant head cocked ever so slightly to one side as though she held a shell to her listening ear. But there was no shell in her hand.

"What was that?" cried the May Girl. "I thought I heard Allan John's whistle!"

CHAPTER VI

WERE you ever in a theatre, right in the middle of a play, on the very verge of an act that you were really quite curious about, and just as the curtain started to go up it was suddenly yanked down again instead, and a woman behind the scenes screamed—oh, horridly, and a man came rushing out in front of the curtain waving his arms and trying to tell everybody something, but everybody all of a sudden was so busy screaming for himself that even God, I think, couldn't have made you hear just what the trouble was?

It isn't a pleasant thing to have happen.

But that is almost exactly what happened to our *Rainy Week* play on this the fourth night of events just as I was waiting for the curtain to rise on the most carefully staged scene which we had prepared, the scene designated as "*The Bungalow on the Rocks.*"

And the woman who screamed was the May Girl. And the man who came rushing back to try and explain was Rollins. And the May Girl it proved was screaming because she was drowning! And if it hadn't been for the silly little Pom dog that Claude Kennilworth had been silly enough to bring way from New York "for a week's outing at the sea shore" just to please the extraordinarily silly girl who occupied the studio next to his, the May Girl would have drowned! It makes one feel almost afraid to move, somehow, or even not to move, for that matter, afraid to be silly indeed, or even not to be silly, lest it foil or foul in some bungling way the plot of life which the Biggest Dramatist of All had really intended.

It was Ann Woltor who gave the only adequate explanation.

Everybody had at least pretended that night the unalterable intention of going to bed early.

Claude Kennilworth of course having absented himself from the breakfast table didn't know anything about the bungalow discussion. But pique alone at the May Girl's persistent yet totally unexcited rebuff of his patronage had retired him earlier than anyone to the seclusion of his own room. And Rollins's unhappy propensity of always and forever butting into other people's plans had been most efficiently thwarted, as far as we could see, by dragging him upstairs and slamming his nose into a brand new and very profusely illustrated tome on the subject of "The Violet Snail."

By half past ten, Ann Woltor confessed she had found the whole lower part of the house apparently deserted.

For the same reason, best known even yet only to herself, she was still very anxious it appeared to get to the bungalow before any of her house-companions should have forestalled her. The trip, I judged, had not proved unduly hard. By the aid of a pocket flashlight she had made the descent of the cliff without accident, and after a single confusion where a blind trail ended in the water discovered the jagged path that twisted along the ledge to the very door of the bungalow. Once in the bungalow she had dallied only long enough to search out by the aid of the flashlight the particular object or objects which she had come for. Startled by a little sound, the sound of a man humming a little French tune that she hadn't heard for fifteen years, she had grabbed up her treasure, whatever it was, and bolted precipitously for the house, not knowing she had sprung the trap of our concealed phonograph when she opened the door. Even once back in the safe precincts of the house, however, she was further startled and completely upset by running into the May Girl.

The May Girl was on the stairs, it seemed, just coming down. And she didn't look "quite right," Ann Woltor admitted. That is, she looked almost as though she was walking in her sleep, or a bit dazed, a bit bewildered, and certainly, dressed as she was, just a filmy night-gown with her warm blanket wrapper merely lashed across her shoulders by its sleeves, her pretty feet bare, her gauzy hair floating like an aura all around her, it certainly wasn't to be supposed that she was just starting off on a prankish endeavor to solve the bungalow mystery. Even her eyes looked unreal to Ann Woltor. Even her voice, when she spoke, sounded more than a little bit queer.

"I—I thought I heard Allan John whistle" she said. "I—I promised, you know, that if he ever needed me I'd come."

Ann Woltor nearly collapsed. "Nonsense!" she explained. "Allan John is in town! Don't you remember? He telephoned while we were at supper. Mrs. Delville delivered his messages and good-byes to us."

"Why, yes, of course!" roused the May Girl, almost instantly. "How silly!—I guess I must have been asleep! And just dreamed it!"

"Why, of course, you were asleep and just dreamed it." Ann Woltor assured her. "You're asleep now! Get back to bed before you catch your death of cold! Or before anybody sees you!"

Ann Woltor, on the verge of hysterics herself, quite naturally was not at all anxious that those dazed, bewildered eyes should clear suddenly and with inevitable questioning upon her own distinctly drenched and most wind-blown and generally dishevelled appearance.

A single little shove of the shoulders had proved enough to herd the May Girl back to her bed-room while she herself had escaped undetected to her own quarters.

But the May Girl had *not* been satisfied, it appeared, with Ann Woltor's assurances concerning Allan John.

An hour or more later, roused once again to a still somewhat dazed but now unalterable conviction that Allan John had whistled, and fully equipped this time to combat whatever opposition or weather she might meet, she crept from the house out into the storm with the little Pom dog sniffing at her heels. Just what happened afterwards nobody knows. Just how it happened or exactly when it happened, nobody can even guess. Maybe it was the brilliantly lighted bungalow my Husband had fixed for the setting of the "Bunga low Scene" just after Ann Woltor's surreptitious visit that incited her. Maybe to a mind already stricken with feverishness the rising tide did suck through the bungalow rocks with a sound that faintly suggested a rather specially agonized sort of whistle. Who can say? The fact remains that to all intents and purposes she seemed to have ignored the ledge that even yet, in spite of its drenching spray, would have been perfectly safe for another half hour at least, and plunged forth down the blind trail, off the rocks into the water below. Resolutely she refused to cry for help. Perhaps the shock of the cold water chilled the cry in her throat. She grasped the slippery seaweed clinging to the rocks—moaning a little—crying a little—the pitiful struggle setting the Pom dog nearly crazy. How long she clung there she couldn't tell. She was mauled and bruised by the threshing waves. Still some complex inhibition prevented her crying out for help. Ages passed, her bruised arms and numb fingers refused to hold the grip on the elusive seaweed forever and she eventually let go her hold. A receding wave took her and tossed her poor exhausted body still struggling against another ledge of rock well out of reach from shore. Then, for the first time, the May Girl seemed to realize fully her peril—and she shrieked for help.

Ann Woltor, rousing sluggishly from her sleep, heard the black Pom dog barking furiously on the beach. Reluctant at first to leave her snug bed it must have been several minutes at least before sheer curiosity and irritation drove her to get up and peer from the window.

Out of that murky blackness of course not a single outline of the little dog met her sight. Just that incessant yap- yap- yap-yap of a tiny creature almost frenzied with excitement. But what really smote Ann Woltor's startled vision, and for the first time, was the flare of lights, which made the bungalow seem as if ablaze. And as she stared aghast into that flare of light which seemed to point so accusingly at her across the intervening waters, she either sensed or saw the May Girl's unmistakable head and shoulders banging into the single craggy rock that still jutted up from the depths saw an arm reach out heard that one blood-curdling scream!

Rollins must have thought she was mad! Dragging him from his bed, with her arms around his neck, her lips crushed to his ear,—even then she could hardly articulate or make a sound louder than a whisper.

Rollins fortunately did not lose his voice. Rollins bellowed. Rushing out into the hall just as he was, pajamas, nightcap and all, Rollins lifted his voice like a baying hound.

In a moment all hands were on deck. My Husband rushed for the dory—George Keets with him, Paul Brenswick, Kennilworth, Rollins!

The women huddled on the beach.

"Hold on! Hold on!" we shouted into space. "Just a minute more!—Just one minute more!"

We might just as well have shouted into a saw-dust pile.—The wind took the words and rammed them down our throats again till we sickened and choked!

Young Kennilworth came running. He was still in his white flannels. He looked like a ghost.

"There's been some hitch about the oars!" he cried. "Is she still there?"

In the flare of our lantern light I turned suddenly and stared at him. He looked so queer. In a moment so awful, it seemed almost incredible that any human face could have summoned so much EGO into it. From those gay, pleasure- roaming feet, it must have come hurtling suddenly—that expression! From those facile self-assured finger tips that were already coaxing the secrets of line and form from the Creator!—From that lusty, hot-blooded young heart that was even now accumulating its "Pasts!"—From the arrogant, brilliant young brain that knew only too well that it had a "FUTURE!"—And even as I watched, young Kennilworth stripped the white flannels from his body. And the pleasure. And the triumph. And all the little pasts. And all the one big future. And he who had come so presumptuously to us to make an infinitesimal bronze replica of the sea—went forth very humbly from us to make a man-sized model of sacrifice.

For an instant only as he steadied for the plunge a flash of the old mockery crossed his face.

"Of course I'm stronger than the ocean," he called back. "But if it shouldn't prove so—don't forget my Old Man's birthday!"

Ann Woltor fainted as his slim body struck the waves.

Hours passed—ages, aeons—before the dory reached them! Yet my husband says that it way only minutes. By the merciful providence of darkness we were at least spared some of the visual stages of that struggle. Minutes or aeons—there were not even seconds to spare, it proved by the time help actually arrived. Claude Kennilworth had a broken arm, but was at least conscious. The May Girl looked as though she would never be conscious again. Against the ghastly pallor of her skin the brutal bruises loomed like love's last offering of violets. The flexible finger-tips had clawed themselves to pulp and blood.

The village doctor came on the wings of the wind! We telephoned Dr. Brawne, but he was away on a business trip somewhere and could not be located! The rest of the night went by like a brand-new battle for life, but in the full glare of lamp-light this time! By breakfast-time, if one can compute hours so on a morning when nobody eats, Claude Kennilworth was almost himself again. But the May Girl's vitality failed utterly to rally. White as the linen that encompassed her she lay in that dreadful stupor among her pillows. Only once she roused herself to any attempt at speech and even then her words were almost inaudible. "Allan John," she struggled to say. "Was trying—to find him."

"Has she had any shock before this!" puzzled the Doctor. "Any recent calamity? Any special threat of impending illness?"

"She fainted day before yesterday," was all the information anybody could proffer. "She is subject to fainting spells, it seems. Last night Miss Woltor thought she looked a little bit dazed as though with a touch of fever."

"We've got to rouse her some way," said the Doctor.

"Oh, if we could only find Allan John," cried the Bride. "Allan John—and his whistle," she supplemented with almost shamefaced playfulness.

My Husband and George Keets tore off to town in the little car! They raked the streets, the hotels, the telegraph offices, the railroad station, God knows what before they found him. But they did find him. That's all that really matters!

It was ten o'clock at night before they all reached home again. Allan John asked only one question as he crossed the threshold. His forehead was puckered with perplexity.

"Is—everybody—in the world going to die?" he said.

They took him directly to the May Girl's room and put him down in a chair just opposite her bed, with the whistle in his hands. "Spring and Youth and the Pipes of Pan!" But such a sorry Pan! All the youth that was left in him seemed to have been wrung out anew by this latest horror. In the grayness of him, the hopelessness, the pain, he might have been fifty, sixty, himself, instead of the scant twenty-eight or thirty years that he doubtless was. A little bit shakily he lifted the whistle to his lips.

"Not that I put a great deal of credence in it," admitted the Doctor. "But if you say it was a sound—a signal that she had been waiting for———"

Softly Allan John fluted the silver note.

A little shiver—a struggle, passed across the figure on the bed.

"Again!" prompted the Doctor.

Once more Allan John lifted the whistle to his lips.

The May Girl opened her eyes and struggled vainly to raise herself on her elbow. When she saw Allan John a vague sort of astonishment flushed across her face and an odd apologetic little laugh slipped weakly from her lips.

"I—I came just as soon as I could, Allan John," she said, and sinking back into her pillows began quite unexpectedly to cry. It was the Doctor himself who sat by her side and wiped her tears away.

Ann Woltor shared the watches with me through the rest of the night. Allan John never left the room. Towards dawn I sent even Ann Woltor to her sleep and Allan John and I met the new day alone. By the time it was really light the May Girl, weak as she was, seemed to have recovered a certain amount of talkativeness. Recognizing thoroughly the presence and activity of both my hands and my feet, she seemed to ignore entirely the existence of either my eyes or my ears. Her puzzled wonderments were directed at Allan John alone.

"Allan John—Allan John," I heard her call softly.

"Yes," said Allan John.

"It's a lie," said the May Girl, "what people say about drowning, that as you go down you remember every little teeny weeny thing that has ever happened to you in your life! All your past, I mean! All the dreadful—wicked things that you've ever done! Oh, it's an awful lie!"

"Is it?" said Allan John.

"Yes, it certainly is;" attested the May Girl. "Why, I never even remembered the day I bit my grandmother."

"N—o," shivered Allan John.

"No, indeed!" insisted the May Girl. "The only things that I thought of were the things I had planned to do!—The—the— PLANS that were drowning with me! One of them," she flushed suddenly, "one of the plans I mean I didn't seem to care at all when I saw it go down and the plan about going to Europe some time. Oh, I don't think that suffered so terribly. But the farm. The farm I was planning to have. The cows. The horses. The dogs. The chickens. The rabbits. Why, Allan John, I counted seventeen rabbits!" Very softly to herself she began to cry again.

"S—s—h. S—s—h," cautioned Allan John. "Things that have never happened you know can't die."

"Of that," reflected the May Girl through her tears, "I am— not so perfectly sure. Is—is it going to clear up?" she asked quite irrelevantly.

"Oh, yes, *surely!*" rallied Allan John. He would have told her it was Christmas I think if he had really thought that that was what she wanted him to say. Very expeditiously instead he began to shine up the silver whistle with the corner of his handkerchief.

With an almost amusing solemnity the May Girl lay and watched the proceeding. Under the heavy fringe of her lashes her eyes looked very shy. Then so gently, so childishly, that even Allan John didn't wince till it was all over, she asked him the question that no other person in the world probably could have asked him at that moment, and lived.

"Allan John," she asked, "do you suppose that you will ever marry again?"

"Oh, my God, no!" gasped Allan John.

"Men—do," mused the May Girl.

"Men do," conceded Allan John. With the sweat starting on his brow he jumped up and strode to the window. From the window he turned back slowly with a curious look of perplexity on his face. "Why—do you ask—that?" he said.

"Oh, I don't know!" said the May Girl. "I was just wondering," she sighed.

"Wondering what?" said Allan John.

"Wondering," mused the May Girl, "if you would ever want to marry me."

For a moment Allan John did not seem to understand—for a moment he gazed aghast at the May Girl's impassive face. "Why—child," he stammered.

"Why Honey-Dear," I intercepted wildly.

It was the strangest wooing I ever saw or dreamed of. The wooing by a person who didn't even know she was wooing—of a person who didn't even know he was being wooed.

"Well—all right—perhaps it doesn't matter," said the May Girl. "I was only thinking how sad it would be—if Allan John ever did need me for his wife and I was already married to somebody else."

When the Doctor came at noon he reported with eminent satisfaction a decided improvement in both his patients. Claude Kennilworth, contrary to one's natural expectations, was proving himself an ideal patient despite his painful injury which he steadfastly refused to acknowledge.

Even the May Girl's more subtle and mystifying complications seemed to have cleared up most astonishingly, he felt, since his previous visit.

"Oh, she's coming out all right," he assured us. "Fresh air, plenty of range, freedom from all emotional concern or distress," were the key-notes of his advice. "She's only a baby, grown woman-sized in an all too brief eighteen years," he averred.

Words, phrases, judgments, rioted only too confusedly through my mind that was already so inordinately perplexed with the whole chaotic situation.

As I said "good-bye," and turned back from the front door, I was surprised to see both my Husband and Ann Woltor standing close beside me. The constrained expressions on their faces startled me.

"You heard what the Doctor said," I exclaimed. "You heard his exact words—'great big overgrown baby,' he said. 'Ought to be turned out to play in a sand-pile for at least two years more.' Just a baby," I protested, "And she'll be tending her own babies before the two years are over! They are planning to marry her in September you know to a man old enough to be her grandfather—almost. To Doctor Brawne," I stormed!

"To whom?" gasped Ann Woltor. Her face was suddenly livid. "To whom?"

A horrid chill went through me. "What's Doctor Brawne to you?" I asked.

"It's time you told her," interposed my Husband, quietly.

"What is Doctor Brawne to you!" I demanded.

"Doctor Brawne? Nothing!" cried Ann Woltor. "But the girl— the girl is my girl—my own little girl—my own big little girl."

"What!" I gasped. "What!" As though my knees had turned to straw I sank into the nearest chair.

With the curious exultancy of a long strain finally relaxed, I saw Ann Woltor's immobile face flame suddenly with amusement.

"Did you think I was talking just weather with your husband all that first harrowing day and evening? In the car? In the bungalow? Oh, no—not weather!" she exclaimed. "Not even just the 'May Girl,' as you call her, but—everything! Your husband discovered it that first morning in the car," she annotated hurriedly. "I dropped my watch. It had a picture in it. A picture of May taken last year. Dr. Brawne sent it to me."

"Yes, but Dr. Brawne?" I puzzled.

"Oh, I knew that May was to be married," she frowned. "And to a man a good deal older than herself. Dr. Brawne wrote me that. But what he quite neglected to mention,—" once again the frown deepened, "was that the old man was himself. I like Dr. Brawne. He is a very brilliant man. But I certainly do not approve of him as my daughter's husband. There are reasons. One need not go into them now," she acknowledged. "At least they do not specially concern his age. My daughter would hardly be happy with a boy I think. Boys do not usually like simplicity. It takes a mature man to appreciate simplicity."

"Yes, but the discovery?" I fretted. "Your own discovery?— Just when?"

"In the train of course, coming down that first night!" cried Ann Woltor. "I thought I should go mad. I thought at every station I would jump off. And then Rollins's bungling remark the next day about my tooth gave me the chance, as I supposed, to get away. Except for that awkward accident to my watch I should have gotten away. Your husband implored me for my own sake, for everyone's sake, to stop and consider. There was so much to consider. I had all my proofs with me, my letters, my papers, my marriage certificate. We went to the Bungalow. We thrashed it all out. I was still mad to get away. I had no other wish in the world except to get away! Your husband persuaded me that my duty was here—to watch my girl—to get acquainted with my girl—before I even so much as attempted meeting my other problems. I was very rattled. I left my broken watch in the bungalow! The picture was still in it! That's why I went back! I wasn't sure even then that I would disclose my identity even to my daughter! For that reason alone I made your husband promise that he would not betray my secret even to you. If I decided to tell all right. But I wished no such decision forced upon me!"

"Oh, Ann, Ann dear," I cried, "don't tell me any more, you've suffered enough. Just Rollins's bungling alone— the impudence of him———!"

"Rollins?—Rollins?" intercepted that pestiferous gentleman's voice suddenly. "Do I hear my name bandied by festive voices?" In another moment the Pest himself stood beside us.

My Husband is by no means a swearing man, but I distinctly heard from his unwonted lips at that moment a muttered blasphemy that would make a stevedore blush for shame.

Despite all her terrible stress and strain Ann Woltor smiled— actually smiled.

My Husband gasped. The cause of that gasp was only too evident. Once again we saw Rollins's ominous gaze fixed with unalterable intent on Ann Woltor's face. What was meant to be an ingratiating smile quickened suddenly in his eyes.

"Truly, Miss Woltor," he said, "*tell me*, why don't you get it fixed!"

For an instant I thought Ann Woltor would scream. For an instant I thought Ann Woltor would faint, then quicker than chain lighting, right there before our eyes we saw her make her great decision. It was as though her brain was glass and we could see its every working.

"All right," said Ann Woltor, very quietly. "All right—you— Damn fool—I *will* tell you! I will tell everybody!"

For the first time in his life I saw Rollins stagger!

But Rollins could not remain prostrate even under such a rebuff as this.

"Why—er—thank you—thank you very much," he rallied with his first returning breath. "Shall I—shall I call the others?"

"By all means, call them quickly," said Ann Woltor.

"Oh, Ann!" I protested.

"I mean it," she said. Her face was strangely quiet. "The time has come—I've made up my mind at last."

From the door of the porch we heard Rollins's piping voice.

"Mr. Brenswick! Mr. Keets! Kennilworth! Allan John!—Come on! Miss Woltor's going to tell us a story!"

With vaguely responsive interest, the people came trooping in.

"A story?" brightened the Bride. "Oh, lovely—what is it about?"

"The story of my broken tooth," said Ann Woltor, very trenchantly, "told by request—Mr. Rollins's request," she added.

With a single comprehensive glance at my tortured face—at my Husband's—at Ann Woltor's, Claude Kennilworth turned sharply on his heel and started to leave the room.

"What, don't you want to hear the story?" piped Rollins.

"No, not by a damn sight," snapped Kennilworth.

"But I want you to hear it," said Ann Woltor, still in that deadly quiet but absolutely firm voice.

George Keets's lips were drawn suddenly to a mere thin white line.

"One has no desire to intrude, Miss Woltor," he protested.

"It is no intrusion," said Aim Woltor.

For a single hesitating moment her sombre eyes swept the waiting group. Then, without further break or pause, she plunged into her narrative.

"I am the May Girl's mother," she said. "I ran away from the May Girl's father. I ran away with another man. I don't pretend to explain it. I don't pretend to condone it. This is not a discussion of ethics but a mere statement of history. All that I insist upon your understanding—is that I ran away from a legalized life of incessant fault-finding and criticism to an unlegalized life of absolute approval and love.

"I cannot even admit, after the first big wrench, of course, that I greatly regretted the little child I left behind. Mothers are always supposed to regret such things I know, but I was not perhaps a normal mother. I suffered, of course, but it was a suffering that I could stand. I could not stand, it seems, the suffering of living with my child's father.

"My husband followed us after a few months, not so much for outraged love, I think, as for vindictiveness. We met in a cafe, the three of us. My husband and my lover were both cool-blooded men. My lover was a Quaker who had never yet lifted his hand against any man. The two men started arguing. I came of a hot-blooded family. I had never seen men arguing only about a woman before. More than that I was vain. I was foolish. The biggest portrait painter of the hour had chosen me for what he considered would be his masterpiece. I taunted my lover and my husband with the fact that neither of them loved me. John Stoltor struck my husband. It was the first blow. My husband made a furious attack on him. I tried to intervene. He struck me instead, with such damage as you note. Enraged beyond all sanity at the sight, John Stoltor killed him.

"Even then, so overwrought as I was, so bewildered with my mouth all cut and bleeding, I snatched up a mirror to gauge the extent of my ruin. John Stoltor spoke to me—the only harsh words of his life.

"Your damage can be repaired in an hour," he said—"but his— mine—*never!*"

"It was at that moment they took him away—almost fifteen years—it has been. He did not have to pay the extreme penalty. There were extenuating circumstances the judge thought. His time expires next month. I am waiting for him. I have been waiting for fifteen years. At least he will see that I have subjugated my vanity. I swore that I would never mend my damage until I could help him mend his."

With a little gesture of fatigue she turned to Rollins. "This is the story of the broken tooth," she finished, quite abruptly.

"Wasn't Allan John even listening?" I thought. With everyone else's eyes fairly glued to Ann Woltor's arresting face, even now, at the supreme climax of her narrative, his eyes seemed focussed far away. Instinctively I followed his gaze. At the top of the stairs, her arms holding tight to the banisters for support, sat the May Girl!

In the almost breathless moment that ensued, Rollins swallowed twice only too audibly.

"All the same"—insisted Rollins hesitatingly, "all the same— I really do think that———"

With a little cry that might have meant almost anything, the Bride jumped up suddenly and threw her arms around Ann Woltor's neck.

Even at twilight time everybody was still discussing the problem of the May Girl. Certainly there was plenty of problem to discuss.

The question of an innocent young girl on the very verge of her young womanhood. The question of a practically unknown mother. The question of a shattered unrelated man coming fresh to them from fifteen years in prison. The question even of Dr. Brawne. Everybody had his or her own impractical or unsatisfactory solution to suggest. Everybody, that is, except Allan John.

Allan John as usual had nothing to say.

Upstairs, in the privacy of her own room, Ann Woltor and the May Girl, without undue emotion, were very evidently threshing out the problem for themselves.

Yet when they came down and joined us just before supper-time, it was only too evident from their tired faces that they had reached no happier conclusion than ours.

George Keets and my Husband brought the May Girl down. Claude Kennilworth, quite in his old form, save for his splinted arm, superintended the expedition.

"It's her being so beastly long," scolded Kennilworth, "that makes the job so hard!"

In the depths of the big leather chair the May Girl didn't look very long to me, but she did look astonishingly frail.

With a gesture of despair. Ann Woltor turned to her companions, as if she had read our thoughts.

"There isn't any solution," she said.

Why all of us turned just then to Allan John I don't know, but it became perfectly evident to everyone at that moment that Allan John was about to speak.

"It seems quite clear to me," said Allan John simply. "It seems quite natural to me somehow," he added, "that you should all come home with me to my ranch in Montana. The little girl needs it—the big outdoors—the animals—the life she craves. You need it," he said, turning to Ann Woltor, "the peace of it, the balm of it. But most of all John Stoltor will need it when it is time for him to come. Far from prying eyes, safe from intrusive questionings, that certainly will be the perfect chance for you all to plan out your new lives together. How much it would mean to me not to have to go back alone I need not say."

Startled at his insight, compelled by his sincerity, Ann Woltor saw order dawn suddenly out of the chaos of her emotions.

From her frankly quivering lips a single protest wavered.

"But Allan John," she cried, "you've only known us four days."

Across Allan John's haggard face flickered the faintest possible suggestion of a smile.

"I was a stranger—and you took me in."

With the weirdest possible sense of supernatural benediction, the dark room flooded suddenly with light. From the window, just beyond me, I heard my Husband's astonished exclamation:

"Look, Mary," he cried, "come quickly."

At an instant I was at his side.

Across the murky western sky the tumultuous storm-clouds had broken suddenly into silver and gold. In a blaze of glory the setting sun fairly streamed into our faces.

Struggling up from the depths of her chair to view it—even the May Girl's pallid cheeks caught up their share of the radiance.

"Oh, Allan John," she laughed, "just see what you have done— you've shined up all the world."

With a curiously significant expression on his face my Husband leaned toward me quickly.

"Ring down the curtain, quick," he whispered. "The Play's done—*Rainy Week* is over."